NICHOLAS EVERARD

MARINER OF ENGLAND: 2

by Alexander Fullerton

STORM FORCE TO NARVIK
LAST LIFT FROM CRETE
ALL THE DROWNING SEAS

timewarner
paperbacks

A *Time Warner* Paperback

This omnibus edition published in Great Britain in 2002
simultaneously by Little, Brown and Time Warner Paperbacks
Copyright © Alexander Fullerton 2002

Storm Force to Narvik first published in Great Britain in 1979
by Michael Joseph Limited
Published in 1996 by Little, Brown and Company
Copyright © Alexander Fullerton 1979

Last Lift from Crete first published in Great Britain in 1980
by Michael Joseph Ltd
Published in 1997 by Little, Brown and Company
Copyright © Alexander Fullerton 1980

All the Drowning Seas first published in Great Britain in 1981
by Michael Joseph Ltd
Published in 1998 by Little, Brown and Company
Copyright © Alexander Fullerton 1981

The moral right of the author has been asserted.

A CIP catalogue record for this book
is available from the British Library.

ISBN 0 7515 3202 9

Typeset by Hewer Text Ltd, Edinburgh
Printed and bound in Great Britain by Clays Ltd, St Ives plc

Time Warner Paperbacks
An imprint of
Time Warner Books UK
Brettenham House
Lancaster Place
London WC2E 7EN

www.TimeWarnerBooks.co.uk

STORM FORCE TO NARVIK

AUTHOR'S NOTE

Storm Force to Narvik is a novel about the naval operations off northern Norway between 8 and 13 April 1940. The destroyers *Intent, Hoste* and *Gauntlet* are fictional, as are the events described as taking place around Namsos, but the general framework of the story and details of the two Narvik battles are drawn from history.

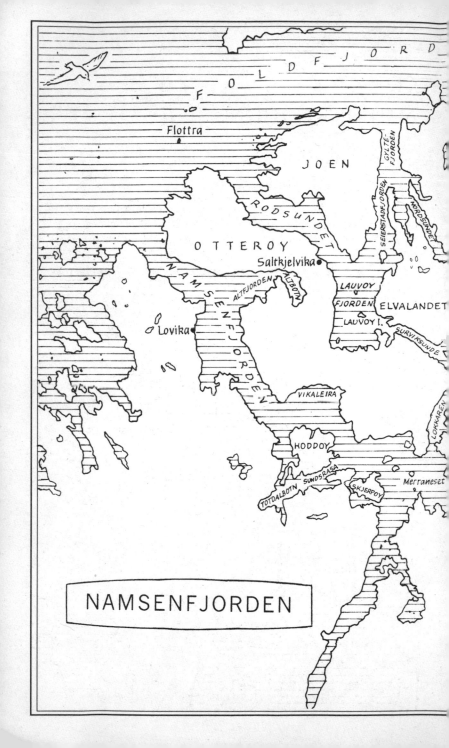

NAMSENFJORDEN

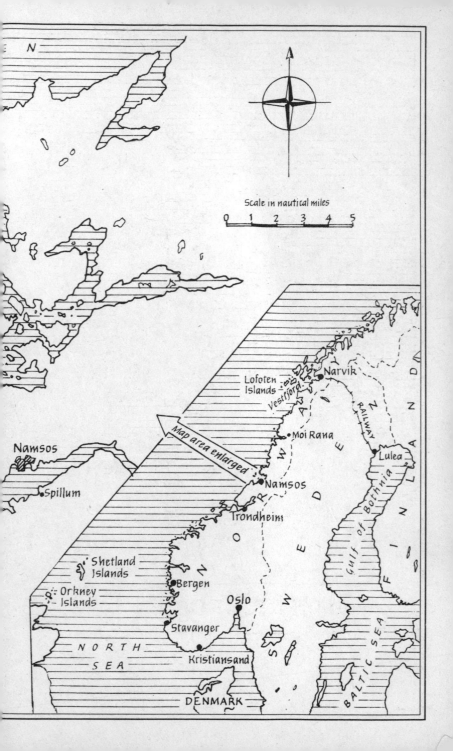

CHAPTER 1

Gauntlet had opened fire. The port-side lookout had reported it and Nick Everard had seen it too, distant yellow-orange spurts of flame, small stabs of brilliance piercing the blanket of foul weather and dawn's greyness still lingering under heavy cloud. Part-lowering his binoculars for a moment he looked across *Intent*'s bridge as she tilted savagely to starboard and bow-down with the quartering sea lifting her from astern, and saw young Lyte with his hand extended to the alarm buzzer, excitement as well as enquiry on his boyish and now salt-dripping face: Nick nodded, and putting his glasses back to his eyes heard the Morse letter 'S' sounding distantly but with dentist's-drill persistence through the ship. 'S' for surface action stations. The destroyer was standing on her tail now, stern deep in white churned froth and her bow and 'A' gun pointing at the cloud: jammed for support against the binnacle he put the glasses back on *Gauntlet* and saw her four-sevens fire again, rosettes of flame that bloomed and faded into smudges and were lost in the surrounding murk. The ship herself was almost invisible and her target, whatever it might be, was completely so: visibility was patchy but at the most four miles.

'Port fifteen.' Acknowledgement came hoarsely from the voice-pipe. He added, into the reek of metal polish and cigarette-smoke which not even a Norwegian Sea gale could clear away, 'Two-five-oh revolutions.' In normal conditions that would give her about twenty-four knots; in this sea it was doubtful whether such high revs could be kept on for long. On most courses it would be out of the question, but as she swung to port she was putting the force of the gale right astern; the dangers now would be of her screws racing as they came up into thin water when she pitched heavily bow-down, and of being pooped – overswept by big seas from astern.

1

Gauntlet was in action, and alone, and *Intent* had to get down there and join her.

'Sub!'

Sub-Lieutenant Lyte, on his way off to his action station in charge of the after guns, turned back, throwing an arm round one of the binnacle's correcting-spheres to hold himself in place as the ship stood on her ear: Nick told him, shouting above the noise, 'If we look like getting pooped, secure "Y" gun until we're on a safer course. And tell the first lieutenant I want him up here.'

The second-in-command's action station was at the after control position; but until he knew what was happening, Nick wanted him within easy shouting distance. He ducked to the pipe: 'Midships!'

'Midships, sir!'

Men rushing to their action stations had to grab for hand-holds as they went, staggering for balance while the ship flung herself about. The helmsman reported he had his wheel amidships; Nick bawled down to him to steer one-four-oh degrees. *Gauntlet* had been just about due south of them and steering north, and she'd been firing to starboard; so this alteration of forty degrees to port – *Intent* had been steering south – was intended both to close the distance and at the same time to bring *Intent* up towards the enemy. Meanwhile communications were being tested, gun receivers lined up, ammunition supply readied, all the set routines of preparing for action being gone through for the second time in an hour. It was only that long since the ship's company had been piped to dawn action stations, no more than fifteen minutes since they'd been sent down again, and the alarm's buzzing would surely have turned the messdeck air blue with obscenities. The off-watch hands would have had breakfast in mind – not *this* . . . Nick saw Tommy Trench, his outsized first lieutenant, oilskins shedding water in streams as he talked over the telephone to Henry Brocklehurst in the director tower, the gun-control position above and abaft the bridge; the tower and its separate range-finder were meanwhile training this way and that over an arc from north-east to south-east – like the raised head of some monster seeking prey.

'Sir . . .' Pete Chandler, *Intent*'s RNVR navigator, former insurance broker and yachtsman, fetched up in a rush against the other side of the binnacle. Tall, pale-faced, hooded in a duffel coat. '*Gauntlet*'s wirelessed an enemy report – two destroyers.'

They'd intercepted her first signal, that she was investigating an unidentified ship to the nor'ard. There'd seemed to be some

2

possibility of confusion then, that she'd been referring to *Intent*; they'd met at just about that time, exchanged the coloured-light challenge and reply and then swapped pendant numbers. But the puzzle was resolved now – partly.

'Tell the first lieutenant. Then see if anything else is coming through.'

Chandler went slithering downhill to join Trench, who'd now tell Brocklehurst the Gunnery Control Officer what he was supposed to be looking for, and Brocklehurst could tell the guns' crews over their sightsetters' telephones. It would be damned uncomfortable down at the four-sevens, and by no means easy to shoot effectively or to handle heavy projectiles on slippery, wildly canting gundecks . . . It could be argued, he realised – one thought overtaking another – that he should be ordering *Gauntlet* to wait for him to join her. But if he did, she might lose contact with the enemy. If the Hun wanted to evade contact it would be all too easy in this weather, and if those destroyers were part of an invasion force, part of the expected German attack on Norway, they *would* want to. The priority therefore was to maintain contact at all costs: not only in order to engage but even more importantly, in the prevailing state of ignorance and confusion, to see what ships were here and then tell the C-in-C about them.

He focused his glasses again on *Gauntlet*. He'd picked her up, to his own and his navigator's great satisfaction, just a short while ago. Dawn, arriving after the four-hour dark period which was what constituted a 'night' this far north, hadn't done more than change pitch black into dirty grey: but suddenly there she'd been, a needle in the North Sea haystack. He stooped to the voicepipe: 'Port fifteen. Steer one-three-oh' – because *Gauntlet* had altered course again, gone round to about 090 degrees, east, which was the bearing of the nearest part of Norway. And there, in fact at three different points on that distant and of course invisible coast, close inshore, minelaying operations were in progress at this minute. *Intent* and *Gauntlet* and half a dozen other destroyers were at sea with the battlecruiser *Renown* as cover to these operations, in case the Germans tried to interfere with them; but *Gauntlet* (Lieutenant Commander J. A. Hustie RN) had turned back to search for a man lost overboard, and subsequently *Intent* (Commander Sir Nicholas Everard, Bart., DSO, DSC, RN) had been sent to find *her*.

God only knew what might be happening elsewhere – whether the Hun was about to invade Norway, or whether the British were.

3

Troops had been embarked in cruisers and transports in Scottish ports, but they were just sitting there, waiting. For what? For the War Cabinet to make its woolly mind up?

And now the Home Fleet had sailed; the C-in-C, Sir Charles Forbes, had brought them out of Scapa last evening. But apparently they were staying out in the middle, not covering the approaches to the Norwegian ports at all. Surely if the Germans were invading that would be the place to find them?

Usual bugger's muddle, Nick thought. *We haven't changed. At Jutland nobody knew what the hell anyone else was doing either.*

Twenty-four years ago, Jutland had been. It felt more like last week . . . At Jutland he'd been a sub-lieutenant, and since then he'd been many different things – including, for about eight years, a glorified labourer on his own land in Yorkshire. The peasant years . . . If it hadn't been for that break in his naval service he'd have been at least a post-captain now. He'd been promoted to the rank of commander – the three stripes they'd given him back now – as long ago as 1926.

Well – it had been by his own choice that he'd left. And in wartime one only needed a bit of luck to make up that sort of leeway.

'Course one-three-oh, sir!'

'Flag signal from *Gauntlet*, sir!'

Acknowledging the wheelhouse report, he looked round: at the back of the bridge, starboard side, Leading Signalman Herrick had a telescope trained on the tiny patch of colour at *Gauntlet*'s yardarm. Herrick bawled, 'Enemy – destroyer flag – bearing—'

He'd stopped, unable to read the numerals under that red-and-white bearing pendant. Blowing down-wind the flags were almost end-on, and when both ships were down in troughs between the waves they were completely hidden from each other. But now it ceased to matter: Trench was yelling with the director telephone at his ear, 'Director has enemy in sight, one destroyer bearing green one-oh range oh-seven-five!'

'Open fire!' Nick called down to the coxswain, 'Port ten.' To turn her so that the after guns, 'X' and 'Y', would bear.

'Ten of port wheel on, sir!'

'Steer one-one-oh.'

It would still be a converging course – with *Gauntlet*'s, and so presumably with the enemy's. Nothing about enemy course from Brocklehurst yet. And it was strange that 'A' and 'B' guns hadn't started shooting. Nick shouted to Trench to ask what the delay was.

'Director lost target!'

He'd got the information at just that moment. Nick cursed, and put his glasses on *Gauntlet* again. She'd gone further round to starboard. Trench called, 'Director reports enemy has turned away eastward, sir.'

Running away. *Gauntlet* chasing him.

'Starboard fifteen.' A sleet-shower was lashing across the bridge. Nick was thinking that two Hun destroyers would hardly be up here in 65 north latitude on their own. They had to be escorting or screening something bigger.

'Fifteen of starboard wheel on, sir!'

'Steer one-three-oh.' He was watching *Gauntlet*, and although the distance between them had lessened somewhat she was becoming harder to see. This sleet didn't help, but where she was the visibility must have closed in during the last minute . . . Escorting *something*, those Huns must be. Troop transports for Narvik, perhaps; or scouting ahead of bigger ships. It would be a normal destroyer tactic to turn away and lead a pursuer into the range of a heavier ship's guns; whereas it was most unlikely that any destroyer man would lead attackers towards a convoy that was in his own protection. This was the analysis that made sense: and you could add a further detail to the picture of probabilities: in these weather conditions any encounter would take place at virtually point-blank range.

And consequently, this was the moment when the right decision for him as senior officer might be to call *Gauntlet* back, not let Hustie press on alone while *Intent* was too far astern to support him.

'Course one-three-oh, sir!'

Wind and sea were just about dead astern again, on this course. He'd acknowledged the coxswain's report: he called down, 'Three hundred revolutions.' If he ordered Hustie to wait for *Intent* to catch him up and contact with the enemy was lost, in this weather it wouldn't be regained. *Gauntlet* therefore had to be allowed to take her chances. Nick yelled at Trench, 'Tell Opie to have his tubes on a split yarn. And Brocklehurst to load with SAP and open fire without further orders.'

'Aye aye, sir!' Tommy Trench was a lieutenant-commander, twenty-nine years old, six-foot four in his seaboot stockings, a very experienced first lieutenant who probably saw his dug-out CO as some kind of ancient mariner. Possibly even as a supplanter. Nick had only taken command a fortnight ago and Trench, who'd been first lieutenant under the previous captain, might have entertained hopes of getting the ship himself.

The voicepipe on the left of the binnacle was the one to the engine-room. Nick called down it to his commissioned engineer, Mr Waddicor.

'We may need to make smoke at short notice, Chief.'

'I'll be ready for you, sir!'

A Devon man, was Waddicor. Short and rather stout – well, say stocky – and always boisterously happy. Extraordinary . . . *Gauntlet* was out of sight, he realised suddenly. In the last few seconds she'd faded, merged into the thick weather, the soupy haze down there where the clouds' lower edges seemed to be throwing roots into the sea. She couldn't be more than 6,000 yards away, and she'd vanished. He was still searching, expecting her to appear again after being hidden temporarily in a squall – they'd endured rain, sleet, hail and snow since midnight – when he heard percussions, heavy as thunder only sharper, more clearly defined. From that easterly direction.

Trench was looking round at him, with a hand cupped to one ear. And there'd been a flash, a diffuse explosive brightness which had flared for about a second and was now extinguished, leaving only drab grey again.

Big-ship guns . . .

'Ask Brocklehurst if he can still see *Gauntlet*.'

Trench turned, ducked behind the glass wind-break which topped the forefront of the bridge, taking the telephone down there with him. Perfectly timed: half a ton of green water burst over, missing him as it plumped into the bridge, bursting in all directions and swirling inches deep to the level of the gratings before it drained away. Trench grinned at Able Seaman Hughes, who'd taken it fair and square and looked like an angry spaniel. Trench rose, slamming the hand-set into its bracket: 'They've lost her, sir!'

Gunfire had become continuous, had thickened into a solid blast with no gaps in it. If Hustie had run into some big ship at close range his reaction would be to turn and fire torpedoes; and the enemy's reply would be to let rip with his big guns as the destroyer swung and exposed her vulnerable beam to him. Guesswork: but it was more than that: he could see it happening – with an accompanying thought in his mind that if *Intent* had been there with her, *Gauntlet* wouldn't have been getting all that vicious attention directed at herself alone. She was there alone because he'd *let* her be . . . More gunfire: but less intensive, separate salvoes again. *Intent* pounding, battering towards the sound of them. Scream of the fans competing with that of the wind: different notes blending into a roar of sound punctuated by the rattling and thumping of the ship's fabric, the battering of the sea.

'*Gauntlet* on green two-oh, sir, on fire!'

Trench, hauling himself over to the starboard torpedo sight, gestured to the communications number, Hughes, to take over the director tower's telephone. And Nick had *Gauntlet* in his glasses. She was coming back, almost bow-on: he saw shell-splashes all around her. The fire was abaft her bridge, he thought probably between the funnels. But now she was beginning to make her own smoke, oily-looking black stuff oozing out and curling away downwind just as another salvo plummeted down and one shell landed on her foc's'l, its flattish orange burst darkening into a red-brown haze with solid pieces flying.

No enemy in sight still. *Gauntlet* swinging hard to port though, lengthening and then shortening again as she turned, belching smoke, revealing the blaze amidships, mainmast gone and after funnel shot to ribbons. The wind was pushing the smoke away to port, between *Gauntlet* and her enemy: her course was something like south now so the German had to be to the east of her.

'Starboard fifteen.'

'Starboard fifteen, sir!'

'Steer one-five-oh.' He added, 'Three-five-oh revolutions.'

The gap had to be closed: the dangers of increasing to full speed had simply to be accepted. And *Gauntlet* was still visible to the enemy, despite the smokescreen: she'd been straddled again, shell-spouts lifting grandly, the wind blowing their tops off as they subsided. Nick saw Trench throw him a glance back across the lurching bridge with a can't-we-do-something appeal on his large, squarish face. He looked over at the suffering *Gauntlet*, waiting for Hustie to turn back behind his own smoke. He *would*, obviously, otherwise there'd have been no point in laying it: and the turn would bring him back towards *Intent*, who meanwhile was straining her steel guts and loosening every rivet in her plates by crashing flat-out across a sea in which normally one wouldn't have

7

attempted more than twelve knots. But she and *Gauntlet* would be closing in towards each other fast once Hustie made his turn: the rate of closing would be the sum of their combined speeds. The enemy had to be somewhere on *Gauntlet*'s bow, since that was the only angle from which he could have her in sight. Unless he was seeing her *over* the smoke: seeing her foretop from his much higher one?

Gauntlet had begun to turn. *At last* . . . He watched her, counting seconds, for her to get behind that smoke barrier. It was already some distance from her, as the diameter of her turn added to the smoke's down-wind drift. But she was round: by now she'd be hidden from the German. Heading back this way . . .

But – still under helm: continuing the turn?

Hustie was going right round, back into the smoke – *attacking on his own again* . . .

'Port twenty, full ahead both engines!'

Maximum revs were already on the clock but 'full ahead' meant emergency, sit on the safety-valves. He shouted to Trench, 'Stand by all tubes port side!' Trench raised a hand in acknowledgement: he'd already crossed to the other sight, having assessed the position for himself and seen that they'd be bound to fire on a starboard turn, since the enemy must be on a southerly course. If he hadn't been, *Gauntlet* wouldn't have laid out her smokescreen that way. Nick called down, 'Steer one-five-oh.'

'Captain, sir.' Chandler, with a signal log. 'New one from *Gauntlet*. She's reported the enemy as a *Hipper*-class cruiser.'

He was watching Hustie's ship straighten from her three-quarter circle and steady on a course of about 110 degrees. She'd be into the smoke before *Intent* could be: and it was too late to recall him. Partly because *Gauntlet* was further ahead but also because *Intent* would be entering this top end of the smoke – which, having been laid first, was further down-wind now than the rest. And thinner, too. He told Chandler, 'Get a signal off, pilot. Same addressees.' That meant the C-in-C in his flagship *Rodney* and Admiral Whitworth in *Renown*, repeated to Admiralty in London. He dictated, *'In company with Gauntlet in position – whatever it is – about to engage enemy cruiser with torpedoes, Gauntlet severely damaged in previous attack.'*

'Course one-five-oh, sir!'

Tremendous racket: wind, sea, and turbine-scream . . . *Gauntlet* was vanishing into the smoke barrier. Nick yelled at Trench, 'Tell

Opie and Brocklehurst the target is a *Hipper*-class cruiser.' The smoke seemed to be holding together remarkably well, down at its southern end; but at this end it was breaking up, leaving gaps that were quite clear of it. *Gauntlet* was blanketed, but the disintegration of the smoke was spreading that way quite rapidly and it wouldn't cover her for long.

She'd have used some torpedoes, presumably, in her first attack; it was anyone's bet how many she'd have left to use this time. No smoke here now to speak of: just patches, and eye-whipping sleet again: and suddenly there was *Gauntlet* – a low, blazing silhouette glimpsed sporadically as she slam-banged through the waves. But the fact that he was seeing her didn't mean the German could. He took his eyes off her: it was the target, the *Hipper*, one had to look for now; and suddenly he heard – with interest and surprise because he hadn't heard it for twenty years and it had the sharp familiarity of something long forgotten suddenly brought to mind – the noise of shells scrunching overhead. Then 'A' and 'B' guns fired, their reports not much more than harsh cracking thuds because of other noise, the smoke and smell of cordite instantly whipped clear on the wind. Hughes, at the director telephone, shouted, 'Enemy cruiser bearing green five, range—'

They'd seen her from up there because they were above the smoke and spray and had that extra height-of-eye: and the German must have spotted *Intent* even sooner. Then Nick had the *Hipper* in his glasses too. Immense, and spitting flame, huge-looking with towering bridge superstructure and single massive funnel. Shell-spouts rose to starboard, a grove of them lifting almost politely from the sea as though rising to watch the destroyer pass: battle experience a quarter of a century old prompted Nick's order to the wheelhouse: 'Starboard twenty!'

Jinking towards the fall of shot. The enemy GCO was bound to make his correction the other way. So you turned your ship one way while he sent his next salvo elsewhere.

But you couldn't dodge for ever: you had to get in close enough to have a fair chance of hitting with one or more torpedoes . . .

Gauntlet: he'd been ignoring her while he watched the *Hipper*, but glancing to starboard now he saw Hustie's obvious intention: he was steering his ship right for her, going to ram!

He must have used up all his torpedoes in the first attack. So he had nothing left to hit the German with except his ship. Fifteen hundred tons throwing itself at ten thousand . . .

'Midships!'

'Midships, sir!'

He should have held him back. They should have been attacking together now, simultaneously.

'Meet her. Steer one-six-oh.'

And now hold this course. No more dodging. Just a little gritting of the teeth. Salvo coming now . . .

It would miss. Because it *had* to. And before the next lot arrived he'd be close enough to turn and fire. A fan of ten fish from abaft the beam mightn't take all that much avoiding, especially with only one destroyer attacking on her own. You needed several, a co-ordinated attack. But – *bad workmen blame their tools*. He decided he'd fire the first five, the for'ard set, then hold on until the enemy began to take his avoiding-action, fire the rest when she'd committed herself and he could see which way she was swinging. There'd be punishment to take in that process . . . Shells ripping over: that tearing-sailcloth sound. A violent jolt flung him forward against the binnacle and he realised she'd been hit aft. He shouted for the general benefit, 'Nearly there!' No point looking round: there'd be flames and smoke and you'd seen all that before. Young Lyte would be looking after things if he was still on his feet: and Opie, please God, would be alive and with his two sets of tubes intact. Stink of burning paintwork and fire-heat in the wind: and Trench pointing . . . *Gauntlet* had rammed the German right for'ard near his starboard hawse-pipe and she was scraping and crashing down his side, ripping off armour-plating as she went. Nick ducked to the voicepipe: 'Steer one-five-five.' Up again: the *Hipper* had blasted off another salvo. Eight-inch shells would be in mid-air now. *Gauntlet* had sheered away from the cruiser's side: she lay stopped, wallowing low in the sea and burning from end to end, and the German gunners weren't even bothering to shoot at her now because they knew she was finished.

They were shooting at *Intent* instead.

'Course one-five-five, sir!'

Shells would be arriving at any moment.

'Starboard twenty-five!'

'Starboard twenty-five, sir!'

Shot was falling close ahead, the splashes lifting like green pillars and from the nearer ones foul, smelly water streaming back across the ship as she drove through them – and beginning, *at last*, to swing. More fall of shot to port: one near-miss, the ship recoiling as

10

from a body-blow. Heeling hard to port as she slammed around across wind and sea. Trench was stooped ready over the torpedo sight. Another crash back aft somewhere. But she was still turning, fighting her way round: in seconds Trench's sight would come on and the silver fish would leap away. More shells scorching down: and an explosion, aft again but – *inside* the ship? On its heels a *whoosh* of flame from aft and, overhead, a crack like a gun firing: then, drowning other noise, the racket of escaping steam.

She'd stopped her swing. Trench looking round, an expression of dismay on his big spray-wet face. A snow-shower sweeping over like a shroud and *Intent* was stopping, slumping in the waves, surrendering to them like a stag pulled down by hounds. No swing now: the momentum of the turn was spent and the sea was beginning to punch her back the other way. She was stopped, and at the mercy of the cruiser's guns.

CHAPTER 2

In London there was no gale or sleet, but it was a blustery day and the tall, grey-haired civilian coming down St James's Street in dark overcoat and homburg strode briskly, keeping the cold out and, by his manner, enjoying the exercise too. An ebony cane with a silver knob swung from one gloved hand; it was a stick that might have gone with a naval uniform and perhaps once had, and as he turned left into Pall Mall he glanced up at the sky with the air of one accustomed to reading weather-signs and making his own interpretation of them. It was a useful knack to have, too, now that for security reasons there were no public weather forecasts.

He'd crossed the road, and presently he turned right into Waterloo Place, where he climbed a flight of stone steps. He was putting a hand out to push the glass front door open when a uniformed hall porter, reaching the door just in time, saved him the trouble.

'Good morning, sir.'

The voice was Scottish, the inflexion faintly interrogative, the tone reserved for someone whom the porter didn't recognise as a member but wasn't *quite* sure about.

'Good morning. Thank you.' He was looking interestedly at the porter. 'Don't I know you?'

That solved one problem: he couldn't be a member. The porter was now battling with the new one. Concentrating, his brown eyes were narrowed to mere slits in a face which, with its corrugations and tan complexion, had something in common with a walnut.

The eyes suddenly lit up.

'Admiral Everard!'

Hugh Everard, nodding, raised the hand with the black cane in it. 'Don't dare tell me . . . You were with me in *Nile*. In '16. And you were – in my gig's crew?'

'I was *that*, sir!'

12

Hugh was still nodding to himself as he regained pieces of lost memory.

'Robertson?'

'Aye, sir!'

'You were a dead-eyed Dick of a marksman, I remember. We were runners-up in the Scapa championships and you were in *Nile*'s eight. Am I right?'

The walnut seemed permanently cracked in that wide smile.

'Right enough, sir . . . Why, I'd never've – my word, it's twenty or more years—'

'I'll tell you another thing, Robertson.' The blue eyes were smiling. 'At Jutland you sustained a slight wound. A shell-splinter in the – er— '

'Aye, sir, I did.' A hand moved as if to rub one buttock, but was then needed for opening the door as some members came up the steps. Hugh Everard moved to the side. Robertson came back to him: 'May I ask, sir – did ye hear anything ever of old George Bates?'

'Dead, poor fellow. Years ago, now. He came with me, you know, when I left the Service. Turned out he had a weak heart – Bates, of *all* men. Wouldn't have believed it, would you?'

'That I would not, sir. Why, us lads were the ones he gave weak hearts to!' He shook his head. 'Sorry – very sorry indeed, tae hear . . .' Away to the door again: and now back, as Hugh began to unbutton his coat. Hugh murmured, 'I'd give a great deal to have old Bates brought back to life . . . By the way, I'm lunching here with Admiral Wishart. D'you know if he's in the club yet?'

'I'd say he's not, sir. But ye could take a seat i' the—' His voice tailed off; he was looking puzzled. 'I'd have thought ye'd be a member here, sir. But unless I'm mistaken—'

'Never bothered to join, Robertson. Always plenty of pals here – and I've a club in St James's Street, d'you see.'

Robertson nodded. 'Aye . . . Sir – your nephew, was it, at Jutland in that destroyer? Is he—'

'My nephew Nick? Yes, he's at sea. He left the Navy earlier on – various reasons of his own – but he's back now. They've given him a destroyer, one of the "I"s . . . And would you believe it, his son's at sea?'

'Och, that's grand!'

'As an OD, what's more!'

'*Ordinary Seaman?*' Robertson looked shocked. Hugh nodded,

smiling as if the thought of it pleased him. 'Joined up without telling his father. A very independent young man, d'you see. Brought up in the United States – well, these last years, his school years, you know. Did you hear that my nephew married a White Russian girl in 1919, when he was messing about in the Black Sea? Well – cutting a long story short – she cleared off to the States and collared a millionaire. Took young Paul with her, of course. But when this war started he came over – worked his passage in some liner – and joined up right away. Didn't want to use his father's influence – or mine, he said. I told him, I've not a *shred* of influence, these days!'

'Well, I'll be—'

'What d'you mean, Robertson, you *will* be?' Another tall man: but younger and bulkier, and in uniform with a rear-admiral's broad and narrow stripe on each sleeve. He told the porter, 'You *have* been. Frequently.' He warned Hugh Everard, 'Shouldn't pay attention to anything this chap tells you, Sir Hugh. Most awful line-shooter in the place.' Robertson was smiling, shaking his head sadly as if he'd given up hope for Aubrey Wishart years ago.

Hugh told his host, 'Robertson and I are old shipmates. *Nile,* 1916.'

'Ah. Jutland.' Wishart's eyes ran over the porter's 1914–18 medal ribbons. He had some of his own, and they started with a DSO. Robertson repeated softly, 'Jutland. Aye.' Wishart put a hand on Hugh Everard's elbow. 'Come along in, sir. Sorry I'm a few minutes adrift. Fact, there's something of a – ' he glanced round, and lowered his voice – 'flap on. Looks like the balloon's going up, up north.'

They'd ordered buckling for a first course, and steak-and-kidney pie to follow, with a bottle of claret to help things along. Aubrey Wishart glanced across the table at his guest: then, meeting his eyes, uncharacteristically looked away again. Ostensibly, he was looking for the waiter who served the tables at this end.

Hugh Everard was about old enough to have been Wishart's father. They'd met through Nick, at a shooting weekend up at Mullbergh in Yorkshire, several years ago; and Wishart's friendship with Nick dated from more than twenty years back, when as captain of an E-class submarine he'd taken the young Lieutenant Everard on a slightly hair-raising jaunt through the Dardanelles

14

minefields to Constantinople. It was a solidly-rooted friendship which had survived Nick's years on the beach.

Wishart murmured, 'Turns out it's a tall order you've sent me, Sir Hugh.'

'What, a sea job for a retired admiral? What's tall about it? Where'd an old goat like me be if *not* at sea?'

'Well, sir—'

'It's got you in a dither, I can see *that*.'

Wishart, fiddling with a crust of bread, could feel those blue eyes opposite boring right into his skull. It was the rottenest day imaginable to have chosen for this lunch, and he was wishing he'd followed his first inclination – to telephone the club and leave a message expressing regrets that Rear-Admiral Wishart was unable to leave his office for the present. If it had been anyone but Sir Hugh Everard whom he'd have been letting down, he'd have done that; and conversely, if it had been anyone else he wouldn't have been feeling so much on edge.

Gauntlet and *Intent*: both gone. *Intent*'s 'about-to-engage-with-torpedoes' signal, and then – nothing.

'You see, the problem is—'

'My dear fellow, I know what the problem is. They'll say I'm too old. Falling to bits and probably a bit dotty too. Eh?'

'No, sir, not *quite*—'

'Look here. Let's talk about my little schemes later. I'm far more intrigued by what you said as we were coming in – about the balloon going up, "up north", you said? Norway?'

Shouldn't one have the guts to tell him straight out what's happened?

But as well as cowardice, there was a strong unwillingness to hurt. Hugh and Nick Everard were more like a very closely-in-touch father and son than uncle and nephew. More like very good friends. Each, Wishart knew, had a profound affection and respect for the other. It didn't make this situation any happier.

Hugh Everard saw his host glance round to see who, if anyone, might be in earshot. *Let not thy left hand know . . .* But here in this panelled dining-room with the oil paintings of Nelson and Jellicoe glaring down at them, mightn't it be somewhat over-cautious, let alone rude, to refuse information to Admiral Sir Hugh Everard, KCB, DSO and Bar? Hugh saw – thought he saw – some such thoughts whisking through Aubrey Wishart's mind; then Wishart had nodded, and begun somewhat unhappily, 'You'll know that

15

Winston Churchill's been pressing Chamberlain for a decision to mine the Leads, to stop the Hun sneaking his blockade-runners, and particularly his iron-ore supplies, through Norwegian waters?'

Hugh nodded. 'Heard that months ago. And it won't stop 'em, will it. Not on its own.'

'The idea is to force them out of territorial waters so we can get at them. If they knew they always stood a sporting chance of finding mines inshore—'

'What the devil are the Norwegians *allowing* them in their territorial waters for?' Hugh tapped the table angrily. 'They raised blue murder when we went in and boarded the *Altmark* – in their so-called neutral waters and stuffed with prisoners out of British ships – and they say nothing about letting the Germans treat the same waters like their own private river!'

'I gather they're going to enormous lengths not to offend the Hun, sir. Not to give Hitler an excuse to invade.'

'While that damned fool Chamberlain daren't so much as cough in church for fear of offending anybody!'

'Yes, well—'

'I beg your pardon. Interrupted you. Were you going to say the mining is going ahead, at last?'

'It is. In fact it was authorised for the 5th, three days ago, and then postponed to today. I believe most of the reason for the postponement was to give time for mounting a contingency plan, called R4, which involved putting our own troops into certain key ports – to forestall the Germans if they look like doing the same thing – which they might, as a reaction to our mining operations. Troops have actually been embarked – in the Clyde and at Rosyth; although in fact—' He checked what he was saying. 'No. I must stick to the point. That was the reason, I think, for the postponement. And the PM imposed a condition on this plan R4 – none of the troop-carrying force should be allowed to sail until or unless Germany actually attacked Norway. He's – as you say – very much concerned to be *correct*, in regard to Norwegian neutrality.'

'He's an old woman, Wishart, in regard to anything you like . . . How would he expect to know German intentions in time to sail the troops?'

'Submarine reconnaissance. We've a number of extra patrols out, in the Skagerrak and Kattegat. And – talking of submarines – Max Horton's quite sure they're on the point of invading.'

Max Horton was the Vice-Admiral commanding the Submarine Service.

'Denmark as well as Norway. He's convinced it's imminent.'

'Their Lordships disagree?'

'It's a matter of how one evaluates and interprets the Intelligence reports. You've got to allow the Admiralty the fact there've been literally months of false rumours: they've been conditioned against crying wolf. Personally I'll admit to bias, because as a submariner and an admirer of Max I'd tend to see it his way. And I don't have the entire picture; I'm without any real base there now, just a sort of temporary hanger-on putting an ear to whatever's audible.'

Hugh Everard looked surprised. 'I thought you were setting up a new section to do with convoy planning and Board of Trade liaison, Wishart?'

'That was the case when Nick wrote to you, sir. But there's been a change. We're all a bit at sixes and sevens, just now. And my own days with dry feet are strictly numbered.'

'Sea job?'

'Mediterranean, is all I know. Andrew Cunningham's asked for me, apparently.'

'Has he indeed.' Hugh sat back smiling. 'I'd say that sounded *very* promising.'

'Can't think of a man I'd sooner work for.' Wishart watched his guest helping himself to buckling. 'And Italy'll be joining in against us shortly, soon as Mussolini feels convinced the Germans have got us licked.' The dish came round to his side; he told the waiter, 'We'll have some thin brown bread and butter with this, please.'

'Of course, sir.'

Wishart said quietly, 'It does mean I'm less well placed than I'd like to be from the point of view of assisting *you*, sir.'

'Obviously. I'm sorry – if I'd known—'

'No, I'd like to help . . . But the snags are the same irrespective of what *my* job is, of course. Frankly—'

'My age.'

'Well, yes. Even for convoy commodores—'

'I did hear that Eric Fullerton has got himself back to sea?'

'But – with respect, he's not sixty-nine years old.'

'Not *quite*. But that, Wishart, is simply a statistic. What they should ask themselves is *can this fellow do the job*? And I'm as fit as many other men ten or fifteen years my junior. I *am*, damn it!' He pushed the bread-and-butter plate across the table. 'Eric, of course, had Dorothy pulling strings for him.'

'Oh now, that's hardly—'

Wishart checked whatever protest he'd been about to make. Dorothy Fullerton was Jackie Fisher's daughter. He'd forgotten, for a moment, the story of Hugh Everard's treatment at Fisher's hands, treatment that had pushed him out of the Navy a few years before the 1914 war. There was a follow-up story too – again, retailed by Nick – of history repeating itself in 1919. Not Fisher's doing, this second time; Fisher by then had been out of it, an old sick man with only a year to live. But – Wishart wondered, studying his guest with interest as well as sympathy – was Hugh Everard a disappointed, *bitter* man? It had never occurred to him before: but wouldn't it be surprising in all the circumstances if he were not?

There was no doubt he'd had a rotten deal. *Two* rotten deals. And no doubt that his nephew, Nick, was now the centrepiece of his life. Knowing this, the prospect of telling him now about what must have been a murderously one-sided action in that North Sea gale only a few hours ago . . . Wishart admitted to himself, *All right: I* am *a coward . . .*

The mind shied away, turned to another difficult but less positively hateful problem. This notion Sir Hugh had of getting to sea as a commodore of Atlantic convoys. Quite a number of retired admirals were being recalled in that capacity, certainly; and as likely as not Hugh Everard *was* as fit as many younger ones. But the line had to be drawn somewhere, and an even worse snag was that he'd been ashore since 1920.

'Something the matter, Wishart?'

'I was – thinking around this problem—'

'Some difficulty you haven't mentioned?'

Only a little thing like your nephew being dead . . .

'None that wouldn't have occurred to you, sir?'

'I've no ties, you know. No old woman to worry about me!'

Hugh Everard had been married once: before the first war, so Nick had told him. He'd been divorced not long after he'd left the Service. Wishart had expressed surprise: all those years, and all the women who surely would have been only too ready to fall for the good-looking, distinguished admiral with the famous name? Nick had said something about Hugh having had his reasons: there was an impression of there being one woman, one particular and un-

18

nameable woman, with whom his uncle had been in love for years and who wouldn't or couldn't marry him.

Someone else's wife?

Sir Hugh put down his knife and fork. '*Very* good.' He looked at Wishart. 'You're thinking of the length of time I've been retired, I suppose.'

'It's – a factor that's bound to be considered.'

'I retired four years ago, Wishart.'

'*Four?*'

'From an active directorship of Vickers. I have never been out of touch with naval matters. On occasion I have even been to sea. I dare say I could tell *you* a thing or two about modern warship design, equipment, weaponry, what-have-you.'

Wishart nodded. 'It's a good point. But it might be argued that sea-going experience, *command* experience—'

'Wishart.' Hugh Everard beckoned to him to lean closer across the table. He whispered, 'As they say in the vernacular – *balls* . . .' Wishart sat back, chuckling. Sir Hugh asked him, 'Anyway, is command at sea so very much changed from my day? If so, in what respect?'

'Well, we now have Asdics—'

'Which virtually any retired officer would have to learn something about. They sent Nick on some course, didn't they?' Wishart nodded. 'What else is new?'

Quite a lot was new. But it was all detail. The basics were the same. Wishart surrendered the point.

'When one thinks about it – darned little.'

'Exactly!' A finger pointed at him. 'And look here. Even if the technical changes were far greater than they are, it's quite irrelevant. A convoy commodore's job is to organise his convoy as it were domestically, internally. It doesn't overlap with the job of the escort commander – that's *another* kettle of fish. The commodore has to jolly his merchant skippers along, get 'em to understand the scheme of things and then play to the rules. More like being chairman of a company – in a slightly unsteady boardroom, eh?' He pointed at his own chest. 'I have all the qualifications and experience that's needed. What's more, Wishart my boy, I shall damn well *do* it!'

'Good. And to whatever extent I can help I'll certainly—'

'No, no.' Sir Hugh swivelled round to contemplate the steak-and-kidney. 'Thank you, but I've plagued you enough. Only got on to you because of what Nick told me, that it was in your new department. Since it's not your part-of-ship at all, however – ' he was helping himself to the pie, and sniffing like a Bisto Kid at the aroma which he'd released from its crust – 'since you're making a move that's entirely in the right direction and which I'm truly delighted for your sake to hear about – ' he put the tools down in the pie-dish – 'no, I'm grateful for what you've already tried to do, but I don't want you going to any further trouble.'

'It's absolutely *no*—'

'I'm considering my own interests, really. It's results I'm after, and I'll attack on a different front now – when I've thought it out . . . This does smell good!'

'Let's hope it is. Thank you, waiter.' He reached for the wine bottle. 'Now then . . .'

When the vegetables had been dispensed and the waiter had finally moved off, Hugh came back to the subject of Norway.

'You said "the balloon's gone up." And "there's a flap on." Mind telling me what it's about?'

'Well . . .' The essential thing was, not to know about this morning's action. There was no reason why one *should* have known. And Sir Hugh would hear soon enough; to keep one's mouth shut now wouldn't be doing him any harm . . . 'Well, for some days – couple of weeks, I suppose – rumours of a German plan to invade Norway and Denmark have been getting stronger and louder. Personally I – well, there is *no* doubt that they've been contemplating it off and on. For instance, they were right on the point of launching an invasion when we and the French were making noises about going through Norway to help the Finns. Then when the Finns chucked their hands in, of course, we shelved our plans and we *think* Hitler did something similar with his.'

Russia had attacked Finland, without declaration of war, on 30 November – about four months ago. They'd expected to make a quick and easy meal of it, but the Finns fought back magnificently; in fact they fought the Soviets to a standstill. Then in February, just two months ago, a new Soviet offensive opened – better-trained troops in enormous strength, and massed artillery; and while Britain and France were still making plans to send men and supplies through Narvik and over the mountain railway to Lulea on the Gulf of Bothnia, Finland capitulated, on 12 March.

'Vian's rescue of our chaps from the *Altmark* may have been another factor. They've certainly used it as an excuse – violation of

20

neutrality by *us*, for heaven's sake . . . Anyway, we've been getting reports of ships assembling and embarking troops, and yesterday we were hearing of fleet movements northwards out of Kiel and Wilhelmshaven. So finally the Admiralty's taking notice.' He glanced round again: nobody else was listening to him. He told Sir Hugh, 'The Home Fleet's sailed. Cleared Scapa yesterday evening.'

'Deploying where? On the Norwegian coast?'

'Well – no. The C-in-C seems to be staying out in the deep field. I'd – ' he nodded – 'as you suggest, or assumed – *I'd* be more inclined to put the whole lot in the slips.'

'But that could be a terrible mistake, Wishart. Even if Horton's right and the Hun's going into Norway, he might well try to kill two birds with one stone – invade behind an offshore covering force which would then pass on out to the North Atlantic. Eh?'

A break-out by German heavy ships was the danger which had kept Jellicoe's Grand Fleet stuck in the wastes of Scapa Flow twenty-something years ago. And it was the same thing now. The sea-lanes to and from North America and the tanker routes from the Gulf, supply and trooping convoys to the Middle and Far East and Australia – the whole strategy of Britain's war depended on keeping the Germans boxed in and those lifelines intact.

'Of course, you're absolutely right, sir. And for Sir Charles Forbes it's a ticklish dilemma, I imagine. But it seems to me that if the Germans get the Norwegian ports our job in maintaining any sort of blockade is going to be twice as difficult. In fact that's probably what they *want* that coast for – as well as safeguarding their iron-ore supplies, which is just about as vital, if not more so . . . But Trondheim, for instance, as a base – even just for U-boats?' He spread his hands. 'My bet is, it's going to happen. While we're covering the Iceland-Faroes Gap and our War Cabinet's murmuring "After you, Adolf . . ."?'

'If I were in Forbes's shoes, *I'd* stay well out to sea. I'd send cruisers and destroyers inshore, and keep the battlefleet's options open until the last minute . . . But – in general terms, what we need is Winston at the top. I mean, as Prime Minister.'

Wishart smiled into his glass. He murmured, glancing up, 'That move wouldn't be at all unwelcome in the Admiralty.'

'Ah.' Hugh Everard nodded. 'Interfering again, is he?'

By 'again', he was harking back to Churchill's stint as First Lord of the Admiralty in 1914 and '15. He was back in the same job now that he'd had then as a young man – a *very* young man who'd driven Jackie Fisher, a very *old* man, half out of his mind and into snarling retirement and senility.

Wishart said quietly, 'He wants to row every boat himself. Despite a tendency to catch crabs.' He shrugged. 'Talking out of turn, of course. And I agree, he'd make a terrific PM. A bit of hard drive at the top is just what the country needs: instead of a wet flannel. And Winston might not have time, then, to play sailors . . .' Wishart snapped his fingers, as a thought struck him: 'Sir Hugh – about this ambition of yours to get to sea—'

'Winston?'

'If you had him on your side – and you probably would have, because what he'll go for every time is positive action—'

'Yes. Yes, indeed.' Hugh Everard frowned, considering the idea. Wishart put in, 'I'm sure he'd see you, if—'

'I dare say. I dare say . . . But – you'll think I'm daft, I suppose, but – frankly, I don't like to ask a favour of a politician. They're not safe hands to let oneself get into. Even if one might be prepared to believe that Winston's a cut above the others . . .' He shook his head. 'I had some experience of politicians, at one time.'

'In 1919?'

'Oh.' The blue eyes sharpened. 'Did Nick tell you about it?' Wishart nodded. 'In confidence, of course.'

'Even in confidence, I'm – surprised.'

'Nick and I are close friends, Sir Hugh.'

Are: or *were*?

'I'll give your suggestion a bit of thought, Wishart.' He poked with his fork. 'This pie's as good as I've ever had here.'

'You've had a good few meals in the place, I imagine, over the years?'

'For a non-member, probably too many.' He watched Wishart topping up their glasses. 'I've belonged to Boodle's since the year dot, you see. Nick uses it too. And like me, when he left the Navy he didn't feel inclined to – so to speak, to hang around the fringes.'

'I can understand that.' Nick had said much the same thing, he remembered. He thought of something else that would help to keep the conversation on safe ground . . . 'I meant to ask you – Nick's son, your great-nephew – any news of him?'

'Yes. He's away at sea now, but he came to visit me a couple of months ago. You know he joined on the lower deck?' Wishart nodded. Sir Hugh went on, 'He was in Portsmouth barracks then.

22

Pleasant lad. Plenty of fire in him – very like his father, you see. Just as damn pig-headed, anyway. And there's a Russian streak in this one, too! *What* a mixture!'

'A Russian Everard in square rig. Ye Gods!'

They both laughed. Wishart added, 'Nick told me he was trying to push him into becoming a CW candidate, and not getting much response.'

'CW' stood for Commissions and Warrants. A CW candidate was a sailor marked as potentially suitable for commissioned rank after a probationary period at sea on the lower deck. But you couldn't be forced to accept a candidacy if you didn't want it. Hugh Everard muttered, 'Nick would be wiser to let the boy reach his own decisions. He isn't the sort to be pushed.'

Wishart was glancing back over his shoulder, trying to contact their waiter. The boy sounded like a chip off the old block, he thought.

'What about the other one, the baby half-brother who went to Dartmouth?'

'You mean Jack.'

Nick's stepmother, Sarah, had surprised everyone by producing a son in 1919. She'd been only thirty-one then, but Nick's father, Sir John, had been a lot older; they'd been married since 1912 and if they'd ever thought of starting a new family there had certainly been no such expectations in more recent years. And it had not been a happy marriage. But Nick, returning from his Black Sea adventures in 1920 and bringing with him his Russian countess wife, was introduced to a year-old half-brother – who at an early age had opted for a career in the Royal Navy and was now just twenty-one and a lieutenant.

Hugh had joined his host in the attempt to catch the waiter. What they were after was a Stilton which had passed by earlier on. Hugh said, 'Jack's done very well, from all I hear. And keen as mustard, apparently. But – ' he shook his head – 'even with twenty-five years dividing 'em, you wouldn't imagine he could be Nick's brother. Or half-brother either.'

'What's he doing now?'

'C-class cruiser, refitting up north. He wants to specialise as a navigator, when he's eligible for the Dryad course.' Hugh had spotted the Stilton, and it was coming this way; some people at a table beyond this one were obviously waiting for it. He told Wishart, 'Coming up on your quarter. *Now.*'

'Waiter – we'll have some of that, please.'

'Well done!'

'Good scouting did it.' He gestured to the waiter, who pushed his trolley up beside Sir Hugh. Presently, as the trolley squeaked away on its interrupted journey, he asked, 'The OD – Nick's son—'

'Paul.'

'Yes, Paul. You said he's at sea now?'

'First ship. *Hoste*.'

'*Is* he, by golly!'

Hoste was one of the 2nd Destroyer Flotilla, who were at this moment somewhere up near Narvik with *Renown*. And with the 2nd Flotilla on this operation were several other destroyers, including *Intent*.

Sir Hugh, with an eyebrow cocked, was waiting for an explanation of that 'By golly'.

Wishart told him, cautiously, about the covering force for the minelaying operations, Admiral Whitworth with the battlecruiser and destroyers screening her. Then he stumbled to a halt: faced with the problem of mentioning or not mentioning Nick's ship. And suddenly the dam burst in his mind: it was impossible to sit here and *not* tell him . . .

'There's something – a subject – which I've been trying to avoid, sir. Largely because we've had only disjointed signals and no confirmation – we don't know for sure at all, but – well, this morning, roughly off Trondheim—'

'*Hoste?*'

He shook his head. '*Intent*.'

The older man's flinch was so quickly controlled that if you hadn't been face to face with him and only three feet away you might not have noticed it.

Wishart told him quietly, '*Intent* and other destroyers were with the 2nd Flotilla for this operation. The other "I"s were doing the minelaying, but *Intent*'s the only one of them not fitted for it, you know.'

'I didn't.'

'*Gauntlet* had to turn back – day before yesterday – to look for a man lost overboard. Hopeless in that weather, but—' He checked that. The hopelessness of survival in that kind of sea was obvious and hardly a point to dwell on, in the circumstances. 'Nick was detached to go back and locate *Gauntlet*. Mainly I suppose because of the stream of reports about German units sailing or about to sail. This morning just after eight *Gauntlet* sent an enemy report – investigating unidentified ship. Then a sighting report, two Hun destroyers, and finally it became one *Hipper*-class cruiser and "engaging with torpedoes". Some little while after that *Intent* signalled – this was the first we'd heard from her – "Am in company with *Gauntlet*, about to engage enemy cruiser with torpedoes, *Gauntlet* damaged in earlier attack." Since then – well, nothing. And no reply to signals addressed to *Intent* and/or *Gauntlet*.' Wishart finished, 'It's gale-force from the north-west and conditions are pretty awful.' He paused, and looked into that blue, unblinking stare. 'I'm – so *dreadfully*—'

One of the hands moved, stopping the offer of sympathy. And the waiter had paused beside them with the trolley, on his way back across the room.

'Touch more of the Stilton while I'm this way with it, sir?'

Hugh shook his head. Wishart cleared his throat: 'No, thank you.'

The waiter began to move the trolley on; Sir Hugh told him, 'That contraption could do with a spot of oil.'

In the ante-room, drinking coffee, Hugh asked him, 'What's being done?'

'Whitworth's turned south with *Renown*, hoping to intercept the cruiser – *Hipper*, whatever the damn thing is – and the C-in-C has detached *Repulse* with *Penelope* and some destroyers.'

'Where's Forbes now?'

'North-east of the Shetlands. He's left now with *Rodney*, *Valiant* and *Sheffield*, plus destroyers. But Admiralty has now ordered the cruisers out too – which means disembarking their troops first.'

Sir Hugh stared at him.

'Disembarking them?'

Wishart nodded. 'They'd been embarked for this plan I was telling you about – R4. The idea was to be on the top line for moving troops into the main Norwegian ports once the Hun showed his intention of invading. Now, R4 seems to have gone by the board. The First Cruiser Squadron's being sailed from Rosyth as soon as the pongoes are all ashore, and *Aurora* and her destroyers from the Clyde. *Aurora* was going to escort the transports that we've had sitting there full of troops.'

'So if the Hun *is* invading, we're giving him a free hand once he gets ashore?'

'I suppose the object is to *stop* him getting ashore.'

'And d'you think we'll manage that?'

'Not if we stay out in the middle of the Norwegian Sea – no, I do not. . . . But as I did say, I'm not as well-informed as—'

'Sounds like the beginnings of a thorough-going mess-up, doesn't it.'

He said no to the offer of a glass of port. And since they'd left the dining-room he hadn't mentioned *Intent* or Nick. He sighed now, blinking, like a man wishing he could escape from his own thoughts.

'Well. Splendid luncheon, Wishart. Most enjoyable.'

'Hardly that, sir, I'm afraid.'

'I'd better let you get back to work now, though. But – if by any chance you did hear anything—'

'I'll telephone. You'll be at home this evening?'

'Later on, I shall be. I've a thing or two to see to before I get back on the train. I may even be in the Admiralty myself, by and by. Twist an arm or two about a job.'

'I wish you success, sir.'

'But they may not give me any news, d'you see. And I can't prompt 'em, because then I'd be letting 'em know you'd blown the gaff. So—'

'You could call me. Here.' Wishart found a card and scribbled a number on the back of it. 'This is my extension – temporarily. I'll try to wheedle any news there is out of Max Horton, if I can get in to see him. He gets shown everything, of course.'

'You've been very kind. I appreciate it.'

'If there's anything I can do at any time—'

'Thank you.' Hugh stood up. Looking round the room, taking long, slow breaths; he seemed to be searching for faces that he might have recognised. And to have drawn a blank: he turned to Aubrey Wishart.

'Nick will be all right, you know.'

The calm, relaxed tone of voice made the assurance almost convincing. But Wishart had a mental picture suddenly of that wilderness of sea and the gale's howl, the ice-grey emptiness: in his mind it *stayed* empty, a wild and bleakly inimical seascape with only the screeching gale-driven gulls as proof that any form of life existed there.

CHAPTER 3

His Majesty's destroyer *Hoste*, 1,490 tons displacement and 34,700 shaft horsepower, was being tossed around like a toy in a bathtub. And Paul Everard, huddled in stiff, ill-fitting oilskins in the lee of 'B' gun, was enjoying every minute of it.

It was the contrast. The fact that he was feeling well, superlatively well, when for the last three days he'd felt that sudden death would have been a mercy.

He'd felt so ill, so locked in sickness that nothing in life, past, present or future, had been anything but nauseating to think about. Taunts and jokes from his messmates and from the others of this gun's crew – well, five out of the six others, because Baldy Percival had been just as sick – had, after a while, become easy to put up with. Just noises in the background, merging into the rattling, thumping, crashing of the ship, pounding of machinery, wind and sea noise. *Try a lump o' pork-fat on a lanyard, Yank – swaller it then 'aul it up again!* You could oblige them with a smile before you grabbed for the bucket: buckets being infinitely safer in this weather than getting anywhere near the ship's side. But what was worse than the gibes was the inner depression, the hopelessness engendered in one's own thoughts and memories. He'd even begun to attach importance to his mother's contemptuous disparagement of his plan to come to England and join up . . . 'Paul, honey, you're no dull-witted sailorman! You're civilised, you're smart, you're going to be *rich* one day!'

He'd told her – fond of her, devoted to her really, but aware that they'd never see eye to eye in certain major areas – 'I'm an Everard.'

'The hell you are. And *if* you are – just a lick of Everard, and that's all it could amount to – do yourself a favour and forget it! Be a Dherjhorakov! Be even a *Scott*, for Christ's sake!'

27

Dherjhorakov had been her family name. Grafinya Ilyana Dherjhorakova. Grafinya meaning countess. She'd had a brother Pavel who'd been murdered by the Bolsheviks during their escape, and one of the earlier battles she and Paul's father had had – this was one of her lines of reminiscence, how she and her first husband had fought all the time – had been whether to christen their son Pavel or Paul, which was the name's English equivalent.

Scott was the man she was married to now. He had a machine-tool business and the war wasn't doing him any harm at all.

His father must have won that row about the name. Paul wondered whether he'd ever won another. He'd met his father briefly in London after he'd first arrived from the States, and then at Christmas at Mullbergh, the family place in Yorkshire; before this, the last time they'd seen each other had been in 1930 when Paul had been just a child. Ilyana had effectively prevented correspondence during the intervening years. Paul's impression – well, one of his impressions – of Sir Nicholas Everard, Bart., was that he was as different from the woman he'd once been married to as one animal species is different from another. It was impossible to imagine him and Ilyana storming at each other. In the face of her outbursts – frenzies, furies or raptures, and all totally unpredictable – wouldn't he just have clammed up, walked away?

If Ilyana's stories were half true, no, he wouldn't. Maybe he'd changed? Or he'd been in an unnatural state of mind: meeting his son, and knowing she'd have told him about the past? Paul wanted to do her justice. Ilyana wasn't anything like the driven snow and the things she said to people weren't always God's literal truth, but in a situation like this, talking to her own son about his father when she'd known they'd be meeting sooner or later, would she have sent up that much smoke without fire?

Listening to old Sir Hugh – Paul had visited him at his house in Hampshire – you wouldn't think there were any weak spots anywhere, on Nick Everard. But nice as he was, the old boy was also strongly prejudiced; he'd gone to considerable lengths, for instance, not to mention Paul's mother's name.

Stay out of it. Yesterday and for two days and nights before that it felt like the weight of the world sitting on your shoulders, and no way out from under. It doesn't have to be like that, though, it *isn't*, it's not your lock to pick. Let it *stay* locked. And render unto Caesar: accept that Commander Sir Nicholas Everard is a hell of a fine sailor and seems a more than ordinarily nice guy. So all right, she wants to project a different view of him, *let* her.

Dozing . . .

Jammed in as close as possible behind the gunshield; not much space between the shield and the gun itself, and several other bodies in there too. At least they all wedged each other against the fiendish pitching and rolling, upward staggers and downhill rushes. Jolting, battering: rather like being in a motor-car that ran into a brick wall several times a minute and, in between the crashes, bounced up and down on solid tyres.

The saying was that the Navy used to have wooden ships and iron men, and now had iron ships and wooden men. But nothing made of wood and getting *this* treatment would have lasted long.

'Oy, you, Yank!'

Waking: aware at once of the enormous pleasure there was in simply feeling *well* . . .

'How's that?'

'Got yer 'ead down, 'ave you, Yank?'

Bow-down, and the vibration of racing screws shaking the whole ship, humming in her steel. Ventilator fans roaring. Solid water smashed against the other side of the gunshield, slashed at the bridge's forefront and the wheelhouse above their heads. He yelled as *Hoste*'s bow began its upward swing, 'Want something?'

It was Vic Blenkinsop, the sightsetter, who'd shouted at him. Vic was sitting under the gun's breech-end with his knees drawn up as far as possible into cover, and as usual he had a length of spun-yarn as a belt around his oilskins. He also wore a red woollen cap under his tin hat, and the earphones of the telephone headset were pushed inside it with the helmet jammed down on top of everything and the curved headpiece hanging down in front, looping under Vic's bright red nose. With that narrow, bony face he looked like Little Red Riding Hood's grandmother.

'What's up, Vic?'

'Char's up, that's what. In the galley. An' you're the lad to nip aft an' fuckin' fetch it.'

'Okay.'

He might have argued, just for the sake of an argument, but he was feeling too damn *good*. Not just healthy, but exuberantly so. His spirits matched – it occurred to him as he struggled out of the heap of men and out behind the gun – matched the ship's dance, the gale's roar. He felt like doing a fandango of his own: or bursting into song . . .

Steady, boy. That's pure Dherjhorakov!

The fanny, tin receptacle for tea: or rather, for the dark brown paint-remover which destroyer sailors referred to as tea: Lofty McElroy was passing the fanny out to him. Tea from the galley was a new idea, some kind of dummy-run for something called Action Messing.

'Thanks, Lofty.'

'Don't go over the side, lad, ay?'

'Lofty, I am profoundly moved – ' he bowed, with a hand grasping the edge of the gunshield – 'by your consideration for the safety of my person. Had I not heard this with my own ears—'

Ducking sideways to avoid flying sea, he'd staggered and fetched up hard against the loading-tray. If his ribs hadn't been padded by two sweaters and the oilskin, they'd have suffered worse. McElroy yelled, 'All I'm considerin', Yank, is the safety of my fuckin' tea. Get a wriggle on, willya?'

Wind and sea were on *Hoste*'s starboard side. Checking on this before choosing his route to the galley, Paul looked out across a heaving grey-white foreground, saw other destroyers strung out in line abreast, battling through the storm. Two, he'd seen then: and far apart, so there'd be one between them and temporarily hidden in a trough. Eight altogether, he thought; there'd been nine before, and now the battlecruiser, *Renown*, had left them and taken one destroyer with her. Nobody knew much about what was going on; and during the last few days he'd been too ill to care. All he knew was they'd come a long way north, so far north that there was hardly any period of darkness. In another month, in these latitudes, there'd be none at all. Land of the midnight sun . . . Well, presumably there *was* land not far off, but if it had any mid*day* sun, even, it was hogging it all to itself. He went down the port ladder, the leeward side, to the foc'sl deck, and turned aft – keeping close in against the wet grey-painted steel of the bridge superstructure – past the screen door and down the ladder at the foc'sl break. The whaler was creaking in its davits, straining against its gripes as the ship rolled over, over – almost *right* over – while he held on tight to the bottom of the ladder. If you went over the side, in this stuff, even if someone saw you go they'd never find you: you'd be *gone*, finished. Now she was rolling back: he reached the galley door, pulled the one retaining clip off it, climbed in over the foot-high sill and slammed and clipped the door behind him.

'Gawd, it's the stars and fuckin' stripes. An' better late than never. "B" gun, is it?' Paul nodded. Perry, the duty cook, was too scrawny to be much of an advertisement for his own art. Crew-cut, and in a boiler-suit draped in loose folds around him but sleeveless, sleeves torn off so that his long arms, stringy-muscled, extruded like white tentacles. A cigarette-stub was stuck to his lower lip. *Hoste* carried two ordinary cooks and one leading cook, and Perry was about as ordinary, Paul thought, as a cook could get to be. Although – when you saw him here in the galley – you had to admire anyone who could cook anything in this cramped black hole: even if the ship stood *still* occasionally . . .

One of the arms came out, clawing for the fanny.

'Right then.'

Two other men were in here, over on the other side. Green, a telegraphist, and a man called Cringle who was either a bridge messenger or a lookout.

'Did say "B" gun, didya?'

'Absolutely, old pip.'

It was intended to sound ultra-British and thus, from someone they all called 'Yank', amusing. But it seemed to annoy Cringle.

'Tryin' to sound like 'is dad.'

'Eh?' The cook, with Paul's tea-fanny under the urn's tap and brown liquid gushing into it in a steamy jet, looked over his shoulder at the messenger. 'Whose Dad?'

Cringle jerked his head. 'The Yank. 'Is guv'nor's skipper of the *Intent*. The one Sparks 'ere says 'as bought it.'

Silence. Perry looking at *him* now as he turned the tap off. Cringle's words sinking in slowly.

'Now wait a minute.' Questions were forming on top of each other, out of complete surprise and – already – an unwillingness to believe . . . How did anyone know about his father? And *Intent* – was she around, even right here with them, one of the ships he'd been looking at? But then – *no* . . . That expression 'bought it'; it was current slang, over this side, for *busted, shot*. Disliking Cringle, he looked at Green: all telegraphists were called 'Sparks'.

'What *is* this? D'you mind?'

Green shrugged, stared blankly at the cook. Perry looked at Cringle, who told him, 'I 'eard 'em 'aving a natter on the bridge. *Intent* got sent off – yesterday, was it?' Green nodded, staring at Paul now. Cringle went on, 'On account that other – *Gauntlet*, ain't she – 'adn't showed up still. Forenoon today there's this palaver goin' on, skipper an' Jimmy, an' Jimmy asks, "What about this Everard lad what's the son of *Intent*'s captain, the OD we got aboard 'ere?" – sort o' thing. Skipper rubs 'is nut a while, then 'e says no, 'e says, don't tell 'im, *Intent* might still turn up, no use warmin' the fuckin' bell, 'e says. Aye aye, says Jimmy. Well, later on I gets talkin' with Subby Peters, an' 'e says yeah, you're right, 'e says, but best keep your fuckin' mouth shut, see.'

Paul took the fanny, hot and heavy now, from Cook Perry. He rested it on his own end of the stove, holding on to it so it wouldn't slide or slop: and one hand on the door, so *he* wouldn't slide. He looked at Cringle as the ship dipped, jolting, stubbing her bow into the sea, shaking as if she was trying to bore her way into something solid.

Did that bastard know what he'd just told him?

'That's what you're doing, Cringle, is it? Keeping your fucking mouth shut? D'you do much of that, with your mouth? Maybe you've nothing *else* to do it with?'

Hate and rage were sudden, overwhelming. A cold rage. Not reasoning: just *there*.

'I'll shut *your* mouth, my little Yanky-lad!'

He was trying to push past Perry. Five or six years older than Paul, a head taller and a lot heavier. It made no odds at all. Everything contributed: the whole damn set-up, and the fact there was nothing he could do about it. What he felt – or did not feel – about his father was a background to the questions that weren't answered, only *raised*: like was any of this story true, had *Intent* been here and where was she now, what if anything had happened while he'd been spewing and feeling sorry for himself. You were born into a situation that wrapped itself around you and you couldn't influence or change: then other things developed out of it and you were still helpless, shut off, impotent.

He could do something about this bastard Cringle, though. That thick, soft-looking throat: hit there first, then—

The cook planted a hand on Cringle's chest and pushed him back. The cook, like Paul, was a smaller man than Cringle; those stringy muscles must have had steel wire in them. One-handed, he'd not only stopped the larger man but actually moved him backwards – as if he'd had castors under him.

Paul said, 'I'd be obliged if you'd let him pass.'

'Don't give a tinker's fart about obligin' you, old son.' Perry hadn't looked round. He told Cringle in just as pleasant a tone of voice, 'Bugger off. Out me galley, pronto. An' when it's me on watch, *stay* out.'

'Never mind your galley, chum, I'll shove you in your fuckin' *oven*!'

Cringle, half-turning his head, for some reason assumed that the telegraphist, Green, was joining the opposition. He swept an arm back, flinging Green against the starboard-side door as the ship rolled that way, helping him . . . But she was holding that steep list. Altering course? Cringle had an upward slope to climb if he was going to reach the cook; he grasped the rail that ran along the front edge of the stove and began to haul himself along it. Paul was clinging to the other door, behind him, to save himself from being thrown downhill, and only Cook Perry, in the middle, was keeping an easy balance.

He'd also picked up a knife. It had a blade about nine inches long. Without looking down at it he was stropping it expertly on the horny palm of his left hand. He asked Cringle, 'Comin', then?'

Silence, except for the racket all around them. The ship was still heeling hard to starboard. Probably had port wheel on, making a biggish change of course. Cringle was staring at the knife, immobile. Perry put it down.

'Your mates 'll be wanting their char, won't they.' He looked round at Paul. '*You* better scram, too.' He waved his arms, like shoo-ing chickens. 'G'arn – sod off, the lot of you!'

'Hey – just a minute . . .'

'Now *look*, I said—'

'This stuff about *Intent*,' Paul asked Green, 'is it true?'

'Didn't you know?'

'For Christ's sake, how *could* I?'

One grey destroyer shape was very much like another. Particularly the G, H, and I classes, which were all practically identical. In any case, he hadn't been doing much looking.

'*Gauntlet* lost some sod overboard and turned back for 'im. Two or three days back. Then they reckon she shouldn't be on her tod like, so *Intent* goes to round 'er up. The pair of 'em fetch up against bloody *Scharnhorst* or something, they gets one message out, and *wallop*.'

Paul stared at him. Why would anyone make up such a story? 'This true?'

It couldn't be. He *knew* it couldn't.

'It's the buzz.' Green shrugged. 'Well, more 'n a buzz, really. I don't see ciphers – we take 'em down coded like. But – you 'ear this an' that, and—'

He stopped talking: the cook, with his boiler-suited back to Paul, must have been making faces at him. Green looked at Paul now as if he was realising for the first time what it added up to.

'Sorry, Yank. If – ' he jerked his head backwards – 'if bloody Cringle 'adn't—'

'It's all right.'

Perry turned round; both of them were looking at Paul with a mildly sympathetic interest. Paul couldn't remember exactly how the row with Cringle had started. He'd wanted to kill him, he knew *that* . . . He wasn't sure some of it hadn't been his own fault.

'I don't know why I lost my temper.'

Perry nodded. 'You want to watch that, lad.'

The Dherjhorakov factor? He'd found it surfacing before, once or twice. And Perry was right, it did need watching.

Green said, 'Buzzes don't always get it right. Shouldn't let it bother you too much.'

'No, I won't.' He picked up the fanny. 'Thanks, Cookie.'

'Oy!'

'What?'

The cook told him, 'We've altered course. Best use the other door.'

'Taken your time, Yank, ain't you?'

'Slight problem in the galley.'

'Yeah?'

'Nothing much.' He stooped, pushing the fanny in towards McElroy. 'It's still hot, anyway.'

'I should fuckin' 'ope so!'

He sat down on the deck with his own mug of the so-called tea. At least it warmed you. He had never, he realised, given much thought to being sunk or blown up. One should, he supposed; there was obviously a reasonable chance of it happening, and if you thought about it in advance it wouldn't take you so much by surprise. You might even subconsciously have some ideas mapped out so that when or if it did happen you'd react without panic or too much dithering . . . He – Paul – happened to be an unusually strong swimmer; at prep – Taft, in Connecticut, where the Scott home was – he'd captained the school team; and swimming hadn't done him

34

any harm, he thought, in Amherst's acceptance of him after he'd graduated from Taft. As it turned out, he spent less than half a year at Amherst, which had been his stepfather Gerry Scott's old Ivy League Alma Mater. Scott had been very decent, despite that, about Paul's insistence on dropping out and coming to England, to England's war. His attitude had been one of regret but resignation: a marked and welcome contrast to Ilyana's hysterical opposition. But it hadn't been a choice, for Paul. And less impulse, he thought now, than instinct, a kind of personal compulsion.

Would a German ship stop to pick up survivors?

You heard and read conflicting stories. He thought it would most probably depend on the character of the individual commander, and perhaps also on the circumstances, whether he'd feel safe in stopping to pick them up.

He remembered an incident he'd read about, where three British cruisers were torpedoed in the English Channel, in the last war, by one U-boat. It had got the second and the third when they were lying stopped, saving men from the first. It had always seemed to Paul quite extraordinary – to treat human beings like bugs, things of no importance, flies to be swatted. . . . And if that was the way they were fighting *this* war . . .

Face it. You no longer have a father.

Running on from that, another thought: *Ordinary Seaman Sir Paul Everard, Bart.?*

The idea was laughable, but he couldn't raise even an inward smile at it. Why, though, should the prospect be so – *disturbing*, to one who'd had no contact with his father in nearly ten years and perhaps wouldn't have been about to have any now if this war hadn't started?

Jammed just inside the edge of the gunshield, half in cover as *Hoste* flung herself about and sea lashed continuously against the shield, ringing hard like hail, he thought about the two days he'd spent at Mullbergh at Christmas. His father, standing more or less eye-to-eye with him – Paul had been surprised to find he wasn't taller, having always thought of him as a big man – saying, 'For what it's worth, this place'll be yours one day. If it still belongs to us at all.'

'Must be quite a – quite expensive to maintain?'

'It is. Even *half* maintaining it as we are now. Costs always tend to rise faster than revenue, you know. But at least the estate's in sound order now, the farms show profits and their tenants have roofs over their heads that don't leak. To that extent we've stopped the rot – given ourselves a bit more time. That's what's kept me busy since I left the Service – making the old place earn its keep.'

'Didn't your – my grandfather, I mean – didn't *he*, in his time?'

'No.' Nick kicked a log in towards the flames. 'No, he did not. He put nothing back, ever, just took out all he could. To no good purpose whatsoever. Well, he ran our local pack of hounds, and paid for it all out of his own pocket.' Nick shrugged. 'Some people would call *that* a good purpose. I don't know.'

Ilyana had told Paul that Sir John had been a sweet old guy. He himself barely remembered his grandfather at all.

'I can't give you much of the family history in just two days. What's more, they'd be better spent enjoying ourselves. And for you, getting the feel of the place. Don't suppose you remember it very clearly, do you? But –' his hand closed on Paul's arm – 'there really is the dickens of a lot to talk about, things you ought to know and understand. When time and Their Lordships permit I'd like you to come here for a good long stay. I suppose that means when you and I have long leave simultaneously.' He raised his eyebrows: '*If*'.

'Or we might win the war, then *really* have time?'

'Better still.' His father had smiled. 'It won't be done in just a year or two, I'm afraid. But tomorrow, I'll show you round the whole estate. Also tomorrow, I have to attend Morning Service. Perhaps you would too?'

'Please.'

'Good. Now then, Paul. I'm not – how shall I put it – I'm not very well house-trained, at this juncture. Domestic and family routines, I mean – I've lived here alone, pretty well, since 1930, and I've acquired – degenerated into – bachelor habits. You may find me a little – well, *rough*, in some ways—'

'Isn't – my step-grandmother, do I call her?'

'Sarah?'

'Sure. Isn't she around – kind of a feminine influence on things?'

'She's "around", as you call it, in the sense that she lives in the Dower House, about half a mile away. I had it done up for her when my father died, and she and her son Jack have lived there ever since. Remember Jack?'

'Ah – not *well*, but—'

'You'll be seeing him this evening. They're dining here – he was due to arrive some time this afternoon, I think Sarah said. But you were asking whether Sarah's presence hasn't kept me civilised—'

36

'Not, if I may say so, that I've noticed anything *un*civilised, so far.'

His father had smiled. 'Early days yet, old chap. But you may be right, Sarah may have stopped me running *completely* to seed. But what I was going to say, Paul – this Christmas business, I'm no use at wrapping things up, sticking candles on trees, all that business. But I do have a present for you. As a matter of fact I've been keeping it for you for quite a long time and rather looking forward to handing it over. So – just come along, would you?'

He'd led the way out into an ice-cold corridor and along it for about forty yards and then down a short flight of steps to an oak door. The room they went into was even colder than the corridor.

'Gunroom.' Nick pointed. 'As you see.'

Most of one wall was occupied by a glass-fronted cupboard which had a whole rack of firearms in it. Nick Everard said, turning a key that had been in the lock to start with, 'We still have some good shooting here – even with only one keeper who should have retired five or six years ago. My father had him and three others under him – *and* they were kept busy. D'you do any shooting over there, Paul?'

'Oh, I've hunted a little. With a college friend whose father—'

'Delighted to hear it. But I was asking about shooting.'

'Oh. Well, we call – I guess what you call shooting, over there is called hunting?'

'How extraordinary.' Nick turned round. He had a shotgun in each hand, double-barrelled twelve-bores that looked as if someone had just been cleaning them. Gleaming, beautiful-looking guns. His father said, 'These are yours. Made by Purdy. It's a pair that was your grandfather's. You won't find better guns anywhere in the world.'

'Why, they're – *lovely*!'

He took one, turning it in his hands, feeling its balance. 'I – really, I don't know what to say. Except "thank you" . . .' He put it to his shoulder. 'Seems about right, too. I—'

'Should be. You're about the same build. But nothing'll beat a Purdy, and this is a particularly fine pair. Look after them, Paul.'

'I sure will!'

'They're quite safe here, for the time being. For ever, if you choose to keep them here . . . D'you realise that if I should get drowned or something silly of that sort, you'd just walk in here and it's yours?'

He'd said something of that kind a short while ago. Must have it on his mind? Paul said, 'I'd prefer it if you did not.'

'Eh?' Over his shoulder, as he put the guns back in the rack.

'I'd sooner you did *not* get drowned.'

'Very decent of you.' Turning back, he smiled. Paul thought it was the first real, deep smile he'd seen on his father's face; he realised too that he was returning it – because it was natural and he couldn't help it. Nick Everard said, 'But it could happen. So there are one or two things you must know about. There's a lawyer-chap in Sheffield, for instance, who's supposed to know all there is to know. And a lot of detail, of course, Sarah could put you on to . . .' He shook his head. 'Later, all that. We'll get back to the fire now and have a snifter before it's time to change . . . You do drink, I hope?'

They were relieved at 1600 by the crew of 'A' gun, who however took over on 'B' gundeck. At this 'degree of readiness' one gun was kept manned for'ard and one aft; torpedo tubes were manned and ready and so were the depthcharge traps and throwers, but two of the four-sevens were considered enough, and 'B' and 'X', being on raised gundecks, were the obvious ones to use.

Paul went down to the seamen's messdecks, two decks below the foc'sl, to shed his wet gear and clean up, warm up. To get to the messdeck you went down the ladder and aft to the screen door that led in below the bridge, and across to the starboard side and then for'ard along a narrow passage which had doors off it to such things as the wireless office and the TS, transmitting station. Then you passed a sliding steel door that led into the washplace, and at this point you were entering the messdeck.

Low-roofed, cluttered, foul-smelling. Lockers ran along the ship's sides port and starboard, and there were racks above them for bulky gear like kitbags and suitcases. Scrubbed-wood tables on both sides, and each pair of them constituted a separate mess. The nearest was 5 Mess, and the next was 4; then came the central, circular support of 'A' gun, and for'ard of that interruption were numbers 3, 2 and 1 Messes, number 1 being right for'ard where the compartment began to narrow. Paul belonged to 3 Mess, the one just past 'A' gun's support.

You had to stoop to avoid slung hammocks. It was like groping your way into a long, narrow, highly mobile cave. The movement was greater here, of course; the further you went from the centre of

38

the ship, the bigger was the rise and fall. The smell was of dirty clothes, *wet* clothes, unwashed bodies, cigarette-smoke, vomit.

Home.

Dripping oilskins – Paul's, for instance, and other men's when they came down off watch – didn't make it any drier. Rubbish – cigarette packets, sweet-papers, crusts, tea-leaves – drifted in a scummy mess, to and fro as the ship rolled. There was an attempt at a clean-up every now and then, but the place was too crowded with men and gear to be got at effectively, when the ship was at sea. Especially in this kind of weather.

'You're in luck, lads.' Brierson, leading seaman of 3 Mess, pointed at the tea-urn. 'Only just wet it.' Brierson was a thickset man with curly yellow hair and rather battered features; he was sitting on the lockers at the end of the table, on the ship's starboard side, reading a torn, week-old copy of the *Daily Mirror*.

'Nice work, Tom.' But he waited, to let Baldy Percival – Baldy being a messmate as well as one of the crew of 'B' gun – help himself first. This was Baldy's first ship too; he was as green to the Navy as Paul was. He smiled courteously; he'd been a Boots librarian, in civvy street.

'After you.'

'Okay.'

Brierson glanced up, stared at Baldy, winked at Paul, looked down at the strip-cartoon of Jane again. On the near-side of the table Randy Philips said to Whacker Harris – they were both regulars, as opposed to 'HO', Hostilities Only ratings, like Paul and Baldy – 'After *you*, Claud.'

'Oh *no*, Wilberforce, after *you*.'

Brierson glanced up again. 'You're after *every* bugger.'

The ship climbed a mountain, tottered on its crest, rolled on to her port side and dropped like a stone. Harris said, 'Gettin' bumpy.' Paul took his mug along behind him and Philips and sat down near the leading seaman.

'Have a word with you, Tom?'

' 'S a free country.'

There was noise enough to allow one to talk quietly, at close range, without being overheard. Paul asked him, 'D'you think I could get to see the skipper?'

Brierson put his paper down, lifted his mug and took a long, noisy sip of tea. Then he smacked his lips, and rested the mug on his knee, tilted his head sideways and stared at Paul.

'What for?'

'It's private. But – okay, but in confidence?' The killick nodded. He told him, 'There was a destroyer with us, not one of our lot, one called *Intent*. My father's in her. But she's not with us now, and there's this buzz that she's been in action and – well, could have been sunk or – ' he shrugged – 'something.'

'Don't want to believe all the buzzes you hear, lad.'

'I know. But – I could ask the skipper, couldn't I?'

'S'pose you could.' Brierson swallowed some more tea. Then he pointed aft and upwards. 'Nip up to the Chiefs' mess, see the cox'n, tell 'im what it's about. 'E might take you to Jimmy, more likely than the skipper.'

'Jimmy' meant the first lieutenant.

'Okay. Thanks.'

'What is he, your guv'nor?'

'He was out of the Navy, now he's back in for the war.'

'Yeah, but I mean, what *is* he?'

'Does it matter?'

'Eh?' Brierson looked surprised. Then he shrugged. 'No. Not to *me*.'

'Thanks. It's just—'

'No skin off *my* nose.'

'Wait here, Everard.'

'Right, Chief.'

CPO Tukes had brought him up to this lobby which was one level down from the compass platform. A door in the for'ard bulkhead led into the signal and plotting office, and the two on the other side were chartroom to port and captain's sea-cabin to starboard.

By the feel of it, *Hoste* was steaming more or less into wind and sea. Or possibly – judging by the amount of roll – the main force of it was just on her bow. The roll, combined with violent pitching, was giving her a sort of corkscrew motion. He propped himself against the after bulkhead, between the two doors. There might be a long wait now, he thought; he'd heard that the skipper hardly ever left the bridge at sea, particularly in rough weather and with other ships in company, and you'd hardly expect him to come rushing down immediately just at the request of some OD.

This was a *hell* of a motion!

Someone was coming up the ladder from below . . .

It was Sub-Lieutenant Peters. Dressed for watchkeeping, by the look of him. Peters was short, round-faced; he paused between one ladderway and the next, and looked at Paul.

'You're Everard, aren't you?'

'Yes, sir.'

Peters was disconcerted. He knew about *Intent* – that fink Cringle had discussed it with him – and who Paul was, but he didn't know that Paul knew. It was awkward for him. Paul said, to give him a hint and make it easier, 'I'm hoping to see the captain, sir. Cox'n's asking him if I can.'

'Oh.' Peters nodded. 'Right you are, then.' He started up the ladder to the bridge. Probably quite a pleasant guy, Paul thought. His own age, near enough. As, of course, was Lieutenant Jack Everard. And if he – Paul – encountered his 'half-uncle' Jack at sea, he'd have to call *him* sir, too!

On the evening before Paul had left home, Ilyana had gone off the deep end about lots of things, including Jack and Sarah. A surfeit of dry martinis had paved the way; then he'd happened to mention Jack, whom he'd last seen when they'd both been children – and come to think of it, hadn't got on with too well . . . Ilyana had accused him, 'You don't *believe* me about your father's darling little Sarah, huh? Don't like to think it of your daddy? Well, you listen, Pavvy boy – if Baby Jack's your father's brother and not his *son* – sure, you heard me – if Jack's not Nick's *son*, so help me I'm the Pope's aunt! When I first set eyes on that kid – and listen, I was bigger than a house with *you*, at that time – I just turned around to Nick and yelled "*Snap!*" And guess what? Little Sarah turned the brightest shade of pink you ever saw!'

But Jack Everard, at Mullbergh this Christmas, had turned out to be quite *un*like Nick Everard. He was taller, slighter, and different in manner and personality too. He had a rather plummy way of talking, and his manner had been condescending, with a sort of shallow jocularity which Paul had found irritating. It was so obviously false. Paul *knew* that Jack resented him; resented his being here, and probably the fact that he was the heir to Mullbergh; this last he only guessed at, because there had to be some reason for that disguised but almost palpable hostility. And as for Sarah – well, what Ilyana had said about her could only be a product of that wild Slav imagination. Sarah was dry, thin-lipped, with a figure like a broomstick and not even a speck of powder on her pale, shiny face. Grey hair drawn back severely into a bun . . .

Sarah was *nobody's* 'little darling'. She never *could* have been! She obviously doted on her son – in a stiff, school-marmy way – and was spinsterishly diffident with Paul. Small, frozen smiles, little bursts of talk for talk's sake. About her late husband, Paul's grandfather; what a fine judge of a horse he'd been, what a great master of hounds, how the whole county missed him. And about local charity committees and war work: she ran some bunch of women who were knitting seaboot stockings and sweaters and sending them off to ships at sea. And decorating the church for tomorrow's service . . . The meal would have been a lot more enjoyable, Paul had thought, if there'd been any possibility of truth in Ilyana's accusations – which all too plainly there could not be. In fact it seemed to him that there was a kind of wall between his father and Lady Sarah: and also as if Jack was a puzzle to Nick, a cuckoo in the nest whom he'd given up trying to fathom.

Paul was certain it had been as much of a relief for his father as it was for himself when Sarah and Jack said goodnight and went back to Dower House. They were alone then: Nick had sent his butler, a very old man named Barstow, away to bed an hour ago. He'd explained, 'I want the old chap to last as long as possible. Shan't ever be able to replace him.'

He suggested now, 'Nightcap?'

Paul had thought he was being offered something to keep his head warm. His father thought this was very funny.

'A final drink before bed, old chap. I'd suggest – I've a rather splendid malt here. Know what that is?'

'I can't say I do.'

'Your education's been neglected, in some areas. We'll have to fill in the gaps. Starting now. A malt is a real Scotch whisky, as opposed to the cheap blends, which are a comparatively modern innovation. This particular malt is called Laphroaig – and I'll lay you half a crown you can't spell it . . . What d'you make of Jack?'

'Jack. Well . . .' Paul stooped to do something unnecessary to the fire. 'I hardly talked enough with him to have much of an opinion.'

'Hmm.' Nick had some bottles on a side-table. He said, with his back to the room and to Paul, 'He's done extraordinarily well, in what you might call the early promotion stakes – courses, exams, and so on. Infinitely better than I ever did. Tell you the truth, I hated every minute of my time at Dartmouth. But he loved it, you see. Extraordinary.' He turned, with a glass of brownish liquor in each hand. Remembering the moment, Paul could see him as if he was looking at a snapshot: a man of medium height, wide-shouldered, a fighter's build. Dark hair with no grey in it yet. A stern, even harsh expression; but it was a harshness that broke up and vanished when he smiled.

'Now then. Try this.'

Liquid gold, he remembered: golden fire. Nectar. Glorious. He'd said, 'If this is how I get educated, I can stand a lot of it.' Thinking back to it, to the whole *ambience* and feel of that evening, made him long to be beside that great log fire again with his father lifting a glass and murmuring, 'Here's to us, Paul.'

Oh, Christ . . .

Like cold grey sea washing over your mind.

And seaboots were clumping down the ladderway. He pushed himself off the bulkhead, pulled himself to attention as CPO Tukes snapped, 'Ordinary Seaman Everard, sir!'

Paul saluted. The skipper – he was a lieutenant-commander and his name was Rowan – said, 'All right, cox'n. Thank you. Come in here, Everard.' He slid back the door of the chartroom and went inside, and Paul followed him. 'Shut the door, so we'll be left in peace.' He pulled back the hood of his duffel, then took his cap off and flung it on the settee which the navigating officer, at sea, used as a bunk. Rowan was swarthy, brown-haired and brown-eyed, in his late twenties or thirty, thirty-one. He told Paul, 'For God's sake, stand easy.'

'Aye aye, sir.'

'Stand easy, Everard, means relax.'

'Yes. I'm – very grateful to you, sir, for—'

'I know what it's about. I only wish I was in a position to give you some kind of reassurance. But – well, all I *can* give you is as much information as I have myself.'

Paul nodded. It couldn't be as bad as he felt in his bones it was going to be. If it was, he didn't want to know . . .

Don't be stupid. You have to know.

'Here we are.' Rowan pulled one chart out of the way, clearing the one that had been lying under it. Paul saw its title: *NORWAY: Lindesnes to Nordkapp.* Rowan pointed with a pair of brass dividers. 'Here's Trondheim. Not so far off it – here – *Intent* and *Gauntlet* were in action between 0800 and 0900 this morning with what *Gauntlet* reported as a *Hipper*-class cruiser.' His pointers moved up the chart. 'We're here. Roughly a hundred and fifty miles farther north . . . Everard, I'd give my right arm to be able to say to you, "Don't worry, your father will be all right." I can't say that, though, because all I know is that the pair of them were about to make a torpedo attack on this enemy cruiser, and from then on we've heard nothing. You must realise – I'm sorry, but it's best to face it – it *could* mean the worst. I'd be lying to you if I pretended anything else.'

'Yes. I appreciate—'

'But it's possible they were damaged and can't use W/T. There've been air searches for them during the day, but in this weather it'd be fifty to one against finding them. We do know *Gauntlet* was badly damaged in the early stages of the engagement – no such indication about *Intent*. There could easily be some good reason for her being off the air.'

'If she'd been sunk – ' Paul heard the artificiality in his own voice, the result of trying to sound unworried – 'would there be much chance of some of them surviving? The action first, and then being rescued?'

'Yes. To both questions. But – it's guesswork, obviously.'

Paul met his captain's eyes. 'On what's known, sir – it's *probable* they were sunk?'

Rowan grimaced: disliking the question. Then he shrugged.

'That's the guess one would make if one had to, Everard. But truly, you can't be sure at all. And remember too – when ships get sunk, nine times out of ten there *are* some survivors.'

'Yes.' He thought, *That's it, then.* And then, *For God's sake, what was I hoping he could tell me?*

Rowan tapped the chart. 'We're here now, as I said. Steering west – on this course. This pencilled track, d'you see?'

They seemed to be heading a long way out from that indented and chewed-up-looking coastline.

'We were supposed to stick around in the entrance to – here, this place, Vestfjord. At the top of it, you see, you come to Narvik. For various reasons Narvik's of particular strategic value, and we don't want the Hun getting any ships in or troops ashore. But now – ' he pointed again at the pencilled line – 'we've had an order direct from the Admiralty in London to come out and rendezvous with *Renown* again. She went off southwards, earlier in the day, in the hope of finding this cruiser we've been talking about – the one that was in action with *Gauntlet* and *Intent*. With this new order, though, she's turned about in order to come back up and meet us.'

'Nobody's left to watch the entrance to the fjord now?'

Rowan, staring down at the chart, sighed.

'A good question, Everard. But ours is not to reason why.' He looked at him. 'I'm extremely sorry about your father. About the uncertainty, that is . . .' Then he changed the subject: 'I'm told you expressed no enthusiasm for being considered as a CW candidate. Is that right?'

It was an effort to switch one's mind . . .

'Well, sir, I felt I'd sooner not put in for it right away, that's all. I'd rather – well, if I could get there on my own showing, so to speak, I'd feel I'd *earned* it.'

'A CW candidate does earn it, Everard. He has a probationary period at sea, and during that time he's under observation. Only if he comes out of it with the right recommendation does he go through for his commission.'

'But wouldn't I have been selected in the first instance on account of – well, my father, and—'

'No, you would not. You'd have been selected because you look like suitable material. We've a huge construction programme, an enormous expansion of the fleet – small ships particularly – sloops, corvettes, destroyers. So we're going to have to train a lot of new officers, and the kind we want are those with the educational background to pick up knowledge quickly and the intelligence then to use it effectively. One or two other qualities as well – some of which, you may be surprised to hear, *are* very often passed from father to son . . . It's not what would or would not be nice for *you*, Everard, it's a question of what the Navy needs.'

Quite a new angle. If you could keep your mind on it . . . Rowan said, 'Think about it. And meanwhile, anything I hear about *Intent* I'll—'

'Bridge, chartroom!'

Disembodied voice squawking from a voicepipe on the centre-line bulkhead. Rowan had slid over to it.

'Chartroom. Captain speaking.'

'*Renown* bearing red three-oh four miles steering north, sir!'

It sounded like Peters' voice. Rowan snapped, 'I'm coming up.' Paul slid the door open and stood aside as the skipper snatched up his cap, shot out and bounded up the ladder.

CHAPTER 4

Intent was coming sluggishly round to the new course, rolling more violently as she turned her quarter instead of her stern into the north-westerly gale. She was a cripple, crawling to find shelter where she could lick her wounds.

And *Gauntlet* was sunk, as likely as not with all hands. Should he have held her back, taken charge of the attack, risking loss of contact with the enemy?

'Course south seventy-three east, sir!'

'Very good.' Steering by magnetic because lack of generator power had put the gyro out of action. What would a court martial decide, he wondered: that the loss of *Gauntlet* was at least partly due to his, Nick Everard's, negligence?

Wind and sea astern had helped *Intent* to make good an average of just over five knots throughout the day. It was 1800 now, 6 pm. That tripod and beacon marking a shoal to port was Nylandskjaer light, and if CPO Beamish managed to keep the screws turning for a few more hours, in about a dozen miles they'd be at the entrance to Namsenfjord.

Beamish was *Intent*'s Chief Stoker. He was in charge of her machinery now for the simple reason that all the other senior men were dead. Mr Waddicor, Chief Engineroom Artificer Foster and ERA Millinger had all been killed when that shell had struck and burst in the engine-room. Leading Stoker Brownrigg had also been killed outright, and the only other men who'd been in the compartment, Stoker Hewitt and ERA Dobbs, weren't going to live. So the doctor, Bywater, said. They were in his sickbay, two ladders down below the bridge. Dobbs wouldn't have been in so bad a state if he hadn't stayed below long enough to shut off steam in an attempt to save the others: he'd been wounded to start with and on top of that scalded almost to death before they'd got him out.

46

Pete Chandler, Nick's ex-yachtsman navigator, came back to him from the chart. 'Twelve and a half miles, sir.'

They'd have to turn down a bit before they entered the fjord, as there was a shoal right in the middle of the entrance. It wasn't an obvious danger on the chart, but the Sailing Directions contained a note that in bad weather the shoal was often awash. And this *was* bad weather. The helmsman was finding steering difficult with the following sea – in which low revs didn't help, either. The sea was overtaking them all the time, great humped rollers racing up astern and lifting her, tilting her this way and that, dropping her back again as they ranged on shorewards; the biggest ones were higher than the ship, so that between the troughs visibility was nil. Grey-green seas mounting, rolling on with spray streaming down-wind from their crests, then toppling and spreading into a wilderness of white where, ahead and on both bows now, the ocean hurled itself against rocks and islands, leaping sometimes against obstructions to a hundred feet or more. *Intent*, with the force of the gale on her port quarter, was like some hard-driven animal with a limp, staggering harder each time to the right than to the left. Funnel-smoke, carried into the bridge by the stern wind, was acrid, eye-watering.

Who'd receive them in Namsos, he wondered – Norwegians, or Germans?

In the first seconds and minutes after the German shell struck and exploded inside his ship, Nick had been preoccupied with two questions. First, whether in her immobilised condition he might still get his torpedo tubes to bear on the enemy, and second, how long it might be before the next salvo smashed down on them.

'A' and 'B' guns, meanwhile, were still firing; but the answer to that first question – and obviously, seeing it in retrospect, to the second as well – had come in a blinding, smothering snowstorm which swept down like a blanket, cocooning the destroyer in her own agony, hissing into the fires leaping from her afterpart.

The guns ceased fire. Brocklehurst reported by telephone from the director tower, 'Target obscured.'

It was no good thinking about getting any signals out. The fore-topmast had collapsed half over the side, taking both the yards and the W/T aerials with it. MacKinnon, the PO Telegraphist, aided by PO Metcalf, the Chief Bosun's Mate, and his henchmen, had rigged a jury aerial since then, using the stump of the foremast

47

and the diminutive mainmast aft, but there'd been no question of trying to transmit. For one thing there were at least one enemy cruiser and two destroyers in the vicinity, and with any luck the Germans were under the impression that *Intent* had been sunk. They must have thought so, because otherwise they'd have arrived through that snowstorm to find her and finish her. So it would have been stupid to have risked alerting them to her continued existence. But in any case, with the ship's main generating plant out of action MacKinnon doubted if they had enough power on the set for it to be heard even five miles away.

The PO Tel was a tall man, black-bearded, with the soft lilt of the West Highlands in his voice. 'It's voltage we're lacking more than aerial height, sir.'

'Have you been listening out since you rigged the jury?'

'Aye, sir, but all we're gettin' is a load o' German.'

There were no British ships anywhere near enough to have a chance of receiving them. And the signals that really mattered, the enemy reports, had been sent out before the action started.

'All right, MacKinnon. Pick up whatever you can, so we hear what's going on. We'll be in shelter in a few hours' time – we'll fix the generator and step a new fore-topmast, and you'll be in business again.'

'We've no spare topmast, sir.'

It was hard to concentrate on one issue for so long, when there were fifty other things to think about. Plugging slowly south-eastward: pitching like a see-saw and losing oil-fuel all the time. The stern tanks were leaking as a result of the main damage, and the port-side tanks for'ard were also leaking, presumably from near-miss damage slightly earlier. So now the only sound fuel tanks were the starboard pair for'ard and the smaller auxiliaries amidships. They were going to need oil as well as repairs.

'D'you know what that topmast was made of, PO Tel?'

'Would it be Norway fir, sir?'

'It would.' Nick pointed. 'And that's Norway.'

But this conversation had taken place several hours later. At the start, with the ship stopped and on fire and no report yet of her machinery state or count of dead and wounded, there'd been no time for anything but coping with such emergencies as one knew about and getting ready for such new ones as might be expected. Like the weather clearing suddenly and the cruiser opening fire again. There'd be nothing to do except to shoot back – for as long as the ship floated.

Tommy Trench had gone aft to take charge of damage-control and fire-fighting. The snow still hid them, hid everything *from* them. Mr Opie, the torpedo gunner, was still standing by his out-turned tubes, and Nick had sent down for Cox, the RNR midshipman, to come up to the torpedo sights, in case visibility *did* lift suddenly and reveal their enemy. If that happened and one was quick enough . . . Well, he knew the cruiser wouldn't be lying stopped as *Intent* was; in fact the probability was that she'd be a long way off by this time. But she might be picking up survivors from poor *Gauntlet*?

Thinking of the possibility of *Gauntlet* survivors, he wondered about sending a boat to search in the direction where they'd last seen her. Both ships had been immobilised, so if there were any that was where they'd be. There'd be none alive in the water, but there might be a Carley float, something or other . . . Risk sending away the whaler in this sea? Throw sound lives after doubtful ones?

Ten or fifteen minutes after the shell had hit them Sub-Lieutenant Lyte hauled himself into the bridge with a report from Tommy Trench.

'Engine-room's a shambles, sir. Chief Stoker's trying to sort things out – *says* it's not as hopeless as it looks. There's a lot of electrical damage, but the LTOs are coping. Only the auxiliary generator's operable – or will be, Beamish says. And we're losing a lot of oil-fuel aft, so he's shut off those tanks. Other damage is comparatively minor – except for the hole in the engine-room casing – first lieutenant's getting that covered with timber and tarpaulins. But everything's in hand, sir, really.' Lyte was panting: he'd paused, getting his breathing under control. 'The four men who were killed are in the officers' bathroom for the moment, sir, and the two wounded – ERA Dobbs and Stoker Hewitt – are in the sickbay.'

'Are they going to be all right?'

'No, sir.' Lyte clung to the binnacle as the ship was lifted and flung on to her port side. 'Doc says not a hope.'

'On your way down, tell him I want a report as soon as possible.'

'Aye aye, sir.' He hadn't quite finished *his* report yet. 'Most upper deck gear's smashed or burnt, sir. The only boat we have left intact is the dinghy. Whaler and motor-cutter are just charcoal. Even the Carley floats have had it. And – Mr Opie asked me to tell you he had to ditch several depthcharges, when everything was burning.'

That seemed to be the lot.

'All right, Sub. Thank you.'

No boat for *Gauntlet* survivors, then; *that* problem had solved itself. No boat for anyone else either. Lyte told him, 'Chief Buffer's clearing away the wreckage of the topmast, shrouds and stuff, in the waist port side, sir, and he's got all the wire inboard now.'

'Good.' Metcalf's first thought would have been for trailing steel-wire rope that might get wrapped round the screws. *If* the screws were to start turning again.

'Sub, I want to know from Beamish, *one*, how long he's going to be, *two*, what revs he thinks he'll be able to give me?'

Visibility was lifting. The snow was changing to sleet and thinning. A minute ago you couldn't see more than ten yards but he could see the ship's stem now – about a hundred feet away. And the sea beyond it, too . . .

'Lookouts!'

Gilbey on the port side and Willis on the other. He told them, 'Keep your eyes peeled now. Weather's thinning. I want to know if anything's there before it sees *us* . . . Mid!'

Midshipman Cox faced round. 'Yessir?'

'Ask Lieutenant Brocklehurst if he can see anything.'

Cox had picked up the 'phone. He was short, sturdy, with a nose like a lump of putty and skin scarred by acne. He'd been a Merchant Navy cadet until 3 September 1939, and he was now just eighteen. His action station was in the plot, below the bridge, and most of the time he was employed as 'tanky', assistant to the navigating officer.

He'd shoved the 'phone back on its bracket. 'Director tower reports nothing in sight, sir.'

'Keep a smart lookout yourself now, Mid.'

Young Cox was a problem. Chandler wanted to get rid of him. But for the moment, the foreseeable future, there were more pressing problems . . . Visibility had stretched to about half a mile, and there was still nothing to be seen. Only the sea heaving green and angry and the clouds pressing low as if they were trying to smother it, and here and there the flurry of a passing squall. *Intent*, soaring and dropping, swinging whichever way the waves and wind pushed her, felt inert and lifeless, with no will of her own.

*   *   *

Some time later, Tommy Trench's mountainous form had dragged itself off the ladderway and slithered across the bridge to join him. Pete Chandler had come up behind the first lieutenant; he was carrying a rolled chart which he took to the small chart table in the front of the bridge. It was a sort of alcove, like a dormer window's recess, with a grey-painted canvas shield that could be let down to keep the weather out and, at night, the light in.

To the left of it, in the port fore corner of the bridge, steps led down to the tiny Asdic compartment.

Trench reported, 'I've got the hole in the engine-room casing adequately covered for the time being, sir. Timber and tarpaulins with a wire lashing to hold it down. The work'll go more easily down below now; Beamish reckons another hour and then slow speed, revs for three or four knots.'

'I see.' He'd been hoping for better things than that. He asked Trench, 'Is it going to be a permanent repair – at that reduced speed – one we can rely on?'

'Afraid not, sir. To make a job of it he says he'd need several days with the ship on an even keel and – well, he's not *up* to it, sir.'

'No.'

It wasn't any of CPO Beamish's fault that he wasn't. He was a stoker, not an artificer.

'I doubt if it was an eight-inch shell that hit us, sir. But in any case it didn't get far in before it burst. Hence the size of the hole.'

It could have been a shell from the cruiser's secondary armament, a four-inch. It had already occurred to him that a direct hit from an eight-inch would almost certainly have sunk them. The engine-room was the biggest compartment in the ship: if it was flooded, she'd go down, to where poor *Gauntlet* was.

The thought of *Gauntlet* was a weight inside him. He thought that in the same circumstances he'd have made the same decisions, but he knew it was arguable and that there'd be plenty of post-mortem experts who'd take a different view.

'How far to the Shetlands, pilot?'

'Roughly – ' Chandler hesitated – 'five hundred miles, sir. D'you want a more accurate—'

'No.' It *would* be about five hundred. And it might as well have been five thousand. He looked at Trench. 'Five hundred miles at three knots – no, not as much, revs for three knots but beam-on to this gale – and with a chance of the engine packing up on us altogether . . .' He shook his head. 'Hardly.'

51

'Might whistle up a tow, sir?'

Nick asked Chandler, 'How far are we from Trondheim?'

'We could just about *drift* there, sir.'

'Let's have a look at it. Take over, will you, Number One.'

You could see a couple of miles now: see *nothing* over a radius of about that. Thank God, he thought, for vast mercies. Despite *Gauntlet*. And don't count on getting many more, not even small ones. Luck, even if one thought of it as intervention by the Almighty, was always a rationed commodity. When you'd had a fairly large issue of it you'd be stupid not to expect some of the other sort thereafter. But for the moment there was still no enemy about. The lookouts and the snotty were all hard at it with binoculars at their eyes, and overhead the director tower was slowly, constantly, traversing around.

So far – *Gauntlet* apart – things might have been a lot worse than they were, he thought. He was staring up at the swaying director tower. Trench glanced up at it too: the motion up there as the ship rolled was terrific. Trench observed, 'If Brocklehurst was a churn of milk he'd be cheese by now.' Best not to dwell on the *Gauntlet* business. Nick knew that *Intent*'s present problems demanded all his concentration. Later, *Gauntlet*'s fate and his own part in the action would be examined through a dozen microscopes, some of them with bureaucratically hostile eyes behind them. If one got through as far as 'later' . . .

Chandler was waiting for him at the chart table.

'DR's here, sir, and here's Trondheim.'

He'd already taken the major decision – to seek shelter and repairs in Norway rather than risk losing the ship and all her company in attempting the very long, rough passage homeward in this unseaworthy condition. With enemy units known to be at sea, and probably a lot more of them than were *known* to be, to stagger off into the gale hoping to find assistance – a tow – wasn't a justifiable gamble. At best, if it worked, it would take other Royal Navy ships from their operational functions, add to the burden of other men's responsibilities. He hunched over the chart: the decision to be made now was which bit of Norway to aim for.

Trondheim was close at hand. It was a major port with full repair and fuelling facilities, and at first sight it seemed the obvious choice.

His eye ran up the jagged coastline, the mass of offshore islands and indentations, the long reaching arms of sea called fjords –

narrow, twisting, deep-water channels. He reached to the back of the table for dividers.

Namsos, he was looking at. At the head of Namsenfjord. The approach to it – from Foldfjorden – was about seventy miles north of the approach to Trondheim. He checked the distances to both places from *Intent*'s present DR position. Nothing in it: they were as close to one as to the other. The only significant difference was that the course to Namsenfjord – he ran the parallel ruler across and saw it would be about 130 degrees – would be exactly down-wind.

Passing a hand around his jaw, he was reminded that he hadn't shaved since yesterday morning.

'Namsos might be our best bet.'

'Wouldn't repairs be easier at Trondheim, sir? And more likely oil-fuel?'

'Let's see what the pilot says. Send Cox down for it.'

Now – think this out . . .

If the Germans were invading – which you could bet on – they'd make landings at four, five, possibly six strategic points. Oslo obviously. Trondheim was probably the next most obvious target. Stavanger for its airfield. And – Kristiansand, Bergen, Narvik. If they had ships and men enough that would be the bones of it. And it made a powerful argument against taking *Intent* into Trondheim. Wherever one went, admittedly there'd be some risk of getting stuck; Namsos *might* be occupied and presumably would be eventually – its strategic position in relation to Trondheim meant it couldn't be left alone for long – but for openers the Hun couldn't spread his forces too thinly, he'd have to concentrate on the more important places.

So if repairs could be made in just a few days there'd be a better chance of getting them done in Namsos and getting away again than there would be at Trondheim.

'Right. Thank you.' Chandler took the *Norway Pilot Vol. III* from Cox, and looked up Namsos in its index. Then he was riffling over the pages. 'Here we are . . .'

'The crucial requirements are repairs and fuel.'

'Yes, here it is . . . "Small repairs can be executed."' His finger moved on, stopped at another paragraph. '"Fuel oil is available." Seems we could do worse, sir.'

'Is that a fairly recent issue?'

'Looks new enough.' The navigator turned to the front and checked the publication date. 'Yes. 1939.'

'Namsos it is, then.' Nick touched the wooden surface of the chart table. '*If* our chief stoker can get us that far.'

Nylandskjaer was well astern now. One bit of bad news since Beamish had got her going had been the discovery that oil was leaking from some of the for'ard tanks as well as the after ones. Problems of that nature could only be cured in dry dock: even if there was a dock in Namsos and engineers who could take on such a job he wasn't going to risk his ship being high and dry when the Nazis might arrive at any moment. So however good a job Beamish might do eventually in the engine-room, with or without shore assistance, *Intent*'s range was going to be reduced by almost half. And she'd only have *that* if the harbour authorities in Namsos came up to scratch with a couple of hundred tons of oil.

Sufficient unto the day, he told himself. For the moment she was, at least, *afloat*.

Trench, lumbering up, caught hold of the binnacle on Nick's left. 'Burial party is standing by, sir.'

'Right. Thank you.' He called to Chandler, who was at the chart table. 'Pilot, come and take over.'

'Aye aye, sir.' The navigator's long, bony frame began to back out of the alcove, letting the canvas down across it to make sure his precious charts stayed dry. He'd got the larger-scale inshore chart of Namsenfjord and surroundings up here now. Midshipman Cox was still at the front of the bridge keeping a lookout, and the watchkeeping lookouts had been doubled up so that there were two each side. The only food anyone had had throughout the day had been corned-beef sandwiches, mugs of soup, and kye. 'Kye' meaning cocoa. Nick stared round, seeing the low encircling rock-grey coasts white-blotched and hung with spray in a continual mist.

Intent had her stern up, foc'sl buried deep in sea . . . The navigator, joining Nick, wiped spray from his long, pale face. Chandler was a cricketer; it was a burning interest which he shared with Tommy Trench. 'With your permission, sir, I'd like to come two degrees to starboard now.'

'All right.' He turned away. 'She's all yours.'

'Then it's six and a half miles to Namsenfjord, sir.'

An hour and a half, he thought. 'How far up the fjord for shelter?'

'Bit less than twenty miles, sir.' Then he re-heard the question, and shook his head. 'Sorry. That's the distance up to Namsos itself. There are sheltered anchorages long before that.'

If they were lucky they'd be met by a pilot boat or some kind of patrol craft who'd lead them in. A pilot was essential, by normal standards, but it might be unwise to count on getting one. For one thing, the ordinary way of getting him would be to radio the nearest pilot-station; and even if the W/T was working he'd no intention of using it. But also, if the Norwegians were expecting to be invaded they'd be chasing their tails a bit – and might not relish being seen playing host to the White Ensign. In fact going on recent form they'd scream blue murder at the sight of it. So – if no pilot was available, as the distance to Namsos was twenty miles and *Intent*'s speed say five knots, they'd be in that narrow fjord when the dark period hit them. Therefore, he'd have to reckon on anchoring before the light failed: and as the fjords were deep – the chart revealed that most of Namsenfjord had more than two hundred fathoms in it – an anchorage would have to be selected in advance.

Well, there'd be time to do so. Now, there were five men to be buried. Five because Stoker Hewitt had died, as the doctor had said he would. Dobbs, the ERA, was surprising him by holding on, and Probationary Surgeon Lieutenant Bywater was staying at Dobbs's bunkside and practically counting every heartbeat. Six months ago Don Bywater had been a student at Bart's.

Nick told Chandler, 'I'm going aft. When it's over I expect I'll visit the engine-room and then the sickbay.'

A small crowd of men had assembled near the for'ard set of torpedo tubes. Mr Opie was there – spidery-thin, grey-stubbled, touching his cap to Nick and then immediately resuming the massage of that long, thin nose. Lyte too – looking soberer, less boyish than Nick had seen him before. This morning's engagement, he realised, must for the majority of officers and men have been a first experience of action . . . Had *he* been changed, he wondered, by his own rather dramatic blooding at Jutland? In career terms, certainly, because at Jutland he'd won himself – by accident, pure chance, he still felt that was all it had amounted to – a future, which he'd not had before. But *personally*?

He didn't think so. Success, approbation, had given him some confidence. That was about all . . . He was looking round at Trench's dispositions for this funeral: at four bodies sewn in canvas and lying under the shelter of the tubes, a fifth on the launching-plank which had been rigged athwartships with its outboard end protruding over the ship's side. Spray flew from mounting curves of green sea, higher than the ship's side: Nick told PO Metcalf, 'Mind you drop 'em in the troughs. Otherwise they might get dumped straight back aboard.' The gunner's mate, PO Jolly, reported, 'Firing party ready, sir.' Four sailors with rifles. The body lying on the plank was shrouded in a Union flag, and the same flag would cover each of the other four as their turns came. Men in gleaming oilskins clung to whatever was solid and in their reach; mostly to the tubes and the gear around them and to the ladder and other projections on the searchlight island. The searchlight itself was *kaput*, non-existent, and the platform it stood on was blackened and twisted out of shape. Nick took up a position under the platform's overhang. One hand for himself, the other for the prayer-book. He was going to have to shout the prayers, to be heard over all the surrounding noise.

I am the resurrection and the life, saith the Lord: he that believeth in me, though he were dead, yet shall he live: and whosoever liveth and believeth in me shall never die . . . We brought nothing into this world, and it is certain we can carry nothing out. The Lord gave, and the Lord hath taken away; blessed be the name of the Lord.

The language was fine but its value here and now was less obvious to him. It wasn't a matter of not believing; more one of believing and caring too much for these ritual mouthings to carry the weight of regret which he felt himself and sensed from the men around him. He looked up from the book: he wanted to say something more personal and more apposite, something these sailors could identify with in their own hearts. Defeated in that, he looked down again . . . *In the midst of life we are in death: of whom may we seek for succour, but of thee, O Lord, who for our sins are justly displeased?* Familiar verbiage: reminding one of other such occasions. A Dover scene, for instance: Christmas of 1917, destroyer men in ranks under a grey drizzly sky, and the flag on the castle at half-mast while a bugler sounded the Last Post. Here there was no bugler, only PO Metcalf and his bosun's call. Metcalf had the little silvery instrument ready pressed between fingertips and palm, and he kept wetting his lips as if he was worried that the prayers might stop suddenly and find him unprepared, lips dried by the wind. Nick paused, to make sure the side-party were ready; then he looked down again and read, *Forasmuch as it hath pleased Almighty God of his great mercy to take unto himself the souls of our dear brothers here departed: we therefore commit their bodies to the deep, to be turned into corruption, looking for the resurrection of the body when the sea shall give up her dead . . .*

For each man the pipe shrilled and a volley of rifle-shots crackled into the sky. Five splashes, and within seconds of each there was nothing to be seen in the boil of sea. He read the Lord's Prayer: and that was it . . . But he saw Tommy Trench staring at him hard, imparting to him by the stare that there might be something else expected of him.

He told them, 'These were our shipmates. When they were alive we took them for granted. Now we know how valuable they were – to us and to the ship. Let's remember it – because it applies here and now to every one of us: we are all dependent on each other, and every single man has his own value and importance.'

Those five had been more valuable than most. *Intent* was not only wounded, she was chronically short of doctors, engine-room staff, technicians. The thought reminded him of ERA Dobbs; he turned the prayer-book's pages back quickly to *Visitation of the Sick*.

'A prayer now for ERA Dobbs. Surgeon Lieutenant Bywater is with him now in the sickbay, but he does not have – very good chances . . . *Oh father of all mercies, we fly unto thee for succour on behalf of thy servant George Amos Dobbs, now lying under thy hand in great weakness of body . . .*' Taking a breath – this shouting was hard work – he saw with dismay that the words which lay ahead were about 'unfeigned repentance' and Dobbs's 'pardon' and a request that he should be granted 'a longer continuance amongst us'. It wouldn't do; he was stopped, totally unable to bawl such stuff into the face of present reality – a crippled ship and a battering sea on a coast which might already be swarming with the enemy, and a man lying close to death because he'd taken it on himself to try to save his mates. It wasn't Dobbs's fault they'd died anyway. The words came suddenly and naturally and with a kind of anger: 'Save him, please God, for us and for this ship and for his family at home. Give him the strength to recover from his injuries. *Please* God – let him *live!*'

This time the 'amens' came sharply, resonantly. And shutting the prayer-book, Nick was suddenly aware of plain *liking* for the men around him: of understanding and respect for them. Instinct told him too that the empathy was two-way: he'd reached them, and they were beginning to feel they knew him. He hadn't thought of it or remembered it until this moment, but it was a phenomenon he'd encountered before and was recognising now from twenty-something years ago. He could see it reflected back at him from a couple of dozen different faces as he looked round at them. They were seeing him as a human being: in time, liking would grow into confidence. It didn't matter whether or not they knew it. The marvellous thing was that it was there, to be tapped and to be built on.

He told them, 'We're going into Namsenfjord, and up to the town of Namsos if the engines hold up long enough, to find shelter and some help in patching up our damage. We need oil-fuel too, and I hope to find some there. It's possible the Germans are on the point of invading Norway; they may even be there ahead of us. In that case, we'll be somewhat up the creek. But – ' he went on, over a burst of laughter – 'but *they* won't be expecting *us*, either.'

A snow-shower obscured the headland. In about half a mile, though, they'd have it on the starboard beam, and the shoal would be well clear to port, and they'd turn down into the fjord.

'Kye, sir?'

'Thank you, Mid.'

Midshipman Cox was offering him a mug of cocoa. It was a pleasure to accept it. The kettle was plugged in on the starboard side of the bridge, on a brass-edged step there. Cox went back to prepare another mug, making a paste of cocoa powder, sugar and condensed milk and then adding the hot water. The cocoa powder was produced beforehand by scraping a block of pusser's (Admiralty-issue) chocolate, and old sailors reckoned that in a good cup of kye the spoon should stand up straight without support; but this involved the addition of custard-powder as a thickener, and was a taste for connoisseurs.

Cox was a problem that Nick would have to tackle sooner or later. Chandler said he was lazy, untidy and sloppy at his work – work which consisted largely of correcting charts and other navigational publications. Also, he was hopeless as a navigator and uninterested in it; a star-sight took him an hour to work out and was usually all rubbish when he'd done it. What made this particularly surprising was that he was RNR, and Royal Naval Reserve officers – even embryo ones, which was what a midshipman really was – were usually the best navigators you could get. Conway, Worcester and Pangbourne, all the merchant-navy training establishments seemed to be way ahead of the RN college in injecting the navigator's art into their cadets.

Nick thought Cox was the only exception to the rule he'd ever come across. And worse than the incompetence was – according to Chandler – the boy not seeming to give a damn about it.

'Aircraft green one-seven-oh!'

Think of the devil . . . Cox had yelled it. Rising from his cocoa bar he'd caught a sight of it, put a mug down and snatched up binoculars . . . 'Almost right astern, sir. Moving left to right, angle of sight – five degrees.'

To be visible under the cloud it would have to be pretty low.

'What does it look like?'

Nick and Chandler were both out on that side, looking aft, and not seeing it yet. Cox said, 'Passed astern, sir.' Meaning it had gone out of his sight. He was moving – uphill, at the moment – over to the port side. He answered Chandler's question: 'Can't tell what it is, sir. In and out of cloud and—' He had it in his glasses again and so did both the port-side lookouts. Then: 'Flown into cloud, sir.'

It had been flying up-coast, northwards from the direction of Trondheim; or it had come from seaward and was doing a leg along the coastline. It could have been Norwegian, or German, or an aircraft catapulted from one of the Home Fleet's big ships and doing an inshore reconnaissance. Whatever it was, if its pilot had seen something way off on his starboard side that was very small and grey, foam-washed and not moving fast enough to be noticeably moving at all, he'd have had no way of distinguishing it at that range from about half a million rocks.

'Well sighted, Mid.' Credit where credit was due. And the corollary too: he called back to the starboard after lookout, '*You* should have seen that first, Kelly.' It had stopped snowing, and the entrance to Namsenfjord was opening out, its westward coast seeming to fall back as the vista opened. The entrance here was about two miles wide; at the limit of present visibility he could see where it narrowed to less than half that. But – he wiped the front lenses of his binoculars and tried again – you could see beyond that too, to a further broadening.

'Can we come round yet, pilot?'

'In about ten minutes, sir.'

A bit stiff-necked, was Pete Chandler. Very good at his job, but sometimes *unnecessarily* meticulous. He'd drawn a pencil track and he was going to stick to it: well, that was his intention. Nick suggested mildly, 'We don't have to go smack down the middle, do we? Isn't it all deep water?'

'It is, sir.'

'Let's come round now, then.'

'Aye aye, sir.' Deadpan . . . The navigator stooped to the voice-pipe. 'Starboard fifteen.'

If that had been a Home Fleet aircraft, Nick thought, it would not, probably, have been searching for *Intent* or *Gauntlet*. They'd have written them off, hours ago. C-in-C and Admiralty and the Vice-Admiral Battlecruiser Squadron – Whitworth – had every reason to assume that both ships had gone down.

How long would Admiralty wait before they notified next-of-kin?

Aubrey Wishart was in the Admiralty and, being Aubrey, would have his ear to the ground when anything was happening. He'd know of that early-morning engagement, the enemy reports and the ensuing silence. And since Nick had recently put Uncle Hugh in touch with him he'd get to hear about it too. He'd keep his mouth shut, though, as long as there was any doubt; basically he'd always been an optimist, and he'd been in love with his young sister-in-law Sarah for – oh, twenty-five years?

Honourably, of course. He'd have kissed her cheek a few times, sometimes touched her hand and found the experience thrilling, something to think about when he was lonely . . . After his brother, Nick's father, had died, Nick had half expected Hugh to propose to her. But he'd overlooked the existence of the Table of Affinity, of course: *A man may not marry his brother's wife*.

She'd have refused him, anyway. Her husband's death hadn't done anything to remove Sarah's hair-shirt, that ghastly outcome of past sins and present rectitude . . . . Whoever put that Table of Affinities together could have expanded it in some directions: he could for instance have added *A man may not go to bed with his father's wife*?

Incredible – to know her, see her now. And she'd been like this – to him – ever since he'd returned from the Black Sea in 1920. Coldly formal, untouchable – actually and figuratively. And at that time she'd still been young and pretty, she hadn't succeeded in turning herself as she had now into an old maid. Caustic, dried up . . . Although Uncle Hugh still seemed to regard her as a raving beauty . . . At first he'd seen her transformation as an act, a cover-up aimed at making sure no one ever guessed the truth: even to

60

destroy that truth, erase it from his mind as well as from her own – the truth being that Jack, supposedly Nick's half-brother, was actually his son. But even if that was how it had started, as a deception that was supposed to last for ever and to cover events that wouldn't be referred to by either of them even if they'd been alone on some mountain-top, it had changed into something stronger and less rational. Now, she hated him. For what he'd done all those years ago, and again for what he'd done more recently.

Above all he remembered the loathing in her eyes ten years ago, on the wide front steps at Mullbergh when they'd returned together from the church, from burying Nick's father, her husband. He'd muttered, speaking his thoughts aloud more than talking to her, 'I feel as if I'd killed him.' Her hand on his arm stopped him, halfway up the steps, and her eyes blazed in that dead-white face inside its frame of black: she hissed, '*Didn't* you?'

Grey-green mounds of following sea still unending, lifting her and tilting her on their summits before they allowed her to slide back and down again and rolled on disdainfully as if they hadn't noticed her or felt her weight.

'Midships!'

'Midships, sir. Wheel's amidships, sir.'

'Steer south fifty-two east.'

'South fifty-two east, sir!'

The engine's thrum had seemed to falter. Chandler had noticed it too, looked round quickly towards Nick . . .

Steady again, and plugging on. He let out a breath of relief. This lee shore would *not* be a place you'd choose for breaking down.

Sarah loathed him, he thought, as a symbol of her own guilt and shame. But there'd been some basis for that accusation.

In 1929, in the autumn, he'd come up to Mullbergh on his own in order to break the news of his impending divorce from Ilyana. He'd been executive officer of a battleship in the Mediterranean Fleet for the previous two years, and now he'd been appointed to the staff of the Senior Officers' Tactical Course at Portsmouth, but he had some leave due to him first. Much of it was to be spent conferring with lawyers and providing Ilyana with 'grounds'. Providing *her* with them, for heaven's sake!

His father had been furious, utterly opposed to allowing a

61

divorce in the family. Nick had expected *some* fuss to be made: as a boy he'd been aware of frightful upheavals at the time of his Uncle Hugh's divorce. But that had been so long ago; divorce in these days had become far more commonplace, acceptable.

Not to Sir John Everard, though. And certainly not when it was his own son and heir who was instigating it. A son and heir whom he could not, incidentally, disinherit, in terms of the entailed estate. He made it plain that he regretted this. Nick might have left at once, but it happened to be the Mullbergh pack's opening meet next day, and it was a long time since he'd ridden to hounds; also, he had the faint hope that if he stayed another day or two some opportunities might arise to make his father understand how he had absolutely no option in the matter of the divorce.

Which was to involve this stupid sham of a convention, that *he* should provide the grounds, allow Ilyana to divorce *him* . . . After Malta, for God's sake! And after – he had to face it now – ten years of shirking the truth . . . He kept remembering a remark he'd overheard at the time of his marriage to her. The marriage had been contracted primarily to save her life, since the Admiralty had decreed that no more White refugees were to be brought out of Russia in HM ships. The only way to get round this had been to turn Countess Dherjhorakov into Mrs Everard: but in any case he'd been in love with her. Or infatuated. Or that and also influenced by the circumstances, the approaching horror of the Red advance and knowing what they'd done elsewhere, the unspeakable savagery and the sheer impossibility of leaving the tiny, exquisite and fantastically *brave* Ilyana to the butchers and the rapists. The fact they barely knew each other hadn't counted: she was there in front of him, he could *see* her, he knew what she'd been through already and what struck him most forcibly was the combination of ultra-femininity and high courage: all he had to do, he'd thought, to make a go of it, was measure up to her. And that snide remark – one young Russian nobleman had said it to another, in French and in Nick's hearing – *Ilyana Dherjhorakov? Yes, I know who you mean. Here, is she? The one they say used to ride horses, until she discovered men?* – he'd dismissed it as clever, cruel, unfounded gossip. It was the way those people talked. Only much later did he remember it and recognise its accuracy. And the last time had been in Malta: where his own captain had summoned him to the cuddy for pink gins and spoken of forbearance, wisdom, the folly of cutting off one's nose to spite one's face; and then an admiral with a famous name had talked paternally of the good name of the Service and the reputation of the Everards. Again it had been a nobleman, of sorts – but an Englishman and a senior officer. The Mediterranean Fleet had gone on its summer cruise; Nick had been with it in his battleship. Back in Malta afterwards he'd found that Ilyana, only just returned to the island, was evasive, uncommunicative, peculiar in manner. It had been the start of Paul's schooling, his first term at prep school in England; she'd gone to collect him and bring him out to Malta for his summer holidays; but she'd left early, the day after the fleet had cleared Valletta, and gone not to England but to a villa at Menton. The villa was owned by a White Russian cousin and had been lent to a certain British officer, a man with aristocratic connections, who until recently had been in Malta. There'd been a photograph in a glossy magazine, and a letter to Malta from someone who'd seen them at some princely party; and then a few more bits and pieces and suddenly it was common knowledge all over Malta, from every gunroom and wardroom in the fleet to the Union Club and the governor's palace . . .

He remembered the admiral, himself not unconnected in high places, telling him uncomfortably – the interview had obviously not been arranged on the admiral's *own* initiative – 'You've a brilliant record, Everard, and potentially a great future in the Service. A little caution now, a few second thoughts, would certainly not be harmful to your prospects. I'm bound to warn you on the other hand that a scandal of such dimensions could be – frankly, disastrous . . .'

The scandal could be avoided. The divorce could not.

In fact he didn't hunt, that day at Mullbergh, and neither did his father. In the morning the head groom came to report that he couldn't saddle Sir John's stallion. The animal wouldn't let him into its box, and it was kicking the place to bits. Nick's father flew into a rage: he shouted at the groom that he was sacked – as of that moment, with no wages, notice or reference. In the first place he didn't know his job, in the second he was a coward; in the third, if the horse was in such a state it was his own, the groom's, fault to start with. Sir John stalked out, taking a crop with him. Five minutes later, with the same groom's help, Nick managed to get his father's unconscious body out of the loose-box. He had extensive bruising, some cracked ribs, a broken wrist and slight concussion.

None of which kept him quiet for long. Within a few days he was shouting from his bed that Nick's behaviour had always been a source of annoyance and embarrassment, and that if he continued with his plans for this divorce he needn't bother to come back to Mullbergh until he – Sir John – was dead.

'All right. If that's how you feel.'

But there was no train he could take that day. And a few hours later, passing by to tell Jack – who was in the sickroom – that Sarah wanted him downstairs, he heard his father lecturing the boy about his future in the Navy. Jack had already expressed the wish to try for Dartmouth.

Sir John was instructing him, 'Model yourself on your half-brother David. If David had lived he'd have been well on the way to becoming an admiral, by now. Brilliant – brave as a lion – why, there's not the slightest doubt he'd have gone to the very top!'

The boy put in, 'I'd like to be like Nick. Get medals like he has. If I could be like Nick—'

'Arrant *nonsense*, Jack! Nick was lucky, that's all – in the right places at the right time! That's nothing to do with *staying power* – which was what David had in such abundance. Determination – grit! And something else – it's called *integrity*. He'd have lived like an Everard, not a creature sliding in and out of marriages and law courts, muck-raking and—'

'I beg your pardon.' Nick stood in the doorway. The door next along from this one he'd seen smashed down – by his father, in a drunken fury, when he, Nick, had been a child and woken in the night to Sarah's screams and come rushing down to help her . . . Today there'd been the earlier row – accusations, threats, and Sarah's tight-faced, mute hostility: and he was looking at a man now who'd never in his life lifted a finger except to please himself. Even in the war he'd found himself a comfortable, safe niche . . . One's own father: a life-long sham! Nick told him, 'David was a coward and a weakling. At Jutland his nerve broke completely – it was the first time he'd been shot at and he couldn't face it. What that padre told Hugh was a lot of bunkum. I heard the truth from a man who was in *Bantry* and took charge towards the end. He had to detail a brother officer to look after David, save him from disgracing himself too obviously in front of the sailors.'

The truth, he'd given him. Like a bullet between the eyes. It was something he'd sworn to himself he'd never tell a soul.

Sir John had his first heart attack that evening. He lived for a few months after it, but that had been the start. Nick had suffered ever since from the knowledge of what he'd done. There'd been no point in it, nothing achieved; he'd let go for a moment, surrendered to a fit of temper. He'd done a dreadful thing. Worst of all was that he'd said it in front of Jack, his own son. All right, *half-brother*. But Jack, who – although one tried hard not to see it – *was* in so many ways like David.

Nothing seemed to be on the move except the sea and the clouds and *Intent* bashing doggedly in towards the land. And a variety of screeching gulls. Namsenfjord lay open now on the starboard bow and Pete Chandler had just taken some bearings for a fix. He came back from putting it on the chart.

'We could come round to south thirty-eight east, sir. Then fifty-five east after two miles.'

'All right. Take over, and bring her round.'

He had to work it out now – times, distances, and the dark period. He went to the chart and leant over it, resting on his elbows. From about midnight to 4 am were the hours when fjord navigation without either a pilot or local knowledge would be too dangerous; so he had two hours – say ten miles – before the ship had to be tucked up in some safe anchorage.

Chandler had laid off courses all the way through to Namsos. Checking on where a two-hour run on that track would take them, Nick found a small, almost circular dead-end of a fjordlet off the main one and on the starboard hand. Hidden and well sheltered. Hoddoy, the island which shut it in was called. But – checking – he found that the run of it would be just *over* the ten miles.

Nearer, then. *This* place . . . He looked up the reference in the Pilot, the book of Sailing Directions. Quay with mooring rings: and inside the distance, certainly. But he didn't want to tie up to the shore: and anyway it was too open to the main channel of the fjord. One had to think of a German invasion force arriving with the dawn, and *Intent* caught there without a hope in hell. She wasn't in a condition to win battles anyway, but if he had her hidden when the enemy arrived there was at least the chance he'd be able to sneak her away later when the repairs were done.

The messenger of the watch brought him a cup of kye. Then Trench joined him.

'Problems, sir?'

'Picking an anchorage.' Glad to share his thoughts with him, he ran a pencil-tip down the length of the fjord. 'If we tried to get right through, the dark period would catch us about here. No good. I'm reckoning on two hours' steaming and then dropping the hook for four to five and pressing on again. Which means *this* is about as far as we can manage.'

'How about here?'

Vikaleira: a bay on the northern shore. Nick dismissed it. 'No anchorage, according to the Pilot. And it's visually exposed.'

'I take that point.' Trench added, 'But – thinking on much the same lines – if we're at Namsos and the Huns arrive, won't we be in a trap?'

Nick straightened, to drink some kye. 'My hope is to get what we need and then away again before the bastards come.' He shrugged. 'We won't get any oil anywhere *short* of Namsos, Tommy.' He put his mug down. 'But for this temporary stop – here, this is the hole I'd like to sneak into, other things permitting.' He was pointing at that gap to the west of Hoddoy, and the anchorage it led to – Totdalbotn. 'In there we'd be tucked away nicely out of sight, and what's more we'd have an alternative exit – this channel, out around the island. But unfortunately it's just outside our range, and that bit's so very narrow that I couldn't risk just not quite making it in daylight.'

Trench thought about it. He suggested, 'Might we persuade Beamish to give us another knot or so?'

It was one answer, perhaps. But Nick didn't want to pressurise his chief stoker into going beyond what his own judgement told him was safe. With Mr Waddicor or Chief ERA Foster it would have been different, but Beamish was less sure of his ground and might agree to something out of ignorance.

But Totdalbotn would certainly be the place to hole up.

'I'll see how he reacts to the suggestion.' He went to the engine-room voicepipe, and got the chief stoker on the other end of it.

'How's it going, Chief?'

'Holding up, sir. All parts bearing an equal strain.'

'D'you think all parts might bear just a little more?'

'More revs, d'you mean, sir?'

'If you could give me one more knot for slightly less than two hours, Chief, I could then give you five hours at anchor. What d'you say?'

'I'd say it's a deal, sir!'

'Good. Up twenty-five revs, then.'

'Well – I'd thought twenty, sir, really—'

'If twenty-five felt like too much you could always come down a bit.'

'I'll see how she takes it, sir.'

There wasn't much shelter yet, because Namsenfjord opened right into the direction of the gale. But as soon as *Intent* rounded the point which the chart called Finsneset she'd begin to get some respite, and it was coming up now on the starboard hand. It was half an hour since Beamish had cautiously increased the revolutions, and so far all seemed well.

To port, eastward, the fjord opened into a V-shaped inlet called Altfjord. It had an island in the middle and the depth of the V was about two and a half miles. What you couldn't see from here but was clear on the chart was that the V's apex was also the narrow entrance to an inner fjord, an almost totally enclosed piece of water that went off at right-angles for about a mile and a half. It would be like a lake, a lagoon in there. He thought, looking at it and wishing he could make use of it, that if only he had some artificers a hideaway like that would be perfect. Nicely hidden, completely sheltered, and just a stone's throw from the open sea.

Lacking artificers, he had to get to Namsos, where there'd be at least *some* kind of engineering help.

Chandler was watching the bearings of the left-hand edge of Altoy Island. When it was abeam he brought the ship round a few degrees to starboard.

'Four miles on this course, sir. Just under eight altogether.'

It was just past ten. *Intent* had been making better than six knots, and as she'd be in calmer water now one might reckon on as much as seven. So they'd be dropping an anchor in that little bay west of Hoddoy no later than 11.30, and sitting down to a hot meal about midnight.

If there was enough power to heat the galley stoves.

'Number One.' He beckoned, and Trench came over to him. 'When we've anchored I want small-arms put out where they can be got at quickly. Revolvers in the chartroom. Rifles and bayonets – well, let's have three or four dumps in convenient places.'

'Aye aye, sir.' Trench was looking at him trying to read his mind. He was like that: he'd work it out, avoid asking a question if he could. Chandler was quite different: he asked immediately, 'Expecting unfriendly natives, sir?'

The engine-room voicepipe squawked: and simultaneously the

note of the turbines began to drop away . . . Nick was already at the pipe.

'Permission to stop engines, sir?'

'*No!*'

'It's bad trouble, sir—'

'Chief, for the moment you *must* keep her going.'

Back into Altfjord, anchor behind the island? He was studying the coastline, remembering the alternatives he'd studied and checked on in the Sailing Directions. Chandler pointed to starboard, where the coastline fell away, opening the fjord to a width of about two miles. 'There's an anchorage in there, sir. Fairly sheltered.'

'Bring her round. And let's have the book.'

Expecting the engines to stop at any second. He bent to the pipe again. 'One mile, Chief, to where we can anchor. We *can't* stop sooner, d'you understand?'

'I can *try*, sir, but—'

'Just *keep her going.*'

He straightened, threw a glance at the rocky lee shore not half a mile away. If the engines stopped now, that was where she'd go, and it wouldn't take long, either. She was under helm and coming slowly round to starboard, and Chandler was telling the helmsman to steer south forty-three west. There'd be at least partial shelter in there, because they'd be in the lee of Finsneset, the last point they'd rounded. He remembered the name of the village near the anchorage – Lovika. He lowered his binoculars: Trench had fetched the Sailing Directions and found the place.

'Lovik?'

'That's it.' Give or take a syllable.

'Twelve to seventeen fathoms, sand and clay bottom.'

That sounded all right, so far as it went. He told Trench, 'Leadsman and cable party, then. I imagine you'll have to work the capstan by hand. And I want Jarratt on the wheel.' He put his glasses up to examine that little bight of coast towards which his ship was creeping. Dying: as if blood instead of oil might be seeping out of her. Anchored there, she'd be in full view of anything passing up or down the fjord. There weren't likely to be any marine engineers in those tiny houses either.

CHAPTER 5

This afternoon Hugh had tracked down one key man and worried at him for an hour like some importunate old terrier; and this evening he'd dined another at his club. Now it was pushing midnight and he was listening to the night-time London silence in an ante-room where 150 years ago a young half-pay captain by the name of Horatio Nelson had waited in vain for an audience with the First Lord. Nelson had been after a sea appointment too.

Hugh Everard had made better progress than Nelson had achieved *that* day. But the commodore's job wasn't what he was here for now. It was still important, and if the worst came to the worst in the matter of Nick and *Intent* it would be vital, would become absolutely imperative to get away to sea. Bad enough to be stuck ashore with things as they were now: but if Nick had gone – he shifted jerkily on his stuffed chair, the thought provoking a sort of stitch – he wouldn't be able to stand it another day.

Cling to hope. There'd always been *such* hope. Getting afloat again would be a kind of escape: he could see that but he saw no reason to be ashamed of wanting it. He could handle it all so much better there than he'd be able to cooped up like an old dog in a kennel.

There was *still* hope, damn it!

He glanced at his watch again, and sighed. Either young Wishart had forgotten he was here or there must be the devil of a lot going on in the remoter depths of this labyrinthine building. People forgot that the Admiralty was an operational headquarters as well as an administrative one. The public probably still thought of it as a place where ancient sea-dogs sat behind vast tables and signed parchments with quill pens: whereas actually there was an Operations Room upstairs, probably going full-blast at this very moment.

Wishart had said on the telephone, 'I'll be here all night, sir. If you'd tell the porter to let me know when you're free, I'll get down to you in my first spare moment.'

Hugh had booked himself a room at Boodle's. One had to keep busy, and in touch. He hadn't liked the idea of the train journey down to Hampshire and then a night at home without news – without a *hope* of news, because nothing could be said over an ordinary telephone these days. He'd have had to have come up again in the morning; there'd have been no point in it.

Strange to think of Nelson kicking his heels in this gloomy hole. He'd failed in his attempt to see Lord Chatham, and hurried over to Wimpole Street to call on Lord Hood instead. Hood had seen him, but told him no, he would *not* intervene with the First Lord. Might one ask why not? Certainly. The admiral had never been a man to shirk an issue. It was because His Majesty had formed an unfavourable opinion of Captain Nelson.

The King, Hugh thought, wouldn't give a damn whether Admiral Sir Hugh Everard succeeded or did not succeed in transforming himself into Commodore Sir Hugh Everard RNR. He'd probably never heard of him . . . But then, he might have. As Prince Albert – or rather, in the alias of 'Johnson' – His Majesty had served as a junior turret officer in *Collingwood* at Jutland: and Hugh had made a bit of a name for himself in that battle. Yes, he probably *would* have heard of him – and forgotten him again long since . . . Anyway, string-pulling, arm-twisting and general browbeating had worked wonders this afternoon and evening, and it would be surprising if in a day or so he wasn't summoned to a medical check-up. He'd pass that as A1, he knew.

Well – near enough A1 . . .

The achievement was less exciting than it should have been. He'd have swapped all hope of it for a reassuring word about Nick.

'Sir Hugh, I am so dreadfully sorry—'

'What?'

He'd jerked upright in his chair: in a kind of shock . . .

'— to have kept you waiting all this time.'

'Oh.' Getting hold of himself again. 'You do seem rather busy, Wishart – for a man with no job to do here?'

'Well, yes. Quite.' The rear-admiral had pushed the door shut behind him. He flipped open a silver case as he crossed the room. 'Cigarette?' Hugh shook his head. Wishart told him, taking one for himself and lighting it, 'I'm helping out on Max Horton's staff.'

His eyes held the older man's as he flicked the match into what must once have been a cuspidor. 'I'd better tell you right away that we've no news of any sort of *Intent* or *Gauntlet*.'

Hugh realised he'd known there wouldn't be. He was aware also that it was a case of no news being bad news. Wishart knew that too, of course. He sat down in a chair facing Hugh's.

'I'll tell you what's going on. The first thing is – we were right, they *are* invading. The first really solid confirmation of it came this afternoon – *Orzel*, a Polish submarine, stopped a Hun transport, *Rio de Janeiro*, and ordered her crew and passengers into the boats before she sank her; then some Norwegian craft came and picked them up. But the passengers were German soldiers in uniform, and they made no bones about it – on their way to "protect" Bergen, they said.' Wishart added, 'On top of a lot of other reports, it doesn't leave any room for doubt. But nobody here – ' he pointed upwards – 'seemed to take much notice. And the Norwegian government won't believe it. They won't even mobilise!'

Hugh commented drily, 'Must have some politicians of our kind over there too, by the sound of it.'

He saw it suddenly: this was going to be the start of the *real* war. We were about to be shown up – to ourselves – as unready and ill-led: it would be so obvious that even the War Cabinet would see it. Britain would get a bloody nose, lose men and ships and strategic advantage: *and be woken up . . .*

An old man's musings . . . The picture seemed real, though. He asked Wishart, 'What *are* we doing? Anything?'

'Well.' Wishart leant forward. 'Early this afternoon a flying-boat 200 miles ahead of the Home Fleet sighted a German force steering west. One battlecruiser, two cruisers, two destroyers. So the C-in-C turned north-westward – to block any Atlantic breakout, of course. He sent off another aircraft – catapulted from *Rodney* – but it never reported back. Either went into the sea or landed in Norway.' He shook his head. 'If only we had a carrier up there. If the Nazis grab the airfield at Stavanger—'

'Have we *no* carriers?'

'*Furious* is in the Clyde but she's not fit for operations yet. *Ark Royal* and *Glorious* are in the Mediterranean. But – other happenings, now . . . Well, first, *Renown* and her destroyers – including *Hoste*, by the way – are heading out westward, for the same reason the C-in-C is. To cut off that force which the flying-boat reported. So Narvik is now left open to the enemy.' He saw Hugh Everard's look of surprise, and nodded. 'I know. I know. And now, anyway, Whitworth's been ordered to turn back and concentrate on blocking the Narvik approaches. It'll take him quite a while to *get* back, though, as it's blowing a real rip-snorter and the destroyers can't make much speed in it. Now – what's next . . . Oh – at about three this afternoon our attaché in Copenhagen reported that two cruisers with either *Gneisenau* or *Blucher* had entered the Kattegat, northbound. Since then two submarines have sighted the same force and one of them made an unsuccessful attack on it, off the Skaw . . . Anyway, it's prompted Sir Charles Forbes to turn south again with *Rodney* and *Valiant*, largely because Admiral Edward-Collins's Second Cruiser Squadron is pretty well in the path of that northbound force, and unsupported. But Forbes has sent *Repulse* and *Penelope* with some destroyers to join Whitworth in the Narvik area.'

'So we've one German force in the north and another to the south'ard.'

'I think others too that we haven't heard about. After all, we know they *are* invading – and there must be inshore forces, assault parties for the different ports . . . But that's the state of things. Admiralty has signalled to the C-in-C that his priorities must be (a) to stop the bunch in the north returning south, and (b) locate and engage the southern force.' Wishart shook his head. 'Between ourselves, I'd say we're making a frightful mess of it. The places we ought to be watching are the Norwegian ports – because that's where the Hun's going, *must* be. In fact we've three cruiser squadrons up there and all out in the deep field, and when the C-in-C just a short while ago ordered the First and Second Squadrons to get into position to start an inshore sweep at first light tomorrow – *really* inshore, in sight of land – our Lordships here in the Admiralty cancelled the order over Forbes's head.'

'That's – incredible . . .'

And utterly depressing. What must it be like for Sir Charles Forbes, the C-in-C?

Wishart drew heavily on his cigarette. Hugh Everard thought, *He's telling me all this to get my mind off Nick* . . .

'I imagine you're staying at your club tonight, sir?'

'What?' He looked up. 'Oh, yes. Yes, indeed.' He frowned. 'I'm being a damn nuisance to you, I'm afraid.'

'You're being nothing of the sort. I only wish I could—' He broke off in mid-sentence, shook his head as he stubbed out the cigarette. 'Sir Hugh, if you were to telephone me here during the forenoon – say about eleven – then if there's any news we could arrange to meet, here or elsewhere, whatever's handy?'

'Very good of you, Wishart. I'll make my call at eleven sharp.'

'You said you'd had some success today, in this scheme of yours?'

'It's a matter of the supply-and-demand balance being tipped my way, I believe. Nobody's admitted it, but I suspect they need more chaps than they've got fit and able to do the job. So – yes, as far as that's concerned it's been a well-spent day.'

Would the day have been missed all that much if the sun had failed to rise?

Careful, he thought. If you get too fanciful they'll rule you out as old and dotty, senile . . . He shivered suddenly: it was a shiver of the mind but it came out through his nerves like a sign of fever. To cover it, he moved quickly, standing up.

'I'll telephone. I am – *most* grateful to you.'

'B' gun's crew took over their own gun from 'A' 's when the watch changed at midnight, and by this time the gale was said to be easing. Down from Force 9 to Force 8 – *that* kind of easing. Trying to sleep on the messdeck had been like taking one's ease in a tin that was being kicked around by a mule; and in spite of it Paul hadn't only *tried* to sleep, he'd slept.

Waking had a new pattern to it. First there was a feeling of relief, of escaping from a disturbing dream. Then the truth bore in: it hadn't been a dream at all, *Intent* was lost and almost certainly her captain would have gone down with her. Reality confirmed itself sickeningly while he dressed for the four hours of the middle watch: sweaters, towel round the neck, oilskins. Depression: this unwashed, unshaven feeling: and the sense of isolation . . . It wasn't only his father's death – he'd lived to all intents and purposes without him, and he could do so again – but the consequences of it, the prospect of becoming a baronet, with Mullbergh to cope with and Sarah and Jack and – *oh, Christ* . . . It wasn't only depressing, it was frightening. Then, feeling the ice-cold sweat, he told himself to snap out of it: *stop acting Dherjhorakov* . . . Old tennis shoes: they were already on his feet but not laced up. He slept in them. Rubber soles were best on the gundeck, when you had to stagger around with projectiles or charges in your arms and the ship was doing its best to dump you overboard . . .

Up top, out of the screen door and in the howling bedlam of the gale on the port side of the foc'sl deck – the wind was on *Hoste*'s starboard bow – he paused with one foot on the ladder and both hands stretched up overhead as high as he could reach; when she started her roll back to starboard he began climbing, up to the top and over the edge of the gundeck quickly, across into the lee of the gun. He clung to the edge of the gunshield, peered round at the sea and as much as was visible of other ships in company. *Renown*'s biggish stern-on shape ahead was a black smudge framed in white; and to starboard in another patch of broken sea another destroyer banged along on *Hoste*'s beam . . . Then he realised how wrong he was. In the dark, with your eyes not yet adjusted and your brain only half awake, sizes and shapes were confusing. That wasn't *Renown* ahead, that was a destroyer; the battlecruiser would be ahead of *her*. Or even *two* up . . . *Hoste* and that ship on her beam each had at least one other destroyer ahead of them; the rest would be strung out astern and invisible from this gundeck.

Bow down, stuck deep into the sea: the ship quivering, shaking, as if she was trying to wriggle or bore her way into it . . . 'That you there, Yank?'

Dan Thomas, gun captain and breechworker, a three-badge killick whose home town was Swansea, was checking to see he had his crew complete. Vic Blenkinsop the sightsetter told Paul, 'Shifted course to nor'-west during the First, Shortarse 'Iggins says. Ride out the worst o' the blow like, 'e reckoned.'

'Which way we goin' now, Vic?'

'*Every* fuckin' way, mate.' Blenkinsop spat down-wind, over Johnno Dukes's shoulder. Dukes was gunlayer. Blenkinsop asked him, ''Adn't you noticed?' He settled the headphones over his ears, easing his balaclava over them before he turned the mouthpiece up and reported to the TS, ' "B" gun closed up.'

'No "B" gun bloody ain't, you bloody ullage you!' Dan Thomas bawled it from inside the gunshield. 'If "B" gun's closed up where's that bald-'eaded bloody bookworm then?'

'I'm – if you mean me, I'm – *here* . . .' Baldy Percival launched himself from the head of the ladder and came slithering across the canting gundeck. Bow out: water streaming back – solid, battering against the shield. She was rolling viciously to port: Paul grabbed an arm and held on until Baldy had his balance and was more or less at rest . . .' Sorry – er – Dan. Fact is I lost a boot, couldn't find it *anywhere*, then—'

74

'Next time come up wi'out the bugger!'

'Ah – yes. Yes, I will.' He crouched down, close to Paul who was edging his way further into shelter, past the sightsetter. The ship was acting like a mad thing: it was a marvel that she was holding together. If it had been worse than this, as apparently 'Shortarse' Higgins – one of 'A' gun's crew – had indicated, it must have been pretty frightening. Percival told him, 'This boot's soaking wet inside – all slushy round my foot. I think – it sounds *ridiculous*, but – I think someone must have peed in it.'

' "B" gun!' Blenkinsop was answering a call through his headset. He was listening now, and the men round him waiting for the message. Then, 'Aye aye. But if I'm not 'ere when you next call, mate – ah, shurrup yourself . . .' He pushed the microphone away from his mouth, and told them, 'In five minutes, ship will be reversin' course – turnin' right around like. They reckon she'll roll like a bastard an' all 'ands is to 'ang on an' say their prayers . . . 'Ear me, kiddies?'

Baldy Percival was muttering, close to Paul's ear, 'All squelchy round my toes. Honestly, some filthy—'

'Who'd have *peed* in it, for Christ's sake.' He was fed up with Baldy's fussing. He should have kept his boots on his feet, like anyone else did if they had any sense. He was thinking about this change of course they'd just been warned about. It was a north-westerly gale and they had it on the starboard bow, so *Hoste* was steering west, and reversing course would mean coming round to east. Heading back towards Narvik, then. Or Vestfjord, whatever it was called.

Having left it long enough for some Germans to sneak in?

He remembered Lieutenant-Commander Rowan's *Ours not to reason why*. If it wasn't for a ship's CO to reason why, it surely wasn't for a raw OD . . . He still did, though. He wanted not only to know what was going on, but to understand it. He'd always had such a need: it irritated him to have to act blindly, or to be fobbed off with shallow explanations that didn't fit or make sense in his own mind. (Shades of childhood: *Because I tell you to, that's why!*) None of his messmates seemed to share this urge; most of the time they didn't even know which way the ship was heading, let alone what for. But in training, the instructors talked about 'initiative': and how could you use initiative if you didn't know what the hell was happening in the first place?

'Here comes the Rose an' Crown!'

Johnno Dukes yelled it: it was his rhyming slang for *Renown*. He'd been looking out through his sighting port, the window in the gunshield above his laying handwheel. Paul shifted back out of the crush, craned his head round the edge of the shield into the buffeting, thumping wind. Eyes more settled to the dark now: in fact it *wasn't* really dark. Baldy Percival squeezing out beside him. Must be more of a kook than one had realised, to suspect messmates of pissing into his boot, for heaven's sake . . . *Renown* – he saw her suddenly, a black mass surrounded by a welter of white: she'd come about and she was pounding back on an opposite course to the destroyers'. Getting on for 40,000 tons of ship – colossal, like a floating town, 750 feet of her and Lord only knew how many decks below the waterline. About a third of that 750 feet was foc'sl, and all of that, as she ploughed bow-down, was buried in the sea: now, rising, bursting out immense, fantastic in size and power: the very size and weight of it made the upswing of that long sweep of bow seem to be happening in slow-motion, breaking out and throwing up a mountain of sea to stream back over her massive for'ard turrets like so much confetti flying on the wind – only it wasn't confetti, it was solid sea, as much as a hundred tons of it tossed back as effortlessly as a man might flick a peanut. The night sky turned blacker with her bulk across it as she thundered past, turrets and superstructure and twin funnels seemingly one mass, bow-wave high and bright underscoring it, curling away aft to pile and then spread out into the morass of foam astern. Bow *down* again now, that enormously long, powerful-looking forepart dipping in with the same slow-seeming grace: there was a look of grandeur, impressive and somehow emotionally inspiring too: it triggered some thought-process at the back of his mind and it was important, a personal thing he had to come to terms with . . . Dan Thomas yelled, 'Inside and 'ang on, lads!'

Paul moved in, shoving Baldy in ahead of him. Thomas was right, of course. The destroyers which had been next-astern of the battlecruiser would be following her round now, and soon it would be *Hoste*'s turn, and when she was beam-on to this murderous sea she was likely to do just about everything except loop the loop. Even crowding in here and jammed tight as they were might be quite hazardous, if a big sea decided to demonstrate its power, to reach in and winkle a few bodies out.

' "B" gun!'

Blenkinsop taking another call. They waited to hear what was new. Probably a warning again, stand by for the rough stuff. Tom Brierson, the leading hand of 3 Mess, had said he'd been in a destroyer when she had her foc'sl deck flattened and pushed in by a sea no worse than this one. There'd been stooping-height only in the upper messdeck, he'd said; and it had happened only a few miles outside Scapa Flow.

'Aye aye.' Vic Blenkinsop shouted. 'Secure the gun, clear upper deck!'

The skipper must have been having second thoughts, seeing just how tricky this turn-about was going to be. Dan Thomas was yelling at them to do this and that; Paul, clear of the scrum, checked that the lids of the ready-use lockers were screwed down tight. The lockers held cordite charges; the projectiles were in open racks, since it didn't matter how wet they got.

'One at a time to the ladder, now. Percival – you first – *move*!'

Baldy went slithering to it, crab-like. One at a time made sense; there wasn't anything much to hold on to at the top of the ladder, if you'd had to wait there. 'All right, Yank!' He shot across, and swung over the edge. Below him Baldy yelped as Paul's foot coincided with his ear or nose, and above Paul's head boots were already clumping down relentlessly. He kept his hands on the ladder's sides, clear of the rungs where fingers could get crushed. Then he was off it and tight-rope walking aft, reaching from one support to the next, vividly aware of the sea roaring fury at him on his right and only a few feet away. The screen door was open, Percival holding it open for him: he pushed inside, and Lofty McElroy leapt in behind him. Paul knew what it was that had been in his mind when he'd been watching *Renown* pass them: the CW business, going in for a commission: what the skipper had told him and also, linking with that, the fact of being alone now, a feeling that one had to move in *some* direction.

'How's the time, Yank?'

Paul shifted aching limbs. A steel deck got to you, after a few hours, and a tin hat didn't make much of a pillow. He squinted at his watch, and was vaguely surprised that there was enough light to make out the positions of the hands. He told Dukes, 'Half three.'

Baldy Percival, mummy-like with the white anti-flash gear covering his head and face, twisted up and on to his elbows. 'What? What's that?'

'Go back to dreamland, Baldy.'

'My foot's *frozen*!'

'Oh dear, oh dear!' The high-pitched exclamation came from Harry Rush, the rammer. He began to warble in a falsetto voice, '*Your tiny foot is frozen. Let me wa-arm it in the fire* . . .'

'Shut up, you fuckin' idiot!'

Dan Thomas's growl, from the huddle of duffel-coats and oil-skins inside the shield. Rush murmured, 'Charming. *Suave*, you might say . . . 'Ow you makin' out, Yanky lad?'

'I'm okay, thanks.'

'Can't you bastards bloody *kip*?'

'No, we soddin' can't. Too bleedin' comfortable up 'ere, for the likes of us. We ain't used to such soddin' luxury, are we, Yank?'

'Sea's gone down a little.'

'Bloody 'ell it 'as. Just the course she's on.'

You could feel the way the following sea was driving her along, lifting her from astern, the destroyer surfing over the big seas and seeming to drop back as well as down as each small mountain rolled on ahead of her. Still going east, Paul realised. Narvikwards. Vibration and ventilator-noise suggested they were doing revs for about twelve knots, something like that.

McElroy mumbled, half asleep, 'Fuckin' 'oggin. Nothin' but mile upon mile of fuckin' 'oggin.'

'Never knew you was a poet, Lofty.' Vic Blenkinsop shifted, pushing himself upright and adjusting the headset under his balaclava. 'Sheer delight to listen to you . . . *What* fuckin' time d'you say it was, Yank?

'Minute or two past three-thirty.'

The sky was brightening ahead. In streaks here and there, where the black storm-clouds had cracks between them, were rifts with a new pale, gale-driven day glittering through. If any Germans had got into Narvik during the night they'd have been damn glad to get inside, he thought, into the shelter of those fjords. He wondered what it would be like inside there. Like a river, probably: flat calm, reflecting the mountain-sides, beautiful. What a change from *this* . . . Keeping one's thoughts on solid things, on present and immediate-future subjects: the aim being to stop oneself indulging in the luxury of worrying, of trying to find an angle that would make everything all right and as it had been. It was *not* all right, and this was something one was going to have to accept and live with, recognise as existing, permanently, behind all the other facts of life.

If the Germans had got into Narvik, what could this force do about it? Sit the gale out in Vestfjord, wait for the Hun to come out and fight?

Couldn't hang around and wait for ever, though. Have to fuel some time. Some time pretty soon, he imagined.

'We're in Indian bloody file again.' Dan Thomas had stepped over some sprawling bodies, crossed behind the breech; he was leaning against the inside edge of the gunshield and staring out over the port bow and ahead. He yawned: it sounded like a donkey braying . . . 'Like a lot of bloody ducks followin' mother . . . *Hey*, what the—'

Vic Blenkinsop screamed, 'Alarm bearing red one-oh, all guns follow director!'

A split second while it hit them and penetrated drowsy brains: then everyone was dodging and barging to the various positions round the gun. Everything happening at once: alarm-buzzer honking away below to get the other watch up, and the sound of the engines changing, turbine-whine rising and the roar of the fans increasing; the ship was swinging to port – but steadying already, course about due east . . .

'All guns with SAP load, load, load!'

SAP stood for semi-armour-piercing, and Baldy Percival, who was the projectile supply number, snatched one of the right kind from the ready-use rack and clanged it into the loading-tray. Paul dropped his cordite charge in behind it and Harry Rush rammed shell and charge home into the breech. The block slid up automatically, its concave curve of silk-smooth steel pushing his fist clear as it rose, and Dan Thomas had slammed the interceptor shut.

' "B" gun ready!'

No fire order yet. Anti-climax. Thomas told them, 'Dirty great battler out there.'

'What, *German*?'

'Wouldn't be fuckin' Chinese, boyo, would she.'

The ship that had sunk *Intent*? But that had been a cruiser, not a battleship . . .

''Aving you on.' Dan Thomas laughed. 'All I seen was *Renown* swingin' off course. Some fuckin' HO on the 'elm, I thought . . .'

Paul had another charge ready in his arms. Until yesterday he'd been the projectile supply number and this job had been Baldy's: they changed you around so you'd learn the different jobs and be able to take other men's places in an emergency. In other words, if some of them got killed. Handling the cordite charges was a lot easier than lumping shells. *Hoste* was in a hurry now, slamming across the rollers, rolling savagely as she plunged in the wake of her next-ahead. She'd have to alter course, he guessed, before they opened fire. The enemy – whatever kind of enemy it was – was somewhere right ahead, blanked off from them by the leading ships. It had to be so, or the guns would have been trained out on some other bearing. He was pulling on his anti-flash gear one-handed and with the tin hat gripped between his knees while he leant sideways against the gun for support. They were supposed to wear the anti-flash hoods and gloves all the time when they were closed up at the gun, but nobody did – except for Baldy . . . Blenkinsop shouted, 'Target is *Gneisenau* with one *Hipper*-class cruiser astern of 'er. Course will soon be altered to port and enemy will be engaged to starboard!'

'Bloody *Gneisenau*, for Gawd's sake!'

''Ere, Dan, you was fuckin' *right*!'

'I'm always fuckin' right . . .'

Hipper-class cruiser, Rowan had said. Here it was again. *Here it was!*

Why couldn't *Renown* have opened fire? Nothing ahead of *her*, was there? Well – she'd want to get her after turret into it too, of course, fire broadsides, not just use the for'ard guns . . . Lofty McElroy bawled, 'Next-ahead's goin' roun' tae port!' He'd be seeing it through the port in the gunshield in front of him. He and the gunlayer on the other side each had one, an aperture with a shutter on it for keeping wind and wet out. In Director Firing – the normal system, which they'd be using now – neither layer nor trainer had to see outside or even know what the target looked like; all they had to do was keep one pointer lined up on another in a brass-cased dial. The director layer did the aiming for all four guns, from up there in the top.

Renown opened fire. Rolling crash of fifteen-inch guns and a flash like lightning flaring briefly, a splash of brilliance overtaken immediately by the dark, which seemed all the darker for it in the racket of wind and sea and the ventilators' roaring, and the turbines' scream. Paul stood with his feet braced well apart, rubbersoled shoes gripping the wet steel platform, one shoulder against the gunshield. Another salvo erupted: explosion and flash, black curtain clamping down again. The ship was swinging, leaning hard to starboard as port rudder dragged her round and turned her port side to the gale's force. Plunging, shuddering, staggering round. As she turned, the gun trained out, staying on the bearing of the enemy. Twenty knots now? Third salvo: count to five and another sky-splitting crash . . . He wondered if the Germans had been caught on the hop: it was possible, with those cloud-cracks in the east putting a light behind the bastards, showing them up to the British battlecruiser who would herself be still hidden in the westward gloom, storm-darkness. Two more salvoes had hurtled away: *Renown* had three twin turrets of fifteen-inch, so they'd be three-gun salvoes, and a fifteen-inch was a huge projectile. *Hoste* was steady now on what must have been a northward course, wind and sea deafening and violent on her port bow, gun trained out on the beam.

'*Commence, commence, commence!*'

Clang of the fire-gong: then the ear-slamming explosion: recoil, breech open, reeking cordite fumes flying as Dan Thomas jerked the lever to send the breech-block thumped down, projectile and charge in, breech shut, interceptor made: fire-gong – *crash* – second salvo, all four guns firing together and a ripple of the other destroyers' guns all down the line and the deeper thunder of the battlecruiser's salvoes in a steady rhythm now, flaming into the dawn-streaked east. No time to look at anything except this job, the loading-tray and the breech, charges and projectiles coming up from below now through an ammo hatch in the deckhead of the Chiefs' and POs' mess under their feet and, before they got that far, from hand to hand up through two messdecks below that. The ship was trying to knock herself to bits, jolting and hammering across the sea, thrashing and flailing like a salmon on a line. The firing was constant now: breech open – filled – shut – *crash*, and flinging back – open . . . Baldy seeming to be in the throes of a little dance as he banged his rounds in and lunged around for the next: it *was* like a dance, a kind of seven-man reel . . .

'*Check, check, check!*'

Stone deaf. Skull ringing. Dizzy from noise and dazed by flash, muscles aching. Dan Thomas's fist hitting Paul's bicep had stopped him as he was about to drop a fresh charge into the loading-tray. The gun's crew was still now, only swaying and weaving to the ship's wild motion. And she was slowing, while from ahead *Renown*'s guns still boomed out, sound muted by distance as well as by one's own temporary deafness. *Renown* had obviously drawn well ahead of the destroyers; so if *Hoste* had been making twenty knots – which in conditions like these was fairly unthinkable, despite the fact that it was what she'd been doing – the battlecruiser must have been working up to – what, thirty?

Enemy running away? *Renown* cracking on full power to stay inside gun range?

They'd run from something their own size, Paul thought bitterly. Different when it had been just two destroyers . . .

Hoste was swinging to starboard. Slowing, and turning back to her former eastward or south-eastward course.

'*Secure from action stations.*'

Dan Thomas yelled to Lofty McElroy, 'Train fore-an'-aft!' Baldy Percival's eyes gleamed at Paul through the gap in his anti-flash hood. He panted, 'D'you realise, we've been *in action*?'

'Yeah. I suppose . . .'

Action was supposed to be something terrific, though. Like getting married or circumcised or something. This had been like a gun-drill. He hadn't caught a glimpse of any enemy and he certainly wasn't aware of having been shot at or in any danger. Technically, Baldy was right – they'd been in action: asked whether one had fired shots in anger, one could now answer in the affirmative. But he didn't feel it counted, really. And it certainly wasn't the kind of action that *Intent* must have been in . . . He was looking out towards the destroyer on their starboard bow – he thought it was the flotilla leader, *Hardy*, Captain (D)'s ship – and there was a signal lamp sputtering dots and dashes from the back end of her bridge. The flotilla – ships from more than one flotilla here, actually, there must have been about nine or ten destroyers altogether – seemed to be in the process of rearranging itself into the two-column formation.

'Right, then.' Blackie Proudfoot, 'A' gun's layer, had come up the ladder and lurched across into shelter. Blue-jowled, scowling, chewing gum. '*Right*, then! Bugger off, you shower o' fuckin' amacheurs!'

Shouts of ritually insulting welcome greeted him. Paul checked the time: it was well past the watch-changing hour, and therefore 'B' gun-crew's watch below now. Lovely! A mug of tea or kye, he thought, whatever's going: then head down, kip until breakfast-time . . . Proudfoot was grumbling, 'Waste o' fuckin' ammo, wasn't it?'

Inside, on their way down to the messdeck, they met Sub-

Lieutenant Peters, and Rush stopped him, asked him something about the action. Peters told them, 'The second German wasn't a cruiser, it was *Scharnhorst*. GCO thought she was a *Hipper* when he first saw her – but we've been engaging two pocket battleships.' He seemed delighted by it . . . 'Last we heard, *Renown* had scored three hits – including one in *Gneisenau*'s foretop, and it's put her main armament out of action. So *Scharnhorst*'s laying smoke now to cover their withdrawal.'

'Mean they're scarpering, sir?'

Peters nodded to Harry Rush. 'Our own gun-flashes will have helped to put the wind up them. They couldn't know we're only destroyers, you see. If they *had* known, they could have got stuck in and knocked the be-Jesus off *Renown*. They're both twenty years newer than she is, you know.'

'They'll 'ave the legs of her, then.'

'Oh, they'll outrun her, I'm afraid.' Peters' round face was scarlet from the wind. 'Unless she's lucky and lands another one in some vital spot.'

Paul asked him, 'What are we doing now, sir?'

Peters turned to him. 'We've orders to patrol Vestfjord, Everard. But if we're lucky – well, there's a signal just in from C-in-C to Captain (D) that he's to send some destroyers up to Narvik. That means right up through the fjords. Apparently some Huns have got in while our backs were turned.'

'Bit late to be much fuckin' use, then.' Rush was pulling a wet-looking pack of cigarettes from some inner pocket. 'I mean, if the sods are *up* there, settled like— '

'*Un*settle 'em, boyo!' The gun captain struck him violently on the back. 'We'll bloody *un*settle 'em!'

CHAPTER 6

'Captain, sir!'

Dragging himself out of sleep . . .

'Unidentified ship approaching, sir!'

He was off the bunk, snatching duffel-coat and cap; *really* awake now, hearing the alarm buzzer sounding surface action stations. Across the lobby outside his sea-cabin, on to the ladder and up it to the bridge.

Very cold, and already daylight. It was four-twenty: he'd had about one and a half hours' sleep. Before he'd turned in the telegraphists had picked up an English-language broadcast announcing that Denmark had been overrun and was now in German hands and that the forts in Oslofjord were being bombarded by German warships.

Tommy Trench was waiting for him on the bridge. He pointed – over the starboard bow.

'Sure she's Norwegian, sir. Better to be safe than sorry, I thought, but – out of the last century, by the looks of her.'

'And practically alongside.' This reproof came as a reflex as he settled his glasses on her and found her so startlingly close. Trench was explaining that when she'd come into sight around the point she'd been only a mile away. A small ship with the lines of an old-fashioned yacht, two raked masts and one high, thin funnel. Clipper bow, cut-away stern, gaffs on both masts and a white painted wheelhouse just for'ard of the funnel. Abaft it there was a longer, lower, dark-coloured deckhouse with ports all along its length. What ought to be a saloon. One could imagine its dark mahogany, red velvet, brass. She was flying the Norwegian ensign and there were no guns on her that he could see. He glanced up over his shoulder and saw that the director tower was trained on her. The four-sevens would be too.

He lowered his binoculars. 'Warn Brocklehurst not, repeat *not*, to open fire without orders. Signalman – give me the loud-hailer.'

Obviously she *was* Norwegian. But since the Germans had taken the whole of Denmark in about half a dog-watch it wasn't inconceivable that they could have pinched a few Norwegian ships by this time. On the other hand he couldn't imagine Germans bothering with such a delicate-looking, totally unwarlike craft; or for that matter that even if she was packed with Nazis from stem to stern she'd pose much of a threat to a well armed, albeit immobilised, destroyer.

He took the loud-hailer from the signalman – who'd plugged it into the socket that was more often used for the kye kettle – and lifted it, aimed it at the stranger. Clearing his throat produced a sound like a seal's bark, fairly cracking across the fjord.

'Do not approach any more closely. Stop and identify yourself!'

He repeated it: his voice boomed over the water and echoed back from the land behind him. Whatever that floating antique was, she must have come round the headland – Finsneset – from seaward, perhaps en route to Namsos, then spotted *Intent* lying at anchor in the shallow bay and turned down to investigate her. *Intent* was lying almost parallel to the shore, with her cable growing straight out into the incoming tidal flow. Beyond the Norwegian – he hadn't stopped yet and he was still heading straight for the British ship – you could see white-topped waves and a drifting haze of spray that was being whipped off their crests, but here in the lee of the point there was no broken water and the ship's motion as she rode to her anchor was comparatively gentle.

He aimed the hailer again.

'Stop, or I shoot!' He glanced at Trench. 'Tell Brocklehurst to load one gun with practice shell.'

A warning shot across the bows was a good way to short-cut any language problems. A practice shell was solid, non-explosive. But he'd no wish to aggravate this Norwegian. If it was true that the Nazis were invading, then Britain and Norway were now allies with a common enemy. And this strange-looking craft might prove to be *Intent*'s saviour, a means of getting shore assistance for the engine-room repairs.

He put his glasses up again. The newcomer was altering course, turning to starboard, and the ripple of bow-wave at her shapely forefoot was diminishing as she slowed. Her captain was doing things his own way, in his own time; either he didn't understand

English, or he was deaf, or he was demonstrating a spirit of Viking independence. And these were, after all, Norwegian waters . . . His ship was beam-on to *Intent* now, and stopping; two hands had gone for'ard to let go an anchor. They were visible only from the waist up, on account of the ship's high, white-painted bulwarks.

The anchor splashed down and its cable rattled out; at the same time a man in what looked like naval uniform emerged from the wheelhouse, and waved.

Nick waved back. He told Trench, 'Fall out action stations, but keep one four-seven and the point-fives closed up. Better send the hands to breakfast while things are quiet.'

The Norwegians were preparing to lower a boat. It was a motor skiff, slung from davits abaft the mizzen mast, and some men were hauling on tackles to turn the davits out on this side.

She was unarmed, and the rigging on those masts and gaffs indicated that she had sails and was equipped to use them. Training ship? Around 200 tons, he guessed, and roughly 120 feet long. No weapons anywhere, not even a machine-gun. But she'd be capable of getting into Namsos and bringing out some plumbers, all right.

He asked Trench, 'Any progress in the engine-room?'

'None at the last enquiry, sir. Beamish is still at it but he's not exuding much optimism . . . MacKinnon's improved the W/T reception though, and he's picked up two or three signals addressed to Captain (D) 2, they tell me. I've been leaving the deciphering until the doctor's had some zizz.'

Nick had told MacKinnon to take in everything he could pick up. He wanted to know what was going on: especially any details of the Hun attack on Norway. But they'd only be able to decipher signals intended for ships of their own size, more or less. Admiralty messages to and from the C-in-C, or signals between flag officers, would be in ciphers which a destroyer didn't carry.

'Have you had any sleep, pilot?'

'Yes, sir.' Chandler took the point of the enquiry. 'I'll make a start on the deciphering.'

'Lyte or Cox can give you a hand.' You needed one man to read out, another to look up and write down. He asked Trench, 'How's Bywater's patient?'

'Stronger, he said. That's why he decided he could get his head down . . . We're about to have visitors, sir.'

The skiff was in the water with two men in her, and the one who'd waved was climbing down to join them. Nick focused binoculars on him. Three stripes: or two and a half. A burly, biggish man. Trousers tucked inside seaboots. Now he was in the boat's stern-sheets, and as he turned around Nick saw a crumpled-looking cap pushed well back and a reefer jacket unbuttoned over a high-necked sweater. Lowering the glasses, he thought he already had a fair idea of the sort of character he'd be dealing with.

'Let's give him the red carpet, Number One.'

Trench nodded. 'I'll have it unrolled, sir.' He went down to organise a Jacob's ladder and a side-party, and Nick sent a message to Leading Steward Seymour to get his day-cabin straightened – after the rough weather it was bound to be in a mess – and to lay on coffee and biscuits. Then Lyte, the sub-lieutenant, came up, sent by Trench to take over anchor-watch on the bridge, and Nick went down to see what was happening in the engine-room.

Beamish and his henchmen looked just about done in. Dull, red-rimmed eyes, faces grey under coatings of oil and dirt. Listening to his laboured explanation of the problems, Nick told himself that one had to allow for that tiredness as a factor in the chief stoker's defeatism. Beamish was winding up his depressing report by explaining what he intended to do about the blast-hole overhead. It was a large, jagged hole; as Trench had said earlier, the shell must have exploded virtually as it pierced the thin layer of steel. And yet the explosion had sounded as if it had been right inside. Echo-effect, perhaps . . . Beamish's plan was to use two of the steel floor-plates, weld them over the hole after the uneven edges had been cut away.

'What'll you stand on, without floor plates?'

'Timber staging, sir. Chief Buffer reckons he can knock some up for us.'

'Sounds reasonable.'

'It was the middy – Mr Cox – as thought of it, sir.'

'What's it to do with *him*, for God's sake?'

'Well, he's been lending us a hand, sir.'

'*Has* he . . .' Extraordinary. But he'd ask Cox about it, not Beamish. 'Just one question, Chief. Could we move now if we had to?'

'Oh, *no*, sir!'

'Second question, then. Do you anticipate that at some later stage we'll be in a condition so we *can* move?'

'I – s'pose so, sir. Somehow or other, like. But—'

'At this stage you can't guarantee it.'

'No, sir.' An oily hand passed round an already well-oiled jaw. 'No. I'm sorry, sir, I—'

'It's not your fault. Anyway, we're about to be boarded by a Norwegian, and with any luck I'll persuade him to carry on into Namsos and bring out some shoreside help.'

The Norwegian would damn well *have* to. Otherwise *Intent* would still be sitting here when the Germans came.

PO Metcalf's bosun's call shrilled as the man came over *Intent*'s side. He was a lieutenant-commander, and in his late forties, Nick guessed. A rugged-looking character with greying hair showing under the battered cap. Wide-set blue eyes in a tanned, muscled face scanned the reception committee and returned to Nick. The salute was casual, friendly.

Nick shook a wide, meaty hand. 'My name's Everard, and this is His Majesty's Ship *Intent*. Glad to welcome you aboard.'

'I am Claus Torp. Kaptein-Löjtnant, Naval Reserve. My ship there – ' he jerked a thumb – 'is *Valkyrien*.'

'A very handsome ship, we've all been thinking.' Nick introduced Tommy Trench. Torp asked him as he shook his hand, 'You got many of such size?' Trench laughed; Nick asked Torp, 'Are you from Namsos, Commander?'

'I – yes. But *Valkyrien* I am bringing from Mo i Rana to Trondheim. Then I am hearing on my radio the Boche is already there, so—'

'The Germans are in Trondheim?'

'I think they are in *every* damn place, you know?'

They could be here at any moment, then . . . It wasn't really a surprise – only confirmation of existing fears. At least he'd been wise not to take her into Trondheim.

'Will you come below, Commander, and discuss the position over a cup of coffee?'

'Sure, thank you.'

'Join us, Tommy?'

'Thank you, sir.' Nick saw Henry Brocklehurst emerging from the screen door, the entrance to the wardroom flat. Short, neat – he'd just shaved – a little cock-sparrow of a man, smart enough for Whale Island, the gunnery school, to which he hoped to return soon for his 'long G' course. Nick introduced him to Torp: and beside Trench, Brocklehurst really did look like a sparrow. Torp grinning down at him and glancing at the bigger man, obviously thinking something of the same sort. Nick told him, 'I'd like you to keep an eye on the bridge, while we're below. Lyte's up there, but we aren't in the safest of spots.'

Brocklehurst nodded. 'Aye aye—'

'Have you had any sleep yet?'

'I kipped in the director, sir.'

'My God . . .' Leading the other two down to his day-cabin, Nick asked *Valkyrien*'s captain, 'D'you have any details of what's happened in Trondheim?'

'The forts are fighting but the town is captured. One cruiser, *Hipper*, and four destroyers with her, they are through the Narrows before alarm was given.' He snorted angrily. 'We are not ready for the bastards, I think . . . Is your wireless not working, Captain?'

'We lost our topmast. Messed things up somewhat. We're on reduced power too.' He led into the cabin and saw that the coffee was already there, set out by Leading Steward Seymour, together with a plate of shortbread from his private store. 'Sit down, please.' Seymour came in behind them, and stood hovering; Nick told him he wasn't needed. He explained to Torp, 'We were damaged in action with a German cruiser. *Hipper*-class – perhaps *Hipper* herself, if she's in Trondheim now.'

'You are lucky to be afloat, I think. Against *Hipper*? One H-class destroyer?'

' "I", as it happens. For *Intent*.'

' "H", "I" – who's giving a damn!' A forthright character, this Norwegian. 'From one look I see what you are. Otherwise I am turning round to run like hell, you bet. *Valkyrien* has no guns, you understand, she is for boys' training. I bring her now from Mo i Rana to Trondheim so they put guns on her for patrol work in Trondheimsfjorden.' He'd stopped his prowling inspection of the cabin in front of a portrait that didn't belong in here. It had strayed – thanks no doubt to the steward's 'straightening' – from Nick's sleeping cabin. Torp let out something between a hiss and a whistle: 'This is your wife, Captain?'

He'd pronounced it 'vife'. Nick told him no, it was not, and invited him to sit down. Torp said, lowering himself into an armchair, 'I suppose you did not hear what has happened in Oslo?'

'Only that Hun ships were bombarding the forts.'

'So.' The Norwegian accepted coffee. 'Thank you . . . Patrol boat *Pol III*, with commander my friend Wielding Olsen – also naval reserve – is in Oslofjord. Sight Boche – make challenge – no

89

answering, so open fire. *Pol III* has one gun – forty millimetre, *one*. She was whaler – very small . . . You know what ships she is fighting? *Blucher, Lutzow, Emden!* Also torpedo boats and minesweepers. Wielding has ram one torpedo boat, then – finish. He himself – listen, I tell you – he is blown in half, his legs – all from *here* . . . He roll himself overboard so the men do not see him and stop fighting. Huh?' Torp's jaw-muscles bulged: his eyes closed, opened again . . . 'Wielding Olsen. My *friend* . . . I have this in Norwegian broadcast. Also our government – listen – they have ordered now to mobilise – and they are sending the calling-up orders today, *by post*!'

'I don't believe it.'

Torp looked at Trench. 'Believe everything, my friend. Anything. So long as a German is not telling it, believe it. We have *idiots* in our government. You too, I think. I think your Navy could – could have been around – not *laying mines*, God damn it, but—'

'Quite.' Nick put his cup down. 'The point is, to decide what we're going to do *now*. And the first thing is, Commander, I very much want your help.'

'Okay, you have it. But the *first* thing is you must move up the fjord much higher. Here you are exposed all ways. If the wind veer one point you have bad conditions and lee shore southward. Also, if I was enemy, I come round the point here and before you can see who I am – *boom*!'

'The problem is that we *can't* move. This is as far as we could get. The cruiser – *Hipper* – hit us in the engine-room. Not only has it done us a lot of damage, but it killed all my artificers and I've no one left who can put us right. What I'd like to ask you to do, Commander, is go to Namsos as fast as possible and bring off some engineers. With whatever gear they might think they'd need. Would you do that for us?'

'Sure.' Torp nodded, munching shortbread. Then he took a swallow of coffee to wash the crumbs down. He blinked at Nick across the table. 'I also have wish to go to Namsos. I *must* go there. But for you maybe I have better plan.' He took a cigarette from the case that Trench was offering him. 'Thank you. I think first I send my boat to *Valkyrien* for bringing my engineer to look at your troubles. You agree?'

It seemed an obvious preliminary. But it would use up *time* . . . And what sort of old Scandinavian shellback would be the engineer of that museum piece?

'Every minute counts, Commander. With the Germans in Trondheim – what, seventy miles from us—'

'Halvard Boyensen is damn fine engineer. This is why I have been taking him to Mo i Rana. That old *Valkyrien* don't work for just any damn-fool mechanic. So I take young – ' he tapped his forehead – '*smart* fellow—'

'All right.' It might *save* time, in the long run. 'Let's have him over.'

'Good.' The Norwegian pushed himself up. 'You stay. I tell them.'

Waiting, finishing his coffee, Nick saw Trench glancing at the portrait. Fiona Gascoyne – a rich man's widow. Thirty, thirty-one. Girl-about-town, and now in the MTC – Mechanised Transport Corps. Hence the existence and presence here of the photograph. She liked the look of herself in the MTC uniform – made for her, of course, at Huntsman. Nick had told her the obvious thing – that he preferred her out of it – and she'd said, 'You're not getting one of me like *that*, my pet!' But there'd be quite a number of those portraits around, he knew that. She made no secret of it, she was far from being a one-man girl. She wouldn't be, she'd added, at least for quite some while. She'd been tied down all her life: she'd been very young when she'd married old Gascoyne, and the marriage had bored her stiff, but now she was free and rich enough to please herself – until she tired of it . . . Which from Nick's point of view was perfectly all right. What seemed to be his mark were brief affairs or longer but essentially light-hearted ones. The long struggle with Ilyana and the continuing background of blind enmity from Sarah – whom he'd loved, twenty-plus years ago, to a degree beyond distraction – well, what was the point, when everyone ended up hurt?

Trench murmured, 'We're in a bit of a spot, sir, aren't we, by and large.'

'Oh, I don't know, Tommy. If this plumber's all he's cracked up to be, we might be running lucky again.'

There'd been some Norwegian sounds up there; now Torp came back into the cabin. 'I have send for Boyensen.' He dropped into his chair, stubbed out the cigarette-end. 'You guess what year my old *Valkyrien* is building?'

Nick made his guess and knocked a few years off the age before he spoke.

'Nineteen hundred?'

Trench said less gallantly, 'Eighteen-ninety.'

'Not so bad.' Torp nodded. 'Ninety-one.'

Nick heard the motor skiff chug away from his ship's side. He told his guest, 'There's one other urgent requirement we have, and that's oil-fuel. I imagine that once we're fixed up and can get into Namsos—'

'Sure.' Claus Torp shrugged. 'If the Boche stay away that long.'

It was a lot to hope for. But there wasn't anything one could do *except* hope for it.

'I suppose there's no chance of a tanker coming out to us with some oil?'

'Yes—'

'What?'

'I say yes no chance. No tanker.'

Trench asked him, 'Have you heard anything of Hun activity elsewhere than Trondheim and Oslo?'

'Sure. Stavanger. Around midnight, one Norwegian destroyer sink one German transport full with guns – artillery. And there were being – ' he moved his big hands about above his head – 'landings by parachute, you know? For the airdrome, I think. Well, of *course* for that . . . But also Narvik – one report say ten or maybe twelve big destroyers—'

'*German* destroyers?'

'Ja – twelve, big ones – on approach to Ofotfjord . . .' He aimed a blunt forefinger at Nick: 'You hear what our government have been saying, that Germans come because you British laying your damn mines?'

'They can say whatever they like. But they're talking through their hats and we all know it.'

The large hands spread. Now that he'd removed his cap you could see that he was completely grey. Nick had amended his estimate of Torp's age, from late forties to early fifties. Torp said, '*I* do not know it.'

Nick thought, *Then you're an idiot . . .* He wasn't sure of him yet: whether there might be a useful ally under that rough exterior or whether he might be backwoodsman all through. He had no enormous hopes, consequently, of the engineer. Torp had a high opinion of him, but what was Torp's opinion worth?

He'd have the answer to that one soon enough. He explained, 'This invasion – Denmark, then most of your ports – is obviously part of a well-planned operation. Separate assault forces, naval covering forces – you can't launch such a project in twenty-four hours. In fact the troops must have been assembled several days ago – let alone the planning before that, the mustering of stores, equipment—'

'Sure.' Torp nodded.

'Well, our mining operation was carried out yesterday morning. At least, so far as we know, it *would* have been. So how can it be said to have precipitated the German assault?'

'Maybe they learn what *you* have been planning and move first, very quick?' He glanced at Trench. 'Is there more coffee?'

'Might be.' Trench felt the pot's weight. 'Yes. Here . . .' He took up the cudgels while he poured out the dregs. 'You realise we *had* to lay those minefields – that you Norwegians made us do it? To stop the Hun routeing all his blockade-runners and ore-ships through your precious territorial waters while your government weren't doing a damn thing to stop it?'

The Norwegian stared at him, half-smiling. He glanced at Nick, then back again at Trench.

'You want to make some fight with me?'

'Lord, no. We want to fight *Germans* with you, Commander.'

'All right.' Torp nodded slowly, still looking hard at Trench. Then he glanced at Nick. 'You got a good man here, I think.'

Chandler had sent Midshipman Cox aft with some deciphered signals, and Nick looked through them while he and Trench waited on the upper deck for a verdict from the engine-room.

Renown had been in action only about an hour ago against *Gneisenau* and a cruiser. Then another signal referred to *Scharnhorst* as being in company with *Gneisenau*. That one faded out: the fault of *Intent*'s poor reception, no doubt. Both were from Vice-Admiral Battlecruiser Squadron – Whitworth – to his destroyers – the 2nd and 20th Flotillas, under Warburton-Lee and Bickford. Then there was another from Admiral Whitworth ordering them to proceed to Vestfjord and patrol to cover approaches to Narvik; Whitworth, presumably, was chasing off in pursuit of those two German ships. So the destroyers would be patrolling Vestfjord on their own.

He turned to the last of the batch of ciphers. It was from the Commander-in-Chief to Captain (D), 2nd Flotilla: *Send some destroyers up to Narvik to make sure no enemy troops land.*

But Claus Torp's information was that there were a dozen Huns up that fjord already. If Warburton-Lee sent just a few ships of his flotilla up, and they found themselves ambushed by twelve of those bigger, newer, five-inch destroyers the Germans had – in fact even if the *whole* of the flotilla went up, because there were only six of them, including *Hoste* with Paul in her . . .

Not a comfortable thought. *So don't think about it . . .* In any case, Torp's rumours weren't necessarily better founded than whatever reports had reached the C-in-C. In this kind of fluid, not to say *muddled*, situation you had to take everything you heard with a pinch of salt.

'Here.' He passed the log to his first lieutenant, and asked Cox, 'That's all we've got?'

'Afraid so, sir.'

'When you go back, ask the PO Tel to come and see me.'

'Aye aye, sir.'

'Is the doctor up and about yet?'

'Yes, sir. He thinks ERA Dobbs is going to pull through, sir.'

Marvellous. And good for Bywater. But if Dobbs hadn't elected to be such a hero he might have been more than just 'pulling through', he might have been on his feet and directing the repair work. The highly recommended Halvard Boyensen hadn't at first sight inspired much confidence; he looked more like a farm-hand than an engineer. Red-faced, with a heavy jaw and small, deep-set eyes. He and Torp had gone straight below with Beamish, after the skiff had brought him. Nick looked at his watch again; it felt like an hour that he'd been waiting.

Trench handed the signal log to Cox. And Nick remembered what Beamish had been telling him . . . 'Mid. You've been giving our chief stoker some technical advice, I hear.'

'Oh, no, I—' Cox had turned pink. 'I only – mentioned an idea, sir—'

'What made you go down there in the first place?'

'Just – wanted to see the shape of things, sir.'

'D'you have a mechanical bent, then?'

'I've always – well, I like using my hands, sir, and' – he glanced down at the signal log – 'that sort of thing.'

'You made yourself useful, anyway. Well done.'

The boy looked surprised. Perhaps he'd expected a reprimand, for trespassing in a department that wasn't anything to do with him. 'Thank you, sir.'

Trench murmured, 'They're coming up, sir.'

Claus Torp, leading Boyensen and Beamish, was wiping his hands on a lump of cotton waste. He stopped in front of Nick.

'In Namsos, alongside, with power from the shore, all that, he fix all good as new in one day.' He raised two fingers, then four. 'Twen'y-four hour, okay? But right here, working with your ship's men, *two* day.' He pointed at Boyensen. 'He say he can do this, but – ' a shake of the head – 'two day here, too damn dangerous, I think.'

'You're thinking of towing me to Namsos?'

'Sure.'

'But is he certain of what he's saying? Can I count on it a hundred per cent?'

'Yes. I tell you, he is damn fine engineer.'

He still didn't look like one.

'I want to be sure of this, Commander. Your man's saying he could do the job here, without other help or gear?'

'Sure. But much better in Namsos, with other help, tools also, and shore power. I think also very bad here if Germans coming.'

Against that, it was also obvious that in Namsos they'd be in a dead-end, trapped. But the priority must be to get the ship back into a state of operational fitness as quickly as possible. If he took the chance of getting bottled up at Namsos, she'd be mended in a single day – and fuel at the same time . . . For fuel, she'd have to go to Namsos anyway.

'What's your ship's speed?'

'Six knots, full speed. We tow at maybe three. You think?'

Behind the Norwegian loomed the burly, bearded figure of PO Telegraphist MacKinnon. Sent aft by young Cox, of course. Mr Opie the torpedo gunner had appeared too: shaved and spruced up, pulling at his nose while he tuned his ears to the proceedings. Nick was thinking that from here to Namsos was about fifteen miles. Five hours then; possibly only four, then twenty-four alongside. Say thirty hours in all.

'All right.' He nodded to Claus Torp. 'I'd be grateful for a tow.'

'Up and down, sir!'

It meant that the ship was up to her anchor so that the chain cable was vertical. Trench, in the front of the bridge, acknowledged the foc'sl report; he glanced enquiringly at Nick, who nodded and told him, 'Weigh.'

The cable began to clank again as the foc'slemen recommenced their circling, leaning on the capstan bars. Weighing was by hand because the auxiliary generator would have been hard put to it to provide enough power. Internal lighting, communications and fire-control systems had priority. Young Cox was down on the foc'sl with Lyte; Nick reckoned he'd been shut away with fine nibs and coloured inks for too long.

Off to starboard, *Valkyrien* was displaying her cut-away stern, and white water under her counter showed that her engine was chugging ahead, already putting some strain on the towing wire which had been led through *Intent*'s bullring and had its eye fast on the starboard Blake slip. Black coal-smoke leaked from the Nor-wegian's tall, pipe-stem funnel as she kept enough pull on the wire to hold the destroyer's bow from falling off landward when the anchor broke clear of the seabed. To start with, Trench had sent one end of a floating coir rope over to *Valkyrien* with the skiff on Torp's return trip to his ship; then the Norwegians had winched it over with a stronger hemp cable attached to it, and finally the hemp had been dragged across, pulling behind it the towing hawser of flexible steel-wire rope.

'Anchor's aweigh!'

Hanging over the flared edge of the foc'sl, Lyte had seen the cable swing, proof that the hook had been wrenched out of its clay-and-sand bed. He'd got back now, out of the way of a man with a hose and another with a broom; it was their job to clean the muck off the chain as it clanked up towards the hawse-pipe. If it wasn't cleaned there'd be mud and weed collecting in the chain-locker down inside the ship, and before long there'd be a fearful stink as well.

Torp had got Nick's signal, and the white at *Valkyrien*'s stern was spreading as she put on more power. Funnel-smoke increasing simultaneously . . . The towing hawser came up out of the water, rising and lengthening as *Intent*'s inertial weight came on it. Trench yelled down at the foc'sl, 'Stand clear of the wire!'

Cox and two seamen jumped away from it: and Lyte, who should have seen it before Trench had, was lecturing them about it. A steel-wire rope under strain was a lethal thing if it parted and found human flesh and bones in the way of its scything recoil.

'She's swinging to starboard, sir.'

'Very good.'

Chandler was watching the ship's head in the compass, checking her response to the pull on her bow. This was the tricky bit –

getting her moving, and particularly at this angle, turning her out across the direction of the wind and the up-fjord tide. On the port side of the foc's'l a sailor crouched with a sledge-hammer over the slip on the port cable; if the towing wire snapped he was ready to knock that slip off and send the anchor plunging down. With no engine power of her own to call on, *Intent* was entirely dependent on *Valkyrien* and on that wire.

'Clear anchor!'

Lyte had yelled it. It meant the anchor was high enough to be visible and it was on its own, not caught in some submarine cable or wreckage. Chandler said, 'Ship's head north thirty-five east, sir.'

Nick had put starboard rudder on to help her round: he didn't give a hoot what the ship's head was. Torp could see to that. She was turning steadily now and the wire looked all right, still had a springy sag in it. They heard the thud as the twenty-eight hundred-weight anchor banged home into its hawser-pipe: the rhythmic clanking ceased. Now they'd put the bottlescrew slip on that cable – because the Blake was in use as a towing slip – and veer to it until the slip had the anchor's weight.

Claus Torp could be seen on the roof of his wheelhouse, out on its starboard edge, with binoculars trained aft on *Intent*. Might have done a lot worse than run into Torp, Nick thought. It was a pity his ship had no guns and wasn't capable of more than six knots. A waste, in present circumstances, of such a man.

But there might be guns ashore that could be mounted in her. Or some less ancient craft that could be taken over and adapted.

'Midships.'

'Midships, sir!'

CPO Jarratt, the coxswain, was on the wheel. Chandler's head bobbed up and down like a hen drinking as he switched his glance between the compass and *Valkyrien*'s stern. Completely unnecessary. If Torp went the wrong way what could *they* do about it? Chandler was – or might be, in some ways, Nick thought – a bit of a pompous ass. Perhaps not the right man to deal effectively with a lad like Cox. A fed-up youngster needed to have enthusiasm imparted to him, not constant disapproval. Enthusiasm, and in extreme cases, chastisement as well. Having spent some years as a fed-up midshipman oneself, one *knew* it.

'Swing's easing off, sir. Steadying towards south eighty east.'

'All right, pilot. I can see what's happening for myself.'

On this course *Valkyrien* would take them out into mid-fjord, where they'd then go round about fifty degrees to starboard. And now that the pull was from directly ahead *Intent* was beginning to pick up a little speed. With no engine noise or fans sucking, the rustle and slap of water along her sides was a peculiar, rather spooky sound.

Spooky was right. Ghost-ship. She'd have been written off as lost by this time. He stooped to the voicepipe: 'Keep us in the middle of *Valkyrien*'s wake, cox'n, and use as little wheel as possible.'

She'd be in rougher water in a few minutes, but only for half an hour. Then they'd turn a corner into a more sheltered part.

MacKinnon had reported that he'd sharpened up the W/T reception, but there was no possibility of being able to transmit over any worthwhile range. Nick wouldn't have used his wireless anyway, even if they'd had full power. One signal out would be enough to bring Germans *in*. Or – worse, or at any rate just as bad – *over*, with their aircraft. If the bastards had been capturing airfields the sky would be thick with their dive-bombers before long. For the time being this low, dense cloud was a blessing, but it couldn't last for ever.

Patience – for one day. Well, thirty hours. Patience and a touch of fortitude. Then, fighting fit, sneak out during the dark hours with either Claus Torp or some other Norwegian as pilot. When *Intent* was well offshore he'd break the self-imposed W/T silence. She'd have generator power and a jury fore-topmast by that time.

There was more motion on her, and on *Valkyrien* too, as they crept out into the less protected water in the middle of the fjord. Chandler was taking bearings – of Sornamsen light structure on the Finsneset headland, and Altoy Island, and a sort of beacon on the Otteroy coast almost right ahead. And now here was young Bywater, the doctor – skinny, dark-haired, smiling his rather boyish smile as he anticipated Nick's question.

'ERA Dobbs is sleeping peacefully, sir. It's a downright miracle.'

'Not medical genius?'

'Ah – perhaps just a *touch* of that, sir.'

'Fishing-boat green three-oh, sir!'

Valkyrien was making the turn at this point, and the towing hawser was angling away to starboard. Jarratt could handle it . . . Nick had the boat in his glasses. Blue-painted, bouncing northward – as they were turning, it would be on the *port* bow in a minute. Nearly ahead now, and for a while it was going to be out of sight. But *literally* bouncing: a beamy, double-ended boat with a wheelhouse amidships painted a paler blue, and the boat was travelling in sheets of spray, moving quite fast, fairly smashing through the lumpy sea . . .

Jarratt had done it well. *Valkyrien* had steadied on the up-fjord course and *Intent* was smack in the centre of her wake.

That boat was in sight again, on the other bow. It looked as if it had sheered away to starboard: and several figures had come out of that little box amidships to stare at the oncoming ships. They'd know *Valkyrien*, presumably. Claus Torp was up on his platform again, waving his cap and his other arm as well, apparently calling the boat towards him . . . Message received there, evidently, and similarly interpreted: the boat was turning, plunging round and heading – by the looks of it – for *Valkyrien*. Perhaps its coxswain had been unsure of what *Intent* was, knowing there could be Germans in the offing?

There was a lot of waving going on, between Torp's ship and the boat. And now a light was flashing from *Valkyrien*. Nick lowered his glasses and looked round. Clash of the Aldis: Signalman Farquharson was ahead of him and had also beaten Herrick to the draw. From *Valkyrien* the calling-up signs ceased, and Nick read the laboriously spelt-out one-word signal: STOP.

'From *Valkyrien*, sir – "Stop".'

'Very good.'

He warned Jarratt of what was about to happen. Meanwhile the blue fishing-boat was closing in towards *Valkyrien* and Torp had put his helm over, altering round to starboard as his ship lost way. Giving the boat a lee on his port side, Nick supposed. One of the boat people was still on the outside beside the wheelhouse, waving frantically: a man in a bright blue oilskin, much brighter than the paintwork of the boat itself. He put his glasses up: it wasn't a man, it was a woman. What he'd thought to be a sou'wester was a lot of dark hair blowing about in the wind. Then the boat vanished, behind *Valkyrien*, who'd gone round about forty-five degrees to starboard, obviously so that the boat could go alongside in that slight shelter.

Trench cleared his throat. 'Popsie in that boat, sir.'

'Yes. I noticed.' He put his glasses up again. The towing cable was sagging to the water but not much more than that. *Valkyrien*, being almost beam-on to the wind now, would drift faster than *Intent* was likely to, so the wire should be kept reasonably taut. He hoped they weren't going to be kept waiting long; he wanted to have his ship alongside that quay, have the work start below, get some oil-fuel flowing into her sound tanks. There was a biting urgency to get her operational again.

Before the bloody Germans come . . .

There was activity now on the Norwegian's upper deck, around her mizzen mast. Several people were clustered on that far side, where the boat would be. He took his eyes off the binoculars to glance again at the hawser; Chandler murmured, 'All's well so far, sir.' Mustn't take too critical a view of Chandler, he told himself. Lumbered with a bloody-minded snotty for an assistant, he'd quite understandably lose patience with him. The more of a perfectionist one was oneself, the more one disliked sloppiness in others; and Chandler as a navigator *was* something of a perfectionist. What else did one want from a navigator but perfection? It was simply that he, Nick, happened also to have some sympathy with bloody-minded snotties.

'By the way, pilot—'

'Sir?'

'I've decided to take Cox out of the tanky job. I want to shake his ideas up a bit by pushing him around to other parts of ship. I think later he'd better come back to you – not as tanky, probably, but just to knock some navigation into his head. All right?'

'Suits me, sir.'

'Tommy.'

Trench came back to the binnacle. Nick said, 'You've got this CW candidate – Williamson, is it, on the searchlight?' Trench nodded. Nick paused: he'd just seen a patch of bright blue on *Valkyrien*'s deck. He focused his glasses on it: and he'd guessed right, it was the girl. He told Trench, 'Your popsie, Number One, has transferred to *Valkyrien*.'

'I've lost her, then. Some chaps have all the luck.'

Torp, he meant. And one could, indeed, imagine . . . Nick said, 'This CW, Williamson – how would he take to a spell as tanky, to widen his experience?'

'I'd say the idea's bang-on, sir.'

'Except – ' Chandler put it – 'that at this stage I hardly need one.'

'You will when we get home and you find a whole raft of Notices to Mariners to deal with. More importantly, it might be good for Williamson.'

When we get home . . .

The boat was leaving *Valkyrien*, nosing out round her stern and

100

turning into the wind, sending up sheets of sea again as she picked up speed. Heading towards *Intent*? It looked like it: and it also looked like Claus Torp standing amidships beside the wheelhouse doorway with one arm inside to steady himself against the roller-coaster motion . . . It *was* him. He was shouting at someone inside and pointing with his free arm towards *Intent*. But if he was planning to come alongside – well, Nick hoped he wasn't. He couldn't give the boat any shelter, unless *Valkyrien* elected to pull her round, and Torp might not appreciate how flimsy a destroyer's plating was, sideways-on.

The boat was turning in towards them. Trench suggested, 'Shall I put a ladder and fenders over, sir?'

'I'd rather not encourage him. Hang on.' The last thing he wanted was that heavy-timbered craft bashing up and down against his ship's side. But it had swung to port and it was heading directly for *Intent*, its stunted mast rocking like a metronome as it rolled, beam-on to the waves. *Damn it* . . . He opened his mouth to tell Trench to get fenders over quickly: then saw the boat going round again – about forty feet from the ship's side, turning to point her stem into the weather, and slowing to a crawl as she came up level with the bridge. Torp had ducked inside: now he was out again with a megaphone.

Trench snapped, 'Loud-hailer, signalman!'

'*Intent*, ahoy!'

Nick got up on the step and put a hand to his ear to show Torp that he was listening. Below him, Herrick was plugging in the loud-hailer. Torp bellowed through his megaphone, 'There are Boches in Namsos!'

Silence . . .

Implications spread quickly through the initial shock. Primarily, *no repairs in Namsos. No oil . . . What ships have they got there, for Pete's sake*? He'd got the loud-hailer up.

'How did they get there?'

'There was one merchant vessel empty for loading cargo. In Namsos lying three day. This morning before light two hundred Boche soldier with guns come out from ship's hold – all surprise, no time for defending. They have control now – *all*.'

Wooden Horse tactics. And Namsos was German. *Intent* wasn't capable of going anywhere. She couldn't stay where she was, either.

He lifted the loud-hailer again.

'What do you suggest we do?'

'I think I tow you into Totdalbotn.'

Totdalbotn. Something familiar about that name. Some small port on this coast? But Torp's earlier remark echoed in his brain: *I think they are in* every *damn place, you know?* Chandler had gone quickly to get the chart and bring it to him. And before he'd looked at it, he remembered – that enclosed anchorage right inside Hoddoy Island. Very sheltered and well hidden. The spot he'd been aiming to reach last night, before the engines packed up. Nearer to Namsos than one would have chosen to be, now that the Germans had taken over, but if they'd come in a freighter and had no naval units with them it might be possible to get away with a short stay – long enough for Halvard Boyensen to work some miracle in the engine-room.

No oil, though. But then, there'd be none – none that he could get at, now – *anywhere* up these fjords. Once the ship was repaired she'd have to sneak out again on as much fuel as was left in the tanks, and when he'd got her well away he'd wireless for a rendezvous with some big ship from whom he could refuel.

It had taken about fifteen seconds to cover that much ground, and to realise that while this was a major setback it didn't have to be exactly doomsday. And in any case his options weren't all that numerous. He pointed the loud-hailer at the fishing-boat, which was holding its station abreast the destroyer's bridge, stemming wind and tide while Torp waited for an answer.

'All right. We will do as you suggest. Totdalbotn.'

Torp bellowed, 'Okay! Very good!'

The conference was over. The blue boat began to surge ahead and swing away to starboard for its trip back to *Valkyrien*. Torp had disappeared inside it. Nick got down off the step, and Leading Signalman Herrick took the loud-hailer from him. Chandler said, looking at the chart, 'Nice private little anchorage, but it's awfully close to Namsos, sir.'

Nick barely heard him. He was staring up-fjord, thinking about the Germans and the ship they'd come in. 'Merchant vessel', Torp had said, but she might be armed; she wouldn't have displayed weapons any more than she'd advertised her cargo.

He told Trench, 'We'll go to action stations, please.'

CHAPTER 7

'Boat's coming off shore, Vic.'

'Yeah?' Blenkinsop's eyes were squeezed half shut in the gap in his balaclava. 'What you got, Yank, telescopic eyeballs?'

'Damn it, look *there*!'

'Blind as a soddin' bat.' Rush glanced critically at the sight-setter. 'Too much you-know-what. Oughter leave it *alone* for 'alf an hour, give the poor bloody thing a chance.' Rush looked shorewards at the tight huddle of houses and the tall, black-looking light-tower, where *Hardy*'s boat had gone in and from where it was now returning. They were in Vestfjord, the inner part of it, the funnel-shaped entrance to Ofotfjord and to Narvik.

'B' gun's crew weren't much of an audience for Rush's jokes this evening. There was increasing tension in the ship as the time for action neared. Paul could feel it in himself: excitement touched with fear, and also an element of frustration at not knowing what was happening or why they were hanging around here, why the flotilla leader had sent that boat inshore.

The buzz was that the tiny village with the lighthouse was called something beginning with 'T' and that it was the pilot station for this area. That would explain the boat being sent in – to bring off a Norwegian pilot for the tricky passage up to Narvik. Particularly if it was true that they'd be making that passage in the dark.

Black water, and a streaky blackish sky. Snow patched the land and blanketed the inland mountains, mountains rising white and steep dramatically against dark sky. Intermittently falling snow was quickly filling the non-white patches; before long there'd be nothing *but* white, anywhere. Because of the cold, most of the gun's crew were wearing greatcoats instead of oilskins. Here in Vestfjord, with the sheltering arm of the Lofotens making a seventy-mile barrier between themselves and the North Sea violence they'd

103

come from, there were no leaping seas to wet them. Only the snow-showers and, in place of discomfort from salt water, the biting cold.

Hostile, who'd been on some detached duty, had just rejoined the flotilla, so now all six destroyers were present. *Hardy* the leader and Captain (D)'s ship, had moved close inshore, and the rest of them had cruised around further out, waiting. Leading them now was *Hunter*; then came *Havock*, and astern of her, *Hotspur*. *Hoste* had dropped back to last place, in order to let *Hostile* slip in ahead of her. *Hoste*'s CO, Lieutenant-Commander Rowan, was junior to the other five captains.

Paul was thinking of applying to join submarines. The idea had been triggered by a broadcast which the skipper, Rowan, had made about an hour ago over the ship's tannoy, telling them about things that had been happening up and down the Norwegian coast. Among the items of news had been details of British submarines' successes off southern Norway, in the Skagerrak and Kattegat. Paul had been left with the impression that the submarines were the real front-liners: in enemy waters and sinking Germans while the Home Fleet in all its glory was – apparently – parading up and down well out to sea.

And something else influenced him too, towards the submarine idea. The talk at that dinner-party at Mullbergh had turned in that direction, and Paul's father had told him how he'd always regarded them not as ships but as *devices* – and nasty, dirty ones at that; but in 1918 he'd had to take passage in one through the Dardanelles to Istanbul, and while he would not, he'd said, want to do anything like it again, he'd come to understand the submariners' fascination with their trade. At this, Jack Everard had definitely sneered. In his opinion Nick's original view had been the right one. Submarines weren't ships, they were *things*: and not the *sort* of thing that one had wanted to join the Navy for. Strictly for oddballs and technical people . . .

So if one did join submarines, Paul thought, one might be fairly sure of not running up against Jack Everard?

There was a superciliousness, an assumption of superiority, in Jack's manner, which he found extremely irritating. There was also resentment, he thought, directed at this half-foreign interloper, an outsider who'd one day take Mullbergh away from Jack Everard the True Blue. Something like that.

He might have to face that hostility very soon. If he was now Sir Paul Everard – HO, OD? There'd be Jack's mother to deal with too. Really a nightmare prospect.

'We're off, lads!'

Harry Rush had made the announcement. There was a light flashing from *Hardy*, the flotilla leader, and *Hunter* up ahead was leading these other five destroyers round to starboard, turning shorewards and right round, reversing course. *Hardy* herself was gathering way westward. You could see her bow-wave rising; her motorboat was inboard, up on its davits and in the course of being secured there.

The light had stopped flashing. Paul guessed it might have been an order to form up on her. The way she was taking them was *away* from Narvik . . . Then he guessed that if the plan was to go through in the dark tonight, it would be much too early to start now – he checked the time – at 1750.

What would close action be like, he wondered. Being shot at; seeing men hit, killed, wounded. He'd asked his father, on the last day he'd had at Mullbergh, what it felt like, the first time you were in it.

'Well . . . You've swum in competitions, inter-school stuff?'

'Why, sure, but—'

'Nervous before the starter's gun, then too busy to do anything but get on with it?'

He saw the point, and nodded. 'I guess so.'

'That's how it is, Paul. The fright comes *before* the action.'

He'd been satisfied with this answer, at the time. Up to a point. With the mental reservation that when he'd swum in inter-College matches nobody had shot at him, and that this must make, surely, *some* difference . . . But now it didn't feel anything like that kind of pre-contest nervousness, it felt more like – *well, damn it*, he told himself, *it's like he said, it really* is*! This is the 'before', and okay, so I'm worried; and he can be right about the 'after' too, can't he?*

In a tizz now, a Dherjhorakov-type tizz, with himself. Recognising it and trying to stifle it . . .

His view of the village – Tranoy, that was the name they'd mentioned – was suddenly fading as if a curtain was being drawn across it. He went back into the shelter of the gunshield and told Baldy Percival, 'More snow coming.' *Hoste* was heeling as she turned behind the rest of the flotilla; she was on *Hostile*'s starboard quarter and from this angle there was a view of the other five ships of the flotilla, in line ahead and all exactly alike, grey ships gliding through the quiet water. Sturdy, powerful. They looked good, he thought; they looked *terrific*. Baldy Percival muttered, 'It might become pretty hot, you know, up that fjord.'

'*Hot?*'

'The fighting—'

'Oh . . .'

'And going up it in the dark?'

'Not *our* worry, Baldy.'

'It will be when we get up there. *Then* we'll be—'

'Worse for them than it'll be for us. Catch 'em on the hop, with any luck.' He looked at him, smiling. 'Hell, Baldy, this morning you were glad you'd been in action. You said—'

'Don't you think this is likely to be rather different?'

Paul shrugged, peered out into the falling snow. It was gathering on the gundeck, whitening the whole ship. Ahead, the fjord widened, white-covered mountains receding into a haze of cloud. *Hoste* heeled again as the flotilla began to zig-zag – to upset the aim of any lurking U-boat.

Vic Blenkinsop answered his telephone headset with his customarily sharp cry: ' "B" gun!'

Listening . . . Then – 'Ah now, bloody 'ell mate, that's a bit bleedin' much—'

Someone had shut him up.

'What's up, Vic?'

He pushed the mouthpiece aside, and told them, 'Ship's company will be piped to action stations at 0030 hours.'

It sank in slowly. This watch now ending was the First Dog; they'd be relieved in about one minute, at 1800, off-watch for the Last Dog, on again for the four hours of the First watch at 2000. That trick would end at midnight. And half an hour after *that* . . .

Rush complained, 'Fuckin' 'ell-ship, this is. The 'uman body 'as certain simple wants—'

'We know about *your* 'orrible body's wants!'

'– such as more 'n five minutes fuckin' kip per fortnight—'

'Don't call yourself '*uman*, do you, 'Arry?'

'If you can't take a joke, boyo – ' Dan Thomas summed it up with an age-old naval admonition – 'you shouldn't've fuckin' joined.'

In *Hoste*'s chartroom, Alec Rowan re-read the operation orders which Captain (D), Captain Bernard A. W. Warburton-Lee, had signalled from *Hardy* to his flotilla.

Final approach to Narvik: Hardy will close pilot station which is close to Steinhos Light. Hunter will follow in support. Hotspur and

Havock are to provide anti-submarine protection to the northward. *Ships are to be at action stations from 0030. When passing Skrednest Light Hardy will pass close to shore and order a line of bearing. Thereafter ships are to maintain narrow quarterline to starboard so that fire from all ships is effective ahead. On closing Narvik Hardy will steer for inner harbour with Hunter astern in support. Germans may have several destroyers and a submarine in vicinity. Some probably on patrol. Ships are to engage all targets immediately and keep a particular lookout for enemy who may be berthed in inlets. On approaching Narvik Hardy, Hunter, Havock engage enemy ships inside harbour with guns and torpedoes. Hotspur engage ships to north-west . . .*

Rowan leant over the chart. It was the best they had on board but he should have had chart 3753, the harbour plan, and it wasn't in the folio. It was only now, to study in advance, that he'd have liked it. He knew that once they got in there there'd be no time for looking at charts of any sort.

Hostile and *Hoste* had freelance roles. They were to be ready to join in the action here, there or anywhere, depending on how it developed.

He read the last part of the orders . . .

Prepare to lay smoke for cover and to tow disabled ships. If opposition is silenced landing parties (less Hotspur) when ordered to land make for Ore Quay unless otherwise ordered. Hardy's first lieutenant in charge. Additional visual signal to withdraw will be one red and one green Very light from Hardy. Half outfit of torpedoes is to be red unless target warrants more. In order to relieve congestion of movements all ships when turning to fire or opening are to keep turning to port if possible. Watch adjacent ships. Keep moderate speed.

Clear enough, Rowan thought, and about as detailed as could be practical. When they got in there, everything would be happening at once and in all directions. They'd be like foxes in a hen-run – except that the hens would be twice their size and better armed . . . He'd turned to the next signal on the log, the one which in fact had preceded the operation orders and in which Captain (D) had passed to Commander-in-Chief and to Admiral Whitworth the information obtained ashore at Tranoy. According to the Norwegian pilots there, there were at least six big German destroyers and one U-boat up at Narvik. The destroyers were of rather more than 1,800 tons, and had an armament of five five-inch guns apiece.

Surprise was going to be important, Rowan thought, to balance that German superiority in fire-power. It was a factor which Captain (D), Warburton-Lee, must obviously have weighed up and accepted, since he'd ended his signal to C-in-C with the words *Intend attacking at dawn high water*.

High water would help to carry them over any moored mines which the enemy might have laid. But then again, mines wouldn't be the only hazard on the way in. Ofotfjord was long and narrow, and despite the *Hardy* officers' attempts at persuasion, none of the pilots from Tranoy had been prepared to come along.

There was a SITREP – situation report – just in. Rowan skimmed through it: noting as he did so that it had not, by and large, been the best of days. The Home Fleet had been under heavy air attack from German squadrons using captured Norwegian airfields. *Rodney*, Sir Charles Forbes' flagship, had been hit – though not hurt, thank God. Several cruisers had suffered minor damage, and Stuka dive-bombers had sunk the destroyer *Gurkha*. Off southern Norway, German air superiority was total; effectively, only submarines could operate against German seaborne traffic down there. Had *anyone* realised, Rowan wondered, until this proof of the pudding was flung in their faces, how impossible it might become to operate surface ships without air cover?

The carrier *Furious* was with the Home Fleet now. But they'd sailed her in such a hurry that she'd come without her fighter squadrons.

He pulled on his duffel-coat and left the chartroom, climbed the ladder to his ship's bridge. He told Mathieson, the first lieutenant, 'You'll find Captain (D)'s orders on the chart table, Number One. Read, mark, learn, etcetera. Then start getting us ready fore and aft for towing and/or being taken in tow. And I want smoke-floats placed on the foc's'l and quarterdeck. And – now – I want to see Gardner and Peters and Mr Stuart – and Mr Braithwaite, please.'

Lieutenant Gardner was his gunnery control officer, and Mr Stuart was the gunner (T). Braithwaite was a commissioned engineer and Peters was officer-of-the-quarters on the after guns. When he'd seen them, Rowan intended to have the coxswain and the gunner's mate and the chief buffer up for a chat. There were various arrangements to be made: for instance, the ship's company were going to have to be fed at their action stations during the Middle, so they wouldn't be going into action hungry as well as cold.

He moved up to the binnacle. His navigator, Tubby Wellman,

was using the hand-held station-keeper, a pocket rangefinder, to check *Hoste*'s distance astern of *Hostile*. Lowering it, he glanced at his captain.

'Right on the nose, sir.'

Rowan didn't comment. He was thinking about those Norwegian pilots, the ones at Tranoy who'd been unwilling to risk their skins. Might it be because they considered this force too weak for the job and hadn't wanted to be associated with losers?

Supper on the messdeck was beef stew, bread without butter, and tea. The duty 'cooks' of each mess had prepared the food by cutting up the meat ration and carrots, and peeling the spuds, earlier in the day; they'd delivered it to the galley for cooking, and now they'd brought it back hot and steaming. There was enough gash gravy to soak your bread in; since 3 Mess had only about five spoons left that was the only way to get it up.

Whacker Harris pushed his empty plate away. He'd wiped it so thoroughly with bread that it looked unused. He mumbled, lighting a cigarette, 'The condemned man ate an 'earty meal.'

'No foolin'.' Randy Philips nodded at him. 'Should've been condemned years ago, you should.' He leant sideways, sniffing the air near Harris. 'Strike a *light*. 'E's fuckin' *rotten*.'

The killick, Brierson, told them, 'There'll be corned dog an' kye dished out sometime in the Middle, lads. Jimmy's orders to the cox'n. 'Eard it meself. So this ain't *quite* your last repast on earth, Whacker ol' son.'

'Yeah, well . . .' Randy turned to Baldy Percival. 'Bein' HO an' only at sea five fuckin' minutes, Percy, I don't suppose you'd appreciate the significance of an issue of corned dog an' kye in the Middle, would you?'

'Well – no, not in any *particular* way . . .'

They never tired of pulling Baldy's leg. It was so easy. He'd demonstrated this on his first day on board when he'd obediently gone trotting along to the chief buffer to ask for some green oil for the starboard navigation light.

'It's extra rations, see. They're takin' a chance there won't be no further stores drawn, like. When it's an odds-on chance of the old 'ooker gettin' sunk, they reckon to build you up for the swim, like.' He shrugged. 'Waste o' time in your case, o' course.'

'What d'you mean?'

'Well, 'ardly last two minutes, in water as cold as they got up

109

'ere. I mean, all bones an' bugger-all else, ain't you . . . Smoke, Yank?'

'Thanks.'

He'd noticed that the old hands liked to have such offers accepted. They were gestures, more than offers. Philips probably wouldn't care if he *ate* the cigarette, so long as he took it. In fact, he lit it too. Randy said, 'We 'eard about your guv'nor, Yank. Tough luck, an' all. Don't want to let it get you down, though.'

He nodded. Several men had glanced at him and away again, as if embarrassed. Obviously they'd discussed it, and Philips was speaking for them all. Paul exhaled smoke. 'Yes. Thanks, Randy.'

'Might turn up yet, lad.' Brierson was wiping his plate with a crust. 'Never say die.' He swallowed, reddening, and began again, 'I mean—'

'Sure, Tom. I know what you mean.'

Baldy Percival said, 'He could easily have been picked up by the Germans. It's really *likely*, when you think about it. And it would probably be quite some while before the news came through.'

'Well, bugger me!' Whacker Harris smacked the table. 'First sensible remark our Percy's made since 'e's been aboard 'ere!'

It was time to get ready for the next four hours on the gun-deck. And really, Paul thought, one could snooze up there almost as easily as down here. *Almost* . . . When they got up top, the gun's crew all looked as if they'd put on a stupendous amount of weight, with the extra sweaters under their greatcoats. Paul was three-quarters asleep when the flotilla went about, heading back towards Ofotfjord, and when the watch changed at midnight they were nearing Tranoy again, the place where *Hardy* had sent her boat in. This time, there wasn't any stopping.

Getting towards 1 am. Pitch dark, and snowing hard. The five destroyers ahead were showing light-clusters on their sterns; without them, it would have been near enough impossible to maintain the line-astern formation.

Alec Rowan leant with his left side against the binnacle. Wellman and Mathieson were vague shapes hunched against the bridge's starboard side, straining their eyes into cold, wet darkness. The flotilla was approaching the island of Baroy, which was on the south side of the entrance to Ofotfjord; when they sighted it, it would be quite close on the starboard bow. The gap between Baroy and Tjeldoy to the north was roughly 4,000 yards.

There was a light on Baroy, but it was unlikely the Germans would have left it shining, even if the Norwegians had. It was mounted on the end of a white timber-built house: which might or might not show up, now that the land behind it would be snow-covered. It would be an advantage to pick it up, because the Sailing Directions described it as the best mark for entering Ofotfjord, and with no pilot or local knowledge one couldn't afford to waste any such aids. It was *Hardy*'s job to lead them all in, of course, but each ship still needed to know where she was; otherwise if the flotilla became separated from each other you'd be lost and groping.

There was nothing to be seen at all except for *Hostile*'s stern cluster and its bluish glimmer on her wake, and the snow like a curtain all round. Thrum of the turbines, subdued humming from the ventilators. *Hoste* was doing revs for about ten knots but the tidal stream would be outflowing and speed of advance would be more like eight. The snow was like a soft, soaked blanket, giving an impression of deep silence all around. Men spoke briefly and quietly, if at all. Below, guns' and tubes' crews slept around their weapons, while in the messdecks and other compartments ammunition-supply and damage-control parties lay on the decks or sat propped against steel bulkheads, dozing or playing cards.

You could only use binoculars for a few seconds at a time; then the front lenses would be clogged with snow and you'd have to wipe them clean. It was a better bet to search with the naked eye. Less time-wasting. And the glasses would still be wet and smeary even when you'd wiped them.

'Captain, sir?'

The voice belonged to Graham-Jones, *Hoste*'s surgeon-lieutenant. 'New one from Admiralty to Captain (D), sir.'

Warburton-Lee must be getting a bit tired of London's chat by this time, Rowan thought. From 1,300 miles away they seemed to imagine that only they could direct this operation. The exchange of messages had been going on all through the night; and if the great men back there at home were poking their fingers into other sections of the pie as well, the Commander-in-Chief must be just about frothing at the mouth by now.

He didn't want to spoil his night vision, reading yet more signals. Once you'd lost it, it took about ten minutes to get it back. He told Graham-Jones, 'Read the bloody thing to me, will you?'

'Aye aye, sir.' The doctor went to the chart table, and leant inside its canvas hood. He called out, '*Norwegian coast defence ships*

Eidsvold and Norge may be in German hands. You alone can judge whether in these circumstances attack should be made. We shall support whatever decision you take.'

He'd switched the light off, and backed out. 'Looks like the decision is we carry on, sir.'

It looked, Rowan thought, like a touch of cold feet in high places.

Mathieson called suddenly, 'Baroy Light, sir. At least I *think*—'

'Where?' Wellman's tone was sharp. Navigators liked to be the first to pick up their marks. The first lieutenant told him, 'It's not lit, but there's a light in the house itself and you can just make out the actual structure. Left from where you're—'

'Yes, I've got it.'

'Well?' Rowan asked him. '*Is* it Baroy?'

'Yes, sir, I believe it is.'

Wellman had recognised it from the little sketch of it in the Sailing Directions. So now they were entering Ofotfjord, and Narvik was about thirty miles ahead.

'Hey, what the—'

He'd been kicked, or trodden on – and it had nothing to do with Mullbergh or—

'Breakfast in bed, you lucky bastards!'

Harry Rush seemed to be talking gibberish. Paul wasn't out of the dream yet. A long, disturbing dream in which—

He'd forgotten, lost it; a second ago it had all been in his mind. Extraordinary. He was sitting up, feeling the ship's movement and the tremble in her steel, feeling the cold too and seeing the swirl of snow outside the gunshield, flakes drifting in and then out again in a kind of spiral. The gun's crew were packed in here like over-dressed sardines. Harry Rush announced, 'Kye an' butties. Any bugger don't want 'is, *I'll* 'ave it.'

'Soddin' 'ell you will.' Vic Blenkinsop's tone was cheerful, though. He added, 'Dump the fanny 'ere an' shove them mugs along.'

'Who asked for *your* 'elp, Victoria?'

'Ah, bugger off, then!'

'Boys, boys . . .' Lofty McElroy wriggled out, feet-first, past Paul. The kye and sandwiches had been fetched from the galley by Rush and Percival, Paul gathered. McElroy was questioning how many sandwiches there were per man, and whether Rush had

112

scoffed a few en route. Paul, remembering what they were here for, where *Hoste* was going, was checking the time, peering at the faintly luminous dial of his watch and seeing that it was twenty-five past two. If they were still expecting to get to Narvik at first light, that would mean some time after 0400; so there was plenty of time yet. He felt himself relax enough to become aware of the cold again: of the wet steel deck inside here and the snow-plastered superstructure abaft the gun.

'Yours, Yank!'

He stretched forward, and his hands closed on thick hunks of bread. Then a tin mug so hot he could barely hold it even in the anti-flash glove. Rush mused, 'Wonder if the bleedin' square-'eads know we're after 'em.'

McElroy mumbled with his mouth full, 'They best *not*.'

'Why?'

'Well – be ready for us, wouldn't they.'

'So what? Ready for *them*, ain't we?'

'Yeah, but – ' there was a long sucking noise as the gun trainer started on his cocoa – 'there's more o' them than what there is of us, an' they're bigger bastards too.'

'What sod told you *that*?'

'Well, it's the buzz, ain't it.'

'*Your* buzz, Lofty?'

That had been Dan Thomas's voice, from the other side. McElroy told him, 'What they're sayin' on the messdecks.'

'Talkin' through their great fat arse-'oles then, aren't they.'

Silence – as if that had settled it, revoked the buzz. *Hoste* had a gentle motion on her, a little rise and fall resulting from the fact that she was moving through sea disturbed by the five ships ahead of her.

Dan Thomas had evidently been brooding on that estimate of enemy strength. He reopened the subject now.

'Wouldn't matter if there *was* more o' them than there is of us. Not if they was bigger boats an' all. We'll be *surprisin'* the bastards, won't we. Likely as not they'll 'ave their 'eads down when we get to 'em. That'll be why we're comin' up in the bleedin' dark, see . . . All right, Lofty?'

'Yeah, well—'

The ship swung, heeling, suddenly. She'd been put hard a-starboard, slanting over. Turbine noise rising sharply: she was shuddering, probably screws full astern, or one astern and—

113

Rush squawked, 'What the *'ell*— '

Both screws, Paul guessed, were going astern. Rush and Percival had moved: he did too, rocking forward on to his knees then pushing himself up: outside the shield he held on to Baldy, peered out round him into the night. He saw one ship about thirty yards to port and another on that same bow with her starboard quarter towards *Hoste*; and a larger but less distinct shape ahead was probably two destroyers overlapping. *Hoste* was going astern, all right; he could see the shine of black, white-flecked water sliding away for'ard.

'Well, strike a soddin' light!'

Harry Rush was pointing. Up ahead, beyond that mixed-up group of destroyers, an enormous white headland towered across black sky. A whole mountain-side – and the flotilla had nearly steamed right into it.

Perhaps if the snow hadn't stopped falling they *would* have?

Hoste's screws had stopped. You could hear the water whispering and thumping along her sides. Those other shapes were drawing away, re-forming into line; and *Hoste* began to swing herself round behind them – starboard screw astern, port ahead, the hum of the turbines and the rattling vibration dispelled those few minutes' unnatural quiet. Then the starboard screw had stopped: you *felt* it, when a certain element in the vibration cut out. She was moving ahead now – still swinging, gathering way eastward behind the others.

'All guns with SAP and full charge load, load, load!'

Baldy slammed a projectile into the tray and Paul thumped a charge in behind it. Harry Rush lugged the tray over with his left hand and rammed charge and shell home into the breech with his gloved right fist. The breech slid up with a metallic whisper and Dan Thomas had banged the interceptor shut.

' "B" gun ready!'

Its crew, tin-hatted and like Frankenstein monsters in their anti-flash gear, waited. Keyed up, tense.

Quiet . . .

Mutter of machinery, swish of sea. The stern lights had been extinguished. Dark, and snow still falling. But it seemed to be thinning out, Paul thought, might even be about to stop. And ahead – he was standing with his feet well apart and the next charge ready cradled in his arms, with nothing to do for the moment except wait – ahead there were seams of brightness showing through dark grey haze.

'*All guns follow director!*'

'B' gun was trained round on the starboard bow, at about green four-oh. No elevation that Paul could see: flat trajectory for point-blank range.

Rush sang out, 'For what you are about to receive, thank—'

No time for thanks. Dawn split into flame and deafening sound as ships ahead opened fire. Gun-flashes, shell-bursts: the sky flickered with red and yellow, orange, white, and suddenly with a much deeper, thunderous explosion, an enormous orange brilliance upwards and outwards. He thought, *Torpedo hit* . . . And immediately, another. A huge roar of sound – torpedo in some German's magazine or fuel tank, he guessed – and the sky ahead seemed to have caught fire. *Hoste*'s guns still silent; but looking across to port, behind the breech and Rush's and Thomas's dark silhouettes, he saw the beginnings of inferno, a whole jumble of ships racked with flame and exploding shells and clouds of smoke billowing out, and in that moment another torpedo struck, an eruption like a vast bonfire suddenly projected skyward. In the light of it he saw the victims – a tanker with a destroyer alongside her, both of them shattered and ablaze.

Fire-gong: 'B' gun fired, recoiled. Reloaded, breech shut: clang of the gong again, and *crash* . . . No idea what they were shooting at. The noise had become continuous, a solid roar instead of individual bangs; in every direction there were ships on fire, exploding, sinking. Two more torpedo hits: a gush of flame as one broke in two. The snow had stopped and daylight was growing rapidly; charges flowed into his arms and out again: he swung to and fro feeding the gun as it belched, recoiled, drew breath, belched again. Ears ringing, eyes half blinded sometimes by the flashes and the sting of cordite; he glimpsed, as he pivoted to snatch another charge from Billy Mitchelmore, one of two stokers who were at the sharp end of the ammo-supply chain, a large merchant ship alongside a jetty blowing up, her centre turning bright red and brightening more, then erupting upwards out of her. Ammunition ship? *Hoste* was swinging and the gun was firing on an after bearing now, so that he and Baldy were going to have to pass *in front* of it to get each charge and shell from the supply numbers at the ammo hatch. You had to duck right down below the level of the blast but there was still nothing between your brain and the explosion except rubber plugs in your earholes.

'Check, check, check!'

Run out of targets?

Just as noisy though. He wondered how long they'd been in action. Narvik's harbour was in flames, with a couple of dozen ships on fire, sinking, exploding. By the looks of it, the flotilla had achieved complete surprise and no small victory. You could only get an impression, though, see this bit of it or that, there was no chance to make sense or a pattern of it. Noise deadened, slowed the thinking-process, and Dan Thomas had them ready and standing-to, gun loaded, layer and trainer following the pointers in their dials, Vic Blenkinsop keeping his range-dial set to TS-transmitted range, deflection-dial the same, everything lined up and ready as *Hoste* swung – heading, presumably, for some new target or target area.

Mist, and drifting smoke. Over the harbour it was dense.

Fire-gong: *crash!* And the same again. How long had the pause been – half a minute, ten minutes? He'd glimpsed two of the flotilla, their two-funnelled silhouettes as familiar as old friends in a crowd of strangers, guns flaming shorewards. It was full daylight – and again the time-element was puzzling . . . He banged a charge down, swung round for another, swinging back a second or so behind Baldy's swing with the heavier burden: the gun had fired, flung back; as he slammed the next charge in he felt the ship lurch violently. As if she'd hit a rock. But the impact had felt as if it was somewhere aft. Another round in, gun fired – firing ahead now, target invisible, hidden by the gunshield. That ship passing was *Hardy*, coming out from the harbour area: she'd been out and gone in again for her second smack at them already. Giving the others a turn or herself a rest, he thought, as he dropped a charge into the tray and swung away and the gun crashed – it was four guns you heard, of course, not just this one, four fire-gongs that rang each time just before the director-layer's trigger completed the electrical circuit that fired the guns. Paul saw a German destroyer with its bows blown off: it was slowly tipping forward into the sea, sliding in. He thought exultantly, *Us? Did we do that?* Hell, this *was* a victory! Swinging back with another charge he found he was having to take a new position on account of the slanting gundeck, a list the ship had developed. And she was slowing. Stopping? You just kept at it, seeing things in glimpses, shut into the confines of your job. 'B' gun fired, recoiled, he slung in another helping and turned back for more, saw *Hardy* passing, going in there again, her

116

leader's pendant snapping in the wind, ensign tattered, her for'ard guns already back in action and a stream of tracer racketing from her point-fives, probably dealing with some gun on shore. They must be field-guns landed from these merchant ships. *Former* merchant ships: wrecks now. *Hoste* was stopped, and the slant on the gundeck had increased. Her engines had stopped, but in fact she had just enough way on to maintain this slow turn to port. Dense smoke drifting; while the noise of battle hadn't lessened except intermittently in surprising pauses, the amount of flame and flash had. More smoke now than anything else. Daylight, of course, and fires having burnt themselves out, burning ships gone down . . . Recoil – breech open – stinking gush of fumes. His eyes were streaming from that reek and he and the men around him were moving completely as machines now, robot-like. Again it was on an after bearing that they were shooting, he and Percival having that quick rush to make for each round, into the muzzle-flash and the mind-crippling concussion. On the bow – starboard, and behind his shoulder as *Hoste* continued her turn to port – two of the flotilla were turning away from some shore target they'd been blasting.

'*Check, check, check!*'

Hardy was coming out again: that was three separate attacks she'd made. Two others of the flotilla were angling in to form line astern of her. *Hoste* still listing – she'd been holed, he realised – that jolt he'd felt. An hour ago? But she was under way again, moving ahead through the water: to tag on astern of those three, perhaps: or leaving a gap for that other pair to come in ahead of her. Withdrawing? He checked the time, fumbling to push back his greatcoat sleeve and pull down the anti-flash gauntlet . . . Five-thirty. One hour, then, since the action had started. It could have been ten minutes: he'd had no idea. He was looking at those other two – *Hostile* and one other – when beyond them he saw a new group of German destroyers emerging from Herjangsfjord.

Three of them. Big, almost like light cruisers.

Jesus Christ Almighty . . .

Fire-gong: *crash*: recoil . . .

Engaging those three now. The flotilla must have sunk or smashed up five or six Hun destroyers already, and now here were three more – fresh, undamaged, with full outfits of torpedoes. All the Second Flotilla ships were engaging them, forming into something like a rough quarterline, fighting as they withdrew

117

westward. Shot from the Germans' guns was whooshing over now – a hoarse, rushing sound – and splashes had just risen about a cable's length to starboard.

Check, check, check!

For God's sake, *why*?

Then he saw. The gun would still bear – just, on that after bearing – but *Hostile* and the destroyer with her – *Hotspur?* – were coming in between *Hoste* and the oncoming Germans, masking her fire. Not for long: they were crossing, turning to port, heading as if to form up astern, or just to get out of the way, clear the range.

And laying smoke, now . . .

Hoste was gathering way. Paul guessed they'd be following on astern of *Hardy* and those other two. Water sliding away faster as she picked up speed, still with the drunken list on. Shell-spouts rose again to starboard, leaping tall and white, collapsing with slow grace. The after guns were in action again. Baldy's eyes were bloodspots and what showed of his face around them, in the gap in the anti-flash mask, was smoke-blackened like a nigger-minstrel's. *Hoste* quivered to explosions aft: not gunfire, shell-bursts. And she was slowing again: you could feel the vibration ease – and then stop, as her propellers ceased driving her.

' "A" and "B" guns follow director!'

She had enough way on to be answering her helm, swinging to allow the for'ard guns to bear on the enemy astern. 'B' was now trained as far aft as it would go, right up against the stop; and loaded, ready.

Fire-gong: *crash* . . .

Back at it again. Like pressing a switch and starting up a machine. Eight working parts: seven men, one gun. It fired again, plunged back, breech opening and stink flooding back: projectile, charge, tray slamming over . . .

Crescendo of gunfire up ahead, where *Hardy, Havock* and *Hunter* were leading westward.

'Check, check, check!'

A very short spasm, that one had been. Paul took a look round the edge of the gunshield; there was nothing to see except smoke. Which presumably was why they'd ceased firing. You could hear *Hostile* and *Hotspur* still in action, though; fighting a rearguard action to hold the attackers off, it must be. The list on *Hoste* was more pronounced and an easterly breeze – the wind had shifted right round during the night – brought a smell of burning. From aft, on this ship? But the whole fjord by this time would stink of burning. Harry Rush, who'd been standing with his back to the gun and looking out the other way, westward, had begun to shout: Paul and Dan Thomas joined him to see what was so exciting.

Hard to see *anything* . . .

Dan Thomas snarled, 'Look at them *bloody bastards*!'

Two more big German destroyers were racing out of a side-fjord to the south, tearing across to cut them off.

How many did they *have* in here, for God's sake?

Hardy, Havock and *Hunter* were already engaging the new arrivals. It was all gun-flashes and drifting smoke, groves of shell-splashes around both groups of ships. Paul, Baldy, Rush, Dan Thomas and Vic Blenkinsop were staring out that way when *Hardy* was hit, her bridge smothered suddenly in a gush of flame and smoke. A flag-hoist had broken at the flotilla-leader's yardarm a couple of seconds earlier: the flames reached up to it and the bunting began to flare. *Hardy* swinging hard a-port: and *Hoste*, steadied from her own swing, was moving ahead through the water again and starting to turn back the other way. It seemed possible that Rowan was taking her to the assistance of his damaged leader.

Paul tried to get a sight of his watch. One gun aft was firing now. *One?*

' "A" and "B" guns follow director!'

Leaving that after gun in local control to engage the Germans coming up astern? He'd only had the barest glimpse of the watch's face but he thought the hands were at just after six: and the fire-gong had clanged, they'd resumed the seven-some reel. Firing directly ahead – at the two new ones. Nothing to see, though; the gunshield limited one's world. Picking up speed: and shaking, rattling more than usual. Heat and stink of burning paintwork – from aft. One of the stern guns must have been knocked out. Fire-gong: *crash* . . . Sounds muffled in numbed or flattened ear-drums. Eyes blurred, and mind blurred too. The clang of shells into the loading-tray and of the tray as it was swung over to the breech was totally inaudible, like a film when the soundtrack's out. Arms were pistons, hands were claws, the gun was the master of seven men who served it. *Hoste* was listing still more steeply, he thought, than the last time he'd noticed. You got into a way of expelling a breath through your mask as the breech opened and the stench flew back. *Crash* . . . Jet of red flame, then black smoke pluming up and back. On 'A' gun, he half realised – below them, just down there . . . 'B' fired, threw back; shell-spouts rose to port quite close, and another explosion down for'ard with a similar jetting flash upwards and sideways out beyond this gunshield. Foul black smoke reeking and flooding back aft. He'd dropped another charge in and turned in that lunging motion to grab the next from Mitch: something slammed into his back with tremendous force and he was aware of sound – *different*, unidentifiable – and tumbling helplessly, the kind of fall that woke one up in nightmares: then darkness and a sense of personal removal, a feeling that one had become a spectator of some battle being continued now at a distance . . . He'd been unconscious, and he came-to in the act of getting to his feet. The ladder to the ammunition hatch and the sight of Mitch told him where he was: he'd been knocked down here, into the Chiefs' and POs' mess. Mitchelmore had been up the ladder and come back down it; he was shouting, 'Whole bloody lot's 'ad it. *All* of 'em!' Shells and charges were arriving from below and piling up. Mitch said, ' "A" gun's the bloody same. Christ, what are we—'

What are we *something* . . . Paul was climbing the ladder and getting out of the ammo hatch. 'B' gun was a twisted wreck and the gun platform itself was slimy, slippery. At first glance it looked like oil but it was blood. He saw bodies and parts of bodies wrapped in the shreds of clothes, and everything burnt black. And some more or less intact. Baldy was one of them: but he wouldn't be putting stickers in any more library books. Guns were firing: a lot of them at a distance, and one much closer. One of the after guns here on *Hoste*, he thought. Over the flare, the leading edge of the gundeck, he saw that 'A' gun had become scrap. One body had been smashed against its breech, which itself had been knocked sideways; it dripped, festooned with what had been the fabric of a man. He saw a leg sticking out of a seaboot, and part of a torso like something on a butcher's slab wrapped in blood-soaked cloth, and one body intact but flattened as if something huge had stamped on it. Turning away, glancing upwards – for relief, perhaps, the only safe direction you could look – he saw *Hoste*'s bridge blackened and smoking, a flicker of flames appearing here and there as the wind fanned them up. Then disappearing, flickering up again . . .

'Yank?'

He whipped round. The voice had come from down there below him, on 'A' gundeck. But they were all—

'*Yank . . .*'

120

He jumped from the edge of the flare to the distorted top of 'A' gunshield and from there in another two-footed hop to land jarringly on the foc'sl deck. Then he came round to the rear end of the gun. It was worse at close quarters, and that voice he'd thought he'd heard could only have been a grisly joke perpetrated by whoever arranged this kind of thing . . . Then – inside the shield, port side – something moved and caught his eye.

A hand. He saw the arm attached to it and a body attached to that, and blood all over everything. Crumpled, flung into that corner; and a dead body which had evidently been smashed down across the layer's handwheel was right above this live one, the corpse's arms dangling down to it and blood flowing in a thick, black-looking and quite slow-moving stream. The hand which had moved and caught his attention was the living man's, attempting to push those dead hands away from his face where they swung to and fro with the ship's motion. Paul knew he had to get in there, get the live one out. *The part one had to play*. It wasn't the kind you'd choose. He'd stepped over an intervening horror and he was dragging the broken and crushed remnants of a human being off the handwheel. Moving it was less difficult than he'd expected it to be. But to be able to reach the man who was alive and pull him out of the corner he'd been jammed into, he'd have to get this one right outside the gunshield, out past two others. The explosion must have been behind the gun, at the base of 'B' gundeck's superstructure; that and the jutting flare above, the angled projection of the gundeck's front edge, would have contained it so that the whole blast would have been *into* 'A' gunshield. Paul let his burden down on the deck and went back inside.

It was Blackie Proudfoot. He rasped, as Paul knelt to get hold of him, 'Can't move me fuckin' legs. Can't feel 'em.'

'Okay. I'll get you to the Doc.'

'Good lad, good—'

'Try to hang on round my neck?'

Prising him up out of it. Blackie was coated in blood – that other man's. Probably shouldn't be moving him: but the doctor couldn't have got to him in that corner, he *had* to be brought out. Blood – clothes saturated – except where he'd been lying, his back on the steel deck. And even *there* – as he began to edge out, dragging the heavily-built gunlayer with his arms locked round him and Blackie's hands clasped together behind his own neck – Paul felt a damp hollow in the small of the man's back. The greatcoat was torn and sticky round the edges of the tear. That was Blackie's *own* blood.

Christ, but I'm lucky to be alive!

The thought hit him so suddenly and strongly that it just about made him stagger. The realisation that he *shouldn't* be alive . . . He got Proudfoot up in a fireman's lift, without having had to look at the wound in his back. The layer had groaned once, and muttered something; either he was incredibly tough or there was some failure of the nervous system and he wasn't feeling anything. Shuffling aft with the heavy body across his shoulders Paul thought not only had the list increased, but *Hoste*'s forepart was higher in the water. Meaning she was down by the stern? Well, obviously there must be some flooding somewhere, or she wouldn't have the list.

Screen door just ahead. Where the hell were the doctor's first-aid parties, he wondered. Weren't they supposed to—

'Who's that?' Someone stopping in front of him, peering into his face. Lieutenant Mathieson, the first lieutenant. Tall, fair-haired . . . 'Everard?'

'Yes, sir. I – ' His voice was like a croak – 'this is "A" gunlayer, Able Seaman Proudfoot. I'm taking him down to sickbay for—'

'The doctor's in the waist, Everard, by the searchlight platform. We're mustering all wounded there. She won't float long now, I'm afraid.'

Not *float*?

'Are you all right, Everard?'

'Yes, I'm—'

'We thought everyone on "A" and "B" was killed.' Mathieson jerked his head. 'Get him along there quickly now. They'll find a job for you.'

He went in through the screen door. Paul moved on – to the head of the foc's'l-break ladder, and slowly, awkwardly down it to the iron deck. Then continuing aft . . . 'Hang on, Blackie. The doc'll fix you up.' Maybe. The for'ard funnel was all chewed up. No fires seemed to be burning now: just smoking, smouldering wreckage. Passing the engineers' store. The point-fives were a tangle of junk on a burnt-out pedestal. Past the second funnel, which had only one shell-hole in it that he could see, to the tubes. They were turned out: but not to fire, because there were no torpedoes in them. To make space on the deck between the two quintuple mountings, he realised. Wounded men lay or sat around. There was a Carley float alongside to port; Petty Officer Rowbottom and a few seamen with him were lowering a stretcher-case down into it.

'Sir – doctor—'

Graham-Jones was fixing a splint to a broken leg. Glancing up, he snapped sharply, 'Put him down, man, put him down!'

A couple of other wounded sailors pulled aside to make room. And Mr Stuart, the gunner (T), came to help. Stocky, red-faced, ginger-headed. Blackie Proudfoot slid into a bloodstained heap which had then to be straightened out. The doctor asked, 'What's his trouble?'

'Hit in the back, I think, sir. He said he couldn't feel his legs.'

'X' gun was still in action, in local control. Sub-Lieutenant Peters was up there, standing out on the side of the gundeck and giving visual spotting directions, watching the fall of shot through binoculars. Paul heard him yell, 'Right eight – *shoot!*' The gun flamed, flung back, and the black-faced men around it went into a spasm of the dance and then froze to the cry of 'Ready!' Paul wished he'd been kinder to Baldy, swapped places with him after half an hour or so of the action, switched to handling the projectiles and given Baldy a break with the much lighter charges – nine pounds a time instead of forty-five. *Sorry, Baldy* . . . Graham-Jones had checked Blackie Proudfoot's heart and breathing, after one look at the hole in his back. He told Paul flatly, 'This man is dead.'

Peters howled, 'Up four hundred, *shoot!*' Stuart had asked Paul something, and now he'd grasped his arm: 'Eh?'

'Sorry, sir, I didn't hear—'

The hair was red but the stubble on the jaw was grey. Eyes grey too and rather close together. Stuart must have been about Paul's father's age but he looked ten, fifteen years older. Up the hard way and a lifetime of naval service, one of the tiny minority who by the standards of the lower deck had made it, to warrant rank . . . 'I asked can you swim, lad?'

'I'm a very strong swimmer, sir.'

'Aye, well, you'll have a chance to prove it now. One bloody float's all we've got. We could fill the bastard three times over wi' just wounded men, but she'll sink long before that, d'you see. Most of 'em's going to have to swim, an' it's a hell of a long bloody way and colder'n *that* – so they'll need help, right?'

'Right – ' he corrected himself – 'Aye aye, sir.'

Staring at the rocky, snow-covered coastline. Three or four

hundred yards, he thought. Ice-water, and then snow. *Then* what –
Germans?

Stuart told him, 'Check they're all wearing lifebelts and see
they're inflated – right?'

Rowan, the skipper, was dead. Everyone on the bridge and in the
director tower had been killed. *Hardy* had run ashore, five or six
miles east of here, and *Hunter* had sunk out in the deep water. The
other ships of the 2nd Flotilla had withdrawn westward now, and
Mr Stuart had said he didn't think the Huns had followed up very
far. The Huns had their own problems, he'd said; he reckoned
they'd lost three destroyers sunk and at least another three badly
damaged, as well as half a dozen store-ships sunk inside the
harbour.

So it *was* a victory, after all. Paul, looking round at the waiting
wounded and the discarded dead, had thought of the Duke of
Wellington's much-quoted words about battles lost and won. Here
was vivid proof of it. *Hoste* sinking, while Stuart, Mathieson and
Peters chatted to the men, keeping spirits up. And they *had* been
up: there'd been singing, jokes, leg-pulling.

The loaded Carley float was clear of the ship's side, being
paddled slowly shorewards.

'Right then. You lot with webbed feet – over the side, and we'll
get these lads down to you.' He remembered stripping off his
greatcoat and sweaters and the tennis shoes. A scrambling-net had
been rigged over the side, for men to climb down. Paul and about a
dozen others who reckoned they were better-than-average swimmers were going to shepherd a whole crowd of poorer swimmers
and lightly wounded men to the shore. He was going to take one
man, a torpedoman with a broken arm, on his back.

Now this was his third trip. Third and a half, really. He'd got his
first man ashore and then swum out again about a third of the way
to help with stragglers from the group. Two had given up, and
drowned; several others had died on the beach. The cold was
unimaginable: in the first minutes of the first swim he'd thought
he'd die of it, then he'd become used to it and stuck it out more
easily, and now it was right inside him, killing . . . *Don't think about
it*. He'd told himself more than once that the sole survivor of two
guns' crews didn't have much to complain about. On his second
trip he'd been out to the ship and brought back that fellow Cringle,
the man he'd had the barney with. Cringle had a head wound and

some cracked ribs, and he hadn't seemed to know who or where he was or what was happening. Third trip now. *Hoste* was slanted steeply in the water, stern right down. She'd be gone soon. Lieutenant Mathieson and Mr Stuart had still been on board, making a final search for anyone left alive, last time he'd been out to her. They'd be able to look after themselves, he guessed, but there'd been men in the water here and there, two or three who'd dropped out, or rescuers who'd gone out again and not come back.

This *bloody* cold. The other thing that was slowing him was the pain in his back – where whatever-it-was had hit him before he'd fallen into the hatch. He'd be bruised all over from that fall, he knew, but it was his back that worried him.

He saw her going. Bow rising slowly and then faster as her afterpart filled, up-ending her . . . He saw a body in the water – about three yards ahead. Frozen black water, liquid ice. Like swimming in a cocoon of ice, a tight skin of it, and it was inside you too, in bone-marrow and veins, all through. The body was hunched, suspended in its lifebelt. Face grey and shiny, like a seal's. Graham-Jones's voice echoed in his brain: *This man's dead.* Looking away from him, seeking others who might *not* be dead, Paul saw that *Hoste* had gone.

He didn't realise at first that she'd been his marker, giving him direction, and that now he'd lost her. He swam slowly to his left. Slow, painful breast-stroke, slower than he wanted it to be. Cold put a brake on you. And he was lower in the water than he had been: to see any distance he needed to get his head up higher. Tremendous effort – just for one second – down again with sheer agony in his back. Can't do *that* again too soon. Relaxing thankfully now in the icy strait-jacket. Arms and legs moving so slowly that it was like swimming in frozen treacle. The mind swam slowly too. It asked him, *Take a rest? Just a little one?*

He wasn't sure which way the coast was. He'd been circling to the left, but he didn't know how much of a circle he'd completed. He tried again to get his head up, catch a glimpse of that snow-bound hillside.

No. Not *this* time. Only falling snow.

Rest. Try again in a minute. He'd strained his back and he had to rest it and gather some strength by relaxing just for a little while: a short rest in this black enclosing ice. Come to terms with it, don't fight it. Face-down, arms outspread – like gliding. Only for a minute.

CHAPTER 8

Dawn had come poking over the low hills, spreading greyish light across Sundsråsa, fingering the southern shore of Hoddoy and applying the beginnings of a shine to the flat, quiet surface of Totdalbotn. Nick had been on deck in plenty of time to watch it happening. Pacing his ship's quarterdeck, hearing an occasional thump or clatter from the engine-room where work had been going on all night, and from time to time still having to push the girl out of his thoughts.

She did have an excuse for getting into them. The plan he was forming in his mind had to involve *Valkyrien* and Claus Torp, and so it had to involve her too.

This wasn't a very extensive deck to pace. About sixty feet each way, from the stern where a sentry with a rifle stood beside the bare ensign-staff, via a slightly curving track to skirt around 'Y' gun and the after superstructure on which 'X' gun stood, to a turning-point at the port-side depthcharge thrower. He'd been up since four and it was getting on for six now. Subtracting from those two hours one short visit to the engine-room – from which he'd learnt precisely nothing – and a much longer spell in the chartroom, allowing for those intervals he must have been pounding this strip of deck for at least an hour. The officers whose cabins were directly under the area of perambulation, if they weren't exceptionally sound sleepers, would be cursing him; their bad luck in having him on their side of the ship was the result of *Valkyrien* being secured alongside to starboard and having a quartermaster of sorts lounging on her stern, hawking and spitting and crunching what sounded like lumps of coal. When Nick had appeared once on that side the man had gone to great efforts to engage him in conversation, despite the fact that he spoke no English and Nick spoke no Norwegian.

Enough distraction without that. The girl kept slipping into his mind, getting between him and the things he *had* to think about. A replay, over and over again, of the impact she'd had on him, and the reflection of it that he'd seen at once in her eyes. Blue eyes, rather wide apart – just like her father's, he'd realised afterwards. But he'd been somehow caught off-balance, taken by surprise, and he'd seen that same reaction, mirrored.

It was partly why he'd turned out this early. There'd come a time, and probably quite soon, when he'd need more sleep than he could get, and then he'd look back with regret on this waste of opportunity. But the girl wasn't the only reason he'd come up on deck. His mind was jumpy, he'd felt an urge to be up and doing. Prowling around, churning the part-formed plan in his brain. The crux of it being that, Germans or no Germans, there was fuel in Namsos.

She'd probably felt nothing at all, he told himself. He'd imagined it. But even if she had, even if she'd been stirred by the most outrageous emotional or sexual upheaval at the mere sight of him – which he didn't flatter himself was likely – this would be neither the place nor time to respond to it. Perhaps one was suffering from the malady to which Fiona Gascoyne sometimes referred as 'sex starvation': which incidentally was something he felt sure *she'd* never had much trouble with. But watch out, he thought: or you'll make an idiot of yourself . . .

He had enough on his plate already. His own share of responsibility for *Gauntlet*'s end, for instance, still nagged him. This *present* situation was what one had to concentrate on, but – Hustie's action had been crazy. If he'd been alone – all torpedoes gone, no hope of his ship surviving, ramming the only way left to him of inflicting damage on the enemy: *then* his action would have been justified, even heroic. But he had *not* been alone.

So Nick as senior officer should have held him back, taken him under his orders and co-ordinated the attack?

However much he thought about it, the conclusion he came to was that in similar circumstances again he'd act as he'd done two days ago. Basically because if he'd held *Gauntlet* back and as a result they'd lost contact with a still unidentified enemy, he'd *undoubtedly* have been called to answer for it . . . So then they'd ask why he hadn't stopped Hustie making his last attack, signalled him to wait behind the smoke: and the answer was that no order should have been necessary. It had been natural to assume certain

127

intentions on Hustie's part: and inessential signals in action were only a distraction, to be avoided if they could be.

But men had been hauled over the coals before this, for doing the right thing. One could think of a dozen cases . . .

Claus Torp's quartermaster had begun to sing some frightful Scandinavian dirge. Nick tried not to hear it. There were quite a few things to keep one's mind off: including the question of what might or might not have been happening up at Narvik, if Warburton-Lee had carried out the attack. There'd been an Admiralty signal in the early hours telling him that the decision was his own, and that he'd be backed whichever way he decided. Nick thought Warburton-Lee would have gone ahead, as long as the odds were reasonable. He didn't know, and there must have been a lot of signals that *Intent*'s operators had missed; but what might reasonable odds be, to himself, say, if he were in that position? Two to one against? It obviously hadn't looked like *even* odds, or the Admiralty wouldn't have sent that up-to-you signal.

The singing had stopped, thank God. There was a mutter of Norwegian conversation over there now. A relief quartermaster taking over, probably.

Gauntlet and *Hoste* apart, the more immediate problems weren't exactly bagatelles. Namsos was in German hands and less than ten miles away by water. Less than eight as the crow – or the Stuka – flew. With a garrison already planted there, it was obvious the Huns would send some kind of naval support as soon as they had craft to spare; they'd send a torpedo-boat or a minesweeper or two up from Trondheim, perhaps. And putting oneself in the shoes or boots of a torpedo-boat commander, one's first sensible move on arrival in a place like this would be to search all the fjords and inlets and hidden anchorages, not only for enemies but also for craft which might be commandeered and used for occupation purposes. Meanwhile, *Intent* was immobilised and helpless, and her chances of becoming operationally fit depended on this one Norwegian, Boyensen. Well, assuming he was as good as he was cracked up to be, he'd mend her. But then – here was the biggest problem of the lot – she'd have fuel for only a few hours' steaming, and there was no source of fuel open to her and within her likely range. His earlier idea, of sailing with near-empty tanks and then signalling for help, had collapsed when he'd subjected it to closer inspection. You needed a big ship to refuel from, so in effect he'd be asking for a cruiser to be sent inshore. The odds were that with the German air superiority which was implicit in so many of the signals they'd intercepted, he'd be asking for the impossible.

Hence the birth of the hare-brained scheme. In the circumstances, he thought it might be near-enough impossible to think up any scheme that was *not* hare-brained. He'd begun to toy with this one – fancifully, not really believing in it then during the tow down Namsenfjord.

Meanwhile, and looking on the brighter side, this anchorage might have been tailor-made for present purposes. *Intent* lay in ten fathoms, in the inlet in Totdalbotn's southern shore. (Botn, Kari had told him, meant 'head-of-fjord', the equivalent of the Scottish prefix 'Kinloch'.) About a mile eastward there was a projecting hook of land, marked on the chart as 'Skaget', which effectively hid the ship from anyone passing up or down the main waterway to or from Namsos. Unless a German ship actually came up into this backwater, the only real danger of being spotted would be from the air. And that was no immediate worry, with cloud-cover intact again.

It was higher cloud, though, and thinner. After such a large shift in the wind direction it was quite possible that the day might clear, later on. And that would be – *not* so good. *Intent*'s point-five machine-guns, two four-barrelled mountings side by side on their platform between the funnels, were her only defence against dive-bombers; and they were short-range weapons, effective up to no more than half a mile. The main armament of four-sevens had a maximum elevation of forty degrees, which made them useless in an AA role. But in fact no matter what guns she'd had, *Intent* would be finished if they once found her here. Even if she'd been mobile, in these restricted waters she wouldn't have a hope.

The point-fives were manned now, and so was 'B' gun. A lookout was being kept from those points and from the director tower and from the bridge, and there were sentries on foc'sl and quarterdeck. Also, a shore lookout had been established on Hoddoy, on a 500-foot ridge a bit less than two miles from this anchor berth. It was manned by Norwegians, a family from a farm somewhere in that area. Nick had picked the spot, after a study of the chart and a careful binocular inspection of the surroundings. From that hill, there'd be a view over land and water from north-west to south-east; really only Namsos port itself would be shut off, by some intervening high ground on the island of Skjerpoy. His idea had been to send young Cox and an OD to camp there, but

Claus Torp had suggested local people might be persuaded to do it and be less conspicuous than British sailors. He'd arranged it yesterday afternoon, when he'd gone ashore in his motor skiff to check on telephone communications and pick up what news he could.

They'd got into Totdalbotn early yesterday afternoon. By 4 pm *Valkyrien* had been secured on *Intent*'s starboard side, and by 4.30 Boyensen had been at work.

There was movement and voices up near the point-fives; and a sailor in a greatcoat and a webbing belt was coming aft, exchanging greetings with *Valkyrien*'s quartermaster. He'd be coming to relieve the sentry: which meant it was now six o'clock.

If there'd been an attack on Narvik at first light, as last night's signals had indicated there would be, it would be all over by now. And if *Hoste* had been in the attacking force – which presumably she would have been – Paul would have some answers of his own by this time to the question he'd asked not long ago at Mullbergh – what did action feel like . . . Nick remembered vividly his own first taste of it: the awful period before it started, when one had been scared stiff of not coming up to scratch; then the relief when there'd been a lull in the fighting and time to realise that one had been in it and not had time to be frightened, only been totally immersed in doing one's job. He wished Paul that sense of relief. He hoped he'd be enjoying it at this minute. Paul's reappearance in his life was the best thing that had happened to him in years: the boy had become a personal reason to want to live, to survive the war – in order to spend time with him, get to know him, have Mullbergh in good shape to pass into his hands.

And simply for the fact that he existed!

If he hadn't turned up, if he'd stayed with his mother in the USA, would there have been *no* reason to care much about survival?

Well, things were different now, and there was no need to think about how they *had* been. But thank God, anyway, for Paul's arrival on the scene. His half-Russian son . . . They had a lot in common, Nick thought. They didn't look much alike – Paul was more athletic-looking, generally *better*-looking than Nick reckoned himself to be – but inside, one sensed the similarities, the common wavelength. The basis of it was that you felt you knew how he'd react to given circumstances or problems: that given the knowledge, training, experience, whatever it took, he'd react very much as one would oneself.

It was something to hold on to, all right. It was a hell of a *lot* to hold on to.

After *Valkyrien* had berthed alongside yesterday, and ropes and wires had been secured and a brow put over from *Intent*'s waist to an entry-port in *Valkyrien*'s bulkhead, Claus Torp had invited Nick to go aboard. So he'd gone over, leaving Trench to see to essentials in the destroyer. Torp had met him at the gangway, and as he'd arrived he'd seen the engineer, Boyensen, and two other characters come sloping aft with tool-boxes. It was more than he'd hoped for, that they'd get on to the job so quickly.

Torp sketched a salute as Nick stepped off the gangway.

'You are welcome aboard, Captain. I have to tell you, however, that since I have only twelve men on board, passage crew you see, with no cook or steward—'

'For heaven's sake—'

'What I do have is Aquavit. Also Scotch whisky.'

'Not for me, thanks. But I'd like to talk to you.'

'Sure. Come, please.'

Valkyrien's saloon was very much as he'd thought it would be. Mahogany, and a dark red carpet, brass lamps in gimbals. Curved-backed swivel chairs were bolted to the deck around a central table which was covered in a green-baize cloth.

'Captain, I introduce my daughter.'

She'd come towards them from the other end of the saloon. Dropping a book – it looked like one of the yellow-jacket English thrillers – on the table as she joined them. This was obviously the female in the bright-coloured oilskins, Tommy Trench's 'popsie'. He'd forgotten about her, until now. Torp was saying, 'Kari, this is Commander Everard of the Royal Navy.'

She wasn't conventionally 'pretty'. But she took all his attention immediately. She was – *very* attractive, in a way that might be difficult to describe, he thought. Except for the striking contrast of dark hair and light-blue eyes there was no feature you'd say was all that special. Very un-fussy, *natural* . . . He felt – immediately – *involved*, and off-balance at feeling any such thing: he saw the same kind of surprise in her face, and then the emergence of that stunning smile.

'Welcome to Norway, Captain.'

'You're very kind.' He glanced at Torp, if only because he felt he had to take his eyes off her for a moment. 'So is your father.'

'Oh, he's not such a bad fellow.'

'You talk very good English, if I may say so.'

'You may say so as often as you like.'

Torp informed him, 'Kari is a teacher. Of English, among other subjects. *My* teacher, of English.'

'Must be a very good one, then.'

'Thank you . . . Knut Lange, the man with the boat – the blue boat you saw? – was bringing her from Namsos to a village; it is called Skorstad, where we have friends. After, he would have come out to stop *Valkyrien* as I am coming into the fjord.'

'I see.' He asked Kari, 'Will you teach me Norwegian?'

'If we have time, of course. But first – ' she pointed – 'won't you sit down?'

He laughed. Sitting, he asked Torp, 'Your friend with the boat was still going on to this village, was he, whcn he left us?'

'Sure. And other places not so far from there. He had two other passengers, who had been in Namsos, to be taking to their homes. But he will come back to us here tomorrow, he was saying.' Torp added, by way of explanation, 'He is our good friend.'

Knut's boat might come in very handy, with the lunatic plan that he was tinkering with. It was going to need a lot more thought before he'd be ready to discuss it with anyone else, though.

He asked Kari, 'Can you tell me what's happening in the town?'

'In Namsos? Our little village, a town?'

'I beg its pardon.'

'Oh, it would be honoured . . . But I was not there myself, you see, I was with cousins who are at a small place called Hals. There is a bay where Knut brought in his boat. What is happening is the Germans have taken everybody by surprise, before daylight this morning. It was an empty ship, they thought, but out of it suddenly came soldiers, guns—'

'What kind of guns?'

'Big, on wheels.'

'Field guns.'

'And also some motor-cars – trucks.'

Nick looked at her father. 'All highly organised, prepared weeks in advance. Just sitting there, waiting.'

Torp nodded. '*Now*, we know it.'

'It must have been planned very well,' Kari said. 'They ran directly to the mayor's house and to the railway station, customs office, police station – to the main roads too, the crossroads have barriers and soldiers – all that. Now all the people must give their names and details for lists to be made and so on. They are being told the Germans are friends of Norway who are come to defend us against you British. This is what I have been told by people coming out of Namsos. Quite a lot of the young men – some old ones too – are making away for the mountains, to organise resistance, join an army or – will your British army come now to drive out the Germans?'

What a question, he thought. Did Britain have enough of an army and weapons, equipment, aircraft, to have held on to the Norwegian ports even if we'd stepped in first, he wondered? Let alone to drive out an entrenched occupation force. Most of the British army was in France, waiting for the war to start, while the French sat behind their Maginot Line, morale crumbling – one heard – almost defeated before a shot was fired . . . *What* army, and who'd send it? Had the War Cabinet in London had a request submitted in quadruplicate; ratified by the League of Nations or initialled by the Almighty?

Nick had some questions of his own. Where had the field guns been set up, was the Trojan Horse ship herself armed, how might the German troops be deployed around the harbour area?

Kari didn't know. Torp said he might be able to find out; he'd go ashore to a farmhouse at Totdal, where he had friends – or one in Sveodden, which was nearer and where he also had friends – and see if the telephones were working. It was too soon for anyone who'd been in Namsos since the arrival of the Germans to have come this far – except by water, which no one had . . .

'They're bound to have taken over the telephone exchange.'

Torp nodded. 'I will be careful.' The Norwegian asked him, 'Why do you want to know about the guns and defences?'

Nick wasn't ready to discuss it. Particularly if Torp was going to be ashore this afternoon, telephoning his friends. He answered vaguely, 'Well, if that ship's armed—'

'I am sure she is not.'

'Like you were sure she was in ballast?'

'I think they have painted false draught-marks, you know?'

He told them, 'I imagine we *will* send troops. So any information we can get while we're here will be useful. If – ' he looked at Torp – 'if the repairs to my ship go as we hope, and we can get away from here, what would *your* plans be?'

'To sail with you, I think.'

'In *Valkyrien*?'

133

'Why not in *Valkyrien*?'

'Would she have the range to reach – well, Scotland?'

Kari said, 'She could be sailed there. With her *sails*.'

'Yes,' Torp agreed. 'But steaming, she would have range to go where on our coast your army is landing.'

'I'm only trying to understand your intentions, you see, how they fit in with mine. It seems to me you're as much at a loose end as I am. More so – you've no operational command in existence, so far as we know, and to the Germans you're an enemy just as I am.'

Torp nodded. 'Yes.'

'So we're in it together. Do you accept the fact that I'm the senior officer here?'

'It's obvious.' Torp glanced at Nick's three stripes. 'You are in command. Although, since I don't have one single gun—'

'That's something we can think about later. But my point – the question of your leaving Norway, coming to England – you accept that it may be necessary?'

Kari told her father, 'I'd like to go. It wouldn't be for *ever*. We'd come back, with—'

'You can go. But if there will be fighting in Norway I want to be here.' He told Nick, '*She* could sail *Valkyrien*. She has done so before—'

Kari put in, 'Illegally, but frequently.'

'—and she has been sailing boats since she is a very little girl.'

That idea seemed a bit far-fetched. But then, it was a day – an epoch, perhaps – for far-fetched ideas . . . He asked Torp, 'What about your crew?'

'They are reservists. They do what I tell them.'

That seems to clear the ground. He could regard the Norwegians, for all intents and purposes, as part of his own force. One snag was the girl: if he was going into Namsos to get his oil, which was bound to be a slightly hazardous operation, he didn't like the idea of having her there with them. But he'd need *Valkyrien* for a landing-party . . . Or perhaps Knut's boat, instead?

'Deep thoughts now, Captain?'

Kari, smiling. He asked her, 'Do you have any close relations or dependants here, whom you'd be leaving behind?'

'No. Only cousins.' Torp had answered the question. Kari told him, 'He was asking do I have a mother, I think.'

'My wife died when Kari was quite small.' Torp explained, 'It is why I left the Navy, to look after her in our home.'

'Consequently he's a big noise in Namsos.' Kari was teasing him as well as giving Nick the information. 'Some great sacrifice, this leaving the Navy was. Timber-merchant, ship chandler, shipping agent, auctioneer—'

'Good man to pick for a father, then. And perhaps with his interest in timber he could get me a spar that we could shape for a fore-topmast and a couple of lighter ones for yards – d'you think?'

'Sure.' Torp thought about it for a moment. Then he snapped his fingers, and told his daughter, 'From old Jens. He will have some already trimmed. If the telephone is working, I give a message to the Korens, and they tell Knut when he is there with his boat, and he will bring them to us tomorrow.'

'Sounds like a smooth piece of organisation.'

'You must tell me lengths, diameters—'

'Yes.' Trench, with Metcalf as consultant, would provide those details. 'But one other thing. If my men bring cables over, would you be prepared to run your steam generator and feed us with power?'

'Perhaps. If I can do it and not make a lot of smoke, I think so. I must speak with Boyensen.'

'I'm most obliged. For *all* your help.'

'You may end with doing some things for *us*, I think.'

'Well, I hope so.' Nick checked the time. 'And to start with, may I offer you both dinner tonight, in *Intent*?'

'Morning, sir.' Trench saluted as he joined him on the quarterdeck. Quarterdeck and CO in one salute: a reasonable economy. Nick looked at his watch, and saw that it was six twenty-five.

'Bright and early, Tommy.'

'Not as early as *you* were, sir, I'm informed.'

'What's this, your intelligence service?'

'Something of that sort.' The big man fell into step beside him. 'Thank you for a most enjoyable evening, sir.'

That supper party with the Torps as guests, he meant. It hadn't been exactly a gourmet's delight – canned pilchards, followed by what the wardroom chef called 'cutlets', which meant shapes of minced corned-beef cooked in breadcrumbs, and a savoury of bacon-wrapped prunes on toast. Afterwards, green Chartreuse, and the men smoked cigars. They'd listened to the BBC news broadcast, which had spoken of air attacks on German shipping in Norwegian ports and of German dive-bombing of the Home Fleet offshore. The Norwegian King and the government had left Oslo in order to direct the fight against the Nazi invaders from a new headquarters . . . Or words to that effect. It wasn't news, actually, since Torp had been getting Norwegian broadcasts during the day. The government and the Royal Family had moved up to a place called Hamar, about a hundred kilometres north of Oslo; they'd moved out only one jump ahead of the Germans, who'd chased them in armoured cars and then bombed and machine-gunned their transport from the air. In order, presumably, to clear the ground for this Norwegian traitor – a Major Quisling – who'd since been heard on Oslo radio announcing himself as the country's new ruler.

Nick had proposed King Haakon's health, and Torp replied with a toast to King George. Nick showed Kari the lovely colour of Chartreuse, the green variety, when it was lit and burning; in the low, yellowish lighting with which *Valkyrien*'s generating plant was providing them, the flame on the glass filled the cabin with an eerie, subaqueous glow. Then for the entertainment of their guests they turned on the Tannoy to a programme of light music, 'Forces' Favourites', and 'A Nightingale Sang in Berkeley Square'.

Kari sighed, 'That's a *lovely* song!'

'As a matter of fact, I know the man who wrote it.'

Eric Maschwitz and his wife were friends of Fiona Gascoyne's. The club which Phyllis was opening, the Gay Nineties, was to be in Berkeley Street, a nightingale's warble from the square. He was telling her about it when Torp asked, 'The photograph of the lovely lady dressed up as a general has been removed, I think?'

Nick saw Trench smother a smile. He told Kari, 'That song's a great hit in a London show called *New Faces*. It's been running months now and it's still packed out every night. Well – every *evening* – our theatres start at six now, because of the blackout. But if you do end up in England, Kari, you should see it.'

Torp asked, 'Have there been air raids on London?'

'No. We expect them, though.' Trench asked Nick, 'Have you had a chance to see *Me and My Girl*, sir?'

'No, I haven't . . .' But it was incongruous – he'd been about to say 'not yet' – to be discussing those areas of frivolity as if one was so sure of getting back to them.

'If I did come to London one day, would you take me to some theatres?'

It wasn't obvious which one of them she was talking to. They both looked at her, and at each other. Nick told her, 'Either of us would be delighted to, Kari.'

'I suppose,' Torp growled, 'that if Mrs Everard does not mind you going about the world with your cabin full of pictures of different girls—'

'There is *no* Mrs Everard, Commander.'

Kari, in a dress, had seemed quite different from Kari in slacks and a thick sweater. She had not only a lovely face now, she had a figure too. One could imagine her – just – in London, dining, theatre-going . . .

Torp had achieved his objectives ashore in the afternoon. He'd arranged for Knut Lange to bring the spars, and he'd got through by telephone to some fishermen friends near the fjord exits, chatted about fish long enough to confuse or bore any eavesdropping Germans, and then asked his friends to telephone to Sveodden if Hun ships entered the fjords. The message would be, 'Tell Claus the animals are on their way.' They were people he'd known for years and he was confident they'd do it. Chandler had christened it 'Torp's Early Warning System', short-title TEWS.

Six-thirty. Wail of a bosun's call, and a muffled bellowing from for'ard. Calling the hands: the duty PO would be roaring through the messdecks, *Wakey wakey! Rise and shine! Heave-ho, heave-ho, heave-ho, lash up and stow! Show a leg, show a leg, rouse OUT!* Nick didn't have to hear it for the noise to start ringing in his head. He'd been thirteen when he'd first woken to those barbaric cries. At Dartmouth: where for sheer bloody hell . . . He shook his head, disliking even the memory of it. He wondered how Paul was taking to the crudities of messdeck life. At least his introduction to the Navy, at nineteen, wouldn't be nearly as unpleasant as his father's had been at a much more tender age.

Trench said, breaking a few minutes' silence, 'My intention is to get the ship cleaned up, sir, during the forenoon. Starting with the messdecks. Do you want to keep one gun and the close-range closed up all day?'

'Yes. And lookouts on the bridge, and the director tower manned. One officer on the bridge and a quartermaster on the gangway. We can do without sentries, though, in working hours. When the spars arrive, let Metcalf have as many hands as he wants. Did he finish the staging for the engine-room, d'you know, in place of the footplates they're using for the patch?'

'He did, sir.'

'Good . . . Tommy, we'll fly no ensign and no Jack. For the time being, let discretion be the better part of valour.'

The shaping, rigging and stepping of a new topmast was a job to be completed as soon as possible, because once Boyensen had done his stuff below and the generator was back in action they'd have full power for wireless transmitting, and the proper aerial height would be needed. If the raid on Namsos went badly at least it would be possible to let the C-in-C know what was – or had been – happening. If it went well, he wouldn't let out a peep. If the Germans could be taken completely by surprise, and if communications between Namsos and the rest of Norway could be cut before the action started, it was possible – with a reasonable share of luck – that *Intent* might get her oil and be away before any alarm went out.

He told Trench, 'I'll be calling a meeting in my cabin this afternoon. I'll ask Torp to attend, and I'll want you, and also Chandler and Brocklehurst. I'll let you know what time.'

He'd have this forenoon, barring interruptions, to work out some details, formulate one cohesive plan out of the jumble of ideas. It could have been done more quickly: if *Intent* hadn't been immobilised, it would have been. As things were, there was time to plan it with some care. And by this afternoon, Boyensen might be able to forecast a time for the completion of his work. If his first estimate had been right, it would be done by some time tomorrow. So tomorrow night for the bust-up. Move in the dark hours: attack in the dark too, if Torp agreed that it could be done. Otherwise, at first light; but the night would be better, in order to get out of the fjords while it was still dark. Check the tides, and the shape of the harbour, and whatever the Sailing Directions had to say. It might be sensible, he decided, to talk it all over with Claus Torp before letting the others in on it. Torp, after all, did know the area and the port.

'Number One.' He stopped near the superstructure door which led down to his own quarters and to the wardroom. 'I'm going down for some breakfast. I'd like you to give Torp a message – not now, but after you've dealt with the hands at eight, say. My compliments, and would he join me at eleven for a cup of coffee.'

'Just him alone, sir?'

Nick glanced at him sharply. Trench began to look as if he wished he hadn't asked the question.

'Yes. Just him.'

*   *   *

He was in his bathroom, shaving, when at 0700 he heard the pipe 'Hands to breakfast and clean.' Scraping the lather off his face, trying to ignore the racket going on up top where engine-room hands were drilling bolt-holes ready to take the steel patch across that hole, and pondering on what part *Valkyrien* might play in the attack on Namsos. He thought the best use for her might be as an escape vehicle, for the landing-parties and others, if *Intent* should – God forbid – get scuppered somehow. *Valkyrien* could then stay clear of the rough stuff; and Kari could be in her. For landing-parties he could use *Valkyrien*'s two motor skiffs or Knut's boat – if Knut was prepared to join in the operation.

Leading Steward Seymour knocked on the bathroom door. 'Surgeon-Lieutenant Bywater would like a word, sir.'

'All right. Hang on there.' He put his razor down and went out, half shaved and with a towel round his waist, into the day cabin. 'How is he?'

'Coming along very nicely, sir, I'm glad to say.'

'Well done . . . He'll be laid up for quite some time, I suppose?'

'Yes, sir. To his own annoyance, he will. I've taken the bandages off his face now – it's nothing like as bad as we thought at first – and he's talking – mostly about the engines and how he ought to be down there getting on with it, etcetera.'

'Good for him.'

'What he needs most is rest. But he'd appreciate a visit from you, sir, if you could spare the time.'

'As soon as I've had breakfast. Anything else?'

'Only this, sir. It's the only one since last evening's SITREP.'

Nick read the signal. It was from Vice-Admiral Battlecruiser Squadron to *Penelope*. The cruiser was being told to take four destroyers with her and proceed immediately to the support of the 2nd Destroyer Flotilla in Ofotfjord.

It didn't look too good. If Warburton-Lee needed support . . .

'We aren't getting much, are we.' He passed the signal log back. 'Anything of interest from the BBC?'

Bywater shook his head. 'There'll be a news at eight, sir, of course.'

When Nick had dressed he went back into the day cabin, where Seymour had his breakfast ready. Cornflakes, and bacon with fried bread.

'Are we out of eggs?'

'I'm afraid we are, sir.'

He decided he'd ask Torp whether there'd be any chance of getting fresh provender ashore here. The invaluable Knut might round up supplies from somewhere. Fresh milk, if there was any to be had, would be a change from this tinned stuff. One wouldn't want to take food from the mouths of Norwegians, but it wouldn't be any crime to put the Hun garrison on short rations.

Seymour had retired to his pantry, which had a service hatch connecting through the after bulkhead, near the door to the wardroom and cabin flat. Nick began to think again about Operation Namsos.

If the attack could be made in the dark hours, there were the alternatives of opening with a couple of rounds of starshell lobbed over the town to light up their objective and/or enemy strongpoints, or of keeping as quiet as possible, concentrating the attack on the oiling jetty alone, silencing any sentries or gunners without disturbing the garrison as a whole. It would be the neatest way of doing the job. Without a shot or a light: only some sentries to be found later with their throats cut – or discovered to be missing, if one took them prisoner – and fuel-tanks lighter by a few hundred tons, *Intent* slipping away to sea before the light came . . .

Dobbs' face wasn't a pretty sight, smothered in some kind of ointment. But it was amazing to recall that such a short while ago he'd been so nearly a customer for that launching-party in the waist. Nick remembered his own impromptu prayer, and he said another now in his mind as he looked out of the sickbay's scuttle across still grey water towards the north-western shore of Totdal-botn: *Thank you, God.* Perhaps it was only a way of hedging one's bets: certainly he couldn't have said whether or not he believed that God might have taken a hand in Dobbs' recovery. But since one had asked for that intercession and then seen – almost miracu-lously, according to Bywater – the desired result, it would be churlish not to follow through.

He'd talked to Dobbs about Boyensen, and his hope that he'd have the ship fit for work by some time tomorrow.

'Only wish I could be on the job meself, sir. Seems *daft—*'

'It's fretting about it that would be daft. The more you can relax and rest the sooner you'll be on your feet. Right, doctor?'

Bywater confirmed it. Dobbs said he knew it: he still hated lying around when there was important work to do, *his* kind of work.

'You made a very stout effort, and it'll be in my report . . . Got anything to read?'

'Be difficult to 'old a book, sir – or turn the pages, like.'

Both his hands were wrapped like an Egyptian mummy's. Nick suggested, 'If you had a rack of some kind – fixed or suspended about here . . . Then to turn the pages – Doctor, a marline-spike would do it. A spike shoved through a cork. You could wedge the cork inside the outer bandage and he'd just prick the pages over?'

'Yeah, if I had *that* . . .'

Bywater was doubtful about how the rack could be fixed up. Nick said, 'We have one *amateur* mechanical genius on board who might turn his talent to it. And who probably hasn't nearly enough to keep him busy at the moment. Midshipman Cox.'

Dobbs grinned. It hurt him: he winced, and straightened his face. 'He's a good lad, sir, is Mr Cox. Very chummy with Mr Waddicor – well, he *was*.'

'I didn't know that.'

'Both Devon, you see, sir.'

Both West-Countrymen, and both with interests in things mechanical and oily. Waddicor, the commissioned engineer, had been a cheerful, easygoing character. A clear contrast to the fussy, very *proper* Pete Chandler. It made sense, all right, and no wonder the boy had enjoyed escaping to the engine-room.

He told the doctor, 'I'll send him along to you.'

Three weeks ago, he reminded himself, he hadn't known anything about anybody in this ship. You began to see them individually, like so many separate pieces of a jigsaw, and then you saw how they fitted in, with the ship's function and with each other, linking this way and that to build the whole picture, the community that was a ship's company. The whole being enormously greater than the sum of the parts.

One of the parts being Randolph Lyte, whom he found on the bridge in charge of the lookout watch. Lyte hadn't shaved yet, he noticed.

'Morning, Sub.'

'Oh – morning, sir!'

He'd made him jump. He asked him, 'Had breakfast yet?'

'Not yet, sir. My relief's somewhat adrift.'

For the change of watch at 0800, presumably. But Nick's watch told him it was still only three minutes to the hour. Then he remembered: just before he'd left the sickbay he'd heard the pipe 'Hands fall in' – and that would have been sharp at eight.

'What's the time exactly?'

'Five and one-half minutes past, sir.'

He'd missed that news bulletin. But someone would have heard it . . . He asked Lyte, 'Everything all right up here?'

'Very quiet and peaceful, sir.'

'We'll change *that*, soon enough.' He focused binoculars on the hill where Norwegians were supposed to be keeping a lookout over Namsenfjord. If they saw anything that looked German, they were to wave a red flag. It would probably be a petticoat, Torp had said. A white one after that would mean 'all clear'.

'You're keeping an eye on that hill?'

'Yessir. Starboard lookout's alert to it as well, sir.'

'Good . . . When you go down, Sub, tell Cox there's a job I want him to do for the doctor. In sickbay.'

'Aye aye, sir.'

Pete Chandler was in the chartroom and on the point of going up to take over from Lyte. It was unlike Chandler, to be late like this. Nick asked him, 'Did you hear the eight o'clock news?'

'Yes, sir.' He seemed cheerful this morning. '*Good* news, for a change. Fleet Air Arm 'planes have sunk the *Konigsberg* in Bergen harbour, and destroyers have smashed up a whole bunch of Huns at Narvik.'

'Tell me what was said about Narvik.'

'German losses were two destroyers sunk and five so damaged as to be unseaworthy. So they're stuck there and presumably we can bomb them – or attack again and finish them off . . . Plus six supply ships sunk or burnt – destroyed, anyway – and one large ammunition ship which our chaps met when they were withdrawing down Ofotfjord. It blew up with an explosion that sent flames to three thousand feet, the man said. British losses were two destroyers.'

'Two *sunk*?'

'One sunk, one beached, sir.'

'Didn't name them?'

Chandler shook his head. 'It said a large number of survivors were thought to have got ashore.' He shrugged. 'Sounds as if we won by an innings.'

Nick was silent, leaning over the chart, giving the appearance of studying it, reading without actually taking into his mind what the words meant, *Namsenfjorden: from the Norwegian government*

142

charts of 1900. With additions and corrections to 1931. He heard Chandler say, 'Good show knocking off the *Konigsberg*, sir.' Six ships, he was thinking, in that flotilla. Two lost. One chance in three. Or rather – he switched to the other way of looking at it, in the process of getting a grip on this – two chances in three that *Hoste* was now out in Vestfjord. Probably fuelling from *Renown* or one of the other big ships they had up there.

'Pilot, I'm going to borrow this chart and the Sailing Directions and the tide tables. Better have the Nautical Almanac as well.' For times of sunset and sunrise. He added, 'We'll be having a meeting some time this afternoon, down in my cabin, and I'll need to have you there.'

Chandler nodded. 'First lieutenant did mention it, sir.'

Six bells: and he had his notes roughed out well enough to go over them with Torp. He had a list of questions for him too. Torp should be here at any minute. From for'ard Nick heard the pipe 'Up spirits!' and from the pantry Steward Seymour's murmured response, 'Stand fast the 'Oly Ghost.' Same old jokes, day after day and all over the world's oceans for – what, two hundred years?

Mr Opie and the coxswain and a few other stalwarts would descend now to the spirit room – it was one deck below this and further aft, between the after magazine and the tiller flat, the steering-gear compartment – and draw the raw Jamaica rum which would then be mixed with water: one gill of water to half a gill of rum. Chief Petty Officers were allowed to draw it neat, and Paul, being under twenty years of age, wouldn't get it at all.

British losses, two destroyers . . .

There was a knock on the door, and he called 'Come in.' Trench announced, 'Lieutenant-Commander Torp, sir.'

'Thank you, Tommy . . . Come on in, Commander.'

Torp said as he entered, 'I must thank you for a wonderful dinner party.' Trench withdrew. Nick told the Norwegian, 'I'm all set to give you a few shocks, to make up for it.' He called to Seymour, 'Coffee please, steward.'

'Shocks, eh?'

'Better sit down and prepare yourself.' He pointed towards the open hatch. 'It can wait for a minute or two.'

'Then while we are waiting, I have an invitation for you to lunch with us, please, in *Valkyrien*. And before you make excuses I warn you we have fresh-caught fish and that Kari is the best cooker of fish that was ever born.'

143

'No excuses, then. I accept with the greatest pleasure.' Seymour had put the coffee in the hatch and he was on his way round – out of the pantry into the cabin flat and then in by the door through which Torp had entered. Nick said, 'I was wondering – talking of fish – whether we could buy any fresh produce for the ship while we're here. Fish, eggs, vegetables, meat? One snag is we've only British currency on board.'

'That would not matter. Only how much time there is. To arrange now for sufficient – is it for your whole crew?'

'Yes. Hundred and sixty-five.'

'Well.' Torp looked doubtful. 'If it had been last week you were asking – before the Boche came—'

'You'd have told me to get the hell out of it. For trespassing in your neutral waters.'

Torp frowned, blinking, watching Seymour carefully setting down the tray. He decided, apparently, to let the point go; he said, 'Halvard Boyensen tells me his work goes well. I think you will not wish to stay here only to have provisions? If he finish maybe tomorrow midday—'

'I want to sail tomorrow night. About midnight.'

Seymour could take *that* buzz for'ard. Nick saw it register – the steward's quick, interested glance. Sailors on the messdecks expected occasional buzzes from the wardroom stewards, and stewards lost face if they couldn't provide some from time to time. Nick told him, 'I shan't be on board for lunch, Seymour.'

'No, sir. I 'eard.'

'And we shan't need anything else now. Shut the hatch, would you, before you leave the pantry?'

A minute later it slid shut, and then they heard the pantry door shut too. Nick told his guest, 'I can't sail without taking in some oil-fuel. You are certain, I suppose, that there's some in Namsos?' Torp nodded. Sudden interest in the blue eyes. Kari's eyes, in that broad, entirely masculine face. Slight pouches under them and thickly matted brows above. Extraordinary . . . Nick pointed at the table on which last night they'd dined and on which he'd now laid out the chart and reference books and signal pads for making notes on. He asked Torp, 'Would you make me a sketch of the harbour layout, quays and oiling jetty, and so on? Use the back of that chart, perhaps, so we can have it on a nice big scale?'

*   *   *

'I think, Kari, I can say without exaggeration or flattery that I've never eaten such fish as this. The sauce is – well, *what* is it?'

'It's secret.'

'She makes up such secrets by herself.' Torp pointed at her with his fork. 'When you see she has a – what d'you call, a *goof* look?'

'Goofy. But I'd hardly—'

'No, you would not, would you. But goofy, yes. She is thinking then about food. Why she is not fat like a pig I do not know.'

'Or why *you* aren't, if she gives you meals like this one very often.'

'He's *quite* fat, don't you think?' Kari poured herself a glass of water. 'Tell me about the plan you've made?'

Torp had produced the sketch which Nick had asked for, and provided answers to all his questions. Then they'd gone over the plan in detail, and made changes here and there. Biggest of all was that instead of an advance party going in by skiff to land and cut the telephone wires leading out of the town – it was a necessity, but it had worried Nick, because of the danger of the men being caught and the Germans alerted to the likelihood of an attack – Torp believed that his friends in Totdal, who had an old Ford truck, would agree to making the journey by road to Sjoasen and from there north up the main coastal highway to a place where the wires could be cut three or four miles south of Namsos itself. The whole road trip would be about forty kilometres, fifty at the outside. And from the torpedo stores the Norwegians could be provided with fitted charges and fuse, to make a real job of it. The rest of the plan hung together with only minor changes, all the result of getting answers to those questions, and by the time they'd come over to *Valkyrien* for this lunch it was cut and dried, ready for presentation to Nick's officers this afternoon.

The oiling quay was on the western side of the harbour. It was made of concrete and about a hundred metres long. There was a railway line connecting to it. Another concrete quay of about the same length was being constructed just beyond it, but was in too rough a stage now, Torp felt, for any guns to have been mounted on it. Plenty of cover, though, among the heaps of sand and concrete blocks. The other jetties, all to the east, were smaller and made of wood, used mostly for loading timber from local sawmills. To the east again was the timber pond, the storage area, and the shallows on that side of the town dried out at low tides.

Kari had asked him to tell her about the plan. Nick glanced at

145

her father. Torp shrugged. 'Why not. You don't want her at your meeting, do you?'

'Well – no, I suppose—'

Kari asked him, '*Why* don't you?'

'Because – ' Torp answered her – 'our friend Commander Trench might not be paying attention to the right teacher.'

'Oh, you're ridiculous!'

'I think he's right.' Nick added, 'And Tommy might not be the only one.' Torp chuckled. Kari was looking at Nick, waiting for some more serious explanation. He said, 'We'll tell you about it now, then this afternoon we can use foul language if we want to.'

'Sure.' Her father nodded. '*I* want to.'

'In a nutshell, Kari, we're going to raid Namsos, take control of the oiling jetty, and hold it for as long as we need to fill our tanks with fuel. Roughly for an hour from the time the oil starts flowing.' That would be CPO Beamish's department, getting the oil in. Beamish would land with the assault party on the main quay. Nick went on, 'While we're doing it – well, look, here's the town and harbour. This is our approach, up Namsenfjord. In this headland here, which is three thousand yards from the quay we'll be at, is a little cove, with a point called—?'

Torp supplied the name: 'Merraneset.'

Kari said yes, she knew it, of course.

'That's where you wait, with *Valkyrien* This ship will be the way out, the escape ship in case *Intent* should get sunk or stuck there. We're borrowing your two motor skiffs, and we're also going to ask Knut Lange if he'll join us with his boat. If *Intent* has to be abandoned we'll blow her up and the survivors will escape by the boats to *Valkyrien*.'

Torp added, 'It would be for you then to take her out and maybe sail her to Scotland. I'll give you a course to steer. The Royal Navy would perhaps find you before you had gone so far.'

She asked him, 'You will be in the destroyer?'

'Sure. As pilot. We do all this in the dark, you see.'

'Who will be with me in *Valkyrien*?'

'Martinsen on the engine, and Kristiansen and Rolf Skaug on deck. Perhaps also young Einar.'

'The old ones and the baby.'

'Exactly. Also any others who do not wish to volunteer. Maybe some of Knut's crew – it depends.'

'Volunteer for what?'

146

'Halvard Boyensen will remain in the destroyer, because they have no engineers. Others – well, you see, Commander Everard's plan is to put ashore two parties of men with rifles and Thompson sub-machine-guns, one on the half-built quay and the other on the most western timber jetty. From there they will cover the approach to the oiling quay also, and maybe derail a railway truck at the inshore end. But the ship's guns will also be used, so for landing-parties we must give more men.'

'Yes.' She nodded. 'More beans?'

'No, thank you.' He told her, 'We'll be tying up loose ends this afternoon. When it's all settled I'll give you some details on paper. Signals, for instance. We'll use Very lights, red and green, to tell you when we've finished and are casting off – so you can then up-anchor and start out – or if things are going wrong and the boats are coming to you. That sort of stuff.'

'I am in charge of *Valkyrien* while you are doing these things?'

'Yes. Your father thinks you'd be better at it than any of his other people.'

'All right.'

Extraordinary. As cool as if she'd been asked to take the history class this afternoon. Nick would have liked to have got up, walked around to that side of the table and kissed her. He had a positive feeling, suddenly, that he was going to end up kissing her in any case; and it wasn't because she'd volunteered so readily. He looked at Claus Torp. 'You've got quite a girl here.'

'Well.' Torp shrugged. 'We'll see how she makes out.'

Kari said, ignoring her father, 'I am sorry there is no pudding now. Only these.' Pointing at a bowl of apples. Torp pushed his swivel chair around and got up. 'Boyensen will be eating lunch now. I will ask him how is the repair progressing.'

'Take an apple with you?'

She'd tossed one to him. Nick declined. The door shut behind Torp, and Kari began to peel her own, concentrating on it as if she was alone and engaged on some particularly intricate task.

'You're terrific, Kari.'

She didn't look up. 'I am glad you should think so.'

'I'm looking forward to taking you to those theatres.'

'You must make sure your raid is successful, then.' She was trying to keep the lengthening strip of peel unbroken. 'It's going to be very dangerous, isn't it?'

147

'It might be, but it might turn out to be easier than we expect. Depends on a lot of things. How old are you, Kari?'

'Twenty-seven.' Munching apple. 'You?'

'Forty-three.'

Mental arithmetic going on. Sixteen years was the answer, and it was an uncomfortably high figure, he thought. But Fiona Gascoyne was only four years older, at thirty-one, and she didn't seem to regard him as decrepit, exactly.

'You don't look as much. I'd have guessed thirty-eight, at very most forty.'

'Call it thirty-eight, then there are only eleven years between us.'

'Okay.' At least she was looking at him now. 'Why are you not married?'

'I was. I was divorced quite some while ago. My former wife lives in the United States and has an American husband now.'

'Did you have children?'

'One son. He's nineteen, and he's at sea. Up off Narvik somewhere, to be precise.'

'In a – ' her apple-hand moved in the direction of *Valkyrien*'s port side, where *Intent* was – 'destroyer?'

'Yes. One called *Hoste*. She's one of a flotilla that was in action at Narvik very early this morning. They sank a lot of German ships, but two of our destroyers were lost in the process.' Kari had stopped chewing: she was watching him intently. He'd already noticed that she was quick on the uptake. He told her, 'The news bulletin didn't mention *which* ships. But—'

He'd stopped because he'd felt her hand on his. She'd leant forward, reached to him across the table.

'I'm so sorry. Of course you are worrying now. But he'll be all right, you'll see. It will not have been *his* ship that—'

'Ah-hah!'

Torp, in the doorway of the saloon, was wagging a finger at them.

'You hold hands, eh? This is what's happening when my back is turned?'

Kari had neither withdrawn her hand nor looked round. She told Nick, 'Your son will be all right. I'm *sure* he will.'

It would have been wonderful to have been able to take her word for it. She truly, genuinely wanted him to: he could see it, feel it. She may even have believed it herself: or been determined to, as if by creating that certainty in herself and for him she could *make* it so.

'Son, did she say?'

He looked up at Torp. 'He's in one of the destroyers in that flotilla up at Narvik. The action we talked about this morning.'

'I see.' The Norwegian crossed two sausage-sized fingers. 'That is for him. For – what is his name?' Nick told him. Torp repeated it: 'Paul. Good luck to Paul.' He swung a chair round and let himself down on to it. 'Boyensen says tomorrow noon.'

Nick looked round at them: at Trench on his left, Henry Brocklehurst beyond Trench, Claus Torp at the end of the table and Pete Chandler on the right.

'That's the picture, then. Summing it up, the timetable will be as follows.' He glanced at his notes. '*Intent* will weigh at 2300 tomorrow and proceed at six knots with *Valkyrien* following close astern and with both motor skiffs on our davits and turned out ready for lowering. We may also have the blue fishing-boat in company. At 0100/12th we'll be off Merraneset, where *Valkyrien* will be detached to remain hidden in that cove. The skiffs will be manned at this point, and *Intent* will increase to twenty knots for the last one-and-a-half miles to the target area. At 0105 we will stop engines, lower the skiffs and slip them, and they will proceed to points A and B as shown on that sketch, land their parties and remain with them in case resistance is such that either or both have to evacuate. Alternatively to bring off any wounded men or messages. The fishing-boat, if we have it, will remain alongside – port side, as we'll be starboard side to the wall – and will be employed as circumstances dictate. "H" hour, for the skiffs' arrival at A and B and *Intent*'s at the oiling berth, will be 0110. Allowing for berthing and connecting up and roughly an hour's fuelling, I would hope to have recalled the landing-parties and be casting off *by* 0230 . . . Are there any questions, now?'

Trench nodded. 'You say telephone lines out of Namsos are going to be cut, sir?'

'At 0100, we hope. Commander Torp is going ashore later this afternoon to make arrangements for it. Which reminds me, Number One – Mr Opie is to provide two one-and-a-quarter pound fitted charges and a good length of Bickfords and some igniters – and a pair of pliers, while he's at it. As soon as this meeting's over?'

'Aye aye, sir.'

Brocklehurst suggested, 'Might it not be as well to blast any shore guns we can see as soon as we do see 'em, before we get alongside, sir?'

'If they open fire on us, yes. Otherwise I'd rather we took them with our assault party, fairly quietly and without waking up the whole town and garrison.'

Tommy Trench was going to lead the assault on the oiling quay. He'd have a dozen men with him. Two of the twelve would constitute CPO Beamish's personal bodyguard until he was back on board with the fuel-hose connected.

'Do you think there's a chance of keeping it all that quiet, sir?'

Brocklehurst again. Nick admitted, 'Not of *keeping* it quiet. But with a bit of luck we might get the oil flowing before the opposition becomes too obstreperous. And they might not realise, then, what we're doing.'

'You mean it may not occur to them that we're fuelling.'

'Exactly. They're pongoes, after all.'

Everybody laughed. Nick looked at Chandler. The navigator said, 'Since we have a highly experienced pilot, sir – ' he bowed towards Torp – 'I don't think I've any navigational problems at all. But the plan for the withdrawal does bother me a little. If we're intending to pick up *Valkyrien* and take her with us—' Nick shook his head. Chandler, who hadn't been looking at him, didn't see it. Torp did though, and raised his eyebrows, staring at him down the length of the table. Chandler was saying, '—her best speed being six knots, if we cast off at your estimated time of 0230, sir, we shouldn't be out of Namsenfjord until something like 0700. As we'll have kicked up quite a rumpus by then it seems to me that such a leisurely withdrawal would be asking for the sort of trouble we can't easily handle. Aircraft attacks, for instance. Even if the telephones are out of action we've no way to stop them screaming for help by wireless.'

'Well.' Nick made a note. 'Perhaps we *have* . . . But – you're right, of course, there's no question of withdrawing at six knots. It's a point which I and Commander Torp haven't gone into yet – although I do have a proposal for him.'

Torp stirred. 'What is it?'

'*Valkyrien* will be there in case we fail. If we succeed, she then has no function to perform. We embark everyone from her, and the last man out opens her seacocks.'

'*Scuttle?*'

'If we don't, it's odds-on the Germans will. And *Intent* with her.'

150

'No.' Torp's face looked as if it had turned to wood. 'I am glad to accept your command, sir, but – no. I don't sink my ship.'

Nick had expected trouble on this issue. It was something for him and Torp to settle on their own.

'I understand your reluctance, Commander. Perhaps we can talk about it after this meeting.'

'Wait. I tell you what I can do.' Torp got up, came round to lean on the table between Chandler and Nick, pointing with a blunt forefinger at the chart. 'Here we will be, off Merraneset. I will come here from shore not in your ship but in one of my skiffs. Or in Knut's boat maybe. I and my own people will board *Valkyrien*. You in this ship can go at your own speed straight out Namsenfjord to the sea.' He put a hand on Chandler's shoulder. 'There are no dangers if you keep your eyes open. Fifteen miles – even at fifteen knots you are out in the open sea at maybe 0330, with darkness for one more hour. Not bad?'

'Not bad for us. But—'

'I take *Valkyrien* this way. Up Lokkaren, Surviksundet, Lauvoyfjord, Rodsundet or Seierstadfjorden. The Germans will be hunting after you and *this* way, not for some old yacht up here.'

'How long will it take you to get clear?'

'Three, four hours. From Flottra then I steer west, five knots. Departure Flottra 0630. When you signal your people you tell them this and they can send a few battleships for escorting me, huh?'

'Of course. The entire Home Fleet.'

But seriously – he *might* get away with it. Nick still had one reservation. He told Chandler, 'Pilot, when we break this up, ask the PO Tel to come and see me, would you. I want to talk about jamming any German transmissions while we're alongside. That was a useful point you made.' He looked across at the GCO: 'Once the shooting starts, we may want to use some starshell. Have one gun lined up for it, with starshell in its ready-use racks.'

'Aye aye, sir.' Brocklehurst made a note.

There was a knock at the cabin door: Nick called, 'Yes?'

Cox stuck his head in. 'Sorry to interrupt you, sir. The blue fishing-boat's just coming through the northern channel.'

'Thank you, Mid.' The head withdrew, and the door shut. Nick said, 'One item not yet detailed is the composition of the two skiff landing-parties. We'll go into that as soon as we know how many Norwegian volunteers we have. Otherwise, I think we've covered everything?'

'Very good.' Torp rose, stood rubbing his behind. 'Sitting so long, I been getting a sore arse.'

Trench murmured, 'Excuse me, sir?' He'd want to see to the reception of the fishing-boat.

Nick told him, 'Best if he berths on *Valkyrien*, Tommy.'

'*My* paintwork, eh.' Torp slapped him on the back. 'First you say I should sink her, now to scrape off the new paint.' Trench had gone up; the others were collecting their notes as Nick and Torp left the cabin. Torp's suddenly raised spirits, Nick guessed, were symptoms of pre-action elation. Something happened to the glands, the blood-stream, with some kinds of men. Some got jumpy and others – Torp's kind – got happy.

Cold air, grey water: the blue boat was carving a broad white track across it, approaching *Intent*'s stern where Trench and the buffer, Metcalf, were waving to Lange to tell him to come around to the inshore side. He'd see what was wanted, because he'd have seen *Valkyrien*'s raked masts and tall funnel sticking up behind the destroyer.

'Claus.' Nick put a hand on Torp's arm.' One suggestion I'd like to make, in regard to this plan of yours, that back-door exit you mean to take . . . You know and I know that while you *may* get away with it, there's a good chance you won't. The Germans aren't all stupid, and they know there's more than one way out to the sea. If I had to bet on it I'd say you'll either be stopped by some incoming surface craft, or strafed from the air. Anything that's moving seaward, after the attack on Namsos—'

'Yes, it is possible.'

'So you'll reduce your crew to a minimum?'

'I guess so. You take the others?'

'Of course. But what about Kari?'

'I thought so.' Torp glanced at him, and away again. He either sighed or took a deep breath. 'She has to be in *Valkyrien* during the attack.'

'But she could transfer after it.'

'Such delay, for one person—'

'Instead of coming off by skiff, you come with me, all of you. I'll put *Intent* alongside *Valkyrien*, and you can make a quick transfer, and away we go.'

'You worrying for Kari, Nicholas?'

'Nick.'

'What?'

'Short for Nicholas. Friends call me Nick.'

'Ah. *Sir* Nick, I think.'

'Who told you?'

'Boyensen. He is talking with your stokers down there. You worry for Kari, Sir Nick?'

'You've admitted the risk. You don't have to run it, you could scuttle your ship. My opinion is you *should*. But at least you don't have to put your daughter's life at risk.'

The blue boat was slowing, chugging in alongside *Valkyrien*. They could see the spars lashed to the cabin-top and along the side. They looked enormous: but Metcalf and his assistants would be paring them down with adzes before they shaped and fitted them. The heel of the new topmast would have to be squared with chamfered corners, and slotted right through for the top-rope sheave; and at two places above that they'd make 'stops', narrowings of the diameter where copper funnels would be fitted to take the upper yard and the rigging. Under the funnels there'd be another slot with a sheave in it for gantlines; and that was just the topmast, the yards would need shaping and fitting too.

Nick said to Metcalf, 'You're going to have your hands full, Buffer, to get it done in time.' Petty Officer Metcalf nodded. 'Keep at it all night if we 'ave to, sir.' The boat was alongside and its lines were being secured. Torp said, 'You take care of her for me?'

'If you'll allow me to.'

'Sure.' The meaty hand patted his arm. 'That is what we do, then.' He broke into Norwegian as he moved forward, answering a yell from Knut Lange which even to a non-Scandinavian ear had asked something very much like *Where the hell's Claus Torp?*

They were talking now. Or rather, Lange was. Unshaven, crop-headed, a triangular face that looked as if it might be all bone under the reddish stubble. He was down on his boat still and Torp was leaning down to him over *Valkyrien*'s bulwark. Lange talking quickly, urgently. Kari had come out of the deckhouse and she was listening: Nick could guess from her expression that whatever this news was it wasn't good.

The spars were being unlashed. Torp straightened, moved aft past the skiff which was still inboard. He'd caught Nick's eye, jerked his head, and now he was waiting for him in the stern.

'We have company.' He pointed northward. 'Three Boche destroyers. They enter Altfjord last evening. At night, two are leaving, one stay at anchor behind the island. Knut told the people

153

not to telephone – he thinks too much risk, better he tell me himself. But this morning one of the bastards is in Rodsundet. One now still anchored there, off Saltkjelvika, the other is going back out into Foldfjorden. Not fast, only – how you say, hanging around.'

The picture was clear enough. One destroyer on each of the two main exits and another one outside. But – it didn't mean they'd still be there tomorrow night. Also, there was still one other bolt-hole.

Torp was as gloomy as he'd been elated a few minutes ago. Scowling, watching some of *Intent*'s sailors manoeuvre the first spar up over *Valkyrien*'s side.

He swung round. 'No raid on Namsos now, I think.'

Nick met the blue stare doggedly. 'There *has* to be.'

'So you get your oil.'

'Exactly. I can't move without it.'

'If you are lucky, okay, you get it. Then you have three Boche destroyers waiting for you. What good is *that* for you?'

More good, Nick thought, than sitting here and waiting for the Stukas.

CHAPTER 9

'How are you now, Everard?'

The short answer might have been, *alive* . . .

Mathieson, *Hoste*'s first lieutenant, wearing fearnought trousers, a woman's embroidered blouse and a tattered red cardigan, was standing and looking down at him, and Paul – wrapped in a blanket – was sitting with his back against the classroom's wooden wall. The schoolhouse was – incredibly – centrally-heated; it was even conceivable now that they wouldn't all die of cold, which a couple of hours ago had seemed almost certain. He told Mathieson, 'I'm okay, sir, thank you.' Trying to get up, because he thought he should: the pain shot through his back, crippling him. It was only bruising and pulled muscles, Graham-Jones had said, nothing permanent or fundamental. Mathieson told him, 'Stay where you are, man.' Randy Philips was singing 'The Last Time I Saw Paris'. If Paris could have seen Randy it would have died laughing: he had on a skirt and a woman's overcoat, a tight, waisted garment of blue woolly stuff. Mathieson was moving on, looking for someone or other in the long, narrow, crowded room, one of several rooms in the schoolhouse into which the ship's company had flowed with the delight and disbelief of men transferred from hell to paradise. They'd trekked seven miles to this place – Ballangen, it was called, and it was about twenty or twenty-five miles from Narvik, someone had said – over rough, snowbound country, the snow in places six feet deep, guided by some Norwegians from the little timber houses near which they'd come ashore. The Norwegians had been marvellous: torn up their own clothes for bandages, deprived themselves of just about everything they possessed – clothes, food bed linen, blankets . . . Like angels of mercy in a frozen purgatory which had begun for Paul on the rocky beach with Timson the SBA – sickberth attendant, Surgeon Lieutenant Graham-Jones's assistant – kneeling astride him and pumping ice-water out of his lungs. About half of Ofotfjord was gushing out and *Christ*, it had hurt, that bastard Timson crashing up and down on his spine which already felt as if it had been sawn through. There'd been a dream which he remembered clearly – if one could have *clear* recollection of something so nebulous. Less dream than series of delusions. As if he was his own father: or with him, but at times actually *him*, Nicholas Everard: and drowned, knowing himself to be dead, which had meant that Paul Everard had also to be dead, to be here with him and part of him. The pumping and the pain had gradually taken over – and even worse, the *cold* . . .

Mathieson had turned back. He had a list of some sort with him and he'd been checking names off, for some purpose. Tall, fair-haired, yellow stubble glinting on his jaw. He said, 'Mr Stuart and I were doing some figure-work, Everard. Your score seems to have been seven.'

He didn't know what the man was telling him. His face must have displayed that lack of comprehension; Mathieson explained, 'Seven men you personally brought ashore.' He added, when Paul didn't react, 'Bloody good effort.' He'd turned aside, gone to talk to Perry, the cook, who was nursing a broken wrist. These injuries didn't count as wounds; the wounded were in the little hospital, which was the reason for having come to Ballangen in the first place. That and the fact that it was farther away from Narvik and its German troops.

Whacker Harris growled, 'You'll be gettin' a fuckin' medal if you don't watch it, Yank.'

'Oh, sure.'

More jokes. All the time, from this pair.

'Reckon you might at that.' Randy Philips didn't look as if it was anything he could approve of. 'You 'eard what Jimmy said. Commen-bloody-dation, that was.' He sighed, glancing at Whacker. 'Bloody HO, not at sea ten fuckin' minutes, an' they're talkin' to 'im like *that*. *I* dunno.'

'I don't either.' Paul really didn't. All he'd been told was that Mr Stuart the gunner, aided by PO Longmore the GM, had been bringing the Carley float inshore for the last time, after *Hoste* had gone down, and they'd found him wallowing face-down in the water. They'd been searching the ship one final time for any surviving wounded who might have been missed in previous searches, and drawn a blank, then loaded the float with small-arms and boxes of ammunition and got clear about a minute before she sank. When they bumped into Paul they'd thought he'd drowned, but pulled him into the float anyway and paddled ashore. After he'd been pumped out and had regained some appreciation of where he was and what was happening, Mr Stuart had torn him off a strip.

'What you got between your ears, lad – solid bone? There's a time to start and there's a time to bloody stop, an' there's such a thing as 'aving the gumption to know when you're done in. What you want's a bit o' bloody savvy, you daft clown!'

Now Mathieson had been congratulating him. One might wonder who was daft and who wasn't. As far as Paul was concerned, the two cancelled each other out. Wondering more about that dream and his father, whether on some other plane they could actually have been together, in such close communication that they'd been virtually one spirit, and then by slipping back into life he, Paul, had deserted him . . . *More* delusion, he told himself. But it had seemed so real: more real than this present scene seemed to him: and the sense of desertion was horrible. Might his father know that it hadn't been his *choice*?

He told Philips, 'I was just helping out, same as everyone else was. I do happen to be good at swimming. Nothing else about it's special that I can see.'

'Yeah, well, Jimmy reckons it was special. An' it's what 'e reckons sticks, ain't it.' He looked at Whacker. 'Besides, if 'e *did* pull seven blokes out—'

'Way we got 'im trained.' Whacker shrugged. He had a mauve shawl around his shoulders. 'Brought 'im up right, ain't we. Now 'e'll go through for C bloody W an' all that 'ard work's fuckin' wasted, ain't it . . . 'Ullo, 'swain!'

'All right, 'Arris, you foul-mouthed bastard.' The coxswain said it quite pleasantly. 'And you, Philips. Jackson, you fit? Course you are. 'Aven't 'ad a dose this year yet, 'ave you? On your feet then . . . And you, Barker. Smith – Daley – Woolley—'

'What's this in aid of, Chief?'

'Guard duty, Smith, that's what. Lovely, out there in the snow. Dream of a white Christmas, can't you. Long as *I* don't catch no bugger dreamin' . . . 'Old off the bloody Germans, lads, that's your job now.'

Paul was struggling to get up, to go along with the others. CPO

Tukes told him, 'You stand fast, Everard. On the sick list, aren't you?'

'Hell, Chief, I'm not *sick*, I—'

'Germans, 'swain?' Green: the telegraphist who'd given Paul his first news about *Intent*. He asked Tukes, 'Coming, are they? Jerries coming 'ere?'

'Green.'

'Yes, 'swain?'

'Does your mother cry every time she sets eyes on you?'

Green's mouth opened and shut: he looked round as if for help. The coxswain told him, 'You make *me* want to cry, Green . . . All right, you lot – in the 'all, draw rifles an' webbing from Petty Officer Longmore, then fall in outside. Shake it up, now!'

Germans: presumably they would come sooner or later, Paul thought. So those rifles and revolvers might come in handy. Although the enemy would be busy around Narvik, one might guess, repairing damage and looking after their own casualties and defences . . . Mathieson was coming back this way. Tom Brierson, who'd been the killick of 3 Mess, went up to him.

'Excuse me, sir. What's likely to 'appen next? I mean, are we staying 'ere?'

'For the moment, yes. It's on the cards there might be a second attack, you see. Even a landing. After all, we gave them quite a hammering, and it wouldn't take much to finish the job off. Also, we'll have to put some troops ashore some time, some place – at least I imagine we will – and Narvik would be as good a place as any. Specially as we've softened it up for them.'

Davis, an Asdic operator, asked him what they'd do if there was *not* a second attack or a landing.

'Make tracks for the Swedish border, before the Huns come for us. As the crow flies the border's only about twenty-five miles, but the way we'd have to go – because of the mountains – it'd be about forty. That's according to a Norwegian here who says he'd guide us.' He turned towards the door. 'But it does depend on the Huns too, of course. Bastards could show up at any minute.'

Brierson came over and sat down beside Paul.

''Ow's it going, Yank?'

'Not bad, Tom, considering.'

'Done yourself a bit of good, they say.'

'I don't know how. What was I supposed to do, sit on the beach and watch?'

'Some might. Goin' through for CW, are you?'

'I don't know that, either.'

'*I* would, in your shoes.' The killick shook his head. 'Bloody shame, skipper buying it. Good 'and, old Rowan was.'

Nick, on *Intent*'s bridge, was studying the hill where the lookout post was. Or where it should have been. Not a sign of any movement there. There could be, though: now that German ships had arrived in the outer parts of these fjords it was only a matter of time before some of them came up to visit Namsos. But for the moment that hill slumped grey and lifeless, with the westering sun vaguely brightening this side of it.

Claus Torp had gone ashore to Sveodden to see about the wire-cutting expedition. And Knut Lange had left them again. He'd taken his boat away through the northern channel with the intention of crossing Namsenfjord and landing near a village called Skomsvoll, in a wide, open bay marked on the chart as Vikaleira. There was a road junction near the village, and Lange's plan – he'd worked it out with Torp – was to send some of his crewmen overland up the east coast of Otteroy to the narrow strip between Altbotn and Lauvoyfjord. From Arnes on the east coast and from the neighbourhood of Alte on the west they'd be able to see into both the anchorages in which the enemy were – or had been – showing interest. From where *Intent* lay now to Lange's landing place was less than five miles, and the trip would only take him twenty or thirty minutes. The hike overland would be roughly another five, for which Claus Torp reckoned one should allow an hour each way, as quite a bit of it was hilly.

'Good for young men.' He'd patted his gut. 'Not for old gentlemen. For them – easy.'

Lange would stay with his boat and send three crewmen ashore. Two would keep watch on the anchorages – or elsewhere, if the German ships had shifted their berths – and the third would be the runner to bring news back to him. He'd return here to Totdalbotn before dark tonight, to let Nick and Torp know how things were shaping up to that time, but he'd go back again during the night to receive his men's first-light report.

Nothing to do but wait. And see which way the cats jumped. The cats were on the exits from the mouse-holes: big cats with five-inch guns . . .

Torp didn't think they'd pull it off now. Nick saw two angles, in the light of this enemy naval presence. First, stealth became much more important. He thought it was just conceivable that the fuelling might be completed without firing a single gun. It wasn't likely, but it was possible, and he was making it his aim now. Cutlasses and bayonets, not bullets; bullets only after – if – the enemy opened fire. The other point he had in mind was that the fact of Hun destroyers having been there earlier in the day didn't mean they'd be there *now* – let alone tomorrow night. Of course, it was also true that by tomorrow night they might be up at Namsos: in which case . . .

Well. *Sufficient unto the day . . .*

His mind jumped three hundred miles: to Narvik. There'd been a signal just after noon from Vice-Admiral Battlecruiser Squadron to the light cruiser *Penelope*, saying *Present situation. Enemy forces in Narvik one cruiser five destroyers one submarine. Troop transports may be expected. Your object is to prevent reinforcements reaching Narvik. Establish destroyer patrol across Vestfjord . . .* So *Penelope* was there now, with some unspecified number of destroyers; and Narvik – if this signal spoke the truth – was still bristling with Germans. It didn't mention whether the destroyers were now operational or still suffering from punishment administered to them by the 2nd Flotilla: it seemed to Nick that if there was a whole clutch of damaged ships in there, anyone in his right mind would nip in double-quick and polish the bastards off.

Guesswork. But carefully not guessing about *Hoste*. One had to keep one's mind on present circumstances, on what had to be done *here*. And whatever had to be done, he'd be running it – men's lives would rest on his decisions. It was necessary to be fit for that, not lose sleep worrying over *private* matters.

He heard a voice behind him: low-pitched, no doubt because *he* was up here. Turning, he saw the snotty, Cox, leaving the bridge, presumably having given some message to Brocklehurst, who had the afternoon watch. Nick called him back.

'Mid – did you fix something up for Dobbs?'

'Yes, I did, sir.' Cox came over to him. 'Wasn't difficult. I made it out of thick wire, just bent to shape and with a couple of screws in the bottom of the upper bunk to hold it.'

'Well done. What are you doing now?'

'Helping with the new topmast, sir. At least, seeing how it's done.'

'Progressing well, is it?'

'Seems to be, sir.'

He put his glasses up quickly: he'd thought he'd seen a movement on the hill. But if there had been, there was nothing to see now . . . 'Mid, we aren't going to allow you to *give up* your navigational studies, you know.'

'No, sir.'

'You must understand that whether it's an activity that appeals to you or not it's as essential to be able to use a sextant and arrive at a decent fix as it is to be able to tie a knot or steer a boat. It's part of your stock-in-trade as a seaman. If you put your mind to it, not as a school lesson but as a practical tool that you've got to master, you may find it a lot easier than you think.'

At Cox's age he'd been pretty hopeless at it himself. Probably for much the same reason: sick of instructors, the Dartmouth atmosphere which, so far as junior officers' training and gunroom life were concerned, lingered on when at sea. He'd been about as bloody-minded, when he'd been fresh out of Dartmouth, as anyone could have been. Then at Jutland – *after* Jutland, when he'd found himself sole surviving officer in his destroyer and that he had to get her back to England, he'd begun to realise that if he'd been less pig-headed in recent years, if he'd ignored likes and dislikes and states-of-mind and just damn well *learnt* it . . .

He was trying to explain this to Cox. Not mentioning the fact that, bringing the shattered destroyer home after Jutland, he'd not known for sure whether he'd hit England or Scotland or miss the lot.

'Yes, sir. I understand that.'

Nick could see that he was *trying* to understand it. He asked him, 'In your cadet days, did they talk at you about leadership?'

'Oh *yes*, sir.'

'What did they tell you it amounted to?'

The boy frowned, trying to remember. Staring at that hillside on the north shore of Sundsråsa. 'Well, just that – well, more or less a quality we're supposed to have, sir.'

'Like Divine Right, holiness or irresistibility to girls?'

The snotty looked surprised. Nick told him, 'It's nothing like that, Cox. No gift of God, and nothing magical about it either. Just common sense. It's not jumping up and shouting "Follow me!" and having all the chaps rush after you because you have this magnetic quality or heroism or something. The reason your instructors never spelt it out is because they're baffled by it

161

themselves because no one ever told *them* either; but not to have this thing is unthinkable, so they daren't look too deeply into it in case they find they haven't got it . . .' He drew breath. During the shore years, he'd had a lot of time to think about such things. 'I'll tell you how you can start working out what it is. First – what made me think of it – this navigation business, as an example. Knowledge and ability, competence – you have to know your stuff. Otherwise you shouldn't be here in the first place, there's no *reason* for you. And your men have got to know that you know it. They'll give you the benefit of the doubt until a time comes when it'll show up one way or the other, and then by God you'd better show it, or else . . . But there's more to it than just competence. They've got to like you. They've got to feel you're honest and fair in your dealings with them. And for that to come about you've got to like and respect *them*. Anyone who can't, or doesn't, might as well go home. When it works, it works because it's *natural*.'

Silence. Staring at the hill. Then: 'Any of that make sense to you?'

Cox nodded. He was looking at Nick now, not at the hill. He had a pleased look, as if he'd been given something.

'Yes, it does, sir.'

'Think about it, from time to time. If you can really digest it, make use of it, you'll find things tend to go well more often than they go badly. But don't think of it as some kind of trick. It's absolutely basic – to what sort of chap you are, or will be . . . Better get back to that topmast, now.'

'Aye aye, sir. Thank you very much, sir.'

Nick focused his glasses on the lookout post again. When he'd been Cox's age he'd had his uncle Hugh to put him straight occasionally. But it had been difficult for Hugh, because Nick and his father were always at loggerheads, and only in much later years had he and his uncle been able to discuss things without a feeling that they were whispering in corners.

Uncle Hugh would be convinced his nephew was dead, by this time.

Still nothing stirring up there. He hoped to God those people were doing what they'd said they'd do. He went back to the binnacle and slung his glasses on one of the spheres.

'I'll be down aft somewhere.'

'Aye aye, sir.' Brocklehurst added, 'Hope that fisherman doesn't run up against any Krauts.'

Nick thought Lange was probably quite canny. He looked it. And he'd surely know how to keep his boat hidden, in these fjords. He told Brocklehurst, 'Might be nicer for the Krauts if they don't run up against *him*.' He went down, avoiding the port side where Metcalf and his team were chopping away with adzes, and walked aft. A Norwegian assistant of Boyensen's and two of *Intent*'s stokers were fixing the steel patch over the engine-room, tightening the bolts all round; and on *Valkyrien*'s stern Kari was watching two of her crew lowering the second skiff out over the old ship's starboard side.

'That's a very economical arrangement.'

She looked round quickly, startled. He meant the single pair of davits amidships, between the two boats' cradles. It could be swung to either side, to lift either of the boats. Only *Valkyrien*'s narrow beam that far aft made it either necessary or mechanically feasible.

'They are going to try out its engine.' She came over to his side. 'For tomorrow night when you need them both.'

'Got plenty of petrol for them?'

'Oh, I think so.' She looked at her watch. 'My father is ashore a long time. Did you know we were invited to dinner in your ship's wardroom tonight?'

'I did hear some such rumour.'

'Will you be there too?'

'They've invited me.'

'Then you will be?'

'I think I'd better let them have you to themselves. I don't want to be greedy and monopolise you.'

'You don't?'

'Well – yes, of course, but—'

'Come too, please?'

'If you put it like *that*—'

'My father says those ribbons you wear on your shoulder – ' she'd perched herself on the white-painted bulwark – 'some are important ones?'

She had a very direct manner. As if they weren't likely to know each other for long and there wasn't time to beat about the bush. Also, she had a way of switching from one subject to another so rapidly that you knew her thoughts must have gone to the new subject while you were still busy with the previous one. Or – in *this* case – she'd been certain that as soon as she said 'Come, please?' he'd give in and agree?

163

He'd told her, 'They're from the last war. Too long ago to remember.'

'You must have been very young, to have won medals in that war. Do you think your plan can still work, with German ships out there?'

'I am hoping that by tomorrow they'll have achieved whatever their purpose is and be gone on their way.'

He would not, he thought, dine in the wardroom this evening.

'You say you are hoping, but do you *think* they will?'

The question was annoying. How the hell could he foresee the enemy's moves when he didn't even know why they'd come here?

'I'd say there's a good hope they'll move on. If they don't, we'll either grab our oil without raising an alarm and then sneak away, or we'll have to fight them on the way out.'

'Yes.' She nodded. 'The oil is necessary. Of course.'

The readiness to accept, again. She'd throw out a lot of questions but she wouldn't question a logical conclusion. Wasn't acceptance of logic unusual in a female? To Ilyana, certainly, logic had always been a strictly male weapon to be either ignored or derided or fought to the last shriek. Sarah – well, that was hard to know. With Sarah he'd never really had an argument: except for one very short, almost wordless flare-up, twenty years ago, and they'd ended that in each other's arms. Which was why nowadays she never spoke to him except in front of other people, when she sometimes had to. He felt he knew nothing, now, about Sarah. Fiona? Well, Fiona would accept logic if it worked out in favour of whatever she was after at the time. Otherwise she'd brush it off: 'My pet, don't be so *boring* . . .' Fiona had just completed her officers' training course: she was an Ensign now, with one pip on her shoulder. Uncharacteristically proud of the oddity that the MTC drills were patterned exactly on those of the Brigade of Guards: and of the quirk that MTC rankers called their lady officers 'Madam' and not 'Ma'am' as was done, apparently, in the FANYS, the nursing yeomanry. He'd made her angry by calling it 'instant tradition': and by laughing at her totally *illogical* frustration at not being allowed red paint on her nails.

This girl – Kari – wouldn't give a damn what she put, or did not put, on her nails.

Why should he think approvingly of that, he wondered? He agreed with Fiona: he *liked* lacquered nails. And he was *not*,

164

definitely, dining with his officers this evening . . . 'Kari, on second thoughts—'

'Here comes my father!'

She ran over to the other side, waving to the motor skiff as it approached from the western end of the little bay. She had a very attractive figure: not a mannequin-type figure like Fiona's, but – eye-catching and eye-holding . . . Claus Torp was standing up in the boat's sternsheets, waving back to her.

Rear-Admiral Aubrey Wishart pushed the door shut as he passed through into his office; he went straight to the desk and flipped up the intercom switch.

'Any messages?'

'Quite a lot, sir. But one is very urgent and personal – from Admiral Everard. He's telephoned twice, and left a number at which he'd like you to call him back.'

She told him the number, and from calls during the last three days he recognised it as a members' extension at Boodle's. He hesitated, drumming the fingers of one hand on the polished desktop. He'd been at a conference for the last two hours, deputising for his chief; he had a stack of work piled up that needed seeing to, and now on top of it, this . . .

Which he'd expected, of course. It was a lousy position to be in. He wished to God that Nick had never written that damn letter, putting the old boy in touch with him.

'Ginny – would you come in here, please?'

'Of course, sir.'

He was sitting behind the desk when she came in. Third Officer Virginia Casler of the Women's Royal Naval Service was blonde and petite. She was also quick-witted and efficient. He told her, 'Sit down for a minute. Something I'd like to explain to you.'

She put herself neatly in the chair facing his, and crossed one elegant knee over the other. Smoothing down her skirt: then the small-boned, well-manicured hands relaxed, folded in her lap on top of a file she'd brought in with her. He told her, 'I don't like to put a man off with excuses, pretending to be tied up or not here, and I dislike having to ask you to tell such fibs for me. Particularly when it's a man like Hugh Everard. But I do have a very good reason why I'd infinitely prefer not to have to talk to him, at least for a day or two.'

'That's about as long as you'll be here, sir, isn't it?'

165

He nodded. His new appointment had come through. He'd be off almost at once, to join the staff of C-in-C Mediterranean. Third Officer Casler's grey eyes rested on his face: she seemed patient – sympathetic, he thought – with his obvious unease.

'Hugh Everard's nephew Nick is an old friend of mine. His ship, the destroyer *Intent*, was sunk three days ago, in action with a cruiser believed to be the *Hipper*. Admiral Everard knows this, but won't or can't bring himself to accept it as fact. Nick was very close to him, more like a son than a nephew. So that's bad enough. The old man's wanting news all the time, and there isn't any and I know there won't *be* any . . . But now on top of it there's something else. In the action at Narvik yesterday morning we lost three destroyers. The communiqué said two, but the three are *Hardy, Hunter* and *Hoste*. And serving in *Hoste* was Ordinary Seaman Paul Everard – Nick's son, aged nineteen, first ship. Hugh Everard had taken a shine to his great-nephew too. So – well, you see?'

'Yes.' The grey eyes were clouded. 'I do. It's—'

'I've been trying to jolly him along about Nick and *Intent*, play up to the wishful thinking . . . But this other thing – well, we do have reason to believe there was a high proportion of survivors, but – ' his hands opened on the desk – 'you can only stretch hope and optimism a certain distance. After that—'

'May I make a suggestion, sir?'

He looked at her quickly. Women were such marvellous creatures to have around when you were tied up in knots. Like oil in jammed machinery. And this one – *well*, he thought, *you've always been a pushover for tiny blondes*. Perhaps because one was such a large, ungainly sort of chap oneself. He stared down at his hands on the desk. 'I'd be grateful if you would, Ginny.'

'I think you should tell him. He's going to find out before long anyway, so keeping it to yourself now isn't really going to save him from it. And if there *are* a lot of survivors – anyway, he's probably a lot tougher than you think. If he's anything like *my* father—'

She'd stopped, catching herself in the act of saying more than was necessary to make the point. Wishart, gazing at a scruffy-looking pigeon which was parading up and down on the stone sill outside his window, thought, *She's right. I'm being kind to myself, not to him.*

'You've got the number. See if they can get him for me, will you?'

'Right, sir. And here's the rest of the intake.'

She passed it to him, a file of signals, memos, reports. He stopped her as she reached the door.

'Ginny – thank you.'

She'd smiled. And now, skimming through the papers she'd left him, he was thinking of what was new that he could tell Hugh Everard about. Nothing on the blower: but if he met with him this evening – which was what he'd better suggest, if the old boy was staying in town again . . . One could hardly just state this thing about *Hoste*, flatly over a telephone.

Sir Hugh had won his private campaign, his battle to become a commodore of convoys, at least to the extent that they were putting him through a medical. At sixty-nine, for God's sake: and all right, so he *was* a tough old bird! But what news could he give him? It wasn't easy to remember what was new, what was this morning's crisis and what was last night's, when you were in the middle of it all the time. However, it was a fact that our submarine captains' hands had been untied since the afternoon of the 9th, when an order had gone out that German merchant ships in the Kattegat and Skagerrak could be sunk without warning. You could operate now as the Germans did: but until this moment one had been obliged to surface, issue a warning and give crews time to abandon their ships before torpedoing them. In effect it had meant that if there was any kind of air or surface escort you had to let the target go – to land its troops and guns in Norway. The first man to benefit had been Jackie Slaughter, the ebullient CO of *Sunfish*: he'd had a Hun ship in his periscope when Max Horton's signal had arrived, and all he'd had to do was press the tit. The submarines had been scoring heavily since then. But what other news, while the submarine service was doing most of the hard work? What else to tell Hugh Everard about?

Well, Narvik was the centre of interest now. Admiralty had told the Commander-in-Chief that the recapture of Narvik was to be given top priority. An expeditionary force was being mounted and despatched for that purpose, and until it got there the C-in-C was to ensure that no enemy reinforcements reached the place by sea.

Until . . . How long, one might well ask. The troops should have been there *now*. Why on earth they'd been disembarked in the first place, when they'd been ready and the ships all set to sail, to carry out Plan R4 . . .

The black telephone tinkled, and he reached for it.

'Wishart.'

'I have Admiral Sir Hugh Everard on the line, sir.'

'Thank you.' He put his hand over the mouthpiece, and cleared his throat. 'Put him through, please.'

'What're you up to, Yank?'

Whacker Harris, in from a spell of guard duty in the snow . . . Rubbing frozen hands together, relishing the school-house's warmth. It was packed to the eaves now, fairly bulging – with another couple of hundred men, here and in the hospital. Paul was squatting in the hallway, cutting up an old motor tyre with a pusser's dirk he'd borrowed from Tom Brierson. He told Whacker, 'Making a pair of shoes. At least, trying to.'

'Make me a pair an' all?'

'Okay. Long as you're not in a hurry for 'em.'

They wouldn't be the smartest footwear ever seen. Not that that would be likely to attract attention here: men were wearing strips of carpet, curtains, women's underclothes, old sacks . . .

Twice in the last couple of hours there'd been alarms that German columns were approaching. The first lot had turned out to be survivors from *Hardy*, and the next – the sentries had been about to open fire on them, then heard a shout in English – were British merchant seamen who'd escaped from their German captors during the early-morning battle. They were lucky – they had all their own clothes, uniforms. But there was very little room to move now. A hundred and seventy men from *Hardy*, and forty-seven merchant navy men.

Hardy's captain – Warburton-Lee, who'd led the attack – had been severely wounded when she'd been ambushed by the last two German ships. His last order had been, 'Abandon ship. Every man for himself. And good luck.' He himself had been *out* of luck: dying. They'd lashed him to a stretcher and the gunner towed him ashore, but he was dead by the time he got there.

The merchant navy group came from several different ships, but they'd been taken prisoner when the Germans had arrived at dawn on the 9th, and held in the *North Cornwall*. There were forty-seven of them, including the *North Cornwall*'s skipper, a Captain Evans. They'd had a ringside view of the battle; in fact they'd been *in* the ring, with ships blowing up and sinking all around them. Then the Germans had ordered them ashore – with one lone Hun to guard them, and not a very bright lad at that. When the boat reached the jetty and he was about to climb ashore, he'd asked one of the sailors to hold his rifle for him.

Whacker Harris, hearing this story for the first time, was convulsed with mirth. Recovering, he suggested, 'Might 'a been related to your oppo, Yank. You know – what'sname. Shitface. I mean *Percy*.'

Paul glanced up from the tyre. It was a tough thing to cut, and if ever Brierson's knife had had an edge on it, it had lost it now. He said, 'Baldy wasn't so bad. He'd have been okay when he'd found his feet.'

'Oh, Christ.' Harris frowned, embarrassed. 'I'd forgot the bugger'd 'ad it.'

By rights, Paul thought, *he* should have 'had it' too. It was a pure fluke that he was alive. And his father – he wondered . . . You never *stopped* wondering, really, whatever else you were doing or talking about, the question-mark and the hope and the despondency were there. Extraordinary: such a short while ago, those few days at Mullbergh, good food and bachelor comfort in that creaky old house, big fires and malt whisky, and the two of them sounding each other out, rather cautiously making friends, a little surprised maybe at finding how well they got on; and now in what seemed like a flash here he was in this timber shack with a blanket for a coat and fumbling to make shoes out of some stinking old rubber, and his father was – *might be* a prisoner of war, *might be* dead.

One of the merchant navy people was telling Harris how the Germans had seized Narvik. All over the room men were swapping stories, recounting personal experiences of the last day or so. This one – he was an engineer of sorts – was describing how three Hun destroyers had arrived off the harbour not long after daylight – a little past 5 am. One of the Norwegian coast-defence ships, *Eidsvold*, had been lying in the harbour entrance. She and her sister ship *Norge* were twins born in 1900, antediluvian-looking twin-funnelled gunboats originally classed as 'Coast Defence Battleships'. *Eidsvold* had flashed an order to the German flotilla leader, *Heidkamp*, that he was to stop: and the Hun commodore had stopped his ships. He'd also sent a boat to the Norwegian, demanding to be allowed to pass into the harbour: demanding surrender, it amounted to. If it wasn't forthcoming the boarding officer was to get himself and his boat out of the way quickly and fire a red Very light. The demand had been rejected, the boat retired and the red flare shot skyward: two torpedoes leapt from the *Heidkamp*'s tubes, blew *Eidsvold* into two halves and killed practically all her crew of more than 250 men. Then they'd sunk

169

Norge in a rain of shells followed by two more torpedoes. Only fifty of her company survived. There'd been no warning: Germany and Norway were not at war: the Germans were still claiming to have come as friends and protectors.

Paul said, sawing at his tyre, 'I guess this may be the first war in history where we don't have any damned options. I mean we *have* to fight the bastards.' He glanced up at the engineer. 'You said the garrison commander turned traitor?'

'So they told us. A colonel by the name of Sundlo. One of Quisling's boys.'

Harris sniffed. 'Sod 'im, then.'

'Why not.' The engineer nodded. 'He ordered the garrison not to resist. The Huns have a general in charge ashore now. We saw him. Twerp by the name of Dietl.'

'Sod '*im*, too.' Harris eased himself down with his broad back against the wall. 'What they givin' us for scoff tonight?'

Claus Torp had arranged that the telephone cables would be blown up near the village of Spillum at 0100 on the 12th. But he had bigger and better proposals too. The men who'd do the job on the telephone wires, if Nick would provide them with firearms, were suggesting they should go on from Spillum to the bridge which spanned Spillumsoren, and if there wasn't a German guard on it they'd go across and make a diversionary attack on Namsos from the east. Probably they'd open fire on a checkpoint which the Huns had set up at some crossroads half a mile outside the town. If there was a guard on the bridge they'd attack that instead. Either way the effect should be to draw enemy troops eastward out of Namsos and divert attention from the harbour while *Intent* was making her approach.

'Not a bad idea.' Nick was studying the chart. The bridge over Spillumsoren was half a mile long. 'For 'bridge', read 'causeway', he thought. The village was one mile this side of it and the Namsos road junction half a mile from its other end.

'They'd have to do the cable-cutting a bit earlier, wouldn't they?'

'Half an hour, yes. Or leave one man there, to follow after.'

'How will they get away?'

'In the truck, same way they go there. But they go to the mountains after, not to their homes . . . They all ask one question: when will your British army come?'

'Be nice to know that, wouldn't it?'

'Will you give them some guns?'

It wasn't so simple, when one had to arm three separate landing-parties already. He asked Torp, 'How many men?'

'Five, maybe six.'

They weren't going to pin down many Germans for very long in that strength. But if they acted as snipers, from spaced-out positions: and they'd know the lie of the land, which the Huns hadn't had time to learn yet . . . He nodded. 'Five rifles. I'll make a saving by reducing the two flanking parties by one man each.'

They were in Nick's day cabin. Knut Lange wasn't back yet; he wasn't likely to show up much before dusk. Nick asked Torp, 'How did you leave the arrangements for all this ashore?'

'I arrange that after Knut's boat is coming back to us tomorrow evening, when you are sure what you are doing, I go ashore to them, with the guns or not, as you decide. They will not move to cut the telephones until I am seeing them again first. All right?'

'Yes. Excellent.'

'Are you with us tonight, in the dinner-party?'

'No.' He hadn't had a chance to tell Kari. Not that *that* should matter. It was the real reason why he wasn't accepting Tommy Trench's invitation: it couldn't be *allowed* to matter. He explained to her father, 'Wardroom table's big enough for two extra but not comfortably for more than that. Besides, you're the guests they want. And – '

'It's a pity. Kari—'

'– *and*, I've work to do . . . Now listen, Claus. Assuming the operation tomorrow night goes as we've planned it, don't you agree that if the enemy's still sitting out there and you try to get your ship out, in daylight and at your slow speed, you're certain to be intercepted and captured or sunk?'

Torp shrugged. 'I think this ship also. I think you don't get far away from the quay at Namsos.'

'I can fight, Claus. I have guns and torpedoes. Also, when your man's done his stuff I can move out at thirty knots. It makes a slight difference, you know.'

'I tell you what *I* can do. I can navigate. Through the fjords, the small ones. I have been thinking about this, you see. Instead of going like I was saying before – Rodsundet or Seierstadfjorden – I go through Lokkaren, and across through all the little islands to Svartdalsfjorden and Nordsundet – that will be into Gyltefjorden—'

171

'You've lost me.' Nick went to the table, where he had the chart.

Torp said, 'I lose the Boche too, I think. Now – *here* . . .'

Nick dined alone. Tomorrow night, before the attack, he thought he might invite Torp and Kari here again, a quiet supper for the three of them. But solitude tonight was useful, a chance to think over the plan in peace and quiet. He had to try to envisage how things could go wrong, what emergencies might arise and what he'd do to counter them. There was also a need for forethought on the question of how he'd handle his ship if he had to fight his way past German destroyers in a narrow fjord. It would be like fighting a battle in a river. Boldness would be the key, he thought: just go straight for them, flat out and no hesitation, hit hard and early, and keep moving fast towards the open sea. Success would build on success: if you could clobber one of them, another might stop or turn back to help him, thus bringing down the odds.

Damn old Torp for his obstinacy. *Valkyrien* was a pretty ship but she wasn't worth men's lives.

'All right, Seymour. I shan't need anything else.'

'Aye aye, sir.' The leading steward nodded. 'Goodnight, sir.' But ninety seconds later he was back. 'That fishing-boat's 'ere again, sir. Just coming across the bay.'

'Right. Thank you.'

No reason to move. Trench would have been told, and Torp was with him. The blue boat would berth on *Valkyrien* and Torp would be down here soon to pass on whatever Lange had reported to him. Doomsday stuff, quite possibly. But even if he came to say there was a whole flotilla of Hun destroyers in the fjord, it wouldn't affect the plans. Whatever the situation might be out there now, it would as likely as not have changed by tomorrow morning and changed again by noon; how things looked at this time tomorrow night – *that* would be what counted. At this stage it was a matter of watching trends, trying to see a pattern and understand what the enemy was up to.

CHAPTER 10

'Our friend the Knut's adrift, sir.'

Trench said it – somewhat unnecessarily. Nick grunted, and checked the time on his wrist-watch, as if Lange's lateness hadn't occurred to him until now, as if his nerves weren't already racked up tight because of it.

Pacing the quarterdeck. Trench pacing beside him because, tired of his own thoughts which had begun to go in circles, he'd invited his second-in-command to join him.

Five minutes to ten. In one hour he ought to be pulling the hook out of the mud, getting set to move out for the raid on Namsos. And before he could do that, Torp had to be sent ashore to see his wire-cutting friends and then get back aboard again: and depending on what news Lange brought with him when he did come, there might be a need to reshape plans. He was cutting it much too fine for comfort.

Last night, the news had been that in Altfjord was one U-boat and that in Rodsundet were two destroyers. Musical chairs, he'd thought, with a submarine now gate-crashing the party. But there had to be a purpose, a reason: and since then a little of it had begun to show, but last night he'd said to Torp, who'd come down to the cabin with Lange's report, 'Let's wait and see what we have out there in the morning, Claus. Who knows – *Scharnhorst* and *Gneisenau* perhaps.' He'd teased him: 'They know you've got your *Valkyrien* here and they're waiting until they've assembled a force powerful enough to take you on.'

'You are so funny you make me want to pump-ship.'

'Your wardroom dinner-party will have given you *that* urge. Use my bathroom if you like.'

He stole another sight of his watch. 2158. The three minutes had crawled like ten. If Lange didn't come, he told himself, he'd let

173

Torp go ashore at 2230 and he'd weigh at 2300. He couldn't afford to waste any of the short period of darkness; he'd have to assume that the enemy were deployed as they had been at noon – which meant one U-boat and one destroyer alongside each other in Altbotn and one destroyer left at anchor in Rodsundet. Between first light and midday one of the two destroyers who'd spent the night in Rodsundet had gone round into Namsefjord and then nosed slowly into Altbotn, the inner fjord, and anchored off its western shore; the U-boat had then moved in too, and berthed alongside her. Guesswork suggested that the U-boat was getting assistance of some kind from the destroyer. Or vice versa: but this was less likely, in view of Mohammed having gone to the mountain and not the other way about. But from Nick's point of view the improvement was considerable. The pair holding each other up in Altbotn probably wouldn't be able to get under way very quickly: one of them must have something wrong with her, and the destroyer might not have steam up now. Also, if no alarm or loud noises were made, it should be possible to sneak past them undetected, as they were blind in there to what was happening in Namsenfjord. In fact, having them bottled up in there, one might do them some damage *en passant*. Nip in: a couple of torpedoes: nip out again. During the afternoon he'd been giving it some thought. But Rodsundet too: with only one enemy destroyer there he reckoned his chances of fighting his way out would be better than evens. He knew the German was there, and the German wouldn't know anything until *Intent* hit him. Depending, of course, on how much fuss was kicked up at Namsos before that.

That had been the lunchtime picture. How it might look now was another question. Where the *hell* was Lange?

Three minutes past ten.

He glanced upwards. Cloud cover was still complete. If anything it was thicker than it had been yesterday. So there'd be no bother with a moon. Twenty-five knots would be a maximum speed down-fjord, after the attack, because at full speed the funnel-glow could give them away.

'Rifles and ammo are in *Valkyrien*'s skiff, sir.'

That, from Tommy Trench, was a display of nerves. They both knew the skiff was alongside and that Nick had given orders half an hour ago for the weapons to be put in it, to save time when Lange did turn up. He didn't answer Trench. That skiff would be hoisted on *Intent*'s starboard davits, after Torp had run his errand

174

and *Valkyrien* had cast off. The other was already hoisted on the portside davits. On both sides Metcalf's upperdeckmen had riven new falls, fitted new gripes and boat-ropes, cleaned, greased and tested the fire-blackened disengaging gear. Petty Officer Metcalf had worked like ten ordinary men since they'd been in here. Thinking of it, Nick told Trench, 'When we're out of here and the dust has settled, I believe we should think about Metcalf going through for chief. Might have a look at his Service Certificate.'

'Absolutely, sir.'

When we're out of here . . .

Lange might have run into trouble. Into a Hun destroyer, for instance.

If he didn't come, Nick thought, he'd use Namsenfjord. There'd been three destroyers altogether in Lange's first report, and the whereabouts of the third was currently unknown. If it returned he thought it would more likely join the one in Rodsundet. The one on the other side was there for the U-boat's benefit and there'd be no point in another joining them. Namsenfjord: and if there hadn't been much of a shindy made, stern-first into Altbotn for a crack at those buggers and then away, *fast*, before the Rodsundet ones woke up.

He liked that. It had a certain neatness.

'I hear your guest-night was a success, Tommy.'

'Guest-night . . .' Trench swallowed surprise. One was hardly expecting to chat about dinner-parties. He nodded. 'I believe it was, sir. We were all sorry you weren't able to—'

'Fishing-boat approaching, sir!'

'—able to be with us.'

'I had a lot of stuff to see to.' No point in dashing about yet. The blue boat would take a little while to cross the bay. However . . . 'Number One, let's have the cable party closed up, and tell Lyte to shorten-in to one and a half shackles. Special Sea Dutymen in half an hour.'

'Aye aye, sir. Bosun's mate!'

Intent's engines were in full working order now, according to Torp's translation of Halvard Boyensen's report. Beamish, questioned by Nick, had agreed with it. They'd run a basin-trial this afternoon, at the Norwegian engineer's request; Nick had consented in return for the man's positive assurance that there'd be too little smoke for a German ten miles away to see. In fact, as he'd expected, the wind had backed to north-west and it blew such

175

smoke as there was directly inshore. And the engines had functioned perfectly. Also, by that time the new fore-topmast had been stepped and rigged. An interesting evolution, which had taken the whole forenoon. A mast-rope was led from an eyebolt on the foremast top, through the sheave in the heel of the topmast, back up again through a block on the other side of the fore-top. Thence it was taken to the capstan on the foc'sl, the slant of it just clearing the forefront of the bridge and the flare of 'B' gundeck. At Trench's order 'Sway away!' and with a couple of dozen seamen all around with hemp guys to steady it, the topmast had risen vertically like some variety of the Indian rope trick. After that, things became more complicated: the yards had to be slung up and secured, and the rigging – stays, backstays and shrouds – of two-inch steel-wire rope, set up. Finally there'd been only the lighter work to do, like halyards and wireless gear. It looked like any other topmast now; but such a very short time ago it had been a tree, snow-covered on a Norwegian hillside.

Nick was thinking as he crossed the plank to *Valkyrien* that his feeling of relief at Lange's arrival might have been a trifle premature. There was no knowing what the Norwegian was about to tell them. It might be bloody awful. And even if the fjords were empty, there was still a tricky operation ahead of him at Namsos.

Torp came out of his deckhouse chewing, wiping his mouth on the back of his hand. The same hand went to push his beat-up cap back to a more comfortable angle. He nodded to Nick, still chewing. 'About times, he's coming, eh?' Kari came out behind him, and went aft without acknowledging Nick's presence. She'd been reserved in her manner with him all day, and he'd decided against issuing any supper invitations. She was cross with him for not having joined them in the wardroom last night, he supposed: which was silly, and also proof that he'd been wise in not going along.

Sooner or later, he thought, one annoyed them all, one way or another. He hadn't annoyed Fiona yet, though. Perhaps by not giving a damn she was annoyance-proof?

The blue boat was curving round, angling to run in alongside. A Norwegian – the young one, Einar – was hauling the skiff farther for'ard to make room for Lange. Kari appeared suddenly at Nick's side: 'We have coffee still hot if you would like some.'

'No thank you, Kari. Kind thought, though.' Peace-offering? When she smiled she was really breathtaking. And she was calmly prepared to sail this ancient heap six hundred miles, with two old men and a boy for crew . . . He had a quick, imaginative vision of Fiona faced with any such suggestion, her huge eyes widening as she uttered a characteristic squawk: 'My dear sweet man, you must be stark, staring bonkers!' Smiling at the mental picture – Kari meeting the smile and taking it as meant for her, smiling back: an unexpected dividend . . . Lange's screws were going astern to take the way off his boat: stopped now, the stream of turbulence between the two wooden hulls quietening as crewmen fore and aft tossed lines to Norwegians on *Valkyrien*.

Lange hauled himself out of the doorway in the side of his wheelhouse, and began to yell at Torp. After a dozen words, Kari turned, glanced back at Nick. He thought she looked startled.

'What's he saying?'

She shook her head: still listening. The singsong recitation might have been going on for ever. Then it ended: Torp had swung round, seen Nick, and he was coming over to him.

'You like good news first, or bad?'

'All of it, and for God's sake let's not waste time.'

'Okay. In Altbotn is still one U-boat, one destroyer. The U-boat has a big hatch open and the destroyer is lifting battery cells out with its torpedo davit. Maybe smashed battery – bad trouble for a submarine, huh?'

It would make sense. They'd need a surface like a pond's, and that was what they'd found.

'Other side, by Saltkjelvika, is now *two* destroyers.'

Two where there had been one, and all three accounted for now. He'd guessed right. And his way out would be via Namsenfjord. With a brief call perhaps at Altbotn.

Torp was grinning at him. 'Now some *good* news. In Rodsundet is not *only* the two destroyers. The one that came brought with it an oil tanker and this has anchored too. Big ship – maybe fifteen, sixteen thousand ton.'

Kari interrupted: 'But with *two* destroyers—'

'Wait.' Nick put up a hand to silence her. If there'd been *ten* destroyers that oiler would still have attracted him. But two was acceptable. *And no need to raid Namsos.* If he took them by surprise: which, coming from inside the fjords, ought surely to be possible . . .

His mind had a picture of that side of it. A snapshot: he'd need to study it closely to extract detail but it was there, complete. The

177

other side – Altbotn – that destroyer would have to be dealt with too. Oiling would take an hour, *after* the tanker was captured, and there'd have been some bangs by that time. Altbotn was less than two miles from the Saltkjelvika anchorage, over that neck of land, and the destroyer would have time to get out and meet *Intent* and the tanker outside, or even to get right round and catch them still alongside, oiling. The U-boat was probably no danger, but the destroyer was.

It could be done. He'd been on his mental toes, keyed up, and everything was whirring and meshing now. It would have to: in the next forty-five minutes there was a hell of a lot of ground to cover.

'Number One – have the rifles taken out of that skiff. Claus, go ashore, please, cancel previous arrangements and get back here as soon as possible.'

'Very well.'

'Then bring Lange down to my cabin with you. Listen – ' he'd stopped the Norwegian as he moved towards the skiff – 'I'm going to need your ship and his boat and all your crews, we move out of here at 2300, and you and your people will accept the dispositions I'm about to make. Right?'

'We going to take the tanker?'

'Yes. But we have to eliminate the ships in Altbotn too, so we've got to be in three places at once.'

Torp threw a glance at Kari, then looked back at Nick. 'Okay. Any way you say.' As he climbed over and down to the skiff he called something out to Lange, and the fisherman laughed, glancing round and up at Nick. Nick asked him, 'Okay?' and Lange laughed again, raised a thumb: 'Hokay!' He had already, when he'd been back here at midday, told Torp that his boat and crew were at Nick's disposal for as long as *Intent* was in the fjords. He didn't want to leave Norway but he'd help out now and he'd join in again when any other British force arrived, he'd said. Kari and he were yelling at each other now, and the other Norwegians were gathering round to listen, while Einar climbed down to join Torp in the skiff.

Nick went over the brow. Ideas developing. *Intent*'s ship's company were grouped around in fair numbers, ears flapping for the buzz.

'Mr Opie here?'

'Here, sir.' The gunner came from aft; he had a Torpedo Log and Progress Book under his arm. Opie had rather the shape of a praying mantis: skinny, stooped. Eyes so sharp and small that they were like skewers stabbing at you.

'Mr Opie, I want two depthcharges provided, with wire slings so they can be slung over the stern either of *Valkyrien* or the fishing-boat. I'll let you know in a minute which one. Also, I want two volunteer torpedomen – one of 'em had better be a killick   to go along with them.'

Opie said, '*I'll* take charge of that party, sir.'

'No, I want you with us. The pair who do go will have to sprint a distance of roughly a mile and a half, possibly being shot at. They're to be warned it'll be a fairly chancy operation. Bloody dangerous, in fact. And I want to see them before we shove off.'

Opie nodded, pulling at his nose. It didn't need any stretching. He must have known he wasn't a man to sprint a hundred yards, let alone three thousand. He said, 'We'll start getting the gear up, sir.'

Nick looked round at Trench. 'Tommy – you, Chandler and Brocklehurst – in my cabin, *now*. Chandler's to bring the chart of the fjords with him.'

He didn't need the chart to work out the next bit, though. He'd checked over the various distances so often that he had them in his head. From here to Altbotn: just under ten miles. From here to the anchorage at Saltkjelvika: about seventeen. Lange's boat would be the most suitable for Altbotn. So *Valkyrien* should come the other way with *Intent*. Sailing at 11 pm, 2300, and making good five knots – her top speed was six, but it was a rising tide and therefore an inflowing stream – three and a half hours in transit meant that the earliest time for zero hour would be 0230. Then an hour and a half for the fracas and the oiling would make it 0400. Dawn, near enough, no darkness left for the withdrawal. *No bloody use!*

Valkyrien would have to do the job in Altbotn. She wasn't as good for it as the fishing-boat would have been, and Torp, who would obviously insist on participating in that expedition, hadn't the youth or athleticism it was going to call for. But – no option . . .

He was in the doorway of his cabin, having thought this out on the way down. Seymour was emerging from the pantry. Nick told him, 'Shin up top, would you, ask Mr Opie to spare me a moment.' Seymour and Pete Chandler collided as the navigator came plunging off the ladder into the flat carrying the chart and instruments. Brocklehurst was with him and, dwarfing the GCO from the rear, Tommy Trench, herding them along. Trench said, 'I've left Lyte on

179

the bridge, sir. Had to leave the foc'sl to Cox. But he's got PO Granger to keep him on the straight and narrow.'

They'd still be shortening-in the cable. And they could shorten it a bit more, now. Mr Opie followed his nose into the cabin, rapping on the door-jamb as he entered. 'Sir?'

'Your charges are to be slung over *Valkyrien*'s counter. With that cut-away stern you'll find it easy enough. You can use our starboard thrower davit to get them over. Haul *Valkyrien* for'ard a few yards if you need to. Wire slings, Mr Opie, a separate sling for each charge, and a slip on each of them which your torpedomen can knock off quickly and easily. They may be doing it under fire so it must be simple and if possible under cover. Leave the charges set to safe until just before she sails – you can arm them either by hanging over the side or from the skiff. I want shallow settings on the pistols . . . Is that all clear?'

Opie nodded. 'Volunteers are Leading Torpedoman Crouch and Torpedoman Surtees, sir.'

'Can they both run?'

'Like bloody riggers, sir. That's why I picked 'em.'

'*Picked* them?'

'The whole lot volunteered, sir.'

It didn't surprise him. If you told matelots an operation was going to be dangerous they all rushed for it. Before the Zeebrugge raid the recruiters had had practically to beat men off with sticks. He told Opie, 'They're to be issued with Tommy guns. Three drums of ammo per gun. Tell the GM, and that he's to see both men know how to use the things. You've got half an hour to be ready, Mr Opie, so you'd better slap it about a bit.'

He turned back into the cabin. Chandler had the chart spread out. Eighteen minutes past ten. He'd been right about those distances, and there was no option as to which of his ragbag squadron did which job. Torp wasn't going to like *Valkyrien* being treated as expendable. He'd have a counter-proposal: Nick could foresee it and he was ready to rule it out. He dropped the dividers on the chart, and told his officers, 'Two separate forces. One is *Valkyrien*, the other *Intent* with the fishing-boat. *Valkyrien* as you heard is being equipped with depthcharges slung under her counter and set shallow; she'll drop them under the destroyer and the U-boat who are alongside each other in Altbotn. Here. Torp will no doubt insist on commanding her. He'll need one engine-room hand and one other crewman, Norwegians, and we are providing two torpedomen for the charges. *Valkyrien* should slip and proceed at 2255. That is, in thirty-six minutes' time. At five knots she can easily reach Altbotn and her target by 0100, which is zero hour. You can check exact timings in a minute, pilot. Now – Tommy. The fishing-boat – for short let's call it "blueboat" – is to be fitted with our own blue stern cluster. Send an LTO over to wire it up. Blueboat will be crewed by Lange and as many of his own men as he needs, and you, Tommy, will go in her to lead the boarding party and perhaps thereafter command the oiler. We shan't just oil from her, you understand, we'll take her with us. Command of her depends on Torp: I'll offer him the job, otherwise it's yours.'

If Torp got there, after the Altbotn operation, he'd obviously accept that offer. He'd be the best man for it, it would be a good use of his Norwegians, Nick would get his first lieutenant back, and everyone would be happy. The doubt was whether Torp would get there, after his action on the other side.

Nick told Trench, 'Pick twelve men for your boarding party. I'll take at least some of them back from you when we're alongside the oiler later on. As well as the twelve you pick you can have all the surplus Norwegians – around ten of them, probably. Then if Torp assumes command of the oiler he'll have his own chaps as crew. But add a leading stoker to your party, to be ready to work with Beamish when we get alongside. Rifles, bayonets, revolvers – and there's one Tommy gun left – help yourself. You'll need a signalman and he'd better take an Aldis and a pair of semaphore flags with him. And I suppose one telegraphist . . . And they'll stay aboard. But look here, we'll be fighting an action, so for God's sake pick your men in a way that won't cripple us in any one department. It's up to you, because we won't have time to consult on it. Take young Cox with you?'

Trench nodded. 'Good idea, sir.'

'Lyte can do your jobs – all from the bridge. Torpedo control is going to be important. Is he competent?'

'He is, sir. But I'll have a word with him.'

Lyte was Trench's action understudy anyway, so he ought to know the job. If things went as they should they'd have sitting targets anyway. Nick went on, pointing out the route on the chart with the tips of the dividers, 'We sail at 2300 and follow blueboat at ten knots through Sundsråsa, over to Lokkaren and up through it, then round this corner into Surviksund and through into Lauvoyfjord. I think you'll find, pilot, that about here – ' his pointer stopped on Lauvoy Island, just inside that much wider fjord – 'we can reduce by a knot or two, provided we're on schedule. I want to get over to this western coast then and hug it right into the anchorage. In case anyone didn't get the buzz, by the way, the anchorage currently holds two Hun destroyers and one tanker of roughly 15,000 tons.'

Henry Brocklehurst raised his eyebrows. 'Ah-*hah*.'

'Sorry. As we're a bit rushed I may be missing other points here or there. Stop me if anyone sees any gaps . . . As I said, pilot, you can work out precise speeds on the various stages, and when Torp's back we'll go over it all with him and Lange. No point bothering Lange on his own, because he doesn't understand English. But his chaps know just how and where the oiler and the destroyers are lying, and we'll get that out of them. What's essential is that everything should happen simultaneously, at 0100: *Valkyrien*'s charges explode here in Altbotn, blueboat puts you and your party into the oiler, Tommy, and I hit the destroyers with torpedoes. Approaches will be dead quiet, slow and not a chink of light. As soon as I've fixed the destroyers I'll berth on the oiler – which will be yours, let's hope, by that time. If not, we'll board and give you some help.'

'Fair enough, sir.' Trench nodded. 'What about Hun prisoners? Lock 'em up?'

Nick rubbed his jaw. 'Ship that size could have a crew of – Lord, forty or fifty. Take a lot of guarding, and we're short-handed enough already.' He shook his head. 'I don't think we can bother with prisoners.'

They were all looking at him. Wondering whether that was all the guidance they were going to get. He pointed at the anchorage, the coast near Saltkjelvika.

'Not a very long swim. Couple of hundred yards, in sheltered water?'

'Ah.' Trench nodded. 'If any of 'em say they *can't* swim, I'll put 'em in the forepeak or some hold that's easy to guard.'

'I'm sure there won't be time to give lessons.' Brocklehurst's contribution raised a laugh. Nick said, 'Final point: having put our boarders into the oiler, blueboat will go inshore – about here, but Lange and Torp can fix the spot – to wait for and then embark the party from *Valkyrien*. They'll have beached her somewhere about here – ' the south-eastern shore of Altbotn, he was indicating – 'and then legged it overland to the beach where blueboat will be waiting.'

Contours on the chart showed high ground to the north and the south of that overland route. It was a valley of sorts and a road ran through it, so presumably it wouldn't be too much of a problem for young, fit men.

He saw Trench glance up: turning, he found Torp in the cabin's doorway. Age fifty-one, and carrying a little weight. Not too clearly one of the 'young and fit' brigade. But if he insisted on staying with his ship – which he would . . .

'All right ashore, Commander?'

'They are disappointed. Here is Knut Lange.'

'Come in.' Nick looked at Trench. 'Better get cracking. Pick your men and arm them, that's the first thing.' He told Brocklehurst, 'You can help him. Get an LTO over to blueboat with the cluster, to start with. And fill Lyte in on what I've been telling you. As far as gunnery's concerned, I can't spell out what'll happen at zero hour, except that I want to hit with torpedoes first. Just have everything on the top line, right?' The GCO nodded. Nick added, 'You can organise your department when we're under way. All right, off you go . . .'

Chandler was bent over the chart, working out speeds and courses. He asked Nick, 'We'll have blueboat to follow but we'll have no pilot actually on board, sir?'

'Well.' Nick beckoned the Norwegians to come closer to the chart. 'We'll have Commander Torp's daughter with us. I gather she knows these fjords as well as he does.'

Ten twenty-eight.

Ten thirty-one . . .

Kari had joined them in the day cabin. Torp asked Nick, 'Why my *Valkyrien*? Why not his boat?'

Nick explained: because *Valkyrien* couldn't make the distance to Rodsundet and leave them enough hours of darkness to get away before the Stukas came. He'd have preferred it the other way round; the faster, smaller craft would have been more suitable for the dash across Altbotn, and *Valkyrien*'s height in the water would have suited the boarding operation better. If the oiler didn't have a gangway or a ladder over her side it might present a problem – an iron wall towering above the boat and no way to scale it. In that event they'd have to wait until *Intent* came alongside. This wasn't a good solution, though, because the tanker's crew would have seen the attack on the destroyers and they'd be ready to repel boarders. One wanted them, if possible, to be sound asleep in their bunks.

Kari was acting as interpreter. Lange mumbled at her, snatched up a signal pad and took Chandler's pencil out of his hand, began to make a sketch. It turned out that he was saying the tanker was a modern ship and very low in comparison to her length. She had a high bridge section amidships and more superstructure aft where the funnel was, but between those two areas of superstructure she had an exceptionally low freeboard. Men could board from the top of the fishing-boat's wheelhouse, and Lange would take some planks to put across.

'Sounds as if he's seen her himself.'

'He has. This last trip he went to look, to make certain. It's why he was late returning.'

'Well, please tell him I'm very grateful to him.' Nick looked at Torp's less-than-happy face. 'You dislike the idea of sacrificing your ship. I understand that. I'm very sorry there's no other way of doing it.'

'But maybe there is. I make the attack, I turn round and come out again, we have – one hour, one and a half? Easy – I meet you here, near Flottra?'

It was the suggestion he'd expected. He shook his head. 'No, Claus. *If* you got away with it, I'd have to find you out there—'

'You don't have to. I go on – right on!'

'But I want my torpedomen back, you see. For one thing because I need them, for another I don't believe you'd get ten miles before you were strafed by German 'planes. You haven't the speed to get away: and we have.' He suggested, 'You don't *have* to go along in *Valkyrien*, Claus. One of your younger men could do it – or I could provide an officer – Pete Chandler here, for instance—'

'*Valkyrien* is *my* ship, damn it all to hell!'

'It'll be hard going, once you're ashore. Frankly, I'd say it was a job for youngsters, but—'

'One and a quarter sea miles. A little more than two kilometres. I am not yet *falling to bits*, you know!' He was red in the face and glaring. 'Okay – how long does it take you to stop, take your men off from me outside?'

'You might not get that far, you see. Once you've dropped those charges, they'll be shooting at you. With only a few hundred yards to go to beach her, you should get away with it, but if you had to go two-thirds of the length of the fjord – and the way they'd *expect* you to be going . . .' He shook his head. 'If you got into trouble and I had to come on round and find you, I'd be throwing my own ship away. I'm not prepared to do that. Whereas when you come overland, we're all in one spot together, ready to start off and not stop – *out*, and in darkness.'

Torp was silent. Simmering down, seeing the common sense of it. He looked at his daughter, and shrugged. 'Man's right.' She nodded: but Nick could see she wasn't happy about the job her father was taking on. Nick asked him, 'What'll you do – put her on the rocks with her seacocks open?'

Torp suggested, 'Perhaps also some of those explosives?'

Fitted charges, with long-enough lengths of fuse to give the five men time to get clear. Half a dozen of them in that old ship's bilges would just about take the bottom out of her. Nick agreed: and his torpedomen could handle that end of it. What he wanted now from Lange was a sketch of the anchorage on the other side, showing exactly where the oiler was anchored and where the destroyers were.

And after that –

Well. One thing at a time . . . But hardly: he was having to think of about *forty* things at a time. He'd had two days to work out the details of the Namsos operation, and he was setting this one up in fifty minutes.

Three minutes past eleven. Eight minutes late, *Valkyrien* was letting go the ropes which had held her to *Intent*. Knut Lange had cast off from *Valkyrien* at five minutes to the hour and dropped astern so that a torpedoman on his boat's bow could set the pistols on the depthcharges which now hung in their wire-rope slings. Then Lange had brought his boat up on *Intent*'s port side, and Trench's boarding party were climbing down a scrambling-net into it. The Norwegians – nine of them – were already in the boat.

Trench wasn't with them yet. He'd be coming up here to report, before they pushed off. Nick went over to the starboard side of the bridge, looked down at the gap of water which had already opened between his ship and *Valkyrien*. Claus Torp was beside the open door of his wheelhouse, chatting to the man inside – a man of about twenty-five, by the name of Larsen. ('Fast runner,' Torp had explained. 'Strong, too. Carry me and run like hell, I think.') He wasn't only talking to Larsen though, he had Kari facing him from

Intent's foc's1 deck, right below the place where Nick was leaning over. She was unhappy, worried for him, and he was keeping up the jokes, teasing her.

She had some reason to be worried, Nick thought. You could hardly expect to pull off a stunt like this one without *some* casualties. And Torp was the most likely candidate. It wasn't only the most odds-against bit of the operation, it was also going to be something of a marathon.

Could he have held him back from it? Stopped him going in his own ship? Nick didn't see how. He was a highly independent character, not a man to betray his principles.

Torp was staring up at him. Nick shouted across the gap, 'Good luck!'

'Look after this woman for me, huh?' Pointing at Kari. Nick looked down, and at the same moment she glanced up: he saw her stiff, unhappy smile. He called to Torp, 'We'll keep her safe for you.' Rather a daft assurance, he realised: the only way to have ensured her safety would have been to have landed her at Sveodden, *now*. Torp had just passed an order over his shoulder to his man Larsen; *Valkyrien*'s single screw was going astern, sliding her away from the destroyer's side and sending a stream of churned, bubbling water seething forward. But she was clear now, and Torp had stopped the engine. *Valkyrien* still slid astern, with port rudder on to turn her bow out.

Torp's and Kari's gear was in Nick's sleeping cabin aft. It was hers now, and she could use the day-cabin and his bathroom too. At sea he only used the little box just below the bridge.

'Captain, sir?'

Tommy Trench, in his tin hat with '1st Lt' painted on the front of it, and a webbing belt with a .45 revolver in the holster.

'Boarding party embarked and ready to proceed, sir.'

'Well done. You've worked wonders. I mean that.'

Trench grinned down at him. 'Needs must, when the devil drives, sir.'

'*What?*'

'Intended, if I may say so, as a compliment. May I tell Lange to carry on, sir?'

'Let *Valkyrien* get well clear first. I'll give you a shout. Best of luck, Tommy.'

'Sir.' Chandler, coming from the chart-table, interrupted. 'Sorry . . . But we must make twelve knots now, sir, to be up to the schedule. Reducing to eight when Lauvoy light's abeam *if* we're up to it.'

'All right. Tommy, see Lange gets that and understands it, will you? Tell you what – ask Kari to translate. She's just down here.'

'Twelve knots, reducing to eight at Lauvoy light if we're on time. Aye aye, sir.' Trench saluted. 'See you alongside *my* oiler, sir.' As he moved off, Chief Stoker Beamish clambered into the bridge. He saluted too. 'Main engines ready, sir.'

'Chief, that's music to the ears.'

'Reckon it is that, sir.'

'Everything on a split yarn for the oiling?'

'Will be by 0100, sir. Leading Stoker Evans 'as gone with the boat party.'

'Boyensen quite happy down there?'

Beamish thought he was. Boyensen would move over to become chief engineer of the oiler, in a couple of hours' time. Meanwhile he was on loan from Torp, to hold Beamish's hand in case anything went wrong or needed adjustment.

Nick told Chandler, 'Ring on main engines.' He crossed to the starboard side again as *Valkyrien*, her engine chugging ahead and black coal-smoke leaking from that tall funnel, came sliding past at a distance of about thirty feet. Torp saluted breezily, and Nick returned it. He called to Randolph Lyte, 'Weigh anchor.' The two torpedomen were standing at attention on *Valkyrien*'s stern; Nick took off his cap and waved it at them, and one hand came up in answer. The light was fading rapidly – outlines blurring, hills merging into the background of low cloud. The two depthcharges slung under the old ship's counter looked like dangling testicles.

He'd shown the torpedomen, Crouch and Surtees, photographs in *Jane's Fighting Ships* of modern German destroyers, pointing out the position of searchlights above and abaft their bridges, fixed to the lower part of the foremast at roughly funnel-top height. The searchlight on the Altbotn destroyer would be an obvious menace to the *Valkyrien* party, and if those two could shoot it out with their Thompsons they'd about double their chances of getting away. Men at guns were also worth shooting at, as was anyone on the bridge, and the time to hit them, he'd suggested, would be immediately after the charges had been released, when they were still at close quarters. But the searchlight should be target number one.

Weighing wouldn't take long now. They'd shortened-in to one

shackle a few minutes ago. So there were twelve and a half fathoms of cable out, and as there were ten fathoms of water here it left very little slack to be gathered in.

Clanking of the rising cable. Power on the capstan – full, main generator power. *Intent* was reborn . . .

And *Valkyrien* was crossing her bow, turning to port to head for the gap into the channel which would take them through into Namsenfjord. Torp was up on his wheelhouse roof, already an indistinct figure in the fading light. Nick wondered if he'd thanked Torp enough, for all he'd done for him. Without Torp, *Intent* would still have been out in that open anchorage – Lovik – when the German destroyers had arrived. Helpless, easy meat . . . There hadn't been time for goodbyes and none for thanks either. There *should* have been. The omission niggled in his mind, tinged with the fear that there might not be an opportunity to make it good. Lyte reported, 'Cable's up and down, sir.'

'Very good.' He leant over the port side of the bridge, looking down at the blue boat. Lange was lounging on the canopy of its wheelhouse, and Trench was perched on it near him. Cox, near the stern, had his tin hat slung on his shoulder. Nick called down, 'Cast off and carry on, please. Best of luck, all of you.' Trench said something to Lange, who gave Nick something between a wave and an offensive gesture; the gleam of his teeth showed up as he smiled. They weren't all that white: just big . . . Some sailors on *Intent*'s iron deck, letting go the blue boat's ropes on Trench's orders, raised a cheer; Trench called up to Nick, 'Knock 'em for six, sir!' A faint blue radiance near the boat's stern showed that the stern cluster had already been switched on. The boat with its low silhouette wouldn't have been easy to follow without it, on a night as dark as this one was going to be.

'Anchor's aweigh, sir.'

'Very good.' He stepped up behind the binnacle and Chandler moved over to make room for him. Checking the ship's head on the gyro repeater. No hurry, though; he'd wait for the report of 'Clear anchor' and by that time the blue boat would have put about the right distance between them. Glancing round, he saw Kari: she was pressed against the port side of the bridge at its after end, near the ten-inch light, and gazing northwards towards a smallish blur and a patch of whitened sea that was all one could see now of *Valkyrien*.

'Kari?'

She was wearing her bright-blue oilskin coat. She came towards him: dark, almost black hair, pale blue eyes with fear in them. He told her, 'Don't worry. Your father's a tough cookie. You'll be entertained with a lot of tall stories from him in about two and a half hours' time.'

She smiled, and nodded. 'Thank you.'

He remembered that she'd offered him a similar reassurance, about Paul. Since then neither of them had mentioned the subject. The anxiety was in his mind but he was keeping it pushed well back, out of the way, where he didn't have to listen to it. He was tempted to tell her that he'd instructed Crouch and Surtees to keep an eye on her father and give him a hand if he needed it. Not to the extent of throwing sound lives after a lost one, but – within reason . . . Lange's boat was forging out on *Intent*'s bow. Moving slowly, waiting for the destroyer to show signs of following. The swirl of the boat's wake showed up clearly, blued by the lights above it. Getting darker every second: by the time they were through Sundsråsa it would be black. Nice timing, in fact. He heard a shout down on the foc's'l, then Lyte's quiet 'Clear anchor, sir.'

'Port ten.'

'Port ten, sir . . . Ten of port wheel on, sir.'

'Slow ahead together.'

'Slow ahead together, sir!'

He felt the vibrations, muted at this slow speed, and the turbines' whisper and the soft, slow-speed sucking of the intakes. Then his ship was gathering way.

'Half ahead together. One-two-oh revolutions.' Lange would see *Intent*'s bow-wave rise, and put on speed to match.

Eleven-eighteen.

'He's – slicing it a bit short, sir?'

Conning his ship round, following the blue glow, Nick didn't answer Chandler. Lange was certainly cutting corners. They'd passed through Sundsråsa and held that same course for about a mile across the comparatively open water of Namsenfjord, and now the blue boat was leading round to starboard within a schoolboy-cricketer's throw of the island of Ytre Gasoy. Meaning *outer* Gasoy, Kari had explained. Whitewashed rocks looked bright to starboard: he was bringing her round carefully, using only five degrees of wheel. There was not much wind, only a lapping on the black water, enough to take the shine off it. Knowing there were rocks off the north coast of the little island,

189

he shared Chandler's anxiety. All you could see was the broken water, but that was enough to make the hairs stand up on the back of a sailor's neck – if not on a Norwegian fisherman's.

'Don't worry.' Kari's voice on his right. 'Knut could be doing this with his eyes shut.'

'I do hope he isn't.' It occurred to him that he and Kari spent a lot of time telling each other not to worry. He bent to the voicepipe: 'Midships.'

'Midships, sir.'

'Meet her.' Keeping her on the outer edge of the blue boat's curving wake. 'Steer oh-eight-oh.' He asked Chandler, 'What's our course to pass the next headland, the one to port now?'

'One-oh-five, sir.'

Kari said, 'He won't cut *that* corner. There is a rock a quarter-mile from the point.'

'How very reassuring.' Nick told the helmsman, 'Starboard five.' Lange was edging round again. He'd probably go right round to that one-oh-five, or something near it. 'How long is the next leg, pilot?'

'Mile and a half, sir.' Chandler added drily, 'Depending on whether he's corner-cutting or rock-climbing.' Kari giggled, and Nick was glad to hear it. He said into the voicepipe, 'Midships.' Breeze on the port quarter and astern now, bringing occasional stink of funnel-fumes. Black, quiet water, darkness enshrouding like black flannel. Damp, iced black flannel. 'Meet her.'

'Meet her, sir—'

'Steady!'

'Steady, sir. One-oh-four—'

'Steer that.'

'Steer one-oh-four, sir.'

'Meet her' meant putting the wheel the opposite way, to check a swing already imparted to the ship. As the rate of swing slowed you had either to give the helmsman a course to steer, or order 'Steady' to inform him that she was at that moment on the course you wanted. A mile and a half at twelve knots would take seven and a half minutes: then there'd be the turn to port into the narrow cleft called Lokkaren, and at the point of entry to it *Intent* and her guide would be less than two miles from German-occupied Namsos.

'Time?'

'Twenty-three fifty, sir.'

If it hadn't been for the news which Lange had brought two

hours ago, instead of turning into Lokkaren now they'd have been steering farther south and rounding the next headland, Merrane-set, to raid Namsos for its oil. Nick wondered whether that might have turned out to be more tricky or less so than the jaunt he was on now. One would never know: it would be something to speculate on in one's old age. If one *had* an old age. All he did know was that the Namsos operation followed immediately by an engagement with superior forces who'd have been actually waiting for him would have been a bit over the odds. He'd have attempted it, because there'd seemed to be no alternative; but now he didn't have to do it he could admit to himself that it had never been a very attractive proposition.

'Steer one-oh-six.'

'One-oh-six, sir.'

He saw Lyte move from the starboard to the port fore corner of the bridge. Trench had found time – heaven knew how – to run over the torpedo-control system with him, and he'd assured Nick that the sub-lieutenant was 'all about' on it. Lyte wouldn't have to cope with the telephone to the director tower: Nick had had a longer lead put on it, so it could be brought here to the binnacle. He could either talk to Brocklehurst himself, or put Chandler on it.

Cold: shivery, bone-penetrating cold, even through a duffel-coat . . . The whitish smear of wake and the blue glow were dead ahead still; he spoke without taking his eyes off it. 'How long to the turn, pilot?'

'About one minute, sir.'

'Bosun's mate?'

'Yessir?'

'Go round the ship, Marryott, make sure there's not a speck of light showing anywhere. Including cigarettes on the gundecks. Take as long as you like, but make certain of it.'

The ship's company had been sent to action stations as soon as the foc's'l had been secured, which had been done by the time they'd been halfway down Sundsråsa. Everything was closed up and ready: they could be meeting Hun destroyers in this fjord – here, *now*. Nothing guaranteed that the Germans would remain where they'd last been seen.

Kari said, 'You can see the rock on your port bow.'

Chandler put his glasses on it. Nick kept his eyes on the blue cluster: it was a circular arrangement of blue light-bulbs fixed in a sort of shallow box so that it could only be seen from right astern.

Lange might alter course at any moment, and he didn't want to overshoot. There was no room or time for errors and corrections or blunderings about, and twelve knots was quite fast enough for negotiating a channel as narrow as the one that was coming next.

'Down five revolutions.'

The light had seemed closer suddenly.

'Down five, sir . . . One-three-five revolutions passed and repeated, sir.'

Chandler reported, 'Rock's abeam, sir, about one cable.'

'Very good.' His eyes were glued to that blue gleam. This was as close to Namsos as they'd come.

'Port five.'

Lange had begun the turn that would take him round into Lokkaren: Nick had seen the light shift away leftwards.

'Midships.'

'That rock is slightly *before* the beam, sir.'

'Very good.' They *were* rock-climbing . . . He stooped again. 'Port five.'

The sense of being behind the enemy's lines: silence and darkness emphasised it, that and the knowledge that in a very short time he'd be creeping up on enemy ships which lay meanwhile in sleepy ignorance of his existence. There was a kind of tight-nerved satisfaction in it: just *being* here, armed and ready and on the verge of action – and unseen, unsuspected . . . He'd felt it before, more than once, but not for – well, twenty years. There was a kind of poacher's thrill about it. That night off the Belgian coast in 1917, for instance, in a CMB – the modern development of which were called MTBs – en route to snatch some prisoners out of a guard trawler known to the Dover Patrol as 'Weary Willie' . . .

'Midships.' They'd be past that rock by now.

'Midships . . . Wheel's amidships, sir!'

'Ship's head now, and the course up here, pilot?'

'Course should be oh-one-five, sir. Ship's head – oh-one-eight.'

Nick didn't want to look at the compass, if he could avoid it, for the sake of his night vision. He told Jarratt, 'Steer oh-one-six.'

'Steer oh-one-six, sir.'

Chandler informed him, 'After a mile and a quarter there's foul ground to starboard, sir, so he'll probably ease over. After that he'll have to come back much more – about ten degrees – to starboard for the slight dog-leg through the narrowest part.'

'All right.' Chandler had courses, times and distances in his brown-covered navigator's notebook, and a pencil torch so that when he squatted down near the base of the binnacle he could use it inside his coat. For all his stuffiness, Pete Chandler made a useful navigator. And the stuffiness might wear off, as he gradually changed from City gent to destroyer man.

'Steer one degree to port.'

'One degree to port, sir!'

'Up five revolutions.'

'Up five revolutions, sir. Course oh-one-five, sir. One-four-oh revolutions passed and repeated, sir.'

It was the feeling of stealth as well as the surrounding quiet that made one talk quietly. As if voices might be heard ashore, or in the next fjord . . . The Germans in Namsos were lucky. A few of them would have died tonight. Perhaps quite a lot of them. But none of ours, please God . . . If this trick could be pulled off without casualties – catch them with their pants so far down that only Germans got hurt – *that* would be something!

Torp and the others, plugging down Namsenfjord at this moment: for all five of them to return would be a bit much to hope for. One did still hope, though . . . Crouch had grinned, and said, 'We'll see 'im right, sir, don't worry!' and Surtees had confirmed, 'We'll 'elp the geezer out, sir.'

Geezer . . . How would one explain that term, to a Norwegian? Literally it meant 'old woman'. One could hardly imagine anyone less womanish than Claus Torp.

The blue spot was moving left, and he bent quickly to the voicepipe. 'Steer three degrees to port.'

'Three degrees to port, sir!'

'Your foul ground coming up, pilot.' Lights in cottages on the coast to starboard. It felt like picking one's way through people's back gardens. Kari said, 'There are shallows and a small island, and half a mile higher there is a ferry crossing.'

'Not crossing now, let's hope.'

'I think it won't be operating at night.'

'Course one-oh-two, sir.'

'Time?'

'Five minutes past midnight, sir.'

'How wide is the narrowest bit of this creek, Kari?'

'About – hundred and fifty metres. Higher up. And before it there is a shoal, right in the middle. What is your ship's draught?'

193

'Twelve-foot six. What's over the shoal?'

'Sixteen, but—'

More, with a rising tide.

'He'll lead us round it, I imagine, sir. Course will still be about oh-one-five. I mean after we've cleared this stuff to starboard.'

'Yes, I think so.' Kari added, 'This would be easy if the lights were burning.'

'Steer two degrees to starboard.' Nick straightened from the voicepipe. 'Except they'd only be burning if your invaders had taken charge of them. Pilot, ship's head now?'

'Oh-one-five—'

'Steer oh-one-five, cox'n.'

Lyte reported, 'Spar buoy to starboard, sir. Green four-oh, fifty yards.'

'It marks the edge of the bad part. Knut will be going to the left of the shoal now. You can make out the high land on your port bow, I think?'

'Yes . . .' There'd be no more than a fifty-yard gap between the shoal and that steep coastline. Without Lange to follow, this would have been a tricky passage to negotiate. Except that Kari could have brought them through . . . A few minutes later, the high ground to port was so close it seemed you could have leant out from the bridge and touched it. Only for a minute: then the blue glimmer was sliding to the right.

'Starboard five.'

'Starboard five, sir . . . Five of starboard wheel on, sir.'

Jarratt wouldn't be seeing much, if anything, through his wheel-house window. He certainly wouldn't see the faint blue glow through sea-misted glass. 'Midships.'

'Midships, sir!'

'Meet her.'

'Meet her, sir . . .'

'Steady!'

'Steady – oh-two-seven, sir!'

'Steer oh-two-eight.'

There'd be a gradual widening now, up to the top of the fjordlet. He asked Chandler, 'Time?'

'Twelve minutes past, sir.'

Forty-eight minutes to zero hour. In that time they had to get around the corner into Surviksundet and through that stretch into Lauvoyfjord and across it to Rodsundet. It seemed like a lot of ground to cover when he pictured the chart in his mind, but it was probably a bit under seven miles.

'Course oh-two-eight, sir.'

'Very good. This is a fiddly business, cox'n.'

'Seems like it, sir.'

Blue light dead ahead, and distance just about the same. The cottages with lit windows to starboard were right by the fjord's edge, a few of them, and the lights were reflected on the dead-flat water. Would Norwegians there be watching them pass? Taking them for Germans? Kari asked him quietly, 'Do you mind if I ask a question?'

'Ask away.'

'I don't wish to spoil your concentration.'

'You won't.'

'Will we hear when they explode the depthcharges?'

'Almost certainly.'

What one hoped *not* to hear from that direction would be the sound of German guns. *Valkyrien* wouldn't stand up to five-inch shells. One had to hope for confusion, the enemy not knowing what had hit them or where from. If they could smash his searchlight . . .

Kari murmured, 'So we will know they have got that far.' Nick was adjusting the course to oh-two-seven, since Lange had drifted off slightly left; he told Kari without taking his eyes off the light, 'We'll be busy too by then. I'll want you to be down below.'

'Oh, but *please*—'

'There's no question of your remaining on the bridge.'

Silence. Except familiar rattles, the steady thrumming of the engines, hoarsely sucking fans. Blue light edging left again: he called down to Jarratt, 'Steer oh-two-five.'

Cutting *this* corner now. Kari asked him, 'May I go in your chartroom, so I can listen to what happens?'

'Yes, you may.' She was a terrific girl, he thought. Torp had done a good job in the upbringing of his daughter. He asked her, 'Any hazards in this next bit?'

'Not in Surviksundet, down the centre. The only shoal is at the other end and it is ten metres, so it won't bother you.'

Chandler muttered, binoculars at his eyes, 'He's going round, sir.'

'Port five.'

Round and into Surviksundet. About three miles of it, with a

195

width of four to five hundred yards all the way through. Three miles at twelve knots – fifteen minutes. Straightening his ship's course into it after a spell of drastic Knut-type corner-cutting, he thought, *After this there's only Lauvoyfjord . . .*

He wanted to be razor-sharp now. *Had* to be. Eight years pottering about with farm-hands and foresters had had a blunting effect, he suspected. The mind rested, took its time. He hoped he'd sloughed the landsman's skin.

'Up five revolutions.'

'Up five revolutions, sir . . . One-four-five revolutions passed and repeated, sir.'

He asked Chandler, 'Are we up to schedule?'

'Just about, sir. We can check it and adjust speed as necessary at Lauvoy Island. But I *think*—'

'Yes, all right.'

In other words, *Don't waffle . . .*

'One mile into Lauvoyfjord –' Kari's voice beside him – 'before we come to the island, there is a one-fathom shoal with a marker-buoy on it. I think Knut will leave it close to port.'

'Right.'

After this – when, touch wood, he'd filled *Intent*'s sound tanks and had possession of the oiler – what next? It was bad luck to count chickens, but one had to think ahead and be ready with the answers. It wouldn't be so long, if all went well, before he was alongside the oiler, with Torp or Trench wanting orders.

Head north, towards Vestfjord?

'Steer two degrees to port.'

'Steer two degrees to port, sir!'

According to the signal they'd picked up, the one Whitworth had sent *Penelope*, Vestfjord was where the action was. And with a number of destroyers up there the tanker and her cargo would be welcome. So – all right, north. It had the additional advantage of being in the opposite direction to the Hun airfields. Head up towards Narvik – where the 2nd Flotilla's action had been . . .

'Port five.'

'Port five, sir. Five o' port wheel on, sir . . .'

No need, when he made his signal, to mention leaking oil-tanks. After all, he'd have his own replenishments with him. If he reported the leaks they'd send him home. As long as this action left the ship in working order and with a few torpedoes left in her tubes, it would be justified. And they'd certainly want the oil up there. 'Midships and meet her.'

'Midships – meet her—'

'Steady!'

'Steady – two-eight-five, sir—'

'Steer that.'

Coming out of Surviksundet, entering Lauvoyfjord. Lyte reported from the front of the bridge, 'Spar buoy fine on the port bow, sir.'

'Ah. Kari's shoal.'

Chandler amplified, 'Should be three cables south of the eastern end of the island, sir.'

At twelve thirty-three it was abeam, forty yards to port. *Intent* was on a course of 286 degrees. Chandler said, 'We're right on time, sir.'

Thanks to Knut Lange's short-cuts . . . Two minutes after they'd passed that marker, Lauvoy light structure was three cables' lengths to starboard.

Going like clockwork. Too good to last.

'Blueboat's going round, sir.'

'Yes.' He put his face down to the voicepipe. 'Starboard ten.' Then, straightening, 'What'll the course be now?'

'Three-three-four, sir. And we ought to be coming down to eight—'

'One hundred revolutions!'

'Hundred revolutions, sir—'

'Midships.'

Getting closer now. And Lange had cut his boat's speed too: in fact the light-cluster was brighter, they'd closed up on him a little. It was all right, though. 'Steer three-three-four.'

This course would take them up close to the western shore, the bulge of land where Lauvoyfjord ran into Rodsundet. The bulge was about one mile below the anchorage where the German ships were lying. The oiler was nearest and the destroyers were about two-thirds of a mile beyond her. All three were lying to single anchors – or had been, when last seen by Lange – and since high water would be at 0414 this morning the inward tidal flow would have them with their bows pointing north, down-fjord.

At twelve-fifty, when *Intent* would be only about one cable's length – 200 yards – offshore, she'd be continuing straight ahead while Lange's boat sheered away to port to follow the coastline round the curve into the anchorage to get inshore of the tanker, in a position to board her over her port side. *Intent* would be passing about 400 yards to seaward of her before turning in and closing the enemy destroyers.

Low coastline to port, dimly visible because of its lower edging of white surf. The hills inland weren't discernible even with binoculars.

'Time?'

'Quarter to the hour, sir.'

He could hear the swell breaking along that coastline. He'd been too busy watching the blue light and the courses and speeds to have noticed until now the increasing motion on the ship. This north-wester, mild as it was compared to the gale they'd had three days ago, would be blowing straight down Rodsundet and funnelling into Gyltefjorden as well, and they'd be feeling it more as they crept round the bulge.

'Comin' up to 0050, sir.'

'Better go down, Kari.' He was watching the blue cluster, for it to disappear. At ten minutes to the hour, 0050, in the position they were reaching now, switching the light off would be Lange's signal that he was branching away to port and would no longer serve as guide.

'Has she gone down?'

'She's on her way, sir, yes. Cluster's extinguished, sir!'

The cold, hard rim of the voicepipe cracked his forehead as he stooped and overdid it. 'Seven-oh revolutions.' He'd straightened. 'Sub, for'ard tubes train to port, after tubes starboard. Stand by all tubes.'

'Aye aye, sir.'

'Give me the director telephone.' Chandler put it in his hand. He told Brocklehurst, 'Have "B" gun stand by with one round of starshell and train on red three-oh. Do *not* load yet.'

Revs, speed and sound all falling away. The wind was whistling overhead, *Intent* pitching gently, waves slapping at her stem. He didn't want to use starshell: he'd order it only if the targets couldn't be seen without it.

'Large ship at anchor red five-oh, sir!'

Lyte had called it: and the for'ard port-side lookout was only a split second behind him. Brocklehurst's voice came over the telephone: 'Oiler bearing two-eight-oh, five hundred yards.'

'Our targets should be to the north of her, right inshore.' He passed the telephone to Chandler. 'Time?'

198

'Fifty-six, sir.'

'Tubes turned out and ready, sir.'

Hope to God those bastards haven't shifted . . .

'Two destroyers to the right of the oiler – red three-five!'

'Port ten.'

'Director target!'

'Steer three double-oh. Load all guns with SAP. Give me my glasses, pilot. Time?'

'Fifty-eight, sir.' Chandler passed the 'load' order to the director tower. Nick called to Lyte, 'Sub, tell Mr Opie I'll turn to starboard in one minute and fire four torpedoes from the for'ard tubes. Can you see both destroyers?'

Lyte had both targets in sight but slightly overlapping. He was talking to Opie now over the torpedo-control telephone. Nick had the enemy in his glasses. *Beitzen* class. Fine-looking ships. They wouldn't look fine for long. After he'd made his turn to starboard they wouldn't be overlapping much either, but they'd present one continuous line of target, which was what he'd planned for in this approach. He asked Chandler, 'Time?'

'Fifty-nine, sir.'

'Starboard fifteen.' He was close enough to be sure of hitting, and swinging now to bring the tubes to bear. Checking the compass. From the west, a rattle of machine-gun fire. Too *soon* . . . Enemy bearing was two-eight-five. He called down, 'Steer oh-one-five.'

'Steer oh-one-five, sir!'

That *had* been from the direction of Altbotn . . .

'Sub – I want four carefully-aimed shots spread over both targets. Don't rush – make sure of it.'

'Aye, aye, sir.' Lyte was hunched behind the sight. With stationary targets the only way he could miss would be if the torpedoes didn't run straight. Which did happen, sometimes. From a westerly direction, shorewards, came a deep, muffled-sounding *whumpf*. Then another. And on the heels of the twin explosions a rattling blare of machine-gun fire. Nick had his glasses on the dim shapes of the enemy destroyers. Silence now: but they'd be stirring, standing-to, alerted by Torp's balloon having gone up a minute early. At any moment there'd be searchlights, starshell, a blaze of gunfire. *Intent*'s swing was slowing as she neared her firing course: with luck Lyte would get the fish away before the enemy woke up enough to—

Searchlight: it flared into life, grew swiftly from the left-hand destroyer, its beam lengthening and at the same time scything round – to search *the shore* . . .

Lyte snapped, 'Fire one!'

CHAPTER 11

Coming through the bottleneck from Altfjord into Altbotn, Torp had brought his ship round so close to the point that he'd almost scraped her timbers on it. Then he'd still hugged the rocky shore. By making the most of its cover he'd aimed to have *Valkyrien* within 500 yards of her target before the Germans had a chance of seeing her.

He'd been outside the wheelhouse on the starboard side, at that stage, with Larsen inside at the wheel. Leading Torpedoman Crouch had been close behind him, and Billy Surtees behind Crouch. Surtees was tall and heavily built, a lot bigger than the wiry, curly-headed killick.

Engine thumping like a pulse, a deep heartbeat banging through the old timbers. Knife-cold air: you had to narrow your eyes to slits to be able to look into it without them watering. Black night, with a light here and there in cottage or farmhouse windows. There was one in the curve of bay which they'd just passed, and it looked as if it must have been right down on the beach. Torp had taken her farther out to round that last point because it had some reef fringing it, a visible rock where the white swirled round it and a lot of other broken water. Now he had binoculars at his eyes and he was leaning with his left shoulder against the door-jamb of the wheelhouse; he had an ancient revolver stuck in his belt, a great heavy thing about a foot and a half long. Surtees had queried, eyeing it earlier on, 'After elephant, are we?' Broken water again to starboard, Crouch saw. Torp lowered the glasses and turned to look at him, his eyes white and glary-looking in the dark. 'Remember what we do?'

'Aye, sir.' Crouch confirmed it. 'All weighed off.'

There was a V-shaped cove ahead, with its open end northwards, facing them, and the Germans were in the widest part of the V. The left-hand arm of it was coastline and the nearer part of the right-hand one was a spur of foul ground, rocks and shallows. Torp's plan was to take *Valkyrien* in between the Germans and the shore and then swing hard a-port to come up across their sterns. As he reached them he'd put his helm over again so that *Valkyrien*'s stern would start a swing inwards towards her victims', and at this point the charges were to be released. The least damage they could do would be to smash the Germans' screws and rudders; in shallow water with the blast bouncing off the bottom of the fjord they might do even better. Internal damage was likely, and there'd be some results too from crashing the two ships together. The submarine's beam tanks, for instance, stood a good chance of getting flattened.

Torp was going to flash a torch aft at Crouch as the signal to knock the slips off the charges. In the stern now with Surtees on his right, Crouch turned half round so as not to miss the flash when it came. Each man had a hand on his own releasing-gear, having located it by feel, by groping for it in the dark. Nobody'd get a *second* chance. One hand on the slip and the other on his sub-machine-gun. After the swing Torp was going to reverse his helm again to steady her and then drive the ship out over the top of that shallow patch. God alone knew how. Well – one might hope that Torp did, too. It was the only way, he'd said, other than by turning up almost alongside the destroyer, beam-on to her, inviting the German gunners to reduce her to matchwood. Crouch hoped the geezer knew his way about it; *Valkyrien*, being a sailing ship, had a deep draught, a keel – she wasn't built for hopping over shallow patches. Torp had said something about the explosions of the depthcharges helping, washing her over.

Peculiar cove. Smashing daughter, though, the one the skipper was keen on. There'd been some bets placed, on the messdecks. He'd said to Surtees, when they'd been chatting on the trip down Namsenfjord, 'Nice bit of stuff, that. Don't blame the skipper 'aving a go, eh?' Surtees had looked vague: 'Thought it was 'er was after 'im. That's 'ow I 'eard it . . . Got a missus already, ain't 'e?' Crouch had shaken his head sadly: 'Bloody 'ell, don't you know *anything*?'

Ahead, a glow of light, startling in the dark . . .

He got up higher for a better look. Floodlight of some kind: on a ship's deck. The Hun destroyer's? The light was shaded, shining downwards. Squinting into the icy wind, standing right up and leaning out on Surtees's side, staring out fine on the port bow: he could see men working around that light and a davit in black, curved silhouette. By its position it would be a torpedo davit. The half-lit picture, vague as it was with the flickering shadows, was cut off vertically with knife-edge abruptness where the ship's superstructure for'ard blanked it off. But *Valkyrien* was edging round to starboard, further inshore, now that she'd cleared the reef: she'd be coming in fast towards her still unsuspecting victims. Crouch went back to his place in the stern, Surtees swearing as he kicked his legs in transit and got down on the other side of him. Watch for the flash now. He told Surtees, 'Won't be long, Billy-boy. Jerries workin' on the upper, got a light on an' all.'

Sharper swing to starboard. And a huge light flaring: searchlight? Jet of brilliance: it had swept *over* them, but there'd been enough spill-off brightness to—

A shout from for'ard. Torp – sounding furious. Crouch put a hand on Surtees' shoulder, pressing him downwards as he passed him. 'Stay there now.' The light's beam had touched the funnel, swung on, then had second thoughts and started to come back. Crouch scuttled for'ard up the port side; he heard the bark of Torp's old pistol from the wheelhouse doorway. *Silly old bugger, might as well fart at it as use that thing . . .* The killick leant with his left arm on top of the port-side bulwark, as a steadying point, aimed his Thompson at the centre of the glare and squeezed its trigger. The gun jumped upwards, as the GM had warned it would: you had to force the barrel down to get it where you wanted. The searchlight was full on them, holding them, and some sort of hooter was blaring from the German. The Tommy shuddering and hammering, its barrel flaming as he brought its stream of .45 slugs down across that blinding glare. Explosion of glass as it smashed and went out. Pitch-black again – worse, he was blinded, couldn't see even his own hands. *Done* it, though. Stumbling aft, groping, pulverising Billy-boy's calves again and *Valkyrien* pounding on, a fine old ship that had never been meant for war, for anything like this. She'd lurched to starboard. Crouch had found the slip entirely by feel. He asked Surtees, 'You set?'

'Yeah. Roll on my twelve.'

Daft bugger . . . Crouch was beginning to see again. *Valkyrien* heeled to starboard as Larsen shoved the wheel hard a-port and she began her turn in towards the enemy's sterns. Two sterns close together. Using the torpedo davit to plumb the U-boat's midships area they'd had to secure them this way.

'Stand by!'

She'd steadied and she was about to pass close astern of them. The wire slips had to work now, and the slings had not to snag. Crouch couldn't see the enemy, the target, because the old ship's deckhouse was in the way. He wasn't trying to anyway, only watching for the torch-flash. The Norwegian would have to be looking about four ways at once: target to port, rocks to starboard, torch signal towards his stern and what Larsen was doing with the wheel. A machine-gun had opened up and tracer was arching overhead and astern. *Valkyrien* leaned over as she went into her zig to starboard.

The torch flashed, yellowish.

Crouch screamed, 'Let's go!' and at the same time struck at the slip in front of him with the stock of his Tommy gun. In the dark he missed it, bouncing off the wire instead: the gun skidded sideways and he'd skinned his knuckles. Surtees yelled, 'All gone!' *This* bastard hadn't. He had to feel for the slip again, shove the barrel of the Tommy under its latch and lever it open. It snapped back and the wires' ends whipped away and the charge fell clear. Surtees' gun began to hammer, banging and flaming at lights and men running on the destroyer's upper deck. Crouch put his gun up too and got one short burst off before it jammed.

The German machine-gun had ceased fire. They'd probably be looking for some quite different kind of target: and they wouldn't know anything about the charges yet. Crouch had the pan off his gun and he was working the cocking mechanism to clear it before he put a new one on. The pistols on the charges would be filling with water now and when they'd filled the hydrostatic valves would be triggered by the pressure in them. Meanwhile nobody was shooting, so why give the sods a mark to aim at? He told Surtees, 'Hold your fire, Billy!' The first charge exploded and astern the fjord erupted, a huge white mushroom-head lifting, with the German ships in it: then the spread of it travelling outwards lifted *Valkyrien*'s stern and drove her ahead bow-down but with the whole length of her up on the enormous outrushing wave, which passed on under her so that she dropped stern-down, almost under water. A succeeding rush was coming, though, overtaking and slewing her off course and right on round, listing hard to starboard, and the second charge went off with a *boom* that sounded bigger than the first, with another swelling mushroom heading skywards: they heard the roar of the approaching wave just as the old ship rocked back to port, practically on her beam ends. She was in a maelstrom of heavy falling and rushing, over-sweeping sea, three-dimensional confusion: spinning her round, the torrent poured right across her, flooded over the bulwarks aft, swirled two feet deep before it drained down. But the engine was still pounding away and she was pitching less already, over smaller waves, follow-ups as the main deluge subsided: it had hit her, mauled her, and swept on. Rolling still but responding to rudder and coming back on course. Astern, the gun began to fire again, something like a twenty-millimetre by the sound of it: but it wasn't shooting in the right direction from any German point of view. *Valkyrien* chugged on: perhaps she *had* been lifted and carried over the shallow patch. The gun ceased fire. It was pitch-black and with any luck the Germans still didn't know what had hit them. It would have done them in, all right, Crouch thought: he muttered, 'Lovely grub, eh, Billy?' and Surtees answered, 'Ah, very tasty, very sweet.' Out of some radio programme. Astern one gun fired once: main armament, one single shot. The crack of it was still echoing round the fjord and surrounding hills when the starshell burst – high and well beyond them, over the land to which *Valkyrien* was pitching over what was now no more than a choppy sea. The shell burst with a sharp thudding sound and the flare appeared and expanded immediately to flood the whole land- and seascape with its harsh magnesium whiteness.

Now they'd seen her. Crash of gunfire astern. Small stuff – pom-poms or Bofors – that kind of thing, and some of it was tracer. Surtees put his gun up, sighted, pressed the trigger: the Thompson banged twice and then jammed. A hand grabbed Crouch's shoulder: Torp yelled with his face down close to him, 'Set the charges! Half-minute only, then we beach!' The top of the old hooker's funnel went, flared and soared away in several burning pieces. Explosive shells ripped in flame and flying timber along the port-side strip of deck. Torp had gone for'ard, luckily for him, up the other side. Crouch grabbed Surtees' arm: 'Charges!'

They were below, ready to be placed and lit. Arne Martinsen, the stoker-cum-engineer, asked Crouch, 'We fix the boggers?' It wasn't clear whether he was referring to Germans or to charges, but an affirmative answered either question. Martinsen was all sweat, coaldust and oil: he'd have stoked her right up by now so she'd have all the steam she needed for this last sprint of hers. There was a crash from up top somewhere: she lurched – either thrown off course or dodging. The fitted charges were all together in an ammo box; he passed three of them to Surtees and took the other three himself. Surtees said, 'I'll do port side, right?' They were tin cylinders about a foot long and three inches in diameter, and Crouch had set them up himself before they'd sailed. It wasn't a difficult operation: you slid the explosive into the tin, which it exactly fitted, and the detonator went into an aperture in the end of the explosive. One end of the fuse you poked through the hole in the tin's screw-cap and then crimped into the detonator, and then you screwed the cap on. It was just a tin, now, with the fuse like white washing-line sticking out of it. On the other end of the fuse, whatever length of it was needed, you fitted an igniter, a tube of tin about the size of a small cigarette; the fuse fitted into one end of it and the other end, if you squeezed it with a pair of pliers or by stamping on it, started the fuse burning. It didn't show, but if it was burning properly and you held it against your ear you could hear it fizz.

Crouch lowered his three charges into the bilge along the length of the engine-space, one for'ard and one aft and one between them, and Surtees was doing the same on the other side. They should have been tamped down, really, but the confined space down there would contain the explosion, concentrate it enough, Crouch reckoned. They were leaving the ends of the fuses with igniters on them up on the footplates, ready to be set going. Torp leant in through the hatch: 'Is it ready?' Surtees nodded: 'Aye, sir.'

'Fuses lit?'

Crouch said, arriving at the after end, 'We'll light 'em now, sir. Billy—'

'Aye aye.' Surtees had the pliers. He went round quickly, squeezing each igniter and checking that it was fizzing, then dropping the whole length of fuse down into the bilge – out of reach, unless you took the plates up. The fuse would burn in water as well as out of it. Arne Martinsen had started up the ladder, leaving the engine unsupervised and lonely, driving itself to its own doom. Crouch pushed Surtees towards the ladder and then followed him up it. Into air even colder than it had been, after the heat below. Surtees asked Crouch, speaking with his mouth against the killick's ear, 'Oughter stay with the gaffer, like the skipper said?' The biggest explosion they'd heard yet – enough to crack the fjord wide open . . . Echoes now. It had been to the east of them – over the land ahead. Now another one exactly like it: this time Crouch saw a flash, a sort of yellow streak, very quick like a light that burns and fuses instantaneously as you press a switch. *Valkyrien* was heeling as she swung to starboard, and a shell burst on her beam – *on land* – a low headland which she was rounding: a fresh starshell had just suspended itself overhead, lighting everything in all directions. Bits of shell or perhaps stones flying, singing away overhead: and another shellburst but astern this time, in the water, he'd heard it scrunch down and then the explosion and after that it was raining, a deluge of heavy rain that stank. They were practically on the beach, he realised. The whole trip across, from dropping the charges to this beach, was only 800 yards. So Torp had said. Five minutes, he'd said it would take them, *All we got to do is stay afloat five minutes. Not too hard, huh?* Norwegian minutes must be longer than the British kind, Crouch thought. Third huge bang: and the yellow flash again: sure of it now, he bawled at Surtees, 'Them's our fish, chum!' Surtees nodded, shouted back, 'I reckon.' They'd helped look after those torpedoes, done maintenance routines on them.

Shells scorched over: a starshell had been fading but another had replaced it. The shells had burst on shore, some way up from the beach. Torp yelled from the wheelhouse door, 'Get for'ard, hold to something, *hold on!*' Surtees moved obediently and Crouch, who was ahead of him on the narrow strip of deck, moved too. He didn't want to get too far from the Norwegian. It was still bright as day from that starshell but no more shells had come, not in the last fifteen or twenty seconds. *Valkyrien* lifted, flinging up, smashing and grinding on to rock. Torp had been thrown back – he'd been holding with one arm to the doorway and he'd been swung so that he'd crashed backwards into the side of the wheelhouse. He shouted at Crouch, 'I say go *for'ard*, damn it!' He'd given Surtees an almighty shove: Surtees blundered into the killick and they both went on towards the bow. The jolting and bouncing had stopped, and the ship was falling over on to her starboard side, subsiding slowly with the water tending to hold her up. She lurched again and Crouch slipped, fell against the bulwark, down on one knee in the swirl of sea that was pouring over now and also rising from astern, up the slope of deck. Larsen gave him a hand up, then went on ahead, and in fading starshell-light Crouch saw him jump over from the bow. Crouch followed him, thinking he could wait for

Torp on the beach rather than hang back now and get sworn at: and Torp's bellow reached him, 'Get a bloody move on – *jump!*' Only the way he said it was 'yump'. Tracer racketed overhead: spraying the beach, now that she wasn't in the bastards' sight? She couldn't be, not in this little cove he'd put her in. Crouch swung his legs over the bulwark, held the Tommy gun up clear of the wet, and slid over, landing in about four feet of icy water. Ahead of him were Martinsen and Larsen, ten- or fifteen-yard gaps between them and between Larsen and himself, and behind him was Surtees and the fellow they were supposed to be looking after. Currently yelling Norwegian: then he put it into English – 'There is a stream in front. Follow it to the road then go left and run!' Another starshell: time they gave up that lark, Crouch thought. More shells scrunching over – bursting on land, so they couldn't be aiming for *Valkyrien*. Wouldn't make sense to now in any case. Chocker, probably, wanting to get their own back, teach a lesson to the unruly natives.

Martinsen had shouted something back to Torp: he had a high, carrying voice, trained by the need to yell over the sound of engines. He was clear of the water, climbing a steep slope with a gully to the right of it. Larsen was still in the water, the shallows, jogging through it. It was still too deep where Crouch was to move fast and he didn't want to anyway, even though Surtees had managed to stay with the Norwegian back there. *Aching* cold water. More shells – falling to the left, exploding in the shallows, sending up sheets of sea and a hail of stones. Then to the left again, that sort of rasping whistle as they rushed down, the crashes of the explosions and the air alive and humming with flying rock and salt water: and now *more* coming. He thought, *Vindictive bastards!* Then he realised: the new salvo was going to pitch *behind* him – where Surtees and the Norwegian were.

Lange cut his boat's speed. The oiler was a dark mass blacker than the night fifty yards off on the bow. A long, low rectangle with two smaller, upright rectangles on it. One of them was the bridge superstructure and there were lights showing from it. Careless: thought they were all right on the landward side, perhaps. Trench looked down, rapped with his knuckles on Midshipman Cox's tin hat: 'Clear about your job, you in there?' Cox said yes, he was. Trench looked past him, at PO Metcalf: 'You, Buffer?' Metcalf growled, 'I'm the bloke as chucks 'em in the 'oggin, sir.' The land was about a hundred and fifty yards to port: on the boat's quarter now as Lange turned directly towards the oiler. Planks were ready on the wheelhouse canopy, to bridge the gap between boat and ship. The boarding party – all in helmets, officers and POs with revolvers and British and Norwegian sailors with rifles – lined both sides of the boat's deck and packed the sternsheets. Riflemen would fix bayonets after they'd boarded.

Trench checked his watch's luminous dial. One minute to zero hour. He leant into the wheelhouse, held up one finger to Lange. The Norwegian blinked at it. 'Hokay.' His engines were turning over very slowly, just paddling the heavy boat up towards its goal.

'Hey, what's—'

Trench said, 'Machine-gun. Keep your voices down, everybody.' That gunfire had come from the Altbotn direction. Metcalf grumbled, 'Warming the blooming bell, sir?' Translated, his comment was that Torp had launched his attack too soon. Then they heard the first depthcharge go off, a deep explosion like subterranean thunder. Trench watched the oiler, dreading that he might see what he now expected – alarm, lights, men rushing about. Practically holding his breath. Forewarned, a couple of men with rifles could make the boarding operation just about impossible. The second deep and distant *whumpf* came: he said evenly, quietly, 'That's both charges. So far so good.' His own voice in retrospect sounded as if he might be slightly bored: whereas in fact his heart was beating like a hammer. More machine-gun fire. *Too damn soon* . . . If those Huns weren't stirred up by now it wouldn't be old Torp's fault. He saw a glow of light to the left of the oiler, silhouetting her vertical stem and the start of the long, low foc's'l; the glow had resolved itself into a swivelling searchlight beam from the destroyer anchorage. For a second or two the oiler was bathed in its light as it swept past, then it had gone round to poke at the beach and coastline of that farther bay. The lights in the houses ashore, Trench noticed, had all gone out. Heads under the bedclothes too?

This boat hadn't been illuminated at all by the searchlight: the oiler had shielded it completely. Which suggested that the inshore approach had been a wise choice. But surely they *must* wake up, realise *something* was going on?

Lange's head came out, like a tortoise's out of its shell. 'Hokay?'

The oiler was dead ahead. To the right, the aftercastle with the funnel growing out of it and no lights showing in the cabin scuttles would contain crew's quarters and galley. A few other things as well. To the left, the bridge superstructure with bridge, chartroom, captain's and officers' accommodation, W/T office . . . Between those two islands of superstructure was the low tank-top section, with catwalks above it, where they were going to board. Trench pointed at that gap, roughly a hundred feet of it.

'There. *Okay.*'

Meaning, *Let's get there – quick, before the stupid bastards pull their fingers out* . . .

'Sure!'

So Lange knew *two* English words . . . He wasn't rushing, though. He'd shut the throttles back as far as they'd go, just about. Dead slow, sliding up towards an enemy who was either daft or unpleasantly alert and waiting to see the whites of the intruders' eyes. Trench ran over some of the detail in his mind. Leading Telegraphist Rose would be taking care of the wireless, ensuring that no calls for help went out. Cox would be attending to the clearing of machinery spaces, then leaving guards on the access points and, with Metcalf, searching the rest of the lower compartments and placing more guards as might be necessary. You had to make sure no bloody-minded Hun could slip down to those bottom areas to open seacocks or place a charge. (Germans were scuttle-minded: witness *Graf Spee*, four months ago.) An LTO, electrician, had been detailed to locate the main switchboard and protect it against sabotage. All cabins had to be searched and firearms impounded, documents and code-books in the chartroom and captain's quarters or elsewhere kept safe from destruction.

If there was anyone up on that bridge, Trench thought, he or they might be fully occupied looking out over the bow, towards the destroyers and the searchlight business. With luck, they might . . . he heard a thump – overhead: saw it was starshell, white light spreading . . . Looking down again quickly, to spare his eyes. Ten yards to go. Too late for the starshell to make much odds, but if it had come five minutes earlier . . . Sea sloshing noisily, violently, between the boat and the tanker's sheer black side. There were to be no lines put across: Lange would keep the boat alongside by its own power, holding it there until they'd all gone over.

'Stand by!'

He'd called the warning aft just loudly enough for the nearer men to hear and pass it on. Gunfire now from the Altbotn direction was something to be welcomed, to hold the Germans' attention during the next few minutes. Trench was up on the timber canopy and so were Cox and Metcalf and the men who'd be first up behind them, including a killick who'd be taking care of the for'ard end of the ship. Men who'd come slightly later were manoeuvring the heavy planks ready for shoving them over. They wouldn't be entirely steady gangways, with the boat's rise and fall on this swell, but at least the oiler was giving them a lee. Another reason for boarding over this side.

Two Norwegians on the deck below this wheelhouse, several feet lower than Trench and others on its roof, were holding up the outboard ends of two planks, as high above their heads as they could reach. They'd launch them upwards and outwards as the boat touched alongside. They were the tallest of the Norwegians.

Three yards – two – one –

'Gangways over!'

The ends of the planks were still bouncing on the oiler's side as Trench rushed over the left-hand one. Other men behind him and on the second plank, and two more bridges crashing over. Not a soul in sight. He was aboard, and no one had shot at him. He grabbed the rail of the catwalk which bridged across the tank-tops in a fore-and-aft direction, hauled himself up on it, ran towards the door into the bridge superstructure: conscious of a whole rush of men behind him, all fast and no noisier than they needed to be. The door was heavy steel, shut and clipped, and he was dragging the clips off. Four, and it still wouldn't open, but Cameron, the killick who was going to lead his party straight through this superstructure and out on to the for'ard section, located a fifth clip low down and heeled it off. The door swung open and they rushed inside, down a short passage, then right into a thwartships passage where, amidships, a ladderway led upwards. Trench went up it. On the next level, cabin doors. Up to the next level with sailors close behind him and the sound of bayonets clicking on to rifles.

He burst into the bridge.

'Get your hands up!'

Three men whipped round to face him: face his revolver and two levelled rifles with bayonets on them. Signalman Lee hadn't stopped, he'd gone straight through and out into the bridge wing, two other seamen following him. Of the three Germans here two were officers and one was a grey-haired petty officer: one of the officers, a short, stout man, had gold-leafing on the peak of his cap. Trench roared again, 'Hands up!' The more junior officer complied. From for'ard came shouting and a single rifle-shot which

211

seemed to have silenced it: Cameron doing his stuff. The PO lunged forward suddenly with some weapon raised above his head: Trench raised the pistol and his finger was tightening on its trigger when the man stopped dead with a bayonet-point about two inches from his throat. All he had in that lifted hand was a pair of binoculars. Now all three had their hands up.

'Captain?'

'Ja.' The short one with scrambled eggs on his hat nodded. 'I am kapitan.' He clicked his heels. Too short and fat to be impressive. 'Grossman. I protest – this is unarmed merchant vessel, in passage through neutral waters—'

'Rotten luck.' Trench nodded. 'Just order your men to surrender, please.' The man stood staring at him, trying to look haughty. Trench added, 'If they resist they're quite likely to be shot . . . What's this, Marsham?'

AB Marsham was prodding a youngster in from the starboard bridge wing, at the point of his bayonet. Some sort of cadet.

'Tryin' to flash a message to the destroyers, sir. Caught 'im in the act.'

The newcomer took his place with the others and raised his hands. The captain nodded. 'You will not get away. You will see in one moment—'

A flash: huge, yellow, reaching from sea to cloud-level, and with it an explosion that shook the deck they were standing on. One destroyer done for: and all the Germans had swung round to look. Trench allowed it, as an exercise that might take the starch out of them. There was a mass of fire now, flames lighting the base of a pillar of black smoke. He'd only spared it a glance but his impression had been of a destroyer broken in two halves and one of them burning.

'Captain!'

He had the man's attention again. 'Will you order your crew to surrender, please?'

A second ringing crash and another leap of fire. No need to look, and the German captain evidently didn't feel he had to either. Behind Trench, Leading Telegraphist Rose reported, 'W/T office is locked up, sir. They didn't get no signals out.'

'Well done, Rose. You'd better stay there for the time being, keep an eye on it.' He raised his gun a little, pointing it at the captain's head. 'Well?'

'You take us prisoners?'

'You and your officers, yes. Perhaps a few others. Most of your crew can go ashore.' He didn't mention *how* they'd go ashore. Officers were to be held prisoner, Nick had decided, because as highly trained men they were better not returned to the German war machine. There might be some technicians who'd be rated similarly. Outside, a third explosion speared the night with flame, rattled the bridge windows. The German captain had shut his eyes and would probably have shut his ears too if he'd had the necessary equipment. He opened his eyes now, blinking, sad, hard-done-by, noble in defeat. He'd have been a real bastard in victory. He muttered, 'I will do as you wish.'

'Excuse me, sir?' Leading Steward Seymour announced from the doorway, 'Remainder of the officers, sir. Winkled 'em out of their beddy-byes, sir.' They filed in, between two fixed bayonets and with Seymour's right behind them – four men of differing ages, shape and sizes but all indignant, confused, frightened. They had coats or dressing-gowns over their pyjamas. Trench waved his pistol: 'Over there, and keep your hands up. Stand in line so I can see each one of you. Captain, tell them that in German.' He saw a new arrival, an OD named Kelly.

'Sir, report from Leading Seaman Cameron. Forepeak is suitable for prisoners, room for a dozen or more. And I'm to tell you 'e's sent 'is prisoners aft to where the other lot is, sir.'

'Thank you, Kelly. And casualties?'

'No, sir. Fired one shot over a bloke's 'ead, and 'e turned all smarmy.'

'Fine. Seymour, what about the chartroom?'

'Williamson's in there, sir. Nobody's touched nothing, and there's a safe that's locked still.'

Williamson was the CW candidate who was going to become Pete Chandler's tanky. Trench had detailed men and parties for these various jobs mainly during the blue boat's passage through the fjords. It seemed to be working out all right. He looked at the captain again: 'Your keys, please. Take them from him, Seymour.' And it was time for that broadcast.

But there was another interruption: a stoker, Ackroyd, from Cox's detail. He reported, 'From Mr Cox, sir: engine-room, boiler-room, generator room, shaft tunnel and steering-gear compartment is all clear and secured with guards on upper access points, sir. Crew's quarters likewise cleared, and search of other spaces is continuing. One German seaman killed, sir, and no resistance is now being offered. Main switchboard's under guard and prisoners are being mustered on the upper deck right aft.'

'Very good, Ackroyd.' It was better than 'very good', he thought, it was bloody marvellous. 'You'd better report back to Mr Cox, and tell him that if you or any other stokers can be spared now I'd like you to join Leading Stoker Evans on the oiling preparations.'

'Aye aye, sir.'

'*Only* if he can spare you.'

'I'll explain that, sir.'

Ackroyd would have the makings of a killick. Trench saw that Seymour had the captain's keys: he told him, 'Take those to Williamson. Tell him to empty the safe, list its contents and parcel everything up ready for transfer to *Intent*. Then come back here, please.' He told Kelly, 'Ask Leading Seaman Cameron to come up here with a few hands to escort these officers to their new quarters.'

'Aye aye, sir.' Kelly shot away. Trench turned to the captain.

'Where's your broadcast system worked from?'

Grossman pointed. There was a switchbox on the bulkhead with a microphone on a trailing lead.

'But why is this necessary? You have my ship: it is not – not *honourable* that a commander should order his—'

'You'll do it though. *Now.*'

He'd gestured with the gun, towards that corner.

'As a sea officer I ask you, sir—'

'I don't *mind* shooting you, Captain.' The German stared at him: then he moved, sluggishly, looking aggrieved. Trench said, 'Keep an eye on him, Gilby.'

'Aye, sir.' Cook Gilby and his bayonet followed the little man to the microphone. Grossman was right, of course, that his ship was now in British control, but lurking in some Teutonic brain might be thoughts of sabotage or other mayhem, and an order from their own CO to surrender could scotch such notions. The German voice was already booming through the ship.

'Sir?' Lee, the signalman, had come in from the wing of the bridge, which connected with the signal deck abaft it. 'Beg pardon, sir, but *Intent*'s circling round on our starboard quarter, looks like we might 'ave 'er alongside soon. Should I shine a light down? There's a six-inch each side, I could—'

'No.' If the Old Man wanted a light he'd shine his own. *Intent* had no searchlight, thanks to that *Hipper*, but she still had her

214

signal lamps and a ten-inch would serve that purpose. 'But – Lee, have you struck the German ensign?'

'Not yet, sir—'

Seymour was back. Trench told him, 'Go and give Lee here a hand. I want the German ensign hauled down with a light on it so *Intent* can see it. Then hoist the White Ensign, also with a spotlight on it. All right?'

'Aye aye, sir!'

The captain had finished his speech. Trench went over to the corner before he could leave it, and told him, 'Switch it so I can be heard all over the ship, please.' Grossman flipped one master-switch up, and nodded: 'So.' Trench slapped the microphone: it was live, all right. He said into it, 'D'you hear there. Petty Officer Metcalf, take four hands as berthing party for *Intent*, starboard side. Leading Stoker Evans, stand by for oiling, starboard side.'

'Stop together. Midships.'

His orders floated back to him out of the voicepipe as *Intent* slid up towards the oiler.

'Slow astern port.'

Five minutes ago they'd seen the German 'State Service' flag – a red rectangle with a black swastika in a white circle in the centre and an eagle-emblem in one corner – come sliding down from the masthead. Nick had said to Kari, 'Tommy Trench is giving us a show.' A few moments later a White Ensign, floodlit, had risen in place of the German flag. There'd been a round of cheering from the guns' crews, and Kari had clapped her hands. 'Bravo!'

She was worried to distraction about her father, and trying hard not to show it.

'Sub – berthing party, port side, and get Beamish moving as soon as we're secured.'

'Aye aye, sir!'

Joy, jubilation in the sub-lieutenant's voice. He'd fired *Intent*'s torpedoes, seen three of them hit, seen both enemy destroyers shattered and sunk. Not one shot had been fired at *Intent* during that short, highly conclusive action. Where the fourth torpedo had gone was a mystery. Dived into the mud, perhaps, if its depth-keeping mechanism had failed, or turned and streaked out to sea if it had been a gyro failure. Failures *did* occur. But those three fish had done the job.

'Stop port.'

215

'Stop port, sir . . . Port engine stopped, sir.'

This sweet smell of success might fade when news came of the *Valkyrien* party. There'd been a lot of gunfire during the starshell period. And it mattered enormously about Torp. It had before, but Nick's concern had been partly smothered in the planning of the operation and in uncertainties of other kinds. Now that the objects had been achieved – would soon have been achieved, if there was no unexpected interference now – that anxiety became stronger and more immediate. Not just for Torp's sake, in the way that one was concerned for the safety of the two torpedomen, for instance, but for Kari's and, selfishly, his own. If Torp had come to grief, he – Nick Everard – was going to be stuck with the girl. By his own sense of responsibility for her – whatever *she* had to say about it, he'd fall into the role of – well, foster-father?

The rescue syndrome? The Black Sea and Ilyana, now the Norwegian fjords and Kari?

No connection. Totally different circumstances: and totally different people. Even *he* was different, after twenty years. *Wasn't* he? And whether he cared for her or not – well, to what extent the care was for her, or for her and her father as an entity, the agency he'd been relying on, he couldn't tell. There wasn't time to think about it properly and for the moment it didn't matter anyway.

Heaving lines flew from *Intent*'s side, were caught by men on the tanker's deck. They had torches to help them see what they were doing. Fenders were in place and hemp breasts were slithering out now, dragged over by the heaving lines bent to them. Nick saw Metcalf down there, bawling at a Norwegian to underrun a spring before it got trapped between the two ships' sides, and the Norwegian, understanding no English at all, saw what was needed and did it. Leading Stoker Evans had an oil pipe triced up, dangling from a boom above and ready to be swung over.

Nick told Chandler, 'I'm going to pay a call next door, pilot. Look after this end, will you.'

'Keep the guns closed up, sir?'

'Yes. We aren't quite out of the wood yet.'

The girl asked him, 'Shall I go with you?'

'Well, I've things to see to. Better wait here until your father gets back, Kari, then it'll be up to him whether you stay with us or move over to the oiler.'

He didn't want her down there when the boat came.

Trench met him at the oiler's side. *Intent* was secured alongside and they'd put a brow across.

'Neat job on those destroyers, sir.'

He nodded. 'What's the score here, Tommy?'

'All in hand, sir. She's the *Tonning*. Naval auxiliary, 14,000 tons, reputedly capable of fourteen to fifteen knots, launched 1938. There's a gun-mounting for'ard but no gun. Six officers – they're under guard in the fore peak – and twenty-eight crew. She has approximately 8,000 tons of oil-fuel in her. Captain's name is Grossman. Inoffensive little chap, knows he's beat, as it were.'

'Do we know if they got any distress call out?'

'They did not, sir. We were in the bridge before they knew anything was happening. It's panned out very nicely and our chaps have done a first-class job.'

Beamish went hurrying past. Nick asked him, 'All right, Chief?'

'Will be, sir, in 'alf a shake. The connections'll do us all right, that was the main 'eadache.'

He'd gone on. Nick asked Trench, 'Steam up? Ready for the off when we've oiled?'

'Top line, sir, according to Cox. And Boyensen's just gone down to get things in hand. One rather useful thing – or it could be – is that there are two engineers, ERA types or possibly more like Warrants, who say they're Danes and want to join us. They say they were pressed into German service. Will you take a look at them?'

'We certainly need plumbers.'

'I meant for *this* ship, not—'

'Naturally. But let's wait for Torp.' *Touch wood* . . . 'They'll be his crew if we take them on, and he may even talk their lingo, or vice versa.'

The oil pipe was across now, linking the two ships. Beamish was back on the destroyer's iron deck with a gaggle of his stokers. Nick asked Trench, 'Have you sorted out swimmers and non-swimmers yet?'

'Cox is attending to that detail, sir.'

'How has he performed?'

'Well, sir – ' Trench smiled, thinking about it – 'I'd hesitate to use the expression "tower of strength" in relation to one of such diminutive stature as Midshipman Cox, but otherwise it might not be inappropriate.'

'That's good news. But you've developed rather an ornate turn of phrase, Tommy?'

'It's because I'm happy, I think.'

He looked round: Norwegians on the oiler's port side were shouting, pointing out into the dark. Nick heard Lange's name among the less unintelligible sounds.

So the boat was coming. No relief in that: only sharpened anxiety, a preference *not to know* . . . Trench said, turning back, 'There's one thing, sir – I promised Lange he could fill his boat's tank with diesel before we all shove off.'

Kari was coming, hurrying across the gangway. Nick nodded to Trench. 'Of course. Better warn Beamish, though.' Lange was intending to take his boat up through the Leads to Ranenfjord, Mo i Rana, about a hundred and twenty miles north. It was the place from which Torp had fetched *Valkyrien*, there were no Germans there yet and Lange had family near by. Nick was watching Kari as she came up to them.

'I heard the boat was coming.'

He'd tried to avoid this, but he was going to have to face it with her. And Torp *might* be in the boat . . .

He took her arm. 'Let's go and meet him.'

Over to the port side, ducking under the two catwalks. There were several Norwegians waiting to take the blue boat's lines. Kari pointed, wordlessly: it was the white bow-wave that she'd seen. Watching it as it approached and the boat began to reduce its speed, Nick felt sick with the conviction that her father would not be in it.

The boat was circling into a position from which to come alongside. The Norwegians along the oiler's side waited silently, motionless as statues, watching it approach. You could see their anxiety in that stillness. An arc of white curled shorewards as the boat swept round, rolling on the swell. Then it had steadied, and Nick could see men standing just abaft the wheelhouse door. Two of them. Then there'd be Lange on the wheel and his mechanic crouched in the little engine-space . . . But he'd *known* this. Right from the start of the operation, when it had become obvious that *Valkyrien* was going to have to do the Altbotn job. There'd been five in the *Valkyrien* party, and Lange and his two men . . . Kari's hand had tightened on his arm. The boat was slewing in, its starboard screw going astern. More men in sight than had been visible before. Then as it bumped alongside two figures moved to launch a plank across, and almost as it crashed down a large-built man climbed on to it and came shambling over with another man

218

on his back. As he entered the pool of light at the oiler's side Kari pulled herself away from Nick and rushed forward. Claus Torp allowed PO Metcalf to take Surtees off him, and Crouch, following, helped Metcalf in lowering the injured torpedoman to the deck.

Surtees announced for general information, 'Two bloody *miles* 'e carted me!'

Crouch told Nick, 'Shell-splinter in 'is leg, sir. I thought the both of 'em 'ad 'ad it, till 'e gets up an'—'

'Get him to the sickbay. Pass the word for a stretcher.'

Kari was in her father's arms, hugging him, sobbing against his chest. The clinch had been her idea, not his: he'd looked surprised as she'd leapt at him and clasped him. Now he was patting her shoulders as he stared at Nick over her dark head.

'You sank them both, huh?'

'Yes. How about yours?'

'Oh, sure. Well, maybe not *sink*, but – you know . . .' He looked down at his weeping daughter. 'What you been doing to this woman – *frightening* her?'

CHAPTER 12

The surface of Ofotfjord gleamed dully under drifting mist. Fir trees formed dark streaks and patches on the high snow-bound slopes and the sky backing the mountains was like dirty cotton-wool. It was a harsh, miserable place, Nick thought, this trap of a fjord where three days ago his son's ship had gone down.

1.30 pm: one German destroyer had already been sunk, although the action had barely started yet. The German had been hiding in Djupvik Bay, on the starboard hand as the British force debouched from the narrows into the wide part of the fjord, and *Warspite*'s Swordfish floatplane, hammering its way up-fjord with the racket of its engine bouncing from the mountain-sides, had radio'd advance warning of its presence. *Bedouin* and *Eskimo* had raced round the headland with guns and tubes ready trained to star-board, and it had needed only a few salvoes to silence the enemy's guns. Then a single torpedo from *Bedouin* had blown his bows off. Finally as *Warspite* steamed by in massive, lordly fashion she'd spared one thunderous blast of fifteen-inch and the already hard-hit enemy turned belly-up and sank.

The echoes died as the force pressed on. Earlier the leading destroyers had streamed their paravanes, minesweeping gear, but no mines had been encountered and they were getting the wires in now, out of the way before the business of destruction started. Leading the force were four of the modern Tribal class – *Bedouin, Cossack, Eskimo* and *Punjabi* – and behind them, screening the battleship which now flew Admiral Whitworth's flag, steamed the smaller destroyers *Hero, Icarus, Kimberley, Forester, Foxhound* and *Intent*. It was a foregone conclusion that when this force withdrew there'd be no German ship left afloat in the Narvik fjords.

Studying that southern coastline, Nick wondered where exactly

Hoste had sunk. Not far offshore, they'd told him last night. 'They' being the captains of two other destroyers who'd come to get oil from *Tonning*. They'd also told him that according to Norwegian accounts quite a number of survivors had got ashore: but later one of them had stumbled into admitting that the ship the Norwegian sources had mentioned had been *Hunter*, whose survivors were reported to have crossed the mountains into Sweden.

So in fact there was *no* news. Except that *Hoste* had been sunk and that before she'd foundered she'd been very badly knocked about. The anxiety was bad now. It had been suppressed, buried under the planning and the action, but now it was in the front of his mind and everything he looked at he was seeing through it. The signals from Admiralty and from C-in-C: or those destroyer captains wringing his hand and showering him with compliments: he'd *felt* none of it.

Last night had been spent off Hamnvik, in Folla, a fjord-complex on the southern side of Vestfjord. The oiler was still there, with Claus Torp as her master and young Lyte in charge of a four-man armed guard on the prisoners. *Tonning* was suckling the fleet's destroyers as they needed it, and in a day or two she was to be moved up to Harstad where a base was being established.

Kari had repeated, last night, 'Your son will be all right, Nick. You will see.'

'I know.' He told her, 'You convinced me two days ago.'

'Did I really?' He'd nodded. He'd been grateful for her attempt to convince him, that was all, her genuine desire to give him that comfort. But she was looking at him now as if she didn't quite believe him: she was anything but stupid. 'I hope I shall meet him one day. With you. Perhaps at your house – ' her hand had moved towards a pocket – 'of which I forget the name—'

'Mullbergh.'

He'd given her his card, given her father one as well, telling them that if ever they came to England they were to make themselves at home there whether or not he himself was around. Which most likely he would not be, of course. He'd written Sarah's name and the Dower House address and telephone number on the backs of the cards, and also the name of his old butler, Barstow.

'This – ' Kari had turned the card over – 'Lady Sarah Everard—'

'My stepmother. My father's widow. She has a house – that address I've put there – which is part of the estate.'

'Is it very big, your estate?'

221

'About four thousand acres. I sold off a lot of land a few years ago to raise cash for putting the rest of it in order.'

'That is still a great deal of land. And you are all sirs and ladies—'

'I'm a baronet because my father was. My elder brother would have been, instead of me, but he was drowned at Jutland. Paul – ' he made himself say this – 'Paul will become a baronet when I die. And when a baronet gets married his wife becomes *Lady* Whatsit. It's of no great consequence, Kari, it makes no difference to the sort of people we are.'

'I am very happy with the sort of person you are. But I should not like at all to become Lady Whatsit.'

'I think I can promise you that you won't.'

'Then I *shall* visit you at Mullbergh.'

'If I'm not there, you'll make another visit later?'

But the Torps might not come to Britain. Troops were at sea, bound for Narvik from the Clyde and from Scapa Flow. Half a battalion of Scots Guards were in the cruiser *Southampton* and the rest of that Brigade plus another one as well were following in five troopships. If a landing was successful, the Torps might elect to stay; Claus almost certainly would.

All that news had come from the destroyer COs last night. And various other bits of information – such as the cruiser *Penelope* having been sent to find a German tanker reported to be in a fjord fifty miles south of Narvik: there'd been no tanker though, and *Penelope* had hit a rock. Nick wondered if that tanker might have been *Tonning*, missed by *Penelope* because it had moved down to Namsenfjord. It seemed quite likely.

Gunfire ahead. A long way off, though, and drifting smoke was combining with mist patches to blind them. There was also *Warspite*'s lumbering bulk ahead. Nick reached for the director telephone and asked Henry Brocklehurst, 'Can you see anything?'

'Three or possibly four Hun destroyers, sir – fighting a rear-guard action by the looks of it, withdrawing towards Narvik. The Tribals and I think it's *Hero* and *Forester* are engaging them. But we've got snow falling up there now and it isn't helping much.'

The Germans couldn't withdraw very far. The fjords behind them were dead-ends. According to what had been said last night there were supposed to be two cruisers somewhere about, and if that was so the destroyers might be falling back to join them. On the other hand *Warspite*'s Swordfish hadn't seen any cruisers or it would have reported them.

222

Chandler said, 'Seems we aren't getting much of a look in, sir.'

The comment, in one's present state of frustration, was infuriating. Nick forced himself to answer equably. He said, 'Things will probably open out presently.'

'But if we're bound to stay astern of the flagship, sir—'

'For the time being, pilot. Not necessarily for ever.'

Those *were* the orders. *Intent* was, so to speak, watching the admiral's back for him. And you couldn't blame him if he felt a bit nervous in taking a 31,000-ton battleship up this narrow waterway, if he took all reasonable steps to protect her. One wouldn't blame him in the least – if he hadn't picked on *Intent* . . .

They'd slipped out of Rodsundet with the oiler just after two-thirty yesterday morning. *Tonning*'s best speed had turned out to be twelve knots, not fourteen, but by six-thirty with fifty miles behind them he'd reckoned he was well enough clear to break wireless silence, and he'd sent for the doctor, Bywater, to come up to the bridge. Nick had been on his high seat in the port for'ard corner, with Chandler at the binnacle and young Cox as assistant OOW. *Intent* had been steering NNE at twelve knots, driving through a low swell and with a light north-west wind on the bow to throw a little spray now and then across the foc's'l, and the oiler ploughing along two cables' lengths astern. Sklinna light-tower had been a pimple on the horizon just abaft the beam to starboard. There'd been no interference, no Stukas coming after them. The cloud-cover would have helped, of course, but he'd been half expecting air activity: the Altbotn destroyer could have got some kind of alarm call out and this had been a weakness in his plan for which he'd had no remedy. The only hope had been that the Altbotn captain might not have guessed at the involvement of a British destroyer: he'd been hit from *Valkyrien* and the attack could have been mounted locally by Norwegians. He couldn't have known until much later, when survivors or men released from the tanker came ashore, what had happened to his two flotilla mates.

Bywater had saluted. 'Morning, sir.'

'Ah, doctor. How are your patients?'

'Dobbs is very happy to have company, sir. He's mending well. To be honest, I think I must have taken too gloomy a view of his chances in the first place. I mean if he'd been as badly damaged as I thought he *would* have died.'

'Better an error that way than the other.'

'I suppose so, sir . . . Surtees will be all right. I took a lump of metal out of his thigh – and he's complaining it hurts now and didn't before I got at him. It's a clean wound, though, there shouldn't be any problems.'

'Good. Now I've got some *real* work for you.' Nick handed him a signal which he'd been drafting. 'Read it out, would you, so we can see if it makes sense.'

Chandler came closer to hear it. Cox too. Bywater cleared his throat, and read: 'To Commander-in-Chief, repeated Vice-Admiral Battlecruiser Squadron and Admiralty. From *Intent*.'

That alone would be enough to create a sensation. *Intent* was supposed to have been sunk four days ago. Bywater read on:

'*In position 65 degrees 22' north 11 degrees 36' east course 020 speed 12 escorting captured oiler Tonning, 14,000 tons, with prize crew of Norwegian naval reservists under Lieutenant-Commander Torp Royal Norwegian Naval Reserve and four Royal Navy ratings under Sub-Lieutenant Lyte RN as guard on prisoners. Tonning has 8,000 tons marine diesel remaining and is flying White Ensign. Two German Beitzen-class destroyers torpedoed and sunk 0100/12 in Rodsundet 64 degrees 36' north 11 degrees 16' east where oiler was taken simultaneously by boarding. Also one destroyer and one U-boat immobilised by depthcharges in Altbotn position 63 degrees 35' north 11 degrees 13' east, the charges being dropped from former Norwegian sail-training yacht Valkyrien commanded by Lt.-Cdr. Torp. Submit air attack on Altbotn would complete destruction of the two damaged vessels. Intent has six torpedoes and 90 per cent ammunition remaining and is now fully operational. Regret have been unable to communicate while in Namsenfjord repairing action damage sustained dawn 8 April. Repairs effected under supervision of Norwegian engineer from Valkyrien. Consider Gauntlet to have been sunk in same action but have no certain knowledge owing to total loss of visibility when about to attack Hipper with torpedoes. Gauntlet had rammed enemy and was in sinking condition. Own casualties 8 April one ERA wounded, all other ERAs and Commissioned Engineer and two stokers killed. In Altbotn action this morning one torpedoman was wounded. Both wounded men's condition is satisfactory. Time of origin 0630 GMT/12.*'

Bywater finished reading. Chandler said, 'That's one hell of a signal, sir.'

Nick thought so too. He still had a sort of lurking guilt-feeling about the *Gauntlet* action but he didn't think he'd be blamed for it. Not now.

'But one thing, sir – ' Chandler's tone was hesitant – 'should there be a mention of our leaky fuel-tanks?'

'I'm not absolutely sure they *are* leaking, pilot.' He told the doctor, 'Get that into cipher, check it very carefully, then tell MacKinnon to bung it out. Mid – you can go down and lend a hand with it.'

Signals of congratulation had come in all through the forenoon. There were also orders to escort the oiler into Folla, where she was to anchor. *Intent* was to remain with her, pending receipt of further orders, and another destroyer would arrive off Hamnvik to oil and also to transfer two ERAs to *Intent* on loan. Commander Torp was requested to provide fuelling facilities to destroyers who would be requiring oil during the next twenty-four hours. Commander-in-Chief and Admiralty both sent Commander Torp congratulations on the Altbotn operation and thanks for the assistance rendered to *Intent*.

Nick had signalled his ETA in Folla as 2200/12, and passed all the messages to Claus Torp by light. He was glad that C-in-C and London had had the *nous* to recognise Torp's efforts.

In London a paymaster commander took a copy of *Intent*'s signal to Third Officer Casler in her office.

'Might this extraordinary communication be what your recently departed admiral was hoping for, Ginny?'

She took it from him. By the time she'd skimmed through it, hardly daring to believe her eyes, he'd left the room. She read the signal again more slowly, making sure that she was understanding it, that it did mean what it seemed to mean. Then she reached for the telephone and asked the Admiralty exchange to connect her with a Hampshire number which Aubrey Wishart had left with her. The telephone was answered by a woman with a strident Hampshire accent.

'Is Admiral Sir Hugh Everard there, please?'

'No, he's not. Who'd that be as wants him?'

'This is the Admiralty in London. When do you expect—'

'Why, he's *there*, where *you* are!'

'You mean he's visiting the Admiralty?'

'I'm sure that's what I said, Missus—'

'Thank you very much.'

Virginia Casler rang off, and called down to the porters' office at the main entrance. The porters were all retired naval men. Yes:

Admiral Everard had arrived half an hour ago, with an appointment in Medical.

'Thank you.' She checked her list of departmental extensions, and got through on an internal line. An SBA confirmed that Admiral Everard was there, waiting for a check-up.

'May I speak to him, please? This is Third Officer Casler calling on behalf of Rear-Admiral Wishart.'

'I'll see if he can come to the 'phone, Ma'am. May 'ave stripped off like.'

'Would that matter terribly?' There was a silence. She added, 'I must speak to him. It's very important to him.'

Now she had a wait of about a minute. Then: 'Admiral Everard here.'

'This is Third Officer Casler, sir. I was Admiral Wishart's assistant, but as I think you know he left us yesterday.'

'I do know, yes. What is it, Miss Casler?'

'He was anxious that I should contact you if there was any news of your nephew, and—'

'And you've *had* some?'

Quick, excited, suddenly a young, *strong* voice . . .

Virginia Casler swallowed, nodding. 'Yes. It's the most marvellous, *wonderful*—'

She was going to cry. Not was going to, *was* crying. She'd felt a bit emotional when she'd read the signal but now suddenly her eyes were full of it and her voice had gone peculiar. She'd had to pause, struggling for control and annoyed with herself, ashamed, but –

'You *are* telling me that my nephew is alive?'

'Yes.'

'His ship was not sunk?'

'*He*'s been doing all the sinking. He's—'

Again, it had stuck in her throat. Swallowing, trying not to weep directly into the receiver, thinking *How ridiculous* . . .

'— been doing the most incredible things, sir. I – oh, I'm sorry, I'm being silly, I—'

'I think you must be a charming and delightful young woman, Miss Casler. Very far from silly. But it might be easier if we were to meet without a telephone in the way? Perhaps after these chaps in here have finished pushing and pulling me about?'

'If you'd ring through when you're free, sir, I could bring this signal—'

'Signal from *Intent*?'

226

'Yes. If we met down at the main entrance?'

'You really are *most* kind. What extension should I ask for?'

She told him. She added, 'It's – a *fantastic* signal . . .'

She'd just managed to get those words out: then she'd fumbled the receiver into its cradle and started looking for a handkerchief. In the medical section Hugh Everard hung up too, smiling to himself. A *young* man's smile . . . He'd fairly fly through this medical now, he thought: then he'd tear down to meet this little Wren girl, who really did sound quite enchanting: and before long – incredibly – he'd be seeing Nick. Nick who might have been dead and by the grace of God was not: and who'd be bound to have quite a yarn to tell! I must not, Hugh thought, get myself sent off into the Atlantic *too* damn soon . . .

Crouch, leaning over number six tube, jerked his head towards the noise of gunfire up ahead. Banks of carved-up sea peeled away on either side. Way back, even farther back than *Intent* was, a couple of destroyers were ferreting along the coast. Crouch grumbled to CPO Shaw, the torpedo gunner's mate, 'The boats up front's 'ogging all the action. Skipper'll be spitting blood.'

Intent was making about twenty knots. *Warspite*'s maximum was twenty-four, and the other destroyers had chased on at more than thirty, so it was hardly surprising that it was distant gunfire they were hearing.

The TGM ignored Crouch's remark. He'd turned to glance up at the ensign, whip-cracking from the mizzen gaff. Joss Bartley muttered as he unwrapped a piece of chewing-gum, 'About 'ad our whack down south, ain't we?'

'Not in 'is book we ain't.' Crouch nodded in the direction of the bridge. 'Be 'alf berserk up there, I reckon. Specially now 'e's lost 'is Sheila.'

Snow swept across the fjord, and there was a lot of smoke as well as swirling fog-patches.

'Aircraft approaching astern, sir, green one-seven-oh, angle of sight two-oh!'

That yell had come from the after lookout on the starboard side. Trench had sprung over to that side of the bridge and he had his glasses trained astern. He told Nick, 'Swordfish, sir. About six – eight . . .'

From *Furious*, somewhere off Lofoten. There'd been a signal

227

that they'd be making an attack. Trench amplified, 'I think *ten* aircraft, sir. But they're in and out of mist and—'

'All right.'

Cutting him short . . . In any circumstances, *any* frame of mind, it would have been frustrating to be stuck behind the battleship while other destroyers were off the leash and doing proper destroyer work. The action seemed to be going in two directions now, north-westward towards Herjangsfjord and east to Narvik. Nick heard the roar of engines as the Stringbags flew over, heading for the harbour area. You saw them in glimpses, one or two at a time here and there as they appeared and disappeared through cloud and fog.

Warspite let loose another salvo and its thunder crashed back in echoes from the mountains. The battleship's turrets were trained to port and on the bow, but it was impossible to know what she was shooting at. A second salvo followed that one: then her guns were at rest again while ahead the intensity of destroyer gunfire thickened. The Swordfish had flown on into the murk ahead and quite possibly some of those explosions could be bomb-bursts. There'd be AA guns in it too. For the moment the snow had stopped. The director telephone squawked: Nick reached for it and Brocklehurst told him, 'One Hun's gone right up Herjangsfjord, sir, with *Eskimo* chasing him, and there's a group of three that seem to be making for Rombaksfjord.'

Nine destroyers up there making hay with them. Avenging *Hardy*, *Hunter*, *Hoste*. Only one out of ten stuck back here where there were *no* Germans. A corollary to that was that there was no danger to *Warspite* from this quarter either. Nick looked round for Herrick.

'Signalman. Make to the admiral, "Am I to remain in this station?" '

He might have forgotten he had *Intent* sitting here doing nothing when with the action going off in separate directions she could have been making herself useful. It wasn't likely but he *might* have . . . Four Swordfish, low to the water, were struggling to gain height on their way seaward. *Warspite*'s big guns flamed and roared. Brocklehurst reported, 'Enemy destroyer gunfire's slackening, sir. Almost as if they're running out of ammo.'

Herrick was clattering that message out on one of the ten-inch lamps, using a big one to beat the soupy visibility. The Germans might be short of ammunition, Nick thought. They'd have used a lot during the 2nd Flotilla's attack on the 10th, and at the end of that battle they'd also lost their ammunition ship. The one with the flames which had risen, according to the BBC, to 3,000 feet. May there have been Germans in those flames, he thought. What about *Hoste*: had *she* burnt? He wasn't sure that his informants last night hadn't known more than they'd told him. Hcrrick had passed the signal and Nick had seen *Warspite*'s flashed 'K' acknowledging it. A yeoman of signals would be taking it to the admiral now. From the north-west, Herjangsfjord, came the solid *boom* of a torpedo hit, and he guessed it would be *Eskimo* finishing off the one she'd chased up there. He had his glasses trained that way and he heard the clash of the shutter on the lamp as Herrick acknowledged receipt of the admiral's reply. It had been a very short one by the sound of it.

'Sir?' He looked round at the killick. Herrick told him unhappily, 'From the admiral, sir – "Yes".'

Bloody hell . . .

'Director – bridge!'

He answered the telephone. Brocklehurst told him, 'One Tribal has been badly hit in Rombaksfjord, sir. Stopped and on fire.'

Nothing *Intent* could help with. *Intent* was wet-nurse to a battleship which was here to look for a cruiser – *two* cruisers – which almost certainly were not in these fjords. The Germans never did leave their ships in positions where they'd be vulnerable to attack if they could help it, and it was a fair bet that any cruisers they'd had up here – *if* they'd had any – would be back in German ports by now.

Director telephone again: 'There's another destroyer, one we haven't seen before, just coming out of Narvik harbour, sir.'

Following *Warspite*, *Intent* was circling to starboard, leaving Narvik off to port. The battleship's guns, trained that way, spurted flame and smoke: swallowing to clear his ears from the concussion, Nick saw three – then four – now *six* destroyers racing towards the newly-emerged enemy. All had their guns firing and the German was surrounded by shell-spouts. And now hits: bursts that blossomed into fires and spread, smoke growing to obscure her . . . *Warspite*'s guns were quiet again as *Intent* obediently fell into place astern of her. Back near the harbour entrance that German destroyer had rolled over, hung for a half-minute on her side then completed the roll and sank. There was only smoke there now, and the British ships circling off to port and starboard like wheeling cavalry. Beyond, on the shoreline and the harbour's fringes, shell-bursts had stained the snow in yellow blotches. *Warspite*'s course was now south-west, and Nick guessed they were going to take a look into the mouth of Skjomenfjord for the mythical cruisers. Glancing back over his ship's port quarter he saw *Cossack* plastered under a sudden deluge of German shellfire. Guns from inside the harbour: range point-blank as *Cossack* had nosed up into the narrow entrance.

Warspite was going about again, probably to use her crushing fire-power on that shore battery. *Eskimo* had come tearing out of Herjangsfjord and she was turning in towards Rombaksfjord where enemy ships had run for shelter. They wouldn't find much: *Hero*, *Forester*, *Bedouin* and *Icarus* were dashing in after *Eskimo*. Like a pack of terriers darting around and routing out their quarry. *Warspite* had already reversed her course, and Nick had to let her pass on her way back towards the harbour before he could put his own helm over to turn astern of her.

Shell-spouts out of nowhere rose in a tight group on *Intent*'s bow. The splashes lifted, hung, then disintegrated into a foul-smelling rain which lashed across the bridge as she steamed through the place where the shells had fallen.

'Destroyer red three-five!'

The German had appeared from behind the cover of the point: she'd been hiding in that southern fjord.

'All guns follow director!'

Clang of the fire-gongs: crash of the four-sevens . . .

If *Warspite* hadn't gone about when she had, the enemy destroyer would have been well placed for a torpedo attack on her.

'Port twenty.'

'Port twenty, sir!'

Another salvo ripping over, *down* . . . Close again. Near-misses like kicks in the ship's ribs as they thumped down and burst and the splashes sprang, one just clear of the quarter but the others abreast the for'ard tubes and collapsing across the iron deck as the ship swung around. Brocklehurst, with work to do at last, had his guns shooting fast and accurately: his first salvo had gone over but the second lot had hit, a splash of red flame on the side of the German's bridge and others amidships around his funnels as he too swung away under helm. As *Intent* turned, heeling hard to starboard, 'X' and 'Y' guns were out of the fight only for a few seconds.

Hugh Everard had saved *Warspite*'s bacon for her at Jutland.

Nick said into the voicepipe, 'Midships.' Odd, to think of that. She'd had a couple of very expensive face-lifts since then, of course.

'Torpedoes approaching starboard bow!'

Quickly down to the pipe again: 'Port twenty-five.'

'Port twenty-five, sir!'

It was the quickest way to get her round because she'd still been swinging. The fish coming at her now would have been intended for the admiral: hence the German's own turn to starboard. They were no danger at all to *Warspite*: *Intent*, in turning to engage and close the enemy, had put herself right in front of them.

'A' and 'B' guns were silent now, unable to bear as the ship swung her stern towards the enemy and his torpedoes.

'Midships.'

'Midships, sir.' 'X' and 'Y' were still banging away. Cox was aft there, doing Lyte's job. Nick called down to Jarratt, 'Meet her.'

'Torpedo passing to port, sir!'

And another track to starboard: the lookouts on that side reported it. *Intent* had combed the tracks quite neatly. Nick stooped and called down, 'Starboard fifteen.' After guns still in action: he'd get 'A' and 'B' back into it now. The German was circling right around, probably trying to get back into that side fjord. The admiral could hardly expect *Intent* to paddle along astern of him like some bloody duck and let the bastard go . . .

Warspite let rip. Hearing the crashing thunder of it Nick looked that way and saw her turrets trained to starboard as she muscled in on *his* German . . .

She'd hit him. Smothering, annihilating. The destroyer exploded upwards in a gush of flame, smoke, escaping steam. Then all smoke, blackness with fire that shot through it like moving scarlet threads. When it cleared there was only litter on the surface.

'Midships. Port fifteen.'

'Port fifteen, sir . . .'

'Three hundred revolutions.' He needed a few extra knots, to get back into station on that floating fortress. There'd been flashing, some signal coming over. A reprimand for having left his station?

'Fifteen of port wheel on, sir!'

Leading Signalman Herrick reported, 'From the admiral, sir – "thank you."'

'What the hell for?'

Chandler suggested, 'For getting between him and that German, sir?'

231

Nick didn't even glance at him. He bent to the voicepipe: 'Midships.' *Warspite* had already been well clear, not in any danger. He was angry, pent-up, feeling the tension like a taut wire in his brain, and knowing at the same time that this *Hoste* business was his own problem, one that he had to face up to on his own, not vent in bad temper on other people. He nodded to Pete Chandler. 'You may be right.'

There was one good thing. After those near-misses he could now discover that his ship had leaking fuel-tanks.

6.30 pm: withdrawing, and still playing follow-my-leader behind the flagship. Steaming westward at twenty-knots. In the fjords of northern Norway, not one German ship had been left afloat. Four lay shattered on the top end of Rombaksfjord, one in Herjangsfjord, one off the harbour and one inside it, another in Djupvik Bay. Considering the odds they'd faced, the Germans had put up a good fight. Three British destroyers had been damaged. One of them, *Cossack*, was aground but would be refloated before long: her wounded had been transferred to *Warspite*.

The troops which were supposed to be on their way should have been here *now*. German troops were pulling out: you could see them, dark snake-like columns winding away across the snow-slopes.

Broad on the port bow as the ships moved westward towards the narrows, in an estuary which had Ballangen village at its head, an 'H' or 'I' class destroyer lay close inshore with boats moving between her and the beach. Trench muttered with his glasses on her, 'Taking men off shore, sir. I wonder –' he glanced round quickly as he thought of it – 'could be survivors from *Hardy* and—'

'It's – possible.'

The thought had hit him, explosively, just before it had occurred to Trench. But then a second thought: that there was nothing he could do about it. He'd made one submission in the matter of having to hang around the flagship, and he'd been snubbed for his pains: he didn't want to try again and have it thought he was behaving like a *prima donna*, trading on his successes. Besides – personal anxieties were – well, *that* – personal, and private.

Fear now, as well as anxiety. He'd been left in doubt too long. '*Warspite*'s flashing!'

Chandler had bawled it, but Herrick was ahead of him and the lamp had clashed before the navigator had shut his mouth. The first word of the message was 'Proceed' . . . Release, then, finally? Nick put his glasses up, focusing on the destroyer inshore, in that southern inlet. A lot of men were being brought off. Boatloads of them. He couldn't identify the destroyer.

Trench had begun to read out the message as the dots and dashes came rippling from *Warspite*'s signal bridge and Herrick acknowledged each completed word with a single flash.

'Proceed – Ballangen – and – join – *Ivanhoe* – embarking – survivors – ex – *Hardy* – *Hoste* – also – merchant – navy – personnel – for – transfer – to – oiler – *Tonning* – stop – You – may – recruit – engineroom – personnel – as – available – and – requisite.'

He'd read the last part of it for himself, and as it ended he was ready at the voicepipe. 'Three-five-oh revolutions!'

'Three-five-oh revolutions, sir!'

'Port fifteen.'

'Port fifteen, sir. Three-five-oh revolutions passed and repeated, sir. Fifteen of port wheel on!'

Turbine-whine rising as the speed built up and *Intent* surged forward: bow-wave lifting, lengthening as she swung away south-westward, pitching out across the battleship's rolling, outspreading wake. Something joyous in that motion and the thrust of speed – as if it came as a relief to the ship herself . . . Nick called to Trench, 'Scrambling nets both sides, Number One. And call away boats' crews.'

One dinghy and one purloined skiff.

'Aye aye, sir. Bosun's mate—'

'Midships.'

'Midships, sir!'

He checked the compass, and told Jarratt, 'Steer two-two-oh.' Then he raised his glasses again to study that activity inshore. He warned himself, in dread of what was coming now, *Don't count your chickens* . . .

The air was like frozen steel, but he'd begun to sweat. For the first time in twenty years he was aware of being truly, deeply frightened.

POSTSCRIPT

The episode of *Gauntlet* ramming a German heavy cruiser is based on *Glowworm*'s single-handed action against *Hipper* at the same place and time. *Glowworm* was, of course, alone and the circumstances were entirely different. Thirty-five of her ship's company survived and were picked up by *Hipper*, but her captain, Lieutenant-Commander G. B. Roope RN, was not one of them. He was later awarded a posthumous VC. The same decoration was awarded, also posthumously, to Captain B. A. W. Warburton-Lee, who led the 2nd Flotilla's attack on Narvik on 10 April.

LAST LIFT FROM CRETE

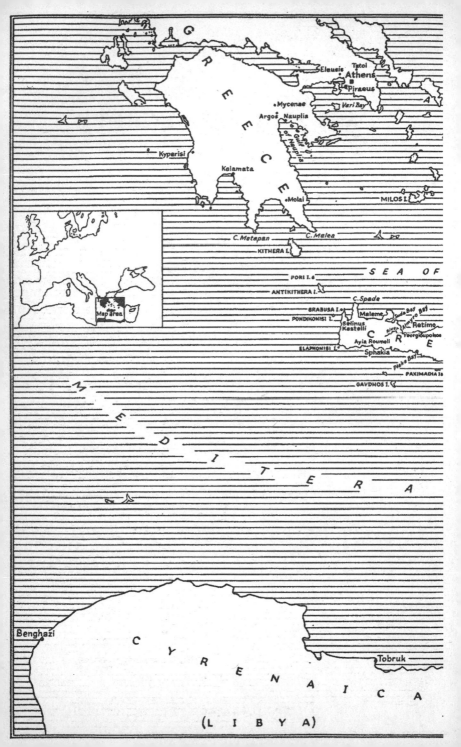

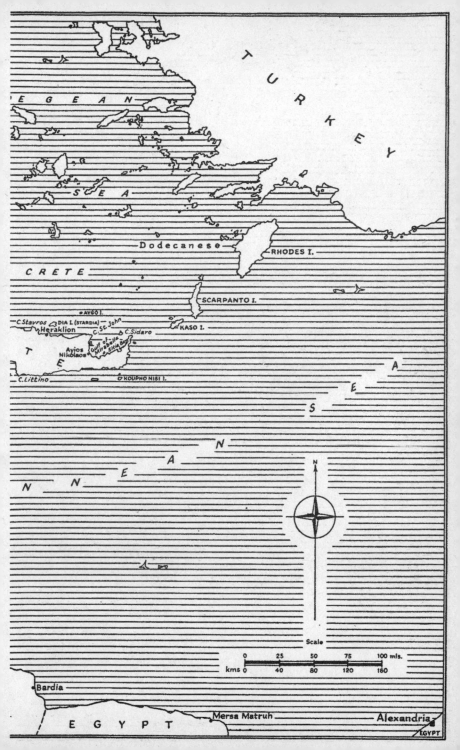

CHAPTER 1

A dark shape looming up ahead with the quarter-moon behind it
was the rearmost enemy, tail-end Charlie of a convoy of transports
almost at its destination and stupidly relaxed, feeling safe, waddling like a brood of ducks into the shelter of the land and keeping,
Nick Everard deduced, a bloody awful look-out. *Tuareg*'s turbines
thrummed in the quiet Mediterranean night, her ventilator fans
hoarsely sucking the cool air, her steel's vibration like the tremble
of excitement in a thoroughbred as she stemmed white-swirled sea
in *Blackfoot*'s wake. Astern, *Masai* and *Afghan* followed, and in all
four ships tin-hatted guns' crews and torpedomen stood by their
weapons. The British destroyers had come down from the north,
found the convoy exactly where they'd expected it to be and
sheered away to starboard to come up on it from astern with
the moon where it would be most useful – as it was now, throwing
the enemy ships into silhouette. At that first sighting, when the
flotilla of Tribals had turned away westward, the Italian escort
commander should have seen them: having failed to, he'd sealed his
convoy's fate.

His own, too, with any luck. *Tuareg*'s captain, Commander Sir
Nicholas Everard, Bart., DSO, DSC*, RN, felt almost sorry for
him. Almost: and if there'd been time for sympathy . . . Rocky
Pratt, the destroyer's navigating officer, reported quietly, '*Blackfoot*'s altering to port, sir.'

Nick swung his glasses to the flotilla leader, saw her low stern
sliding to the right, pushing round the mound of white wake
seemingly glued to it. And from the director control tower's
voicepipe another report came now: Harry Houston's emotionless
tones informing him, 'Two escorts in sight to port of the convoy,
sir.'

From the level of this bridge the Italian destroyers were not yet visible, but they'd have been spotted from *Blackfoot* half a minute ago and they'd be the reason for her swing to port. Nick stooped to the wheelhouse voicepipe: 'Port ten.' Bringing his ship round in *Blackfoot*'s track. There were supposed to be three escorts shepherding this convoy – according to the report from a Fleet Air Arm reconnaissance flight – and as two of them were on the convoy's seaward side you could reasonably assume that the third, most likely the senior man, would be up front. He told the helmsman – CPO Habgood, *Tuareg*'s coxswain and senior rating – 'Midships and meet her.'

'Midships and meet her, sir. Wheel's amidships . . . Ten o' starboard—'

'Steady!'

'Steady, sir. Oh-eight-three.'

'Steer that.' His voice and the coxswain's were both low, echoey in the metal tube, backed by the hum of the ventilator fans and engine noise, the ship's vibration and the constant underlying rush of sea along her sides. He could see two of the transports quite clearly now as *Blackfoot* overhauled them and *Tuareg* followed her: farther ahead, up-moon, a less distinct huddle of blackness would be the other three. Five transports, the Walrus recce report had said: they'd been much farther west then, having crossed the Sicilian narrows and then hugged the coast around the Gulf of Sirte, and they'd be deep-laded with troops, weapons, ammunition and stores for Rommel's eastward drive. Those stupid bastards *must* be blind . . . The night air was cool with a hint of land-smell in it, the sweetish tang of the desert littoral. He told Houston through the voicepipe to the director, 'Your first target is the nearest transport. Open fire when *Blackfoot* does. As we move up, shift to the next without waiting for my orders.'

'Aye aye, sir.'

'Be ready with torpedoes either side, Sub.'

'Standing by, sir.' That was Ashcourt, the RN sub-lieutenant, at the torpedo control panel. It probably hadn't been necessary to tell him he'd need to be looking both ways at once: the reminder had been precautionary, a warning to a young officer who hadn't seen all that much action yet – except against the Stukas, which was a different thing altogether – against becoming mesmerized by whatever might be happening in one particular direction . . . It was extraordinary how familiar and how   could the word be 'pleasurable'? – was this tension that bound them all, the silent

240

ultra-tense expectancy, the careful hold on pre-action nerves. There was a thrill in it, a sense of arrival after long preparation, interminable waiting; he thought, his mind going back to take in another war as well as the first eighteen months of this one, *It was always like this, probably always will be* . . . The flash and thunder of *Blackfoot*'s guns came as a relief and brought a reek of cordite flying back over his own bridge: *Blackfoot* had engaged the Italian destroyer over her own port bow and *Tuareg*'s guns flamed and roared now, one half-second later, to starboard, blinding light giving a photo-flash view of the ship's side and the smoking out-trained barrels of the twin four-sevens, then darkness utterly black for about a second before the salvo struck below the transport's bridge and in her waist. The guns had fired again and the pompoms were in it now, raking the already blazing ship with their streams of two-pounder shells. Explosions on her stern would be shellbursts from *Afghan* or *Masai* or both: there was a constant din of firing and *Tuareg*'s four-sevens had shifted their point of aim to the target's side, the waterline, while on her waist-deck you could see motor transport, jeep-like trucks, burning fiercely. There'd be some petrol there perhaps, to help things along. Glancing away to port Nick saw the Italian destroyer stopped and on fire, *Blackfoot* leaving her and engaging a new target somewhere ahead; he yelled up to Houston, 'Shift to the next transport, don't waste time on that escort.' And into the other pipe, 'Steer five degrees to starboard.' He told Ashcourt, 'Enemy destroyer on red three-five. One fish into her' – *Tuareg*'s guns fired, and he paused fractionally until he could almost hear his own voice again – 'as we pass, Sub.'

'Aye aye, sir!'

'Three-six-oh revolutions.'

'Three-six-oh revs, sir!'

Ahead, it looked as if *Blackfoot* was now in action with *two* Italians: Reggie Marsh, Captain (D), might be in need of some assistance. Three-six-oh revs would give *Tuareg* thirty-four knots, about her maximum, even if she wouldn't have time in covering that short gap of sea to work up to such a speed. The second transport was burning: she'd swung away to starboard and Houston was pumping shells into her stern as they swept past her, vibration worse and noise increasing as revs built up: and now he'd shifted target to the next ship, the third in the line. Way back astern, tail-end Charlie was a blazing wreck, a firework display as minor explosions shook her apart. The burning and immobile destroyer was coming up to port and about to be given its come-uppance. *Tuareg*'s guns were hard at it, with a fast rhythm to the firing now, pompoms just as busy and very noisy and the point-fives rattling away as well, arcing tracer traversing a seascape lit by gun-flashes, shellbursts, burning ships. Dramatic, even beautiful, if you'd an eye for this sort of thing and time to take it in. Ashcourt had reported, 'One torpedo fired to port, sir.' Another salvo crashed out, guns trained abaft the beam now as they moved up to join the flotilla leader, leaving three ships now well on fire. Nick told Houston, 'Shift target. Two enemy destroyers engaging *Blackfoot* ahead of us. Take the nearest.' *Masai* and *Afghan* would be pushing on to round up the rest of the convoy: the ones astern could be finished off later if they were still afloat, but those which hadn't yet been attended to had – predictably – turned away to starboard, running for the beach. They wouldn't get there. Explosion to port: a vertical column of black water illuminated by the Italian destroyer's fires. Ashcourt exultant: 'That fish hit, sir!' There'd have been answers called for if it hadn't. But *Blackfoot* had been hit too: Nick had had his glasses on her and seen a shell burst abreast her for'ard funnel: then *Tuareg*'s A and B guns fired, at the nearer of the two Italian destroyers. It was coming *this* way, with *its* for'ard guns spurting flame: shells scrunched whistling overhead and some of *Tuareg*'s burst shatteringly in the forefront of the Italian's bridge. He was swinging away to starboard, turning very slowly – for lack of steerage way, Nick thought. More hits blossoming amidships and one of his boats ablaze in its davits lighting his upperworks in flaring yellow. A shell clanged off *Tuareg*'s foc's'l, hurtled away without exploding, and X and Y guns were in action now, trained about as far for'ard as they'd go, and the pompoms opening up again as well. Nick had been concerned not to expose his beam to enemy torpedoes, but the Italian's bridge was all flame now and the fires were spreading aft very quickly as he turned into the north-west wind; only one of his after guns was firing. Nick told Ashcourt, 'I'm going to turn hard a-starboard. Give him one fish when your sight comes on.'

'Aye aye, sir!'

Into the wheelhouse voicepipe: 'Starboard—'

That last salvo from the four-sevens hit the Italian amidships, all four shells close together. With his face lowered to the voicepipe Nick saw, under the rim of his tin hat, the flash of one shell bursting on the torpedo tubes and then the eruption from inside as the others penetrated and exploded in the boiler-room. Deep, thunderous explosion: no flames, only a dark mushrooming cloud of smoke or steam or both billowing up, enfolding. From the outer pipe he heard Houston's flatly-spoken order to the guns, 'Cease firing.' He finished his own order to the coxswain in an amended form: 'Starboard ten. Two hundred revolutions.'

'Starboard ten, sir. Two hundred—'

'Belay that last order, Sub.' No need for a torpedo now. *Blackfoot*'s other opponent was done for, too: the Italian's stern was awash, bridge smashed, guns silent, flames dancing here and there. The sea would soon drown those flames. The flotilla leader was turning away, about fifteen hundred yards north-east of *Tuareg*, turning towards the continuing action eastward, inshore. Benghazi lay north-east and about six miles away: eastward there'd be about four miles of sea with deep water right up to the coast. Benghazi had been in British hands until only about a month ago: Wavell had flung the Italians out of it early in February, lost it to the new German drive two months later. The Germans were outside Tobruk now. Nick had his glasses on *Blackfoot* and he couldn't see anything wrong with her, any damage from that hit.

'Midships. Steer one-two-oh.'

The guns' crew were cheering, for some reason.

'Midships, sir. Wheel's amidships, sir. Two hundred revolutions passed and repeated.'

'Our joker's sunk, sir.'

Rocky Pratt was referring to the destroyer they'd been engaging, the one whose boilers had gone up: that explosion would almost certainly have blown her sides out too. Anyway, she'd disappeared, and it would account for those cheers from the gundecks. CPO Habgood's voice floated from the tube: 'Course one-two-oh, sir.'

Nick had his glasses on the transport which had been third from the rear – the centre ship of the convoy, in fact – and was now alone, with the first two burning and sinking a long way astern of her. This one's fires seemed to be dying down: she'd had less attention given to her, probably, because there'd been some urgency to push on quickly and prevent the escape of the other two. He saw now, as he inspected her through the binoculars, that she was getting under way, a white bow-wave seeming to flicker in the dark as she began to move ahead.

'Starboard fifteen. Three-six-oh revolutions.' Straightening from the voicepipe, hearing his coxswain's repetition of those orders, he saw that *Blackfoot* was calling him up by light. Beyond her, gunfire and the flashes of shellbursts still broke the darkness. The moon was hidden at this moment: he heard the turbines' rising note, the slap of sea against his ship's side as she swung.

'Signalman?'

'Aye, sir!' A flash from the port-side Aldis proved that *Tuareg*'s V/S department weren't asleep. Nick called down to Habgood, 'Midships and meet her,' and transferred quickly to the other voicepipe. 'Bridge, director!' Houston answered, 'Director,' and he told him, 'Target that steamer ahead of us. When we're closer I'll come round to port.'

'I'll engage with A and B now, sir.'

A and B were the two for'ard mountings; turning would allow the after ones, X and Y, to bear as well. From *Masai*'s and *Afghan*'s area of operations the deep *crump* of an explosion and a single leap of flame was probably a torpedo ending one Italian's bid to escape – or to put his cargo on the beach where at least some of it might have been salvaged by the Wehrmacht.

'Steady as you go, cox'n. One-four-oh revolutions.'

No need for high speed now: one-four-oh would produce about twelve knots. He heard the fire-gongs clang, down for'ard, a split second before the guns flamed and split his eardrums – that was how it felt – and in the ensuing, ringing silence before the shells smashed into their target, Yeoman Whiffen reported, 'From Captain (D), sir, *Your last bird was only winged, I see.*'

The explosion was magnificent. A great shoot of fire, vertical at first but starring outwards: orange and yellow with a shade of green – a delicate, Chartreuse tint – in its centre. Black objects hurtling skyward, disappearing as they passed out of the multi-coloured circle of illumination, reappearing in the form of splashes, some of them very large: that was a cargo of ammunition going up, ammunition that would *not* be thrown at Wavell's army. He saw a truck airborne, silhouetted against a sheet of copper-coloured fire: it seemed to rise slowly, turning end-for-end, and then begin to fall just as gradually, as if it wanted to stay up but couldn't quite make the effort: it fell into a bed of black smoke that was swelling now with the central fire contracting to an orange core inside it.

He ducked to the voicepipe: 'Port twenty.' Then to Houston in the tower, 'You hit the jackpot that time.' He didn't hear the ex-bank official's answer, only Petty Officer Whiffen's question, 'Any reply to Captain (D), sir?'

Burning or burnt-out wrecks: sea loppy, broken up by the wind and patched with moonlight where it leaked through scudding clouds. There was one point of burning inshore but no gunfire now; the entire convoy must have been accounted for, and the flotilla would shortly be re-forming. There'd be time, possibly, to scout around for survivors.

Nick told the yeoman, 'No. No reply.' That column of flame had been as much answer as Reggie Marsh could need. Marsh had been a fool of a man when Nick had been his senior – *and* had had to kick his arse for him, more than once – back in 1929; and he was still – Nick suspected, privately – not exactly bright . . . But there were other things to think about, here and now – such as the fact that picking up survivors mightn't be all that easy. *Tuareg* had one of her two motorboats left, and its engine wasn't reliable; the other motorboat, the whaler and the dinghy had been lost or smashed during the last fortnight while the Mediterranean Fleet had been struggling to get an army off the beaches of southern Greece. The other ships in this flotilla were about as badly off: *Afghan* didn't have a boat at all. There'd be replacements to be had from the dockyard in Alexandria, presumably, but this flotilla had come directly from Suda Bay in Crete and the odds were they'd be going straight back there now, to help in the final stages of the Greek evacuation. It wasn't anything to look forward to.

'From Captain (D), sir, *Order One, executive*.'

'Right.' Bending to the wheelhouse pipe, he ordered, 'Midships the wheel.' Straightening, hearing CPO Habgood's acknowledgement, he focused his glasses on *Blackfoot*, to estimate her speed: 'Order One' meant line-ahead, and he had to take *Tuareg* into station astern of her. Re-forming, and *not* bothering to look for survivors? It had been a clean sweep, anyway: five transports and three escorts reported, five plus three destroyed.

'Steer one-two-five.'

'One-two-five, sir!'

He didn't see how the army, now it had been pushed out of Greece, was going to hold on in Crete. That was the intention now, but he couldn't see it happening. Since the beginning of this year – it was May now, actually May Day of 1941, and had been for the last hour or so – since January the Luftwaffe had been building up its strength in the Mediterranean. *Fliegercorps* X had come first, moving into Sicily to put the heat on Malta: and now *Fliegercorps* VIII was operating in Greece and over the Aegean, commanded –

according to the last WIR, War Intelligence Report, by a man called von Richthofen, cousin to the fighter ace of the '14–'18 war. He had nearly a thousand front-line aircraft in his command, and from this flotilla's recent experience you could reckon about half of them were dive-bombers. How many aircraft did we have in Crete now, Nick wondered; a dozen?

'Three hundred revolutions. Steer five degrees to starboard.'

Blackfoot's shaded lamp was passing a message to *Afghan* and *Masai*: you saw only a faint blue leak of its radiance, from this angle. Telling them to rejoin, re-form, probably. One transport was still burning, so far inshore that it might be on the beach, he thought; the absence of other fires suggested that all the other targets had been sunk. It felt good, made a welcome change, to have dished out some punishment, after weeks of being on the receiving end, giving the Stukas and Ju88s target practice . . . Sheer exhaustion was a major problem for both men and ships: they'd spent March putting the army into Greece, and now April taking it out again: and at the same time there'd been this immensely long desert coast to look after, and Malta to be fed and the Italian fleet to be contained – plus a few lesser tasks.

'Sub – tell the first lieutenant I'd like a word.'

'Aye aye, sir.' Ashcourt could pass the message aft over his torpedo-control telephone. Tony Dalgleish, *Tuareg*'s second-in-command, had a roving commission at action stations but his base was the after control position on the searchlight platform. In less than a minute he'd arrived in the bridge.

'Nice party that, sir.'

'Nothing came near us, did it?'

'One scratch on the foc'sl where a dud bounced off. Nothing else. It's put new heart into the lads, sir. Could you hear them cheering?'

With extra sweaters under his duffel-coat as well as the regulation Mae West, Dalgleish looked about twice his normal size. He was a lieutenant-commander, young-seeming for the rank: dry-mannered, self-contained. Nick said, 'We seem to be re-forming. I don't know if we'll be looking for survivors or not, but you'd better be ready for it anyway. Motorboat, scrambling nets, lines, and warn Gallwey. I shan't use the boat unless we have to.'

It might be necessary. Wounded men couldn't be expected to climb nets or ladders.

'Doc's all set up for it, sir.' Surgeon-Lieutenant Gallwey,

RNVR, was the doctor. Dalgleish asked, 'Will we be going back to Suda, d'you expect?'

Nick called down, 'One-eight-oh revolutions. Follow *Blackfoot* now, cox'n.' *Tuareg* was sliding up into station on the flotilla leader. Straightening from the pipe, he said, 'We might be sent to Alex. After all, tonight's the last of the pick-ups, or supposed to be.' The last troop-lifts off Greek beaches, he meant: according to the signals, and reading between the lines of some of them, you could guess that any soldiers they didn't get out tonight wouldn't get out at all. Pratt called from the front of the bridge, '*Masai* and *Afghan* red one-oh, sir, rejoining.' And *Blackfoot* had begun to flash again, in *this* direction. Dalgleish muttered, 'I'll go down and—'

'Wait. See what this is about.'

If he was in Reggie Marsh's shoes, Nick thought, he wouldn't hang around looking for survivors. Not only because of the lack of boats – which really wasn't much of an excuse – but more because they were on an enemy-held coast with enemy-occupied airfields, and the priority must be to get as far offshore as possible before daylight brought the bombers over. Not to mention the even closer danger of E-boats, which by now the enemy might have brought up to Benghazi.

'From Captain (D), *Nine blue*, sir.'

'Nine blue' meant 'alter course in succession ninety degrees to port'. In other words *Blackfoot* would shortly turn left and wanted *Tuareg* to follow in her wake. The other two would then be roughly on the starboard beam and they'd steer across to tag on in line astern.

'Executive signal, sir!'

'Very good.' And he could see the leader turning: the sudden heel of that slim, black shape, the sharp elbow in the white wake. He bent to the pipe: 'Steady as you go.'

Cancelling his last order, which had been for the coxswain to follow the ship ahead . . . The new course would be oh-four-oh. It could be either for a straight dash across the Mediterranean to the Antikithera Channel and into the Aegean, or a course to round the bulge of Cyrenaica and then head east for Alexandria. He heard a telephone buzz in the front of the bridge: Rocky Pratt began to back out of the chart alcove but PO Whiffen was there ahead of him, snatching the phone off its hook.

'Repeat that last bit?'

Whiffen had edged into his own hooded table's light, with the phone at his ear, reaching inside the canvas flap to scribble on a signal pad. Nick, watching *Blackfoot*'s wake, called down, 'Port fifteen.'

'Port fifteen, sir!'

Whiffen called, 'Signal from D.37 to C-in-C, sir, reporting convoy and escorts destroyed, flotilla withdrawing north-east-ward. Then reply, C-in-C to D.37, *Well done. Proceed to rendezvous with First Battle Squadron noon May 1 in position 180 Cape Littino 25*. Time of Origin—'

'All right, Yeoman.'

Cape Littino was on the south coast of Crete, about halfway along.

'Fifteen of port wheel on, sir!'

Watching the turn, Nick thought about that signal – which would have been received in cipher and translated into plain language in the plot, one level below this bridge and adjoining the signals office, by young Chalk, the RNVR sub-lieutenant . . .

'Midships.' He straightened again: 'How is a course of oh-four-oh for that rendezvous position, pilot?' Ducking back to the pipe: 'Meet her!'

'Meet her, sir!'

'Follow *Blackfoot*.' Pratt answered that last question: 'Need to come round to about oh-six-four when we're round the bulge, sir.'

'Distance?'

'Two-eighty miles, sir.'

With about ten hours in hand, it would mean making good twenty-eight knots all the way. Hard on fuel consumption; but they'd be able to replenish from the big ships when they reached them – or from the oiler in Suda Bay, if it had got there, replacing the one that had been sunk a few days ago . . . First Battle Squadron consisted of the battleships *Barham* and *Valiant* with the aircraft carrier *Formidable* and a bunch of escorting destroyers, all under Rear-Admiral Rawlings. They were up there first to provide cover for a big convoy that was being run from Suda Bay to Alexandria, and then to support, in case of interference by Italian surface ships, the last three lifts of troops from Greece.

'From Captain (D), sir – *Speed three zero, executive.*'

He called down, 'Three-one-zero revolutions.' Then he asked Pratt, 'Remind me, pilot, would you – there's the Suda convoy going to Alex, but what are the three Greek pick-ups?'

'Well, *Hotspur* and *Havock* are collecting a load from Milos, sir, and *Hero* with *Isis* and *Kimberley* are fetching some from Kalamata. The other's – well, you know, *Carnarvon* and—'

'Yes. Thank you.' He certainly did know about *Carnarvon*'s trip. She was a light AA cruiser and a new arrival on this station, up through Suez from the Red Sea, and his own young half-brother, Jack Everard, was serving in her. Being fresh, in good order compared to most of the Mediterranean ships, she and the destroyers *Highflier* and *Halberdier* had been given the trickiest of the final troop-lifting jobs to do: right up at Nauplia, where the last lift was supposed to have been the one two nights ago, to bring out a rearguard battalion of New Zealanders.

Dalgleish murmured, 'We aren't looking for swimmers, I don't think.'

'No. Sorry, Number One.' He'd forgotten he'd told him to wait. And leaving men in the water wasn't a *happy* necessity: it just did happen to be a necessity sometimes. At least one didn't turn machine-guns on them, as the Luftwaffe did. He told his first lieutenant, 'Soon as we're off the coast a bit, one watch can get their heads down. Say in half an hour.'

They'd sleep at their action stations, while the other half of the ship's company stayed awake. Dalgleish said, 'I'll have the galley organize some hot soup meanwhile.'

'Splendid. And don't forget the bridge.'

Dalgleish cleared his throat. 'What they all need really, sir, is a night or two in harbour.'

That throat-clearance was a habit of his first lieutenant's, Nick had noticed, before advancing an opinion. But what he'd said then was more a statement of fact than an opinion: in the last seven weeks they'd had – what, three nights in harbour? It wasn't anything that anyone could help: the fleet had been at full stretch even before the Greek adventure started . . . He breathed cold air, taking deep breaths of it to freshen mind as well as body. The wind was almost on the beam, not enough of it to make the sea more than choppy, but at thirty knots it was bringing bursts of spray that swept across the foc'sl, slashed and drummed against the for'ard gunshields and the forefront of the bridge. *Blackfoot* was still easy enough to see, with the mound of wake bright under her counter, but the moon had hidden itself behind thickening cloud. A bit of cloud-cover for tomorrow, for those last trips out of the Aegean, might be worth praying for.

He didn't want to keep thinking about *Carnarvon*: or rather, about Jack. For a mixture of reasons, some of them old, private history, and some he couldn't easily have explained even to himself, he'd have preferred to have had the boy anywhere but on this station.

Jack Everard – lieutenant, Royal Navy – had just checked his anchor-bearings on *Carnarvon*'s softly-lit gyro repeater. The cruiser's captain, Howard Napier, lowered the binoculars through which he'd been staring at the Dutch ship, the *Gelderland*. Napier was a tall man, about Jack's own height, and slim, wide-shouldered: normally rather quiet-spoken, easy-mannered, he was fidgety now with impatience. 'Might send someone over there, sir?' Bell-Reid, Napier's second-in-command, suggested it. Talking about the *Gelderland*, the transport, and exasperated at the unexplained, inexcusable delay . . . Napier put his glasses up again: 'What the *bloody* hell's the matter with him?'

The Dutch ship hadn't moved or even begun to prepare to move: one of her lifeboats was still in the water – you could see the falls dangling there, on her quarter – and there'd been no activity at all on her foc's'l, at the anchor gear. Napier had twice signalled to her captain to weigh anchor: the signals had been acknowledged but nothing had happened. *Carnarvon*'s own boats were hoisted, her messdecks were full of New Zealanders – most of whom had simply collapsed and fallen asleep, still in tin hats and boots and with the packs strapped on their backs – and the three destroyers had already weighed and moved out south-eastward to wait a mile or two down the gulf.

It was vital to get out of the Stukas' backyard before daylight, at least to get far enough south to have some hope of air cover from the RAF in Crete. *Gelderland*'s best speed was sixteen knots, seventeen if they sat on all the safety-valves and prayed: so there'd be seven hours' steaming from here to the Kithera Channel. If they started now, this minute, they'd be there at about 1030. With Morning Civil Twilight coming at 0528 you could reckon on broad daylight well before six: so even now it would be a miracle if they didn't get *some* attention from the Luftwaffe.

Jack Everard told himself, *We might not. They might not find us* . . . He checked the time: three twenty-five. At the same moment Napier swung round, lowering his binoculars.

'Very well. Everard – go over to the Dutchman and give him my direct order to pull his anchor up and sail immediately.' He looked at the commander: 'Which boat, John?'

'Motorboat's still turned out port side, sir.' Bell-Reid raised his voice: 'Bosun's Mate, call away the second motorboat!'

'Take whatever action's necessary, Everard. Just get him moving.'

'Aye aye, sir!' He was already on his way, rattling down the steel ladder. Two more ladders after that one: skimming down them at a speed that came with long practice, hearing the shrill pipe and the wailing cry, 'Aw-a-ay second motorboat's crew! Aw-a-ay second motorboat's crew!' It was abreast the foremost funnel, just abaft the bridge superstructure, and as he burst out of the screen door Jack saw the boat's coxswain and three crewmen there ahead of him, already climbing up into the boat where it hung in its outturned davits. Tom Overton, the cruiser's first lieutenant, arrived at the same moment from the foc'sl where he'd have been standing by with his cable party, ready to weigh anchor; he was mustering the lowerers, one leading hand and two seamen to each fall. Climbing up into the boat, Jack heard Overton's order, 'Turns for lowering!' Bell-Reid was bawling down at him from the after end of the signal bridge, telling him to get a move on; Overton called back patiently, 'Aye aye, sir!' and added in a quieter tone, 'Start the falls.' In the boat's sternsheets Jack felt the jerky start, the boat dropping a few inches; then the next order, 'Lower away', sent them down fast towards the sea. The motorboat's coxswain, a leading seaman, asked him where they were going; Jack told him, 'To the Dutchman. Find out why he hasn't pulled his hook up.' Then they were in the water and the engine puttered into life, with Overton's shout of 'Light-to!' up above their heads and down here the bowman and sternsheetman hauling at the falls to get some slack so they could unhook the boat. He told the coxswain, 'Near side of her, long as there's a ladder. Fast as you like.'

Several hours of Stukas, he thought. It would be his baptism of dive-bombing. Even to himself he was unwilling to admit that the prospect did, truly, chill him.

There was a first time for everyone, of course, and it was the time you dreaded most. Brother Nick had told him, *Not so bad once it starts . . .* Well, he'd heard the same line from other people too: but Brother Nick acting big-brotherly, acting kind, for God's sake!

'There's plenty of ladders there, sir. 'Alf a dozen of 'em!'

Ladders the Dutch had put over for embarking New Zealanders, who'd been brought off from the open beach in lifeboats and naval whalers in tow of motorboats: the harbour was blocked by the wreck of the assault ship *Ulster Prince*, who'd grounded during a previous night's lift and then, at daylight, become a sitting target for the Stukas. How would Nick handle *this* job, Jack wondered. He'd be sure of himself, he'd know instinctively how to take command . . . Jack told the coxswain, pointing, 'That one.' It dangled below the *Gelderland*'s bridge, a long chain-sides ladder with flat wooden rungs, reaching to the water. He heard a voice raised, on deck above him somewhere, then a flicker of torchlight grew into a beam directed vertically down the ladder as the boat slid up to it.

'Wait alongside, cox'n.' The ladder was an awkward thing to climb. But it would have been worse for the soldiers, weighed down with packs and weapons and just about dropping from exhaustion. The Germans were only a few miles behind them, they'd said.

'Is your captain on the bridge?'

An elderly seaman in a blue jersey, the man with the torch, had tried to help him over the rail. As if he thought a 22-year-old RN lieutenant might be some kind of cripple. He'd got into the habit, perhaps, dragging pongoes aboard earlier on.

'*Kapitein*?'

'Yes. On bridge?'

The man didn't look too bright. Jack went inside the superstructure, pushing through a double flap of blackout canvas: the sailor gabbled something, following him in, and one word stood out.

'In his cabin?'

'Ja. I show.' In his quarters, when his ship was supposed to be getting under way? The sailor had passed him and he was banging on a polished hardwood door: he'd opened it, and stepped aside.

Now, Jack thought. Act like Nick might . . . 'Captain?'

A squat, pale-skinned man with a close-shorn grey head: *Gelderland*'s captain wore white flannels and a food-stained reefer jacket. Jack had a fleeting memory of the Royal Naval College at Dartmouth, the daily working rig: except that if a cadet had appeared in flannels even half that dirty he'd have been flogged.

'I am Kapitein. Anton Beukenkamp. What you want?'

'You're to weigh anchor and sail, Captain. *Now*. We've signalled you twice. What's—'

'I wait.' Beukenkamp had tobacco-juice stains running from the

252

corners of his mouth, a left eye that wandered, and he was so short and broad he made Jack feel like a flagpole. 'Little while, must wait. Peoples coming – from shore, peoples . . .'

'My captain' – Jack pointed in the direction of *Carnarvon*'s berth – 'the force commander, Captain Napier, orders you to weigh immediately. Otherwise—'

'No, mister, please!'

A woman in a red dress: long, greasy black hair and swarthy skin: she'd emerged from what must have been the sleeping-cabin. Beukenkamp muttered defensively, 'This lady – her peoples – her brother and uncle and also—'

'You've been waiting for – for *this lady*'s family?'

'I have boat inshore, you see.' Incredibly, the man was trying to smile about it. 'Coming very soon now, I think.'

It was unbelievable. Thousands of lives, several ships, the whole operation . . . The gypsy woman was jabbering in what sounded like Greek. Jack cut across the babble to tell the captain, 'Sail now, this minute. Otherwise we put the lady ashore, put you under arrest and take over your ship. D'you want to be shot, Captain? Because if you don't move now—'

'My boat . . .'

'You'll have to leave it.'

'But – I *ask* you . . .'

'Give the order, Captain!'

He made sure it was actually happening: that Beukenkamp was on his bridge, main engines rung-on, capstan turning on the foc's'l. Then he went down into the boat and waited, lying-off, until he saw the Dutchman's anchor break clear of the surface streaming mud, and then a swirl of movement at the stern as his screws began to turn.

'Back to the ship, cox'n.'

In *Carnarvon*'s bridge, he told his CO what had been going on. Napier said, 'When we get back to Alex, I'll see if I can't have him shot.'

'I did mention it as a possibility, sir.' He thought, *If* we get back to Alex . . . You could hear the cruiser's cable clanking up, and the stench of the mud that it was shedding as it rose. Napier added, 'You did a good job, Everard. Never mind his boat's crew – they're on *his* conscience . . . Why, look at that!'

Some kind of flare-up: and now the thump of an explosion: a few miles inland, to the north. There was a spreading glow with a halo

253

to it, diffuse and orange-tinted. Fading now . . . Bell-Reid suggested, 'Probably the railway junction. One of the pongoes did say they'd mined it.'

It was ten minutes to four. It would be daylight by, say, 0550. Two hours, at perhaps a little better than sixteen knots; they'd have covered at the most thirty-five miles before the bombing started. More than that if the Luftwaffe didn't find them at first light, of course; but luck of that sort wasn't anything to count on.

He went to the chart. He was acting as navigator now. He'd been appointed to this ship as an ordinary watchkeeper, but the navigator had been landed in Aden suffering from stomach ulcers and Napier had shuffled the jobs around. He was keen to get the same navigator back when the ulcers were cleared up, and if he'd had a new man appointed he'd have made that impossible. Jack let down the canvas flap behind him, leant over the chart and switched on the inside light, marked the EP, estimated position, thirty-five miles down the pencil track. He saw they'd be just about on latitude thirty-seven north: which to all intents and purposes was beyond the range of any RAF or Fleet Air Arm support. Even if there were any on thirty-*six* north, which wasn't by any means a certainty.

He switched off the light and backed out. There was a yell from Tom Overton down on the foc's'l, and the commander, who was looking down over the front of the bridge, reported, 'Clear anchor, sir.'

'Half ahead together. Port twenty.'

Following astern of the *Gelderland*. Time – he checked it, took a reading of the log and entered both figures in his notebook – was 0358. One hour later than it should have been.

'Morning, sir.'

'Morning, pilot. All well?'

'No problems, sir.'

Rocky Pratt, his navigator, had the watch. A former P & O Line deck officer, Pratt was short and stocky, and gnome-like now with the hood of his duffel pulled up. It was cold enough to need it, in this pre-dawn hour: *too* cold, Nick thought, for the first day of May. Wind was still from the north-west, which meant that with the ship on a course of 063 it was slightly abaft the beam, and *Tuareg* was rolling as she thrashed along in *Blackfoot*'s wake. He'd slept, in his fold-away canvas bridge chair, from three-thirty to just after five; hoisting himself on to the high seat now and feeling like something recently disinterred, he almost wished he hadn't. You had to get some rest when there was a chance to, though, or you'd be at half-cock when you needed to be wide awake: so he'd dozed somewhat uneasily with the Cyrenaican land-bulge only fifteen to twenty miles away to starboard, and now as dawn approached he was fit – or would be, in a minute – to cope with whatever daylight might bring. There were airstrips, for instance, on that desert coastline, and the aircraft on them now were German, whereas the RAF had a total of twenty-one serviceable Hurricanes in the whole of the Western Desert and there was an army as well as a fleet needing air support.

Even Norway hadn't taught the powers in London that ships couldn't operate for long under skies dominated by the enemy. Until the Norwegian fiasco nobody had really thought about it: which was partly why most destroyers' guns – *Tuareg*'s included – could only elevate to forty degrees. Fat lot of use that was, against bombers diving almost vertically. Luckily these Tribals had multiple pompoms as well, which was *something* to ward off Stukas with: and when the opportunity occurred there was an intention of replacing the twin four-sevens at X position with a four-inch high-angle mounting. But many of the older ships – of the H-class, for instance – had nothing but point-five machine-guns for close-range protection. That was all he, Nick Everard, had had in *Intent*, in the Namsos fjords when he'd been trapped there with the Germans invading Norway and his ship crippled, immobilized: if the dive-bombers had found her she'd have been there still, as scrap-iron. He'd been lucky, though, he'd been able to bring her out and do some worthwhile damage to the enemy en route. Then, back in England, he'd been hauled over the coals because in an earlier action he hadn't prevented another destroyer committing hara-kiri.

When he'd first got back, there'd been congratulations and applause. The Press had made an overnight hero of him: so much so that the new Prime Minister had expressed a wish to have Commander Everard brought before him. It was at this interview that Nick's troubles must have started. Winston had remarked that it was saddening to see a campaign which had opened with such an impressive performance by the Navy going so dismally now on land; Nick had agreed, adding that the soldiers, sent in so late and so ill-equipped and unsupported against the Luftwaffe, really hadn't ever had a dog's chance. It so happened that he had a great admiration for General Carton de Wiart, VC, and he'd spoken as much as anything out of respect for him; he'd also been speaking the plain truth, but forgetting that the Prime Minister in his former role of First Lord of the Admiralty and as a member of Chamberlain's cabinet had been closely concerned with the mounting of the Norwegian expedition.

At the time, all he got was a cold stare. But twenty-four hours later he was facing an inquisition in the Admiralty. It wasn't an 'official' inquiry: it started with 'Look here, Everard, we need your help. There've been some questions asked, and we have to produce some answers . . .'

So he was still a commander. He'd hoped, after the Norwegian success, to have won a fourth stripe and a flotilla, to make up the leeway he'd lost by retiring from the Navy in 1930. He'd spent eight years 'outside', and now he was back in the rank he'd reached in 1926, just before his thirtieth birthday.

All right – so he'd been an idiot . . .

Eastward, there was a silvery streak on the horizon and, above it, a faintly lighter section of sky. No cloud: last night's hope of cloud-cover for today had been wishful thinking. He swung round to see what was happening in the bridge behind him: he'd been lost in his thoughts, searching the horizon with his glasses but seeing and hearing nothing close at hand. Houston, the gunnery control officer, touched his cap.

'Morning, sir.'

'Morning, Harry.'

Houston was an RNVR lieutenant. He was of medium height, like Nick himself, but corpulent. Nick was broad, strongly built, but Harry Houston was fat: if he put on any more weight, Dalgleish had warned him recently, they might have to get rid of him because he wouldn't be able to shoe-horn himself into the director tower. He was going aft now, to the ladder that led up to it. Ashcourt, the RN sub-lieutenant, was yawning over the torpedo control panel. He was tall and slim, willowy; if he'd been dark instead of fair he'd have been rather a Jack Everard type, Nick thought. Yeoman Whiffen was in the port after corner of the bridge, lecturing the young signalman of the watch. And now Tony Dalgleish, the first lieutenant, hoisted himself off the up-ladder into the bridge's after end and came for'ard, nodding to Rocky Pratt who was at the binnacle. Dalgleish stopped beside his captain.

'Morning, sir. Darned cold.'

'Be less so, Number One, if you had a coat on.'

'Oh, soon warm up.' Dalgleish was wearing a polo-neck sweater under his reefer jacket. He reached to the alarm buzzer, held his thumb ready over it. 'Close the hands up, sir?'

'Yes, please.'

The noise of the alarm was muted up here, but a harsh, sleep-penetrating racket down in the messdecks. Dalgleish kept it going in short sharp bursts for about half a minute. Then he turned away. 'I'll go on down, sir.'

'Make sure they know this isn't just routine. There's an airfield at Benghazi, and we stirred things up last night.'

'Aye aye, sir.'

Ashcourt was testing his communications with Mr Walsh, the gunner (T), whose action station was at his torpedo tubes aft, and from the director tower Houston would be lining up his sights with the receivers at each of the four twin four-seven gun-mountings. He'd be checking his connections with the TS too, the transmitting station two decks down and below B gun; and higher than Houston's steel box up there, above his head and a bit aft, Petty Officer Wellbeloved and Able Seaman Sitwell would have settled into the combined rangefinder and HA director; they'd be testing their circuits too.

Reports were coming in now. Main armament closed up and cleared away, circuits tested. Torpedo tubes and depthcharge crews closed up, communications tested. Close-range weapons closed up . . . Dalgleish would be moving round the ship, seeing that men on the upper deck were wearing their anti-flash gear, lifebelts and tin hats, and that everyone was alert and ready, wide awake. Nick reached for his own helmet and put it on. Light was flushing up that eastern sky, greying upward from an horizon which in that quarter – on the starboard bow – could just be made out now with the naked eye. Light growing steadily: you could see the sky's greyness reflected on the sea now, on that bow. This was the period when light was confusing and attack most likely, and when the range of visibility suddenly expanded so that an enemy who hadn't seemed to have been there one minute might be in gun-range the next. Nick, Pratt and Ashcourt all had binoculars up, searching sea and sky: farther aft the look-outs, two men on each side in the bays where the eighteen-inch searchlights stood like huge, closed eyes, were dark, tin-hatted silhouettes slowly turning as each swept his own ninety-degree sector through high-powered glasses. And overhead the director tower trained slowly round, like the head of some animal wary of its surroundings.

In London, it would be dark for another hour or more. He wondered if the bombers had been over again: nights were London's *bad* time, while here they provided intervals of near-safety. He hoped Fiona was all right. *Please, God* . . . Here, light would come rapidly, in a minute: and it would be exactly like this 200 miles away in the Aegean, where *Carnarvon* must be hurrying her convoy down from Nauplia. There too the curtain would be going up on a new Stuka-infested day.

CHAPTER 2

In *Carnarvon*'s bridge McCowan, the gunnery lieutenant, banged a telephone back on to its hook and told Captain Napier, 'All quarters closed up and cleared away, sir.' McCowan was a thin, bony-faced man in his middle twenties, with deepset eyes and wiry black hair; he was a Scot but he didn't sound like one. Ahead of the cruiser the Dutch transport lumbered stolidly south south-eastward, following *Halberdier* and with the other two destroyers, *Huntress* and *Highflier*, on her bow and beam to port. The mainland of Greece was a humpy grey division, touched by early daylight now, between sea and sky to starboard; a quarter of an hour ago, when Cape Turkoviglia had been abeam, the convoy's distance offshore had been as little as 3,000 yards. It was twice that now, but the closeness of land was Napier's reason for having kept his destroyers only ahead and on the seaward side; by hugging the coast he was making the trip as short as possible, and as soon as it was fully light he'd be shifting the escorts into a more regular formation.

Pretty soon now, in fact. It was already almost day. They were well out of the Gulf of Nauplia but for another hour that land would be close to starboard.

'I'll go up, sir.' Up to the ADP, McCowan meant. The letters stood for Air Defence Position; it was the partly enclosed platform up on the tripod foremast above the bridge, with the rangefinder-director above that. When *Carnarvon* had been launched in 1918 as an ordinary light cruiser the ADP had been known as the Spotting Top, but in an extensive refit from 1939 into 1940 she'd been re-equipped as an AA cruiser, with high-angle four-inch guns and a whole lot of modern fire-control devices in that ADP.

It was light enough now for Jack Everard to be able to see *Gelderland* easily without glasses, and *Highflier* and *Huntress* as

259

silhouettes against the flush of dawn. The wind was a light breeze on the starboard quarter, but here in the land's shelter the sea was flat with that dawn shine on it: it was going to be a beautiful, classic Aegean day. Bell-Reid must have had the same thought: he murmured with binoculars at his eyes, 'Splendid flying weather. Wonder if they'd let me change sides.'

'You'd make a rotten Nazi . . . Pilot, what's that?'

Napier was pointing at a white lighthouse on a minor headland. About a minute ago Jack had been studying the chart, memorizing landmarks, and he was able to trot out the answer: 'It's a light called Aspro Kortia, sir.'

'Sounds like something for a headache.'

'The inlet to the south of it is Port Kyparisi.'

Bell-Reid snorted: derisively, perhaps, a comment on a young man showing off, offering more information than had been asked for. Bell-Reid was a caustic and impatient man, entirely different from the quiet, easygoing Howard Napier, whose last pre-war post had been as naval attaché in an embassy.

Irvine, a bearded RNR lieutenant who was action officer-of-the-watch, was at the binnacle. Jack Everard lingered near the chart table; as navigator his duties were divided between bridge and plot. Napier – perched up on his bridge chair – and Bell-Reid and the midshipman of the watch, Brighouse; all had their glasses up, probing the circle of visibility as it expanded. Elsewhere in the bridge were the chief yeoman of signals, a leading signalman and a bridge messenger; right aft at the base of the tripod mast which formed a circular steel shelter housing the Tannoy broadcast equipment, a very young Royal Marine bugler conversed in whispers with the commander's 'doggie', an Ordinary Seaman by the name of Webster; while behind them, leaning against the shelter, loomed the bow-legged figure of Able Seaman Noble, the captain's servant.

Jack took his eyes off the Dutch ship and glanced again at the coastline. It was a bleak, barren-looking landscape. Within days it would be overrun by Germans. To port, the sea was like a mirror throwing light into the sky: the stars had vanished and there was a loom of brilliance from just over the horizon. An empty, cloudless sky, half-lit: the question in all their minds was how long it would *stay* empty.

'Chief Yeoman!'

'Sir!'

CPO Hegarty came forward: he was a smallish man with a flat, sharp chin like a paint-scraper. Napier told him, 'Hoist *Destroyers form close screen round convoy*.'

'Aye aye, sir!' Hegarty went aft, yelling down to his men on the flagdeck, one level below the bridge, for the flags he wanted to have bent on, then leaning over the back end of the bridge and watching to see each one whipped out of its pigeon-hole in the big, grey-painted locker. The signalmen could tell from the toggle-fittings on each flag which was the top or bottom of it . . . 'Hoist!' The string of bunting ran up swiftly, led by the yellow-blue-yellow of the destroyer flag, and the destroyers' red-and-white answering pendants shot up in acknowledgement within seconds, pausing momentarily at the dip and then rushing close-up to the yardarms, signifying 'signal understood'. Napier called, 'Executive please, Chief Yeoman', and Hegarty roared, 'Haul down!' The hoist tumbled, to be gathered in on the flagdeck and the flags restowed in their slots. *Highflier* and *Huntress* were on the move at once, *Highflier* increasing speed and angling inwards to close up on the Dutch ship's port beam, *Huntress* also cracking on more revs and at the same time going over to starboard, heeling to the turn, passing ahead of the Dutchman and astern of *Halberdier* in order to take station on the landward side.

To all intents and purposes it was day now. That eastern glow had acquired a hard, hot centre growing upwards out of a strip of sea so bright you couldn't look straight at it without being blinded. Bell-Reid asked Napier, 'Might send one watch to breakfast, sir?'

Napier didn't answer immediately. He'd lowered his binoculars and he was looking around, swinging his high chair around as he examined the sky astern and on the quarters.

'Yes.' He nodded to the commander. 'And get 'em up again and the others down there as fast as it can be done. You go down too, John; I'll have mine up here.' He glanced at Jack. 'And you, Everard. Don't take longer than you need.'

On his way down, he met Overton, the first lieutenant, coming up to take over from Willie Irvine as OOW. Tom Overton's action job was damage-control, below decks, and on this trip he was also responsible for looking after the army passengers. He smiled amiably at Jack: 'Nice quiet morning, eh?'

Quite a pleasant old goof . . .

The breakfast on offer consisted of cornflakes, scrambled eggs made of egg-powder, and toast and marmalade; in the interests of speed he decided to do without cornflakes. The wardroom was littered with bed-rolls, and some of them still contained slumbering New Zealanders. Jack sat down opposite Bell-Reid, who was chatting over his shoulder to a major with a bandaged head.

'Steward'll give you chaps some breakfast in half an hour or so. We have to be rude and eat first so we can be ready to receive the Luftwaffe.'

'Don't worry about us, Commander.' The major put a hand to his lightly bearded jaw. 'Might even get to shave before I eat.'

'Use my cabin. The steward can show you where it is, and you'll find all you need there . . . Here, come and sit, have some coffee to go on with. Jenkins!'

'Coming sir.' The steward was at the hatch at the end of the long, rather narrow wardroom. There was a sideboard under the hatch, connecting to the pantry. Bell-Reid told the soldier as he pulled a chair out, 'Leading Steward Jenkins will attend to all your wants. He'll be single-handed once we're closed up, because we need the others elsewhere, but just tell him what you want. Right, Jenkins?'

'Do me best, sir.' He was a large, happy-looking man; he told Jack over Bell-Reid's head, 'Your eggs is coming, sir.'

'Good. Make it snappy, please.' He nodded to the soldier. 'How d'you do, sir. I'm Everard.'

'Our navigating officer.' Bell-Reid told Jack, 'This is Major Haskins, OC troops.'

'Glad to know you, Everard. Reckon to find the way home, do you?'

'Oh, with a bit of luck . . .'

'No fooling.' Melhuish, the surgeon commander, flopped into a nearby chair. A boozy-looking man with greying hair. 'Luck's the word for it. He spins a coin, then we bounce our way off the headlands. I've just been up for a breather, and we're practically on the bloody beach.' He looked at Jack. 'Didn't know that, did you?'

'You don't mean there's land in sight?'

They all laughed – except for Bell-Reid, who only raised an eyebrow. Robson, a lieutenant-commander and electrical specialist, asked Melhuish, 'How are your patients doing?'

He meant the military wounded. Melhuish told him, 'All responding nicely, touch wood.'

Jack had his eggs now. The powdered stuff had seemed uneatable when it had first appeared, but you got used to it: surprising what you *could* get used to. Including, he wondered,

262

Stukas? He asked Major Haskins, 'Must have been pretty awful, the last few days?'

'Well.' The New Zealander sipped at his coffee. 'I'll admit there've been happier times.'

'On the Corinth Canal, we heard—'

'Christ, *that*.' He shook his bandaged head. It was like a turban only with short hair bristling from the top of it. 'That was *something*.' A very large, younger man, a captain with one arm in a sling, came and stood behind him and took over the answering as Haskins seemed to dry up. The newcomer told Jack, 'They sent 88s over first to draw our ack-ack so they could spot the batteries. Then Stukas came after to dive-bomb the guns first and then our positions, fifty or sixty bloody Stukas routing around like mad dogs and I'd say maybe a hundred Messerschmitts strafing anything that moved. It just went on and on like that. I tell you it was plain *unbelievable*, and when they had us about cooked the gliders and paratroops came over and went down behind us.' He turned away. 'Damn right it was something. Something like I hope to God I never—'

The action-alarm bell silenced that single voice. The bell was ringing short-long, short-long, As for aircraft alarm, action stations.

Jack was getting out through the doorway and the bell was still sounding off when the four-inch guns opened fire overhead: the noise of them, down here inside the ship, was something you felt as well as heard, as if it jarred the bone of your skull. Like an incredibly violent impact of iron on iron: solid, ringing. But he was up the ladder now and out of the screen door, turning for'ard, hearing a burst of fire from the multiple pompoms at the other end of the ship as he ran that way: the four-inch fired again and he felt the blast from the midships mounting as he passed below it. Up the ladder at the foc'sl break, level with the second funnel and between the whaler and the starboard motorboat, then in the door to the bridge superstructure, taking the ladder several steps at a time, racing up towards whatever . . .

The guns had ceased fire. He was in the bridge, and he could see no aircraft anywhere. Napier told Bell-Reid, who'd arrived a few yards behind, 'One Messerschmitt – a 110, the twin-engined kind. It came out of the sun' – he pointed – 'and we didn't see it in time to get a barrage going. It aimed two bombs at *Gelderland* and missed by fifty yards or more.'

Bell-Reid, panting from the fast hundred-yard run, leant against the side of the bridge, shielding his eyes and staring towards the sun. AB Noble came lurching from the ladder, bringing a tray with the captain's breakfast on it.

'Sorry I got 'eld up, sir. Trouble was—'

'Doesn't matter, Noble.' Napier told Bell-Reid, 'We'll stay closed up now. Action messing henceforth.' Jack was checking the ship's position by land bearings, and Irvine was saying to Overton, 'I've got the weight, sir. Many thanks for my breakfast.'

'My dear boy.' Overton stepped down from the binnacle platform, the slightly raised bit in the centre of the bridge. He was a lieutenant-commander but before the war he'd twice been passed over for promotion, and he was older than Bell-Reid. His only burning enthusiasm was for golf.

Course one-five-nine: revs for sixteen and a half knots. *Halberdier*, the leading destroyer, was in sight to the left of the Dutchman, who must have swung off course during that surprise attack. There was nothing for *Carnarvon* to do about it: *Gelderland* was the one out of station and it was up to Anton Beukenkamp to get back into it. One might imagine that the Messerschmitt's visit would at least have got him out of bed? Glancing round, Jack saw the snotty, Brighouse, leaning against the starboard searchlight sight and picking his teeth with a matchstick. Brighouse was an untidy, rather hairy little lad, with small sharp eyes and an insolent manner, and Jack wondered whether brother Nick might not have been something like Brighouse when he'd been a snotty. According to Nick's own stories he'd been constantly in trouble – disciplinary trouble – in his early years at sea. It would certainly delight this little brute, Jack thought, to be told he might have anything in common with a brass-hat baronet who had a DSO and two DSCs . . .

Coming up from Suda Bay they'd had air cover, Fulmars, until dusk, and until dusk they'd steered a course well away from the Nauplia direction, so as to mislead the enemy in case one of his recce flights did get past the Fulmars and see the ships. The point of an air escort was more to keep the Hun reconnaissance flights away than to shoot down attackers *after* you'd been spotted.

But the Luftwaffe would know where they were *now*, all right.

Napier was in his bridge chair; he was munching his breakfast, but his eyes were on the sky. Bell-Reid was leaning against the port side of the bridge, thumbing tobacco into his pipe. Jack checked the time: it was six fifty-eight.

'All guns follow ADP!'

There was a loudspeaker in the bridge so that Napier could hear what Jock McCowan's team up on the foremast were saying to the guns. He could have it switched on or off, loud or quiet, and when he wanted to he could chip in on his own sound-powered telephone line to McCowan. But the voice from the speaker had been that of Paymaster Lieutenant Clutterbuck, whom McCowan had trained to operate the HACS, high-angle control system. Clutterbuck had been telling the layers and trainers at the cruiser's four twin four-inch guns to line up the pointers in their dials with the pointers which were controlled electrically from the sight in the ADP.

A red air-warning flag fluttered at *Carnarvon*'s yardarm. Bell-Reid murmured, his glasses trained almost right into the sun, 'Twelve of 'em. Four flights of three. About 6,000 feet.'

Twin-engined, black against the sky and with the sun behind and under them: Junkers 88s. Clutterbuck would have a chance to go through the HACS drill this time. The system involved the feeding of information such as height, range, course, speed and angle-of-sight to a machine down below called a Fuse Keeping Clock, which then provided the guns with fuse-settings and aim-off, but it wasn't often of much use because attacks tended to be made in a less orderly way: aircraft jinked, dived, dodged about. There was a type 285 RDF set up there as part of the system, but it was no good for anything but ranging; you had to see your target and then point the aerial at it. It was mounted on the director above the ADP platform and it looked like three broomsticks with small cross-pieces all down their length.

'Open fire!'

Highflier had opened up with her four-sevens at that moment. Some of the 'H' class – including *Huntress* – had been fitted with three-inch AA guns in place of their after tubes, but this one hadn't. The low-angle four-sevens could really engage only approaching aircraft, or put a barrage over other ships. Now *Carnarvon*'s high-angle four-inch opened fire, brown smoke and cordite fumes blowing back from A gun, down for'ard; the Ju88s seemed to be rising across the sky as they came over on a straight course towards the ships. Shellbursts were opening below them and to the right. You saw the smoke-puffs appear and only

265

afterwards, if surrounding noise permitted, you heard the thudding sounds of the bursts: by which time there were a lot more of them, all the ships shooting fast now, the sky a mass of shellbursts and the bombers not wavering at all, coming on and rising into the littered sky-bowl overhead. The first flight of three had gone into shallow dives – going for *Gelderland*, the biggest and most obvious target for their bombs.

'Pompom open fire!'

Noise-level leapt as the multiple pompom, eight-barrelled, added its fast thump-thump-thumping to the general din. It was immediately below and in front of the bridge, where in former days the old cruiser had had her B gun-mounting. The destroyers were shooting at the succeeding flights of bombers, the ones still coming in behind this first bunch, but *Carnarvon*'s guns were throwing a barrage over the Dutchman and ahead of the three front-running Junkers, who seemed to be flying straight into the mass of shellbursts. Tracer was flaring up from *Gelderland*'s own close-range weapons; by the look of it, one Bofors and several lighter machine-guns. You could see the black-cross markings on the bombers' wings and the shine of the early sun on them, and then the bombs falling away, a tight black rain of high-explosive slanting seaward, quite slow-moving it seemed when they first started but then speeding – obeying, Jack mentally noted, the formula of thirty-two feet per second per second, the acceleration due to gravity: hardly surprising that one lost sight of them. Paymaster Lieutenant Clutterbuck's even tones were ordering *Carnarvon*'s four-inch to shift target and engage the second flight of Junkers. Jack could visualize him up there with his pale face and bluish jaw, pale eyes blinking surprisedly through his spectacles: he wondered if they steamed up – the spectacles – as they did when Clutterbuck drank pink gin. Either the Dutch ship had discovered she had reserves of speed or *Carnarvon* had slowed down: Irvine bent to the voicepipe and called down, 'Up four revolutions,' just as Napier turned to draw his attention to the increasing gap and three geysers of water – four – towered astern of the Dutchman, momentarily blotting him from sight. Another stick fell short, closer to *Highflier* than to *Gelderland*, and the rest were out ahead, a short avenue of waterspouts out on the transport's bow. Three more flights to come.

'X and Y guns shift target, Messerchmitts green one-five-oh, blue barrage, *fire*!' Clutterbuck's voice sharp and urgent . . . The number three look-out on the starboard side had seen the new

266

threat at the same time as the paymaster had given tongue: he was up on his feet, pointing and shouting, no words audible, only a mouth open in the middle of ginger beard. They were fighter-bombers, 110s, slanting in low, curving over towards *Carnarvon*. The starboard point-fives were letting rip, tracer streaming out on the quarter and seeming to curve away behind the oncoming planes: Bell-Reid had rushed to the back of the bridge to tell that look-out to get down – he was bawling now at everyone to take cover – *down*! There wasn't really any cover but you could duck, throw yourself flat in the stupendous noise as the Germans tore over with their guns flaming, hammering, sparks flying from the side of the bridge and torn steel where a nest of voicepipes had been smashed. Everyone was getting up now: but Napier had never left his seat. Clutterbuck's voice was cool, back to normal as he told X and Y to follow ADP. Bomb-splashes were lifting in quick succession beyond the Dutch ship. The Messerschmitts had flown over *Huntress*, raking her with machine-gun fire as they crossed and then banked the other way to swing left, swooping upwards with the land behind them: bombs were falling from the third flight of Ju88s, and *Carnarvon*'s four-inch were shifting to engage the last flight as it approached. And one Messerschmitt had been hit: there'd been a burst beside it as it turned, and the end of the raised wing disintegrated, the aircraft rolling over and going down, upside-down and falling sideways towards new bomb-splashes rising ahead of *Gelderland* – the Dutch ship was steaming into them, passing through them with salt water raining down across her. More bombs were falling close to *Halberdier*. A dozen things happening at once, and in all directions . . .

The Messerschmitt had gone into the sea: it must have been *Huntress*, he thought, who'd got that one: and she'd suffered, there was movement around her B gun, it looked like men had been hit and were being lowered from the gundeck. The gun was still in action though. Napier called out, pointing, '*That*'ll larn 'im!' He was pointing up at a Ju88 trailing smoke, losing height and diverging to starboard while his two companions held to their straight course. There were flames coming out of him now as well as smoke. Clutterbuck's voice came out of the speaker: 'Check, check, check . . .' The other Messerschmitt had turned back over the land, climbing as it circled northward. Below *Carnarvon*'s bridge the pompom gunners were cheering: that Junkers was in a dive, all flame and smoke, and it was going to crash in Greece,

267

not in the sea. Either the pompom crew were just glad to see it, or they reckoned *they*'d hit it. Looking at his watch, Jack saw they'd been in action for six or seven minutes. It had felt more like half an hour: it was all one, now, a smear of violence wrapped in noise, but at the time each picture had been frozen in your mind as in a frame. It felt marvellous to have it over, threat and noise so suddenly removed: he felt an urge to laugh, chat . . . Napier looked around at Bell-Reid and pointed up towards the ADP: he said, 'They were beginning to get the hang of it.'

Bell-Reid was inspecting the side of the bridge, the smashed voicepipes to the plot, captain's sea-cabin and signals office. He glanced round at Napier and nodded, and Clutterbuck's voice came booming from the loudspeaker, 'Alarm port! All guns follow ADP, red one-seven-oh, angle of sight two-oh, large formation of Ju87s, closing!'

Christ. Not a bloody *moment* . . . And Junkers 87s were Stukas. Jack thought, putting it to himself calmly, rationally, that his advisors had been right, that there always *was* a first time, and the anticipation was probably worse than the actual experience. He told himself, There'll be *hours* of this . . .

'Red barrage . . .'

Red was the long fuse-setting, blue the short one. There was a fuse-setting machine at each gun and also a few shells with these pre-set standard fuses, dabbed with coloured paint to make them easily recognizable, in the ready-use racks. *Highflier* had opened fire with her four-sevens: and Jack had the attackers in his glasses. His first sight of Stukas: a big group of them, squat and evil-looking. Like vampire bats, he thought: not that he'd ever seen a vampire bat . . . They were splitting up, some circling off one way and some the other, just one pair flying straight towards the convoy, shellbursts opening in front of them, brownish puff-balls flowering in irregular batches and the Stukas racing in through them and between them, ignoring them, bat-like and yellow-nosed, beginning to weave now as the anti-aircraft barrage thickened: some of the others who'd swung off to circle the ships at a safe distance were turning in.

He looked over to the other side, saw it was happening there as well. *Huntress* on that side was throwing a barrage ahead of the ones approaching from that landward side: the whole sky was already pock-marked with shellbursts and full of weaving, jinking bombers. Clutterbuck had ordered a switch to blue barrage and

Carnarvon's were bursting over the *Gelderland*, roofing her with a layer of explosions through which no pilot in his right mind would consider flying: but Jack saw the first two Stukas suddenly tip over and go screaming down in steep dives towards the Dutch ship, their sirens screaming through the racket of the guns, which was now one continuous roar. There were more Stukas coming in from starboard, pompoms and point-fives blazing at them, the Dutch close-range guns all busy, *Huntress* making a violent course-alteration as a plane dropped down at her like a plunging eagle. He saw bombs falling towards the *Gelderland* and the first Stuka pulling away out of its dive, streaking away to the right with the second one following some way behind it. He hadn't seen that one's bomb go but it burst now, the sea erupting on the Dutch ship's bow so close it could as easily have hit as missed. Stukas everywhere you looked, weaving between bursts of shells and streams of tracer: one on fire spinning away to port and another diving over *Carnarvon*, coming down right on top of her and almost vertically. Napier shouted 'Port twenty-five!' and Irvine passed the order down the pipe to CPO Partridge: crouching with his beard touching the voicepipe's rim he watched the Stuka, seeing shells bursting all around it as it came rushing in that dead-straight dive with its angled wings and the undercarriage like a vulture's legs and claws: a bomb dropping from it was turning over and over with the sun's glitter on its fins, Irvine scowling up at it and Jack Everard guessing it was going to land in this bridge – and nothing anyone could do about it. The noise was enclosing, isolating; *Carnarvon* was swinging fast to port, heeling as her rudder dragged her round, and the bomb went into the sea off her starboard bow, a sheet of water leaping and the thud of the explosion like a hard kick in her belly. Napier shouted, 'Bring us back on course!' Irvine called down, 'Midships', and Partridge acknowledged the order, then confirmed, 'Wheel's amidships, sir.' Irvine told him, 'Starboard twenty.' The destroyers were under helm too most of the time, but the barrage over the Dutch ship never slackened much. It was keeping the Stukas high, or high-ish, and the Dutchman's own close-range weapons were helping too, but another Stuka was diving on her now and higher up were two more just at this moment tilting their yellow noses down. Bell-Reid was talking into a telephone, getting reports from below about possible damage from those near-misses. Napier was on the phone to the ADP, conferring with Jock McCowan; bombs were splashing in

269

astern of the Dutch ship, and one Stuka was careering away landward just a few feet above the water, passing so close to *Huntress* they could have thrown spuds at it. Another was coming down – *now* – on top of the Dutchman and one on *Carnarvon*, and *Highflier* was swinging hard a-starboard with a bomb-splash rising just ahead of her: he saw the muzzle-flashes of her for'ard four-sevens as she shifted target and began to put a barrage over *Carnarvon* to ward off this attacking Stuka. It was silvery-grey against bright smoke-stained sky, yellow-snouted, disgusting, screaming hate: Irvine was ready at the voicepipe, waiting for Napier's order, when a shell burst close to that yellow nose and the machine exploded, wiped out in mid-air in a spread of smoke-trails and debris. A Stuka was pulling out of its dive over *Gelderland*, its bomb on the way down, tracer arcing up to converge on the plane as it flattened and presented a broader and perhaps temporarily slower-moving target; *Huntress*, inside her station and very close to the Dutchman, was turning her point-fives on it. And that bomb had hit the *Gelderland* . . .

Port side aft: a burst of flame and smoke, and the Stuka was flying out of all that concentration of close-range weaponry, escaping landward. There was another one too, going for her now, approaching in a shallower dive from the other quarter, astern of *Huntress*. The Dutch ship was still plugging on and seemed not to have slackened speed. Clutterbuck had directed *Carnarvon*'s two after four-inch to go for the shallow-diving Stuka, and Napier had come to the binnacle himself: he called down, 'Port twenty-five!' He was staying there: Irvine had moved over, off the step. The pompoms were roaring away at a new one coming in from the port bow, diving steeply across *Highflier*, screaming down with its sights obviously on the cruiser's bridge. The for'ard and midships four-inch were pumping a barrage into the sky right in front of that yellow nose: for a moment you couldn't see it for shellbursts, but then it was in sight again and still diving on its target – *this* target. Napier called down, 'Midships and meet her!' His object was to steady her on a course directly towards the diving bomber: if its pilot was to have a chance of hitting with his bomb he'd have to steepen his dive, take it even nearer to the vertical and thus to suicide: he'd chosen not to, he was pulling out prematurely – which was his only alternative – and the multiple pompoms' concentration of two-pounder shells was reaching eagerly towards him as he levelled across the stream of it: *and shells were hitting* . . .

270

Clutterbuck's voice came urgently from the speaker: 'Shift target right, green one hundred, Stuka over *Gelderland* . . .'

The one the pompoms had hit had gone into the sea in a sheet of flame. The other, the last to come, had dropped its bomb short of *Gelderland* and broken away landward, pursued at first by shellbursts and machine-gun fire from *Huntress*.

Now it was quiet again and the sky was empty. Smoke leaked thinly from the Dutch ship's stern, but the fire was out and the bomb didn't seem to have hurt her much. The convoy was maintaining its previous course and speed: they were two-thirds of the way across the twenty-mile half-moon formed by the coast of the Elos Peninsula. In about twenty minutes Cape Malea would be abeam to starboard, and from there roughly three hours' steaming would see them into the Antikithera Channel, at the western end of Crete. But long before that, Jack guessed, with any luck at all and if there were any RAF or Fleet Air Arm planes at all left in Crete . . .

It was a lovely thought. *Too* lovely, and dangerous to reckon on. The odds were, he told himself, that before they saw a Hurricane they'd see a lot more Stukas. The German airfields were so close that the bombers had only to fly back and land, refuel and refill their bomb racks, and come back for another go. Over and over again: yellow-nosed bastards in pursuit of Iron Crosses.

Bell-Reid had gone for a tour of the ship. He'd chat to guns' crews and ammo-supply and damage-control parties, look in at the Marines in the TS, have a word to the engineers and give the pongo passengers news of what was happening up top. Guns' crews meanwhile would be clearing away the clutter of empty shellcases, replenishing the racks with fused shells, relaxing tired muscles, lighting cigarettes and drinking the dark brown liquid that sailors called tea; the pompom and point-five gunners would be re-ammunitioning, oiling and cleaning their somewhat temperamental weapons.

It might start again at any moment: that it would start again before long was inevitable. So far they'd been lucky. Only poor *Huntress* had suffered any casualties: two dead and one wounded at her B gun-mounting. Jack had a feeling that *Carnarvon*'s and *Gelderland*'s luck couldn't last: sooner or later the other side would get some. But looking round the bridge he noticed the snotty, Brighouse, scratching like a dog and looking bored, and beside the bridge shelter the Marine bugler – Sykes, that one's name was, and he looked even younger than the midshipman – was laughing at some remark made by Durkin, the leading signalman. Jack thought, If *they* can stand it . . . But there was no question, none at all, of *not* standing it. Not to be able to stand the stress of action because of some defect in oneself had been the fear, the nightmare of the recent years: if one could give it the boot, there *was* no fear.

Like hell there wasn't.

Well, not real fear: not that deep, recurrent dread . . .

No, he assured himself, not that kind. He smiled, making a private joke of it to himself: *Just pure terror, that's all.*

Half-brother Nick, he knew, expected him to lose his nerve. Nick had a private theory about Jack being a reincarnation or facsimile of the older, dead half-brother, Nick's own elder brother David who'd gone into a blue funk at Jutland – gone *mad* at Jutland, and then drowned . . . Nick had told the story, years ago, to their father Sir John Everard. He'd apologized for it since, or half-apologized, admitting he'd only burst out with it in a rage, stung by the old man's goading. All anyone knew for certain was that David's ship had been sunk and that afterwards the ship's chaplain, a survivor, had told their uncle, Admiral Sir Hugh Everard, that David had died a hero's death trying to save wounded men. Sarah, Jack's own mother, swore this must be the truth. She'd known her stepson David and admired him, adored him. Nick had spoken out of spite, she said, because he'd always resented David for being the older son and their father's heir. It was the shock that Nick had given her husband, Sir John, with that pack of lies about poor David, that had given the old man his first heart-attack and finally killed him. Jack had been only a little boy, then, his half-brother Nick already a grown man.

Sarah had added, 'In any case, you aren't really at *all* like David!' But he was: there was an oil painting at Mullbergh of David in naval full-dress, and some old sepia snapshots that she hadn't wanted him to see. She'd persisted, 'If there's some superficial resemblance, that doesn't mean you're . . .'

'No.' He'd tried to make it easy for her. 'No, of course not.'

The second lot of Stukas, the ones who'd arrived just when the convoy had been altering course to 170 degrees, had made their attacks and been beaten off; *Highflier* had been near-missed, stopped for about one hair-raising minute and then got going again, to everyone's intense relief. Napier had signalled to her *Are you all right?* and she'd flashed back, *Never better, thank you, it was just a temporary indisposition.* And in *Carnarvon* three men of Q gun's crew – Q was the midships four-inch mounting – and Sub-Lieutenant Ramsden, RNVR, who was the officer of the quarters there, had been hit by machine-gun fire from a Junkers strafing them. That had been the end of it so far as the 87s were concerned, but just as they'd finished and the last of them had winged away a crowd of 88s had appeared, coming from the same direction – from over the land on the quarter. They'd made their shallow-diving runs, a few quite low but mostly fairly well up, and the action had been quite hot for a while but ended with the convoy still intact and plugging on, no ships damaged and no aircraft hit. Then there'd been a breather – quite a good one, ten or twelve minutes – before this last Stuka attack had started. Now it was eight minutes past nine and there'd been a whole quarter of an hour of peace. *Carnarvon* was back where she belonged, close astern of the Dutch ship, and the destroyers were in station ahead and on either beam. The sea's surface was ruffled by a light wind on the quarter; it was coming to them through the Elaphonisos Channel, the gap between the mainland and Kithera Island. The lighthouse on Anti Dragonera bore 243 degrees, nine miles away; he could still see Cape Malea, and the 0900 fix using these two landmarks showed they had thirty-five miles to cover, to reach the Antikithera Channel.

Bell-Reid suggested, puffing at his pipe of pusser's best – Admiralty-issue tobacco – 'Shot their bolt, d'you think, sir?'

'Doubt it. If I know anything about 'em they'll be grinding their teeth with fury, by this time, and mad to get back at us.' He was looking at the sky over the Grecian mainland. He added, 'Although it's conceivable we might get some help from our own air boys before much longer.' He'd sent a request for air support, after that first attack. He shrugged: '*Conceivable* . . . Pilot, how far are we from Maleme airfield now?'

Jack went to the chart and measured the distance. Maleme was in north-west Crete, about ten miles west of Suda Bay.

'Fifty-three miles, sir.'

'Close enough, you'd think.' Bell-Reid pointed with the stem of his pipe at the *Gelderland*. 'And by this time, mark you, we'd be clear out of it, if it hadn't been for that bloody woman.'

A telephone buzzed: Midshipman Brighouse, who was nearest to it, snatched it off its hook. 'Bridge.' Then: 'Hold on, sir.' He looked at the captain: 'PMO would like to speak to you, sir.'

Napier slid off his seat and went across the bridge; PMO stood for Principal Medical Officer. Jack Everard was thinking that the attacks *might* be over: the Germans might reckon they'd be under their own air cover by now. So even if the RAF didn't show up soon, the Stukas might stay away. Napier said, 'I see. Thank you, Doctor.' Jack thought about the Stukas not coming back. Pigs might fly, too . . . Napier told Bell-Reid as he went back to his chair and got up on it, 'Ramsden's dead. The loading number, Richardson, has only a slim chance. The other two will be all right.'

'Aircraft, right astern!'

Number three look-out on the port side had yelled it. Napier reached down for his telephone to McCowan: before his hand had closed on it Clutterbuck's voice came sharply from the speaker: 'Alarm astern! All guns follow ADP, aircraft, angle of sight two-five – red barrage, load, load, load!'

Then he came through again: 'Aircraft astern are Stukas.'

Napier murmured, settling his tin hat on his head, 'On battle bowlers.' He beckoned: 'Pilot, let's concoct another signal. Pad?' Jack got one from the chart table, and a pencil. Napier began, 'Same addressees as last time. Prefix "Most Immediate". Start – *Since my* – time of origin of the last one—'

'0719.'

'*Since my 0719 I have been under almost constant air attack. New force of Stukas is now arriving. My position* – whatever—'

The two after four-inch mountings had opened fire: Clutterbuck was ordering A and Q to load with the shorter, blue barrage settings. Napier went on quickly, 'Put in the position: then, *course 170 speed 16*' – he paused as the guns fired again – 'and time of origin. Fix that up and send it in plain language.'

'Aye aye, sir.' He yelled for the chief yeoman as he ducked to the chart, filled in the missing bits and added time of origin 0921. Hegarty was waiting: he tore the top sheet off the pad and passed it to him. All the guns were firing now: coming up from the chart table, Jack saw Stukas overhead and on both sides, shellbursts under them and all around them: one bomber diving now at *Gelderland*, and the pompoms had opened up just as it turned its snout down. He recalled a thought he'd had earlier, about luck changing, the unlikelihood of having a monopoly of it: and it was as if he'd seen it before it happened, knew beyond doubt that it was about to happen: *a hit on the Dutch ship, in her bridge superstructure* . . . Then another in the sea just over, a near-miss, but already her bridge was a mass of flame, and she was swinging out to port with a third bomber going for her, dropping on her in shrill cruelty. Every gun – *Carnarvon*'s, *Halberdier*'s, *Highflier*'s and *Huntress*'s – was in action to shield the transport from this fresh attack, but she'd been hit again, a column of smoke and flame bursting upwards from her forepart as she circled, out of control. *Highflier* was turning outwards to give the Dutch ship sea-room, *Huntress* beginning to turn too, in towards her. There were Stukas everywhere and the sky was plastered with shellbursts, laced with tracer. Napier had taken over at the binnacle: Irvine moved around to stand beside his vacated seat within reach of the telephone to the ADP. The noise of the pompoms was head-splitting as they fired vertically at a diving bomber and the bridge caught all the sound of it. *Gelderland* was still circling, with smoke and flames pouring out of her. Napier was stooping to the voicepipe to pass a helm order and at the same time looking upwards, seeing the Stuka coming down at them – vicious, horrible . . . The pompoms were hitting him or it was the Stuka's guns firing, or both, there were flame-spurts anyway in that blur of movement: flames expanding suddenly, whooshing out: but the *thing*, still diving, still had its bombs . . . Noise a crescendo, mind-numbing: there was a moment's passing, scorching heat and then the Stuka had plunged into the sea a dozen yards from the cruiser's side and exploded as it went in: sea cascaded across the ship.

The Dutch ship must have got her rudder centred because she'd stopped circling, but she was going the wrong way, back along the convoy's tracks so that she was steaming into the wind and it was helping to drive the flames aft, spreading the fires along her decks. *Carnarvon* was under helm, turning to stay with her: *Highflier* had gone right round to port and was beyond her, on her starboard beam, and *Halberdier* had also gone about. *Halberdier* was having to defend herself at this moment, speeding up and zigzagging to dodge a Stuka in its dive, but her four-sevens were still contributing to the barrage over *Gelderland*. *Gelderland* was slowing – stopping . . . Jack focused his glasses on her and saw that the only section of her not on fire was her stern part, roughly one-fifth of her at that end, and both tiers of deck there were thronged with men. Some of them were trying to get her boats away: only four boats, *if* there were two intact on the other side, where he couldn't see; the others were in the flames. The two he could see, still high in their davits, were already full – *too* full . . . Stukas were diving on her again: and now one racing across her stern with its machine-guns blazing, and men in khaki jumping from that stern into the sea. He saw a Stuka diving now to bomb, straight into the barrage, through it: bomb falling away and the plane curving out and away below the shellbursts: behind it the bomb struck *Gelderland* amidships, bursting inside her, the ship's guts spilling skywards. More men were jumping from her stern into the sea as the flames spread back towards them: she was listing to starboard and at a standstill and another Stuka plummeting down above her.

'Midships. Signalman . . .'

Carnarvon was moving up on the doomed ship's port quarter. Ringing with noise . . . Eardrums mercifully part-numbed, but down below in the enclosed compartments it must, he thought, be unbearable. *Huntress*, who'd turned in from what had been the convoy's starboard side, was now astern of the cruiser and closing up towards her, a bit out on the starboard quarter. *Highflier* was on *Gelderland*'s starboard beam and *Halberdier*, circling back now, was right astern of her. A Stuka was tearing across over *Halberdier* with its machine-guns sparking and the destroyer's point-fives missing astern of it, the tracer's curve seeming to fall back on itself and the Stuka away and clear, lifting higher as it flew off northward. Napier had shouted to Durkin, the leading signalman, 'Make to *Highflier* by light, *Close Gelderland and pick up swimmers.*' The order was going to her now in dots and dashes from the starboard Aldis lamp. He'd ordered port wheel and an increase in revs, and called the chief yeoman and given him a signal for the other two destroyers: *Act independently while Highflier collects survivors.* They would circle, dodging, using their guns to shelter the rescue operation as far as was possible. But the noise of the guns was slackening: just as he noticed it, it increased again, every weapon back in it suddenly as one last Stuka came screaming down and every gun that could bear concentrated on that one target, one last enemy symbolizing all of them, all the ferocity of the past few hours. Jack Everard watched it with a kind of astonishment in his own *enjoyment* of it: enjoyment coming from anticipation, the *certainty* that the Stuka would be hit, explode, go like those others had in a flash and roar of bombs, gas-tank, human blood and bone: watching, expectant, *longing* for the sight of it . . . The Stuka came straight as a dart, loathsome, a vulture plunging on an already dying victim: the bomb fell away and he saw the levelling-out process begin, knowing it was the stage at which several of them had been destroyed. But the plane wasn't touched and its bomb struck, hideously, landing on that packed

stern deck. Bodies and objects flying outwards from the burst . . .
The Dutch ship was *all* flame now, and the Stuka was racing away
north-westward across the blue Aegean.

'Midships. Slow ahead together.'

There were no enemies overhead and the guns were silent. You
could hear clangs from the gundecks and splashes alongside as the
crews ditched shellcases; from across the water came the roar and
crackle of that giant floating bonfire. She was listing now, lying
almost on her side. Napier called down, 'Stop both engines.' Jack
Everard was stooped against the side of the bridge in order to rest
his elbows on it and hold the glasses steady despite his hands'
tendency to shake. He was counting heads, or trying to, as
Highflier nosed up towards the swimmers, *Halberdier* joining
her now in the rescue work. *Highflier* had a scrambling-net down
on this near side; she'd slipped her whaler and she had men
standing by with lines all along her sides from stem to stern. He
trained his glasses left, to *Gelderland* herself. The whole ship was on
fire: at her stern one lifeboat, suspended vertically from only one
fall, was resting against the ship's raised side, lying on it, and the
boat itself was smouldering. Then he caught his breath: he was
seeing arms, some bare and some in khaki shirt-sleeves, waving
from open scuttles in the Dutch ship's side. Signalling for help,
rescue. But she was going. He saw the final movement start, the
downward wash and froth of sea as she rolled right over, turning
her keel up first and then the stern lifting before she slid bow-first
into something like 500 fathoms.

Gelderland had sunk at 0937. It had taken *Highflier* and *Halberdier*
half an hour to gather the survivors, and at 1010 the force had got
under way on course 170 at twenty-five knots, which was *Carnarvon*'s best speed. *Highflier* had eighty-four survivors from the
Dutch ship and *Halberdier* had thirty-one. At Nauplia *Gelderland*
had embarked twelve hundred soldiers.

At 1025 two aircraft had appeared ahead and were identified as
Hurricanes. They'd hung around, patrolling to the northward, for
about an hour, and when the ships were in the channel between
Crete and Antikithera Island one of the aircraft had flashed a
message to *Carnarvon*: *Have to leave you now. Good luck.* They'd
flown off eastward, presumably to Maleme. It had been half-past
eleven when they'd left, and at that time the force had been steering
due south with Agria Grabusa, the north-western point of Crete,

seven miles abeam to port. At 1220, by which time Elaphonisi lighthouse was coming up on the port bow, a signal thumped up in the pneumatic tube from the office down below; the yeoman of the watch, PO Tomkins, extracted it and brought it to the captain.

Napier read it, then held it out to his navigator.

'We're to rendezvous with the First Battle Squadron ten miles south of Gavdo at 1430. How does that look?'

Jack went to the chart to check distances and courses. He had in mind that there was a much earlier signal on the log – it had been repeated to *Carnarvon* for information – ordering the 37th Destroyer Flotilla to meet the battle fleet south of Cape Littino at noon. 37th DF was the Tribal flotilla with brother Nick's *Tuareg* in it, and presumably that rendezvous would have been effected by now. There'd be *Barham, Valiant, Formidable*, plus the destroyers they'd had with them already, and now this bunch, and presumably after they'd joined up they'd all be heading back to Alexandria.

He told Napier, 'We can hold these revs, sir, and alter to one-three-five when Elaphonisi bears oh-five-eight. That'll be in about ten minutes.'

'Good.' Napier looked round. 'Yeoman – bend on, but do not hoist yet, *Course one-three-five*.' He told Jack, 'Warn me when we have three degrees to go on that bearing, would you.'

Jack nodded. 'Sir.' He moved to the pelorus, where he could keep an eye on it. He saw that Napier was still looking at him, either critically or thoughtfully.

'Everard.' Speaking quietly . . . 'It's not the end of the world, you know.'

'No, sir.' Lining up the sight on that lighthouse. 'I know.'

You didn't have to talk about it. Everyone in the ship felt the same despondency. Napier added, lifting his binoculars, 'It's the end of Demon, though.' 'Demon' had been the code-name for the Greek evacuation. He added, training his glasses slowly left to study the rocky coastline and the Cretan mountains that rose behind it, 'The Germans will be going for *this* place now.'

CHAPTER 3

Tuareg was rolling in quite a lively fashion as, with *Masai* and *Afghan* following, she zigzagged astern of *Blackfoot* towards the Kaso Strait. Tribal-class destroyers did tend to roll, in any kind of a beam sea; but it was a small fault to put up with, Nick thought, for the pleasure of driving such a lovely ship. Resting his eyes from binoculars, he was looking for'ard over the front edge of the bridge. The flare of B gundeck hid A gun from his sight; beyond B's twin muzzles and that jutting flare was the narrow foc'sl and sharp prow splitting the sea ahead, carving deeply into it and sending it curling out and back, the white of the broken water vividly bright against varying shades of blue. Harry Houston, who was officer of the watch, informed him from the step behind the binnacle, 'You have a – ah – visitor, sir.'

Nick was on his bridge seat, a wooden-based affair in the port fore corner behind the chart-table alcove: he glanced round and saw the young Royal Marine captain, Brownlees, lurching for'ard from the ladder, grabbing hold of fittings here and there for support as he approached. Captain Brownlees looked uneasily aware of the destroyer's motion.

'I wondered if we might take a shufti at that chart now, sir, as you suggested earlier. Hope you don't mind me barging up like this.'

'You've timed it well. We'll be going to action stations in twenty minutes.' He told Houston as he slid off the seat, 'I'll be in the chartroom.'

A haze of land on the port bow was the mountainous eastern end of Crete, and a more nebulous but higher haze to starboard was the ridge of mountain which ran like a spine along the lizard-like shape of Scarpanto. A smaller island, Kaso, lay this side of Scarpanto, but it was lower as well as smaller and from this distance you couldn't see it. The flotilla had sailed from Alexandria at six this morning – having got into harbour at ten the night before and spent several hours fuelling and ammunitioning. They'd steamed all day at twenty knots, and at 8 pm this evening, by which time they'd have passed through that Kaso gap, they'd be stopping the A/S zigzag and increasing to thirty knots for the night dash to their target area.

Putting in marines, he thought, who in a few days' time would have to be brought out again. He didn't mention the thought to Brownlees.

'Is *that* Crete?'

The Marine was pointing. Nick, pausing near the head of the bridge ladder, nodded. 'Yes. And the high ground on the other bow – *there* – is Scarpanto. Italian.'

'Scarpanto where they've based a Stuka group?'

'Right. Not a bad reason for going to action stations before we get too close to it, would you say?'

'Perhaps' – Brownlees staggered, caught at something – 'perhaps you've a point, sir.'

There'd been no let-up for the fleet since Operation Demon had ended three weeks ago. It had been logical and obvious that Crete would be the Germans' next objective: so Crete had to be supplied, and the waters to the north of it patrolled; and down in the south Tobruk was under siege and there was a desert army to be supported. Two destroyers, for instance, operated what was known as the spud run out of Alexandria up-coast to Tobruk every single night with ammunition and stores, leaving for return to Alex the same night with the army's wounded. You couldn't let yourself be caught on that coast in daylight now. And just as the Greek evacuation ended – 50,000 men had been lifted, most of them from open beaches – London had decided to run a convoy from Gibraltar right through to Alexandria, bringing tanks and aircraft for the defence of Egypt. A German panzer division had been identified in the desert, and without tank reinforcements Wavell would have been at a hopeless disadvantage. The Admiralty had pointed out that with powerful Luftwaffe forces now based in Sicily – Malta was under day-long, day-after-day attack – the chances of getting a convoy through without appalling losses were extremely slim: Churchill had overridden the objection, insisted on the convoy being sent. Incredibly, it had turned out well: low cloud and bad visibility, conditions never heard of in the Mediterranean at this time of year, had come like a gift of God to protect a wild gamble. It had been a complicated operation, code-named 'Tiger': Admiral Sir Andrew Cunningham hadn't just sailed his Mediterranean Fleet to meet the convoy, he'd also run two convoys of his own into Malta and carried out two bombardments, *en passant*, of Benghazi, and he'd brought the tank convoy from Gibraltar into Alexandria harbour on 12 May.

The fleet had benefited from 'Tiger'. With the convoy had come reinforcements, the battleship *Queen Elizabeth* and the cruisers *Naiad* and *Fiji*.

After five days of heavy air attacks on the airstrips and on Suda Bay, the German military assault on Crete had opened thirty-six hours ago with parachute and glider landings. Twenty-four hours before that, all RAF and Fleet Air Arm operations finished. On 15 May there'd been three Gladiators, three Fulmars and three Hurricanes working from Maleme: they'd fought virtually to the last man and the last aircraft, and now the fleet had no air support at all, no hope of any – only the certainty of German air assault from fields at Scarpanto, Tatoi, Eleusis, Mycene, Molai and Argos. And from Crete itself too, when they captured Maleme – which they might have done already. After the first day's fighting they'd already had part of the airfield in their hands. Other airborne forces were fighting furiously for the airstrips at Retimo and Heraklion.

Brownlees unfolded his own map. He'd wanted to see the naval angle, relate map to chart. There were about 150 Marines in each of the four destroyers, and their colonel was in *Blackfoot*.

'We're to be landed about' – he pointed – 'here?'

'Right in that corner. Armyro Bay – also called Almirou Bay, on some charts. I'll show you the detail in a moment on a different one, but you'll be landing beside a village called Yeorgioupoleos . . . Look, here's Retimo. Alternative spellings Rethimnon or Rhithymno, take your pick. But it has an airstrip – fairly primitive, I gather – about here.'

The Marine nodded. 'Germans are on a hill that commands both the airstrip and the road south-west out of Retimo. On and around it. There's to be an attack by Aussies from Retimo itself at the same time as we barge up the other way . . . Why are we having to start so far west?'

'Is five miles *far*, for leathernecks?'

Brownless smiled patiently. 'I'm thinking of the delay, possible hold-ups.'

'It's the best spot. The only one, probably. The pilot' – he reached to a shelf above the table and tapped the spine of *Mediterranean Pilot vol. IV* – 'this tells us that for five miles east of our village there's a wide coastal bank with hidden rocks in it. Then it gets openly rocky from about where your hill is right up to Retimo.' He pulled the marine's map closer and bent over it. 'I wonder why we haven't planned to bombard the German positions – lob starshell over that hill and then plaster it with HE before your attack. It wouldn't have presented any problems.'

Brownless shrugged. 'Colonel mightn't go for that. Rather do it softly, softly, I should guess.'

Nick thought that if he'd been in Reggie Marsh's place when the orders came . . . Well, he hadn't been, and wasn't. He pulled another chart out from under the one they'd been looking at. 'Now – here's your landing area . . .'

'Speed thirty knots, sir!'

'Very good.'

Blackfoot was flying the signal. Nick leant out to port and looked astern, saw *Masai*'s and *Afghan*'s answering pendants going up. *Tuareg*'s was already close-up. Cape Sidaro, Crete's north-east corner, would be abeam before much longer; Kaso was behind them, about twenty miles on the starboard quarter. They'd come through without even a sniff from the Luftwaffe. Not that one should count chickens yet: it was eight o'clock, and it would be an hour before it was dark enough to start feeling safe.

'Executive, sir!'

He glanced at Pratt, who called down to the wheelhouse, 'Three-one-oh revolutions.' Now he was taking bearings: and Ashcourt had got a pad ready, to write the figures down for him. The ship was still at action stations, and would be until the light went. Pratt said, 'Paximada two-eight-one. Plaka – two-one-three.' Then he took the beam bearing last, because that was the one that changed fastest: 'Sidaro, two-five-three.' He straightened from the pelorus and put a hand out for the pad. 'Thanks.'

'My pleasure.'

'Your pleasures don't bear thinking about, chum.'

'Don't they, hell. They're all I have to keep me warm.'

'Sub.'

He turned quickly. 'Sir?'

'Go down and bring me the pilot, would you.'

282

Nick met Pratt's glance, and winked. But he did want the book of sailing directions. Sooner or later – it was a certainty, he felt, not speculation – they'd be told to start getting the army out of Crete, and he might as well start familiarizing himself with details of the few small ports and the coastline.

It would be a matter of taking them off beaches again, he supposed. Such ports as existed – Suda Bay, Retimo, Heraklion – were all on the island's north coast; and even at this stage it was chancy enough to be on the northern side in daylight. All right, so you'd make your pick-ups in the dark: but you'd have to get to the embarkation point in darkness, load the troops – which wasn't always the smoothest, fastest evolution – and then back either to Kaso in the east or to Antikithera in the west: two or three hours' steaming at full speed, and you'd still be in those straits at daylight, with no air cover and your ships crammed with soldiers. Like the Dutch transport that young Jack had seen go down.

Nick had seen Jack in Alexandria, just before they'd sailed for 'Tiger', the convoy operation. He'd been – well, his usual self. Polite, but under the politeness, hostile. Or defensive? Yes, defensive: and you couldn't blame him for that. Nick *didn't* blame him: only wished, as he'd wished for years, that he could cut through the barriers.

Was every man allowed one truly colossal failure?

'*Blackfoot*'s altering to port, sir.'

Cutting the corner. Midnight was zero-hour for landing the marines; a few minutes saved now might prove valuable later. Nick told Pratt, 'Follow him round.' Pratt was a reliable navigator and a good man to have around. He'd make a good first lieutenant before long. There'd be plenty of opportunities coming, with the rate at which destroyers, sloops and corvettes were beginning to pour out of the yards at home. None too soon, at that.

But Jack, Sarah's son . . .

It was a safe way to label him, in your mind. Your stepmother's son, when his name was Everard, was obviously your half-brother; people took it for granted. You couldn't tell anyone the truth, ever, but out of your own need to be honest or loyal – something like that – you couldn't deny it, deny him either. Nick hadn't been able to get close to him, help him or really talk to him; Sarah had made it impossible, and he'd been forced to accept the situation – accept, without really understanding it even now, her fierce, long-standing hatred. Only Nick and Sarah knew that Jack was his own son, not

283

his father's. It was Sarah who'd worked the deception, fooled the old man completely and left him, Nick, to guess in silence at how she'd managed it.

It was now 2200 and pitch dark. Standia Island three and a half miles abeam to port. Everyone in the bridge was dressed for the cold. The Mediterranean Fleet had shifted into summer whites several weeks ago, but once the sun went down there wasn't much feel of summer.

Beside Nick in the dark bridge, Dalgleish said, 'Must be a lot of ships plugging around tonight.'

'Yes.' Nick asked Pratt, 'Are we on the ball with recognition lights?'

'All checked, sir.'

There were lights fixed to the lower edges of the fore-yard, and a locked steel box in the chartroom where you could change the combination. To challenge an unidentified ship at night you pressed a key here in the bridge, and the pre-set sequence of colours flashed out at her. You'd have your guns loaded and trained before you made the challenge.

As Dalgleish had remarked, something like half the Mediterranean Fleet was in the Aegean tonight. A lot of ships: and also a truly vast number of aircraft squatting, ready bombed-up and fuelled, on the German airfields all around, waiting for first light, knowing they'd have the sky all to themselves. A Stuka pilot's dream of heaven: plenty of targets and no airborne opposition. They'd be getting in a good night's rest – to be fresh and eager for the dawn.

The Luftwaffe had made only one kill today; they'd bombed and sunk the destroyer *Juno*, who'd been with Admiral King's Force C. But there'd been air attacks all through the daylight hours, and the cruiser *Ajax* had been damaged by near-misses. *Ajax* – with *Orion* and *Dido* and destroyers – was part of Force D, under Admiral Glennie. By the sound of things, tomorrow would see a lot more action – there'd been reports of German troop convoys from the Piraeus and from Milos island heading south for Crete, and several squadrons were being deployed to search and intercept.

Including – later tonight – this flotilla. After they'd put the marines ashore the Tribals were to make a sweep north-westward before turning down to pass through Kithera and join the battle-fleet – Force A1 as it was now being called – under Admiral

Rawlings with his flag in *Warspite*. The C-in-C, directing operations from Alexandria, was keeping a force of big ships in that south-west area in case the Italian fleet should so far forget itself as to venture out to sea.

Carnarvon, Jack's cruiser, was down there with the battle squadron.

What else had been happening . . . Well, the 14th Destroyer Flotilla had bombarded Scarpanto airfield last night, the cruisers *Gloucester* and *Fiji* – Force B – had made a night sweep up to Cape Matapan, and King's Force C had had a brush with Italian torpedo-boats in the Kaso Strait. During the day *Gloucester* and *Fiji* had joined Rawlings' battleships, and so had Glennie's Force D, *Orion* and company; and tonight Forces B, C and D would all be up here in the Aegean looking for those invasion convoys. Force C had been scheduled to pass northward through Kaso about two hours astern of this flotilla; the three groups had orders to foregather off Heraklion at dawn, after their night sweeps, and hunt north-westward towards Milos island.

In daylight, with no air cover. Evidently all risks were to be accepted, to stop seaborne invasion forces reaching Crete.

'Captain, sir. Signal . . .'

'Read it to me, Yeoman, or tell me what it's about.'

He didn't want to ruin his night-vision by going to the light. PO Whiffen told him, 'Bad news, sir. Gerry's got Maleme airfield. It's a general signal to all ships.'

'Gerry' could fly in his heavy stuff now, in the big Junkers 52 transport planes. Men, weapons, ammunition, stores: he'd got the back door open and he could expand, consolidate. Even if the fleet *did* stop all surface invasion forces – which they would, of course.

'Messenger!'

'Sir?'

'Give him that signal, Yeoman. Harris, take it down to the wardroom and show it to the captain of marines.'

2350: *Tuareg* lay stopped and silent 400 yards offshore, and only about half that, a cable's length, from the little island of Ayios Nikolaos. On the shore opposite the island, which had a church on it and a rough, narrow causeway connecting it to the beach, a huddle of white buildings which comprised the village of Yeorgioupoleos gleamed in the darkness. Rocky Pratt was hunched at the gyro repeater, checking shore bearings, and the echo-sounder was humming as it recorded the depth of water under the ship's keel; in this sheltered bay, with every star reflected in its surface, it would have been a waste of time to anchor. It would have been noisy, too. Crete wasn't a German stronghold – not yet – but there were pockets of invaders everywhere and the marines were treating this landing as a raid into potentially enemy territory.

For the last twenty or thirty minutes – since about the time they'd turned for the run down into Almyro Bay – there'd been outbreaks of gunfire to seaward. The sound of it came from the north-west, where the flotilla would be heading when this landing job was done. Admiral Glennie's ships, he guessed: they'd have been sweeping eastward on a track to the north of the Tribals' westward one, and they must have run into something . . . He thought, waiting for the all-clear signal from the shore, *Come on, come on* . . . The boats were alongside, full of men and ready to shove off. On the port side one motorboat – with Sub-Lieutenant Chalk, RNVR, in charge – had the whaler astern of it in tow, and to starboard the other motorboat waited on its own. All the boats had been scrounged or 'borrowed' from Alexandria dockyard by Dalgleish – who was down there on the iron deck now, waiting to send them away. Nick had his glasses trained on the islet, the causeway and the land behind it, and Ashcourt was at the after end of the bridge acting as a link between Nick and Dalgleish. Half a cable's length to starboard *Blackfoot* was a low, rakish silhouette, and *Masai* lay beyond her; one motorboat-load of marines had already gone inshore from *Blackfoot* to check that the immediate surroundings were clear of Germans, and the destroyers were at action stations, their guns ready to respond instantaneously to any opposition.

Afghan was guard-ship, two miles out in the bay and keeping an Asdic listening watch. She'd come in and land her troops when the first of these three finished and moved out to take her place.

Ashore, across that gap of starlit water, nothing moved. Gunfire in the west – ashore – was a sporadic crackling like the sound of fireworks at a distance. It was quite different from the heavier explosions that came from seaward – *still* came, although less frequently.

Ayios Nikolaos . . . Ayios, according to the pilot, meaning 'saint'. Where the causeway reached the beach was the mouth of a river, the Almiros, and its westward-reaching valley carried a track which later curved northward to the southern shore of Suda

Bay. Suda, which Winston Churchill had thought should be turned into a Mediterranean version of Scapa Flow, an impregnable naval base. Royal Marines were improvising defences for it now, marines of the MNBDO, Mobile Naval Base Defence Organization, under a General Weston.

Nick saw the all-clear: a morse K on a blue lamp from the shore. And now a second later it had been repeated from the island. He told Ashcourt, 'Away boats!'

Ashcourt called down to Dalgleish, 'Away boats, sir!'

Nick asked Pratt, 'Depth all right still?'

'Yes, sir. We seem to be static.' Pratt added, 'That action's still—'

'I know, pilot, I've got ears . . .'

Pratt had been talking about that gunfire: and Nick was wanting to finish this quickly, get out there . . . The motorboat from the starboard side was chugging out ahead of the ship, waiting for the other one with its whaler. Nick had given orders that they were to stay together, move to and fro as one unit. Motorboats' engines were notoriously unreliable, and by doing it this way you ensured that if a boat broke down there'd be only a minimal delay before it was added to the tow. As a last resort, if both power-boats failed, the whaler had its oars and would tow *them*. There were fifteen marines in the 27-foot whaler, thirty in each of the motorboats, so two round trips would complete the job. The boats were all clear now, moving shoreward, and he could see the other destroyers' boats off to starboard, the phosphorescence at their sterns and their dark shapes against the shiny surface. *Blackfoot*'s and *Masai*'s would be landing on the north side of the islet, while *Tuareg*'s had this side to themselves. In both approaches, the seaward extremity of the island had to be widely skirted, because of off-lying rocks; *Tuareg*'s boats had farther to go than the others had, but the lack of competition for landing space ought to give their coxswains an advantage.

Apart from the desire to get out to sea and to where the action was, he wanted *Tuareg*'s boats to finish first: in particular, to beat *Blackfoot*'s. He'd have made sure of it, he knew, if he'd put Ashcourt in charge of the operation, instead of young Chalk; Ashcourt had two years' experience of boat-handling as an RN midshipman behind him, whereas Chalk had come straight from Oxford via the Joint Universities' Recruiting Board. He needed experience, the feel of responsibility, though, and it was in the ship's interests as well as his that he should get it. Besides, with a first-class killick coxswain in each boat he couldn't go far wrong.

'Boats returning, sir!'

Ashcourt sounded as if he'd caught the regatta spirit too. Or he was thinking about that gunfire. Anyway, those *were Tuareg*'s boats: the others must still be behind Ayios Nikolaos.

Blackfoot's having put the advance party ashore hadn't given her any advantage, because the marine colonel had a few extra men in his contingent anyway. And unless *Tuareg*'s boats did something silly now – like breaking down – they'd win easily: they were more than halfway from the shore, and the first of the others had only just come in sight.

'Sub – tell the first lieutenant to stand by with the second flight.' He went to the engineroom voicepipe and told Redmayne, the engineer lieutenant, 'About three minutes, Chief, then I'll be turning the ship.' The boats were making their approaches; down on the iron deck Dalgleish, aided by Mr Walsh the Gunner (T) and PO Mercer the Chief Buffer, would have the rest of the landing-force ready at the top of the nets.

Nick thought that if he'd been in Reggie Marsh's boots, he'd have been flashing to *Afghan* now, telling Pete Taverner to start moving in.

There'd been no flashes or colour in the sky, nothing visible to accompany that gunfire. No sound for the last few minutes, either.

Reggie Marsh had had a pat on the back, apparently, for snapping up that convoy off Benghazi, at the beginning of the month. Aubrey Wishart, who was a rear-admiral on A. B. Cunningham's staff in Alexandria, and who'd been a close friend of Nick's for more than thirty years – since a somewhat hazardous submarine patrol to the Golden Horn, back in 1918 – Wishart had told him that the C-in-C had been impressed by the neatness of that interception and the clean-sweep of the convoy.

Well, it *had* been an efficiently handled affair. Perhaps Reggie Marsh wasn't as muddle-headed as he'd been in earlier days. Perhaps one should accept him now at apparent current value, forget the longer-standing, less favourable impressions?

Tuareg's boats were going to beat *Blackfoot*'s hollow. They were clear of the ship, heading away shorewards and going well, and the other two destroyers' boats were only just getting in alongside. Dalgleish – or rather Mercer, his right-hand man – would be getting the scrambling nets up now and overhauling the boats' falls, ready for all three to be hooked on and hoisted. *Tuareg* would be under way and gathering speed seaward the moment those boats' keels were clear of the water.

'Sub, tell the first lieutenant I'm about to turn the ship.' He went to the wheelhouse voicepipe. 'Port twenty-five. Slow astern starboard.' Straightening, he asked Pratt, 'All right for water?'

'Three and a half fathoms, sir. Fine as long as we don't go any closer in.'

That was why he was turning her astern. The ship was trembling now as the one screw churned, driving a swirl of water up her starboard side. He could see her stem against the land, moving to the right as she began to swing around with stern way on.

'Slow ahead port.'

Pratt said, 'We've made Captain (D) look a bit slow off the mark, sir.'

'We had the best billet, pilot.' He stooped to the pipe again. 'Midships.' *Tuareg* was turning nicely, spinning on her heel. For ten minutes now the only gunfire had been from the land fighting, the westerly direction. He guessed that the sea action, whatever it had been, must have been about thirty miles offshore. Ashcourt reported, 'First lieutenant says they're standing by and ready to hoist the boats, sir.'

'Very good.' He told Pratt, 'See if you can spot *Afghan* out there.' And into the voicepipe, 'Stop both engines, cox'n.'

'Stop both, sir . . . Both engines stopped, sir!'

The swirl of sea would settle now, leaving calm water in which the boats would shoot up to the dangling falls and hook on.

0230: one watch slept around their weapons or at their stations below decks, while the other half of the ship's company stayed awake. Pratt was sleeping in the chartroom and Nick had told Dalgleish to get his head down in his – Nick's – sea-cabin, which was next to the chartroom, just one ladder down from the bridge. Ashcourt was at the binnacle as officer of the watch.

The flotilla had formed up six miles east of Cape Malea three-quarters of an hour ago; they'd idled northward across Almyro Bay while *Afghan* had been landing her quota of Royal Marines and then come racing out to rejoin them. The four Tribals were in line-abreast now, steaming at thirty knots on a course of 336 degrees, north-northwesterly. Marsh in *Blackfoot* had put *Afghan* to port of him and *Masai* to starboard, with *Tuareg* out on the sweep's starboard wing; *Afghan* and *Masai* kept station on *Black-foot* and *Tuareg* kept station on *Masai*. The ships were five cables, half a sea mile, apart from each other. If it had been a decision for Nick to have made he'd have had one-mile or even 3,000-yard gaps, to widen the coverage of the sweep; there was no moon, but stars gave light enough for the flotilla to keep in visual touch without much difficulty.

Nick thought he *should* try to dismiss his reservations about Reggie Marsh. They were based, after all, only on recollections of the man as he'd been more than ten years ago. Pete Taverner of *Afghan* and Johnny Smeake of *Masai* seemed to think well enough of him as their Captain (D), and he passed muster – presumably – with the great A. B. Cunningham . . .

Poor old ABC. It irked him badly, Aubrey Wishart had told Nick, that he had to run this widespread battle from a shoreside headquarters. He'd sneered at it as 'soft-arsed accommodation' . . . Cunningham was 100 per cent seaman and seagoing commander: but obviously with so many ships involved and over such an area, with the desert coast and Malta to look after as well as the Aegean, and the Italian fleet still a *potential* menace lurking in its harbours, and having to keep in close touch with Army HQ in Cairo as well as with what existed of the RAF – it was obvious that he couldn't be stuck out at sea.

About now, Nick guessed, the flotilla was passing through roughly the area where that action must have been. It was a reasonable guess that Admiral Glennie with *Dido* and *Orion* and the other ships of Force D might have run into an invasion convoy and disposed of it, then continued their eastward sweep. Whether that made it more or less likely that this flotilla would meet any other invasion groups farther north was an open question; but the orders were that they should sweep as far as a position 36 degrees 30 north, 23 degrees 45 west – it was the mid-point of a line drawn between Cape Malea and Milos island – and then come about to course 190 degrees so as to be down in the Antikithera Channel by first light.

Having, as likely as not, seen damn-all.

He planned to take an hour or two's rest after they'd turned to the southerly course, which would be at about 0400. Dalgleish and Pratt could be up here then, and he'd sleep in his bridge chair and be back on his feet, rested and fit for another day's work, by dawn action stations.

In the cocoon of ship and sea noise, using binoculars to study a hazy, vague horizon while the four Tribals' hulls lathered white tracks northward into the Aegean, your mind could slide from one thing to another without interrupting the concentrated effort of looking out. He was thinking again about Jack: Jack saying, when he'd consented to dine on board *Tuareg* as Nick's guest in Alex about three weeks ago, something about war reducing men to the state of wild animals. It was the Stuka attacks he'd been thinking about, the impression of ferocity, blood-lust.

'Oh, those people could teach wild animals a thing or two,' Nick had agreed with him. 'But several million decent people in Europe, in countries they've invaded, have been shut up in cages in conditions you wouldn't inflict on any animal. Those Stukas you didn't like the look of have already flattened cities and bombed columns of helpless refugees. They've struck at countries who were falling over backwards to stay clear of war – it's like a gang of thugs walking up to innocent passers-by and attacking them. They're gangsters. You either surrender, or look the other way until it's your turn, or you fight.'

'I'm not saying we shouldn't be fighting. I'm only saying – well, it's a revelation, people who preach that war's foul are right – even the Oxford Union—'

'No, Jack. The foulness is in instigating war, making it necessary, not in standing up against it. It would be degrading *not* to be fighting them.'

'Well, as things are, certainly. But . . .' Shaking his head, perhaps confused by the contradictions of it . . . Nick wondering whether Jack remembered anything of the David-at-Jutland business, the truth he'd told their father – wishing immediately afterwards and ever since that he'd kept his mouth shut; whether Jack could have remembered it, and if so, whether he'd have allowed it to worry him. Because the physical likeness to David was unmistakable. Even his manner, his way of looking at you . . .

But perhaps he'd changed, in recent weeks? Wasn't there a degree of new self-assurance behind that defensive reserve? And the talk about war – wasn't it possibly the nearest thing to a conversation they'd ever had?

Hopes, to counter fears . . .

But they hadn't talked all the time about war. Jack heard regularly from his mother, with reports of Mullberg, the Everard house and estate in Yorkshire, and some items from her letters he'd

291

been prepared to pass on. Sarah, and Jack when he was at home, lived in the Dower house; Mullbergh and its land was Nick's now. It had been taken over by the War Office as some sort of training centre, while Sarah kept an eye on the management of the four farms and also accommodated some girls of the Women's Land Army in her Dower house. It had been an exceptionally hard winter: when she'd last written, at the end of April, the whole West Riding had still been deep in snow.

And London lay in partial ruin, with bombers over night after night. But *Blithe Spirit* and *Arsenic and Old Lace* were still showing to capacity audiences, and Carroll Gibbons and his orchestra still played at the Savoy. There had been a Communist-organized demonstration at the Savoy a few months ago: because Cabinet ministers, foreign press representatives and diplomats still ate well there despite shortages and rationing. The Communists, whose Soviet masters were of course allies of the Nazis, were calling it a 'bosses' war.

'Object in the water green four-oh, sir!'

He swung his glasses to it . . .

'Looks like a caïque, sir.'

Nick thought Ashcourt was right. And there was no bow-wave or wake; so it was stopped, and probably damaged. About 3,000 yards away.

'Bring her round, Sub.'

'Starboard fifteen!'

'Signalman – make to *Masai, Investigating object bearing*' – he checked the bearing quickly and roughly – '*bearing oh-one-five.*'

Ashcourt said into the voicepipe, 'Midships.'

'Midships, sir . . . Wheel's amidships, sir.'

'Steer oh-one-five.'

No need to rouse the other watch. The invasion troops had been reported as coming in convoys of caïques, and this was as likely as not one of them, but it was alone and quite probably holed, half full of water: that was how it looked. He'd been hearing the clacking of the lamp, and now the familiar rhythm of the *AR* end-of-message sign: *Blackfoot* would probably have read the signal, and if she hadn't *Masai* would anyway be passing it on. He told the signalman, 'Stand by the eighteen-inch, starboard side.'

The searchlight, he meant. There was an eighteen-inch diameter light on each side of the bridge and a twenty-four-inch one on the platform aft . . . That 'object' *was* a caïque: almost certainly a victim of the action they'd heard earlier. But not necessarily: caïques had been used extensively during the Greek evacuation, ferrying troops from shore to ships, and this one could have drifted from any of the islands . . . The purpose in taking a close look at it now was to check whether there might be anyone alive in it.

'Messenger – go to my sea-cabin and shake the first lieutenant.' He glanced round to see what the rest of the flotilla was doing. *Masai* was following, about a mile astern, and he could see *Blackfoot*, when he used binoculars, in silhouette; Marsh hadn't altered course, but he'd reduced speed.

About half a mile to go. Nick told Ashcourt, 'Two hundred revs, Sub. Steer to leave it close to starboard.'

'Aye aye, sir.' Ashcourt called down, 'Two hundred revs. Steer three degrees to port.'

'*Ship green nine-oh, sir!*'

A second look-out amplified: 'Destroyer, sir!'

He was at the binnacle, displacing Ashcourt. 'Sound surface alarm, Sub.' He called down, 'Full ahead together, starboard ten.' Dalgleish was in the bridge: 'Challenge, sir?' Nick told him, 'No. Stand by the searchlight sight.' He wouldn't expose its beam until he told him to, he'd just have it trained ready to illuminate the target: which was showing two red and two white lights, fixed, on its foreyard. The surface alarm S's were jarring through the ship, and Nick was telling Houston in the director, 'Unidentified ship starboard—'

'I'm on it, sir. Eyetie, I think.' The merchant banker up on the foremast was talking into his headset before Nick had moved from the voicepipe: 'All guns with SAP load, load, load . . .' Nick called, 'Signalman, make to *Blackfoot, Enemy destroyer bearing one-one-oh.*'

'Searchlight ready, sir.'

'Searchlight *on!*'

The light's beam sprang out across the sea, fixed immediately on an Italian torpedo-boat of the *Partenope* or *Climene* class. Short, high foc'sl, long and lower afterpart, single funnel. Afterpart all smashed: mainmast gone, wreckage where the deckhouse and a stern gun-mounting should have been . . . the fire-gongs clanged, and the four-sevens flashed and roared. Eyes blinded, ears stunned. Fire-gongs again, a distant tinny sound, and shells exploding, orange explosions in the Italian's bridge, an Italian caught up in his second action of the night. Those hits had set his bridge on fire:

but he was speeding up – you saw the bow-wave rising – and coming round to port: the gun on his stubby foc'sl spurting flame. Just that *one* gun, all he had left: it would be a 3.9. He'd reversed his helm – turning away now, *Tuareg*'s four-sevens firing fast, plastering him. It was conceivable he was turning to fire torpedoes.

'Starboard fifteen.'

If torpedoes were coming, *Tuareg* would point her nose between them, comb their tracks. *Masai* was coming up to port with her A and B guns in action: it was astonishing that the diminutive Italian could take this much punishment and remain afloat. Well, he wouldn't, not for much longer. *Tuareg*'s two for'ard mountings were the only ones that would bear now she'd pointed her stem at the enemy, but with *Masai* in it as well that still amounted to four twin four-sevens pumping semi-armour-piercing shells at the six- or seven-hundred-ton torpedo-boat.

'Midships.'

'Midships, sir . . . Wheel's amidships, sir!'

If he'd turned to fire torpedoes, he'd done it. He was coming round to port now. Bridge and midships section burning brightly.

'Port fifteen.'

'Port fifteen, sir!'

Houston called down the voicepipe to tell him he couldn't fire: the Italian was about to pass between *Tuareg* and *Masai*. Giving himself a few minutes' extra life: he'd kept that wheel on and spun right round – like a speedboat, dodging shells. Dalgleish shouted, 'He's going to ram *Masai*!'

The Italian had flung his wheel hard a-starboard just as he entered the gap between the two Tribals: choosing *Masai* probably because she was the nearer. *Masai*'s X and Y guns fired right over her just before the crash came, and shells whirred only a few feet over *Tuareg*'s bridge as Nick called down, 'Midships!' The Italian had struck *Masai* right aft as she swung hard in an effort to avoid him, and now the two ships were locked together, circling, *Masai*'s way carrying them both along, circling like dancers, flames on the Italian dazzling bright and a wide streak of their reflection reaching to *Tuareg* across a couple of hundred yards of sea. Movement slowing: all guns silent. *Masai* had stopped her engines: or her screws were done for. Near one would have been anyway. Losing the forward impetus, she'd ceased the process of tearing her own stern off with the Italian embedded in it.

'Meet her. Steer north. Slow ahead both engines.'

The Italian was sinking, sagging low in the sea, probably only supported by her stem's grip on *Masai*. The sea was washing across her afterpart, rising in a pale fog of steam where it lapped her fires. *Masai* seemed to be on an even keel: it looked from here as if the damage would be all in the stern twenty feet of her: just the tiller flat, the steering-gear compartment, then. The port screw and shaft *might* have survived: but one screw and no steering wouldn't be much help . . . He ducked to the voicepipe: 'Starboard ten.' Up again, with his glasses on that stern, in time to see a sudden lurch and an upheaval of white foam: the Italian had broken loose, dragged out by the weight of his flooded hull. As the torpedo-boat slipped back he saw its bow lift vertically before it disappeared.

'I'll want the loud-hailer, Yeoman.' It had only to be fetched and plugged in. He stooped: 'Midships.' He put his glasses back on *Masai*'s stern: the only way she'd get home, he guessed, would be under tow. She'd float, all right; there was a watertight bulkhead immediately for'ard of the tiller flat, and even if that one was ruptured there was another through the centreline of Y gun-mounting's support. It was a matter either of towing her, or of taking her crew off and sinking her. Towing would mean a slow-speed withdrawal southwards, and a lot of Stuka attention from first light onwards – with a towing ship who couldn't dodge.

It was a decision for Reggie Marsh.

CHAPTER 4

'One-three-five revolutions on, sir.' Pratt reported it from the binnacle. Those were revs for about twelve knots: Nick was building the speed up gradually, with Dalgleish on the quarterdeck watching the tow and the strain on it. *Tuareg* had a shackle of chain cable out astern, and *Masai*'s towing wire was shackled to it, the weight of the cable acting as a spring to absorb the stresses on the wire and on the gear on *Tuareg*'s stern and *Masai*'s foc'sl.

Sub-Lieutenant Chalk, on the bridge end of the depthcharge telephone, reported, 'First lieutenant says all's well, sir.'

An absence of any protests from *Masai* indicated that she had no problems either, from the last step-up in speed. Nick let it settle down for a few minutes, then told Pratt, 'One-five-oh revs.'

Thirteen knots.

It was past 4 am. *Tuareg* was towing *Masai* on a course of 227 degrees, south-westward, with thirty miles to go to the Antikithera Channel. Not that reaching Antikithera would mean any lessening of the Stuka threat: with no air cover and with the Luftwaffe ranging freely over the whole area in enormous strength you'd be bombed as thoroughly down there as you would be here. It was simply a step in the right direction, the direction of the long route south.

'One-five-oh revs on, sir.'

Marsh had made a wrong decision, Nick thought. The right one would have been to take *Masai*'s crew out of her and sink her, then carry on with the ordered northward sweep before turning south to join the battle squadron. All right, so it would have resulted in one fleet destroyer lost. But in terms of this battle for Crete she was already lost: she'd be out of action for many months. This effort to get her away turned her from a loss into a liability; air attacks were inevitable from dawn onward, and with the sitting-duck target of

296

two unmanoeuvrable destroyers chained together, and tied to a straight course and a set speed, the hungry Stukas would be competing for sky-space to get at them. So there'd be a distinct possibility of losing more than just *Masai*, and in present circumstances here in the eastern Mediterranean that was a risk no one could afford.

'One-six-oh revolutions.'

Blackfoot was on the beam to starboard, *Afghan* to port. Marsh had wirelessed a signal a quarter of an hour ago, to C-in-C and repeated to the various force commanders now at sea, telling him what had happened and that the flotilla was withdrawing via the Antikithera Channel; he'd given an 0400 position, their course, and speed twelve knots.

'Signalman.'

'Sir?'

'Lever . . . Make to *Masai, Are you quite comfy?*'

When the attacks started, he thought, *Masai* might not be able to use her after guns. Almost certainly not Y gun, the quarterdeck mounting, with the strain it might impose on the stern bulkhead. She'd lost her starboard screw and she had no steering: rudder gone, tiller flat smashed and flooded. The port screw and shaft were undamaged, but that wasn't going to help her without steering. The signalman was just finishing that message. Nick went to where young Chalk was propped in the bridge's starboard for'ard corner with the depthcharge or A/S telephone in his hand; its lead came up from the door of the tiny Asdic cabinet, so that when you were hunting a submarine you could stand behind the operator and talk over the line to Mr Walsh the Gunner (T) back aft at the chutes and throwers. He took the telephone from Chalk and asked Dalgleish how the tow was looking. You looked for the cable's sag in the water, and for vibration: you could put your hand on it and feel any change.

'Think we can stand a bit more?'

'Certainly looks all right, sir.'

'Good.' He put the phone back on its hook. The signalman told him, 'Reply from *Masai*, sir, *Snug as a bug. Let's step on the gas.*'

Nick told Pratt, 'One-seven-five revolutions.'

The wind was about Force 2 and north-west; there was hardly any movement on the ship. When they were through Antikithera, of course, conditions might be quite different. He thought, *Sufficient unto the day . . .*

There'd be some evils to *this* day, he guessed.

Pratt had been checking the automatic log, timing its ticks against his stopwatch; he told Nick, 'Fifteen through the water, sir.'

Not bad, with a 2,000-ton destroyer in tow.

'Let's go up another notch. One-eight-five.'

Four-thirty, nearly. Dawn in about an hour. With so many ships in and around the Aegean, the Luftwaffe would be out in force. They'd every reason to be: the Germans wanted to push surface convoys into Crete, and while the Royal Navy was in these waters they weren't able to. It would be a straight fight between something like 2,000 German aircraft and a couple of dozen British ships, more than half of which were already suffering from defects that in normal times would have put them in dock. Engine-room staffs were having to improvise and make-do, handle their own problems as best they could – anything to keep the ships at sea. Ships' companies weren't exactly fresh either: for a long time nobody had been to sea without being bombed, and as they were only allowed into harbour for long enough to refuel, re-ammunition and top up with fresh water and stores they'd begun to equate salt water with high explosive. What with that and the lack of sleep, it was hardly surprising that one saw, here and there, signs of strain.

Thinking of the dawn and of the bombers jogged him into a change of mind. He'd been hoping to work the speed up to twenty knots, but it struck him now that fifteen to sixteen, which they were already doing, wasn't at all bad. The round figure of twenty wasn't worth running risks for: one of those risks being the backwash effect, *Masai*'s exposed after bulkhead and the forces sucking at it as she was pulled through the water, a suction force directly related to the speed. If that bulkhead collapsed it would mean not only more damage to *Masai* and perhaps some lives lost, but the sudden jerk and increase in weight would almost surely part the tow; then you'd be at a standstill, picking it up and making it fast again just as the light came – and the bombers.

He reached past Chalk for the A/S phone again. 'Number One?'

' 'Alf a mo', sir.' Then Dalgleish came on. 'Sir?'

'I'm going to settle for these revs. Leave one hand to keep an eye on the tow.' He hung up the telephone and told Chalk, 'You can leave it now.' Chalk was sturdy, freckle-faced, boyish-looking. Nick told him, 'You did a good job with the boats, Sub.'

He grinned: 'Thank you, sir.'

Pratt said, 'Just under sixteen knots, sir.'

'It'll do.' He called to the signalman, 'Lever, make to *Masai, I think this is fast enough*. Then to *Blackfoot, Intend maintaining present speed.'*

Marsh could object if he wanted to. But there'd been a night in the English Channel in 1917 when Nick had been first lieutenant of the destroyer *Mackerel* and his captain, Edward Wyatt – who died a few months later on the mole at Zeebrugge – had been greedy for more speed than the ship's shattered bow could stand. He could remember vividly the lurch and rumble as the bulkhead went: and he could see, as clearly as if he was standing in front of him now, the face of the man who'd been trapped in the for'ard messdeck when the sea burst in. A chief petty officer by the name of Swan.

He often thought of Swan. And of others like him.

It was a relief to have come to that quite ordinary, logical decision. So much so that he realized he must be more tired than he'd recognized. He saw Dalgleish just coming from the ladder. With him and Pratt up here – and they'd both had a stand-off – and with dawn about an hour ahead and then hours, even a whole day if it lasted that long, of the Luftwaffe . . . He made up his mind that half an hour's cat-napping in the chair would be better than no rest at all.

'I'm going to have a snooze, Number One. Give me a shake at five-fifteen, and we'll close the hands up at five-twenty.'

'Aye aye, sir.' Dalgleish poked Rocky Pratt. 'I'll see this bloke stays awake.' Someone else had arrived behind him: as he came forward into the bridge, Nick saw that it was Simon Gallwey, the doctor.

'Can't you sleep, Doc?'

'They won't let me, sir. Cruel men keep bringing me signals to decode. Like this one.' He had a sheet of signal-pad in his hand. Nick thought, *Twenty-five minutes now, if I'm lucky* . . . He took the signal to the chart table, elbowed his way inside its canvas hood and switched the light on.

It was to D37 – Marsh – from Admiral Rawlings, commanding the battle squadron somewhere down in the south-west; it informed Marsh that *Carnarvon* was being detached to join them five miles west of Cape Grabusa at 0600.

Well. Perhaps they had a chance of getting away with it, now. He came out, and handed the signal to Pratt.

'We're having company. *Carnarvon*'s meeting us in the Anti-kithera soon after dawn.'

Pratt clasped the sheet of paper to his heart . . . 'Saved, saved!'

Laughter in the back of the bridge. But the AA cruiser's eight high-angle guns *would* make a difference.

Fighting to wake up, to crawl out from under a deadweight of heavy sleep . . . The voice broke in again: 'Five-fifteen, sir.' The voice was like a rope let down to you: you needed to grab hold of it before sleep closed over your head again, to let the rope haul you up into the light and air. Or you could let go, slip back, forget . . .

'Captain, sir – it's five-fifteen, sir!'

The rendezvous with *Carnarvon* was set for 0600. But the signal Marsh had sent carlier had given this flotilla's speed-of-advance as twelve knots, not sixteen. Unless he'd amplified it since then. If Rawlings' staff man had based his orders on that information, the flotilla would be eight – no, six – miles farther south than anyone expected.

But it wouldn't make all that much difference.

'Captain, sir, it's five—'

'Yes, I know. Thank you, Number One.'

Collecting thoughts . . . This was Thursday. Thursday, 22 May 1941 . . .

'Kye, sir?'

'Thank you. What the doctor ordered.'

It was marvellous – the 'kye', or cocoa – thick, hot and sweet, life-restoring . . . Marsh might have sent another signal amending the speed he'd given before. Otherwise there could be a delay in effecting the rendezvous. In full daylight six miles wouldn't make much difference at all, but it wouldn't be fully light until just before the time they were supposed to meet.

Before long all ships would be fitted with RDF, new types that were being developed and which even destroyers would be getting – so one heard – in a year or so. It would remove a hell of a lot of problems if they did get it. The Americans were working on it too, but they called it radar.

He'd finished the kye, at the cost of a burnt tongue, and he felt alive again. Pulling off the hood of his duffel-coat, and reaching down beside the chair for his cap . . . It was a cap he'd owned in 1926, and the oak-leaves on its peak were distinctly the worse for wear. The badge was tarnished too, and he could feel ragged ends of gold wire with his thumb. This was his seagoing hat: he also had a new one, smart and shiny, which had been posted by Messrs Gieves to him at a pub in Hampshire where, last autumn, he'd spent a few days with Fiona. She'd opened the parcel during breakfast in bed: then put the cap on her dark, tousled head and pranced around the room stark naked, uttering what she'd imagined to be nautical phrases.

But think about Stukas now: not about Fiona Gascoyne with her clothes off. Fiona had *her* bombers to cope with, too: the night raiders on London, where she was stationed in the MTC – ambulances, despatches, driving for the Army or civilian ministries. He thought rather frequently about Fiona, nowadays: ever since a chance meeting in a restaurant, each of them with someone else – an accidental meeting but a watershed in their relationship . . .

He got up out of his chair, and stretched. He hoped to God she was all right, after the 11 May raid. The Germans had sent 500 bombers over, and set 700 acres of London on fire. He hoped and prayed to God he'd hear from her soon.

'Tow all right?'

'No change, sir, and no problems. May I close the hands up?'

'Go ahead. Pilot, did you check the rendezvous position?'

'Yes, I did, sir.' Pratt told him, 'We'll be six or seven miles to the south of it, at this rate.'

'He hasn't amended that signal, then.'

'No, sir. There's nothing new of any interest on the log.'

Thinking it out – the flotilla would be passing through the rendezvous position at, say, twenty minutes to six, and at that time *Carnarvon*, if she was coming at her flat-out speed of twenty-five knots, would be something between six and ten miles to the west. It would be pretty well light by that time, and they'd be looking out for each other, so they should make contact all right. Marsh probably hadn't wanted to go on the air again: the more signals you sent, the more clearly you advertised your presence. Although the Germans had to know, surely, that the whole area was crawling with ships, that any bombers taking to the air this morning were bound to find targets?

On that basis, they wouldn't be hanging around their airfields waiting for reconnaissance reports. They'd be airborne at first light, and bottlenecks like Kaso and Antikithera would be obvious places to take an early look.

'Ship is at action stations, sir.' Dalgleish had been taking reports through telephones and voicepipes. 'I'll go on aft.'

There was a familiar greying in the east. Cape Spada was in that direction, about nine miles away, and the sun would rise there, behind the land. Much closer than Spada and roughly on the beam now, south-eastward, Cape Grabusa was a mound of black rock which was staying inky-black while its surroundings lightened.

'When should we be altering, pilot?'

'If it was up to me, sir, when Grabusa lighthouse bears oh-eight-four. That'll be in about twenty minutes. Then one-nine-five would clear Pondikonisi.'

Pondikonisi was a small off-lying island. *Blackfoot* would be ordering the change of course, when it pleased Reggie M. Just on five-thirty now.

The Italian commanding that torpedo-boat had displayed a lot of guts, last night. Whatever they had as the equivalent of a VC, he deserved one. As a nation they weren't militarily impressive, they weren't really significant – at Matapan for instance, two months ago, when the 10,000-ton cruiser *Pola* had been immobilized by a torpedo from one of *Formidable*'s aircraft, destroyers found her lying in a state of helpless panic, her upper deck littered with baggage, bottles and drunken sailors. How to deal with her had been something of an embarrassment, but eventually she'd been sent to the bottom – joining the heavy cruisers *Zara* and *Fiume* and two destroyers – and 900 of her crew were saved. Rescue work was interrupted by German aircraft – Ju88s – and had to be broken off; so A. B. Cunningham signalled the Italian admiralty telling them where to find the rest of their survivors, and they sent out a hospital ship which for some reason the Germans didn't attack. But there'd been some other interesting signals exchanged between the destroyer flotilla who picked up the 900 Italians, and the Commander-in-Chief in *Warspite*. One had reported, *Prisoners when asked why they had failed to fire at us replied that they thought if they did we would fire back*. Then, when ABC had called for details of any wounded men picked up, he was told *State of prisoners: six cot cases: fifty slightly injured: one senior officer has piles*. The Commander-in-Chief flashed in reply, *I am not surprised*.

But the *Pola* and last night's torpedo-boat seemed hardly to have belonged to the same navy.

Five thirty-five. In a quarter of an hour it would be daylight. Start of the bad time here, end of the bad time in London . . .

When Nick had got back from Norway, his uncle Hugh had been in London, wreathed in smiles at his nephew's recent successes. Admiral Sir Hugh Everard had retired years before the war, but like many other retired admirals he'd rejoined as a convoy commodore. He was doing that now, in the Atlantic: no sinecure, for a man of seventy. He'd been dressed in his new rank of Commodore RNR when Nick had met him in London, in the late spring of last year. Hugh had asked him to lunch, and produced another guest as well, a Wren Third Officer called Virginia Casler. She was small, blonde, smart and very pretty, and she was working in the Admiralty; Hugh had come across her at the time when there'd been no news of Nick or of his destroyer *Intent*, when everyone had been assuming the worst. Hugh Everard had been highly impressed by the WRNS Third Officer, and when the great news had arrived – *Intent* still afloat and with a string of successes behind her – the gaunt old admiral and the curvy little blonde had gone out to celebrate; and Hugh had resolved to introduce Nick to her when the chance came. Match-making, Nick had guessed; the old boy had been on at him for years about settling down with a new wife. But the night before this luncheon, his first night in London, he'd spent with Fiona. He'd arrived late, learnt that there was no room for him at his club, telephoned her and found she was alone. (He wouldn't have taken a chance on it. She wasn't a one-man girl: she'd been married, not too successfully, to a rich man nearly twice her age, and when he'd died she'd decided that the one thing she wasn't going to do was tie herself down again in any hurry. Nick had happily accepted this situation: he'd concluded a long time ago, after the divorce from Ilyana, that he wasn't cut out to be a husband.) He'd asked her, in her flat that night, to join him next evening for dinner and a nightclub, but she'd said she couldn't because she'd be on duty. So he invited Ginny Casler instead, and Ginny said she'd love to, which was fine. A 'stunner' was how Hugh Everard had described her, when he'd been asking Nick for lunch: he'd also referred to her as a 'corker'.

Nick booked a table for that evening at the *Jardin des Gourmets*. London's ordeal by bombing hadn't yet started, in May 1940, and all the restaurants and nightspots were still open and intact. The table they'd reserved for him was one of a pair at the far end of the long, rather narrow dining-room: there were just those two 'banquette' tables facing this way, down the room's length as you approached them. He hadn't been taking much notice of his surroundings as he and Ginny followed the waiter to it; it was only when the man had pulled one end out for Ginny to slip in behind it that he noticed the occupants of the other one – Fiona Gascoyne, with an RAF wing commander.

There'd been no reason to be upset about it: he'd known she went out with a lot of other men. Why shouldn't she? He was surprised she'd made that excuse, though: there'd been no reason to. Looking at her, showing his surprise, seeing her take in all there was to see of Ginny Casler in one swift feline appraisal before she glanced back at him – *puzzled*, almost – he'd felt a new element in the air between them: there was something disturbing about it but at the same time exciting, a feeling – which he couldn't have described there and then – of make or break. Afterwards he'd wondered if he and Fiona hadn't been struck simultaneously and separately by the same feeling: that it was – surprisingly – wrong to see each other out with other people. The corollary, of course, would be that they belonged together.

In the next few days he'd telephoned her several times, both to her flat and to the MTC headquarters in Graham Terrace, but failed to catch her. Then he had to go back up to the Clyde, where he'd left *Intent* in dock. He was on his way north when news came that the Dutch army had surrendered; and for the next fortnight there was a whole series of evacuations from various points in Norway. By that time *Intent* was fit for sea again, and he was bringing her into Harwich after a fast dash around the top of Scotland when a BBC broadcast announced the collapse of Belgium. There was just about time to refuel, and they were away to take part in the Dunkirk evacuation. After that there was hardly any leave for anyone: invasion was expected at any time, the Battle of Britain was being fought over southern England, and the flotillas and squadrons waited with intentions that were entirely clear: whether the air battle was won or lost, the Navy would die in the Channel before a live German landed on an English beach.

The all-night raids on London started at the end of August; in his destroyer during the patrols and anti-invasion sweeps and bombardments of the invasion-launching ports, he prayed for Fiona to be alive each morning. It wasn't until October that he had some leave – before taking over *Tuareg* in Portsmouth – and spent nearly all of it with her in Hampshire. They'd laughed about that chance meeting in the *Jardin*: she explained that she *had* been on the duty roster, but another girl had persuaded her to swap, for

304

some reason, and then this friend-of-a-friend had called: and she hadn't known where Nick was . . . That she'd bothered to explain was unusual, out of character with their relationship as it had been. And on their last night together he'd been woken by her crying on his shoulder. She'd asked him, 'You *will* come back, Nick? Please? Promise me?' He'd thought of her expression when he'd seen her in the restaurant, remembered how he'd felt and felt now even more, and he'd had a sickening glimpse of what it would be like not to have her to come back to.

Nearly fifteen hundred people had been killed in London on the night of 10/11 May.

There'd be a letter from her soon. There might be one now, at this moment, lying in the Fleet Mail Office or in *Woolwich*, the destroyer flotillas' depot ship in Alexandria. Even if there wasn't, she might still have written: mails were unreliable, particularly out of London. And at least she didn't ride a motorbike now. Without any help from Germans she'd twice nearly killed herself on that machine . . .

The light was coming rapidly, pouring up from behind a range of mountains which slanted jaggedly southwards from the low cape to port. It was five forty-five: they were in the position ordered for the rendezvous with *Carnarvon*.

If the cruiser was inside visibility range, she ought to see them before they saw her. She'd have them silhouetted against the dawn – if the land's shadow didn't hide them – and she had a greater looking-out range from that old spotting-top of hers.

Pratt said, 'Should be altering at any time now, sir.'

It was up to Marsh: and as if he'd heard what Pratt had said, *Blackfoot* started flashing. Nick was looking out that way, in the faint hope of an early sight of *Carnarvon*, and he saw it start: and Whiffen had his signalman ready and waiting for it, so that the answering clash of *Tuareg*'s lamp came with pleasing promptitude.

'You must have a carrying voice, pilot.'

'Perhaps Captain (D) and I are on the same wavelength, sir.'

Ashcourt, beside his torpedo-control panel on the starboard side, read the message aloud as it came rippling over in fast dots and dashes.

Alter course to one-nine-seven. I will wait here for Carnarvon and then catch you up.

Tuareg's signalman had rapped out a K in acknowledgement. Pratt said, 'There's an answer to the speed discrepancy, sir.'

Nick glanced at him: it was light enough to see the navigator's slightly rueful smile, as if he was thinking that Marsh had been a jump ahead of them all the time.

'Bring her round gently to one-nine-seven, pilot.'

Nick could hardly believe Marsh was doing this. What if there was some delay in *Carnarvon*'s arrival, and the Stukas found him first? The only effective weapon ships had in this battle against dive-bombers was *collective* firepower. A single destroyer with low-angle main armament, alone and unsupported, didn't stand a chance.

'How far are we from them now, pilot?'

Jack Everard went down to the chart to check on it. *Carnarvon*'s best speed now was twenty-two knots. She was no chicken, and a month's hard driving plus quite a few near-missing bombs to shake bits loose had taken its toll despite extraordinary efforts by her engineers. She'd been on the move and at sea, without any break at all lasting more than a few hours, since she'd arrived in the Mediterranean near the end of 'Demon'. She'd had *one* whole night in harbour – in Alexandria, just before 'Tiger', the convoy trip to Malta and back. There were three other AA cruisers on the station – *Coventry, Carlisle* and *Calcutta* – and all four of them were wanted here, there and everywhere else, simultaneously.

At four-fifty this morning, after a breakdown lasting half an hour, the engineer commander had told Napier, 'If you can keep her down to revs for not more than twenty-two knots, sir, I can keep her running for a week or two. If we have to exceed that for more than a few minutes I can't answer for the consequences.'

It wasn't light enough for chart-work: Jack pulled the screen down behind him and switched the light on. About time he replaced this chart anyway: the bridge charts always got harder use than the ones in the chartroom, and there were so many rubbed-out workings from the past month's operations that the paper had barely any surface left on it. *Carnarvon* was steering a course of 106 degrees, aiming to meet the 37th Flotilla at 0700 instead of the ordered 0600 rendezvous farther north; Napier knew that the Tribals would push on southwards, and he'd had to make the adjustment for his ship's reduced speed. It did mean the destroyers would be on their own for the first hour of daylight, but that was beyond his control; he'd be joining them eight or nine miles south of Pondikonisi at seven instead of four miles north of it at six.

Jack came up from the chart and told him, 'At their 0600 position they'll bear oh-seven-eight, range twenty-six miles, sir.'

Napier looked ten years older than he had a month ago. Thinner, greyer, eyes deeper set.

So long as the Stukas didn't arrive too soon, Jack thought, everything should turn out all right. Even if they did find them the four Tribals would be able to fend for themselves for a while, with luck. They'd be handicapped, of course, by only two of them being free to take avoiding action; *Tuareg* and *Masai*, confined to a steady speed and straight course, would obviously be the bombers' target.

But brother Nick, for God's sake, was more than capable of looking after himself . . .

By five-past six it was daylight. The Cretan mountains, thirty or forty miles ahead, were an uneven scar of indigo against a burning sky. Clear sky: in that quarter, burning bright. Here in the cruiser's bridge, unshaven faces with binoculars at their eyes. From the constant looking-out your eyes acquired rims, circular depressions that you could feel with your fingertips.

Bell-Reid muttered, 'Enemy's late this morning. Ought to be ashamed of themselves. A good German's never late.'

'Let's not object too loudly.' Napier's glasses traversed slowly across the horizon on the bow. 'And you know what they used to call a *good* German.'

A dead one . . . There'd be a few floating around, too, after last night. Just after four o'clock this morning there'd been a signal to C-in-C from Force D, Admiral Glennie with *Dido, Orion* and *Ajax*, reporting that earlier in the night they'd run into an invasion convoy of caïques and steamers and one Italian escort, and destroyed it. Glennie was withdrawing westward now, towards Rawlings and the battle squadron, because his cruisers were low in ammunition; Admiral King's Force C was thus alone in the Aegean, carrying out the C-in-C's earlier orders to conduct a daylight sweep from Heraklion northwards to Milos island, looking for more invasion convoys. The one thing they could be absolutely sure of finding was Stukas.

Other signals on the log showed that the 14th Destroyer Flotilla, the ships who'd bombarded Scarpanto airfield two nights ago, were heading for the Kaso Strait from Alexandria, where they'd have fuelled and ammunitioned; and the 10th, comprising three rather ancient Australian destroyers, was on its way from Alex to join Admiral Rawlings. Also the 5th – Louis Mountbatten's flotilla, which Cunningham had been keeping in Malta as a raiding force against Rommel's supply convoys from Italy to the desert – had sailed from Valetta last night and would be joining Rawlings during the forenoon.

Able Seaman Noble brought Napier a cup of coffee. He muttered in that low growl of his, turning pale slit-eyes up towards the sky, 'Gerries must be 'aving a lie-in, sir.'

'Long may it continue. If there's any more of that, Noble, perhaps you'd spare the commander a cup.'

'Aye aye, sir.' Noble asked Bell-Reid, 'One lump in coffee is it, sir?' Bell-Reid nodded, and said to Napier, 'Very kind, sir.' Napier's ADP telephone buzzed, and he reached down for it. 'Captain.' He was listening, and at the same time drawing himself up on the seat, tall in the saddle to get a better view of the horizon on the port bow or the dark blue mountains crowning it. 'Are you sure of that bearing?'

He put the phone down and told Jack Everard, 'McCowan reports what he says looks like the flotilla on bearing oh-nine-five, but one ship less than there ought to be. We don't expect 'em to be as far south yet, do we?'

Jack told him – the Tribals should have been thirty degrees on the bow, not ten.

'That's where they are, anyway.' Napier pointed. 'And McCowan's got an RDF range of fourteen miles. Visibility's poor against the land, I dare say they're all there . . . Giving 'em twelve knots, what's an adjusted course to intercept?'

He went to the chart and worked it out. On the present showing he'd have given them about fifteen knots, not twelve.

'One-four-oh, sir, to bring us up with them at 0700. But they may alter course before that, in the process of rounding Elaphonisi.'

Napier told Willy Irvine, 'Come round to one-four-oh.'

'Aye aye, sir.' The black beard touched the voicepipe's rim: 'Starboard ten.' Jack checked the time of the alteration: it was six twenty-two.

'Aircraft astern, sir!'

One of the look-outs had yelled it. Nick slid off his seat: he told Yeoman Whiffen, 'Red warning flag,' and joined Pratt at the binnacle. Ashcourt had gone to that look-out, to check on the report. Nick told Harry Houston up the director voicepipe, 'Alarm astern, aircraft. Be ready with your barrage and for God's sake watch the sun.'

They liked to make use of the sun when it was low. It was lifting over the mountains: like an enormous, blinding searchlight aimed into the destroyer's bridge. Ashcourt shouted from where he was leaning over the look-out bay, 'Long way off, sir, hard to see. They're circling, I think – can't see 'em at all now . . .'

They'd be circling over or round *Blackfoot*. Like bloody vultures, Nick thought. He heard B gun's fire-gong clang, and there was a split second in which to notice that the barrels of both the for'ard mountings were tilted up to port – into the sun – and then four guns had thunderclapped, recoiled smoking, and the second gun in each mounting fired, and it was continuous now, a fast barrage straight into that blind sector. With his eyes squeezed three-quarters shut Nick tried to see their attackers, but he couldn't: the guns were shooting fast and steadily, and it wasn't just Houston being edgy because the other ships were in action too; *Afghan* slanting across ahead from starboard to port with her guns cocked high spurting flame, disgorging smoke; and *Masai* on the end of her lead also giving tongue, at least with her for'ard guns. And now he heard it – the Stuka's siren, the banshee howl that was supposed to break men's nerves. With the tow astern, there was nothing to do except keep shooting. Every gun was doing that: pompoms thump-thumping, point-fives clattering. There was one four-barrelled pompom between the funnels and another on the platform aft which also supported the big searchlight and the after control position: over all the din, the growing volume of the Stuka's shriek.

'Flashing, starboard side, sir!'

Carnarvon, at last . . . He put his glasses up. The winking light was on the beam and a long way off: Mason, a leading signalman, was at the starboard eighteen-inch, sending his single answering flash just as a bomb splashed into the sea ahead and the Stuka levelled, tilting on to his starboard wingtip as he swung away towards the north.

'What's happened to the bunch astern?' He was asking Ashcourt – who like everyone else had been concentrating on things nearer at hand. That last one had come from nowhere: out of the sun, of course, but one minute it hadn't been visible and the next it had been in its dive. There was another one behind it too . . . If Ashcourt had heard that question, he hadn't answered it. The guns were thundering again, and the cordite stink was as eye-watering as the sun, smoke flaring over in brown throat-filling gusts with each salvo from the for'ard guns. Pratt yelled in his ear, 'From *Carnarvon*, sir – *Joining you at my best speed which is twenty-two knots. Are you one ship short?*' A Stuka was screaming in, black and bat-like, just to the right of the sun's blaze: it was banking, to come in on *Masai*'s beam, in a dive quite shallow by Stuka standards – making full use of the sun, of course. The port-side point-fives had opened up as the range closed in: *Tuareg* had quadruple point-five machine-guns each side of the bridge, on the wings of the signal deck, one level down. Petty Officer Whiffen was looking at him with a question-mark on his broad, pink face: Nick shouted, 'Make to *Carnarvon*, *Blackfoot is ten miles astern and under attack. Her need may be greater than ours.*' The Stuka was howling in, gun noise rising to a peak, starboard point-fives joining in for a snap shot as the machine roared low over *Masai* and a bomb went into the sea to starboard of her; the four-sevens were still shooting after the plane as it pulled away. Nick called up the voicepipe to the director tower and told Harry Houston not to waste shells on enemies who'd completed their attacks, that it was vital to conserve ammunition.

Because it was going to be a long, long day. If *Carnarvon* got a move on they might last through it. *Might.* The silence came, lasted about twenty-five seconds before the next attack developed, a batch of a dozen 88s coming up high astern. Houston could give the HACS a run this time, with planes coming straight and high as peacetime expectations had allowed for: you could estimate height, speed, inclination, wind, et cetera, feed it down to the machine below decks – a machine presided over, like the Admiralty Fire Control Table next door to it, by Petty Officer Eustace Roddick, Gunner's Mate – and the machine would feed back its instructions to the layers, trainers, fuse-setters at the guns. The system's pre-war designers had only reckoned on aircraft being able to fly at 125 knots, so all the figures had to be doubled (roughly) to make the equation come out right: and there was a long sheet of paper stuck on to the machine to extend its scale.

Astern, *Masai* had opened fire. Nick got up on his seat for extra height-of-eye, and trained his glasses westward to where *Carnarvon* had until now been only a flashing searchlight. At first he couldn't pick up anything: *Tuareg*'s X and Y guns opened fire, the hard crashes of the explosions drowning nearer sounds, and there was other gunfire – *Masai*'s astern and *Afghan*'s from the landward bow. Now he had the cruiser in his glasses, he'd moved them to the right and picked up her foretop, bridge and both funnel-tops: as he'd expected, she'd gone round to port, steering to close *Black-foot*. Gunfire was one continuous blast again as he got down off the seat, and Pratt was shouting something, pointing astern: his expression was one of alarm and Nick thought the tow must have gone. It wasn't that, thank God: the navigator had yelled, '*Black-foot* is coming up astern, sir!' Thank God again: for tiny, though very much belated, sparks of sense. But probably *much* too bloody late. The Junkers 88s were coming up astern too, not only *Black-foot*: they were almost overhead now – twin-engined, black, big-looking against the bright morning sky: the other half of the formation had circled away eastward and were turning in now to make their attack from the direction of the land. Nick leant out over the side of the bridge and put his glasses up for a glimpse of Marsh's ship chasing up astern, but all he was looking at was gunsmoke hanging over his own ship and *Masai*. The report must have come down from the director, which had the advantage of being above most smoke and all but the biggest splashes. He'd thought of the tow first when Pratt had shouted because it was what he most feared – a hit on *Tuareg* aft or *Masai* for'ard, to snap the wire or the cable. Then they'd be done for. Bombs raised humps of sea all up the port side and on the bow; the pompoms were pumping away at the 88s overhead and the four-sevens were engaging the next crowd, the detachment coming in on the beam.

He went to the binnacle, rested a hand on Rocky Pratt's shoulder as he checked ship's head and glanced at the revolution indicators: everything was as it should have been. The first flight of 88s had gone on over and swung north and the other lot was rising across the sky from the Crete side: going into their dives now, more downhill runs than dives. He saw shellbursts high astern, right up and way back behind *Masai*'s masthead, a couple of miles back, and those bursts led his eye to Stukas, two flights, one of five and one of four: he heard the whistle of the 88s' bombs falling, saw the first go up to port – short – in a thick upheaval of dark sea, and a second, then four others closer and a batch of four still nearer but off *Masai*'s stern: then the much closer rush of the next one coming and a thought flashing through his mind, *Here comes ours* . . . Pratt's face in shock, mouth open and eyes upward then momentarily screwed shut: water-mountains rose to starboard, thirty

311

yards clear, explosions like blows against the Tribal's hull and more bombs falling farther off, receding like huge footprints splashing in puddles as some vast beast plodded on. Pratt was looking up over the stern as the first of the newly-arrived Stukas went into their dives, one pair starting down while others circled left and right: he thought, *They have to hit us some time, they'll go on all day until they do* . . . Ashcourt came from the back of the bridge and told him, 'Captain (D)'s about three miles astern, sir, he's on fire and he seems to have slowed – he *was* coming up quite fast but—'

Gunfire drowned the end of it as the pompoms opened on the diving Stukas.

'Going to be too late. Why the blazes he had to go and—' Napier shook his head, bit off words spoken in sudden anger. He had his glasses on *Blackfoot*, who'd just been hit again. She was about four miles ahead of the cruiser. She'd slowed down and smoke was belching from her afterpart, but that last hit had been on the for'ard part of the bridge. Clutterbuck's voice boomed from the speaker: 'X and Y shift target, Stukas red one-three-oh angle of sight four-oh, blue barrage—'

'Port twenty!'

'Port twenty, sir . . .'

Napier was at the binnacle: he'd taken over the ship from Irvine a few minutes ago, about the time they'd started having to fight off their own Stukas. McCowan still had A gun, the mounting for'ard, throwing shells up over *Blackfoot*. When she'd slowed and they'd turned directly towards her, to get in close and try to save her, the other three guns wouldn't bear. In any case the cruiser had to protect herself as well. Now with the swing to port he was using Q again, as well as A, keeping only the after mountings and the pompoms for self-defence.

'Midships and meet her.'

He'd turn his ship back now: the jink had been to fox the Stukas, at least make their job less easy. There was a cloud of them in and out of a haze of smoke over *Tuareg* and the other Tribals: like flies round a distant runner's head. *Tuareg* couldn't do any dodging, with *Masai* strung on astern of her. Napier had ordered starboard wheel, and Clutterbuck was telling Q to follow ADP; the multiple pompoms were trained as far aft as they'd go, blazing at the yellow face of a diving 87. *Blackfoot* had been very badly hit . . .

312

She was about twenty degrees on the cruiser's port bow as Napier checked the counter-swing, steadying on this interception course which also allowed the midships gun to bear. Jack's glasses had been focused on the Tribal leader and he'd watched a Stuka pressing its attack home almost to deck level, breaking out of its dive only when the pilot must have been certain his bombs must hit. Amidships, somewhere abaft the bridge, a yellow-orange brilliance sparked and bloomed inside outspreading petals of black smoke, then the smoke was all you could see, the destroyer's forepart protruding from it and her B gun still firing at maximum elevation, its small flame-spurts winking in the shredding eddies of the smoke. There was something both desperate and pathetic in that one gun's puny-looking effort. Napier had doubled to the voicepipe again, a bomb had thumped into the sea to starboard and a Stuka had dived straight in after it, its siren shrieking right up to the moment of explosive impact: another, trailing smoke, was wobbling away just a few feet above the water, and the cruiser's guns were blazing furiously at two others screaming down. Jack looked back towards *Blackfoot* as Napier steadied the ship directly towards her: and *Blackfoot* had blown up. The sound reached him as confirmation just as his mind grasped what had happened, watching the huge expanding cloud which had hidden her and a Stuka branching out through its upper fringes, arcing away towards the mountains: a stab of flame quickly smothered in the centre of the cloud was the Stuka's bomb exploding on a ship already killed.

Napier called down, 'Starboard twenty.' Grim-faced, knowing his duty now: to get his ship and her guns to the others, leave the dead to bury the dead, seek the salvation of the living. 'Midships.' A Stuka was boring down on the quarter and Clutterbuck had all the guns poked up at it, spitting flame and smoke and noise: Clutterbuck who at breakfast yesterday had blinked pale-faced across the wardroom table, that strangely calm, deliberate way he had of blinking through shiny steel-framed glasses while he buttered a piece of toast and piled Oxford marmalade on it from his own private jar, and answered a remark which Jack had made to the effect that gunnery control, even a half-arsed procedure like *HA* gunnery control, was a peculiar employment for a paybob.

In fact, half the fleet were using paymasters for the job. Brand-new RNVR officers, straight out of the knife-and-fork course at

King Alfred, were being drafted to Whale Island for a course of instruction in the new art, but there weren't many such people at large yet.

'Peculiar, do you say?' Clutterbuck had raised an eyebrow towards the paymaster commander, his boss. 'Not if you give the matter a moment's thought, my dear Everard. It's a job requiring gumption, d'you see. Brains. It's not at *all* a job for bone-headed bloody salt-horse ullages such as—'

He'd stopped short as his eyes had met those of Commander Bell-Reid, who was a salt horse if there'd ever been one. Clutterbuck had smiled disarmingly. 'Good morning, sir.'

Crescendo of gunfire: then Clutterbuck's voice from the speaker intoning the ritual 'Check, check, check', and an isolated last shot from one of the stern mountings. Silence, now.

Blackfoot had disappeared, and *Carnarvon*'s attendant Stukas had – for the moment – left them. Fine on the cruiser's bow the cluster of surviving Tribals was almost stern-on, the air above it murky with shellbursts: sunlight flashed there on circling and diving Stukas. About five miles away, Jack thought. Chasing after them now at twenty-two knots, less the twelve knots or more that the destroyers would be making southwards, would close the gap at no more than ten sea-miles per hour; so it was going to take a minimum of half an hour.

Nick hadn't seen *Blackfoot* go. Houston had reported it, from his perch in the director. Gloom wasn't much lessened, if at all, by having been aware for some time of the possibility, even likelihood, of it happening, but one's own predicament left little time for ruminating on the fate of others. One was aware of the loss of a fine ship and of some proportion of her company of 230 men, and that it had not been necessary. *Tuareg* was leader now, because Nick was the senior of the remaining COs; and now that the Luftwaffe had eliminated *Blackfoot* he knew that *Tuareg* and *Masai* would become the priority target in this area.

Not quite yet, though. There was a lull in progress, and every second of it was being used: clearing gundecks of the litter of shellcases, overhauling guns, getting up stocks of ready-use ammunition and setting more barrage fuses.

The Luftwaffe would be busy too, refilling their bombers' tanks and bomb racks.

He'd sent young Chalk aft to make himself useful to Dalgleish.

With the tow to keep an eye on as well as his other responsibilities, Dalgleish could probably use some help.

'Alarm port – aircraft, red nine-oh!'

Houston was on them too: the director had just swung round, settled on the port beam, and the barrels of A and B guns had swung to the same bearing. You could see them now slowly lifting as the angle of sight increased, and shifting in small amounts this way and that as layers and trainers followed the pointers in their dials, pointers that moved in step with the one in the director-layer's dial up in the tower. Nick had the Stukas in his glasses now, and it was the biggest group he'd seen this week. Three flights of six planes each, then a space and then another three flights of six.

Pratt muttered, lowering his glasses, 'Bastards could do with some thinning out.' He glanced round into the bridge behind him: casually, then sharply: 'Sub, put your bloody hat on!'

Ashcourt grinned as he reached for his tin helmet. Pratt turned back, grumbling, 'Cooling his fat head.' *Afghan*, weaving ahead of them, opened fire. Fire-gongs rang down on *Tuareg*'s gundecks and the show was on the road again, the guns' crashes and the ringing in her steel and in men's heads and, up around the oncoming yellow-snouted bombers, puff-balls opening like brown woolly fists with the Stukas streaking on, flying straight and level at the moment so that Houston had the HA director above him controlling the guns, shooting by the book, an AA shoot at this stage and not a barrage. After each salvo there was a pause, and just as deafness seemed to be easing off in your eardrums there'd be another thunderclap, and just as regularly a new group of shell-bursts that broke open against the blue background of the sky, adding to those from *Afghan* and *Masai*. Now they were splitting up, some one way and some the other, others coming on but weaving, jinking, rate of fire increasing as the guns switched to barrage fire. Deafness was cumulative, building while the action lasted. The first two planes were tipping over, lowering their yellow noses as if to inspect for the first time the shellbursts that were plastering the air they were about to dive through. He saw one explode: a flash, black smoke-burst, cloud of debris scattering: only one plane diving now: the next pair tearing in, dodging and bucketing through the bursts, this front-runner half-hidden in them, its siren's ear-splitting note rising as it swept down at the ships. Pompoms giving all they had, point-fives stammering from both sides. Ammunition wouldn't last the day out if this went on –

it wouldn't even last till noon. The Stuka was hit, flaming, on its back and falling away to port, but there were two others – no, *four*, two beyond them – in their dives and no pause in the barrage, in the huge expenditure of shells, two more bombers coming in shallowly from astern and yet another brace steeply from right ahead, so there was no question of shooting at individual attackers – except at close range, for the pompoms and point-fives. The best you could do was fill the air with shells and pray for the things to fly into them.

A bomb had gone up astern of *Masai*: about eight Stukas were diving on her and half a dozen on *Tuareg*, one levelling out over *Afghan* now with its bomb raising the sea ahead of her as she swung hard a-starboard: you glimpsed pieces at a time, saw bits here and bits there through a blanket of noise and smoke: behind it was the recurrent and sick certainty that it couldn't last. *Afghan*, being free to dodge, was not a favourite target and she was having a comparatively easy time, contributing her firepower mostly to the barrage above this tow. Flame shot up in a streak like a gas-jet, and as the top of it seemed to pinch inwards a fireball rose from that: burning gas – ammunition, a cordite fire? *Masai* – from her stern, where a bomb had burst. Smoke now erupting: her after magazine, he guessed. Magazine and shellroom, respectively port and starboard sides, were under the X gun-mounting, and immediately for'ard of that was an oil-fuel tank. He had to think it out, get facts and probabilities straight in his mind, thinking of what *Masai*'s position would be now and what could be done about it, if anything. The tiller-flat bulkhead was already exposed to the sea, and that would have been an internal explosion about twenty-five feet for'ard of it. But it was whether the bulkhead for'ard of the explosion held that would decide whether she sank or floated.

The bombers' siren-screams were howls of exaltation piercing bedlam: another Stuka had gone down burning, spinning, and the sea was lifting all around as planes hurtled in from all angles and all directions, plummeting through the cloud of shellbursts screaming for blood to dip their yellow beaks in. One disintegrating, flung over as a shell burst under it, two others weaving as they flew off towards the mountains, one of them trailing smoke: and one right ahead now, coming down near-vertically, pompoms blasting up at it from all three destroyers. It was beginning to pull out, bomb falling clear, shiny like a toy with the flicker of the sun on it as it turned over in the air: the Stuka had flown into converging streams of pompom shells, and flames were licking round its cockpit. The bomb went into the sea but so close to *Masai*'s stem that its fins might have scraped it: sea mushroomed up from the explosion, raining across both ships: Nick felt *Tuareg*'s sudden lunge and it was the thing he'd dreaded, the tow parting.

CHAPTER 5

'Stop both engines. Port twenty-five.' Over the blare of guns he heard the swelling volume of a Stuka's siren: it wasn't his business, it was Houston's and the gunners'. He yelled at Pratt, 'Tell them to slip the tow!' Pratt was at the A/S telephone. The pompoms had allowed him to make that audible but now they drowned the voicepipe acknowledgements from CPO Habgood: a Stuka was pulling out of its dive higher than usual, he heard the whistling rush of its bomb and then the hard *whumpf* of it exploding in the sea, not in his field of view but too close for comfort. Then in slackening gunfire he caught Pratt's shouted report, 'All gone aft, sir!' That meant the tow, they'd knocked the slip off: he told the coxswain, 'Half ahead together, three hundred revolutions. Midships.' The stop-engines order had been a precaution against getting wire wrapped round the screws: if there was a wire trailing and a screw turning that was what invariably happened, and this wouldn't have been the best time or place for it; but with the slip knocked off the cable would have gone straight down, taking the wire with it into about 4,000 feet of water. Taking stock now: tow gone, *Masai* on fire aft, stopped and down by the stern: *Masai* was a dead loss, in fact. He had no options, really. He called down, 'Starboard ten.' The crippled Tribal was on his port quarter, two cables' lengths away, with *Afghan* circling round her stern, guns just ceasing fire as a Stuka – the last of this batch, perhaps – batted away towards the land. Nick shouted to Mason, the signalman, 'Make to *Masai*, *Prepare to abandon ship over your starboard side for'ard. I am coming alongside bow to bow.*' He beckoned Ashcourt: 'Go down and tell the first lieutenant I'll be putting the starboard side of this bridge alongside the starboard side of hers. I want her people over like greased lightning and straight below. Then—'

318

'Alarm starboard – Stukas green five-oh!'

'—then stay down there and help, Sub.'

'Aye aye, sir.' Ashcourt took off. Nick told Pratt, 'Warn the doctor.' It was only a matter of calling down the voicepipe to the plot, but *Masai* had been hit by two bombs and Gallwey would surely have some customers and might get some more during the transfer operation, if this was a new attack about to start. He looked up and saw them, another drove of Ju87s coming high and bloodthirsty over Crete, obviously from Scarpanto. Only half a minute between assaults now: the Luftwaffe's organization must be sharpening up. He stooped to the pipe: 'Starboard twenty.' He told CPO Habgood, 'Cox'n, I'm circling to go alongside *Masai* and take her ship's company off. There'll be some close manoeuvring and I expect we'll have some Stuka interference while we're at it.'

'Aye, sir. Twenty of starboard wheel on, sir.'

Nick explained to Houston what he was doing: he made it brief because Houston was about to get busy again. Even when they were alongside *Masai* the guns could still be used – all except the starboard point-fives, which otherwise might blow the heads off men in both bridges. And Houston would need to be careful which way he pointed A and B guns. *Masai* had acknowledged the signal and *Afghan*, on her port beam, had just opened fire at the approaching bombers.

'Midships. One-two-oh revolutions.'

Tuareg's four-sevens opened up. About two dozen Stukas up there, in three groups. 'Steer oh-one-oh . . .' There was more way on the ship than he'd have been happy with in normal circumstances, but it was essential to get alongside fast, get those men out of *Masai* before things got worse. It wasn't the easiest thing to do while you were being dive-bombed.

'Course oh-one-oh, sir, one-two-oh revolutions.'

It was time to cut the speed. 'Slow ahead together.' Gunfire getting faster, heavier; above the noise of it, like the beginning of some weird descant, he heard the first Stuka in its dive. He wondered whether there'd be many survivors from poor *Blackfoot*. Or any at all. The German flyers didn't seem to like survivors, judging by the prevalence of machine-gun attacks on men helpless in the water. It seemed pointless as well as barbarous: they must be very young, he thought, mindless, really rather horrible people. It could be that they were under orders to terrify, break their enemies' spirit, shatter morale. There was another theory, that the pilots were fed drugs of some kind. But no time now for speculation: pompoms had opened fire.

'Steer two degrees to starboard.'

Masai's for'ard guns were hard at it. A Stuka swept so low as it levelled that it passed right through the narrowing gap between the two ships, then banked to the left and curved away down *Tuareg*'s port side, getting a parting burst from the point-fives as it swept past. There was a medley of sirens overhead and all the guns were cocked up and blazing. He bent to the voicepipe again: 'Stop starboard.' *Tuareg* was sliding up almost stem to stem with *Masai*: by doing it this way he was reducing the risk of new explosions in the other destroyer's stern spreading fire or damage to his own ship: and he was keeping his screws well clear of trouble too. By now Johnny Smeake should have most of his men waiting under cover, ready to rush out of the screen door at the foc'sl break and flood over into *Tuareg*. Habgood reported that the starboard telegraph was to 'stop'. Gunfire was at its peak, about as loud and continuous as it could get, and the ship was ringing to the percussions: by the noise of sirens there must have been two or three Stukas diving now. Looking quickly over the side of the bridge, down at the foc'sl deck, he saw Tony Dalgleish and Petty Officer Mercer, the buffer, standing with heaving lines looped ready in their hands: two other men, one a killick called Sherratt, were dragging up a coil of steel wire rope. He saw Chalk down there, and a man securing a line to the end of a ribbed gangplank: two other planks were ready near it.

'Slow astern both engines.'

'Slow astern both, sir!'

Bombs were exploding in the sea astern. This wasn't going to turn out too badly, he thought . . . 'Stop starboard.'

'Stop starboard, sir . . .'

'Stop port!'

A bit more of a bump than one would normally have been proud of: but the object hadn't been to show off any ship-handling ability, only to get there as quickly as was possible without bumping hard enough for the ships to be thrown apart again. Lines, wires and planks had gone over, and sailors were boarding thick and fast. Johnny Smeake in *Masai*'s bridge was waving and shouting something: Nick waved back but he couldn't hear Smeake's words. He looked down to see two wires made fast: and that at one of the gangplanks a line of *Masai*'s men were forming with a gunner's mate organizing them and shells being passed from hand to hand: there was an outsize stoker on the plank as link man. It was four-seven HA ammunition and boxes of pompom, all worth its weight in gold. Pratt pointed northward and shouted something about *Carnarvon* coming: a Stuka was shrieking down, wild fury in the hideous noise, guns doing their best to shout it down, *Masai*'s A and B guns cocked up to port and barraging in front of a group of about six weaving, high-up bombers. *Afghan* was out on that side too, and all three ships' pompoms were pumping vertically at the closer, more immediate threats, the planes already in their dives. Nick was looking down at the foc's'l deck again, at the rapid transference of men and ammunition: he heard the bombs coming – two Stukas diving simultaneously . . . The first eruption was right ahead, not more than ten yards from *Tuareg*'s stem and about five from *Masai*'s burning afterpart: the second plumped in well clear, farther out on the other side. There'd been the usual thick upflinging of sea as the first bomb splashed in and exploded: now a wall of sea flung back against the bow and into the gap between the ships, sluicing aft. The ammunition handler on the plank staggered, swaying wildly with a shell clasped in his arms: like a high-wire artist, he was on one foot and doubling backwards, but he'd somehow managed to throw the shell towards *Tuareg* – or it had simply happened, ejected from his grasp by his own strenuous efforts to avoid falling between the two ships and being crushed – and PO Mercer, leaning out from *Tuareg*'s side, had caught it. It weighed fifty pounds, that shell. The other man was sitting on the plank, his long legs dangling in the gap then whipping up out of the way as he saw his danger a second before the two destroyers lurched back together. A roar of cheers was drowned in gunfire and the shrieking of more diving Stukas: Nick shouted to Whiffen, his yeoman, to get the loud-hailer rigged so he could tell Johnny Smeake to send the rest of his men over, forget the ammunition.

From *Carnarvon*'s bridge all you could see of *Tuareg* and *Masai* was a muddle of bomb-splashes, smoke, shellbursts and diving bombers. *Afghan* was more easily visible as she dodged around the other ships at high speed, zigging to and fro to foil her own attackers while keeping far enough from the maelstrom in the centre to be able to keep her four-sevens barraging over it.

Stukas hadn't bothered the cruiser much. They'd made a few attacks, but with her high-angle four-inch guns she wasn't as soft a target as the destroyers were, and the Germans tended to pull out of their dives well up, which considerably reduced their accuracy. During the last ten minutes there'd been a procession of flights of Ju88s coming over, and this had kept everyone busy; but they'd left now, having churned the sea up all around, and McCowan had switched all his guns to a long-range barrage above the Tribals, twenty degrees on the port bow; Napier was steering this course so as to allow all the guns to bear.

The director telephone was calling: nobody heard it, but Brighouse, the snotty, saw its light flashing and jumped to snatch it off its hook and offer it to the captain. Bell-Reid stared at Brighouse with his bushy eyebrows raised, as if amazed that the lad should have done something useful. Jack thought again of the possibility that brother Nick might, a long time ago, have been rather Brighousian . . . He was feeling no anxiety for Nick, no more than one would have felt for anyone else in that fairly desperate situation: less, in fact, because he'd little doubt that when the smoke cleared *Tuareg* and her captain would emerge like muddied players from the bottom of a rugger scrum. Nick was a sort of indiarubber character, a bouncer-back: and didn't he expect everyone else to be just as tough, just as uncaring?

Sarah said he was like flint. She said Nick was so inconsiderate, so lacking in normal human compassion that it was astonishing his marriage had lasted the few years it had . . .

Napier still had the director telephone at his ear: now, pushing it back on its hook, he was looking round and beckoning to the chief yeoman. Hegarty moved over quickly: his narrow face under the tin hat sharp, terrier-like. Napier told him, 'That's *Tuareg*, there.' He pointed at the right-hand edge of the smother of smoke and ships; Jack put his own glasses up again, and he could see *Tuareg* drawing out to starboard. Napier told the yeoman, 'Make to her, *Course one-eight-oh, twenty-two knots*.' Hegarty had scrawled it on his pad: he began to shout it back, but the pompoms opened fire and drowned his voice. A Messerschmitt 109, a single-engined fighter, roared over from port to starboard, machine-guns racketing. Now another: and a third . . . Bell-Reid was using a telephone to get a first-aid party up to attend to a casualty in the pompom's crew, and a replacement for him. The fighters had come over without anyone having sighted them, and now Bell-Reid was at the after end of the bridge blasting the port-side look-outs. Messerschmitts making a pass at the Tribals now . . . Putting his glasses on *Tuareg* again, Jack saw the single flash of her light telling *Carnarvon*'s signalman to go ahead, send his message. *Tuareg* had gone astern until she was clear of *Masai* and now she was circling away, gathering speed under helm, her pom-poms engaging the oncoming fighters and her four-sevens in action too, pumping shells up at Stukas diving on *Afghan*: she looked magnificent, angry and defiant. One of the Messerschmitts had flopped into the sea on the far side of *Afghan*: *Afghan*'s bird, by the look of it, he guessed.

A sudden upheaval took his eyes back to *Masai*, as a flash and a spout of water shot up beside her. That had been a torpedo, he realized, from *Tuareg*. Gunfire drowned the sound of it: the high, dark column of sea collapsed right across the abandoned ship, and literally within seconds she'd gone down.

Forenoon wearing on, sun high and hot now, blue sea, blue sky. Mean course south-east: the three ships were zigzagging in unison, following an ordered pattern of regular course alterations to fox any lurking submarines. There'd been only one attack – ineffectual, by high-flying Ju88s – since the force had left the Antikithera Channel.

The engineer commander had just been up to report to Napier on the machinery problems he was having to cope with now. Jack, thinking of enginerooms and other cramped compartments below decks, wondered whether it would be as unpleasant as he imagined, to be shut down in the ship's guts during action. He imagined that to be below the waterline, hearing the noise of battle and knowing you had two or three decks and armoured hatches between you and the daylight would be fairly nightmarish . . .

Perhaps it was only a fear of the unknown. Perhaps one's imagination would always balk at the idea of being shut-in below decks. And in fact it was something he'd never be called upon to experience. One could be glad of that, to be spared it, but also regret that since one would never be put to any such test it would remain a potential weakness, a suspected Achilles' heel.

He had a fleeting thought of Nick, of brother Nick's expectations, the David syndrome. He told himself quickly, *Don't think about it. There's no point . . .*

'What?' He glanced round: startled, as if the interrupter might have read his thoughts. It was PO Tomkins, bringing him the signal log, which Napier and Bell-Reid had already perused. Jack rested it on top of the binnacle, leafed through the wad of signals.

Admiral King's Force C, up in the Aegean still, had been under attack since seven o'clock this morning. Three solid hours of dive-bombing: and it was still going on. *Calcutta* – an AA cruiser like *Carnarvon* – had sighted a transport, and it had been sunk by King's destroyers; now the force had 'numerous small vessels' and one Italian destroyer in sight: the destroyer was laying a smoke-screen to protect its convoy's retreat northward and the cruisers *Perth* and *Naiad* were pursuing. All this under constant bombing.

Admiral Glennie's cruisers – *Dido*, *Orion* and *Ajax*, who'd destroyed the invasion convoy last night – had joined up with Admiral Rawlings' battle squadron west of Kithera. But there was a signal from C-in-C with time of origin 0716 recalling Glennie's force to Alexandria. There was also one from C-in-C to Force B – the cruisers *Gloucester* and *Fiji* with two destroyers, *Greyhound* and *Griffin* – ordering them to a position off Heraklion. They'd been steering west, though, at 0700, and under heavy air attack; *Fiji* had been damaged by near-misses. *Gloucester* had reported that she had only 18 per cent of her outfit of ammunition remaining.

There was also a copy of Napier's signal earlier on about the loss of *Blackfoot* and *Masai* in the Antikithera Channel, reporting too that *Carnarvon*'s maximum speed was now down to twenty-two knots.

Like a peacetime cruise, Nick thought. He'd been down to his sea-cabin for a shave, earlier on, and he was on the bridge now with Ashcourt as officer of the watch. Even if it had been Dalgleish or Pratt at the binnacle he'd have been up here: he was very much aware that as they slanted across the Mediterranean on this south-easterly course they were drawing nearer to Scarpanto and its nest of Stukas all the time. They'd be closest to it at 1600, when they'd be 140 miles south-west of it, and after that the range would be increasing until dusk.

He heard the zigzag bell ring, down in the wheelhouse, and *Tuareg* heeled very gently to five degrees of starboard rudder as the quartermaster of the watch brought her round to the next leg of the pattern. He had the diagram down there in front of him, the book of zigzag patterns open at the one *Carnarvon*'s captain had selected. On this one you lost 15 per cent of speed-made-good; but it was a lot better than being torpedoed, which was what tended to happen to ships that steered straight courses.

He slid up on to his seat, and thought about Fiona. Human problems tended to get buried, when you were having to concentrate on staying alive, afloat. The problems stayed in men's minds but at the back of them, possibly influencing them indirectly in some ways but in storage until pressures eased. Problems like – he lit a cigarette – Fiona's silence.

If anything happened to her, an MTC friend of hers, a Mrs Stilwell, would have written to him. *Was to have* written to him. Fiona had promised to arrange it: and similarly there was a letter addressed to her, back in HMS *Woolwich* the depot ship, that would be posted only if *Tuareg* ran into bad luck. The idea had been to set each other's mind at rest: he could hear her telling him now, *If you don't hear, don't worry . . .*

Pretty silly instruction to give anyone, that had been.

He wondered about marrying Fiona. Not that either of them had ever referred to such a thing, but – well, it could come to marriage. Because – all right, because it was what he wanted: wanted – his worry for her brought it out and faced him with it clearly – very much indeed.

Old Hugh Everard might not take too happily to the idea. Hugh was a splendid man, but he was also rather strait-laced, a product of his own age: none the worse for that, but Fiona might be too modernly sophisticated for his taste. Once he got to know her it would be all right, but he wouldn't fall for her as easily as he had for Ginny Casler. He'd try to, he'd do his best to like her, for Nick's sake; they'd always been close, more like father and son than uncle and nephew. Many years ago, when Nick had been something of a rebel and the Navy hadn't thought much of him, Hugh had given him his one big chance: he'd grabbed it, and had some luck, and as sole surviving officer of the destroyer *Lanyard* he'd brought her back – so badly damaged that she'd been unrecognizable – from Jutland. If it hadn't been for that helping hand, Nick knew he wouldn't ever have got anywhere at all.

Sarah? Sarah would hate any woman that Nick married. Any woman he *knew*, she'd loathe. No good trying to reason it out: it was simply how Sarah was. Perhaps because he'd married Ilyana? Because he should have stayed single, Sarah's devoted and remorseful slave?

The zigzag bell rang again, and the quartermaster applied port rudder. Lowering his glasses, Nick watched the stem swinging, slicing round through blue water and edging it with white. On the beam, *Afghan* was also under helm, and on *Tuareg*'s quarter *Carnarvon* was taking part in the same stately waltz.

When Jack came up from lunch there were some new messages on the log. At 1225 Admiral King, still up in the Aegean with his Force C, had signalled Rawlings to the effect that he was in urgent need of support against the ceaseless air attacks. King had broken off his pursuit of the invasion convoy some time before that, earlier in the forenoon, and turned his ships to head for a rendezvous with Rawlings in the south-west; but the attacks had continued and his flagship, the cruiser *Naiad*, had been damaged. Her speed had been cut to sixteen knots, she had two turrets out of action and some internal flooding.

Carlisle, sister-ship to *Carnarvon*, had been bombed in her bridge and her captain had been killed.

Jack glanced up from the log. He could imagine how things must be up there. Like all the attacks they'd been through themselves, only a lot more intense and with no breaks in the action, bombers on them all the time, hour after hour. It would be totally exhausting as well as nerve-racking. Napier, on his high seat and with a luncheon tray in front of him, was staring at Jack across the bridge, probably to see his reaction to those signals. Napier called over his shoulder, 'Noble, you can take this now.'

The tray, he meant. He was reaching for a cigarette. A thump from the pneumatic tube announced the arrival of yet another signal from the office down below. Petty Officer Hillier, the signal yeoman of the watch, was removing it from the carrier; Napier watched him through narrowed, deepset eyes as he flicked a lighter to the cigarette. Behind him, where a tall snotty named Burk was taking over the bridge watch from a short one called Wesley, you could see weld-marks where voicepipes had been patched up by the ERAs after that Messerschmitt had jumped *Carnarvon* during a Nauplia lift.

Hillier had clipped the new signal to the log and taken it to Napier, who was studying it. He nodded, expelling smoke. 'Show it to the navigating officer, please.'

And another thump in the tube . . . Jack took the log from Hillier as he passed: the signal on top was from Rawlings to King and to the C-in-C: Rawlings was taking his battle squadron into the Aegean to support Force C. Jack, imagining the scene up there again, thought how extremely lucky *Carnarvon* was to be out of it,

326

gently shepherding the two Tribals home to Alex. PO Hillier had taken the new signal straight to Napier: he told him, 'It's addressed to us, sir.'

Carnarvon was to leave the destroyers, and proceed at her best speed to join the battle squadron, Force A1, via the Antikithera Channel.

'Course, pilot?'

He was already at the chart, getting it: and thinking, *I should have touched wood . . .* He answered Napier, 'Three-two-oh, sir.'

'Yeoman – make to *Tuareg: Proceed independently to Alexandria. I have been ordered to return to Antikithera.*'

Tuareg wouldn't have had those signals, because she didn't carry the code books for them. As a destroyer and a private ship, not a flotilla leader, she'd only take in plain-language signals and ones intended for her or for other destroyers. Durkin, a killick signalman, was already at the lamp and calling *Tuareg*. Napier told Bertie Tyler, who was officer of the watch, 'Come round to port to three-two-oh.'

'Aye aye, sir.' Tyler lowered his tanned face to the voicepipe. 'Port fifteen.' Jack took a reading of the log and noted the time, and went to the chart to mark it up. Seventy-five miles to Antikithera: best part of three and a half hours. By that time they might tie up with the battle squadron and Force C as they came *out* of the Aegean.

1.30 pm . . . Nick watched the cruiser swinging away on to a north-westerly course, the course for Cape Elaphonisi and the Antikithera Channel, the Stukas' playground. He glanced round, and told the signalman on watch, 'Make to *Afghan, Speed thirty knots.*'

He'd cut the revs again after dark. It would be necessary to idle away some of the dark hours anyway, because you couldn't enter harbour until the sweepers had cleared the channel at first light. German aircraft were in the habit of planting mines at night in the Great Pass, the Alexandria approach. But it would be as well to get past the Scarpanto airfield's close radius as quickly as possible, now that *Carnarvon*'s reduced speed wasn't tying them down.

'Make that executive, signalman.'

Lever was already passing the speed order. Nick told Pratt as the lamp stopped its clattering, 'Three-one-oh revs, pilot.' Behind him a voice murmured, 'Burning the midday oil, are we?'

Johnny Smeake, *Masai*'s captain. Pratt had called down for the

327

speed increase. Smeake was a commander, recently promoted. 'Mind me cluttering up your bridge?'

'You're welcome.' The former captain of *Masai* was fair-haired, skinny, with eyes that looked gleamingly blue in the reddish colouring of his skin. It was the kind of face that turned red when others tanned. Nick asked him, 'Your chaps all being looked after?'

'Doing us proud, thank you.' He'd taken the loss of his ship hard, though. He said now, 'Should have sunk her last night, you know. Pointless, trying to tow her out. I was glad of it at the time – who wouldn't be, but . . .'

'Yes.'

The point didn't have to be elaborated. Very few of *Blackfoot*'s company could be alive at this moment. Smeake turned away, stared out over the quarter at the cruiser's diminishing shape. 'Going back for another dose of it. Won't be too healthy up there by this time.' He looked at Nick – 'My chaps are going to be okay, incidentally. Mending well. Frightfully lucky, all things considered.'

Only three of the *Masai*'s crew had been wounded, and none killed. It did seem like a lot of luck. Smeake added, 'Wonder what they'll find for us to do now.' He brought out a cigarette case: 'Smoke?' Nick shook his head. Smeake said, 'Bloody shame, only two ships left out of four. If there'd been one more – mine – we'd still have looked more or less like a flotilla, and they might have given it to you.'

Oddly enough, that thought *had* occurred. Nick said, as if it didn't much matter to him, 'They'll tag us on to some other lot.' Chalk was just coming off the ladder and there was a signal in his hand. Bad news, Nick thought, guessing it from the boy's expression.

'*Greyhound*'s been sunk, sir, and *Warspite*'s been badly damaged. Two plain-language signals—'

'Let me see them.'

Warspite, 30,000-ton battleship, was Admiral Rawlings' flagship. She was more than that, she was floating history, a famous and distinguished ship. But the import here and now was that Rawlings and his battleships must have linked up with King's Force C: which meant that Force C must have run into very serious trouble, or Rawlings wouldn't have taken his ships into that rain of bombs: and it was obvious now why they'd turned *Carnarvon* back.

'Then there's this one, sir.'

Plain language again: an order from Flag Officer Force C to the destroyers *Kandahar* and *Kingston* to go and rescue survivors from *Greyhound*.

You could guess how it would be. Men in the water, German aircraft diving to machine-gun them, ships under constant air attack struggling to get them out of it but facing the huge risk of presenting stationary targets when they stopped at each boat or raft or individual swimmer . . . The signal office telephone buzzed, and Nick took it off its hook: 'Bridge.'

'Plain language signal, sir, Flag Officer Force C to *Fiji*, sending her to the support of *Kandahar* and *Kingston*.'

He put the phone down. In bits and pieces and from a distance that felt almost criminally safe, he was witnessing what sounded unpleasantly like the beginnings of defeat. Like a tide starting to come in: swirls here and eddies there, a movement gathering momentum and force, compounding on itself, building a sense of looming disaster. Personal issues flickered inside the wider, vast ones . . . With an effort, he pulled himself together. He told himself that he was overtired, overstrained: that this was a time for strength, purpose, not for letting one's imagination drift: that he was a professional and that in the long run professionalism and staying power, not drugged Stuka pilots, would win and come out alive.

'What was it?'

'*Fiji*.' He told Smeake, 'Being sent to support—'

'Alarm port! Red eight-oh – Stukas, sir!'

One of the port-side look-outs had shouted it. Nick had caught the first two words and his thumb was already on the button stabbing out A's for air action stations. At the same time he was looking out on the port beam and seeing those unpleasant, mosquito-like things glinting in the sky, a small high cloud of them coming from Scarpanto.

4.30 pm . . .

Carnarvon pounded steadily north-westward. There was still a long way to go to Cape Elaphonisi but the ship was already at action stations. Twenty miles was no distance to a Stuka, and just over the horizon Stukas would be as thick as flies.

An hour ago the cruiser *Gloucester* had been hit. Badly, by the sound of it. Half an hour before it happened there'd been a signal ordering her and *Fiji* to withdraw from the area where they'd been

329

sent – separately, one after the other – to support attempts at rescuing *Greyhound* survivors. Both cruisers, as Napier had observed to Bell-Reid, must by that time have been extremely short of ammunition for their four-inch AA guns.

Things looked pretty bloody awful. Jack was at the chart, putting on it such information as could be gleaned from the recent signals. All the heat of the action seemed to be in the Kithera area: *Greyhound* had been sunk near Pori island, which was about five miles north-west of Antikithera. The air attacks were constant, with no let-up at all, and it had been like that since early morning. Hour after hour: bombers overhead all the time . . .

Gloucester was obviously in a bad way. She'd reported boiler damage and reduced speed and suffered a series of internal explosions. *Fiji*, who'd been damaged earlier in the day, was standing by her, and they were both under constant attack.

Bell-Reid growled, 'No air cover, and now no ammunition. Luftwaffe must think it's Christmas.' He rounded on Buchanan, the engineer commander, who'd just arrived in the bridge and was hurrying towards Napier. 'Can't you make this tub go faster?'

'Going too fast already.' The Commander (E) wasn't joking. Tin-hatted and wearing a lifebelt outside his white boiler-suit, he stopped beside the captain's seat. 'Sir, I'm sorry to have to tell you this, but—'

'I can't slow down any more, Chief. There's all hell loose up there, and we're wanted in a hurry.'

One of the signals on the log was from the C-in-C to all ships at sea: *Stick it out. Keep in V/S touch. Navy must not let Army down. No enemy forces must reach Crete by sea.*

Buchanan cleared his throat. He said quietly, 'If we don't slow down, sir, we won't get there at all. I'm extremely sorry, and we've been doing everything we can, but—'

'What speed?'

Napier's question cut across the apology: Buchanan looked surprised, as if he'd expected a longer argument.

'Fifteen knots maximum, sir. If we exceed that, we'll break down altogether. Then . . .'

He'd shrugged, glancing skyward. Napier growled, 'The consequences of a breakdown, Chief, I do not need to have pointed out.'

'Sorry, sir.'

He shook his head. Grey-faced, ill-looking. 'All right, Chief.' He told Willy Irvine, who'd been waiting for the order, 'Revs for fifteen knots.'

'Aye aye, sir.' Irvine called down, 'One-eight-oh revolutions.' CPO Hegarty was removing a new signal from the carrier; on his way towards Napier he paused to let the engineer commander, leaving the bridge, pass ahead of him.

The pointers were dropping in the rev indicators; the chief quartermaster reported from the wheelhouse, 'One-eight-oh revolutions passed and repeated, sir.' Napier said, looking up from the new signal to meet Bell-Reid's questioning stare, '*Valiant*'s been hit by two bombs. Only superficial damage, thank God.'

Valiant was the one battleship with Rawlings. Like *Warspite* she was *Queen Elizabeth* class and another Jutland veteran. They'd all had at least one expensive face-lift since *that* war, of course . . . As the speed fell off, *Carnarvon* felt as if she was crawling. Napier told Hegarty, 'Take down a signal, Chief Yeoman. To Flag Officer Force C, Flag Officer Force A1, and C-in-C. From *Carnarvon*. *Engine defects have reduced my speed to fifteen knots. Present position – course* . . . In code, please.'

Hegarty came down to the chart table, where Jack was getting the position for him, a bearing and distance from Cape Elaphonisi. The course was still 320 degrees. It would be dark, Jack thought, before they got close enough to anyone to be of use to them: and before that they'd almost certainly get a ration of attention from the Stukas. He wondered whether *Tuareg* and *Afghan* were getting any as they passed through the Scarpanto area. Yet another signal had come up: Napier glanced back almost fearfully as CPO Hegarty, who'd sent *Carnarvon*'s signal down for ciphering and transmission, went to unload the tube – beating Midshipman Brighouse to it by a whisker. Hegarty glanced at the signal as he crossed the bridge with it, and Jack thought he saw him flinch. Then he was passing it to Napier.

Napier had glanced at it; now he was holding the signal out to Bell-Reid. He saw Jack staring at him and he looked away with a slight shake of the head. Bell-Reid was scowling down at the flimsy sheet of paper with the blue-pencil scrawl on it: Bell-Reid furious, Napier sad. Hegarty murmured to Jack as he squeezed past, '*Gloucester*, sir. She's sunk.'

There had been nine Stukas in that afternoon attack, and eight of them had flown back to Scarpanto after they'd dropped their bombs. One had fallen to *Afghan*'s four-sevens dur... proach run, before any of them started diving, and th... had seemed to put the others off their stroke, so that... weren't pressed home as hard as usual. Perhaps that o... the leader.

Houston was officer of the watch, with young C... number two: Chalk had no watchkeeping certificate ye... he'd learn the trade by standing watches with the more... officers. Nick had sent half the ship's company b... because he thought it was unlikely there'd be any... visits now; it was getting on for seven-thirty, Scarpant... 200 miles away and the 87s would have bigger and b... well inside that range. In an hour and a half it woul...

The end of a rotten day. He thought perhaps they h... or heard – the last of it yet. He was at the chart, makin... as he could of the scraps of information that had been...

They'd had A.B. Cunningham's exhortation about... the army down; then the news of *Gloucester*'s sin... recently there'd been a signal to some of Force C's... telling them to rendezvous with the cruiser *Fiji* twent... north-west of Cape Elaphonisi: *Fiji* had been steering s... twenty-seven knots. Until *Gloucester* had sunk, those... had been together. And the battle squadron, one co... from other plain-language messages, must be about... west of *Fiji*'s position and steering either south-east or... still trailed by swarms of Stukas. He guessed that *Carn*... have joined the battle squadron by this time, and that t... heading north again as soon as it was dark, to resu... invasion sweeps.

Depending, of course, on which ships had any amm... *Gloucester* must have been down to about her last shell... sunk her, and *Fiji* couldn't have much left. The destroy... low on fuel too; the need for bursts of high speed whe... dodging bombers sent consumption soaring. There'd be... ships who *couldn't* be sent back into the Aegean: it wa... you had to be wary of, being caught up there short of oi... ammunition . . . Dawn was a bad time anyway, he thou... days were worth living through for the dusk at the e... Even a day like this one.

'Captain, sir.'

He glanced round, knowing from that throaty voic...

told Willy Irvine, who'd been waiting for the order, 'Revs for fifteen knots.'

'Aye aye, sir.' Irvine called down, 'One-eight-oh revolutions.' CPO Hegarty was removing a new signal from the carrier; on his way towards Napier he paused to let the engineer commander, leaving the bridge, pass ahead of him.

The pointers were dropping in the rev indicators; the chief quartermaster reported from the wheelhouse, 'One-eight-oh revolutions passed and repeated, sir.' Napier said, looking up from the new signal to meet Bell-Reid's questioning stare, '*Valiant*'s been hit by two bombs. Only superficial damage, thank God.'

Valiant was the one battleship with Rawlings. Like *Warspite* she was *Queen Elizabeth* class and another Jutland veteran. They'd all had at least one expensive face-lift since *that* war, of course . . . As the speed fell off, *Carnarvon* felt as if she was crawling. Napier told Hegarty, 'Take down a signal, Chief Yeoman. To Flag Officer Force C, Flag Officer Force A1, and C-in-C. From *Carnarvon*. *Engine defects have reduced my speed to fifteen knots. Present position – course* . . . In code, please.'

Hegarty came down to the chart table, where Jack was getting the position for him, a bearing and distance from Cape Elaphonisi. The course was still 320 degrees. It would be dark, Jack thought, before they got close enough to anyone to be of use to them: and before that they'd almost certainly get a ration of attention from the Stukas. He wondered whether *Tuareg* and *Afghan* were getting any as they passed through the Scarpanto area. Yet another signal had come up: Napier glanced back almost fearfully as CPO Hegarty, who'd sent *Carnarvon*'s signal down for ciphering and transmission, went to unload the tube – beating Midshipman Brighouse to it by a whisker. Hegarty glanced at the signal as he crossed the bridge with it, and Jack thought he saw him flinch. Then he was passing it to Napier.

Napier had glanced at it; now he was holding the signal out to Bell-Reid. He saw Jack staring at him and he looked away with a slight shake of the head. Bell-Reid was scowling down at the flimsy sheet of paper with the blue-pencil scrawl on it: Bell-Reid furious, Napier sad. Hegarty murmured to Jack as he squeezed past, '*Gloucester*, sir. She's sunk.'

There had been nine Stukas in that afternoon attack, and eight of them had flown back to Scarpanto after they'd dropped their bombs. One had fallen to *Afghan*'s four-sevens during the approach run, before any of them started diving, and the early loss had seemed to put the others off their stroke, so that the attacks weren't pressed home as hard as usual. Perhaps that one had been the leader.

Houston was officer of the watch, with young Chalk as his number two: Chalk had no watchkeeping certificate yet, of course; he'd learn the trade by standing watches with the more experienced officers. Nick had sent half the ship's company below again because he thought it was unlikely there'd be any more Stuka visits now; it was getting on for seven-thirty, Scarpanto was nearly 200 miles away and the 87s would have bigger and better targets well inside that range. In an hour and a half it would be dusk.

The end of a rotten day. He thought perhaps they hadn't seen – or heard – the last of it yet. He was at the chart, making such sense as he could of the scraps of information that had been coming in.

They'd had A.B. Cunningham's exhortation about not letting the army down; then the news of *Gloucester*'s sinking. More recently there'd been a signal to some of Force C's destroyers telling them to rendezvous with the cruiser *Fiji* twenty-four miles north-west of Cape Elaphonisi: *Fiji* had been steering south then at twenty-seven knots. Until *Gloucester* had sunk, those two cruisers had been together. And the battle squadron, one could deduce from other plain-language messages, must be about thirty miles west of *Fiji*'s position and steering either south-east or south-west, still trailed by swarms of Stukas. He guessed that *Carnarvon* would have joined the battle squadron by this time, and that they'd all be heading north again as soon as it was dark, to resume the anti-invasion sweeps.

Depending, of course, on which ships had any ammunition left. *Gloucester* must have been down to about her last shell when they'd sunk her, and *Fiji* couldn't have much left. The destroyers would be low on fuel too; the need for bursts of high speed when you were dodging bombers sent consumption soaring. There'd be quite a few ships who *couldn't* be sent back into the Aegean: it was the dawn you had to be wary of, being caught up there short of oil and out of ammunition . . . Dawn was a bad time anyway, he thought. Dusk – days were worth living through for the dusk at the end of them. Even a day like this one.

'Captain, sir.'

He glanced round, knowing from that throaty voice that he'd

find himself looking at the broad, cheerful countenance of PO Whiffen. But this evening it wasn't all that cheerful: and he had a signal in his hand.

'It's *Fiji*, sir.'

'What about her?'

Guessing it: just giving himself time to adjust to more bad news.

'Hit an' stopped, sir. *Kandahar* an' *Kingston*'s standin' by her.'

London believed that a fleet could operate 400 miles from its base in the face of total enemy air superiority. Or they were pretending to believe it, because they hadn't the aircraft to send out or didn't want to spare them from the defence of Britain. Which might be difficult to argue with, but brought one back to the basic, underlying failure, the failure to be ready for a war which everyone who wasn't blind had seen coming.

Chalk looked twitchy, and even genial Harry Houston had a graveyard look. Nick told them as he came up from the chart, 'It's what we're *for*, you know.'

Houston nodded. As a former merchant banker he ought to know something about risks, Nick thought. What annoyed him about their obvious gloom was that they were showing what he was feeling and *not* showing. Houston murmured, 'But *Gloucester* was such a lovely ship. Practically brand new, and ... .' He checked, shaking his head.

Fiji was even newer. Nick didn't bother to mention it, but *Fiji* had been launched in 1939, two years later than *Gloucester*. Houston said, 'Rather a good chum of mine in her.' He glanced round, as Dalgleish came towards them from the ladder.

'News isn't so hot, sir.'

'No.' But it could get worse, he thought, and it very likely would. 'Are you up here to take over, Number One?'

'Thought I might, sir. Unless our city slicker here doesn't want any supper. I did hear he was going on a diet.'

Houston glared at him. 'I heard *you* were seen in Mary's House, last time in.'

Mary's House was one of Alexandria's more exclusive brothels. Nick snapped, 'Shut up, both of you . . .' He was too tired and it had been too foul a day to stand listening to their backchat. One minute they were glum as hell, the next pulling each other's legs like children. Compared to him, he thought, they *were* practically children . . . He told Houston, 'When you go down, tell Mr Walsh I want his return of ammo expenditure tonight, not after we get in

333

in the morning. You might give him a hand with it.' Mr Walsh, the torpedo gunner, was responsible for the magazines: and Houston might as well work a bit of fat off. Nick looked at Dalgleish, 'And everything else, Number One, is to be on the top line before we dock. I want a word with Chief, too, about his defect list. We'll almost certainly be coming straight out again, and I don't want any hold-ups. All right?'

'Aye aye, sir.'

'Tell Chief I want the tanks dipped *now*.' Dalgleish nodded. Nick added, 'I'll be in my sea-cabin.' He glanced at Chalk. 'When you go down, Sub, tell my steward I'm hungry, will you?'

He was eating supper in the cupboard-sized cabin below the bridge when Petty Officer Whiffen brought him the news that *Fiji* had sunk. Lying stopped, she'd been attacked again. The destroyers *Kandahar* and *Kingston* were picking up survivors. Then five minutes later there was another signal: it was an order to the destroyers *Hero* and *Decoy* to go to Ayia Roumeli at the western end of Crete's south coast and bring off the Greek king and the British minister and his wife, and various other personages. There was no harbour or jetty at Roumeli, he knew, so these important people would have to be taken off the open beach: and to get there they must have trekked on foot or perhaps mule-back right across the mountains.

The word 'evacuation' hadn't been used yet. Not publicly.

CHAPTER 6

The minesweepers had come out at first light to sweep the two-mile length of the Great Pass, Alexandria's main entrance and exit channel, and now *Tuareg* was leading *Afghan* down it with the early sun a hot glare fine on the port bow. At this range you could smell Alexandria quite distinctly: the smell was a blend of many compounds, but you'd get a fair approximation to it by mixing horse manure with rotting vegetables, joss-sticks and swamp water. It was quite a different aroma from Port Said's, which had more blocked drains and cheap perfume in it, or from Haifa's, which with an offshore wind was loaded with the scent of wet hides. It wasn't exactly a *nice* smell, Alexandria's, but it was a comforting one in its familiarity and its promise – almost certainly illusory, in present circumstances – of rest and relaxation.

Two mines had been exploded on the sweepers' trip out north-westward, and they'd just set off another right on the edge of the channel, between North Shoal and the port-hand buoy half a mile beyond it. Dead fish floated belly-up where that one had gone off; *Tuareg* was passing through them now at fifteen knots, her pendant numbers fluttering from the port yardarm. She'd identified herself already, from much farther out, to the Port War Signal Station.

Over the jagged stone top of the outer breakwater, which was a couple of miles long, the upperworks of the demilitarized French warships stood out as a foreground to the more distant montage of roofs, cranes, masts and minarets, all vague in the soupy haze of building heat. Drawing the teeth of the French squadron without bloodshed or much worsened relations had been an individual achievement of A. B. Cunningham's, last July. If Cunningham hadn't decided to ignore at least one utterly inept instruction from Whitehall there *would* have been bloodshed – as there had been at

335

Oran – and quite possibly Alexandria would have been blocked with scuttled ships as well. They looked pretty now, with the new day gleaming on them. Pretty, and also sad. But at least they were afloat and intact. There was one battleship – the old *Lorraine* – four cruisers and three destroyers; the French admiral's flagship was the heavy cruiser *Duquesne*.

Looking farther to the left, over the northern part of the long breakwater, the lighthouse of Ras-el-Tin was a white finger trembling in the haze. Most of the naval administrative offices were in the buildings grouped near that lighthouse. Beyond it to the northeast lay the walled palace of King Farouk.

'How's her head, pilot?'

Pratt glanced quickly down at the gyro compass . . . 'One-one-three, sir.' It was as it should have been: Nick had thought she was slightly askew to the line of the channel. Pratt added self-righteously, 'We're between the centreline and the southern edge, sir.'

About 3,000 yards astern of *Afghan*, Admiral Glennie's cruiser flagship *Dido* was leading *Orion* and *Ajax* into the top end of the Great Pass. Nick hadn't any idea what might be happening now in Cretan waters or in the Aegean; there'd been no signals that *Tuareg*'s code-books could have coped with, and nothing of interest in plain language. The only ships the Tribals had encountered during the dark hours had been a northbound force comprising the assault ship *Glenroy* escorted by the AA cruiser *Coventry* and the sloops *Flamingo* and *Auckland* . . . The stunning, really frightful news had come last night in a BBC broadcast, and it had nothing to do with Crete. It rang now in his mind, that calm newsreader's voice: *The Admiralty regrets to announce the loss with all hands of the battle-cruiser* Hood . . . *Hood* had been sunk in the Denmark Strait by *Bismarck*. She'd blown up, apparently, just as three other battle-cruisers had blown up at Jutland a quarter of a century ago. Coming on top of yesterday's losses in the Aegean, there'd been a shock effect to the news: it left you winded, groping for some reason to believe that things weren't quite as hopeless as they seemed.

'Shall I come round now, sir?'

Tuareg was passing the last of the port-hand buoys; the course to the harbour entrance would be 090 degrees, due east. He nodded to Pratt: 'Yes, please,' and told Dalgleish, 'Fall the hands in, Number One. I'll berth starboard side to.'

'Aye aye, sir.' Dalgleish moved aft. 'Bosun's mate – pipe hands fall in for entering harbour.'

336

Special Sea Dutymen had been closed up ten minutes ago; the rest of the ship's company would have been getting themselves cleaned and smartened for the formality of entering harbour. *Tuareg* and *Afghan* would be berthing one each side of an oiler that was moored near the coaling arm, on the Gabbari side of the harbour near the battleships' berths. Near ABC's headquarters too: he might well have his telescope focused on the destroyers as they slid by. Later they'd have to shift berth from the oiler to buoys farther in, near the depot ship, and have their ammunition brought out to them in lighters.

At some early stage, mail should be delivered to them. Dreading disappointment, really frightened that there'd be no letter from her, he was trying not to think about it . . .

'Course is oh-nine-oh, sir.'

'Very good.'

The next turn would be to port, to about 015 degrees, to enter the gap between the outer breakwater and the quarantine mole. At that point Nick would take over the conning of the ship. He looked astern, and saw *Afghan* following round. Two returning, where four had left. These would be sad days for A. B. Cunningham – sending his ships out, seeing fewer and damaged ships come back, wishing to God he could be at sea with them himself, and caring as fiercely as everyone knew he did for both men and ships. *Tuareg* was crossing the foot of the other channel, the Boghaz Pass, where the mine-sweepers were doing their stint now; the Boghaz was the more northerly-leading channel, the one you'd take if you were leaving harbour bound for Port Said or the Levant.

Johnny Smeake asked him, 'Mind if I hang around up here?'

Nick glanced round: he hadn't immediately recognized the voice.

'Johnny – no, of course I don't mind. Make yourself at home.'

'Thank you.' Smeake flicked a half-smoked cigarette away to leeward. 'Never thought I'd be coming back in someone else's ship.'

Aubrey Wishart glanced at Fiona's portrait as he answered Nick's offer of some coffee. 'Thanks, but I've just had a bucketful.' He stooped, peered closely at her. 'Must say, Nick, you do pick 'em.'

There was a mail on board, two sacks of it that had come over from *Woolwich*, the depot ship, by skimmer. Nick had seen the little grey-hulled speedboat coming bouncing round the end of the coaling arm just as Wishart, in the Commander-in-Chief's barge, had been approaching *Tuareg*'s gangway; he'd been waiting to receive the rear-admiral with the pipe and side-party due to him, while oiling continued on the other side. A. B. Cunningham's barge was a thing of beauty, green-painted and ornamented at the main cabin's sides amidships with brass dolphins that gleamed golden in the sun, and crewed by sailors whose boathook drill was impressively precise. *Tuareg* had only been secured at the oiler for about five minutes before the barge had come into sight, sliding out from behind the far side of *Queen Elizabeth*, the flagship; at first it had looked as if the C-in-C himself had been about to pay them a visit – until keen eyes had checked that ABC's tin 'Flag' wasn't mounted in its socket for'ard.

Queen Elizabeth was moored with her stern to the jetty at Gabbari, just a few hundred yards away, and ABC's headquarters was the rectangular building behind the quay to which the jetty led. Wishart had murmured to Nick as he'd followed him in through the screen door, 'Been let out of school for ten minutes. Thought we might have a chat. You've had a rough time, I gather.'

They'd be sorting the mail in the ship's office now, under the supervision of young Chalk. Most of the noise, shouting and clattering that one could hear, came from the oiling operation, the stokers and the oiler's men. This day-cabin – with the sleeping-cabin and bathroom aft of it – was on the ship's starboard side at upper deck level, in the raised after superstructure. The scuttles looked out on to the oiler's deck and, across that, to *Afghan*.

Wishart lowered himself into an Admiralty-pattern armchair, and shook his head at Nick's offer of a cigarette. He was a big man, heavily built, with shrewd eyes behind a genial expression; if it hadn't been for the war, he'd have been retired by this time. He looked tired, and Nick thought there were more lines in his face than there had been a few months ago. He explained, 'Trying to cut down. One smokes too much, ashore. Can't stay long anyway, old lad. As you can imagine, we're slightly on the hop.'

Nick asked him, 'Can you tell me what orders I'm getting now?'

'Yes. You've got today and tonight to lick your wounds. You'll sail at 0600 tomorrow, escorting *Glenshiel* to Plaka Bay with Special Service troops. You'll be senior officer of the escort, which will consist of you, *Afghan, Highflier* and *Huntress*.'

A whole day in harbour . . . It was all he needed to know until, later in the day, the operation orders would come in sealed envelopes, by hand of officer, to the captains of the ships involved.

He reached for the bell. 'If you'd excuse me, I'll pass on the glad tidings.' One watch could go ashore this evening, if the men wanted to. If they had any sense, he thought, they'd stay aboard and get some sleep. The engine-room department would be busy anyway, attending to the numerous defects that couldn't be worked on when the ship was at sea. Leading Steward McEvoy knocked, and came in; Nick told him, 'Ask the first lieutenant to spare a moment, please.'

'Sir.' The door clicked shut. McEvoy was Nick's personal attendant; the other two stewards, the wardroom pair – one of them a petty officer – were Maltese. Nick asked Wishart, 'How are things up there now?'

'Well, starting with your relations – *Carnarvon*'s on her way here at twelve knots. Engine-trouble. Repairable, her plumber says, but she's going to be *hors de combat* for a day or two. Which is *not* all that convenient. Before long we won't have many ships *un*damaged . . .' He shook his head. 'We've recalled Force C – at about midnight, that was – and now the battle squadron too. It's slightly complicated, because Rawlings sent Lord Louis's flotilla to look for more *Gloucester* and *Fiji* survivors and then sweep the north-west coast, and one of 'em – *Kipling* – had trouble with her steering-gear. So she's lame too, and Rawlings was taking his ships up to Kithera to meet the rest of that flotilla as it came south. Should all have been extricated by now, with luck.'

'So everyone's recalled to Alex?'

'Except for what's heading north. And *Jaguar* and *Defender*, who're running ammunition into Suda. But – yes, mostly. No point leaving 'em up there when they're out of ammo, is there.'

'*Carnarvon*?'

'She got a real bollocking yesterday evening, not far short of Elaphonisi. Near-missed three or four times, apparently. She'll be here tomorrow at first light.'

Dalgleish arrived. Nick told him, 'We're under sailing orders for six tomorrow morning. Tell Chief, please. So long as ammunitioning's completed you can give leave to one watch from 1600 to midnight.'

Dalgleish nodded. 'That's marvellous, sir.' The whole day and night in harbour, he meant. 'Here's your mail, sir.'

Nick took the bunch of envelopes – about eight or ten, he guessed – and put it down on the corner of the table without looking at it more than he could help. It scared him, that the answer was so close, that he had only to put his hand out again and collapse the pile to see what was in it – or what wasn't.

'Thank you, Number One.'

Wishart said, 'Perhaps you'd tell the barge's cox'n that I'll be out there in three minutes.'

'Aye aye, sir.'

'You might mention it to Commander Smeake too.'

Nick asked, when Dalgleish had gone, 'By the fact we're carrying troops to Plaka, do I gather there's no immediate likelihood of having to bring the army *out* yet?'

Aubrey Wishart hesitated, his eyes on the pillars of sunlight slanting through the scuttles. Dust-specks swirled in them: the Egyptian flies avoided them, buzzing and circling in the darker areas. There was a reek of oil-fuel. Wishart shook his head. 'No.' Nick was still keeping his eyes away from those letters. 'In strict confidence, old lad, you can't assume it. If we were evacuating, we'd aim to do it from Heraklion, from Sphakia and from Plaka Bay. The Suda Bay lot would cross to Sphakia and the Aussies from Retimo would cross to Plaka: those garrisons would fall back across the mountains and we'd lift them from their respective beaches – 90 per cent of it from Sphakia, probably. But you see, the beaches and the withdrawal routes do have to be secured.' He sighed. 'I *will* have a cigarette, if you've one to spare.'

Nick opened the box and pushed it across the table.

'So in fact we're preparing to evacuate?'

'On the contrary. Orders from London are that Crete is to be held at all costs.'

'Does London understand anything about the Crete situation?'

'That might be a very pertinent question, Nick. But—' he leant forward, as Nick flicked a lighter for the cigarette. 'Thanks. Things aren't going at all well ashore. Morse, who's NOIC at Suda, is pretty sure we can't last. The army are fighting like mad dogs but they're in the same boat we're in – they can't fight dive-bombers with bayonets. Every time they get the upper hand – and they've had it, several times – in come the blasted Stukas. They've really done incredibly well, but in the long run it's the bloody air that counts.' He nodded. '*Only* that. If we'd had a few squadrons of Hurricanes and proper airfields to operate from we'd have had the Boche licked hollow.' He sent a cloud of smoke spiralling through a wedge of sunlight. 'The tide could still turn, you know. I'm not

340

saying we *will* evacuate. Certainly Whitehall's still expecting miracles.'

'ABC must have his problems.'

'Believe me, Nick, he's got 'em coming out of his ears.'

'Getting the pongoes out of that island is going to be a lot trickier than Dunkirk was. Distance, lack of air cover . . .'

'It'll be perfectly bloody, old lad.' Wishart paused, thinking about it. Then he added, smiling, 'Not *much* worse than sneaking through the Dardanelles minefields in a shaky old E-class, though?'

'It might be. As I remember it, we all got quite a bit of zizz-time in. In *this* lark sleep's what you *don't* get. You have to be closed up at action stations three-quarters of the time, and when you take a chance and let one watch get their heads down the Stukas seem to hear of it and come running. I imagine the whole fleet's about shagged out.'

'It is. ABC's only too well aware of it.'

'Well, we'll pull it off, of course we will, but – how many pongoes will there be to lift?'

'About 22,000 . . . Now, listen. What I came to tell you, Nick, is that ABC wants to see you. Lunch – in *QE*, twelve forty-five for one o'clock. To spare your chaps the effort I'll have one of *QE*'s boats sent for you at twelve-thirty. All right?'

An invitation – or command – to lunch with ABC in his flagship was very *much* all right.

'It won't be formal or elaborate. And the C-in-C may not be present for much of the time. Lorrimer of *Glenshiel* will be there, though, and perhaps one or two others. Creswell, possibly – you know him, don't you?'

He did, from way back. Hector Creswell was now Rear-Admiral (Alexandria), in charge of the port and its security and all movements in and out; but he was a destroyer man, he'd had the first Tribal – *Afridi* – that came off the stocks, and he'd been Captain (D) of the flotilla of Tribals that Philip Vian had now.

Wishart said, 'Now I must push off . . . I'm taking Smeake ashore to tell his story, did I mention that?'

'Yes, you did.'

He'd also said there'd be a tender coming to collect *Masai*'s ship's company, who'd be accommodated in a transit camp.

'Sorry. Going daft. Tell you the truth, *we* don't get all that much sleep, either.' They were both on their feet, and Nick was looking down at the letters, seeing the edge of one dark blue envelope that

341

could – just *could* – be from Fiona. Wishart was saying, 'Tell you frankly, old lad – I know you're at the sharp end of it, but I'd rather be in your shoes than mine. Except—'

He'd cut himself short, remembering something else . . . 'One thing. At lunch, don't mention *Juno*.'

'Why not?'

'You know she was sunk, day before yesterday? With King's ships, Force C?' Nick had nodded, 'Well, her first lieutenant was Walter Starkie, and he was lost with her. He was married to ABC's favourite niece, and his previous job was the old man's flag lieutenant. He thought the world of him, and—' Wishart frowned. 'It's been quite a blow to him. On top of all the other things, *Gloucester* and . . .' He stopped, put a hand on Nick's shoulder. 'One thing you'd like to know. When your troubles were in full flood yesterday, *Blackfoot* and all that, your name was mentioned as being the senior CO left in the flotilla, and ABC asked me why you were still a commander, with your record.'

Nick smiled. 'I liked him before you told me that.'

'He knew a certain amount about you, anyway. I answered that it was because you were an outspoken cuss with a penchant for insulting Prime Ministers.'

Nick wondered what he *had* said.

'In fact I told him the bare facts as I know them. Norway – he knew all about that – and the interview you had afterwards with Winston. He's – er—' Wishart smiled – 'rather on your side. He's had a number of extraordinarily offensive signals from that quarter. Now look, I must be off.'

On the quarterdeck, the side-party fell in quickly as the Rear-Admiral appeared. Half a minute later Nick lowered his arm from the salute as the last wail of PO Mercer's bosun's call faded into silence. He watched the green barge slide away, its powerful twin engines rumbling as it turned out from the destroyer's side. What Aubrey Wishart had told him was distinctly encouraging: and it was also an honour to be invited for lunch aboard the flagship. On top of which, there was a dark blue envelope on the table in his cabin, and he could go back there alone now and—

Redmayne, *Tuareg*'s engineer lieutenant, saluted him.

'Tanks'll be full in another thirty minutes, sir.'

'All right, Chief. After we get to the buoy, you can get cracking. You'll make good use of this break, I imagine.'

Redmayne – thickset, a rugger player and a graduate of Keyham engineering college – held up two thick, crossed fingers. 'I'll have her running like a two-year-old. Twist of wire here, lump of chewing-gum there . . .' His grin faded. 'But we're lucky – whole day and night in – aren't we, sir?'

'Most of the fleet's on its way south. Besides, they have this job for us tomorrow.'

'Is it to Suda, sir?'

'You know better than to ask me that, Chief.' He went in quickly through the screen door: he'd seen the coxswain hovering, and whatever Habgood wanted, Dalgleish could deal with it. Redmayne said, 'No shore leave for *my* department. I need every man jack of 'em.'

Dalgleish shrugged. 'So long as I have at least a dozen stokers to help with ammunitioning, old cock.'

'Sorry.'

'What are you apologizing for?'

'Sorry I can't spare any stokers.' The engineer's eyes were coldly belligerent. 'Out of the question, I'm afraid.'

'Now listen to me, Chief, God damn it—'

Nick shut the cabin door behind him, went to the table and picked up the wad of letters and lettercards. He stood, shuffling them like playing cards and discarding the chaff – a Gieves bill, a letter from his bank, another with a Sheffield postmark that would be from the Mullbergh estate's solicitors. And a couple more of even less interest . . . End of obvious chaff. Now, one from Paul, recognizable by the slanting, very even handwriting, and with its PASSED BY CENSOR stamp on the front. He hadn't looked at the dark blue one yet: by sleight-of-hand he'd fiddled it to the bottom of the pack without seeing its face . . . There was an air lettercard from his uncle Hugh: that small, neat hand identified it immediately. For the time being, he dropped it on top of the others, and looked at the blue one.

He sat down slowly. He felt winded, knocked sideways by disappointment deepening into fright. Sure that it would be from Fiona, he'd been saving up the pleasure, the thrill of confirming it: but he'd never seen this handwriting before. London postmark: he thought, *Mrs Stilwell* . . . But – it had been sent to him care of Mullbergh: *she* wouldn't—

Turning it over, to look at the 'Sender's name and address' space, he saw the name – Miss K. Torp.

Kari Torp, for heaven's sake! Claus Torp's daughter, and

343

formerly of Namsos, Norway. It had been in Norway – in a fjord called – memory slipping . . . Folla? Off Vestfjord, the approach to Narvik. That was where he'd last seen Kari Torp.

She'd addressed the letter to him at Mullbergh, and Nick's old butler, Barstow, had re-addressed it in his shaky copperplate to HMS *Tuareg*, c/o GPO, London. Barstow, well into his seventies now, was staying on at Mullbergh during the army's occupation of the house, looking after the small wing that Nick had insisted on keeping for himself and Paul. At least that bit of the house wouldn't be trampled by pongoes' heavy boots: and Barstow, who was of the same vintage as Nick's late father and had been in service at Mullbergh since the beginning of the century, had a roof over his head and a wage to live on.

Well. At least there'd been nothing from Mrs Stilwell.

By the time he'd read all the mail, oiling was finished and it was time to shift *Tuareg* to her buoy. Then he walked round the ship, looking into most compartments and chatting with everyone he met, in the course of it keeping an eye open for signs of stress. There were signs, all right, but none that were chronic, he thought. It was a relief to hear all the usual jokes, all the usual grouses disguised as jokes. He asked Leading Seaman Duggan, 'Going ashore this evening, Duggan?'

'Might stretch me legs, sir.'

Duggan was a CS rating – Continuous Service, as opposed to HO for Hostilities Only – and bright, likely to make Acting PO after his year as a killick. Goodall, a three-badge Able Seaman and pompom gunner, explained that Duggan's presence ashore that evening was essential, since the Afghans had challenged the Tuaregs to a darts match, and Duggan was the *Tuareg* star player.

'I'd have thought you'd all want to get your heads down.'

'Well.' Goodall shrugged. 'Change is as good as a rest, sir, they say.'

At stand-easy, the break from work in mid-forenoon, he had a glass of squash in the wardroom. The ammunition lighter hadn't turned up yet, and with the amount of sea-time they'd been putting in there'd been few opportunities recently of meeting his officers *en famille*. He asked Mr Walsh, the gunner (T), 'Is Chief arranging for those cannons to be mounted?'

'We're 'oping so, sir.' Chief was at work, down in the engine-room. Mr Walsh, with his seamed, reddish complexion and balding head, looked at least as old as Nick although he was still in his middle thirties. He'd glanced sideways at Dalgleish. 'Not too mad keen on it, but—'

'It'll be done this afternoon, sir,' confirmed Dalgleish. 'The ERAs *have* got their hands full, but Chief reckons to get some help from *Woolwich*.'

The job was to mount two pairs of Vickers GO machine-guns, one each side of the searchlight pedestal, between the after pom-poms and X gun. The four machine-guns had been removed from a badly damaged trawler, and the depot ship's armourers had already mounted them in pairs by the time Mr Walsh – who had a nose for treasures lying in dark corners – had discovered them in some workshop and arranged a deal. A lot of destroyers had mounted extra close-range weapons – Brens, Lewis, Spandaus, Hotchkiss and a dozen other varieties, all makes and nationalities and mostly scrounged in the desert ports of Mersa and Tobruk, which the Tribals had never visited for long enough for anyone to get ashore and tour the arms dumps.

Mr Walsh asked Nick, 'Who'll man 'em, sir?'

'I'd say your after tubes' crew could look after one of them. Not getting much to do these days, are they?' It was a fact: when the enemy came in bombers, torpedoes weren't in great demand. 'Let 'em take turns at it, if you like.' He looked past Dalgleish – at young Chalk, hovering diffidently in the background. 'You need a change too, Sub. Been cooped up in the plot long enough, I think.' He asked Pratt, 'Sinclair could work the ARL on his own now, couldn't he? And help Doc with ciphers?'

Rocky Pratt agreed. Sinclair was a CW candidate, and the ARL was the inertial navigation system, a machine wired to the gyro and to the Chernikeeff log so as to trace a record of the ship's track on a plotting diagram. Nick told Chalk, 'Your action station is now with the first lieutenant at the after control position. Under his direction you can use the other Vickers, or act as OOQ, as circumstances demand.' Chalk seemed pleased about it. Nick told Dalgleish, 'Roddick had better clue him up – and the torpedomen, Mr Walsh – before we sail. How to use the guns and how to clear them when they jam. All right?'

He put down his empty squash glass. Dalgleish began to talk about machine-guns and other close-range weapons: Oerlikons, which everyone was crying for but weren't in adequate supply yet, and Bofors, to which the same thing applied. Nick gave the impression of listening to the discussion, while he thought about

345

Fiona. The relief at not hearing from Mrs Stilwell had faded into renewed worry at not hearing from Fiona herself. It was a whole month since he'd had a letter from her.

The newspapers and magazines that had arrived in that mail had come by surface transport round the Cape, and they were weeks old, so there was no mention of the big raid on London on the night of 10/11 May. There'd been a talk about it on the BBC, though, which Johnny Smeake had heard and told Nick about, in which the point had been made that more people had been killed in that one night in London than had died in the San Francisco earthquake of 1906. But – again according to the BBC – there'd been no raids of any size *since* that night. The suspicion was that the enemy might be saving up for another huge one.

Kari Torp had written, *I am in England, and I am being taught some things to make me useful, which my father has said is about time too* . . . She'd given him the Norwegian embassy in London as a contact or forwarding address, and reminded him of his promise, made in a Norwegian fjord, to take her to the London theatres. Her father was at sea again and very well, she said. But as to her being made 'useful', she'd been *extremely* useful up in Namsenfjord, he remembered. She'd acted as local pilot for *Intent* all through those narrow, twisting fjordlets, in pitch darkness and under the noses of the Germans. She was a pretty astonishing female, when you thought about it: and an astonishingly pretty one too.

Not in the way that Fiona was. Fiona wasn't just pretty, she was exquisite. Why the *hell* she hadn't written . . .

Paul was enjoying his submarine training course at Blyth. The trainees, a mixture of RN, RNR and RNVR sub-lieutenants and a handful of lieutenants, were accommodated in Nissen huts inside a wired perimeter; he felt a bit like a POW, he wrote, except that the mess was Duty Free and there was entertainment to be had 'ashore', in Whitley Bay just down the coast and farther down at Newcastle. The work intrigued him, and he thought he was doing reasonably well.

Uncle Hugh had written cheerfully too; but everyone knew what it was like now in the Atlantic, where in the month of March alone over half a million tons of British shipping had been lost to U-boats, raiders and long-range aircraft. And when you thought of the Atlantic conditions – and the fact that it wasn't just one trip now and then but one after another, on and on, in all weathers and all through the year – re-reading his uncle's letter and reaching with his free hand for a cigarette, Nick thought, *What a job for a man of seventy* . . . And arising from that, *What have any of us got to grouse about?*

A bugle-call floated across the water: some big ship ordering 'Hands to dinner'. Noon. Time to change into Number Sixes, ready for his lunch aboard the flagship.

Andrew Cunningham said, 'So you're the fellow who ticks off Prime Ministers.'

'Quite inadvertently, sir.'

The blue eyes smiled, humour-lines deepening on each side of the straight, decisive mouth. Tanned skin, short grey hair. 'Don't spoil it. You've had my admiration ever since I heard about it.' He glanced at Aubrey Wishart. '*Envy* might be the word.' Now he'd turned to shake hands with Captain Lorrimer of the assault ship *Glenshiel*. 'You'll be lunching without me, I'm afraid. I've a stream of bloody nonsense pouring out of London – as well as some more essential business . . .' He'd checked, looking back at Nick. 'Has Admiral Wishart told you what's happened to the 5th Flotilla?'

'No, sir?'

'*Kelly* and *Kashmir* were both sunk by Stukas at about half past eight this morning. *Kipling*'s been picking up survivors all forenoon, with bombers on her all the time.'

Kelly was the 5th Flotilla leader, Lord Mountbatten's ship.

'Would you like my job, Everard?'

He shook his head. 'No, sir.'

'Well, I'd like yours.'

'I believe you, sir.'

'Yes.' Staring at him. The blue eyes had a penetrative quality. 'We'll see you in a better one before long, I dare say. For the time being, we've all got our work cut out, haven't we? Your ship's company in good heart?'

'They're well up to scratch, sir.'

'Good.' He'd nodded, turned to Lorrimer. 'Everard'll get you there and back all right. Only doubtful point's the weather – I'm told there's a blow coming. Anyway, you'll manage. Sorry I can't stay now – Wishart here'll play host for me.' Scanning them both again . . . 'Good luck.'

'Sir—'

'Yes?'

Nick asked him, 'Is Lord Louis—'

'Oh, yes. He's in *Kipling*, drying out.'

Wishart murmured, when the door had shut behind their Commander-in-Chief, 'He's – well, he's splendid, d'you know?'

Lorrimer said, 'We're damn lucky to have him, if you ask me.'

'What I was saying earlier, Nick – I'd give my right arm to be at sea, except for the fact that that's the man I'm working for.' He smiled, lowered his voice so the stewards wouldn't hear: 'Did you know he was given an adverse report after his course on Whale Island, in days of yore?'

'He *was*?'

'Conduct generally unsatisfactory, it said. He's got it framed.'

CHAPTER 7

Tuareg steadied, aiming her rakish bow up the line of the Great Pass out of Alexandria. Minesweepers moving out west-north-westward, a mile ahead of her and with the first light of a new day growing out that way with them, were trembling mirage-distorted objects floating in a shivery, bluish haze. Saturday, 24 May. Nick heard CPO Habgood's report float from the voicepipe: 'Course two-nine-three, sir', and Rocky Pratt's quiet acknowledgement. On *Tuareg*'s quarter and a cable's length away, right in the glare of the sun that was scorching up out of Egypt, *Afghan* was nosing into the swept channel, under helm to turn in *Tuareg*'s wake; astern of her at the same 200-yard intervals came *Huntress* and *Highflier*. Farther back still, half a mile astern of *Highflier*, the assault ship *Glenshiel* was just emerging from the harbour, wallowing out through the gap between the breakwaters, bulky and gaudy in her camouflage.

The Glen-class assault ships were converted merchantmen, and in the Greek evacuation they'd proved invaluable. But they'd been sent out here on orders from Winston Churchill, bringing 'Lay Force' – commandos under Brigadier Laycock – with the idea of capturing the Dodecanese islands, Rhodes in particular. Among the officers of Lay Force were Geoffrey Keyes, Randolph Churchill and Evelyn Waugh.

ETA Plaka Bay was 0200 Sunday morning. None of the destroyers was carrying troops: late yesterday it had been decided to send only about half the force that had originally been intended for this Plaka Bay landing, and that half could very comfortably be accommodated in the assault ship. What was more, her twelve landing craft – LCAs – would be able to land the 650 commandos in one single flight, if Lorrimer and the men's colonel chose to do it that way. Nick thought it might have been to make up numbers in two other expeditions that their own force had been reduced; *Abdiel*, the forty-knot minelayer, had sailed during the night with a detachment for Suda Bay, and three destroyers – *Isis*, with *Hero* and the Australian *Nizam* – would be leaving Alexandria during the forenoon with Special Service troops to be put down at Selinos Kastelli, at Crete's western end.

Rawlings' battle squadron and King's force and the 14th Destroyer Flotilla were all in Alex harbour now. With the battle squadron had come *Hero* and *Decoy*, their passengers including the King of Greece.

One other force would be sailing from Egypt this morning. There'd been Intelligence reports of an Italian-manned invasion fleet from the Dodecanese islands heading for Sitia Bay in north-east Crete, so Cunningham was sending *Ajax* and *Dido* with the destroyers *Kimberley* and *Hotspur* to search for it. They were due to sail at 0800, pass through the Kaso Strait and sweep the coastline in the Sitia area, and if they met no enemy they were to push on westward and bombard the Maleme airfield.

It was by no means certain, Nick guessed, that *Glenshiel*'s soldiers would get ashore. The rather similar force – *Glenroy*, escorted by the AA cruiser *Coventry* and two sloops – which had been on its way yesterday to Timbaki, some twenty miles from Plaka Bay, had been carrying 900 men of the Queen's Royals, but after a conference with General Wavell about the intensity of the air attacks and the chances of the assault ship being sunk with the troops in her, ABC had ordered the force to return to Alexandria. Then, during the afternoon, someone in London – it was tempting and not difficult to guess who – had stepped in over the C-in-C's head and sent a signal direct to *Glenroy* that she was to reverse her course again and continue to Crete. *Glenroy*'s captain, Captain Sir James Paget, put his ship about again. But as this would have brought her to the Cretan coast at daybreak, which would have been suicidal, Cunningham reasserted his authority and ordered the force to withdraw.

Ashcourt arrived in the bridge and reported that the foc'sl was secured for sea. Hands had fallen out as soon as the ship had passed the breakwater. Nick glanced up over his shoulder, then round at PO Whiffen: he told him, 'Down pendants.' In the dancing heatwaves astern, all the ships were now in the swept channel. Within a few minutes *Tuareg* would be out of it, passing

350

the sweepers who were already waiting at the top end to let this force get by. They'd found no mines this morning.

Nick saw his ship's pendants, her signal letter and numbers, tumble from the yardarm. There was no sign yet of the blow that had been forecast. He thought it might well be localized, a strictly Aegean wind, and according to the Sailing Directions the most likely wind in Cretan waters at this time of year would be from the north-west. This didn't guarantee there'd be shelter in Plaka Bay on the south coast, because one also knew that squalls driving through the valleys could strike suddenly and savagely; there was no place on that coast that was really sheltered. Nor would flat-bottomed landing-craft be very handy, he imagined, in bad weather.

Well, it might *not* blow.

Dalgleish joined him. 'Upper deck's secured for sea, sir. May I fall out Special Sea Dutymen?'

'Yes, please. And let's have a demonstration of the new guns. As soon as we've cleared the channel and before we form up, chuck something over for them to shoot at.'

'Aye aye, sir.'

'We've lost a motorboat – is that what you told me?'

The one Dalgleish had scrounged some time ago had been reclaimed by its rightful owners. Dalgleish nodded. 'But we've an extra whaler in its place.'

'How about the others – *Afghan* and—'

'She's the same as us – one motorboat, two whalers. Same with *Huntress*. *Highflier*'s been craftier – she's won herself a motor-cutter.'

'Where'd they steal that?'

He didn't know. But there'd been a bit of a free-for-all, over boats, after so many had been lost on the Greek beaches. Nick was thinking that a motor-cutter, thirty-two feet long, would be a tight fit in a twenty-five-footer's davits. They must have adapted the stowage somehow: and that boat would hold up to fifty men, at a pinch.

Five minutes after Dalgleish had left the bridge some empty paint-drums were thrown overboard, and *Tuareg* circled to give each pair of guns in turn a few bursts at the floating targets. After an unimpressive start they got the hang of it, and with his third burst Chalk just about cut his drum in half. One of the other pair jammed, but the torpedoman cleared it quickly and then sank his target. Nick told Dalgleish over the telephone, 'Secure from target practice.' Hanging up, he told Pratt, 'Come up to two-four-oh revs.' The destroyers were deploying into their screening positions across *Glenshiel*'s bow, Asdics were closed up and pinging and *Glenshiel* had the signal flying for 'Commence zigzag'. The force had 350 miles to cover, and at dusk they'd be only a hundred miles from Scarpanto; but they'd be in range of the Stuka base long before the light went.

'Commence zigzag signal down, sir!'

'Port five. Continue the ordered zigzag, quartermaster.' The telegraphman would have started the clock as the wheel went over. Nick, with his glasses on the still hazy horizon on the bow, spotted cross-trees: then more, a ship's superstructure strangely distorted by the mirage. He'd suspected it would turn out to be *Carnarvon* and now, seeing a C-class cruiser's spotting-top sort itself out of that peculiar object, he knew it was. A minute later recognition signals were being exchanged. There was a destroyer, one of the H class, with her. Astern of *Tuareg, Glenshiel* was flashing to the cruiser, *Good morning. Please book me a table at the Auberge Bleu for next Saturday night.* After a few seconds the reply came winking: *Shall I warn Fifi to expect you?*

Lorrimer and *Carnarvon*'s captain must be close friends. Nick couldn't see – using his glasses as they passed the cruiser – any external damage. There were two tall figures in the front of her bridge, and either of them could have been Jack. Two days in harbour, Wishart had reckoned *Carnarvon* would be allowed now. Lucky devils . . .

Noon: and the force was eighty-five miles from Alexandria, 215 from Scarpanto. A north-west wind, which had been no more than light airs an hour ago but had already increased to about force 3, was putting a lop on the sea's surface, pushing up small white-edged waves through which *Tuareg*'s stem smashed continuously with spray streaming back across her foc'sl. Wet steel gleamed in the sun, and the spray was brilliant white; the sound of it lashing across the gunshields and superstructure was a constant drumming. The wind was still rising and it was driving wisps of cloud across the high blue of the sky.

Rum had been issued, and one watch sent to dinner. Tony Dalgleish was at the binnacle, and Chalk had just gone down; he'd been up with a file of official correspondence with which there hadn't been time to bother when they'd been in harbour. No time, and even less inclination . . . Nick reached for a cigarette, as *Tuareg* swung to a port leg of the zigzag pattern. He'd slid the case back into his pocket and pulled out his lighter when, behind him, Dalgleish barked 'Alarm starboard – aircraft – green five-oh—'

Nick was off his seat, his thumb on the alarm button, sending morse As racketing through the ship. He'd yelled at Mason, the signalman on watch, 'Red flag – hoist!' Houston told him, 'Junkers 88s, sir. Flying right to left.'

'Yes, I see them.' Black against the blue, and flying at this moment through shreds of cloud. They *had* been flying from right to left – westward – but they were turning to port now, this way. They'd probably been on a sweep, just hoping to run across some target. Six of them. He'd been holding the binoculars one-handed while he used the other on the action stations buzzer, but that was finished now, the ship humming and clattering with movement as her crew closed up, and he had both hands free. Pratt was at the binnacle, Dalgleish had gone aft, and Houston was dragging his dead weight up to the director tower, where his team were already busy, with A and B guns' barrels lifting and traversing outwards on the bow. Six 88s were *not* anything to get worked up about – not after the experiences of recent weeks – but they would already have wirelessed a sighting report to their colleagues on Scarpanto and to the other airfields, and that was something else again.

Huntress – on *Tuareg*'s starboard quarter – opened fire. Too soon, Nick thought. Waste of shells. Houston was holding his fire, but the guns were following director and on target, their barrels still moving slowly upward and inching left, tracking the black twin-engined bombers as they droned in towards the ships.

You could imagine the scene on Scarpanto, when the sighting report came in: the ranks of yellow-nosed 87s, their pilots racing out to them . . . Fire-gongs: the double, tinny clang, and immediately the head-splitting crash as the four-sevens fired. Fumes choking for a second, clearing immediately as the wind and the ship's forward motion whisked the stink aft and away. Shellbursts opened ahead of the attackers: *Huntress*'s had seemed to be on the right from this angle, which meant short, but Houston had put his straight under the Germans' noses. They'd begun to weave, the formation splitting as they dodged and bucketed. The Glen ship had opened fire, and now *Afghan* had too: two bombers were going for the big ship in the centre, putting themselves into shallow glides and crossing in the sector between *Huntress* and *Tuareg: Tuareg*'s rate of fire increased sharply as Houston gave up his controlled shoot and switched to barrage, browning the sky ahead of the Junkers' dives.

Bombs away . . .

The other four were boring in, flak all round them, black crosses plainly visible on white panels on wings and fuselages. Bombs leaving them now – leaving two of them just as the first ones raised thick humps of sea astern and on the quarter of the Glen ship. Rather like shallow-set depthcharges exploding, only smaller in diameter. More bombs coming now, from the last two attackers: a double line of splashes rose astern again, well clear. Compared to Stukas these 88s were so unfrightening that they were almost benign. The first lot of bombs must have fallen on *Glenshiel*'s far side, hidden by her not inconsiderable bulk. All six Junkers had banked away to starboard after their attacks, and all six were still in sight but nobody was wasting ammunition on them now; they were drawing together, gradually re-forming as they flew away north-westward at about 2,000 feet.

The red flags were sliding down. Pratt suggested, 'Just a curtain-raiser, I suppose.' Nick had got through to Dalgleish, on the telephone to the after control position. 'We'll remain at first degree, Number One.'

It would mean action messing for the watch who hadn't fed yet. Even those who'd been sent to dinner probably hadn't got much of it inside them before the buzzers went. But this sort of thing was Dalgleish's problem. Nick lit the cigarette which he'd been about to light when Houston had spotted the bombers; he'd taken his first drag at it and he was letting smoke trickle gently from his nostrils, deliberately relaxing while he had the chance, when Yeoman Whiffen reported, 'Red warning flag on *Glenshiel*, sir!' Turning, he put his glasses up – to the danger sector, the starboard bow: he saw them at once, fine on that bow, high up, a big crowd of them. Stukas – as evil-looking as ever.

Guns were already following the director to that alarm bearing. The Stukas were flying south. Nick tossed his ill-fated cigarette away to leeward. They were flying across the force's bows, from right to left. They'd circle, he supposed, and attack from the port side on a northward – homeward – course, using the sun behind them to blind the gunners. There seemed to be a couple of dozen of them in roughly equal groups, two groups at different heights. No – *three*. There was a third lot behind the higher one, on a closing course towards the others as if they'd been out on their own. A sky sweep, and homing now on the target they'd found; about thirty bombers in three groups of ten. He'd been wrong with his mental picture of Scarpanto: these things must have been in the air long before the 88s had arrived.

Houston was telling the four-sevens to load with long-fused barrage. Nick was watching that force of bombers as it crossed ahead, circling its intended victims; he was thinking that with eight hours to go before the light went, if the Luftwaffe was going to hound them in this kind of strength they'd be bound to draw *some* blood. Better not to dwell on it too much: best to live from one minute to the next, from one attack to another. Although one might imagine that now the bastards had located them, going by recent Aegean experience the attacks might soon become continuous – the kind that poor *Gloucester* and *Fiji* were subjected to, the kind that made ABC recall *Glenroy* yesterday. Cunningham wouldn't want to recall this expedition if he could possibly get it through: after the *Glenroy* business he'd be under enormous pressure from London to get these troops in.

All right, come on, let's get on with it . . .

Vultures still circling: mean, sharp-eyed, crossing the ships' line of advance and edging round, moving down the port side now. Pratt muttered, 'Wonder what it feels like. They must know *some* of 'em won't get home.'

Each would count on it happening to the other man, Nick guessed. And they'd be thinking of killings and Iron Crosses, not of their own casualties. Yeoman Whiffen reported, at Nick's elbow and with his tin hat at a rakish angle over his bony face, 'Signal from *Glenshiel* to C-in-C, sir, repeated *Ajax*: *Under attack from Ju88s, in position—*'

That would have gone out ten minutes ago. Nick nodded. 'Thank you, Yeoman.'

'Sir.'

Tin hats, binoculars jutting below them, revolved slowly as the bomber force drew aft down the port side with the sun flashing on a wing here, a tailplane there. Guns traversing too, loading numbers peering out round the edges of the gunshields, hands shielding narrowed eyes against the sun. Pompom gunners squinting upwards, rotating themselves on their seats as the whole mounting swivelled, turned by handwheels rather like pedals on a bicycle. *Tuareg* seesawed rhythmically, splitting the choppy sea and spraying it out on either side as her bow dipped smoothly into it, smashing the waves one after another without noticing them, flinging sea back over her foc's'l and the for'ard guns. Everything white and blue gleaming in the wetness of salt spray, the shine of painted steel. The bombers were far out beyond *Afghan*, who was on *Tuareg*'s beam; farther out and two cables' lengths astern, *Highflier*'s single-barrelled four-seven mountings were cocked up, waiting, ready on the target: one group of which seemed for a moment to be stationary, suspended in mid air, floating . . . Then Nick realized that they'd turned inwards – while the other groups continued steadily from right to left. The batch who'd turned were splitting up: separating, some of them climbing . . .

'What the hell?'

Bombs were falling, over there. Out there halfway to the horizon, over no kind of target, he saw a desultory rain of bombs. And Stukas climbing, swirling out in a general break-up of the formation. He moved his glasses to the left again: a thought had occurred to him, an explanation of the Stukas' strange behaviour, but he wasn't putting any trust in it, no more than he believed in fairies. Settling his binoculars on the other two groups of Stukas, the ones who'd flown on down the port side, he saw them turning in now: the far-back lot were all over the place but two other groups of ten were turning to attack.

A Stuka out of that mix-up on the beam was falling, streaming smoke. And another – watching it, he was beginning to believe in fairies after all – exploded, sending a third over on its back and spinning downwards. Others scattering in all directions: and he saw another in flames, gliding seawards.

'All guns follow director. Red barrage, stand by!'

Highflier and *Afghan* had opened fire. But the second group of bombers seemed to be in trouble now – as if they'd caught the same infection. Bursts of HA shell were to the left, ahead of and below the flights approaching from the quarter: looking up at his own ship's director tower Nick saw Houston shifting left as well, swinging about ten degrees and settling on that left-hand attack. And the reason was – extraordinarily, but beyond doubt now—

Pratt began it.

'Sir – I hesitate to suggest such a thing, but—'

'We've got an air force.'

'Thank God. Thought I was getting DTs or—'

Tuareg opened fire. But Pratt hadn't been seeing pink elephants, he'd been seeing Hurricanes. And Stukas were falling like autumn leaves. At one point he saw four dead ones in the air at the same moment: all burning, going down. Poetry of motion, he thought, beauty unsurpassed: but the left-hand flight was coming over now and all the ships were in action, barraging ahead of it as it approached. To the right, three Hurricanes were making hay, making the Stukas look as clumsy and as vulnerable as barnyard fowls, as helpless as the half-drowned sailors they liked to shoot at in the water. No time to watch that circus, though; weaving, dodging bombers were overhead, *Tuareg* throwing up a short-fused barrage now, all four destroyers putting an umbrella of shellfire over *Glenshiel*, whose own guns were shrouding her upper decks in smoke. Shooting into the sun, which the enemy was trying to make use of; pompoms opened up just as the first siren-screams rose to cut through the din of gunfire. Glancing to the right he saw a Hurricane chasing a Stuka in a shallow dive: he saw the blast of the fighter's guns, bits flying off the bomber. Come-Uppance Day, he thought, glimpsing it in one ecstatic glance: looking back quickly at the danger zone he saw a Stuka picking *Tuareg* for its target, flipping over at this moment into its dive: he was already at the binnacle, displacing Rocky Pratt. The attack was coming from the port side, from high up across *Afghan*.

'Port twenty-five.'

'Port twenty-five, sir!'

Turning his ship into the direction of the attack. Guns pounding solidly: and he heard, as one bomber pulled out of its dive and curved away from *Glenshiel*'s bow through the gap between *Tuareg* and *Huntress* – out of his sight as it passed astern – the new Vickers guns' strident blare. He hoped *Huntress* wasn't in the line of fire of one trigger-happy RNVR sub-lieutenant. He was watching the Stuka, its dropping, screeching, vulturish descent.

'Midships!'

'Midships, sir . . .'

By turning towards it he was making it dive more steeply: break its bloody neck, if it could be persuaded to go just a *little* steeper . . . Or else make it let go of its egg from high up, with consequently poor aim, before *Tuareg* passed under the line of steepest-possible trajectory.

'Steady as you go!'

'Steady, sir!'

The bomb fell clear of the thing's spread legs. Tumbling in the sun: 1,000 pounds of high explosive gathering the pull of gravity while the Stuka pilot fought to defeat that same pull, the aircraft flattening and shellbursts and close-range fire all around it as it pulled out high and the bomb went wide. Nick called down to CPO Habgood, 'Starboard fifteen.' *Tuareg* was right ahead of *Glenshiel* after that swing off to port, and he had to get her back into station. There were Stukas in all directions, gunsmoke, shellbursts, noise. The one who'd attacked so ineffectually was legging it away northwards, half a mile away and about 500 feet above the sea. *Tuareg* heeled to port as she turned to regain her position in the screen. A Stuka was dropping on *Glenshiel* – it was through the barrage and only close-range weapons were shooting at it as it came on down, down . . . Bomb leaving it now: and the Stuka was sliding away to port, banking as it dragged its yellow nose up, and flames streamed suddenly from that raised starboard wing: then he'd lost sight of it in smoke, and he'd no idea where the bomb went. Gunfire was easing off: *Tuareg* had just ceased fire altogether. The only Stukas in sight were three scurrying northwards with two Hurricanes in pursuit.

1630: with four and a half hours of daylight left, the ships were alone again. Two Hurricanes had stayed with them for about an hour after that air battle, then another had arrived and that pair had departed. The single aircraft had been relieved by yet another, after another hour, and he'd been the last. End of luxury, of the sensation of being pampered.

Three times during the afternoon enemy reconnaissance machines had come to look at them. Twice Hurricanes had chased the snooper away, and once it had been shot down. But the Germans would know that when the force got to a certain distance from the desert airfields the fighter escort would be withdrawn; once a recce flight came and found them unescorted, it wouldn't be long before the dive-bombers returned.

There was quite a lot of movement on the ships now. The wind was force 4 and the sea was up to match it. But it seemed to have got no worse during the past hour; if it stayed like this and there was some degree of shelter inshore, it ought to be possible to get the troops in.

On his high stool, Nick drank tea and munched biscuits. Pratt came up from the chart, bringing a tea-mug with him. He murmured, looking round at the sea's frothy, jumpy surface, 'Might be a bit tough for the landing-craft, sir?'

'They'll have to cope with it. It's important to get this lot ashore.'

The appearance of the Hurricanes might have been an indication of the importance attached to it. For the sake of the cut-off Retimo garrison, presumably. A garrison – Wishart had said – that included women, for God's sake: an Aussie field hospital with twenty or thirty nurses in it, evacuated from Greece. Well, they'd be worth their weight in gold, no doubt, but there'd be all hell to pay if they couldn't be got out when the crunch came . . . There'd been a heated exchange of signals, Wishart had told him privately, between Whitehall and ABC during the last day or two; the C-in-C had had to point out that the Navy wasn't afraid of incurring losses, only of losing so many ships that there'd be too few left operationally fit for the Eastern Mediterranean to be held. Then Malta would fall, and Suez would be lost, and the Levant and the whole Middle East and its oil . . . London still seemed blind to the facts of life in terms of air power and the lack of it. One trouble was that 'Tiger', the big Malta convoy operation, had succeeded; it had only got through by a fluke of weather, but as a result of it London – or Churchill, anyway – did believe in miracles and the performing of the impossible.

Wishart had mentioned the hunt for *Bismarck*, too. The entire Home Fleet was at sea, and so was Force H from Gibraltar. *Hood* had to be avenged. Britain and the Empire were fighting the war alone: the German propaganda machine under Dr Goebbels was going full blast – *Bismarck* was unbeatable, cock of the oceans, and where was the Royal Navy? The world sitting on the sidelines had to be shown *Bismarck* destroyed and Goebbels answered. Here and now as *Tuareg* and her consorts zigzagged towards Crete and prepared to receive the Stukas, the job was to get *Glenshiel*'s troops ashore in Plaka Bay: but at the back of one's mind there was also a picture of the bleak Atlantic weather and the great ships dipping through it, searching for a needle in that enormous haystack.

The Stukas didn't come until half past six. When they opened the attack, which was to be non-stop from that time on, the ships were about 140 miles from Scarpanto and the same distance from their destination. The first sign of the ordeal that was coming was not the usual cloud of dive-bombers but, on the starboard bow, a single twin-engined aircraft which Houston identified as a Heinkel. It came in to a range of about six miles, flew parallel to their course for a few minutes, then swung away and dwindled towards Crete. Nick sent the ship's company to action stations, knowing what must be coming.

'We'll get the full weight now.' Pratt said it, behind Nick, to Ashcourt. 'Unless they've also found *Ajax* and *Dido*, perhaps.'

Ajax, Dido, Kimberley and *Hotspur*, heading for the Kaso Strait and about two hours astern of this force, would be on the quarter to starboard and roughly sixty, seventy miles away. From the Scarpanto Stukas' point of view one target might be about as attractive as another, since both would be at about the same radius from their base. They'd more than enough aircraft to take on both targets, anyway.

Nick saw them first, ordered the red warning flag to be hoisted and alerted Houston to that bearing – fifty degrees on the starboard bow, about due north and the direction of Scarpanto. A cluster of black specks, high, crossing an area of clear blue. About a dozen, he thought. But after about a minute Houston called down his voicepipe to the bridge that there was another bunch not far behind that first one.

And there was another behind *that*, although it wasn't visible yet. Ten minutes later, by which time it was obvious that the action was going to be continuous until darkness came, no one bothered with the reporting of new formations as they came into sight. The Stukas were coming in a constant stream, a dozen or sometimes eighteen or twenty at a time, with only a few minutes' flying time between waves.

Nick guessed how it was going to be. He slid off the seat and went to the binnacle.

'I'll take her, pilot.'

Pratt made room for him. The navigator's tin hat was green with a red-and-yellow unit flash on it; it had been left behind by some pongo in one of the Greek rescue operations.

All the ships' guns were poking skywards and on the bow, waiting.

'Red barrage – load, load, load!'

Nick heard, from X gun, the clangs of the first fused rounds dropping into the loading-trays and then the thuds of the trays as they were swung over to the guns' breeches.

'Signal most immediate from *Glenshiel* to C-in-C repeated *Ajax*, sir. *Stukas approaching in large numbers from Scarpanto. My position 160 Kupho Nisi 95.*'

'Very good.' He called up to the tower, 'Harry – if this becomes as fraught as it looks it might, you'll probably be better off with the after guns in local control.'

'Aye aye, sir. May I see how it develops?'

'Up to you entirely.'

But dividing the fire-control would make it easier to ward off more than one attacker at a time. Otherwise Houston would need eyes all round his skull and two separate brains. Nick glanced at Pratt: 'D'you agree with *Glenshiel*'s position?'

'Near enough, sir.'

The last time Lorrimer had sent such a signal, the reply had come in the form of three Hurricanes. You couldn't hope for anything of that sort here, though, so much farther from the desert. That signal had been only to let ABC know what was happening, and to warn the cruisers who were heading towards Kaso.

Tuareg was rolling now as well as pitching. It didn't take much to make a Tribal roll, on account of the rather high centre of gravity. He could hear the sea's drumbeats slamming against her stem, the rush of water heaving and thumping against her sides as she drove through it, the roar of the ventilator fans and the wind's howl in the foremast rigging. Within seconds these familiar sounds would be drowned in the noise of battle.

'Signal flying from *Glenshiel*, sir – *Negative zigzag*.'

'All guns follow director. Red barrage: stand by—'

'Signal's down, sir!'

Tuareg was on her mean course at this moment. He told Habgood, 'Stop the zigzag, cox'n. Steer three-one-oh.' The Stukas, a squad of them in four flights of three, were bouncing about in the wind. He watched through his binoculars as they rose across the sky, in and out of whorls and streaks of fast-driven cloud.

At seven-forty, *Glenshiel* was hit for'ard. The assault had been continuous, with bombers overhead all the time and no moment when planes weren't diving to attack, bombs in the air and others bursting in the sea.

Glenshiel's forepart was in flames. The ship's course into the wind had helped the fire to take hold, and now it was expanding it, driving the flames aft. Bunting was running to her fore-yard:

Whiffen, with his glasses on the flag-hoist, bawled through the noise of gunfire, 'Red one-eight, sir!'.

An about-turn. To give Lorrimer's people a chance to get that blaze under control, of course. Then they'd turn back, press on towards Crete. Turning stern to wind would confine the fire to the for'ard end of the ship, where it could be got at with foam and hoses. He saw the string of flags drop: Whiffen saw him see it, which saved him the effort of making himself heard again above the din. Two Stukas were diving on *Glenshiel* and one on *Tuareg*: but there wasn't anywhere you could look in the sky without seeing at least one yellow nose. As he bent to the voicepipe he felt the jar of a bomb exploding in the sea somewhere abaft the beam: he called down, with his mouth inside the wide funnel-top of the pipe, 'Starboard twenty!'

All the ships were under helm, reversing course. A 'red' turn was a turn on your heel, an immediate about-turn instead of the follow-my-leader kind that would have been ordered with a blue pendant. The figures one-eight meant 180 degrees, right round. *Tuareg* and *Afghan* would find themselves astern of *Glenshiel* now, with *Highflier* and *Huntress* roughly on her beams. *Tuareg* rolling like a bottle as she turned broadside-on to the sea: a bomb plunked down on the quarter, raising a mound of erupting sea so close that her stern almost swung into it before it collapsed. All the guns were firing, and their barrels would be about red-hot by now: four-sevens, pompoms, point-fives and the new Vickers GO too: those Vickers pans had been loaded with one tracer bullet to every five others, which were a mixture of armour-piercing and incendiary, and the tracer made their double streams of shot easy to identify. It also allowed the gunners to 'hose-pipe' their shot on to the targets.

'Midships!'

'Midships, sir . . .'

Habgood's tone in action became so calm that he sounded like a man drifting into sleep. Nick told him, 'Steady on one-three-oh degrees.'

'Steady on one-three-oh, aye aye, sir.'

Pratt was talking into the plot voicepipe, telling Sinclair, the CW candidate, to get the ARL plot-table going. Then he'd be able to adjust his dead-reckoning position by however much this course alteration put them off the track. A Stuka had gone straight into the sea, between *Tuareg* and *Huntress*. *Huntress* had a three-inch AA gun mounted where her after set of torpedo tubes had been removed, and she was making good use of it. There was already less smoke coming from *Glenshiel*'s fire: with any luck they'd be able to get back on course quite soon. To be going the wrong way like this felt like conceding victory to the Stukas, and any delay to the schedule would mean that tomorrow morning the force would be in range of the bastards for longer than they need have been. And by tomorrow morning ammunition might not be all that plentiful. A bomb was coming down from a Stuka that had broken off its dive high up: Nick had done a deep knees-bend to the voicepipe. 'Port twenty-five!' Another yellow-faced horror up ahead, half obscured by shellbursts and just tipping over now into its dive: *Tuareg* swinging hard a-port, listing and rolling violently, swinging halfway back then rolling again to starboard so far over you'd imagine she'd turn turtle. The bomb had raised the sea off the starboard bow and the other Stuka had corrected the direction of its dive: coming from the bow, screaming in as the first swept out of it, low to the surface of the sea . . . 'Midships. Starboard twenty-five.'

Flags on *Glenshiel*: it was the same hoist as last time, red one-eight. They'd beaten the fire, then.

'Executive, sir!'

Tuareg already had full starboard rudder on as she fought round across wind and sea, sheets of water flying as she turned, to head in towards the diving Stuka. 'Midships!' That dive was close to the vertical. Any steeper, the pilot wouldn't be coming out of it. *Come on, just a little more* . . . Pratt's mouth was opening and shutting as he pointed: all one could hear was gunfire and sirens, the fast booming thuds of the pompoms and the higher racket of point-fives: the Stuka which Pratt was pointing at was coming in a shallow dive straight towards the bridge. Pompoms switching their attention to him now: and the German's machine-guns spitting yellow flame . . . 'Starboard twenty-five!' One bomb was falling from the Hun he'd been trying to push into a vertical descent: he hadn't pushed him far enough, unfortunately; the hideous thing with its black-cross markings was pulling out, arcing upwards and away through woolly-looking shellbursts. The other one almost on them now, pompoms and other close-range weapons blazing right in its face and *Tuareg* turning fast right under it: Pratt lurched sideways, cannoning into Nick then throwing his arms around the binnacle, sliding down on to his knees. There was blood all over Nick's left side. 'Midships.'

'Midships, sir.'

Pratt had toppled, gone over on his back; half his face was missing. Nick saw that Ashcourt was at the voicepipe to the plot, which was the way to contact the doctor or one of his first-aid parties. PO Whiffen was kneeling in Pratt's blood. *Tuareg*'s swing was easing too fast, and he ordered ten of starboard wheel to get her round to the course of three-one-oh. *Glenshiel* wasn't much more than halfway round: he saw a bomb-splash go up very close to the big ship's starboard side, and the Stuka, breaking away over the top of *Huntress*, burst into flames. Tail down, stalling, about to fall into the sea. Several more overhead, one in its dive above *Glenshiel* and the next wave coming up from the direction of Scarpanto.

'Steer three-one-oh, cox'n.'

'Three-one-oh, sir . . .'

They were taking Pratt down on a stretcher. Gallwey, with 'MO' stencilled on his tin hat, was standing in the middle of the bridge, swaying against the roll and pitch, staring up at the weaving Stukas with his mouth open. Nick shouted, 'Go on down, Doctor!' and Gallwey turned, only half hearing: Nick was already busy again with another attack developing, a Stuka starting into a dive from right astern. 'Port twenty-five!' The doctor was moving away, still staring upwards as if he couldn't believe what he was seeing: and the Stuka pilot had shifted his aim, hauling his machine to port as he saw the start of *Tuareg*'s swing. Waiting now, counting seconds, to get the timing right . . . Quick glance away towards *Glenshiel*: there was one going down on her too: but nothing else, only this one immediate menace to his own ship that he could see. The after guns were shooting at it, while A and B barraged over the assault ship.

'Midships.'

'Midships, sir . . .'

'Starboard twenty-five.'

'Starboard twenty-five—'

'Bring her back to three-one-oh, cox'n.'

Gallwey had left the bridge. Pratt's blood was everywhere. The Stuka attacking *Glenshiel* was through the layer of exploding AA shells, and the other one's bomb had missed to port of *Tuareg* by about twenty yards as she swung hard a-starboard. That one on top of *Glenshiel*, though – he saw its bomb fall away, the first slow-looking moments of its drop, the Stuka itself roller-coasting up and away on the other side. Lorrimer had put his wheel over, but the broad-beamed assault ship wasn't as manoeuvrable as a destroyer was . . .

'Course three-one-oh, sir.'

A sort of cloud – like the dust from a beaten carpet – rose over *Glenshiel*'s foc'sl as the bomb plunged into her.

Waiting for the explosion, eruption deep inside her. Glancing round: no other immediate dangers. There'd still been no visible explosion. Men were running for'ard along the assault ship's upper deck: her forepart was already blackened from the earlier fire. *Tuareg*'s guns and all the other destroyers' guns as well were barraging at Stukas circling and dodging high overhead: seven or eight of them, but nothing diving at the moment: then he saw two of them push their noses downward. Farther back, another squad was approaching from the north-east. Darkness was the only hope of an end to this, and darkness was still the best part of an hour away.

'Yeoman!' Whiffen saw him beckon and hurried across the bridge. 'By light to *Glenshiel, Are you all right?*' Silly question, he thought: still, let it go . . . He saw Ashcourt, and beckoned *him*: 'Sub, you're navigator. Get the DR up to date from whatever Sinclair can tell you.' He saw a Stuka on the bow tilt over, pointing its nose down at *Tuareg*, and as he bent to the voicepipe the thought flashed into his mind that it was no wonder ABC had recalled *Glenroy* and company yesterday . . . He waited with his face down at the pipe, staring up under the rim of his tin hat at the down-rushing bomber, and not liking it all that much.

'Starboard twenty-five.'

'Starboard twenty-five, sir . . .'

'Reply from *Glenshiel*, sir—' Whiffen bawling into his ear – '*One in fore peak failed to explode. Hold your breath while we perform extraction.*'

The Stuka was angling off, adjusting its aim to *Tuareg*'s use of rudder. Nick ordered, 'Midships. Stop port. Port twenty-five.' He nodded to the yeoman of signals, looked back at the Stuka and saw its wings tilt again: he thought it was because it was coming in a comparatively shallow dive that it could keep adjusting its aim like this: perhaps he'd passed the port helm order a bit too soon. Reaching for the telephone to the ACP: 'Number One, can you shift the pompoms to this fellow on the bow?' He'd hung up without waiting for an answer. A and B guns couldn't have elevated enough to reach it, and if he checked the swing again he'd have been playing into the German's hands: with one screw stopped she was fairly whizzing round, heeling hard over. Pom-poms suddenly: and point-fives, and the distinctive tracer-streak of the starboard Vickers GO. The Stuka was diving right into those converging streams and he was being hit, smoke and flames gushing suddenly, bomb released and falling short, the pilot trying to level out . . . 'Midships. Half ahead both engines.'

'Midships, sir . . . Half ahead both, sir. Both telegraphs half ahead, sir. Wheel's amidships, sir!'

'Starboard fifteen.'

'Starboard fifteen, sir.'

'Steer three-one-oh. How are you doing down there, cox'n?'

'Fifteen of starboard wheel on, sir. Steer three-one-oh. Happy as larks, sir . . .'

A Stuka was going for *Glenshiel*, who at the moment was on *Tuareg*'s quarter, but Dalgleish had shifted his guns to it. The local-control arrangement seemed to be working rather well, Nick thought. He saw some men on *Glenshiel*'s for'ard well-deck: putting his glasses on them he saw they were bringing out a Neill-Robertson stretcher, the kind you could strap a wounded man in to pass him through hatchways or down into a boat. They were taking it to the ship's side: tipping it over, letting the whole stretcher go . . . He realized they must have had the unexploded bomb in it. He looked up and around, at a sky still full of Stukas, smoke, shellbursts; two more 87s were diving towards *Glenshiel*: there were others higher, circling, watching for openings, he supposed. Ammunition ought to last out until sunset, with luck, but there'd be precious little for any sustained action of this kind tomorrow. One Stuka above *Glenshiel* had let go its bomb high up, but the other in contrast was pressing its attack right home, diving straight into the umbrella barrage and through the streams of close-range stuff: and still intact, still diving . . .

Bomb released. The Stuka was pulling out rather gradually: scared perhaps he'd tear his wings off.

A spout of sea leapt up, right against *Glenshiel*'s starboard quarter. Its blast flung one of the landing craft upwards, wrenching the for'ard end from the davit: what was left of it dangled from the after davit, and the ship's side was blackened, its paintwork scorched and smoking. There'd almost certainly have been some damage done inside, from that one. Now there was another Stuka diving at *Tuareg* from astern: Nick was at the voicepipe, watching it come down . . . A minute later, when the bomb had thumped into the sea and Habgood was bringing the destroyer back to her course, he found *Glenshiel* out on the quarter, much farther away than he'd expected. At the second glance he realized her speed had been cut by half.

'Starboard fifteen.'

To close in, get back to her. A light began to flash from that high bridge; this would be a crucial signal. He had one eye on that fast-winking lamp and the other on the Stukas. Leading Signalman Mason was at the starboard ten-inch, taking the message in. A Stuka right in the sun was tilting into its dive, and the fresh team, refuelled and bombed-up in Scarpanto, was just arriving.

Starboard shaft damaged. My best speed now ten to twelve knots.

In other words, the end. Victory to the Stukas . . . No bad dream to be shrugged off, it was reality. They'd have to turn around, admit defeat, get as far south as possible during the dark hours, pray for fighter cover some time tomorrow.

'From *Glenshiel*, sir—'

'Yes, I read it.' That one had gone for *Afghan*, but two more of the circling vultures were going into their dives now. Having hurt *Glenshiel* – her sudden slowing would be obvious to them – it would be her they'd concentrate on now. Vultures plummeting, shrieking, scenting victory and blood. *Glenshiel* couldn't possibly reach Plaka Bay with the troops now. At twelve knots it would take ten hours from here, it would mean arriving in full daylight. Lorrimer had begun to flash again: that last signal had only answered Nick's question, but now he'd had time to confirm the damage and it was obvious what he was about to say. The only thing he *could* say – turn about, withdraw.

CHAPTER 8

The thought came to him suddenly, mainly out of distaste for the prospect of conceding victory to the Luftwaffe, that perhaps there *might* be some way . . . The light was still flashing from *Glenshiel.* Lorrimer would be talking plain horse-sense, not wishful thinking: Nick told himself he was being silly to allow himself the luxury of imagining that anyone could wave magic wands. Merit lay in knowing when you were beaten: in not throwing away lives and ships when there wasn't a hope in hell of—

'From *Glenshiel,* sir – *It appears we have no option but to withdraw.*'

Peculiar signal to make . . . 'Port twenty.' Stuka coming. He beckoned to PO Whiffen, without taking his eyes off that yellow nose. 'Pad, Yeoman!' Signal pad, on which to take down a reply to Lorrimer – who was delaying the decision, inviting the submission of ideas. Crouching by the voicepipe and watching that foul thing hurtling down at his ship, Nick wondered whether the troops *might* still be got ashore . . .

'Ready, sir.' Whiffen, with the pad, right beside him. When he'd told him to stand by he hadn't known what message he'd be dictating to him: only giving himself a moment's grace, as Lorrimer indeed had given himself some latitude by not having passed the about-turn order yet. But it came now, born of necessity and urgency: Lorrimer could accept it or reject it, might spot some weakness in the proposal that he hadn't yet seen for himself.

'Midships.' He heard Habgood's acknowledgement and added, 'Stop starboard. Starboard twenty-five.'

'Stop starboard, sir. Starboard twenty-five . . . Starboard engine stopped, sir. Twenty-five of starboard wheel on, sir . . .'

He tapped Whiffen's pad. 'To *Glenshiel. Submit it should be possible after dark to transfer all troops to* Tuareg, Afghan *and*

Highflier, *using your landing craft*. Huntress *would escort you homeward. On completion of landing operation I would withdraw at full speed rejoining you during forenoon tomorrow.*'

With that engine stopped she was fairly spinning round. He called down, 'Half ahead both engines,' and asked the yeoman, 'Got that?'

Whiffen began to read it back: Nick cut him short. 'Send it, quickly.' Before Lorrimer ordered the reversal of course: once he'd passed the order it would be less easy for him to accept this proposal. It wouldn't be *easy* to accept it anyway: the weather would make the transfer of men to the destroyers and also their landing in Crete a fairly tricky business, and it wouldn't be helped by the shortage of suitable boats. Another drawback, perhaps in the long run the biggest, was the splitting-up of this force before the inevitable air assault tomorrow morning. He had suggested *Huntress* as the assault ship's escort because she had that high-angle three-inch gun.

'Ease to ten degrees of wheel.'

'Ease to ten, sir!'

He was reducing the amount of rudder on her, but continuing right round, which was the shortest way back now to the course of three-one-oh. The bomb had gone wide and it was *Glenshiel* who was getting attention now. Lever, the killick signalman, was passing Nick's message, *Glenshiel*'s lamp winking acknowledgement word by word. One Stuka diving on her: several more weaving about above the barrage, waiting to pick their moments. Nick thought Lorrimer *might* accept this plan: the fact he hadn't already hoisted a 'red one-eight' signal did suggest reluctance to throw in the sponge. 'Midships. Steer three-one-oh.'

'Three-one-oh, sir . . .'

'Two four-oh revolutions.'

Lever reported that he'd passed the message: Nick heard Habgood's 'Two-four-oh revs passed and repeated' and he thought, *Poor old Pratt . . . Glenshiel* was flashing: Lorrimer hadn't taken long to sort out the pros and cons. *Tuareg* was steadying on course again, the course for Plaka Bay alias Ormos Plaka: dipping to the head sea, bridge aslant and wet as he looked back across it at the Glen ship, at that dot-dashing light: then quickly upwards again and all round, for Stukas.

'From *Glenshiel*, sir—'

'Port twenty. Three hundred revolutions.' He stayed close to the top of the pipe with his eyes on a Stuka that had seemed to be going for *Huntress* but was now aiming itself at *Tuareg*. A quick glance towards the yeoman: 'Well?'

'Message reads, *Concur with your 2027. Transfer of troops will take place at 2200 without further signal. I will stop but maintain steerage way on course 045 degrees. One destroyer at a time is to come close into my lee with scrambling nets down port side. On completion of transfer of approximately 220 men to each of your three ships you are to proceed independently in execution of previous orders.* Time of origin 2036, sir.'

'Midships!' Gunfire thickening again, pompoms joining in. 'Starboard twenty-five!' In less than half an hour, he thought, watching the bomber rushing down, it would be dusk. Plenty of time between then and 2200, 10 pm, for Dalgleish to make arrangements for the reception of the troops, and by that time it would be fully dark. One thought of 'the troops'; a mass, khaki-covered, seasick . . . As well to remember that they were also men, individuals, lives, people with other people who loved them, worried about them . . . He shook the thought away: what he had to do now – when his eyes and mind had a moment clear of Stukas – was work out some orders to be passed to *Afghan, Highflier* and *Huntress*.

Darkness was a blessing, a priceless benefit, resting to the mind and soothing to the spirit . . . *Tuareg*, with her quota of troops safely inboard now, nosed out around the assault ship's bow, feeling the effect of wind and sea immediately as she left the patch of shelter.

'Steer three-oh-six.'

'Steer three-oh-six, sir!'

'Cox'n, you can take a few hours off, now.'

'Aye aye, sir. Thank you, sir.'

A relief quartermaster would already be down there with him, ready to take over. The ship wasn't at action stations, but Nick had wanted that expert hand on the wheel during the transfer operation at close quarters with *Glenshiel*. He'd want it again in a few hours' time when they got in towards the landing place.

Tuareg was rolling and pitching, sliding her foc'sl into the black water and flinging it back in white sheets at the bridge. Astern, hidden now behind *Glenshiel*'s bulk as Lorrimer held her broadside to the direction of wind and sea, *Afghan* was getting her troops up out of the plunging landing-craft while *Highflier* waited for her turn and *Huntress* circled on anti-submarine guard. Darkness was velvet, a surrounding comfort: it was only when it came down around you that you realized how much you'd come to hate the daylight. Checking the luminous face of his watch, Nick saw that it was now ten twenty-five. He heard arrivals in the bridge behind him: then Dalgleish announced in his clipped, dry tone, 'Lieutenant-Colonel Oswald, sir.'

A tall figure groped up beside him. 'Commander Everard?'

'Welcome, Colonel. Your men being made comfortable?'

'Absolutely, thank you. Good as the Ritz any day.' The colonel laughed: he had a young man's voice, Nick thought. These Special Service warriors did tend to get promoted young, he'd heard. The soldier added, 'Even if a few of us do have a touch of *mal de mer*.'

According to a report from Mr Walsh, who'd been helping Dalgleish during the embarkation, half the pongoes had been 'puking like cats' as they came aboard. Possibly an exaggeration: but it couldn't be too pleasant for them, even less so if they had to land and go into action in that condition. The colonel told him, 'I've a message from Captain Lorrimer. He wanted me to tell you that your idea for carrying on like this is absolutely bang-on, and he's grateful to you for coming up with it. He wishes you the best of luck and says for God's sake get a bloody move on.'

Nick had every intention of getting as much of a move on as he could. But the inshore work wasn't likely to be all that simple.

'*Afghan*'s closing astern, sir.'

'Very good.' One more to go. He told Oswald, 'I'm praying we'll find some shelter in Plaka Bay when we get there. If we don't, we won't get you ashore. It's quite a wide bay, but it doesn't go far in, and the only bit clear of rocks is right in the centre at the back end. It'll mean one ship going in at a time, taking it in turn. In calm weather we could probably do it faster, but with this wind and in the dark – well, we'll see how it is when we get there.'

'I'm sure you'll do the best you can for us.'

'Another problem is we only have ships' boats, not landing-craft. In this ship we've one motorboat and two whalers.' He looked round into the dark of the bridge behind him. 'Number One? Listen – Ashcourt can take charge of the boats, this time. I want one whaler each side of the motorboat, and all three lashed together. It ought to make for stability, so that even if it's a bit bumpy inside we could still load all three boats to something like

371

their life-saving capacity. Then we'll put the whole lot ashore in three trips.'

The soldier murmured, 'More of a business than I'd realized.'

'Depending on what it's like inshore, I'll get as close to the beach as I can. Number One, work out how the boats are to be secured together, and set up whatever gear you need. Ashcourt'll need a few good hands with him. And think about capacities – it may call for four trips, not three.'

'Aye aye, sir.'

'And I'll want an anchor ready for letting go. I'll need Chalk up here with me: and I think Houston should stay up top, in case we run into any opposition, so either Mr Walsh or the buffer could take charge for'ard. Up to you. But now take Colonel Oswald down to the wardroom and give him a large whisky, on my wine-bill. Ditto his officers.' He told the colonel, 'Sorry I can't join you.'

Houston muttered, when Dalgleish had led their guest away, 'Likely to be an awful lot of dampish khaki socks . . .'

At 0148 Cape Littino was abeam to starboard at a range of five and a half miles, the high ridge of land behind it a black interruption to the starry sky. With this wind and the cloud-patches they'd had earlier Nick had entertained faint hopes of cloud-cover for the return journey tomorrow, but it didn't look now as if they'd get any.

'Sharp look-out to starboard now, Sub.'

He'd said it to Chalk but the gunner, Mr Walsh, also grunted an acknowledgement. Nick had sent Dalgleish, Houston and Ashcourt to get some sleep: he didn't need them at this stage, and rested men would be more use later than tired ones. He himself had been off the bridge for about five minutes – when they'd buried Rocky Pratt, at midnight. He doubted if he'd be leaving it again before they were back in Alexandria.

The reason he'd called for a sharp look-out on the starboard bow was that eight miles after Littino was abeam they'd be coming up to the Paximadia islands, rocky outposts of Crete which were the reason for his having led the flotilla this far out. He reckoned to have the islands two miles on his beam at ten minutes past two. It was part and parcel of the same thing: he'd needed the running fix on Cape Littino so as to be sure of passing at a safe distance from the Paximadias but also in sight of them, in order to use them as a point of departure for the fifteen-mile run from there to the landing spot. The Sailing Directions suggested no landmarks in or near Plaka Bay, and it was essential to arrive at precisely the right bit of coast.

He moved out to the side of the bridge, and trained his glasses astern. He could see the splodge of whiteness that was *Afghan*'s bow-wave: it changed shape, expanding and contracting as her bow rose and fell in *Tuareg*'s wake. The destroyers were in close order, only cable's-length gaps between them. He came back to the binnacle; Mr Walsh asked him, 'What's the height of this rock supposed to be then, sir?'

'About eight hundred feet.'

'Eight twenty-seven,' Chalk corrected him. The gunner muttered, 'Oughter be stickin' up like a sore what d'you call it, then.'

Chalk picked them up at that moment: 'There they are! Green five-oh, sir!'

'Well done, Sub.'

The islands were abeam at eight minutes past two. He brought *Tuareg* round to 326 degrees.

Fourteen and a half miles now, from that turn to the entrance to Plaka Bay. He had it clearly in his mind's eye, an entrance two miles wide between Cape Stavros to port and Kako Muri – whatever *that* meant – to starboard, and he wanted to take *Tuareg* in just slightly to the left of centre. He'd memorized the land heights behind the bay and on each side of it, too, and this would be a help when he got in there.

'Messenger—'

'Sir?'

'Shake the first lieutenant and Lieutenant Houston and the sub-lieutenant. Then go aft and tell Colonel Oswald that disembarkation will commence at 0240.'

2.30 am. It was Sunday now, 25 May.

'One-four-oh revolutions.'

Salt-washed rocky headlands lifted on either bow, and a welter of foam boiled right across where *Tuareg* was heading. The offshore wind was strong and gusty, and the general run of the sea was from the west and along the coastline.

'One-four-oh revolutions passed and repeated, sir.'

CPO Habgood was back on the wheel now; Nick was taking his ship in alone while the other two waited close offshore. Dalgleish had the boats and gear organized and a scrambling-net ready at the ship's side, ready to be cast loose, with men standing by to help the soldiers over the side with their weapons and equipment as soon as the boats came alongside the net.

'There'll be a cross-current, cox'n, by the looks of it, as we enter.'

'I'll be lookin' for it, sir.'

Might turn out to be bloody awful, in there. On the other hand, it might be easy. *Tuareg* was acting as guinea-pig for the others; and it wouldn't be very clever to have beaten the Stukas and then end up on the rocks.

'Steer three degrees to starboard.'

'Three degrees to starboard, sir . . .'

Due north, that would make it. *Tuareg*'s stem was moving up close to the welter of sea that was pouring over itself in a sort of tumbling action from around the left-hand promontory. Entering it – now . . .

'Course north, sir!'

She was being pushed round to starboard: swing increasing fast. Habgood grunting curses as he got hold of her head and yanked her back like a wayward horse. She was as much as forty degrees off course before he got her under control.

'Carrying port wheel, sir.'

'You'll have to lose it quickly as we get through this.'

'Aye, sir . . .'

A few miles inland and on either side, rising ground loomed high across the stars. Wind was gusting through the gap between those mountains: it would be blowing clear across the island from Retimo.

Chalk's attention was on the whirring echo-sounder. According to the chart there'd be plenty of water here, but local charts weren't detailed or reliable. And there'd very likely have been silting, in recent years.

Ship's head swinging away to port: Habgood whipping off the port rudder she'd been carrying, then hauling her back to her course of due north.

Ahead, conditions looked patchy: more sheltered than it was outside, but with a ground-swell and areas of whitened surface where wind-gusts from gaps in the mountains scored it. He guessed there'd be a circular flow around the bay, probably an eastward or south-eastward set so far as *Tuareg* would feel it. Likely as not a strong one . . . The most obvious hazard was over to starboard where a long spur of rocks a mile inside the headland extended south-westward from the shore. Through binoculars Nick could see a heave and swirl of broken water close inshore: but it was in two separate areas, and where the land came out in a flattish promontory between them might be a likely aiming spot for the boats. For want of an alternative, it would have to do: as long as they could get in that far, across however much of a current there might be. Lacking time as well as alternatives and information, you couldn't dither: you had to make a quick choice, then stick to it. He reached for the telephone to the after control position, where Dalgleish would be waiting to hear from him.

'Number One. I'll be stopping in about three minutes' time. The landing area for the boats will be where our stem will be pointing when we stop – a minor promontory with broken water to each side of it. Due north, distance about one cable when we stop. Tell Ashcourt to look out for an easterly set, could be quite strong.'

Dalgleish would start getting the boats down close to the water now. One whaler, being the seaboat and having Robinson's disengaging gear on its davits, would be slipped quickly, with a bang, actually dropped into the water. But the other one and the motorboat would have to be lowered right into the sea before their falls could be released: an extra two or three minutes, because the weight had to come off the falls before the pins could be unscrewed. And every single minute counted now. From one problem to another: first it had been the Stukas, then the uncertainty of shelter from the north-wester, and now it was time: which made a vicious circle, bringing one back to Stukas – tomorrow morning's. Four return boat trips, each taking, say, fifteen minutes including loading and off-loading time, were going to fill an hour. Then if he sent the other two in here together – there'd be room for them, and if the weather didn't go mad suddenly it would be safe enough – that would add another hour. So – 0445 at the earliest, before the job was finished and he could start getting off the coast again. One hour after 0445 would be 0545 and daybreak, Stuka time . . .

It wouldn't do.

'Yeoman.' Whiffen appeared quickly out of the darkness behind him. Nick told him, 'Take this down.' Whiffen was moving to his hooded signal table on the starboard side. 'To *Afghan* and *Highflier. Join me now. Enter at slow speed with caution for tide-rip off Stavros point and stop near me one cable south of landing beach. Commence landing troops immediately on arrival.* Got that?' Whiffen, scribbling rapidly, said he had. Nick added, 'Blue shaded lamp. You'll raise them somewhere astern.'

It was going to crowd the place, but it would save an hour. He called down, 'Stop both engines.'

'Stop both, sir!'

'How much water, Sub?'

'Six fathoms, sir.'

'Good.' At the voicepipe again: 'Slow astern together.' Just to get the way off her. He told Chalk, 'White houses off to starboard – see them?' Chalk said yes, he did. 'That's a village, marked on the chart as Plakias. Use that and the edges of the headlands for shore bearings.' Into the pipe: 'Stop both engines.' He added to Chalk, 'When we drift I want to know which way and how fast.'

Engine and ventilator noise died away. From the back of the bridge he could hear the rapid clack-clacking of the shaded Aldis lamp, and from down near the boats orders, voices shouting to each other. It was 0246 now: it would be at least an hour before he could hope to be getting under way again.

'We're drifting astern, sir. South-east – quite fast, sir.'

'Slow ahead starboard. Port ten, and steer three-one-five, cox'n.'

One engine slow ahead, and her nose straight into it, might hold her. He told Chalk, 'Watch the bearings constantly, now.' He could have been anchored, but time and his instincts were against it. He sent the messenger, Crawford, down to Dalgleish to tell him that he was stemming the tide on 315 degrees – for Ashcourt's information.

The other two destroyers were in position with their boats in the water by 0301. *Tuareg*'s own boats had returned by that time, crabbing awkwardly across the current, for their second load. Nick had his glasses on *Afghan*, and felt considerable relief when he saw her motorboat and two whalers draw away and head for the shore – in a slightly circular route, as they found out about the cross-current. From down on the iron deck he heard Dalgleish yell, 'Carry on, Sub!' That was the second lot of soldiers going in. Should complete by 0400, with luck: but it was the performance of the slowest ship that would count. *Highflier*'s motor-cutter was away now, thick with men and towing a whaler that looked dangerously low in the water. Now there was nothing to do except hold the ship in her position and wait for the boats to reappear.

He'd increased the revs slightly on the starboard screw, and he thought he'd got it about right now. The other two ships were to starboard and slightly on his quarter: they were coming back to where they'd started from, having both drifted astern to start with and then woken up to what was happening.

'Are you watching that bearing, Sub?'

'Yes, sir. We're all right, still.'

Nick put his glasses up, searching for the boats, wanting to see them coming *now* . . . But it was deep shadow in there under the loom of the mountains. You could see where the water was broken and where it wasn't, but that was about all, except for the mountains themselves against the sky and those white cottages.

Chalk had taken a closer look, thinking better of what he'd said a moment ago . . . 'We're – about one degree *inshore* of it, sir!'

Nick bent to the voicepipe. 'Down four revolutions.'

Boats were approaching . . . And a second lot to the right: one of the others catching up a bit . . . The time was 0319. *Tuareg* was moving quite a lot to the ground-swell but it was also getting noisier and he thought the wind was freshening, humming and whining in the shrouds. He thought he'd probably been lucky to get in here now and not any later, when slightly worsened weather could have changed the situation quite dramatically. So long, he thought, as it doesn't happen before we finish. When the boats came alongside this time it would be the halfway mark, so far as *Tuareg*'s soldiers were concerned. And that was at – 0323 . . . About forty minutes since they'd started, so adding the same time-lapse again you could still reckon on completion by 0400. Allow another twenty or thirty minutes for the others, and it would be 0430. Not much better than the original estimate, the one he'd thought to improve on by bringing them all in here at once. One hour of darkness was all they'd get, for putting distance between themselves and the Cretan coast.

Then, at 0348, four minutes after the boats had left with the fourth and last party of soldiers, *Tuareg*'s motorboat broke down.

Going by the timings of the first three runs, the boats should have returned one or two minutes before 4 am. They arrived at fourteen minutes past, in tow of *Highflier*'s motor-cutter. It had been coming off from shore, seen *Tuareg*'s contraption being carried away rapidly south-eastward on the current, chased after it and caught it, towed it inshore to off-load and then brought it back out to the ship. It was now a quarter past four, and *Highflier*'s cutter still had two more parties of men to land.

At *least* an extra half-hour . . . Nick forced himself to stay calm, control jumping nerves. *Afghan*'s boats, meanwhile, completed their landings and embarked *Highflier*'s final load, so that the last two lots of soldiery in fact reached shore practically simultaneously.

Nick had turned *Tuareg* around while her boats were being hoisted and secured, and he was in position to lead the others out of the bay.

'Boats are coming from shore, sir!'

'How many?'

'Both lots, sir, I think . . .'

His fingers were drumming on the binnacle: he caught them at it and stopped them. It felt as if he had wires inside his brain, all strung tight. *Too* tight: and it wouldn't do, a man who was too tense and too tired was a man who made mistakes.

'Cox'n, is Leading Seaman Duggan there with you?'

'Aye, sir, he's here.'

'Put him on the voicepipe, please . . . Duggan?'

'Yessir?'

'I meant to ask you earlier – who won that darts match?'

'We did, sir.'

'Well done!'

'Thank you, sir.'

Nick straightened, checked the time. Four thirty-one . . .

'Three-one-oh revolutions.'

'Three-one-oh revolutions, sir!'

That was Leading Seaman Sherratt on the wheel now; one watch had been stood down and CPO Habgood would be getting some well-deserved rest.

'Three-one-oh revs passed and repeated, sir.'

Afghan and *Highflier* were in station astern of *Tuareg*, on course 143 degrees. Thirty knots, those revs should provide: he'd have liked to have made it 360 and squeezed an extra two or three knots out of her, but thirty was *Highflier*'s best speed.

It was a quarter to five. The two hours inside Plaka Bay had felt like two weeks. Now Plaka was astern, Alexandria 300 miles ahead. One hour of darkness, therefore, then dawn and a whole day within easy distance of the Scarpanto airfield.

There was satisfaction in having got the troops ashore, particularly as the wind was rising astern of them now, nearer force 5 than 4. He'd thought it had been past its peak, but he'd been wrong; and he doubted whether the three destroyers who'd been taking a similar batch of commandos to Selinos Kastelli would have got them in. It was right on the island's south-west corner, with no kind of shelter at all; the full strength of wind and sea would be sweeping along that curve of coastline.

The Praximadias were twelve miles ahead. Ten miles beyond them Cape Littino would be abeam, and course would be altered to 130 degrees – adjusted for the one-knot easterly set – the straight heading for Alexandria. There'd be an eight-hour gap, roughly, before he'd catch up with *Glenshiel* and *Huntress*: eight hours during which each small force would be on its own. Just about all the losses so far had been from small, detached forces . . .

He was tired, suddenly: or suddenly conscious of being tired. It came from this temporary relaxation of the tension, probably; for about fifty minutes one could *afford* to feel tired. Better make the most of fifty minutes, he thought. There was a day of Stukas coming now; then a quick turn-round in Alexandria and another job to be done, troops to be taken in or brought out. Before much longer it would be all one way – out.

He got into his chair. He'd expected to do no more than doze, but he slept at once, and dreamt. Fiona was there somewhere, and he was reaching to her: touching emptiness: but then it switched, and he was at Mullbergh with a high wind in the trees outside the window where they were dining – Paul and Jack on his left, Sarah stiff and old-maidish on his right, staring disapprovingly at Paul. Jack was talking on and on, sounding pompous and condescending, making sneering remarks about submarines, and Paul was watching him across the table with an air of guarded reserve, silently critical. Nick urged Paul, 'He isn't like this really, you know. He's like you and me. It's only the effect this old bitch has on him, don't you see that? Damn it, he's your *brother*—'

'Five-thirty, sir . . . Captain, sir?'

The dream had changed. That wasn't Paul's voice.

'Sir, it's half past five!'

He didn't believe it. It was obviously part of the same stupid dream. He'd only just slumped down and shut his eyes.

'Captain, sir. About time for dawn action stations.'

It was Tony Dalgleish beside the chair. *Tuareg*'s dark bridge and the noise of sea and wind, the roar of the ventilator fans. Wind and sea were still astern, he knew it immediately from the motion.

'Right. Thank you, Number One.'

'Here's some kye, sir. I think the cox'n got at it.'

Nick took the mug of cocoa that Dalgleish was offering him, and sniffed at it. Rum. Illegal, of course. He straightened in the chair. 'My compliments to the chef.'

Daylight growing: with the coast of Crete thirty miles to the north, Scarpanto sixty north-eastward. All three ships were rolling and pitching as the eastern sky turned rose-red and its glow spread across the lively, wind-whipped seascape. Stars were fading rapidly in a clear dome of sky, and the destroyers astern were plunging end-on shapes wedged in high-curving, flying sea.

'Signal to us, sir, from C-in-C!'

PO Whiffen was beside the chair, his jovial face redder than usual from the wind. Ashcourt was beyond him at the binnacle, where Pratt should have been. Nick missed Pratt's stolid, pragmatic personality. He told Whiffen, 'Read it to me, would you.' He was watching the sky, the eastern and north-eastern sectors in particular, the direction of Scarpanto and of the rising sun. It was already three-quarters daylight and he doubted if they'd be kept waiting long.

'To *Tuareg*, from C-in-C, repeated—'

'Just the message, Yeoman.'

'Aye, sir . . . *Report position course speed and whether troops still on board.* Time of origin—'

'All right. Here.' He slid off the seat, beckoning Whiffen to join him at the chart, so that he could give him their position. He hadn't intended to break W/T silence at least until the enemy had found him, by which time it wouldn't have made any difference, but now he'd have to. He could understand ABC wanting to know where his ships were, anyway, and presumably the army command would want to know what had been done with their commandos, too . . . The position was 237 Kupho Nisi 50: course 130, speed 30. He added, for Whiffen to scrawl on his pad, *Landing operation was completed at 0430.* 'Send that, Yeoman. To C-in-C and the same repeateds.' The 'repeated' addresses were authorities to whom the signal was sent for information; in this case they included *Glenshiel* and the force that had been sweeping Crete's north coast during the night – *Dido* and *Ajax* and two destroyers.

It was fully daylight now. Leaning against his chair he studied the horizon and the sky. Nothing: except for the sun coming up red and angry, rather like a hot tomato. He got through to Dalgleish at his station aft, and told him to have one watch piped to breakfast. 'While you're at it, tell McEvoy I'll have mine up here, would you.'

'Think our friends may be busy elsewhere, sir?'

It was possible. *Dido* and company would be somewhere in the Kaso area.

At 0640, by which time he'd had his breakfast and there were still no bombers, another signal arrived from C-in-C. Nick was ordered to turn his three ships north-eastward and join up with the cruiser force – *Dido* and *Ajax* – which was now steering south-west out of the Kaso Strait. The force was also to be joined by three other destroyers, *Napier, Kelvin* and *Jackal*, who were on their way north from Alexandria.

He went to the chart and marked the rendezvous position on it. The new course would be 050 degrees, which required an eighty-degree turn to port. He told Whiffen, 'Hoist eight blue, Yeoman.' Back in his chair, he thought about this change of plan: that – probably – it meant reprieve. He'd have his destroyers in close company with the cruisers and their batteries of high-angle AA guns in about one hour flat. And today's chances had been slim: *now*, he could admit it. When one thought about what had happened to Mountbatten's ships . . .

'Answering pendants are close up, sir!'

'Haul down.' He told Ashcourt, 'Come round to oh-five-oh.'

Jack Everard had got all the information he'd come down to the plot for. He shoved the notebook into his pocket, yawned for about the tenth time in the last half-hour, and went back to the bridge. He told Napier, 'We were right, sir. Should sight them any minute now, probably fine on the port bow.'

He'd had no sleep at all last night. He felt all washed out: and for the best of reasons. Inside the condition of physical exhaustion, he'd never felt so good in his life. Or so – *dumbfounded* . . .

Carnarvon had sailed from Alexandria at 0800: the sailing orders had come late at night, when Jack had been ashore on night leave expiring at 0600 . . . Ahead of the cruiser a destroyer, *Halberdier*, was zigzagging and pinging for submarines. There was a long swell running and she was making heavy weather of it: each time she plunged her bow down into the sea you expected to see her screws come right up out of it, but each time they just stayed hidden. She and *Carnarvon* were making eighteen knots; one full day in harbour, plus last night with the engineers working until about midnight, had got her back into running order.

'We need a good long spell in dockyard hands, sir.' Buchanan, the engineer commander, had warned his captain this morning when they'd been coming up the swept channel out of Alex. 'In anything like normal circumstances I'd have to tell you she wasn't fit for operations. So if you *can* keep the revs down, sir, treat her gently—'

'Depends on the enemy, Chief.' Napier had shrugged: Buchanan hadn't told him anything he hadn't known already. 'We shan't dash about when we don't have to . . . But look here, Chief, you've done extremely well, you and all your people. The C-in-C's pleased as punch, I can tell you. D'you realize that in just three days he's had two cruisers and four destroyers sunk, and one battleship, two cruisers and four destroyers badly damaged? Every ship he can get, he needs.'

'Argument rather on my side, sir, if I may say so. I mean for treating her like an old lady with a weak heart.'

She certainly wasn't a *young* lady. But you wouldn't have thought there was anything weak about her, looking down on her forepart as she smashed powerfully through the long, blue-white swells, heading out north-westward to meet the crippled assault ship *Glenshiel* and bring her back to Alexandria. *Glenshiel* had caught a packet yesterday, when she'd had brother Nick's destroyers with her, and this morning she'd already fought off three separate attacks by Junkers 88s. She was down to eight knots, now.

Fullbrook, an RNVR lieutenant, was just handing over the watch to Tom Overton. Old Tom, for God's sake, who *did* have interests other than golf – as Jack had witnessed, last night . . . Overton met Jack's eyes, and winked: Jack nodded, still astonished by everything that had happened, and thinking of a girl with blue-black hair who was the cousin of another rather like her but more beautiful and a few years older, this older one being Tom Overton's girlfriend and the wife of a very rich French-Egyptian. Overton beamed at Fullbrook: 'All right, dear boy, I have the weight.' The weight of the watch, the ship, he meant. But Alexandria was an extraordinary town: and it had taken on entirely new fascinations now for Jack Everard, Lieutenant, Royal Navy.

Napier was looking at him, seeing him lost in daydream. And he could, just about, have fallen asleep on his feet, gone on dreaming . . . He went down to the chart table instead, pulled the log towards him and leafed through the signals on it.

The ones directly affecting *Carnarvon* – the changed rendezvous position when *Glenshiel* had reported her latest speed reduction, and the assault ship's signals about air attacks and requests for fighter cover – fat chance she had of *that* – were familiar, things he'd worked with during the forenoon. But there was also one from C-in-C to brother Nick in *Tuareg*, ordering him to join the cruiser squadron up near Kaso: the cruisers were being sent back up through the straits for a second night's sweep of the north coast, a repeat of last night's operation. It would be a day or two before *Tuareg* could be back in Alex, then. All the talk was of evacuation: in the Union Club last night, for instance, in the crowded downstairs bar where Jack had started his evening with Overton . . . It was no secret that the fighting was going badly: troops were holding out strongly at Heraklion and at Retimo – although at Retimo they were said to be cut off – but at Suda and in the Maleme-Canea area, which was where it really mattered, the situation was reported to be hopeless. The Germans were pouring supplies into Maleme airfield in Ju52 transports, so that hour by hour the balance was tipping further in their favour.

Other signals: *Isis, Hero* and *Nizam* were returning from their attempt to land commandos at Selinos Kastelli. Bad weather had forced them to turn back; *Nizam* had lost both her whalers in the heavy seas. But *Tuareg* and company must have got their troops ashore: brother Nick, Jack thought wrily, coming up to scratch – as usual . . . Meanwhile *Glenroy* would be sailing later today for Timbaki, escorted by *Coventry* and two destroyers: she'd been turned back from a similar operation a couple of days ago. And last, but very far from least, a battle squadron under Vice-Admiral Pridham-Whipple was sailing from Alexandria at just about this moment, escorting the carrier *Formidable* for an air attack on Scarpanto airfield. The carrier's escorting force consisted of the flagship *Queen Elizabeth*, her sister-battleship *Barham*, and eight destroyers.

At lunch yesterday in the wardroom, Jack had remarked to Tom Overton, 'Rather funny exchange of signals, our skipper's and *Glenshiel*'s, on the way in.'

Overton hadn't heard about it. Jack told him about Fifi and the Auberge Bleu. Overton chuckled: 'Great spot, the old Auberge.'

'Oh, d'you know it?'

He wouldn't have thought nightclubs were the first lieutenant's line of country. Overton had murmured, 'Used it once or twice, you know.'

Then they'd met in the evening, in the Union Club. Jack had gone ashore with Willy Irvine for a drink and a snack, a change of atmosphere. Leave had been granted until 0600 Sunday morning; the ship was 'under sailing orders' but no specific orders had been received by the time he'd come ashore, and the engine-room department had still been at work down in the bowels. So she hadn't even had steam up, and no early departure had seemed likely.

In the bar he'd found himself standing next to old Tom. *Carnarvon*'s first lieutenant had a glass of Stella beer in his sunburnt fist: Jack had looked at it in surprise.

'I agree. This horse is not fit for work. But the night is yet young, dear boy, and at this stage easy does it, eh?'

'I dare say, if you're making a night of it.' He wondered if Overton played golf in the dark. Luminous balls? He laughed, spluttering into his gin. But Overton ignored that: he was looking at him rather intensely as if he'd just had some bright idea. 'Everard. I say.'

'What?'

'Did I understand you to say that you had never sampled the pleasures of the Auberge Bleu?'

'I haven't, no.'

'Like to? Tonight?'

'Right ahead. Just her masthead.'

Glenshiel had been spotted from the director platform ten minutes ago but now Commander Bell-Reid had sighted her from the bridge. He added, 'You can see her spotting-top when she rises on a swell or we do. *There—*'

'Yes.' Napier, ramrod-straight on his seat, had got on to it too. There was a certain relief in having made the rendezvous with the assault ship before the bombers came back to her.

Then they had the destroyer, *Huntress*, in sight too. A quarter of an hour later, when they were at close quarters and *Carnarvon* was being put about to turn in astern of *Glenshiel*, Jack could see the assault ship's fire-blackened upperworks, bomb damage aft, several landing-craft shattered in their davits and paintwork scorched black from near-misses. He could imagine her as she'd have looked yesterday evening, on fire, and this morning with the 88s' bombs raining down around her: for all that, she'd got off lightly. With only one destroyer in company, and so slowed-down that from the

384

bombers' point of view she must have looked like a sitting bird, at their mercy . . .

No – not mercy. You couldn't use that word, here in the eastern Mediterranean in the spring of 1941. Certainly not in relation to Stuka pilots. And despite that, last night one had – he thought, *It's incredible* . . . To think of himself last night in that nightclub, and later in the small hours in the cousin's bed: and this wounded ship struggling south while others nearer to Crete waited for the dawn and for the arrival of the bombers: there was a harsh incongruity, a sense of two identities, two worlds.

Napier had given the yeoman a signal that was to be flashed to *Glenshiel*'s captain but not recorded on the log: *Fifi is filing a paternity suit. Now which way do you want to go?*

Overton chuckling at the binnacle, looking round at Jack . . .

At the Auberge last night he'd been a different man entirely. His girl – she'd be about twenty-eight or -nine, he guessed – had turned out to be about the most beautiful woman Jack had ever seen. In a city of beautiful women, she outshone them all. The cousin, Gabrielle, could have walked into practically any room and stopped the conversation, but beside Tom's girl she'd been eclipsed, made to look quite ordinary. She wasn't ordinary: when her cousin was out of view she was sensational. And very lively, warm, outgoing: within minutes they'd been having fun, and even right at the start there'd been an edge of tension, expectation . . . Overton quick-witted, amusing, taking it for granted that he should have this extraordinarily beautiful, extremely rich man's wife hanging on his words, taking no notice of anyone but him . . . And again, thinking back to it, he was struck by the nightmarish contrast – the girl's lips and lithe, sweet body, enclosing arms, whispers in the scented darkness and the first faint light of dawn outside – dawn that had also begun to light this long rolling swell and the bomb-scarred ship, the battle raging in the north.

At 1800, when they'd brought *Glenshiel* to within seventy-five miles of Alexandria, they met the battle squadron on its way out north-westward for the attack on Scarpanto, and *Carnarvon* was detached to join it. Jack's mind stayed full of the girl: his memory of the extraneous events which followed was like a film shown fast but with occasional stills of incidents and conversations that weren't necessarily of particular importance. There was the run northwards, *Carnarvon* acting as AA guardship and stationed between the battleships and *Formidable*: *Queen*

Elizabeth impressive in her dazzle-camouflage, with the Vice-Admiral's flag at her foremasthead and a huge ensign flapping at the main. He was watching her through binoculars when Overton asked him, just before they closed up for dusk action stations, 'Wish it was this time yesterday, Jack?'

Lowering the glasses, he shrugged.

'Don't tell me you didn't enjoy yourself.'

He took a breath. 'No. I won't tell you that.'

'Seeing her again, d'you think?'

He had to. He said, 'Of course.'

'She won't always be available, you know. Matter of luck and timing.'

'What d'you mean?'

Action stations: the Marine bugler, Sykes, splitting the air with it, and the same call floating from the flagship and from *Barham* and the carrier. It felt good, he remembered, being part of such a powerful force – and being on the offensive, too. It was a disappointment to learn next morning that the 23,000-ton aircraft carrier had only ten operational aircraft with which to attack the hundreds on Scarpanto and then fight off the inevitable retaliatory attacks. At dawn action stations on the Monday morning – it was 26 May – he watched *Formidable* turn into the wind to launch her aircraft. Two of the ten that took off turned out to be defective and had to land-on again, but the other eight, four Fulmars and four Albacores, formed up and winged away towards Scarpanto. All eight returned, with reports of Stukas destroyed on the ground and damage inflicted on the airfield installations. They had to get airborne again almost at once, as the Stuka counter-attacks began to come in; and at about the same time the battle squadron was joined by the cruisers *Dido* and *Ajax* and destroyers which included *Tuareg*, *Afghan* and *Highflier*.

Thinking about Gabrielle – between Stuka attacks, and sometimes even while they were in progress – Jack wished his involvement with her hadn't stemmed from Tom Overton's affair with another man's wife. That was a bit over the odds, he felt; it stuck in the gullet, rather, and he was aware of having consciously to turn a blind eye to it.

Still fighting off Stukas and 88s, the fleet withdrew south-westward. Then at noon there was a signal ordering them to provide cover for *Glenroy*, who was trying to run troops up to Timbaki, and course was altered to due west. At 1320 a force of twenty Stukas arrived from the direction of the desert, and attacked, most of them going for the carrier while she was still in the process of getting her fighters up. She was hit by two bombs and badly damaged, and at the same time the destroyer *Nubian* had her stern blown off.

If a girl went to bed with you so readily, the very first time you met her, did it mean she'd do it with anyone?

Of course it didn't. He told himself not to be stupid, not to waste time thinking about it. It kept him awake, though, even when he was dog-tired.

Glenroy had been badly mauled by the bombers: she'd been forced to turn back again without getting her troops ashore. Air power, nothing else, was allowing the Germans to pour their troops in and keep British reinforcements out. Nothing was going well: if you faced it squarely you had to admit that all the Navy was doing was losing ships . . . Destroyers were oiling from the battleships during the 26th, that Monday. It was at dusk that evening that *Formidable* was detached to limp away to Alexandria. At daylight on Tuesday the 27th the battle squadron was ordered to close in towards the Kaso Strait again, to cover the withdrawal of *Hero*, *Nizam* and *Abdiel*, who'd run the gauntlet with commandos and ammunition into Suda Bay and were now bringing out about a thousand other personnel who weren't needed on the island. But the battle squadron was still a couple of hundred miles short of Kaso, just before 9 am, when a mixed force of Junkers 88s and Heinkel 111s attacked. Jack saw the almost solid descent of bombs: it was a well-executed, highly-concentrated attack, and the battleship *Barham* got the worst of it. One bomb hit her on Y turret; near-misses, enormous blasts of sea flinging up close beside her, holed and flooded two of her anti-torpedo bulges. She took on a list, and had a fire inside her which her ship's company were fighting all that forenoon.

He could imagine what it must be like inside there, in those cramped, smoke-filled compartments, airless, suffocating, and the fire taking hold and spreading . . .

'Everard – are you in love, or something equally ridiculous?'

He looked round quickly. The commander, Bell-Reid, was glaring at him from a couple of feet away.

'The plot is calling, Everard.' Bell-Reid pointed. 'The plot voicepipe?'

It was right beside him. He hadn't heard a thing. He answered it now, and Midshipman Brighouse, who was taking a turn as his Tanky, navigator's assistant, had some footling thing to ask him. He gave the snotty a short answer. Bell-Reid growled at him as he straightened from the voicepipe, 'Ever since we left Alexandria two days ago, Everard, you've been giving a close imitation of a dying duck in a thunderstorm. Are you sick?'

He shook his head. 'Perfectly fit, sir.'

'Woman trouble?'

'No, sir.' There was no trouble that couldn't be solved by getting *back* to Alexandria. Bell-Reid muttered, 'Well, pull yourself together, for God's sake!'

At least he'd had the decency to keep his voice down . . .

At 1230, the C-in-C recalled the whole force to Alex. Jack's last memory of that trip – the last still picture in the blur of ships' movements, signals, Stuka attacks and the sickening sight of bomb-bursts – was of Petty Officer Hillier's face as he goggled at a signal which he'd just removed from the pneumatic tube. Hillier was yeoman of the watch. It was early afternoon, and the battle squadron was steaming south-westward. He'd been taking the signal over to Napier, unfolding it as he crossed the bridge: glancing at it, he'd stopped in his tracks, mouth open.

Napier asked him, 'What is it, Yeoman?'

'Sir, they've—' Hillier gulped, swallowing emotion. 'We've sunk the *Bismarck*, sir!'

In Alexandria, Aubrey Wishart left ABC in the Operations Room and went down the passage to his own office. The wires had been humming all day between this headquarters, Army HQ in Cairo and the Chiefs of Staff in London.

Wishart picked up the telephone and asked the exchange to connect him to the extension which was Rear-Admiral Creswell's office at Ras-el-Tin.

'Creswell.'

'Aubrey Wishart here. It's on, Hector.'

At the other end, George Hector Creswell took a deep breath. 'It' meant the lifting of 20,000 troops from Crete.

'Right. Thank you.'

He put the phone down, on a battle lost.

CHAPTER 9

'Something wrong, Nick?'

It was stuffy in the day-cabin, despite open scuttles: all they seemed to let in was the smell of Egypt, and Egypt's flies. The urgency now, the need to be seeing to about forty things at once in order to be ready to sail again at dawn, might be adding to the sense of airlessness. And he didn't want to seem fidgety to Aubrey Wishart, who must have had a thousand matters to deal with but had still found time to call by and see him.

He answered that question: 'Not – necessarily.' He'd had a feeling there *would* be a letter from Fiona, this time. He told Wishart, nodding at the totally uninteresting mail scattered on the table, 'I'd hoped for one that isn't here, that's all.'

'When you get back on Thursday' – Wishart smiled: genial, confident – 'she'll have written then, old lad.'

'Well.' He glanced at her portrait. 'I hope so.'

'*That* one, eh?'

'She's stationed in London. MTC. Since that bloody awful raid three weeks ago I haven't heard from her.'

'Mails are fairly erratic, you know.'

'Mr Gieves gets his bills to me regularly enough.' He flopped into the armchair facing Wishart's. There wasn't time for this kind of chat, for talk of personal matters and the outside world. They mattered as much as they ever had, but here and now they had to be pigeon-holed: to get back to the real world, or be any use to Fiona – if she'd let him – he had to see this through first. It wasn't going to be any joy-ride.

Tuareg had entered Alexandria with the rest of the force a couple of hours ago; they'd oiled and then shifted to a buoy, and now as daylight faded they were taking in ammunition from a lighter on the starboard side. On the other side there was a lighter with stores and fresh provisions, and a water-boat beyond it. Lights had been rigged on the upper deck and the work would be going on for some hours yet; then there'd be an interval in which to get some rest before sailing at 0600 for Heraklion via the Kaso Strait.

The object of this expedition was to lift 4,500 men, the entire garrison of Heraklion, from under the Germans' noses and into destroyers and cruisers between midnight tomorrow and 2 am on Thursday the 29th. Embarkation would have to be completed by 2 am, or the warships with their loads of soldiers would be caught by daylight on the wrong side of Kaso.

He reached over with a light for Wishart's cigarette. This was the evening of Tuesday, 27 May, but it felt as if it could easily have been last Friday, when he'd sat in this same chair and Wishart had filled the one he was occupying now; the ensuing days could have been one long disjointed dream. Another dream haunted him too, when he let it: that apparently inconsequential one of Jack and Paul at Mullbergh. He had a sense of important things left undone: of time running out, no chance now to put matters on any better footing. He or Jack or both of them might so easily not survive this next phase of the battle – survival even this far seemed vaguely surprising – and he'd have liked to have cleared things up, at least to have had a shot at bridging the gulf between them.

Too late now. And even with time and opportunity, he knew it might well have been a wasted effort. He shook it out of his mind again . . . 'It's good to see you, Aubrey. I hope one of these days we'll be able to spend more than five minutes talking to each other.'

'Not this evening, anyway.' The admiral shot a glance at his watch. 'As I need hardly tell you, there's a lot going on. I'm on my way over to Ras-el-Tin, actually. Main reason for stopping was, as I said, to tell you that having got those chaps ashore at Plaka Bay has impressed ABC considerably.'

'I was lucky. The weather only just held up long enough.' He changed the subject. 'Who's this navigator I'm getting?'

'*Masai*'s. A VR lieutenant, name of Drisdale. Smeake says he's good.'

'And what's the overall pattern for the evacuation, can you tell me that? Apart from tomorrow's outing?'

Force B, the ships heading for Heraklion tomorrow, was to be commanded by Rear-Admiral Rawlings with his flag in *Orion*. There'd be three other cruisers – *Ajax, Dido* and *Carnarvon* – and the destroyers *Tuareg, Afghan, Decoy, Jackal, Imperial, Hotspur,*

Kimberley and *Hereward*. But the Tribals and *Carnarvon* wouldn't be embarking troops; they were to sweep north of Heraklion to fend off interference by Italian torpedo-boats.

Wishart told him, 'Mostly it'll be from Sphakia on the south coast. All the troops from the Suda-Maleme area have been told to fall back across the island to Sphakia, and the first lift will be tomorrow night, same time as yours on the other side. There'll be a bigger one the second night – 6,000 men, it's hoped – and about another 3,000 on each of the two nights after that. There's also Retimo . . .' He frowned. 'That's much less simple. We want them to pull out and get across the Plaka Bay, but so far it hasn't been possible to get a message through.'

'No W/T there?'

'There's no military wireless anywhere, old lad. All army communications for some time now have been passed through our NOIC Suda – one Captain Morse. He's now shifting to a cave above the Sphakia beach, and the pongoes are setting up their HQ there with him. But we sent a Hurricane with long-range fuel tanks on it, to drop a message to the Retimo garrison, and nothing more's been heard of it. We've twice tried sending submarines in, too; but the Eyeties are patrolling that coast with their torpedo craft every night, and we damn near lost the first boat we sent in. The second simply didn't get her landing-party back. And as you know we're having to use every submarine we've got, to sit on the Italian ports in case they get a rush of blood to the head and send their fleet out—'

'The people I landed at Plaka may have fought their way through. Would they know what's wanted?'

'Well.' Wishart spread his large hands. 'They were to secure the route. There'd been no order to evacuate, though, at that stage.'

'Retimo's where you said the field hospital is. All those women?'

Wishart took a long drag at his cigarette.

'Nick, it's a bugger.' He shook his head. 'Yesterday General Freyberg reported that the Suda troops had reached the limit of endurance. It's the air thing again, you see . . . Only hope, he said, was withdrawal to the south coast. He also reported Retimo cut off, Heraklion surrounded. Same day, Churchill signals Wavell, "Victory in Crete essential, keep hurling in all you can."'

'Are they mad, in London?'

Wishart shrugged. 'They don't know their arses from their elbows. Wavell explained it to them yesterday, though, in words of one syllable, and they do seem finally to have glimpsed the realities of the situation. Better late than never.' He slapped his hands down on his knees, and stood up: a bulky, towering man. 'I'm off now. Late already. Nick, don't worry about that girl. She's *much* too pretty to come to grief.'

On deck, ammunition boxes were being slung up out of the lighter on the torpedo davit, and seamen working at high speed under the direction of Petty Officer Roddick were uncasing the shells and cordite charges and sending them on down to the shellrooms and magazines. Pompom and point-five ammunition went straight down in its boxes, except that on the gun platforms gunners squatted, loading belts. Mr Walsh was darting to and fro, ticking off items on his clipboard, and on the other side of the ship CPO Habgood and assistants were doing the same with sacks and crates of stores. Up ahead of the stores lighter, the water-boat was just casting off. Dalgleish had a stranger with him, an RNVR lieutenant with a beaky nose and deepset eyes: a cadaverous, gloomy-looking man. After Wishart had left, Dalgleish introduced him to Nick.

'Lieutenant Drisdale, sir, formerly of *Masai*.'

Most of *Tuareg*'s officers would already know Drisdale, of course, and it would make things easy. Nick asked him, 'Are you an experienced navigator?'

'One year in *Masai*, sir, and before that I was in a minesweeper.'

'Glad to have you, anyway.' He looked at Dalgleish. 'Ashcourt could show him where everything is . . . You'll find all the corrections are up to date, I expect, Drisdale. Pratt was a very conscientious fellow.'

'Yes, sir.' Drisdale nodded. 'A very nice one too.'

There was a letter to be written, to Pratt's family.

Redmayne, the engineer, was waiting to have a word with him. And PO Whiffen, the yeoman, was hovering with a log of signals. A lot of the routine stuff wasn't transmitted but came by hand, on paper. Too much paper by half: and there wasn't time now to bother with anything but essentials: there was a fresh and mounting sense of urgency as the new task loomed.

Jack Everard had gone ashore, to collect new charts, replacements for worn-out ones and also some inshore charts that weren't in the folio and might be needed in the course of the evacuation. His most pressing need, in fact, was to get to a shore telephone.

While they were looking out the charts he'd asked for he borrowed an empty office with a phone in it, lit a cigarette to calm his nerves and then asked the dockyard exchange to get him Gabrielle's number.

Her telephone was ringing, ringing . . .

'*Oui?*'

'Gabrielle?'

'Who is it who asks for her?' French, and female, but not Gabrielle. Some visitor to the apartment . . . He spoke in his own halting, Dartmouth-accented French, 'This is Jack Everard. May I speak to Gabrielle, please?'

She laughed, as if he'd said something funny. Then she said, 'Oh, *Lisa* . . . It's Martine here, my dear.'

'I don't understand, I'm sorry. Martine—'

Martine was Overton's girl. She broke in, in that rapid French gabble, 'Lisa dear, how sweet of you to ask us. Gabrielle and I would *adore* to, but I'm so terribly sorry, you'll have to do without us. Her beloved is returned, you see, *and* my own, and—'

'Beloved? Who—'

'Oh, you're right, these husbands *do* get in the way.' She'd laughed again, and called out to someone else in the room: a string of French, with more hilarity mixed up in it. There was a man's voice then – from some distance – and then – his nerves jumped – Gabrielle's, unmistakable . . . She'd laughed too, and answered – incomprehensibly. Martine said into the phone, 'I'm truly sorry, Lisa, joking apart. Both our wretched husbands are insisting we must dash away with them to Ismailia. So Lisa, pet—'

'Look, my name is *not* Lisa—'

Shriek of laughter: 'But we know this so *well*, my dear!' He could see that lovely, laughing face: and somewhere in the room behind it he could imagine Gabrielle's too, Gabrielle asking her cousin with the enquiry in those wide, dark eyes of hers, who this really was . . .

'Lisa, do you hear me? Are you still there?'

'What?'

'I said Gabrielle would like a little word now.'

'Hello?'

'Gabrielle – what on earth is—'

'I'm so sorry, my darling. We'll be away at least a few – well, I suppose as much as a week, or—'

'*Husband?*'

'Oh, never mind that. What's a little week matter? In about seven or eight days I shall be here again and this wretch will have deserted me again, and – oh, just one moment . . .' He heard the man's voice, closer now: then Gabrielle's quick, high note of protest: 'You certainly may *not* speak with her! All you wish to do is flirt, and I won't have it! Lisa – goodbye, darling.'

Click. She'd hung up.

Gabrielle had a husband?

She'd gone to a lot of trouble to keep it quiet . . . In the boat again, on his way back to the ship, he tried to remember details: how, for instance, there'd been no signs of a man's clothes or shaving gear, anything masculine at all. In fact the apartment and its decor and atmosphere had been so entirely, positively feminine that no such possibility had occurred to him. Of course, he hadn't looked inside any cupboards . . . Had she worn rings? Yes, he remembered a small clicking shower of them on the glass top of her dressing-table as she'd shed them.

Another man's wife?

Overton wasn't in the wardroom, and Jock McCowan said he'd gone to turn in early – most people had. So tonight he couldn't question him about Gabrielle. Couldn't do a damn thing – not for eight days. Or seven . . . But – he put the question to himself, and shirked answering it – would he go to see her then? Ring her, in a week's time?

He'd been privately censorious of Overton's affair with a married woman; he'd been careful to ignore it. That had been the first step – looking the other way because if he hadn't it might have upset his own apple-cart. Now, the *second* step?

He was in the chartroom, stowing away the new ones. Then he went on to the dark and empty bridge to change the one on that table, the chart for the Alex-Kaso run tomorrow. He'd put the light on, pulled the old chart out and begun to roll it, glancing at its clean replacement: he was looking at the Kaso Strait, with Scarpanto like a lizard flanking it to the north-east. Tomorrow – by this time tomorrow night, he thought – we'll have fought our way through that gap. Touch wood . . . The mental shiver told him that he was tired and that it would be sensible to turn in. He put his hand to the light-switch, and his eyes went back to the charted shape that was Scarpanto: it was truly lizard-like, reptilian, and you could think of its Stukas as reptiles too, the spawn of that large, sprawling parent – poisonous, yellow-faced, massed and waiting for the victims . . . Crossing the bridge with the rolled chart under his arm he paused, leant there for a moment, looking over towards the destroyer moorings and all around the big, quiet expanse of harbour. Lights burned on ships still ammunitioning or storing. Others besides the Heraklion force would be sailing in the morning: there was to be a lift at the same time from Sphakia on the south coast, a small one presumably, only destroyers. Reflections of those lights grew out like spears across the dark water: a snatch of music in the breeze was from one of the French ships, lying demilitarized with only skeleton crews on board. A sentry's hail of 'Boat aho-o-oy!' was answered by a shout of 'Guard!' Guard-boat doing its rounds: the officer of the guard from the duty battleship toured the harbour several times during the night to check there was a sentry awake and alert on each ship's upper deck.

Turn in now, he thought. He pushed himself off the side of the bridge, headed for the ladder. He'd have to be up by five-thirty; and for some time after that there might not be many opportunities for sleep.

Gabrielle, married? Just – amusing herself, then?

He woke – shaken by the snotty of the watch at 0530 – with the same thought in his mind, and a strong desire to talk to Overton about it. But he wasn't able to until late in the afternoon, just after 1630, by which time the force was only a hundred miles from Scarpanto. They'd been zigzagging all day with revs for twenty-three knots on, making good twenty on the mean course, and there'd been no sign of the Luftwaffe. The four cruisers were in line ahead, the flagship *Orion* leading and *Carnarvon* bringing up the rear, and the eight destroyers were spread in a screening arc across the line of advance, wing ships tailing back far enough to be on the flagship's beams; on the starboard side of the screen the wing ships were *Tuareg* and *Afghan*. It was an arrangement that made sense, since the Tribals were to be detached, with *Carnarvon*, after dark and after they'd all passed through the Strait. While the others raced westward to Heraklion, these three were to diverge north-westward and patrol a line twenty-five miles north of the evacuation port. Then they'd rendezvous with the main force north of Kaso at 0430, for the run south.

At 4.30 pm Tom Overton had come up to confer with Tyler, who was officer of the watch for the first dog, about some change in the watchkeeping roster. Conference over, he'd drifted across to the side of the bridge and begun to fill a pipe. Jack went to join him: it was the first time he'd seen Overton today when there hadn't been other people hanging around.

Overton looked up at him. 'May this peace and quiet last, eh?'

'Fat chance . . . Tom, I – er – went ashore last evening, to get some charts. Happened to find myself near a telephone, with a few minutes to spare, so—'

'Tickled to hear from you, was she?'

'Her husband was there with her.'

'Crikey!' The pipe-stuffing stopped for a moment. 'Who did you tell him you were? You should always have some yarn ready, you know.'

'You aren't surprised, then.'

'How d'you mean?'

'You knew she had a husband, didn't you?'

'My dear boy, most of them do have. I suppose if I'd *thought* about it—'

Bell-Reid shot a hard look at the pair of them as he stalked past, heading towards Napier in the front of the bridge. 'Shall we close the hands up, sir?'

'I suppose we should.' Howard Napier lowered his glasses, and checked the time. Now he was looking round for his navigator . . . 'How far are we from the Kaso Strait, pilot?'

'About – ninety miles, sir.'

'We *had* better, then.' He nodded to his second-in-command. 'Close 'em up, please, John.'

Bell-Reid swung round: 'Bugler! Sound action stations!'

Just before five o'clock the red flag ran up to *Orion*'s yardarm, and within half a minute the cruisers were doing a controlled AA shoot at a flight of three Italian high-level bombers. Their pilots seemed more interested in survival than in getting their bombs anywhere near the ships: as the last bomb splashed into an area of unoccupied salt water, Drisdale spread his arms horizontally and intoned, 'Wide . . .'

Despite his appearance of deep gloom, Drisdale had been *Masai*'s resident comedian. So Dalgleish said.

'Should we remain closed up, sir?'

'Until dark, yes,' Nick answered Dalgleish over the telephone to the ACP. 'Better lay on action messing, for supper.'

To port, *Orion* was a handsome sight. Low, powerful-looking with that single wide-based funnel, four-inch AA batteries abreast it, main armament of six-inch turrets fore and aft. *Ajax*, famous for her part in cornering the *Admiral Graf Spee* at the battle of the Plate in December 1939, was *Orion*'s duplicate. Astern of her came *Dido*, elegant-looking with the two slightly raked funnels and the tier of three for'ard turrets, two more aft. By contrast *Carnarvon*, plugging along behind those three, had a decidedly old-fashioned look about her. But her engineers seemed to have done a thorough job in record time on those recently defective engines of hers. Nick saw tin hats in her bridge, in place of white cap-covers: so she too was staying closed-up at action stations.

'Alarm starboard! Green four-oh – Stukas!'

'Red flag, Yeoman!'

But *Tuareg* hadn't beaten the flagship to it: *Orion*'s red warning signal had shot up just at that moment. All the fleet's guns swinging round and lifting . . .

'*There*, lad!'

Mr Walsh yelled it as he grabbed the killick torpedoman's shoulder, pulling him round and at the same time pointing aft – at a single Me 109 coming at them from astern at wavetop height, now rocketing upwards to sweep over *Afghan* with its guns flaming: *Tuareg* next in line on that same flight-path . . . Overhead, the rising note of a Stuka's siren suggested that a co-ordinated attack might be developing. The torpedoman bent his knees, settled the stocks of the twin Vickers against his shoulders, took aim: the Messerschmitt was coming straight towards the ship, so there was no deflection. Walsh had shown the other Vickers gunner the target: he was a torpedoman too, and he was on it, whipping round and sighting and opening fire in one swift movement. Two double streams of tracer were flying at the fighter's nose, and point-fives joining in now too from farther for'ard. The German didn't like it, he was banking away, twisting his plane to starboard, dragging it up and round with flames visible inside it then gushing out, streaming right to the tail with the black cross on it: the Messerschmitt went over on its back before it hit the sea, sea leaping in a long, low, moving fountain as it skidded in upside-down. Cheering from the guns' crews aft: and the pompoms were thundering at the Stuka – which was pulling out high, letting its bomb go wide. But the leading torpedoman was pointing, his mouth open as he shouted – inaudibly, the words drowned in noise. Mr Walsh saw what he was pointing at: a bomber going down nearly vertically at the destroyer *Imperial*, out ahead. She was under helm, and nearby ships were barraging to keep the attacker high: *Imperial* had no pompoms, only point-fives. The Stuka pilot seemed to know it and to be taking advantage of it, plummeting down through the canopy of shellbursts – still diving . . .

They saw the bomb detach itself: and the Stuka levelling, not far above the sea's brilliant blue. The bomb burst just about alongside its target: a mountain of sea shooting up right against *Imperial*'s stern. Almost for sure, she'd be stopped by that one . . . But she hadn't even faltered. The waterspout had crashed down across her afterpart and she'd steamed on out of it. Mr Walsh shouted in Dalgleish's ear, ' 'ighly adjacent, that was!' He was scanning the sky again, getting ready for the next attacker.

Nick checked the time: an hour had passed since *Imperial* had survived her near-miss, and the force was still intact, well inside the Kaso Strait and with land in clear sight to port. They were up to schedule, maintaining the ordered speed of advance under constant, concentrated attack. It was astonishing, he thought, that ships could be bombed so determinedly for so long and that none of them should be hit: should *yet have been* hit . . .

'Port fifteen.'

Attending to business: turning towards the direction of a Stuka's dive, and looking all ways at once. It was rather like a game of squash, except that if you missed a squash-ball it didn't kill you.

'Midships.'

The attack had been going on for three hours now. Another half-hour and the sun would be sliding down behind the Cretan mountains. Thirty minutes, and several bombs per minute . . . The Stuka was hidden in shellbursts: emerging now, yellow snout bright with the sun's glint on it. He watched it closely and at the same time retained a peripheral awareness of the possibility of being jumped on simultaneously from another direction. The Stuka boys had evidently been putting their cropped heads together, planning synchronized attacks; he'd seen it half a dozen times in the last hour.

Bomb releasing *now* . . .

'Stop starboard. Starboard twenty-five.'

Spin her away from it: and with a quick glance round at sealevel for the positions of other ships, all of them dodging bombs. *Tuareg*'s thumped in thirty yards to port, close enough

398

to feel the jar of its explosion through the wood grating under his feet.

'Midships. Half ahead both engines.'

'Midships, sir. Half ahead both, sir . . . Wheel's amidships, sir . . .'

Lilting tone: a voicepipe litany. Nick told him, 'Port fifteen. Steer three-two-five.'

The sky over the cruisers was filthy-grey with shellbursts. High up and to the west, flying north, he saw the group of Ju88s which had attacked from astern a few minutes ago. Their bombs had gone down like rain on the other side of the cruisers, a long grove of splashes with the last ones rising only a short distance astern of the destroyers in the centre of the screen. Perhaps one small miscalculation – of wind or drift – had made the difference between that clear miss and having all four cruisers hit or near-missed. Pilots had problems, no doubt, but from down here it looked as if it ought to be so easy . . . 'Starboard twenty.'

He was pleased with his ship's gunnery performance. Separating the control of the guns was paying off, in terms of flexibility, and also he'd been impressed by the way they all united, as if all the gunners' brains were connected telepathically, when one particular attack looked more threatening than others.

'Midships.'

It left him free to concentrate on handling the ship . . . '*What?*'

Drisdale repeated, '88s coming up astern, sir!'

He nodded, concentrating on this Stuka. In any case you couldn't dodge the high-level attackers as you could the point-blank rushes: luckily they weren't as accurate in their aim, either. The 88s were getting round astern of the northward-moving force and attacking on their homeward course towards Crete – or Greece, wherever their base was . . . The sun was inching down: and the Scarpanto Stuka base was now less than forty miles away. Wouldn't it be shaming for the arrogant, murderous bastards to have so many ducks waddling through their backyard and not be able to hit a single one of them?

Don't count on it, he thought. Still fifteen or twenty minutes of light, or partial light, left.

'Port twenty-five.'

'Port twenty-five, sir . . . Twenty-five of port wheel on, sir!'

Bomb on its way down. One single Stuka, about an hour ago, had let go five small bombs from one dive. An experiment, presumably, that hadn't come to anything. Several times he'd seen two bombs, though, two splashes, probably two 500-pounders instead of the more usual 1,000-pounder. Splash going up now, nicely clear to starboard; he called down for the rudder to be centred, then shot a glance at the compass to see how far round he'd come: then, looking up, he saw one of Drisdale's 88s trailing black smoke like a scar across the sun.

Within a few minutes the lower rim of that sun would touch the mountain peaks. Stukas were still coming up from the Scarpanto direction, perhaps desperate for last-minute success. At this moment three were diving on the cruisers: on *Orion*. Gunfire increasing, shellbursts thickening over the centre: he took his eyes off it, aware of the danger of looking at one sector for too long, and glanced round for nearer threats. The sky was colouring as the sun sank and the blackness of the mountains made them seem to lean out across the sea: there was violet growing, and deep blue, a whole spread of colours deepening and blending, flooding outwards; over the other horizon, the Scarpanto side, first stars were pinpricks in a darkening sky. The colours growing out from behind the mountains were mixed rose-pink, gold and violet. Gunfire was at a peak again, the Stukas' sirens screaming through it, and the action was all concentrated in the centre, against the garish backdrop. Nick swung around with his glasses trained to starboard, swept to the right into dimmer, opalescent light that was fading and at the same time reflecting – from the sea's surface probably, the image refracted in layers of warm air – a distillation of the colour in the west: through it, *in* it, he saw the Savoias, five or six of them, sneaking in towards the ships like big wave-hopping moths.

'Alarm starboard – torpedo bombers, green nine-oh!'

He added, for Houston's benefit, 'Flying right to left, Harry, angle of sight zero—'

'Director target! Red barrage—'

'Starboard twenty-five.' The guns were swinging around and depressing at the same time as layers and trainers followed the pointers in their dials. Clang of the fire-gongs: the four-sevens flamed and crashed, the amount of flash showing how dark it was getting suddenly. This turn towards the bombers would shut X and Y guns out of the action but it would also help to avoid any torpedoes which the Italians might already have dropped. He saw one Savoia pulling upwards and banking, sheering away to the left and its torpedo dropping very much askew: to the right a flare-up, one plane hit: *Afghan*, astern, had joined in, and that burning plane had flopped into the sea . . . 'Midships.'

'Midships, sir . . . Wheel's amidships, sir.' Gun-flashes and shell-bursts were bright now as night closed in. A fire burning on the sea was the wreckage of that Savoia: the attack had been broken up and the others had disappeared, but they might be circling for another attempt in some other sector and Nick had a signalman flashing to the flagship, *Savoia bombers attacked with torpedoes and some may still be with us*. Over the rapid click-clacking of the signal lamp he heard Houston's order to the guns, 'Check, check, check!' A sudden silence had allowed him to hear it – the Aldis lamp, and Houston's voice from the tower carrying down the voicepipe. No targets, then: it was bewildering, after so long. He said into the voicepipe, 'Port twenty', and the yeoman reported, 'Message passed to *Orion*, sir.'

The wind was right ahead, on this course. Spray swept over constantly, whipping like hail over the glass wind-deflector on the leading edge of *Tuareg*'s bridge; binoculars needed frequent wiping.

Ajax had been near-missed and damaged in that last Stuka effort against the cruisers. She'd reported damage that included a fire and twenty men wounded, and Admiral Rawlings had detached her with orders to return to Alexandria.

Now it was 2200, 10 pm. Half an hour ago *Orion* and *Dido* and the other six destroyers had increased to twenty-nine knots without zigzag and headed west for Heraklion; *Carnarvon* had turned off on to a course of 281 degrees, maintaining revolutions for twenty-three knots, and *Tuareg* and *Afghan* had taken station thirty degrees on her starboard and port bows respectively.

Nick asked Drisdale, 'What time should we raise Ovo island?'

'About 2300, sir. It'll be abeam at a quarter past.'

'And the turning spot?'

'Near as dammit 1 am, sir.'

Pretty well what his own mental arithmetic had already suggested. If it hadn't been, he'd have checked Drisdale's figures. There was to be a small adjustment of course when they passed Ovo island, in order to reach the ordered position of 35 degrees 45 north, 24 degrees 50 east; then they were to turn and patrol a line due eastward, which would cover the approaches to Heraklion from the Milos direction. Then at 2 am they'd turn south-east,

401

eventually rejoining the rest of the force at about four-thirty just north of the Kaso Strait.

Presumably some Intelligence source had suggested that interference by light surface forces was to be expected. The Italians certainly *had* had some destroyers at Milos – which was where they'd mustered those caïque-borne invasion forces – and MAS-boats in the Dodecanese, Scarpanto and elsewhere. With the evacuation starting, they *might* decide this was the time for some offensive action – such as catching *Orion* and company speeding eastward, loaded with battle-weary troops.

Tuareg and *Afghan* were primarily the patrolling force. *Carnarvon* would have been added to the party in case they failed to link up with the main force before daylight; then they'd have the AA cruiser's guns to protect them, and some chance of getting through. And *Carnarvon*'s limited speed would also have earmarked her for this job: she couldn't have kept up with the others on their fast passage from Kaso to Heraklion and back.

Ajax's departure wouldn't affect the operation much, Nick thought. 4,500 men, which was the maximum number of troops expected to be there for lifting, could easily be fitted into two cruisers and six destroyers. Rawlings would miss *Ajax*'s firepower when the air attacks began again in the morning, but that was about all; the admiral had been right to disembarrass himself of a lame duck at this early stage, because the one thing the evacuation force could not afford was to be slowed down.

2345: the main force would have reached Heraklion and the first ships ought to be inside the little port by now. 2330 had been the estimated time of arrival, based on departure from Cape Sidaro after the passage through the Kaso Strait. Jack Everard came up from the chart, and answered a question Napier had put to him half a minute ago: 'Exactly thirty miles to go, sir.'

Thirty miles to the western end of their patrol line, to the point where they'd change course to east. At this moment, Heraklion was twenty miles to the south: and those thirty miles, at twenty-three knots, would be covered in one hour and a little over twenty minutes. They'd been intended to reach the turning point at 0100, so in fact they were about twelve minutes astern of station.

It didn't much matter, Jack supposed. And just as well it didn't, because there'd have been no question of speeding up. According to Tom Overton there'd been a decidedly frosty exchange between

Napier and his engineer commander on the subject of maintaining these revs all through the night – all through tomorrow as well, come to that. In Alexandria, Buchanan had agreed that there was no reason to expect problems now; he'd been proud of the way his staff had coped with the earlier difficulties, and confident the repairs would hold out. Napier had reported accordingly, and *Carnarvon* had therefore been included in the operation. But a short while ago Buchanan had started worrying again and brought his worries to the captain, who had – according to Overton – blown his top. Buchanan had been sent off with a flea in his ear and instructions to look after his own problems.

Jack had been down in the plot, clearing up Midshipman Brighouse's inept attempt at working out some earlier star-sights; Overton had been on the bridge when he'd come back to it.

He hadn't reopened the subject of Gabrielle: and Overton had seemed relieved that he hadn't. It was in his mind all the time, though . . . Morally, there was no doubt what he ought to do: and the urge to cut adrift wasn't just a moral thing either, it was the fact of having been deceived, tricked into this. And that telephone call: the husband unsuspecting in the background and the women laughing – worst of all, making him a party to that laughter. Unless he cut loose, he *would* be a party to it.

But – not see her? Ashore in Alex in a week's time would he be capable of not calling her?

Carnarvon ploughed on, deeper into the black Aegean.

'Captain, sir . . .'

He was awake at once, hearing Dalgleish telling him that it was ten minutes past two and that they were coming up for the next alteration of course.

'Right. Thank you.'

'Kye, sir. Just common or garden, I'm afraid.'

'Can't always be lucky, can we?'

He'd dreamt he'd had a letter from Fiona; it was disappointing now to know it had been a dream. He sipped his cocoa and thought about their position now, the distances and the timing of the rendezvous with Rawlings' ships down near Kaso before daylight.

They'd reached the north-western limit of the sweep at thirteen minutes past one, and altered course to 090 degrees, in accordance with operation orders. At two-fifteen, by which time they'd have been steaming due east for an hour, they'd be coming round two

403

points to starboard for the two-hour leg down to Kaso. According to the orders there was supposed to be some fighter cover over the Kaso area at 0530: but Nick thought he'd believe that when he saw it. Long-range fighters from the desert, they'd have to be; or imaginary ones from never-never land.

Coming to the end of the west-east patrol line didn't mean the screening job was finished. All the way down to Kaso they'd still be to the north of the evacuation force, covering it against surface raiders.

Dalgleish called suddenly, 'Signalman!'

'Aye, sir . . .'

Dalgleish told Nick, who still had his nose in the cocoa mug, '*Carnarvon*'s flashing, sir.'

That blue lamp would be winking out the order for the change of course. When they'd turned, Nick thought, he'd go back to sleep.

A thump in the port side of *Carnarvon*'s bridge was a signal arriving up the tube. Petty Officer Tomkins, yeoman of the watch, retrieved it and took it to the hooded signal table.

He read it out to Napier. Flag Officer Force B was announcing that the Kaso rendezvous was to be delayed by one hour, from 0430 to 0530.

Napier gave it a moment's thought. Then he asked, 'To what speed can we reduce now, pilot, and keep that rendezvous?'

About seventeen or eighteen, Jack guessed, as he went to the chart to check on it. He also guessed that the question of rpm and Buchanan's fears must have been worrying Napier all this time. At the chart table, he found they could come down to sixteen knots, and he reported this to Napier.

'Yeoman. Make to the destroyers, *Speed sixteen*.'

Probably it was taking longer than the admiral had expected to embark the troops. The ones ready for embarkation when the force had arrived would be taken aboard fast enough, but the soldiers actually holding the perimeter against the surrounding Germans would only be able to slip away in small groups, a few at a time. And it was possible, Jack guessed, that with the wind as strong as it was the cruisers might not have been able to get inside that very small harbour; then they'd have to lie off while the destroyers ferried soldiers out to them.

Napier cut into his thoughts: 'You'd better get some sleep, pilot.'

*   *   *

404

At four-eleven, Jack woke with the bridge messenger bawling at him from the chartroom door, 'Captain wants you on the bridge, sir!' Flinging himself off the settee, he realized that the ship was rolling – which she hadn't been when he'd turned in – and also, judging by the vibration, that she was again doing something more than twenty knots. His first thought was that perhaps they'd run into some Italians and turned to engage or chase them: but there'd have been an action alarm, in that case . . . He was on the bridge within seconds: Napier told him, 'We're on two-four-five, pilot, twenty-three knots. Altered three minutes ago. You'll see some signals on the log. Get an up-to-date DR on, will you?'

PO Hillier gave him the signal log, and he took it with him to the chart table. The first thing was to establish the dead-reckoning position and mark on the new course, extending it south-westward. Then, to find out what it was all about.

The signals told the story clearly enough. One: *Imperial*'s steering had failed: she'd run amuck, just before 4 am. A total breakdown. *Imperial* was the destroyer who'd been near-missed last evening and seemed none the worse for it, he remembered. When her rudder had jammed, Rawlings' ships with the troops from Heraklion on board had been steering east at twenty-nine knots. Two: *Hotspur* had been ordered to take off *Imperial*'s crew and sink her. Admiral Rawlings was continuing eastward: with his ships full of troops he'd have no option. But he'd reduced speed, so that *Hotspur* should catch him up later – with any luck, before daylight. Three: *Carnarvon* and the Tribals were steering south-westward now to provide cover to *Hotspur* as she withdrew alone, with two ships' companies and an unspecified number of troops on board.

Following that misfortune, it made good sense. But at about four-thirty, when he was fiddling around with courses and distances at the chart, Jack saw that *Carnarvon* and her destroyers had no hope at all now of getting through the Kaso narrows before dawn. The same of course applied to *Hotspur*. There'd been that earlier delay of one hour, and now another ninety minutes had been lost.

At 0446 the order came to alter course and withdraw towards Kaso. *Hotspur* had torpedoed *Imperial*, and was on her way. There was to be a rendezvous two and a half miles north of the Yanisades lighthouse at 0545.

'Course, pilot?'

He was at the chart, getting it . . . 'One-oh-two, sir.'

Napier gave Hillier, the yeoman, a course-alteration signal for the destroyers.

At twenty-three knots, by 0545 they'd be several miles short of the rendezvous position. The run to it was twenty-five miles, and it was now 0450. They'd be three or four miles short. Jack reported this to Napier; the captain nodded, but did nothing about calling for more speed. He had accepted, right from the beginning, Buchanan's prognostication that if he exceeded revs for twenty-three knots she'd almost certainly bust a gut.

Now, they'd be entering the Kaso Strait at dawn. It wasn't good, but it was less bad than it had looked a short while ago – being caught well this side of the bolt-hole. And if the promised air-cover should by chance materialize, all might yet be well. In fact it would be absolutely marvellous . . . Jack put the time of the alteration, and a reading of the Chernikeeff log, in his notebook. The time, as *Carnarvon*'s wheel went over, was 0452.

At 0503, the port engine stopped.

CHAPTER 10

Light grew like a cancer in the east. Guns were cocked up, trained towards that brightness: from the destroyers' bridges binoculars swept horizon and sky: on the gun platforms men in tin hats, lifebelts and anti-flash gear had their eyes fixed on the coming of a day that no one wanted. *Carnarvon* was struggling eastward at less than seven knots, on one engine and carrying enough rudder to counter the single-screw operation. She was a cripple, painfully dragging herself across the sea: you could think of a mouse being played with by a cat, with no chance of escape but still trying to get away, following blind instinct but aware of the imminence of a savage clawing. Waiting for the cat . . .

There was a faint chance of escape, perhaps, if they got that engine going. At any minute her engineers might work the miracle: after three-quarters of an hour of 'any minute now . . .' The Tribals zigzagged, using their Asdics and watching the sky, that streaky silver leaking up from behind a mauve horizon. Twenty-eight miles eastward, according to Drisdale's calculations, the rest of Force B would be just about entering the Kaso Strait, and *Hotspur* would be rejoining, panting up from astern into the shelter of the cruisers' guns.

Drisdale murmured, with his glasses on *Carnarvon*, 'Glad I'm not a plumber.' By 'plumber' he meant engineer; Nick had glanced at him and away again, not understanding what else he meant. Drisdale added, 'Thinking of *her* blokes. Slaving away at that engine, with everyone else cursing at 'em to get a bloody wriggle on—'

'Red flag on *Carnarvon*!'

Ashcourt had reported it. Instinctively you looked for a threat in the east, where both the sunrise and Scarpanto were. All Nick could see in that sector was an irritatingly *pretty* sky.

'Alarm port, red seven-oh, 88s!'

'Starboard fifteen.' To get closer to the cruiser. 'One-four-two revolutions.' Fifteen knots, that would give him. He put his glasses up and found the bombers: there were two flights each of four aircraft, flying on a course of about 130 degrees at something like 5,000 feet. He told Houston, up the voicepipe to the tower, 'Open fire when you're ready.'

When they're in range, he'd meant; but if they held on as they were going they'd pass about a mile astern. Going somewhere else, perhaps. Could be: that course would bring them over the Kaso Strait, if they held to it . . . But one flight of four was veering off, swinging away to port. Nick told CPO Habgood, 'Midships. Steer one-double-oh.' Then, glancing round at Ashcourt, 'Keep your eyes peeled on the sun while I watch this lot.'

'Aye aye, sir.'

Tone normal: eyes slightly more expressive. Ashcourt had had enough experience of battle recently, of this kind of battle, to realize they'd be very, very lucky now to get away intact. It wasn't just a threat from those four bombers, or from those eight, but from the hundreds that would be coming very soon. The ships had been spotted – which had been inevitable, but it had happened sooner than it need have – and one of them was lame, and the Stuka base was only sixty miles away.

You could see the land clearly now, from south-east to south-west, and the sun's first rays were spotlighting the higher inland peaks. The nearest bit of coastline was a promontory called Spinalonga, ten miles away. One lot of 88s seemed to be going straight on, still, while the other four aircraft circled round astern: if they kept circling they'd be coming up on the port beam in a minute.

'Alarm ahead – Stukas! Right of the sun—'

'All guns follow director. A and B with red barrage – load, load, load!'

The 88s were coming up on the port quarter in a loose straggle and in shallow dives: ahead, the Stukas were above the sun and hard to see. Nick heard the fire-gongs from down for'ard as Houston launched an up-sun barrage from A and B guns, leaving X and Y in the control of PO Wellbeloved from the open-topped HA director-rangefinder up behind him. All noise now . . . Stooping near the voicepipe with his eyes slitted against the glare, watching for Stukas attacking, he heard *Carnarvon*'s guns and

408

Afghan's: then Ashcourt's noise-piercing yell, 'Alarm port! Port quarter – Messerschmitts!' Nick had the ACP telephone – fumbling it as he still watched for Stukas . . . 'Port quarter, Messerschmitts!' The racket of a fighter's engine confirmed it: an Me 110 out of nowhere, blasting across ahead and banking round to starboard towards the cruiser: and others were over her already in swallow-like swooping rushes, one bomb just short then one hitting near the base of the foremost funnel: there'd been a flash and a burst of smoke and debris and now a plume of smoke trailing back. Stukas coming now – and *they*, like the Messerschmitt fighter-bombers, were also going for *Carnarvon*. She'd been hit again, for'ard, and the last of the Messerschmitts had straffed her bridge with its guns. Stukas' sirens swelled in triumph over the bedlam of gunfire. A spout of sea rising close to the cruiser's quarter was a bomb from an 88: she seemed to stagger as a second struck her, right aft. The raised four-inch gun-deck amidships – the gun-mounting on it – had been blown clean out of her in the blast of yet another hit; and she was on fire aft, more bomb-spouts rising on the far side of her, in the sea but near enough to hurt. One Stuka was diving steeply at her, another close behind it, both sirens screaming: the first one's bomb tumbling clear, shining as it turned over in what looked like slow motion with the new day's brilliance flashing on its fins. New day dawning in a rush of disaster, precipitate and stunning, a nightmare bathed in sunrise, drowned in noise. *Carnarvon* lay stopped, stricken, like a boxer overwhelmed before anyone had heard the bell for the new round: you had an urge to appeal to some non-existent referee, ask for a new start . . .

'I'll see if I can find him, sir.' Jack heard himself shout it over the thunder of guns and the howl of Stuka sirens. Napier looked round with a suggestion of a smile that was noticeable because this wasn't much of a time for smiling. He'd nodded. *Carnarvon* was on fire and had some flooding on the port side aft, several other areas of damage below and above decks, and Stukas still swarming over. It was eight or ten minutes since the first bomb had hit.

It was Bell-Reid, his second-in-command, whom Napier wanted found. He'd glanced round, as Jack moved away: 'Clear the bridge!'

There was a general movement to obey: look-outs, signal staff, messengers. Willy Irvine nodded at Midshipman Wesley: 'Go on, Mid.' Jack stopped at the plot voicepipe to tell young Brighouse to clear out too; going on aft to the ladder he found himself joined by McCowan, Clutterbuck, Midshipman Burk and the rest of the director's and ADP's crews, who'd been ordered down when the power circuits had failed. Clutterbuck shouted in Jack's ear, 'Last man over the side's a sissy!' Pompoms and point-fives roaring: Jack hurried on down into the ship, and Napier, glancing behind him into the near-empty bridge, found Able Seaman Noble, his servant, still standing there.

'Away you go, Noble!'

'Ready when you are, sir.'

Napier told him, 'I'm waiting for news from the commander. You carry on, now.'

'All the same to you, sir, I'd as soon as—'

Both men staggered as the ship lurched from an explosion. You could hear the rising shriek of another diving Stuka. Noble shouted, 'Oughter blow up your lifebelt, sir.' Pointing at Napier's dark blue covered Mae West. Napier looked down at it and nodded, and one hand moved to free the inflation tube. The other gestured brusquely: 'Off the bridge, Noble. Do what you're bloody well told, will you?'

Jack had gone down two ladders: to the lower bridge, then to the level of the for'ard gundeck. Now another, to the foc'sl deck: and another still, to the upper deck but under cover, inside the foc'sl deck's shelter. It felt as if he was forcing himself to keep on going down. Men were mustering in here by divisions, here and up for'ard in the seamen's messdeck; until the order came to abandon ship, it was healthier to be under cover. Down again: the PMO and the younger doctor, Holloway, were using the lower-deck crew space as a dressing-station and operating theatre. There'd been casualties among ammo-supply and damage-control parties, and there were sights one tried not to look at; on the upper ladders Jack had heard McCowan say that two of the four-inch guns' crews had been wiped out.

Several minutes ago Napier had given the order to prepare to abandon ship, but he'd been unable to contact the commander, Bell-Reid, who'd gone down earlier to visit various trouble spots and should have reported over the sound-powered telephone from the lower steering position. That was on the platform deck, almost in the bottom of the ship and vertically below the bridge. In the lower deck, emergency lanterns glowed, hoses had been run out and men were struggling to manoeuvre stretchers up through hatches,

410

through thickening smoke and the reek of fire, the ship's compartments booming and shuddering to bomb-explosions in the sea around her. Like a dark, noisy, enclosing cavern. Damage-control parties were getting out, getting up towards the air and daylight: they'd been told to, with the stand-by to abandon order. Buchanan, the engineer commander, was on his way up to report to Napier; Jack asked him if he'd seen Bell-Reid, and he had not. When the commander had gone down, *Carnarvon* hadn't been in quite as hopeless a state as she was now; the only fire inside her then had been the one right aft, and Buchanan had still been trying to get her engines going. While there'd been that degree of hope, plus the expectation of getting her under control in emergency steering control, there'd been no talk of abandoning her. Everything had got much worse very quickly: in something like six minutes she'd been hit by four more bombs, there'd been an explosion in No. 1 boiler-room, the steering-gear compartment right aft had been wrecked and flooded, and a fire somewhere between No. 2 boiler-room and the for'ard engine-room was threatening the midships four-inch magazine. That magazine should have been flooded by now, but no report had reached the bridge.

On one of the ladders, Jack met a stoker petty officer named Berwick. He asked him if he'd seen the commander anywhere.

'Can't say I have, sir.'

'He was supposed to be going down to the lower steering position, I believe.'

'Ah, but we shut it off, sir, that section . . . *Christ*, then—'

'Why did you—'

'Fire, sir, very fierce, started in the LP supply room – so the 'atch over that lobby—'

'He may be down there.' Nightmare, suddenly. But real: and he was in it. With the peculiar feeling that he was down here on his own orders, his own victim . . . 'Listen, Spo – if we can't open that hatch, we could get to him from aft along the lower passage. With a couple of hoses going to hold the fire back—'

'What's the fuss, Everard?'

Commander Bell-Reid: and he had his doggie, OD Webster, trotting faithfully at his heels. No need for the rescue attempt, then: relief was huge. The stoker PO actually laughed with the relief of it: Bell-Reid glared at him, and Jack explained, 'We thought you'd been shut in, sir, in the lower steering position. We were working out how to try to get you out.'

411

'Very civil of you.' Bell-Reid nodded. 'Thanks. But where the hell's Overton, d'you know?'

'Afraid I don't—'

'Mr Overton's dead, sir.' Berwick added no detail. Jack gave Bell-Reid the message he'd come down to deliver: 'The captain's anxious for you to get in touch, sir. He sent me to find you. He's ordered stand by to abandon ship, and—'

'I know *that*, damn it.' But with telephone circuits mostly dead it was hard to know who knew what. Bell-Reid had spotted someone he wanted: he shouted, 'Mr Brassey!'

Brassey was a warrant officer, gunner. A scrawny man with skin like yellow parchment; he looked now as if he'd just been down a coal-mine. Bell-Reid asked him, 'Is the bloody thing flooded now or isn't it?'

'What I'm after, sir. Should 'a been, but I just got the buzz there's lads in there wounded.'

'Inside the magazine?'

'I dunno, sir, but that's what I 'eard. If it's right I could use some 'elp.'

'How did you hear it?'

'Young Clark, sir. He's a good 'and but he was – well, shook up. And he couldn't shift 'em, not on his own. Weren't making all that much sense like, sir.'

Bell-Reid looked at Jack.

'Give Mr Brassey some support, Everard?'

He nodded. 'Aye aye, sir.'

It hadn't been his own choice, this time.

'There's your help, Mr Brassey. Get it flooded double quick. If it blows up she'll go down like a stone before we've got the wounded out of her. Petty Officer Berwick here'd like to go along too, I expect.'

How men might have been wounded in a magazine deep inside the ship, without the magazine itself having exploded, was a mystery. But with fires near it, it did have to be flooded, obviously . . . 'Here, Everard!' Bell-Reid called him back, handed him a box; there was a hypodermic in it and a flask of some fluid. 'Morphine. Up to that mark *there* is one effective dose to kill pain. All right?'

He nodded, stuffed it inside his shirt so he'd have his hands free. Blundering aft through smoke, darkness and the noises of the tortured, dying ship. *Sinking* ship. Well, not yet: there *might* be time to get down there, do whatever had to be done and get back

412

up again. *Don't think, just do it* . . . The only torch they had was Mr Brassey's: they were three decks down and moving aft along a passage that ran down the ship's side – the starboard, higher side – flanking the two boiler-rooms and engine-rooms. It was narrow, and with the list on her the deck slanted so that their shoulders bumped along the inboard bulkhead as they moved from one watertight door to the next, having to stop to open each one and then shut it again behind them. The farther aft they got the hotter and smokier it was: it was the eye-watering, lung-racking reek of burning paint, corticene, rubber. The bulkhead on the left, the inboard one, was hot to the touch. Behind him, Berwick called out something about smoke-helmets in the damage-control headquarters beside the engineers' store – *if* the damage-control parties hadn't taken them all up top with them when they'd evacuated. But that meant lower deck, back aft. There was a transverse bulkhead with the wardroom and officers' cabins aft of it, warrant officers' mess and gunroom – the gunroom being an unusual feature in a cruiser of this class – this side of it, and various offices and stores for'ard of that before you came to the marines' messdeck. Smoke-helmets were going to be a necessity: Jack already had a wadded handkerchief – cotton-waste, Berwick had – to breathe through, and they were going to have to get right inside the magazine, which extended down into the hold and had the seat of the fire somewhere close to it. The noise of the guns was muted this far down, but each near-missing bomb was like a kick in the head.

Carnarvon lurched suddenly, just as they were getting through a door: it was as if there'd been a big shift in ballast that had increased the list to port, and the heavy door swung back on the gunner. Brassey cursing: the stoker PO shouted, 'Now then, 'old steady there, old girl!' Keeping his own spirits up . . . A bulkhead had gone, probably, letting sea flood into another section of the stern. For one blind moment Jack did let himself think about it, *feel* it: the hatches and ladders overhead, hatches slamming and ladders twisting under distorting strain as one end of her filled and the sea rushed thundering through: he knew what it looked like from outside, but here he was *in* it: he could have let his nerve go, turned and made a break for it: but he'd allowed himself that flash of imagination deliberately, to prove to himself he *could* master it, and he'd already wrenched his mind to another area – to the fact that there were wounded men down here, helpless men who'd drown like kittens in a sack if they weren't brought out. Behind it

413

was a memory – it would last him all his life – of the Dutch transport *Gelderland*, with men waving from her scuttles as she sank. He'd regained purpose, balance, a sense of direction and of urgency outweighing fear. Breathless still, and shaking inside, but it was the answer, the antidote to fear, having purpose and having to concentrate on the detail of achieving it: it enabled you to tolerate the fear, live with it.

Through what seemed like hours . . .

They got two wounded men. Flash or blast – Mr Brassey reckoned – had passed down the shell-hoist from the midships four-inch mounting to the ammo lobby twenty-five feet below it. A single shell had exploded in there, probably in the arms of the handler. It had blown that one man to pieces, plastering him over the lobby's bulkheads, and badly wounded two others inside the magazine. One had had an arm torn off and one side of his head scalped to the bone, the other multiple punctures and broken ribs, perhaps lethal internal injuries. The morphine acted quickly, but getting them up and out of the magazine and then out of the flat up to the next deck wasn't easy. It was greenhouse-hot, stifling, the deckheads raining condensation. The fire had reached the battery rooms, and the switchboard room was a furnace behind its clipped steel door. The way up from this section was by a vertical steel ladder to an armoured, watertight hatch in the deck above: up there, they were above the edges of the fire. Berwick had left a hose running, to safeguard the line of retreat; the canvas of the hose was steaming from the deck's heat and the water might have been gushing from a hot tap. But worst of all, they found that the fire had broken through on the starboard side, upwards from below to this higher level: the realization that there'd be no getting back the way they'd come hit all three of them at about the same moment.

Berwick had opened the magazine flood-valves: she wouldn't blow up now, not from *this* cause: and now they'd got the two wounded men up, dumped them for a moment in a swirl of hot water that reddened around them. Like corpses: and by flickering yellow torchlight their rescuers looked to each other like ghouls: bloodstained, sweating, filthy. Bombs were still exploding and close-range weapons were in action, but it sounded as if all the four-inch had been knocked out. Or no ammunition getting to them now. Jack took Brassey's arm and tilted the torch upwards so its light would shine on the underside of the big armoured hatch at the top of the next ladder: there was a manhole-size smaller hatch

414

in its centre, oval-shaped and held shut by the usual heavy clips. Steel an inch thick. Brassey grunted, '*You're* a big bastard, Spo.' Berwick went up the ladder, Brassey shining the torch up past him at the hatch. He got two of the clips off: then the third wouldn't budge as easily. Jack thought, watching upwards, *It's got to . . .* Berwick was straining at it now, using all his weight and grunting with the effort: he was braced with his feet well apart on the ladder, shoulders bunched, both fists locked on the handle of the clip. He was a very powerfully built man: Jack knew that if he couldn't move it neither he nor Brassey need even try.

'Sledge-'ammer.' Panting, chest heaving, Berwick stared down into the torch beam. The ship rang from an explosion for'ard. She'd go – they all knew it – at any moment: there'd be a movement, a sudden shift in her angle in the water, and she'd go in one swift slide. Berwick said, 'Won't do it wi'out a sledge.'

'Won't do it, then.'

Brassey stared at Jack. He looked like something dug up out of a wet grave. The stare dredged an alternative, the only one, out of Jack's mind.

'We'll have to try to get for'ard up the port side.'

The low side, where the flooding was. Berwick was clambering slowly down the ladder. Brassey growled, 'What if it's up to the fuckin' deckhead?'

The answer was, *Then we shan't get through.* There was incipient terror in his mind but he had a hatch jammed shut on that too. And he'd told himself, while he'd been waiting in an agony for Berwick to open the other one, that you could drown outside the ship as easily as inside. All right, so in here you'd be trapped, you *were* trapped, but—

Shut up . . .

The ship had a pronounced list already, and she was deeper by the stern than she had been when they'd started this. That port-side passage *might* be flooded right to its roof, and even if it wasn't, if she tipped over by another degree or two when they were in it, they'd *stay* in it. But with that hatch stuck – you could guess, from bomb-damage up top when the mounting itself had been blown over the side and flash had penetrated to the magazine – there wasn't anything else left to try.

'We'll be lucky, you'll see.' He told them, 'Let's keep close together. Mr Brassey, you come in the middle with your torch. I'll go first with this chap.' The man with no left arm: the badge on the remaining one was a star with the letter 'C' in it, marking him as a cook.

'Might bloody fry before we're swimmin'.' Getting aft, out of this lobby, Brassey meant. Water swirled steaming on the deck. Water from the shattered stern would drown the fires eventually, but by that time it wouldn't do anyone any good, she'd be on her way to the sea-bed. Meanwhile in the wet area where flooding had approached the edges of the fire and where damage-control parties had had hoses running to cool decks and bulkheads, it was less fire than progressive scorching, smouldering, heat and fumes. A battle between elements, and the sea would win it: in the end, the sea won everything. They'd left the smoke-helmets one deck down, he realized . . . One-handed, he dipped his handkerchief in water and held it against the lower half of his face: he needed the other hand for steadying the cook, who was across his shoulder in a fireman's lift. He was soaked in blood from him already, and moving into greater heat, through the short midships passage between the two fan rooms and then turning right out of it, down the slope with really blistering heat radiating at him now, truly man-burning heat, and paintwork beginning to bubble on the bulkheads.

On the port side he found himself moving into water that was knee-deep, thigh-deep, then up to his waist, and over it: by the time he was actually in the passage and had turned for'ard it was around his chest and the man he was carrying had his face an inch from the darkly swirling surface. He was unconscious now: he might even, for all Jack knew, have been dead. The length of the passage they had to get through was something like a hundred feet, he thought, with four watertight doors which he'd have to open and Berwick shut again behind them. Brassey's torch-beam glinted on the water, throwing grotesque shadows on white-enamelled bulkheads as they shuffled forward: Jack burdened, sticky with the cook's blood, trying to keep his breathing slow and even, forging slowly through black water that deepened as they got nearer to the ship's middle section where her beam was widest. First door now. He spread his feet on the slanting deck, got the cook well balanced across his shoulder so as to have his hands free for working off the clips. If she listed one degree more, he thought, it would drown them. *If* . . . The knowledge was in Brassey's face too, close up beside him: yellow, blood-streaked, smoke-blackened here and there from some earlier excursion. Easing the last clip off, he felt the pressure

416

of the water on this side of the door and above its two-foot-high sill forcing it open, away from him. The weight on the clip made it hard to move and he had to hammer at it now with the heel of his hand: but if it had been a door that opened the other way, *this* way, nobody could ever have opened it against the pressure. *Christ*, he thought, *but we're lucky* . . . The clip banged up and the door crashed open: water was sluicing over the sill like a river over a weir, deluging into the next section, foaming and roaring. His ears ached from the rise in pressure: he shouted, turning and at the same time bracing himself against the flood's pull, 'Shut it quick as you can, Spo.' Berwick wouldn't manage it until the level on the other side had risen so that the flow slackened; by that time, with luck, it mightn't be at much more than sill-height. But the door had to be shut behind them: it would have been a relief to have simply hurried on, but you had to think of the risk of a new flood pouring up behind them from the stern. Air out, water in: if all these doors were open at once it could send her to the bottom. They were all through, and Berwick was leaning hard against the door, Brassey helping to support that other wounded rating. The flow of water was quite gentle already, and Jack hoped that at the next door it might even be contained by the sill.

'Next section ought to be dry, I'd say.'

'Like *I'd* say I oughter be 'ome in me bed.' Like a dog snarling, only it had been intended as a smile, Jack thought. He told him, 'You may not have noticed, Guns, but so far we're doing pretty well.'

Even in this section the water was only going to be about three feet deep at the higher end: so there'd be a little to spill over at that next door, but it was a terrific improvement. In fact it felt like a miracle. *Touch wood* . . . There wasn't any, only enamelled steel. *And don't get too cocky too soon*, he warned himself. She could still go in this next second: roll over, or there'd be a split, a suddenly collapsing bulkhead, the roar of inrushing sea: Berwick had the door shut and a clip on, and they began the wade to the next door, which was in the bulkhead that made the after end of No. 2 boiler-room. The water was about eighteen inches higher than the sill and there was that much to cascade through, but it amounted to nothing much, because it was pouring from a short section of passage into a long one. The air was cooler too. It was about forty-five feet to the next bulkhead, the one dividing the two boiler-rooms: he'd stopped there, waiting for the others, and the man on

417

his back said, 'Florrie – Christ's sake, Florrie luv, what y' *doing?*'
Brassey said, 'Takin' 'er knickers off, I shouldn't wonder.' He
cackled with laughter. 'Come on, Spo, let's get a bloody—'

A deep *boom* from aft: a shudder that ran right through her. He
felt the deck angle more as her stern settled. He was wrenching at
the clips: he shouted, 'Leave it open! *Run!*'

Still one more door.

This wasn't a cave they were trying to get out of: it felt like it but
it was a steel carcase hanging at the top of 350 fathoms of sea. And
it *would* go soon: you could sense or feel how it was just hanging,
how the next thing would be the stern-first slide, the fast and
sickening slipping-away you'd seen quite a few times now. He had
the clips off the last door, and it wasn't opening. It was stuck. He
couldn't—

'Bloody 'ell—'

Brassey had pushed up beside him, added his not very considerable, scrawny frame to it. Muttering obscenities . . . Stoker PO
Berwick suggested mildly, 'Let *this* dog see the bone, sir?' Jack
edged one way, Brassey the other, and Berwick came in between
them. Now five men's weight – including the unconscious ones
on their backs – still wasn't moving it. But there was a deep
rumbling noise from the stern and the door gave suddenly, swinging open . . . 'Go on, Spo. Straight up top!' Another, similar
rumble: it could only be water breaking through her, and he
thought, *Here it comes* . . . He'd guessed all along they'd never
get away with it: hadn't he?

'Carry on, Mr Brassey. See you somewhere.'

Slitted eyes gleamed out of the fiendishly ugly face. Brassey
growled, 'You're a right good 'un, Everard.' Then he'd gone
through into the lobby where the up-ladder was.

'Starboard twenty-five, sir . . .'

CPO Habgood sounded as calm as always. Nick told him, 'Two-
five-oh revolutions.' There'd been another upheaval or explosion
in *Carnarvon*'s stern, but she was still afloat. There must still have
been a lot of men to come out of her. A Stuka's bomb missed to
starboard, the fountain of it breaking right across her: she'd go at
any moment, and in the circumstances he knew what he was going
to have to do. Nothing he did would save her, and if he stopped to
pick up survivors he'd as likely as not lose his own ship and another
230 lives, quite probably adding *Afghan* and *her* 230-odd to that.

And the survivors he rescued would simply be sunk twice instead of once.

The facts were simple but the decision wasn't easy.

A Stuka was aiming itself at *Tuareg.* 'Midships.' He had Dalgleish on the ACP telephone. 'Get the lashings off half our Carley floats. Stand by to ditch them when we're closer.'

He bent to the voicepipe again.

'Meet her.'

'Meet her, sir . . .'

'Steady!' Yellow beak predatory, loathsome: but it was pulling out, high among the shellbursts, tracer curving away short of it. Its bomb had seemed to start with a slanting trajectory to port: when it had splashed in he'd put on wheel to close the cruiser. Drisdale was pointing: at more 88s arriving . . . 'Port fifteen.' The bomb had gone in forty yards away. Another Stuka was about to start its dive: and there'd been another hit, in that second as he glanced at *Carnarvon,* in her bridge. He'd seen it and flinched from it . . . 'Midships.' Then, into the telephone, 'Stand by to ditch the floats.'

'Standing by, sir.'

Chalk's voice, very calm. *Carnarvon* was almost right over on her side and men were sliding down the exposed slope of hull. The cruiser had got her own Carley floats over and he saw some boats in the water too: the Stukas and Messerschmitts weren't likely to leave them alone for long. In fact there – now – a Stuka flying low, parallel to the ship's side, guns flaming . . . The spectre behind his eyes was of his own elder brother, twenty-five years ago, in a shattered, sinking cruiser: David starkly mad, jabbering incoherently. Memory wrapped in shame and infinite regret was heightened by knowledge now of personal responsibility: what you'd made yourself, you couldn't blame, couldn't stand aside from . . . 'Stop both engines!'

His own voice had passed that order. *Tuareg's* screws would stop now – were stopping – but she still had a lot of way on, pitching as she drove up towards the expanding area of survivor-dotted sea. The gleam on the water and the stink was oil-fuel. He told Chalk over the telephone, 'Scrambling-nets both sides!'

Chalk was yelling the order to Dalgleish. The nets were rolled up and lashed along each side of the iron deck; all you had to do was cast off the lashings and they'd tumble down . . . 'Slow ahead together.'

Chalk reported that the nets were down.

'Ditch the floats.'

Dropping them out here rather than closer in where they might fall on top of swimmers. From all round the ship's afterpart the heavy life-saving rafts were toppling over, crashing into the sea. The guns were engaging yet another Stuka that was going for *Carnarvon*.

'Stop both.'

'Stop both, sir.'

'Port twenty.'

There was a group of about twenty men on and around one of the cruiser's own floats: they were waving and cheering as *Tuareg* slid up towards them. But thinking more clearly now, he knew he had no business to be stopping, risking his own ship and all her company. That group around the float would be all he'd take: twenty-odd out of nearly 500. No business to be taking *any* . . . From the foc's'l break a heaving line soared out and fell across the float; they'd got hold of it, and now the men on *Tuareg*'s deck would haul them in alongside. Nick was looking round for Stukas, shocked at the wrongness of his decision: but it hadn't been a decision, only an unthinking reflex. He shouted to Drisdale, 'Tell me when I can move!' The navigator raised a hand in acknowledgement, and leant over the side of the bridge to monitor the rescue operation. A Messerschmitt 109 swept low over the sea, firing bursts at floats and the heads of swimmers. Bombs from some Ju88s were raising mounds of sea around the foundering ship's hulk: men would die from the shock-waves of those explosions.

'All inboard, sir!'

'Half ahead together. Three-six-oh revolutions. Starboard twenty-five.' He felt sick. A Stuka was diving on *Afghan: Afghan* lay stopped, as *Tuareg* had been, and *Tuareg*'s four-sevens were barraging over her.

'Yeoman' – he had to yell into PO Whiffen's ear – 'make to him, *Course one hundred, speed thirty-four knots, executive.*'

Dalgleish reported by telephone, 'We have twenty-three survivors on board, sir. No officers.' Nick passed the phone to Ashcourt and told the coxswain, 'Steer one-oh-oh degrees.' *Afghan* was getting under way, circling to starboard through a man-dotted sea, bow-wave rising as she picked up speed; and Houston was shifting target to a new group of Stukas approaching from right ahead, high above the sun.

*   *   *

420

Napier had been killed when a Stuka's bomb had hit the bridge, and the fire from that hit was still blazing, would be until she sank and the sea put it out. You could feel the heat from it down here on the upper deck beside the starboard whaler's davits, where the last of the wounded were being got away. Jack and Brassey had been helping with them, getting them aft to this point and then down the side to waiting Carley floats. The whaler itself had been lowered fifteen or twenty minutes ago when the order to abandon ship had been given, and the system – presided over by Bell-Reid – was that a stretcher with a man in it would be lowered from the for'ard davit and the empty stretcher brought up again on the after one. There were several stretchers in use, so it wasn't too slow a process. Jumping ladders had been shackled together and hung over the side, resting on its slope, and men at intervals on the ladders were guiding the stretchers as they came slithering down.

It was nearly finished now. At the ship's side, Bell-Reid asked one of the men who'd brought the last customer, 'How many more?'

'Three, sir. One's strapped in an' ready, then two to go.' The SBA turned back, to re-enter the ship through the door under the foc'sl break. Brassey sloped in after him. 'I'll give 'em an 'and inside.'

It wasn't all that safe *out*side. One man had been shot off the ladder, and another killed on the upper deck, both by Stuka machine-guns.

Bell-Reid helped to detach an empty Neill Robertson from the after fall. Then he leant over the side, and called down to the two men on the ladder to go on down, get away. Straightening, he told Jack, 'You go down, steer the next one when it comes, then carry on. Someone else'll replace you.' He'd turned to Fullbrook, the RNVR lieutenant. 'You too. And well done, both of you.'

Jack was about a quarter of the way down the ladder when the ship began to move. Bow rising: then the ladder began to slide, scraping across the ship's side as she tilted. This time she wasn't fooling. And old Brassey was inside her – and Bell-Reid, Melhuish, half a dozen others. Above him Fullbrook shouted something, but a Stuka was roaring over and the shout went with it: next moment something came crashing down past him and it was Fullbrook, jumping . . . Jack looked down, saw where he went in, saw also an area of sea clear of heads or floats: *Carnarvon*'s long bow was lifting, lifting faster . . . He twisted himself round on the ladder and pushed off from it in a sprawling sort of dive.

'Course one-four-six, sir.'

It was the course for Alexandria; and the first twenty-five miles of it, starting now, was the run through the Kaso Strait. At the moment *Afghan* was more or less back in station astern; both ships had been dodging like woodcock under the Stuka rushes.

They *might* get through. It was possible – given an outsize allowance of continuing good luck.

The sun was well up now. Sidaro had been abeam before 0700 and they'd held on to the old course for two miles beyond that in order to clear Elasa island at a safe distance. Ahead, about twenty-five miles south-eastward, a discoloured patch of sky like a dirty thumbprint on a glass marked the position of Force B – Admiral Rawlings with *Orion* and *Dido* and destroyers. Force B was just about out of the Strait now; and a signal from the admiral to C-in-C a quarter of an hour ago had reported a near-miss on the destroyer *Hereward*, and that she'd been slowed down. She was dropping astern and the rest of the force was pressing on, under constant attack.

One more carcass to the vultures. Alone, a single destroyer couldn't possibly survive when it was already winged.

For the moment, *Tuareg* had no bombers overhead. It was the first respite since the attacks had begun on *Carnarvon* at first light, and you could bet it wouldn't last many minutes. But even *one* minute gave you time to draw breath, gave guns' crews a chance to clear the gundecks of shellcases, ammunition-supply parties to get more shells up and into the ready-use racks.

Unfortunately it also gave you time to think.

'We seem to be still here, sir. Once or twice I didn't think we would be.'

Dalgleish had taken advantage of the lull to come up on the bridge. He was offering him a cigarette. Nick took one. 'Thanks.' Dalgleish said quietly, 'About *Carnarvon*, sir. Difficult to know how to say how *bloody* sorry—'

'All right.' He shook his head: he knew how well-meant it was, but – he didn't want it. 'Thank you.'

'I promised some of the lads, sir – they wanted me to tell you how they felt.'

'Thank them for me. Number One – are you doing something about organizing breakfast?'

'Sandwiches and tea, sir. I've sent cooks to the galley . . . I'd better get back aft—'

'Alarm port! Stukas, red nine-oh!'

'Signal, sir—'

'Give it to the navigating officer.' How *they* felt . . . They meant it kindly and he appreciated it, but none of them could even begin to guess at how *he* felt. He had his glasses on the new attackers: about a dozen of them, in three flights. And any moment now, back to routine . . . Drisdale told him, '*Decoy*'s been near-missed, sir. Speed of the force is reduced to twenty-five knots.' *Afghan* had opened fire: now *Tuareg*'s guns crashed: Nick lowered the glasses from his eyes, watched the ugly-looking bombers spreading out for their attacks. The near-miss on *Decoy* was an ill wind: they'd be catching up at an extra five sea-miles per hour now. It wouldn't be anything like *safe* down there with the admiral but it would be less *un*safe than it was here. Pompoms had opened fire and the whole circus was in action: diving, shrieking bombers, guns thudding, crashing, flaming. *Afghan*'s pompom flashes were mixed blue and white. Some of the pompom belts would have been reloaded during that lull: they were two-pounder shells, each the length of a man's forearm, and handling the belts was heavy work. They'd put more tracer into the point-five belts now, taking that tip from the point-fives' little brothers farther aft. Same family name of Vickers. *Tuareg* heeled as he turned her hard a-port and a bomb thumped in to starboard: each one that was dropped could be the one that would hit or near-miss, stop her, give her to the pack to finish off: behind recognition of that distinct possibility was an out-of-focus image of *Carnarvon* on the sea-bed with 2,000 feet of water over her. 'Midships.'

'Midships, sir . . . Wheel's amidships, sir.'

'Starboard twenty-five.'

Glimpses: of *Afghan* away to port with two Stukas going for her at once, *Afghan* heeling so far over under a lot of helm that he was looking almost straight into her bridge; a bomb-burst flinging up sea ahead and *Tuareg* driving through it, dirty water drenching down on them, swirling down through the gratings; Drisdale doing a little dance, shaking first one foot then the other, his white buckskin shoes filthied from that torrent. Cursing: and PO Whiffen advising him in a piercing yell, 'Shouldn't 'a joined, sir!' Then the far-off sight of a destroyer on her own, steaming towards Crete under a cloud of shellbursts, bombers trailing her like flies. That would be *Hereward*, closing the Cretan shore to give her soldiers and ship's company a chance of reaching it when she sank. *Four* Stukas now attacking *Tuareg*: *Afghan* helping with her pompoms: *Afghan* with all her guns poked up and flaming, defiant, angry-looking, beautiful. The Stukas seemed to be ganging up against one ship at a time, and each time you came out of one of the onslaughts it was a surprise to find you'd got away with it.

At 0730 Houston had Force B in sight from the director tower. Even from the bridge you could see the bombers over them, a constant procession of them to and from Scarpanto. Soon afterwards, a new signal to C-in-C reported that *Orion* had been near-missed and damaged and that the force's speed was now twenty-one knots. *Orion*'s captain had been severely wounded by a Stuka's machine-gun bullet. Nick remembered that fighter-cover had been promised for 0530 over this Strait. But at that time Force B hadn't been *in* the Strait: the fighters might have come, found no ships to cover, flown home again? Then he remembered – Rawlings had signalled that one-hour delay, last night . . . Anyway, the only fighters here had black crosses on their wings.

'Flight of 88s coming up astern, sir!'

Ashcourt: he had a telephone, at the back end of the bridge, to the point-fives and the for'ard pompom deck, and he was directing them to fresh targets after each one had passed over. He was spotting for himself and also getting reports from the tin-hatted look-outs each side of the bridge.

'Midships.'

'Midships, sir . . .'

You lived by the minute but you had to reckon on hours, on a day-long battle. Dodging, you held as closely as you could to the south-easterly course, getting back to it each time as soon as possible. Every yard made good in that direction was a *good* yard. Habgood had reported the rudder centred: Nick told him, 'Starboard fifteen. Steer one-four-six.' He was watching one that looked like attacking at any moment. Up ahead there seemed to be a lull, with Force B's ships in sight now from *Tuareg*'s bridge and pushing on under a clearing sky-cap, an absence of shellbursts or attackers. One quick glimpse through binoculars had told him this: another now confirmed it. Bomb-splashes rising like geysers between the two Tribals were from the Ju88s, three of them at about 5,000 feet.

424

That Stuka was going for *Afghan*, not *Tuareg*: *Tuareg*'s pompoms and point-fives flaming at it. And it was the last of them: there was nothing up there now but the muck hanging, shredding away in the wind. One Stuka, its bomb somewhere in the sea, was departing, and gunfire had petered out.

Peace was uncanny. There were ship and sea noises instead of the roar of guns: there was time to take note of being alive, ships unharmed, on course, catching up on the main body up ahead. Blue sky, blue-and-white sea, *Afghan* sleekly impressive as she wheeled back into station.

Swimming slowly: becoming aware of himself doing it – of having been doing it, semi-consciously, for some time. Cold water. *Very* cold.

'Give us a tow, sir?'

A Carley float, thick with men, and other men in the water round it holding on. A few of them laughed at the comedian's request, and the same man called, 'We could accommodate one more, sir.'

It was a kind thought, but the float was already overcrowded. He swam on, looking for a float where there *would* be room for him. He'd been pretty well whacked out before this swim had started. Oil in the water here: the sea was loppy but it was probably the oil that was holding it down, preventing the small waves from breaking. The waves were high enough to prevent one seeing far, though: a radius of five to ten yards, he thought, was about his field of vision.

Clutterbuck swam into it. Blinking steadily: he'd lost his spectacles, poor chap. When he saw Jack, he stopped swimming.

'Why are you going that way, Everard?'

'Good as any, isn't it?'

'Ah.' An eyebrow lifted. 'You pays your money and you takes your choice . . . Hey, look out!'

An aircraft was approaching, low. Jack waited, just dog-paddling slightly, otherwise motionless in the water, and the thing roared overhead. Live men attracted bullets, he'd seen that time and time again. There was aircraft noise a lot of the time but it was mostly high up, and one had only to be careful of the low ones or of a circler that might be looking for something to use its guns on. Wave-tops were breaking in his face: he was out of the oil-patch, then. Clutterbuck was swimming slowly away, going towards the sun; it was easier to go the other way, so it didn't blind you. Might have suggested that, if one had thought of it.

425

Brassey's face, Brassey's rasping voice: *You're a right good 'un, Everard.*

As if he hadn't reckoned on living: and at that, he'd most likely reckoned right. But frankness in the face of extinction: things not mattering that *had* mattered, rank-consciousness no longer operating. Face like a squeezed lemon with stubble on it, a man with a lifetime of naval service behind him calling you a right good 'un, for God's sake . . . The mind roamed free while the body remained trapped in the swimming stroke and another aircraft zoomed low somewhere close: the sudden stammer of its guns came like torture to the brain, as if the brain could feel the bullets that would be ripping into helpless swimmers or a crowded float. He'd stopped moving again while it passed, until the sound had faded. Not all that many of the pilots did it, and perhaps only a minority of them enjoyed the killing, but there had to be a fair proportion of psychopaths up there, he thought.

Getting bloody tired. Waves breaking in your face didn't help much, either. Might be why Clutterbuck swam east? The hell . . . Poor old Brassey: right good 'un *he* was . . .

He'd stopped swimming, his body telling him it was a pointless as well as painful exercise. Slumping with his face down in the water: holding his breath and then expelling it through pursed lips as the sea washed over him. All that exertion earlier . . . Drifting into thoughts of brother Nick: whether he and his destroyers had got away with it, or been sunk too. Aircraft noise again: he pulled his face up, gulped air mixed with salt water: it wasn't a low-flyer, he thought, not one of the blood-lust merchants, just one passing over. Keep swimming, you've had your rest. Swim all the way to that—

All the way back to Gabrielle. Of *course* he'd ring her . . .

That *boat!*

Making his eyes focus: one hand up quickly to clear them. It was a whaler he was looking at, clinker-built, greyish-blue, full of men. But room for more, he thought, certainly for *one* more. It was rising and falling, rocking, by no means overfilled. He'd turned himself towards it, water breaking in his face again in stinging whiteness, and one man in the boat had seen him. He was pointing, shouting.

Three yards – or ten, it might have been. Some of the men were trying to paddle the boat towards him with their hands. No oars, then. The one who'd spotted him was standing, leaning forward with his hands on the boat's gunwale; he seemed to be about to launch himself over, come and fetch him. Talking over his shoulder to a stir of men behind him as the boat rocked over.

'Hang on there, sir, I'll—'

It was young Brighouse, for God's sake. Beside that first chap: Brighouse was clambering over, coming for him. Pausing to shout, 'Shan't be a jiffy—'

Roar of an aircraft engine suddenly very close: a fighter dipping, swooping at the boat. He heard the hammering of its guns, saw flashes, a wave broke in his face. The Messerschmitt had swept over, banked in a sharp turn, engine-noise thunderous as it hurtled over in another pass. He was face-down in the sea, jarring underwater thumping in his ears. Head up again, sucking at the air: noise fading . . . The boat lay a few yards from him, broadside-on and low in the water with its upper strakes in splinters, no sign of human movement in it. One man's body was slumped over the bow, head and shoulders in the sea as if he'd been trying to drag himself away.

'*Dido*, sir . . .'

Nick couldn't pay attention to whatever his navigator was telling him. He was aiming *Tuareg* at a diving Stuka. Stooped above the voicepipe, ready to jink her away when he saw the bomb coming. A quick glance now, though, at Drisdale – he was staring out towards the cruisers – and back quickly to face this obscene attacker.

The lull was over and the storm had broken. *Tuareg* and *Afghan*, rejoining Force B, were thrashing up into station on the wing of the destroyer screen, under waves of attacks by 87s and 88s. During that lull the Luftwaffe must have been reorganizing, girding themselves for this all-out assault. Nick had thought he'd seen concentrated attacks before: but *this* . . .

The bomb was falling away from that shrieking, spread-legged horror.

'Port twenty-five. Two-four-oh revolutions.' He looked over at the cruisers, saw more diving Stukas, ships' guns all flaming up into the permanent haze of smoke, the self-renewing clouds of shell-bursts. There was something wrong with *Dido*'s for'ard guns, though: he put his glasses on her, and saw that she must have been hit on her B turret. She had three twin turrets for'ard, and in the turret in the centre one of the pair of barrels simply wasn't there, the other was twisted up, bent nearly double.

Bomb-splash to starboard. 'Midships.'

'Midships . . . Wheel's amidships, sir.'

'Starboard fifteen.'

'Alarm astern – Stuka!'

He could hear its howl rising over the din of gunfire. Even now *Carnarvon* was in the back of his mind, a shattered hulk in the deep-sea darkness. Habgood had reported fifteen degrees of starboard wheel on: he told him, 'Increase to thirty degrees of wheel. Three-six-oh revolutions.'

'Stone the crows . . .'

Back aft, Mr Walsh had grabbed Dalgleish's arm, pointing: at a Stuka diving vertically on *Orion*. Literally vertically: like a dart dropped out of the sky. Dalgleish had to look away, attend to other business, barrage-fire from X and Y guns at a flight of 88s coming up on the quarter: Mr Walsh goggling, seeing the bomb come away and the Stuka go straight on, straight into the sea in a huge fountain-splash right ahead of her. The bomb burst on her A turret, turret dissolving in flash and smoke, then the smoke clearing to show that pair of guns wrecked and naked to the sky, the turret's armoured casing blown right off. *Orion*'s B turret had been knocked out too, in the same explosion: so now she had only her after six-inch turrets and the midships four-inch mountings on each side. None of that A turret's crew could possibly have survived.

Dalgleish was looking over at the flagship now: he hadn't seen it happen but he could see the results of it now. The sudden roar of pompoms and point-fives brought his attention back to things close at hand: a Stuka that had attacked *Dido* and levelled out down on the sea was racketing clumsily up across *Tuareg*'s stern, exposing its whole disgusting underside as it banked and lifted. *Tuareg*'s close-range weapons – *Afghan*'s too now – were all at it, seeing the chance of a kill and wanting it, *needing* it . . . You could see the tracer converging, hitting, the little flashes and then the start of fire as the incendiary rounds ripped in, and the Stuka was suddenly a flying torch with a German frying in its cockpit: Mr Walsh hit the port-side Vickers GO torpedoman on the back – ''Old your fire, lad!'

Bullets and shells were precious, not to be wasted. There'd be hours of this yet, before they got out of the Stuka radius.

*   *   *

Battling southward: still praying, minute by minute, for the promised air support.

Orion's captain had died of his wounds at about 0930, soon after she'd been near-missed in a multiple attack. Now, just over an hour later, here was another one: eleven Stukas were going for the flagship. They came over through a heavy barrage, dipping their yellow snouts one by one and close on each other's tails.

A minute later, from *Tuareg*'s bridge the flagship was invisible among the bomb-splashes, her 7,000 tons and 550 feet of length completely hidden in the bomb-churned sea. Nick thought, *She's gone* . . . As if the whole world was going, piece by piece. All the guns in all the ships barraging to protect her: and the Stukas still getting through. Then she was in sight again, steaming out of the holocaust: but stricken, swinging away off course with smoke pouring out of her. Steering gone, or jammed: out of control and badly hurt. Some of those bombs must have burst inside her, and she had more than a thousand troops on board as well as her own complement of about 600.

'Port fifteen. One-eight-oh revolutions.'

All the other ships were turning, dropping back to stay with the flagship. You could imagine the struggle inside her, the desperation to smother fires, tend wounded, get her back into control. You had to try *not* to think about the troop-filled messdecks.

Jack Everard lay across the whaler's bow, resting on a dead man's body, half in and half out of water. He'd clawed up over the body, using it as a bridge while the whaler tipped, heavy with sea and dead men inside it.

Sea washed red over and around the bodies. There were about eleven of them. The boat had been riddled with bullets and it was waterlogged, waves slopping over the shattered gunwales; the weight of the bodies inside it was lessened by the fact they'd all been wearing lifebelts, some of which had not been punctured. It was also the reason for a few of them floating near the surface, only barely restrained by the top edges of the boat as the whole mass lurched sluggishly to and fro.

The only face he could recognize was that of a leading signalman named Durkin. He lay on his back, partly supported by an inflated Mae West, and as the boat and its contents rocked so did the killick's head. When it faced to its right it looked quite normal, but each time it flopped over you could see where the back of the head had been smashed. Durkin's head wasn't the only thing you didn't want to look at twice.

There was no reason for it, no way to understand it, no advantage to anyone in these men having been turned into corpses. With time to think, not much strength in him for the moment, and the horror all around him, under him, Jack wondered whether the Messerschmitt pilot could have explained it.

Brighouse, the snotty, wasn't visible. He'd be in the sea, Jack guessed. Brighouse had been in the act of climbing over the side to come and help him; he'd have been hit then and gone on over, and if his Mae West had been perforated he would have sunk. They floated afterwards, brought up after a certain time by the expansion of internal gases.

He'd got his breath back, more or less. He shifted, to get himself up higher and look around. The whaler's bow went down deeper and the body under his left knee shifted: he had nearly all his weight on the other foot, on the top of the stem-post. The boat was like a half-rotten log, only just on the positive side of neutral buoyancy. There were two drowned or shot men not far away, supported by their lifebelts and with waves breaking right over them, but neither of them was small enough to be young Brighouse. The best thing to do now, he decided, would be to get these bodies out of what was left of the whaler. If its timbers remained buoyant it would be better than nothing to hold on to.

Orion was turning back again, recovering. She was magnificent, Nick thought: a wounded lion refusing to lie down and die, crawling back into the fight.

'Midships, sir!'

'One-four-two revolutions. Steer one-four-six.'

The destroyers were gathering round their flagship, and *Dido* had dropped back too. The Luftwaffe was at this moment conspicuous by its absence, but it was likely to return at any moment. When it did, *Orion* would have her hand held tightly.

Italian MAS-boats – torpedo craft – might pick up *Carnarvon* survivors. The MAS-boats, one had heard, had saved a lot of men from other sinkings – from *Gloucester* and *Fiji*, for instance.

Drisdale was looking at him expectantly: as if he'd said something to which he now expected a reply.

'Say something, pilot?'

He'd shaken his head. 'Only being wildly humorous, sir.'

'Sorry I missed it.' He put his glasses on *Orion* again: she'd just spewed another cloud of yellow smoke from her funnel, and her speed had dropped to almost nothing: you could tell at once by the way her bow-wave dropped. He cut *Tuareg*'s speed to match: the others were all doing the same, and watching for the flagship to gather way again.

Still no Stukas.

'How far are we from Scarpanto?'

'Hundred and twenty miles, sir.'

At noon, two Fulmars appeared from the direction of the desert. It was a marvellously comforting thing, to see aircraft that weren't enemies. They stayed with the ships for about an hour and then flew south again. *Orion* was still in trouble, with sudden speed variations and gushing multi-coloured smoke; each time she slowed the whole force fell back, clustering around her, praying she'd get going again and knowing she might not. Junkers 88s attacked at 1300, and again half an hour later, and the last attack came at 1500 – by which time the force was only about 100 miles from Alexandria. Several of the destroyers in the screen had been damaged by near-misses. Most of the ships were very low in ammunition: *Orion* had only a few rounds left.

'It's a mercy the Luftwaffe decided to call it a day, sir.'

Dalgleish said it, after he'd leafed through the signals on the log. *Orion* had 260 dead inside her, and rather more than that number wounded. Nick was thinking of a letter he was going to have to write, to Sarah. Saying – what? *I had no option but to leave our son to drown.*

Who'd understand it, who hadn't seen this kind of war? Sarah, of *all* people?

431

CHAPTER 11

When he woke, opening his eyes slowly to the growing Aegean light, it took a few moments to remember where he was and what had happened.

Pain in his back: he shifted, easing himself over on the caïque's hard timber, and immediately the young Italian began jabbering at him. He hadn't got as far as remembering the Italian until he heard that voice start up again. He was up on the cabin roof, grinning like a wolf.

Jack sat up. 'Morning, Alphonso.'

Gabble-gabble-gabble . . . Alphonso – whatever his name was, Alphonso suited him and he didn't seem to mind being called it – had sprouted more black beard during the dark hours. He'd been on this caïque when Jack had seen it and eventually decided to leave the whaler's wreckage and swim over to it. He hadn't realized until he got quite close to it that the caïque was wrecked too; it had been hard to make out what it was, and he'd studied it for a long time before he'd started out, wondering how long the swim would take him and whether after he'd committed himself to the transfer it might start moving away. In fact it had been closer than he'd guessed, and it wasn't in any condition to move except by drifting. Its hold, occupying about half of its normal below-water bulk, was full of water, the bow actually under water and gunwales awash from right for'ard to about amidships; only the stern part was dry. There was a wheelhouse-cabin, and a lower cabin down a short ladder from it, and also an engine space right aft; these were sound and watertight and were providing the buoyancy for the caïque to remain afloat. The engine was smashed; he'd been down there yesterday before the light went, and it looked as if there'd been some kind of internal explosion.

The Italian had helped him aboard, over the gunwale amidships

432

– which was more or less at water-level – and then up to the stern. Treating him like some long-lost brother, or at least as a welcome guest. He'd given him bread, cheese, and a cup of peculiar-tasting wine. Greek, probably. It had come out of a very large, wicker-covered jug; if it was full there'd be about three gallons in it.

Alphonso was round-faced, soft-looking, not at all badly fed. About twenty or twenty-one, probably. He was beckoning to him now, wanting Jack to join him on the cabin-top. And why not: there'd be more of a view from up there. He stood up, looking round at the sea as the light of a new day grew across it. It was almost fully daylight: roughly as it had been yesterday when the assault on *Carnarvon* had begun.

He clambered up to join Alphonso, who greeted him with easy friendship. Looking around from this higher viewpoint he could see nothing floating, no boats or Carley floats to interrupt the bright gloss on the sea's surface. To the south the mountains of Crete were pink-washed in the lifting sun; they seemed closer than they'd been last evening.

Fiona had written, *I have been in contact with someone at the Admiralty whom you do not know – incidentally he's a friend of Jane Derby's, not mine – and he swears that up to this moment of going to press a certain destroyer and its captain are in perfect nick. (No pun intended.) So what the hell is said person doing ignoring my letters? No answers to the last three, and really it's a bit damn much, I sit here writing my heart out and not a word from you for week after week. How do you think I was feeling, before Jane went and found this out for me? How do you think I feel NOW, you rotten swine? What is it, some Egyptian belly-dancer? If it is I'll get myself sent out there somehow and dance on her belly and on her boyfriend's with my Army boots . . .*

'Clear this away, sir?'

He glanced up at Leading Steward McEvoy, and nodded. 'Yes, please.' 'This' meant the breakfast things. Outside on the iron deck the hands were being detailed for the forenoon's work. Last night had been spent in the usual way – oiling, ammunitioning and storing – and *Tuareg* with others would be sailing at noon for Plaka Bay.

They'd entered Alexandria yesterday evening at 8 pm. *Orion* had had only eight tons of fuel and two six-inch shells remaining. Below decks she was a shambles, a butcher's shop.

He left the table, to get out of the steward's way. He'd answered Fiona's letter last night, with a telegram saying *Just received your first letter for a month. Have written innumerable times and will write again now. Love, Nick.*

He hadn't in fact done much letter-writing lately; he'd been waiting to hear from her, and he hadn't wanted to express anxiety as forthrightly as she'd done now. That angry and possessive note, faintly disguised as humour, brought feelings into the open, where until now neither of them had wanted – or allowed – them to be. In a way, it was rather marvellous.

But he had to write to Sarah too. It was a hellish job to face: not only because of what he had to tell her, but also because there was not the slightest point in even trying to express, to Sarah, his deepest, sincerest feelings. Nothing he could say to her, now or at any other time, could help the situation; it was a fact of life that one had to face, accept . . . Beside that unpleasant prospect, Fiona's letter – this flimsy sheet of pale blue paper in his hand – was a life-saver, one item of relief and pleasure to rest the mind on. It was also thrilling, wonderfully promising for the future; if it hadn't been for the loss of *Carnarvon* and the odds-on death of Jack Everard, Sarah's son, he'd have been glowing with it. And it *was* marvellous . . .

Wasn't it?

If there was going to be a future – yes. He had a stronger motive for personal survival now: so yes, it was terrific . . . But this was hardly a time for counting chickens. In the past fourteen days, the Mediterranean Fleet had been reduced to just one quarter of its operational strength; and there were still thousands of soldiers to be brought out of Crete. You couldn't last for ever. Any more than a tossed coin would always fall the same way up. There was a certain amount of skill in avoiding bombs, but there was a damn sight more luck in it than skill.

While Force B had been lifting men from Heraklion on Wednesday night, four destroyers had been at Sphakia landing rations for 15,000 troops and taking off an advance party of 750. The Australian destroyer *Nizam* had been near-missed during the withdrawal. Also on Wednesday Force D, comprising the Australian cruiser *Perth*, assault ship *Glengyle*, AA cruisers *Coventry* and *Calcutta* and three destroyers, had sailed from Alex; they'd have been taking a biggish load of troops from Sphakia during this past night, and now, this morning, they'd be fighting their way southwards. Then in about an hour Force C again – *Napier, Nizam, Kelvin* and *Kandahar* – would be sailing; and at noon *Tuareg* and *Afghan* with two H-class were to set off for Plaka. With so few ships intact, nobody could expect much let-up; nobody was asking for it, either.

It was a bit much to believe that Fiona, bless her heart, had written *three* letters that had gone up in smoke. He guessed that in the last few weeks she'd have been waiting to hear from him – just as he'd been waiting to hear from her.

A knock on the cabin door announced PO Whiffen, with the signal log. He announced, tucking his cap under his arm as he came into the cabin, 'There's an "immediate" to us, sir.'

It was the one on top. Their sailing orders were cancelled. *Tuareg* and the three others who'd been earmarked for the Plaka Bay lift were to remain at immediate notice for sea.

'Ask the first lieutenant to come and see me, would you.'

It would be diplomatic, he knew, for him to go over to the depot ship and call on RA(D), the Rear-Admiral (Destroyers). But in the present state of upheaval RA(D) had been spending a lot of his time at sea commanding cruiser forces, and he wouldn't be an easy man to find or have much time to spare. Also, Nick's position was an irregular one, since he was neither commanding a flotilla nor attached to one, and as CO of a private ship he had no natural direct access to the Rear-Admiral. The division of four ships of which he'd have been senior officer on the cancelled Plaka expedition was only a temporary grouping of bits and pieces: for whatever job replaced the Plaka one they might well be split up again. Another point was that in *Woolwich*, however helpful RA(D)'s staff might be, he wasn't likely to get much of a clue as to what was happening: it was from Gabbari, from ABC's War Room, that the decisions were coming now.

So thank God for Aubrey Wishart and the Old Pals' Act.

'Want me, sir?'

'Come in.' Wishart would be just about standing on his ear, at this stage. He'd sent Nick a very hurried, private message last night about *Carnarvon*, but obviously the Staff was being worked twenty-four hours a day. But then – he was a *very* old friend . . . Nick was lighting a cigarette, and he offered Dalgleish one. He'd seen him briefly earlier on, on the quarterdeck at Colours, before he'd come in again for breakfast. He told him, 'Our trip's

435

been cancelled. No midday sailing. But we stay at immediate notice.'

'As Mr Walsh would say, sir' – Dalgleish expelled a cloud of smoke – ' "Stone the perishin' crows" ' . . . The evacuation can't be *over* yet?'

'Some snag at the place we were going to, I'd guess.' A snag like the Germans getting there first, perhaps. He added, 'I'm going over to Gabbari to see if I can find out what's cooking. I'd like the motorboat alongside in' – he checked the time – 'at a quarter past nine . . . How's Redmayne getting on?'

'Still hard at it, sir. I don't know, I'll—'

'Tell him I want to hear from him before I leave the ship, would you.'

Some of the nearer misses had shaken things up in the engine-room, and Redmayne and his staff had been working down there all night.

'Admiral Wishart will join you shortly, sir.'

'Thank you.'

The marine orderly went out and shut the door, leaving Nick in Aubrey Wishart's office. He'd waited in the lobby, to start with, while Aubrey had been contacted in the War Room.

Lighting a cigarette, he stared down at the now familiar pattern of Chart 2836a – *Grecian Archipelago, Southern Sheet* – which was spread on a trestle table. Crete – Kaso – Scarpanto: for an age now it seemed one had lived with this picture. Leaving it, he sat down in the visitor's chair, took Fiona's letter out of his pocket and re-read it. It was possible, he thought, that she was pulling a fast one: that she hadn't written at all – for some reason at which it might be unwise to guess – and so he hadn't either, and now this was her way of breaking the deadlock?

She'd sent him a copy of *The Last Tycoon* by Scott Fitzgerald, she said. An American edition. He wondered where she might have got it from.

Wishart broke in like a charging elephant.

'Did you get my note, old lad? More sorry than I can say. We've had no news about survivors – if that's what you've come about. But a lot of 'em are sure to be picked up, and we *wouldn't* hear, not for a while.'

'No, I realize—'

'It was a pretty dreadful spot you were in. You did the right thing

436

though, Nick.' He flopped into the chair behind the desk, and glanced at his watch. 'Anything I can do for you, while you're here?'

'Yes, please. Tell me why my trip to Plaka's been put off, and what *is* lined up for us.'

Wishart's smile faded.

'You've bust in here just to ferret that out? Not about *Carnarvon*?'

'I wouldn't have expected you to have news of survivors yet. But we're all getting a bit frayed around the edges, and if we could know how long we're likely to be here in Alex—'

'Christ Almighty!'

'What?'

'I think you've got a bloody nerve, that's what!'

No smile.

Nick stood up. He said quietly, 'I'm sorry. I hadn't intended—'

'Really, a *bloody* nerve!'

Wishart was right, of course. He did have a bloody nerve. He nodded. 'Yes. Very sorry, Aubrey. I'll—'

'Look, sit down.'

Aggression had faded into sudden weariness. Nick said, 'No, you're perfectly right, I should have thought before I—'

'Sit *down*, damn it.' Wishart was pointing at the chair. He looked exhausted. 'We're *all* – frayed round the edges, aren't we . . . ? I'll tell you what's happening, Nick. Otherwise I suppose I'll never get to meet that slant-eyed female who's on display in your cabin . . . Heard from her yet?' Nick nodded: Wishart smiled. 'Told you so . . . Now, listen. We aren't sending you to Plaka Bay because it seems the information we had yesterday was all balls and there won't be any troops there to lift. We're getting a lot of conflicting reports. For instance NOIC Suda, from his cave at Sphakia, told us there'd be 10,000 men for Force D to embark last night; then the Army said there'd be only 2,000 plus stragglers, and no hope of holding out until the night of the 30th – tonight – so last night's lift would be the final one. Cutting confusion short, Force D is now on its way back here with 6,000 soldiers on board, and there'll be certainly one more lift, possibly two . . . *Perth*, incidentally, was near-missed about twenty minutes ago, and she'd had one boiler-room knocked out. We're risking lives and ships – soldiers' lives as well as sailors', once they're at sea – and the dividend isn't always clear. You saw what it was like, on your own last trip, and it's getting worse every hour.'

'Arliss is sailing now for Sphakia?'

'Yes.' Captain Arliss, RAN, was commanding Force C from his destroyer *Napier*. 'And subject to developments it's likely there'll be one last, bigger lift tomorrow night. If it's approved you'll probably sail at dawn tomorrow with *Phoebe* – flying Admiral King's flag – plus *Abdiel* and a bunch of whatever destroyers are still seaworthy by then. That's what you're being held back for now. Satisfied?'

'Grateful for the information. And I do apologize—'

'It's a damn shame about Plaka. But obviously we can't send ships out to get bombed when it's unlikely there are any troops to bring off. And the north coast's finished now, of course; Kaso's a closed door.'

'What happens to the Retimo garrison, then?'

'They remain there.' Wishart looked down at his hands. 'With orders to capitulate – if we can get an order to them, which so far's been impossible.'

'The field hospital, and its nurses?'

'There's nothing we can do, Nick. They shouldn't have been there in the first place, mind you. When they were pulled out of Greece they were supposed to come back here; some mix-up stuck them in Crete, and by the time we heard of them – well, Retimo was already cut off.'

'So we have to leave – what is it, twenty women—'

'Nearer thirty. Plus the wounded men they've been nursing.'

'We leave thirty women in a garrison that's about to be overrun by Nazi paratroops?'

'Nobody likes it, old lad.' Wishart's large, tired face was rather like a Saint Bernard's, nowadays, Nick thought . . . 'ABC is very deeply concerned about it. Apart from one's personal feelings, I can tell you – in confidence – that it's being alleged in very high places that we aren't getting enough Aussies out. This is being hung round ABC's neck, and obviously he'd give his back teeth to bring out more. Point of fact, there were five Australian infantry battalions in Crete to start with, one has already been lifted from Heraklion and two others are now on their way – or will be – from Sphakia. Leaving two out of five, and they're shut up in Retimo, or possibly between Retimo and Plaka. The RAF's sent planes to drop messages at Retimo no less than three times now, and so far as we know not one of the messages has got there. Hence the fact they haven't pulled out to the south coast as ordered.' He sighed, looked at his watch again. 'ABC's got Prime Ministers and all sorts of people yammering at him. I suppose they have to clear their own yardarms before the Press starts on it and there's some political storm back home. What's more, they don't seem to have heard about the girls yet. And we're helpless, Nick, we can't do a bloody thing!'

'No hope of another shot at getting a message in by submarine?'

'Pointless.' The big man got up, lumbered over to the chart, and Nick joined him at it. 'However – just to show you we aren't absolutely stupid here, I'll tell you, for the record, that I've arranged for another boat to be off Retimo tonight. *Tamarisk*, from this Alex flotilla. She's been doing a cloak-and-dagger job up in Vari Bay.' He pointed: Vari Bay was in Greece, about ten miles south of the Piraeus. 'Consequently she has commandos with canoes on board, so she could have been used for a Retimo reconnaissance. In fact, we've decided against it . . . She's had an interesting patrol, though. She sank a steamer and two caïques full of Germans about *here* – and had a look right inside the harbour at Milos island, and one or two other places, and found them all empty. They did have MAS-boats at Milos, but obviously they've brought them farther south now. And hence the little troop convoy – Huns are bringing 'em down straight from Greek ports, instead of mustering them at Milos.'

Being an old submariner himself, Aubrey Wishart was proud of his fellow submariners, and inclined to ramble on about their exploits. Nick brought him back to the subject.

'Why would it be pointless?'

'Because it's too late for any troops there to get across to Plaka Bay – which was the purpose of contacting them. And there's no question of any more runs through Kaso. There's simply nothing to be gained.'

'You couldn't bring the women out by submarine?'

'For Christ's sake, Nick, talk sense. You know the size of our boats. Thirty women – even if we could get them off from shore? In what – canoes, one at a time? Not to mention the wounded – and they'd as likely as not be unwilling to just walk out on them . . .'

'Yes. I see . . .'

Something Wishart had said a minute ago was fermenting in his brain. He was probing, worrying at it: and his nerves jumped suddenly.

'The enemy's moving reinforcements down by sea from Greece?'

'From the Piraeus.' Wishart nodded. 'Long haul, but safe for them now.'

'Into Suda, I suppose.'

'They may be using Heraklion as well.'

'But Suda'd be the main base for their destroyers and MAS-boats.' He ran his finger around the crescent-outline of Crete, Scarpanto, Rhodes. 'This is their front line now. North of it, up here, anything of ours that moved they could bomb the hell out of. So they'll forget the backwaters, concentrate on securing Crete.'

'We'll be operating submarines up there, of course.'

'This one – *Tamarisk* – she'll be off Retimo tonight, and you can get a signal to her when she surfaces after dark?'

'It's already drafted, I imagine.'

'Recalling her to Alex.'

'Precisely.' Wishart checked his watch for the twentieth time. 'And *now*, Nick—'

'Could we sit down for a minute?'

'Christ Almighty!' Wishart, flushing, pointed at the wall. 'My boss is in there with two generals and one air vice-marshal, and he's expecting the Prime Minister of New Zealand and Field-Marshal Wavell at any minute. London's screaming its head off, our ships at sea are being bombed round the clock, I've given you ten minutes I can't spare, and—'

'Give me two more.' He wasn't apologizing this time. 'I believe I could get your women and wounded out of Retimo. Two minutes, to tell you how?'

It took four minutes. Then another at the chart, checking distances and times. Finally Wishart threw down the dividers.

'It's bloody chancy. I think it's probably idiotic. But if ABC agrees, and you pull it off, you could ask for the Crown Jewels.'

'If I was looking for rewards I'd settle for a flotilla. In point of fact it looks like a job worth doing.'

'I'd guess you'll be getting a flotilla in any case. If ABC didn't have such an enormous load you'd probably have it already.' Wishart stopped talking. He stared at Nick for a couple of seconds: then he nodded. 'Wait here. I'll see if I can get a word in.'

Nick sat down, lit a cigarette, went on thinking about it. It *was* risky: there were certain things that could only be left to chance. But nowadays you were taking a gamble every time you poked your ship's nose out of harbour. You took an almost suicidal risk

440

when you tried to pass through Kaso in daylight. Risks were commonplace, routine: and he didn't think his plan was all *that* chancy. It was unconventional, certainly.

He sat back in the chair, thinking about details. He'd smoked three cigarettes before Wishart came back.

He looked grim. Bearer of rotten news, Nick guessed. He was well aware there could be some fundamental snag he'd overlooked, and that ABC's hawk eye would have spotted it right away. Or the hawk eyes of the Chief of Staff or Staff Officer (Operations) . . . He got up, watched the Rear-Admiral push the door shut and move over to the desk.

He cleared his throat.

'We are to work out an operational plan. You and I. Then the Staff will look it over. To start with' – he sat down, reaching for signal-pad and pencil – 'let's decide what orders we'll ask S/M(1) to pass to *Tamarisk* when she pops up at 2200 tonight.' By S/M(1) he meant the commanding officer of the 1st Submarine Flotilla. '*Tamarisk*'s CO is a Commander Rivers, by the way. Got a cigarette?'

'Here—'

Wishart used Nick's lighter. Then, leaking smoke from his nostrils, he pointed the cigarette across the desk. 'Nick – hold on tight to that chair, will you.'

'Why?'

'So as not to fall off it. Listen – I'm instructed to inform you that the 37th Destroyer Flotilla is now reconstituted. It consists of *Tuareg* as leader, with *Afghan, Highflier* and *Halberdier.* Captain (D) is Captain Sir Nicholas Everard. To be precise, *acting* Captain, since this'll need a rubber stamp from the Board of Admiralty. Now, let's get down to your hare-brained scheme . . .'

He was back at *Tuareg* at eleven-thirty, climbing the gangway into the screech of the bosun's call. The news had come aboard ahead of him: there'd been a signal from C-in-C to RA(D) repeated to various people including D37, which now meant Nick Everard. On the quarterdeck, faces were smiling as the call's wail died away.

'This is terrific, sir!'

'Glad you think so, Number One. Any problems here?'

'No unusual ones, sir.'

'Chief?'

Redmayne had washed the oil off, he noticed. 'Top line, sir.'

441

'Well done.' He asked Dalgleish, 'Did you get a message about COs coming aboard at noon?'

Dalgleish nodded. 'Your steward's preparing for them, sir.'

He'd invited the captains of *Afghan, Highflier* and *Halberdier* for a midday gin. The gins would in fact be small ones; the object was to give them a preliminary briefing on tomorrow's operation. Written orders wouldn't reach them until shortly before sailing time; there had to be a lot of information from the submarine, *Tamarisk,* before details could be established, and they wouldn't get her report much before dawn tomorrow. But the basic plan was worked out, and there were certain preparations to be made now.

He told Dalgleish, 'If you're happy to, you can pipe a make-and-mend.' A make-and-mend was a half-day free of work; it was a term deriving from older times, when such occasions were used by sailors for making and patching their clothes. 'But no shore-leave. And there's one job – some stores to be drawn. Paint and timber.' He enjoyed the look of mystification that crossed his first lieutenant's face. It was reflected in some others too, notably in CPO Habgood's and in the Buffer's, PO Mercer's. He asked Habgood, 'All right, cox'n?'

'Yessir. And if I may, sir, on be'alf of chief and petty officers and all the ship's company, I'd like to offer most 'earty congratulations.'

Mercer growled, 'Hear, hear, sir.'

'Thank you very much, cox'n.' He glanced at Mercer. 'You'd better stick around, Buffer. First Lieutenant'll have a job for you in a minute.'

'Paint and timber, sir?'

'Right.' He looked at Dalgleish. 'Come and have a word, Tony, would you?' They went round to the starboard side, and in the screen door; in the day-cabin he pulled out some sheets of Wishart's signal-pad on which he'd made various jottings. He asked Leading Steward McEvoy, who was mustering glasses near the pantry hatch and had the whole cabin shiny-bright, 'Are we allowed to sit down in here?'

'Och, I might permit it, sir.'

'Very kind.'

'Like tae say congratulations, sir.'

'Thank you. Sit down, Tony. Smoke?'

'No, thank you, sir.' Nick was aware that he himself had been smoking far too much, lately, and that he'd have to cut it down.

After this jaunt . . . He saw that Dalgleish had a notebook and pencil ready: he told him, 'What we need is – in total, to take into account whatever's on board already – paint, as follows . . . Black, six gallons. Red, four gallons. Green, four gallons. White, also four. And have them ready before we sail in two separate lots of each colour, each lot one half of the total quantity.' He waited while Dalgleish wrote it down. From the far side of the cabin Fiona's eyes were fixed on him, and he wondered whether she'd have had his cable yet. He told Dalgleish, 'Make sure we've got a dozen wide paint-brushes. Widest obtainable. And the other item is timber. We need one dozen planks twenty-five feet long, and about six fifteen feet long. Usual sort of planks, about a foot wide.'

Dalgleish listed it all.

'The depot ship's been warned they're to meet our requirements without argument, by the way. Have Mercer start checking on what he's got already – get it done with, then he can enjoy his make-and-mend . . . But also there'll be some crates of medical stores arriving, and a lot of cots or camp-beds. Gallwey can take charge of the drugs and stuff; stow the beds aft somewhere. That's the lot, and if you're back here before my guests arrive I'll give you a glass of gin.'

'I'll make it snappy, then.' Dalgleish got up. 'Actually the wardroom would very much like the pleasure of your company this evening, sir, to wet the fourth stripe. Would you honour us with your presence, sir?'

'If I'm not summoned ashore, I'd like nothing better. Thank you . . . Look, one other thing. Tell Drisdale he's to check that we have chart 1658 on board, and that it has any recent corrections applied to it. It's a large-scale plan of Suda Bay.'

'Suda!' Nick just looked back at him. The first lieutenant nodded. 'Aye aye, sir.' He added the chart number to his list.

That might provide a good red herring. Leading Steward Mc-Evoy had visibly absorbed it. It so happened that chart 1658 had the Suda Bay plan as its main content, but it also had plans of five other places including Retimo, alias Rethimnon.

Let not the left hand know . . . Nearer the time, he'd tell them. News travelled on the winds – on the khamsins, mistrals, gregales. One man's ignorance could mean another's life.

He was positively enjoying this. His own plan, and his own flotilla about to put it into action. Unless of course whatever *Tamarisk*'s landing-party reported put the kibosh on it. The submarine's signal, which would come at some time before dawn tomorrow morning, would be the trigger to action. Or the other way about, the stopper on it. Nick was due to go ashore at 6 am to Wishart's office at Gabbari: by that time they should have the answers. But he felt guilty for enjoying the prospect of this – 'lunatic operation', Wishart had called it at one stage. Smoking now, prowling the spacious day-cabin, pausing at a scuttle to watch a felucca sliding past with its lateen sail barely holding any wind, then stopping to look into Fiona's eyes: thinking about *Carnarvon*, about the letter he had to write to Sarah. Did he *have* to describe all the circumstances, including the fact that by his own decision he'd had to steam away from her survivors?

Yes. Fiona told him flatly, *Yes, you do*.

It wasn't a job to funk. It wasn't anything to be ashamed of – unless you *did* funk it. And it was a fact that, by and large, the odds were in favour of survival, in warmish waters . . .

There'd be a heap of problems facing him when he got back from this jaunt. Assuming the mantle of a Captain (D) meant taking on a mass of administrative work. It meant embarking a staff – with consequent crowding of wardroom and cabin accommodation – of specialists: flotilla torpedo officer, communications officer, and so on. And a secretary, a paymaster to cope with the paperwork. Extra communications ratings, both V/S and W/T: and a PO steward in McEvoy's job, damn it . . .

Fiona's look was expectant, demanding. He hadn't noticed it until this moment, but he knew what she wanted. He nodded at the portrait, and murmured, 'I'll write to *you* this afternoon.'

'Sir?'

McEvoy was looking at him enquiringly down the length of the cabin. Nick thought it might be possible to push him – McEvoy – through for the PO's rate. Something to discuss with Dalgleish . . . He admitted, 'I was talking' – he touched the frame – 'to her.'

'Oh. Aye.' Unsurprised. Setting the Angostura and lime-juice shakers on the silver tray, near the new bottle of Plymouth gin. He nodded. 'I'd not blame ye for *that*, sir.'

The caïque had been drifting south-eastward, Jack thought, and was now in a different current that was taking it more or less due south. A finger-like object on the horizon – it had been to the north of them when he'd first seen it and now it was about north-west – was almost certainly Ovo island, which he knew was about fifteen miles north of Malea Bay and had a 170-foot light-tower on it. He guessed they'd either drift ashore somewhere in the Malea Bay or Cape St John area, or be transferred to the western-flowing current as they came nearer the coast. If that happened they might run ashore on Standia island, or pass it and carry on for sixty or seventy miles to Suda Bay.

He and Alphonso were keeping off the cabin-top now, because three times Messerschmitts had buzzed them, obviously looking for signs of life – in order to end it if it existed, presumably. From the caïque's sternsheets, where they spent most of their time now, they could dive into the cabin and out of sight at the first sight of an approaching aircraft. Alphonso seemed to have no illusions about the Luftwaffe, even if they were his country's allies.

Through being taken sparingly, the bread and cheese were lasting well. Alphonso was a generous host, taking it for granted they'd go halves whenever they allowed themselves a snack or a drink of wine. The bread was hard, like grey rusk, and the cheese was made from goats' milk: no mistaking *that* rank flavour. In the circumstances, no objecting to it either.

Apparently the caïque had been attacked and damaged by a British submarine. Jack had asked Alphonso what had happened – by pointing at the sky and at the caïque, making aeroplane and machine-gun noises, and so on. Alphonso had shaken his head, gabbled away in Italian: then, remembering that Jack couldn't understand him, had sprung to his feet and embarked on an elaborate charade. First he'd used his hands in the sea over the caïque's side to indicate the surfacing of a submarine. *Boom* . . . A ship blown up: then he began to fall about, jumping up and falling down again, in one place and then another. A lot of men falling dead: passengers: soldiers? Alphonso drew a swastika in the salt crust on the cabin door. Then, pointing at himself, he went through the motions of diving overboard and swimming. Looking at Jack: eyebrows raised to ask him, *understand?* He began a new mime: of a man resembling Jack – he pointed at him – coming aboard. From the submarine, it had to be. Going down for'ard to the hold which was now flooded: doing something or other: then coming aft here and down through the trap-door into the engine space. Alphonso dropped down into it and showed Jack the damage he'd already noticed: smashed machinery, holed and charred deckboards. Jack guessed that an officer from the submarine had boarded this craft in order to place charges, which would be the simplest way to sink a ship built of heavy timber, but hadn't found any heavy, movable object with which to tamp down the stern charge. So the force of the explosion had been dissipated instead of directed down through the bottom. And of course the bottom would be particularly strong here, reinforced to carry the engine's weight.

Back on the caïque's stern, Alphonso had finished his story. First, a couple of *boom-booms*: then he'd shown the submarine gliding away: gone! Flashing smile from the narrator. Then himself swimming, and climbing back on board. Heaving objects overboard: dead German soldiers was a fair bet. Finally Alphonso climbed to the cabin roof and reclined on it. He spread his hands: understand? Jack had given him a standing ovation. Then he'd had to tell *his* story. Himself in a big ship – spreading his arms and looking upwards and from one side to the other, to suggest its vastness. Alphonso got that all right, and he was enjoying this game like anything. Jack gave him Stukas swooping, guns shooting up at them, bombs whistling down, bombs bursting all around him, Alphonso was screaming with laughter, rocking to and fro. Jack swimming, climbing aboard . . . Alphonso, having laughed himself almost sick, clapped him on the back and shook his hand. He wasn't at all a bad companion to be stuck on a half-sunk caïque with.

At about 10.30 pm, Nick added the final lines to his letter to Sarah. He'd redrafted it twice: it still wasn't perfect, but it would have to do. He addressed it, and added 'sender's name and address' to the space on the back, remembering as he did it to write 'Capt.' instead of 'Cdr.'

He'd already written to Fiona: he'd done that before he'd gone along to the wardroom to 'wet his stripe' and accept his officers' hospitality at dinner. He'd told her nothing about his promotion; there was only that small panel on the back to catch her eye and frustrate her with the lack of news of it inside. She'd have to write back immediately now, to question him about it.

From outside on the quarterdeck he heard the quartermaster of the watch give a sudden, high-pitched yell: 'Boat aho-o-oy!' Challenging some approaching or passing ship's boat in the darkness. The answer came immediately: 'Aye aye!'

It meant two things. One, the boat was coming to *Tuareg*: otherwise the answering cry would have been 'Passing!' Two, the boat was carrying an officer of wardroom rank, a lieutenant or above, but not a ship's captain or an admiral. If whoever was arriving had been junior to a two-striper, the answer would have been 'No, no!', while a commanding officer in the boat would have produced the name of his ship, or for an admiral a yell of 'Flag!'

Nick was about ready to turn in, but he waited to see what this might be about. Hoping his guess would be right . . . He heard the boat coming alongside; Harry Houston, officer of the day, had been fetched from the wardroom to receive the visitor. There was a murmur of conversation out there: and presently a knock on the door of the day-cabin.

'Excuse me, sir.' Houston's bulk filled most of the frame. 'Officer with a message for you from Gabbari.'

'Bring him in.'

An RNVR paymaster lieutenant came in sideways around Houston. Removing his cap, he handed Nick a brown OHMS envelope with BY HAND OF OFFICER stamped across it. Nick thanked him. 'Who are you?'

'McCartney, sir. I work for Admiral Wishart.'

'Lucky man.'

'Yes, sir. I'd sooner have a sea job, though.'

The tone had suggested it wasn't an entirely casual observation. Nick took the envelope and tore it open: he murmured, 'So would Admiral Wishart.' Then he read the brief, handwritten note.

Our signal was passed and acknowledged at 2210. See you here at 0615. A.W.

He nodded. 'Thank you. There's no answer.'

At this moment, *Tamarisk* would be moving in towards the coast at Retimo, running on her diesels and trimmed-down so as to present as small a silhouette as possible. Inside her, the commandos would be blacking their faces, checking weapons and readying their canoes. And depending on what they learnt ashore and then reported, there would or would not be a lift from Retimo tomorrow night.

CHAPTER 12

He'd got her in his glasses: a black hump in the dark, quiet sea on *Tuareg*'s port bow. And she must have picked them up at about the same moment: he'd only just settled the glasses on her when the challenge came winking on a blue-shaded lamp. Leading Signalman Lever was beside him in the front of the bridge and he had *Tuareg*'s shaded Aldis ready: he was aiming it, with his eye to the back of the sight on it, and now he was clicking out the reply, the recognition letters for this watch.

'Yeoman – pass astern "S" for sugar.'

'Aye aye, sir!' Three blue flashes was the code in the operation orders for *I am stopping engines*. Lever reported, 'Challenge answered, sir.'

'Make to him, *Please transfer passengers over my port side*.'

The lamp began to click again. It was a quarter past midnight – Sunday morning now, the first day of June. The rendezvous had been ordered for 0020 (with the object of making it by not later than half past) so they were five minutes ahead of schedule; it should be easy enough now to embark the commandos and get under way again by the half-hour. *Tamarisk*, her job completed, would continue her delayed return passage to Alexandria.

The calm conditions were ideal. If there'd been any sea running this transfer would have had to be done by boat, and it would have taken longer. Timing, keeping right up to the schedule, was vital to the plan.

'Message passed, sir.'

'Stop both engines. Where are the others, pilot?'

'Hauling out northwards, sir.'

The other three were to patrol to seaward while *Tuareg* picked up her passengers. Nick trained his glasses on the submarine again. Last night she'd landed her commandos at about midnight and

448

embarked them again a few hours later, and before she'd dived for the daylight patrol she'd signalled the report that Wishart had shown him before breakfast.

Reconnaissance completed. Approximately 800 personnel including 26 nurses and 230 wounded will be ready for embarkation from sandy beach between longitude 24 degrees 29 point 1 and point 3 east 0130/1 June. Beach party will be transferred at rendezvous as ordered.

It had been a huge relief, getting that message; not only for the sake of this operation, but because of earlier failures to contact the garrison by submarine.

'Slow ahead port, slow astern starboard.' He was turning the ship, to make it easier for the submarine to come alongside. There'd be no need to secure her: she'd only be there long enough for four fit men to rush over. 'Stop both engines.'

'Stop both, sir . . . Both telegraphs to stop, sir.'

Just abaft the beam now, the submarine was a low black silhouette, its length shortening as it turned. Bridge and conning-tower were easy enough to see, but you needed to look hard to make out the low, dark line of casing that swelled upwards at the bow, a curve up over the for'ard torpedo tubes. Evil-looking object . . .

'Take over here, pilot.'

Drisdale came up beside him at the binnacle, and Nick moved to the side of the bridge to watch *Tamarisk* slide up out of the night. Down on *Tuareg*'s waist PO Mercer and his gang would be ready with a plank to shove over; and Rivers would probably only lay his bow alongside the destroyer, because amidships the bulge of the submarine's saddle-tanks would make for a wider gap to bridge.

The flotilla had come up from Alexandria on a course that would have taken them to Plaka Bay if they'd continued on it; if a Luftwaffe scout had spotted them, it would have seemed they were heading for somewhere on the south coast. In fact no German had come anywhere near them: they'd had cover from Fulmars to start with, and then Beaufighters. How the aircraft had been spared to work with ships was something best known to ABC, air command in Cairo and possibly a Dominion prime minister or two.

Tamarisk's forepart slid up to overlap *Tuareg*'s quarterdeck. The submarine was at a slight angle to the destroyer: Rivers was keeping his screws well out and his tanks clear of any bumps. Men were standing on the casing, ready to come over: there was a forward-rushing swirl of sea as her screws went astern and stopped her, then a warning shout and a thump as the end of gangplank banged down to bridge the gap. The men were moving to it: the first one hesitating for a moment, making sure of his balance then coming swiftly across. A voice called, 'Everard?'

Nick shouted back, 'Yes. Rivers?'

'Morning. Listen – you've got *five* passengers. Extra chap's a leatherneck who says he knows you.'

That would explain itself in a minute, no doubt. Nick called, 'Many thanks for your help!'

'My pleasure. Good luck now!'

The men had all come over and the plank was being dragged back. A couple of submariners were retreating along their casing towards the conning-tower. And the submarine was backing off, white water lathering through the widening gap. Nick told Drisdale, 'Half ahead together, three-one-oh revs.' The course from here would be due west to clear Cape Stavros, with small alterations later to bring them down to the coast at Retimo. It was twenty-five minutes past midnight: so they were right on the schedule, so far. As *Tuareg*'s screws began to drive her ahead he aimed his glasses out to starboard and saw *Afghan* leading the other two down on a converging course to get back into station.

There was a clattering at the back of the bridge. Dalgleish announced, as he came for'ard, 'Captain Brownlees, Royal Marines, sir.'

Brownlees . . . He remembered: the marines they'd landed on the other side of Retimo, to relieve German pressure on the Retimo airstrip: Brownlees had been OC *Tuareg*'s detachment. They'd been one of a flotilla of four Tribals then: looking back on it, it seemed like a year ago.

'I gather I should congratulate you, sir.'

'Very good of you. I expect you've had a rough time since we last saw you. Perhaps you'll tell me about it later. Who have we here, now?'

'Lieutenant Haggard – Lieutenant Scott – Sergeants Davies and Foster, sir.' They all shook hands. Haggard said, 'I'm in charge of our party, sir. We brought Captain Brownlees out, though, with the idea it could be useful to have a Retimo local, as it were.'

'Might well be. Do you people need feeding, or anything?'

'We've been very well fed, sir, thank you.'

'Then we'll go down to the chartroom and tie up loose ends.

Number One, stay up here, will you? Sub,' he told Ashcourt, 'we'd better have you down there.' He explained to Haggard, 'Sub-Lieutenant Ashcourt will be in charge of our boats . . . Lead on down, Sub, and I'll be there in a moment.'

There was one hour to go before 0130, when the boats' keels were due to scrape on sand. Then one hour for the embarkation. It would mean smart boat-work and no delays at all. Joining them presently in the chartroom he asked Haggard – recognizing him by his shape, which was short and square – 'The extent of the beach, according to the signal, is about three hundred yards. Right?'

The commando nodded. He had close-cropped ginger hair and a face that suggested he laughed a lot. 'Wider than that, actually, but that's a stretch where your boats can get right up to the sand-shelf instead of sticking fifty yards out. We gave you the location, incidentally, in case something went berserk and we missed this rendezvous.'

He and Wishart had guessed it. And of course they *could* have made the lift without these men's help; it was just easier with guides who'd already been there. And he had another use for the commandos, at dawn, which as yet they knew nothing at all about . . . Ashcourt had spread out the Retimo chart: Nick reached for a pencil to use as a pointer.

'Embarkation beach – here to here. We'll use the whole length of it. The advantage is that our four ships can stop at the three-fathom line at hundred-yard intervals, giving the boats bags of room to get to and fro without getting in each other's way. It should speed things up, and time is a very important factor on this one.'

Lieutenant Scott nodded. 'We'll organize our Aussies into four widely separated queues. Nurses and doctors with wounded will come first.'

'Do they realize ashore we'll be showing no lights at all?'

'Very much so.' Brownlees said, 'If you showed any they'd quite likely shoot them out. They've had Germans heavy-breathing in their faces for quite a while now; the bastards are very close all round them. Also, they put up a starshell or two every so often. We may very easily get some interference.'

'Let's hope we don't . . . Is 800 the sum total?'

'For lifting, yes. By no means the total garrison. For the reason I've mentioned, mostly – there's constant pressure on the perimeter and the blokes holding it simply couldn't move.'

451

'Will they capitulate in the morning?'

'Well.' Brownlees shrugged. 'It's a decision for their commander. None of them *wants* to surrender. They reckon they could hold on for ever. They question why *anyone* should be jagging in.'

'The CO's an Aussie?'

'Certainly. There aren't more than a dozen of my lot left. My colonel was killed three days ago.' He leant forward, to the flame of Ashcourt's lighter; Nick had passed his case round. 'If the Hun does catch on to the fact we're pulling out and starts making a nuisance of himself, I take it you'll want to join in with your ships' guns?'

'Only if we're certain they know we're there. And not if we can possibly avoid it. Nine-tenths of our chances of success depend on them *not* knowing we're here. Didn't that come across in our signal to *Tamarisk*?'

Hammond nodded. 'Loud and clear.'

'I'm only talking about what *could* happen.' Brownlees breathed smoke out. 'The principle's accepted – we try to do it softly, softly. But *if* it blows up in our faces, you'll want to know where the Hun positions are. I've got it all marked out on this, anyway.' The map he pulled out of his pocket looked as if it might have been used for wrapping fish and chips. 'Shall I transfer the essentials to your chart?'

'That could be useful. Thank you. But I want to make this point about secrecy very strongly to you. Wouldn't be much point crowding people into ships just to be drowned when the Stukas come looking for us at dawn, would there?'

Sergeant Foster nodded. '*There*'s a thought, now.' Davies muttered, 'Sooner *not* think about it, thanks.' Nick was saying to Ashcourt, 'If you've any questions to ask them about the beach and approaches, Sub, now's your time. After that I've something quite different to talk about.'

He checked the time. It was 0040. But the point he'd made about not being caught by the Stukas: he didn't think any of them had really followed the implications to where logic took them. Dalgleish had, though. When Nick had been explaining the operation to him, here in the chartroom early yesterday, when he'd got to the point of 0230 being the latest they could afford for departure from Retimo with the troops on board, Dalgleish had gone on staring at the chart for about half a minute. Then he'd reached for the dividers and checked the distances from Retimo to Kaso and from

452

Retimo to Antikithera. Then he'd looked puzzled, and gone through his throat-clearing routine.

'Hesitant as I am to look on the gloomy side of things, sir, or quibble over paltry detail – if we leave Retimo at 0230 and leg it away at thirty knots, won't we be on the wrong side of Kaso at sunrise?'

There'd been a lot of gunfire ashore, to the west and south: machine-gun fire and heavier explosions – mortars, he guessed, but there were no soldiers up here now to ask.

'Course two-oh-oh, sir.'

Drisdale was stooped at the pelorus, watching bearings – a church about 250 yards inland of the beach and the dome of Retimo's ancient fort off to starboard. The town, or village, was built on an out-jutting piece of coast with a little harbour tucked in this side of it; it was a tiny harbour without quays or any jetty and apparently it was always silting up. Drisdale said quietly, 'Bang on for the approach, sir. Perfect.'

'Slow together.'

Aware of how close the Germans were, you tended to speak in whispers. The quiet area behind the beach was if anything more worrying than the more lively western sector: you found you were waiting for the silence to be shattered . . .

A mile offshore he'd positioned himself so that by running in on a course of 200 degrees with that church exactly ahead, its spire even at that distance easy to pick out with binoculars, when he stopped her and sent the boats away Ashcourt would only have to steer for the church and he'd hit the beach right in the centre of the strip they were going to use. *Afghan* was slanting out to starboard now, on *Tuareg*'s quarter, and the other two were diverging to port: when they all stopped roughly on the three-fathom line, their boats would have about 500 yards to cover. *Tuareg*'s were already manned and lowered almost to the water.

'Fifty yards to go, sir.'

Drisdale had only the dome's bearing to watch; Nick, conning the ship in, was keeping the church dead ahead.

'Stop both engines.'

'Stop both, sir . . . Both telegraphs to stop, sir.'

'Thirty yards . . . Twenty . . .'

'Tell 'em to stand by, Sub.' Chalk passed the order by telephone to the for'ard pompom deck. Drisdale intoned, 'Ten yards—'

453

'Slow astern together.'

'In position, sir!'

He left the screws working astern for just a little longer, to get all the way off her.

'Stop together. Away boats.' He told Drisdale, 'Watch that bearing like a hawk.'

The boats would be in the water now, and their crews would be securing them together: at any moment they'd be moving off towards the beach. He could see the other ships' boats in the water too, but *Tuareg*'s had a bit of a start on them. Time – exactly 0130.

'Boats are on their way, sir!'

So were *Highflier*'s. She was lying on *Tuareg*'s port side, *Halberdier* beyond her. *Afghan*'s boats moving away inshore now: and *Halberdier*'s. Not bad at all.

Seconds ticking by . . . Drisdale was muttering numbers to himself at the gyro repeater. Nick imagined that the waiting troops would be formed up in one mass: there'd be an initial delay while Brownlees and the commandos split off the first four loads, but by the time the boats went in for their second loads things should be better organized. Embarking lame men and stretcher-cases would be a fairly slow process, naturally.

He'd told Brownlees and the cut-throat merchants, half an hour ago and after the details of this bit of the operation had been settled, 'When we clear out from Retimo, we're going to take an island.'

0148: one lot – all women and wounded, Dalgleish had reported – had been embarked, and the boats had gone inshore again. Fighting was heavier now – judging by noises and flashes – inland and to the right, the west. It was too close to feel comfortable about, even if it might be farther inland than it seemed to be. Nick asked Houston up the voicepipe whether he could see anything ashore.

'Only when flares and things light bits up, sir. I'd guess most of the action's five or six hundred yards behind the town.'

It was rising ground there, but not all that steep: if an enemy had a sea view at all it would be from several miles away. There was a modest hill about three miles inland, and a lower one to the right, but the real heights on this slim waist of the island were near the south coast, the Plaka-Timbaki area.

Drisdale was putting the port screw ahead, to maintain the

position. The drift was north-westward, and every few minutes there had to be an adjustment. He put his glasses up towards the beach again: things were going to have to speed up, now. Otherwise—

Drisdale had called down quietly, 'Stop port.'

There was no 'otherwise' about it. The time-limits were rigid. The next part of the operation, nearly a hundred miles away, had to be completed by first light: hence the need to be off this coast by no later than 0230. There were forty minutes left and three round-trips still to go . . .

'There, sir!'

Chalk was pointing. 'Bit off to the right—'

'Must be *Afghan*'s.'

'No, sir, hers are in sight too – to the right again.'

'Are we in position, pilot?'

'Within a few yards, sir, yes.'

And the boats were swinging round: Ashcourt must have just seen the dark shapes of the ships and realized he'd gone off course. 0152: he'd be alongside now in – say, five, six minutes. It would take a few more minutes to get his passengers inboard, and it would then be just past the half-time point, with two more trips to make. Perhaps it wasn't as bad as he'd thought: perhaps they *would* do it in the time. He wondered how the women were settling into his quarters back aft.

Hare-brained . . . Aubrey Wishart wouldn't be getting much sleep tonight. If Ashcourt hadn't mucked this trip up they'd have been inside the schedule. There was nothing in hand for this kind of cock-up, or for any more of them: they'd started off five minutes to the good and now that had been thrown away.

A starshell broke overhead. He'd heard the thump of it bursting, and looked up just as the bleak magnesium brilliance sparked and expanded to flood the whole coastline, seascape, town, beaches, ships . . .

Drisdale muttered, shielding his eyes, 'That's torn it.'

Like a false daylight: shiny sea with boats chugging towards their ships, weighed-down, slow with their loads of passengers, sitting ducks if anyone was there to shoot at them. Nothing was happening for the moment, though, except the flare hanging right overhead, drifting lower and slightly westward on its parachute. Its stark brightness made the scene unreal, unnatural: light too bright and shadows too black, one of those nightmares when you were held in treacle or your limbs wouldn't move. He heard the motorboat's engine as the three linked boats ran in alongside: an Australian voice bawled, 'Put the bleeding light out, Ethel!'

He didn't get a single laugh.

The flare died. Suddenly, as if it *had* been switched off. Odd: the British kind burned right down to the sea. The Aussie called, 'That's my girl!' A gush of men's laughter rose as the boats bumped alongside.

Last trip now: and it was 0225. All four ships' boats were inshore. *Highflier*'s had had a slight lead when they'd last been in sight. *Tuareg* had lost ground – probably impeded *Afghan*'s boats too – through Ashcourt's earlier misjudgement.

Anyone could make mistakes: the trouble was that *everyone* could pay for them.

The shore action was still heavy, but sporadic and still mostly behind the town. The Germans must have been trying to light up some shore sector, not the sea, with that starshell.

'*Highflier*'s boats are in sight, sir.'

Whiffen had spotted them, on the port bow. Drisdale was checking *Tuareg*'s drift, bringing her back into position for the umpteenth time. Whiffen added, 'And again. *Halberdier*'s, sir.'

'Boats in sight starboard bow!' Chalk, this time. They'd be *Afghan*'s, over there: Ashcourt surely couldn't have done it *twice* . . . Sweating with impatience, Nick reminded himself that Brownlees, who was to command the next phase, was coming off in *Tuareg*'s boats on this last trip and that he'd have wanted to see the others get off the beach first.

Afghan's boats were well out now, two-thirds of the way to her.

'Time, someone?'

Leading Signalman Lever told him, 'Half past, sir.'

Should have finished: should be clear, getting off the coast . . . Houston was calling 'Bridge!' into the voicepipe. Nick ducked to it. 'Captain.'

'Our boats are in trouble, sir, I think. About halfway out or nearly, and stopped. I'd guess the motorboat's seized up again.'

Jesus Christ Almighty . . .

'Bearing now?'

'Just about right ahead. Bearing now is – one-nine-eight, sir.'

'Distance?'

'They're roughly halfway, sir.'

250 yards, say . . .

'Slow ahead together.' He straightened. 'Chalk.'

'Sir?'

'*Run* to the first lieutenant. I want two strong swimmers ready on the foc'sl with all the grass line we've got, and power on the capstan to haul the boats in when the line's fast. When I'm as close in as I can go I'll give them a shout, and they're to wait until they get it. Understood?'

'Aye aye, sir.' Chalk was throwing himself down the ladder at the back of the bridge as he yelled it. Whiffen reported, 'Torch flashing from the boats, sir!'

'Don't answer it.' He wasn't flashing lights that could be seen ashore. The engines were going slow ahead: he told Habgood, 'Steer one-nine-eight.' Then to Drisdale, 'How close in can I get without going on the putty?'

'Another half-cable, sir. *If* the chart's reliable.'

It probably wasn't: he recalled the stuff about silting on this coast. But you had to take your chances. He told him, 'Watch your bearing on the dome and tell me when I must stop.'

'Better just check it.' Drisdale dived for the chart alcove. The other destroyers' boats were all alongside their respective ships, or at least so close as to be hidden by them. Nick told Whiffen, 'Blue lamp to *Afghan* – and don't let any of it leak shorewards – *Proceed in execution of previous orders.*'

'Aye aye, sir!'

Drisdale had done his checking and he'd put the bridge messenger, Crawford, to watch the echo-sounder: he himself was back at the pelorus. 'Three degrees to go, sir.' Chalk came back, out of breath. Nick told him, 'Keep a look-out for'ard, tell me when they're ready on the foc'sl.' He called down, 'Stop starboard.'

'Two degrees to go, sir.'

Chalk reported, 'They're on the foc'sl, sir.'

'How much water under us?'

The messenger said, 'About four feet, sir.'

Nick had remembered that he had 180 or so extra men on board. Extra bodies, anyway. She wouldn't be drawing *less* than usual. 'Stop port.' He asked Chalk, 'D'you know who the swimmers are?'

'PO Mercer and Leading Seaman Sherratt volunteered, sir.'

Nick guessed, focusing his glasses on the boats – they'd swung broadside-on now, and the torch was still flashing seawards – that the swim would be roughly a hundred yards. But Mercer and

Sherratt could manage more than that, he thought, rather than have their ship smash her Asdic dome on some obstruction. 'Slow astern together.'

'Still one degree to go, sir.'

She still had forward way on, too, and he aimed to take it off her. Grass line was actually coir rope, made from coconut fibre and so light that it floated. Paid out properly from the foc's'l it wouldn't impose much drag, if any, on the swimmers. He'd called for two of them in case one got into any difficulty.

'Ship's stopped, sir.'

'Stop both engines.' He shouted at Chalk, 'Go!', and Chalk yelled it down to the dark foc's'l; a second later two splashes were clearly audible. Action behind the beach now: it seemed to have spread this way from the area behind the town . . . 'What are the other three doing, Yeoman?'

'Moving off, sir. *Afghan*'s turned round and the other two's getting round astern of her.'

He went to the front of the bridge, and put his glasses on the boats. Fireworks flickered along the coastline: flashes of small-arms and machine-gun fire. Drisdale reported, 'Bearing's steady, sir, and there's three feet of water under the sounder.'

They were all right as long as they didn't drift sideways: on either side there could be shallower patches, silt deposits.

'How's the ahead bearing?'

'As it should be, sir.'

Chalk began suddenly, 'I think—'

Then he was silent. It had been wishful thinking, and he was thinking better of it. It was never difficult to imagine you were seeing what you were waiting to see.

Minutes passing. *Slow* minutes . . .

The torch from the boat flashed slowly and clearly, *O . . . K . . .* Nick shouted down at the foc's'l, 'Heave in!' and Dalgleish's 'Aye aye!' floated back to him. The sky had been lit for a second by an explosion among the houses: now it was dark again and he was temporarily blind from it. He told Chalk, 'Nip down and remind the first lieutenant to bring the tow in very steadily with no jerks or straining. Otherwise the grass could break.' The breaking-strain of coir was only one-quarter that of hemp: Dalgleish wouldn't be unaware of it but it could be as well to remind him. Nick checked the time: twenty minutes to three. By cracking on full speed, thirty-four or thirty-five knots, he'd catch up on the flotilla's thirty or

458

thirty-two. But they'd only just beat the light: in fact they might *not* beat it, now. It was a three-hour passage to that deep harbour in Milos island.

En route, there'd be some painting done.

He was awake: what had woken him was the lurching and scraping of the caïque running aground on rock. It had roused Alphonso too: he was panicking, in Italian.

'All right, all right . . .'

The sunken forepart seemed to have anchored itself: the caïque had been swivelling on that pivot so that the stern was now pointing at the land. He could see it through the darkness – high, and higher still behind that, a hill or mountainside blacking out the stars. Alphonso was still chattering like an excited monkey: he told him, feeling the total contrast of his own Britishness, 'Wait a mo'. Steady on. *Attendo – momento!'*

He had no idea what time of night it was, except that he felt as if he'd slept for a long time.

Sorting out some stars, he got his bearings roughly. This had to be an east-facing coastline they'd fetched up against: and that made sense, because at dusk they'd been moving into a westerly drift. The only place that fitted this was the shoreline south of Cape St John, in the Gulf of Mirabella.

The distance to the actual shore and from where the caïque had stuck on its submerged rock was hard to make out, in the dark. It might be two yards and it could be twenty. But the thing was, obviously, to get ashore, before the caïque either washed off again or sank: more likely, both. Five, ten yards, he thought. The sea was washing regularly over a rock ledge there, sluicing over and pouring back each time in a miniature white waterfall; it might be an easy place for getting out.

'Come on, Alphonso.' He sat on the transom, swung his legs over; there was a list on the caïque and he was at the lower, starboard side. The sea felt warmer than it had when he'd last been in it: probably because the night air was so cool. Alphonso hung back, muttering what sounded like a prayer. Jack reached back, grabbed a handful of his shirt and tugged at it. 'Come on. *Venez. Allez oop!'* Alphonso pulled back, protesting. 'All right, suit yourself, I'm off.' He let himself down into the sea; he was expecting his feet to touch bottom, but they didn't. He let go of the transom, dropped right in and began to swim; he was climbing

459

up on to that shoreside ledge when he heard a splash and then gasping noises as Alphonso floundered after him.

'Time now?'

'Five thirty-six, sir.'

And as near as damn it, daylight: except that the bulk of Milos island close to starboard was keeping the flotilla in shadow as they raced northward within spitting distance of the rocky coast. Black, forbidding: it didn't look like a place the Venus could have come from. It would look prettier, no doubt, when the sun was up and shining on it, and by that time they'd be tucked away inside the inner harbour, the landlocked dead-end of the splendid bay called Ormos Milou which was in fact the ancient crater of a volcano.

He said to Dalgleish, 'We're going to make it by the skin of our teeth.'

'Please God.'

'Let's not rely on him *too* heavily.'

Drisdale said, 'Time to come round, sir.'

'Bring her round, then.'

And the three other destroyers would follow, one after the other heeling as they put their rudders over to turn in *Tuareg*'s gleaming wake. She'd only caught them up at a little after five, about ten miles south of Psalis Point. Now at thirty-two knots, creaming up along the sheer black coastline, they were about to round the corner which the chart called Akra Vani. Then they'd turn again, first east and then south-east to enter the bay, which might or might not have Italian destroyers or MAS-boats in it. He'd suggested to Dalgleish that they shouldn't try to saddle the Almighty with too much responsibility for the outcome because he had a feeling that the Deity's concern might be more for grand strategy than for tactics. Saint Paul, after all, did find himself having to 'cast four anchors out of the stern and pray for the day' when he arrived at Malta, and even for the Saint that prayer neither brought the day any closer nor saved the ship from being wrecked. He shouldn't have got himself on to a lee shore in a force 8, that was all.

Any more than Nick should have allowed his flotilla to be half an hour behind schedule, the one thing he'd sworn must *not* happen.

'Course is oh-six-five, sir.'

Akra Vani would be abeam in about one minute, distance 400

460

yards. Then they'd alter round again. There was plenty of water here and it was safe enough, but so close to the rocks thirty-two knots felt like an enormous lick of speed. It was necessary, and so was corner-cutting, if they were to have any chance at all of getting in there before the enemy knew they'd arrived. He wondered if there might be anyone up on those slopes to see them, see the rushing ships and the white bow-waves curling, the wash rolling away powerfully and fast to break in surging foam along the steep-to, rocky coast. In the villages – one hamlet at the little harbour and the main village higher up, inland – there'd be *some* kind of garrison. Probably Italian, possibly German. He'd gone into the idea of putting landing-parties ashore on their way into the bay, to take the main village from its rear, the north-west, but he'd decided against it, for several reasons that still seemed sound. Primarily because of the delay involved and the difficulties of finding a landing-place on that area of coast; and as things had turned out, there certainly wouldn't have been time.

The cape was abeam. He nodded to Drisdale's unspoken ques-tion, and said again, 'Come round.' Drisdale called down for fifteen degrees of starboard wheel.

Growing light showed them the entrance now, a gulf about two and a half miles wide narrowing to no more than one mile farther in. In just a few minutes they'd be tearing through those narrows into what would then be a widening, figure-of-eight-shaped harbour, a wonderfully sheltered and spacious bay which the enemy had used as an assembly point and jumping-off place for those caïque convoys which the Navy had broken up or turned back. Nick's plan was a gamble on the theory that now the Germans had Suda Bay, and there was no Royal Navy north of Crete to threaten their south-bound convoys, they'd have allowed Ormos Milou to relapse into the peace and obscurity from which they'd disturbed it.

He was also gambling on the accuracy of Intelligence reports which indicated an almost total lack of liaison between the Italian navy on the one hand and the Luftwaffe and Wehrmacht on the other. And on one other hope: there'd been an incident recently when German aircraft had attacked an Italian destroyer. There might still be minimal contact between the Master Race and its lackeys but it was a reasonable bet that after that fuss the German planes would shy away from Italian markings.

All the same, a week ago there'd been five Italian destroyers in

461

this harbour. And the flotilla ought to be making a quiet approach in semi-darkness, not galloping in in broad daylight.

'Midships.'

'Midships, sir . . .'

The water was absolutely flat. *Afghan* under helm astern of him, tucking her forefoot neatly inside *Tuareg*'s outdrifting wake. *Highflier* about to follow round . . . Behind him Brownlees, the Captain of Marines, said, 'I'll go down and get my chaps ready, sir.'

'Good. Best of luck.'

'Steer one-one-oh.'

Dalgleish suggested, 'Cable party, sir?'

'Have them piped, but only to stand by down there.' He looked round, and beckoned to Ashcourt. 'We're cutting this so fine I shan't anchor until the boats have got to the jetties.' He thought, And *that*'s if there's no shooting . . . But it was the racket of cables running out and waking the garrison from its beauty-sleep that he was thinking of – as well as counting on there being no Italian ships in the inner harbour. If there were, nobody ashore would sleep on much longer. He told Ashcourt, 'Muster your cable party behind A gun, to start with.'

'Aye aye, sir.'

'And watch out for the wet paint. We don't want Mercer's artistry all buggered up.'

Ashcourt would be taking charge on the foc's'l while Dalgleish got the motorboat away with twenty-five Australian soldiers under their own lieutenant and with Captain Brownlees and Sergeant Foster as well. The two commando lieutenants and Sergeant Davies were now in the other three destroyers as liaison officers between Brownlees and the three other detachments of the landing-force. There'd been written orders for the soldiers in each ship, but the commandos had been used to explain Brownlees' own intentions for when they got ashore. There'd be roughly a hundred men landing, more than enough to take and police the two villages and keep the lid on tight until dusk this evening.

Dalgleish said, 'I'll go down now, sir.'

'Yes. Tell Mr Walsh to train the tubes out on both sides.'

'Aye aye, sir.'

Guns' crews were closed up, circuits tested, ammunition-supply parties standing ready. The ships would be stopping to send their landing-parties away in less than ten minutes. Running straight into the gulf now, and daylight reaching down inside the bowl of hills.

'I'd like to come round a bit more, to hug that next point, sir.'

He nodded. 'All right.'

'Starboard ten.'

'Starboard ten, sir!'

'Steer one-two-oh.'

Nick hoped the artificers' night's work on the motorboat was going to prove effective . . . The point Drisdale was about to embrace was called Akra Kalamaria. And the time was 0544, already a quarter hour past the deadline for having all four ships at rest in the inner harbour looking like Italians, and the soldiers in possession of the harbour village – Adhamas – and of the larger village of Milos a mile and a half up the road.

The paint was spread in three colours – green, white, red, the colours of the Italian flag – right across the foc'sl of each ship, and duplicated on their quarterdecks between Y gun and the depth-charge chutes. It had been done in a hurry and in the dark on the way up from Retimo, and as artwork it might be a bit rough, but it should pass inspection from the air. Planks had been put across the painted areas so men's feet wouldn't smudge them, particularly on the foc'sls during the anchoring.

Akra Kalamaria was 200 yards abeam to starboard. And on about red three-oh, up on the hill and right against the background of brightening eastern sky, he saw the village: houses, two church spires . . .

'Yeoman – hoist the Italian ensign.'

'Aye aye, sir!' They were all ready with it: almost in the same breath Whiffen confirmed, 'Eyetie flag's up there, sir.'

'Very good.' He didn't particularly want to look at it. 'Now make to *Afghan, Will postpone anchoring until boats have reached shore.*'

0547: the point coming up to port now was called Bombairdha. Just around it – they'd be turning to port, circling it – was the anchorage and the harbour, with two jetties of sorts. The nearer one would be used by *Afghan*'s landing-party, who were to take control of the waterfront and the houses near it, and the other three contingents would land at the eastern jetty, which was where the road up to Milos and to its subsidiary village of Tripiti started.

Chalk said, 'Mr Walsh reports tubes trained out both sides, sir.'

'Very good.'

He hoped there'd be no use for them. He'd know in about ninety seconds' time.

Jack had been right when he'd guessed they'd landed on the western shore of the Gulf of Mirabella. It was getting light now and he could see the Spinalonga peninsula offshore to the south, and the little islet this side of it. Here, behind them, a spur of mountains ran south-westward and another, less dramatic, formed a coastal ridge. Calm sea, with nothing in sight on it except the wreck of their caïque a few yards away, edged a high, stony landscape which would become a hot one when the sun was up.

Alphonso sat hugging his knees, facing the sunrise and Jack Everard. He was silent, for the first time since they'd become shipmates. Perhaps he was realizing that now they hadn't the sea to isolate them and to contend with, they'd become part of the world again and therefore enemies. But they still had needs in common: food, drink, perhaps shelter. The biggest difference between them would be that Jack's ambition was to avoid meeting Germans, while Alphonso would probably like to find some.

Quite a *large* difference, when you thought about it. It would be sensible, Jack thought, for him and Alphonso now to go their separate ways. He bent down and offered his hand.

'So long, Alphonso. *Au revoir. Bon chance, amigo.*'

Alphonso shook his hand warmly enough, and with a flash of the old happy smile, but there was still cogitation in progress behind those dark brown eyes. Jack had just done his own thinking: it would be a good idea, he'd decided, to head for the south coast. If there was any evacuating still going on that would be the likely area for it. Alternatively one might be able to pinch some sort of boat and sail south. To kick off with, if he followed the shore of the gulf until the coastline curved east, then he'd be able – with luck – to find a way on through or over the mountains, and he'd have to chance his luck along the way in the matter of food and drink. Water, he supposed, would be the most important thing.

He'd gone about five yards before Alphonso caught him up. Jack stopped, looking round at him and frowning.

'Me go. You stay. Or go *that* way.'

He tried to mime it, putting the flat of his hands towards Alphonso as if to bar the way to him. But this was the sort of game the Italian enjoyed. He was smiling, pointing south and nodding violently, then pointing at both himself and Jack, linking

464

them together. Then he was going through the motions of eating, stuffing food into his mouth and chewing, and taking a drink – he was thinking of it as wine, by the way he smacked his lips – again, apparently it was something they were going to do together.

'Alphonso, I believe you're bonkers.'

Nodding, laughing . . . '*Si, si!*'

He gave up, started off again, trailed by his Italian. Ten minutes later, he saw the houses. A hamlet: a fishing village, perhaps: there were boats and nets. He stopped to let Alphonso catch up with him. The sight of the white houses – cottages – obviously pleased the Italian: he started towards them at a trot, and Jack followed. He thought they might at any rate get a drink of water.

An old woman, in black and with her head covered rather like a nun, turned and scuttled away, round the back of the first house as they approached it. Alphonso laughed, turned to wink at Jack, then walked up to the front door and knocked on it. Jack stood waiting, glad to have Alphonso take the initiative now, a dozen yards behind him. He was conscious of looking like a tramp: bearded and none too clean. Well, say like a shipwrecked RN lieutenant. Alphonso looked like a circus acrobat down on his luck.

Right behind him, a harsh voice barked some sort of question.

Jack turned quickly, startled. A man of about thirty, brown-skinned and heavy-set, a peasant or a fisherman, had materialized from God only knew where. He repeated the same question: in Greek, presumably, or Cretan. Jack waved a hand towards the sea, then pointed to himself. 'English navy.' He made a swimming motion, and the man nodded, jerked his head in a beckoning gesture and then turned away. Jack, trailed again by Alphonso, stumbled after him along the uneven, stony path. If anything wheeled moved here it wouldn't be more than a donkey-cart. At about the third house, which seemed to be a small farm or smallholding, the man turned in and beckoned again. He led them past the house, heading towards a barn, and when he got close to it he waited for Jack to get there before he pushed the door open and went in.

Hard-baked earth floor: circular, a threshing-floor. But there was a big rough table at the back, with glasses of wine and a stone jug on it, a group of people vague in the half-light. Early in the day for boozing, he was thinking: then he'd focused on the people. A corporal with a New Zealand shoulder-flash, a dark girl – Cretan,

465

he guessed – and a solid-looking male local who might have been the girl's father. She looked about seventeen.

The corporal, surprisingly, got to his feet. The girl half-smiled, dropped her eyes. The man who'd brought them in was explaining something to the other one. The girl looked up again, and as Jack met her eyes the smile came back. He said, 'My name's Everard.' His epaulets marked him for *what* he was. He added, 'I was sunk in the cruiser *Carnarvon* three days ago. What's the form here?'

'We're foraging.' The corporal held out his hand. 'I'm Chris McGurk. Glad to meet up with you, Lieutenant, sir. This here's Maria. We come down on the scrounge – they're s'posed to be gettin' us some fish. Stuck here till it gets dark again now, can't bloody move in daylight.' He pointed at the Cretan. 'We're with *his* lot, dozen of us, up in the mountain there. He's her brother – Nico, he's called.' The girl was attractive, in a direct, uncaring way. Long skirts and shapeless wrappings, but she'd have a good figure, he guessed, under all that. The corporal said, 'The *Carnarvon*, you said? We got a rum little bloke with us, name of Brighouse . . . he come off—'

The brother interrupted, muttering in his own language; he'd lifted one hand, to point. Eyes followed the thick, pointing finger to Alphonso.

'Hey. What's *this*?'

They were all staring at Alphonso. Jack said, 'He answers to the name of Alphonso. Unfortunately I can't speak Italian and he doesn't understand a word of—'

'*Italian?*'

The brother looked suddenly very angry. Corporal McGurk had a Luger in his fist and it was aimed at Alphonso. The Cretan reached across, grasped its barrel and pushed it down. He growled something to the other man, the one who'd brought them in. Alphonso found himself grabbed suddenly from behind: both his arms were twisted up behind his back, and his young, swarthy face in its fringe of black beard was screwed up in pain. The brother spoke again, and the other one turned Alphonso round and rushed him out: he'd found his voice and he was protesting, pleading in shrill Italian. Nico touched the corporal's gun again: 'No shoot. Shoot no good.' He touched his own ear. 'No good. Germans come.'

'Yeah. Okay.'

'Okay. Good!'

466

'Look,' Jack told the corporal, 'he's perfectly harmless! He and I have been sitting on a half-sunk caïque together for three days and nights, he's really—'

'Save it, Lieutenant.' McGurk nodded at him. 'Believe me, it's best.' He looked away, staring up at the rafters, and began to whistle between his teeth. Jack came to life: 'Christ, they aren't going to—'

Alphonso screamed. The sound came from somewhere round behind the shed: then it cut off abruptly. The girl leant forward, crossing herself and whispering. The corporal explained, 'We're liable to be hunted. We've no choice, sir.' Maria's brother leant over to pour Jack a glass of wine.

The director-tower voicepipe called; Nick answered it, and Houston told him, 'Harbour and anchorage is empty, sir.'

From up there he could see clear across the point of land. Nick straightened from the pipe, and glanced at his navigator; Drisdale said, 'Phew . . .'

They could have wiped up a few destroyers or MAS-boats; normally one would even have hoped to find some, but noise and fireworks were very definitely to be avoided if possible in this operation. Perfect peace and not a raised voice anywhere was what was wanted. There might quite possibly be a radio set with a German or Italian operator up in the village; to find such a radio and destroy it was a priority job for the landing-parties. *Tuareg* swept past the point, and Nick said, 'I'll take her now.' He called down, 'Port fifteen.'

The inner harbour gleamed like an enclosed lake on a gentle, dewy morning. Light pouring over the eastern hills confirmed that it was completely empty: there wasn't even a caïque afloat in it.

'Midships.'

'Midships, sir!'

'Yeoman – pass the signal for *Am stopping engines*.' He stooped to the pipe again: 'Steer oh-six-eight.'

Afghan would come inshore of *Tuareg*, as she closed in to her own landing-place.

'Message passed, sir!'

'Slow together. Sub, tell Mr Walsh to train his tubes fore and aft.'

It was like a picture postcard. Shabby little fishing harbour: wisps of chimney smoke: some old lobster boats moored close

467

inshore. *Afghan* was hauling out to port and slowing, her boats lowered close to the water and her waist crowded with khaki and tin hats. Once they'd got control of the place the soldiers were to lie low, stay inside the houses.

'Stop together.'

'Stop together, sir . . . Both telegraphs to stop, sir.'

The ships were rolling and pitching as their own wash overtook them: they'd entered at high speed and over the shallows it really stirred things up. Another forty or fifty yards and he'd stop her, about one cable's length from the jetty. There wasn't a sign of life anywhere, except for bluish smoke drifting up in still air.

'Slow astern together.'

'Tubes are trained fore and aft, sir.'

Sand-stained water swirled up *Tuareg*'s sides as her reversed screws took all the way off her.

'Stop both engines.' He glanced at Chalk. 'Away motorboat.'

Nine minutes to six. She was still bucking around, to her own and other ships' disturbance of the water. But apart from that it was as smooth as glass, and barring enemy interference it promised to be a very quiet, peaceful day. The messdecks would be jammed solid, and therefore hot, but exhausted men wouldn't find it impossible to sleep. Half of the main-deck crew space had been screened off as a hospital; the nurses had Nick's quarters aft, and Aussie officers had the wardroom. The two doctors who'd come with them were being accommodated in Gallwey's sickbay. Upper decks were to be kept clear; close-range weapons' crews would stand normal watches but keep under cover, out of sight. It was all in the orders.

'Motorboat's alongside, sir.'

The other destroyers' boats were in the water too, but it would be five or ten minutes before the troops could be ashore. That wasn't long, but if the Luftwaffe chose to pay a visit now, saw the ships lying off and the soldiers landing, the Italian colours might not impress them all that much. This should have been finished before daylight.

Waiting: controlling impatience. The ship's movement was lessening as the water calmed. He glanced at Drisdale. 'If we wanted to look 100 per cent Italian we'd have chickens pecking around on the quarterdeck.'

'Might get some from shore, sir?'

Drisdale had taken it seriously, for God's sake . . .

'Boat's left the side, sir!'

About bloody time . . . He bent to the pipe: 'Slow ahead port. Starboard twenty.' She was in as good a spot as any, and it would leave plenty of room for the others to anchor to the north-east of her in a line parallel to the waterfront: all he had to do was turn her round and drop the hook. 'Stop port. Midships.' *Tuareg* was already swinging nicely. He told Chalk, 'Up here, Sub, and tell the cable party to stand by.'

Afghan's boat had reached the nearer landing-place. He asked Drisdale, 'How much water?'

'Seven fathoms, sir.'

Two shackles of cable would be plenty, then. He stooped: 'Slow astern together.'

'Boats are at the other jetty, sir.'

Troops would be landing, hurrying up towards the village. So far, so good . . . He was waiting to get some sternway on her, so as to lay the cable out neatly ahead of the ship. 'Stop together.' He told Chalk, who was in the front of the bridge with an arm raised for Ashcourt to see from the foc's'l, 'Let go!' Chalk dropped his arm. Nick heard the clink of a sledge-hammer knocking the slip off, and then the roar and clatter of chain cable running out. His mind was moving on, meanwhile, to the next stages . . . The landing-parties would re-embark at nine-thirty, by which time it would be dark enough, and by ten he'd have his flotilla outside and well clear. The black paint would be used then, for blanking out the Italian colours while the ships sped south across the Aegean; four hours at thirty knots to Kaso, with another three and a half hours southwards from the Strait before the blessed darkness lifted. By sunrise they'd be not much more than 200 miles from Alexandria, and there'd be Beaufighters to meet them.

In Alexandria, please God, there might be news about *Carnarvon* survivors . . . He told Chalk, as he heard the cable's rush slow and then stop, 'Tell him to veer to two shackles, and secure.'

'Aye aye, sir!'

He had his glasses on a column of troops doubling up the road. With the delay he'd run into, he thought he was extremely lucky to be getting away with this. Touch wood . . . Dalgleish said, beside him, 'Captain, sir. Deputation here from the medical party. You did say as soon as we'd anchored—'

'What?'

Lowering the glasses, turning: Dalgleish had an Australian

major with him – a doctor – and two Australian-uniformed females. The one pushing forward beside the major was short, stocky, decidedly plain. The other—

He took his eyes off the other one, as the major said, 'Wanted to say how grateful we all are, Captain. I'm sure you're busy, we'll clear off again now, but—'

'Captain – you've done us proud, you really have, sir.'

That had come from the short, thickset woman. The other, who was willowy with light brown hair and a distinct resemblance to Ingrid Bergman, only nodded as she looked at him very directly out of wide, grey, appraising eyes. About twenty-eight, he guessed: and what a business for someone like her to have been through, for heaven's sake . . . Then he was telling them, 'Kind of you to feel like that. But—' he shrugged, shook his head. Dalgleish shouldn't have let them up here this soon, and there wasn't time for speeches. Nick told him, 'See they have everything they need.' The Bergman-type girl hesitated as the others turned away: she asked Nick quietly, 'Tomorrow – at sea, if it's okay – could I come up here? Little while, just to see how—'

'You'd better,' he warned her. 'If you don't come up of your own free will, I'll send an armed escort to collect you.'

'Cable's secured, sir.'

'Thank you, Sub.' Surprise on young Chalk's face. The girl had paused at the ladder-head, looking back at him across the bridge: and Fiona would have her eyebrows raised, he guessed. But what was Fiona doing with her spare time – except not writing letters?

Boats were returning to all the ships. Signalmen had been landed with the soldiers, sailors with battery-powered Aldis lamps and semaphore flags; there'd be some 'all-clear' messages soon, please God . . . Beaufighters in tomorrow's dawn: he warned himself, *Better not count chickens. We can't have* all *the luck*. He yawned – and caught himself in the act, realizing how tired he was. Then a follow-up thought hit him – a really marvellous one: once those signals had been made there'd be no reason at all why he shouldn't retire to his sea-cabin below the bridge, and sleep like a dog all day.

Postscript:

There was no last lift from Retimo (or Rethimnon). There was no 37th Destroyer Flotilla, cruiser *Carnarvon*, destroyer *Huntress*, assault ship *Glenshiel*, nor transport *Gelderland* either. But all the other ships mentioned in the story were present and engaged in the operations as described.

'There is rightly little credit or glory to be expected in these operations of retreat,' wrote Admiral of the Fleet Viscount Cunningham of Hyndhope in his autobiography *A Sailor's Odyssey*. He also said, during the course of the evacuation of Crete, 'It takes three years to build a ship, but three hundred to build a tradition.'

The tradition held up. And bringing sixteen and a half thousand soldiers out of the island cost not only ships but the lives of two thousand men of the Royal Navy. With the greatest respect for the memory of ABC, *I'd* say there was glory.

A.F.

ALL THE DROWNING SEAS

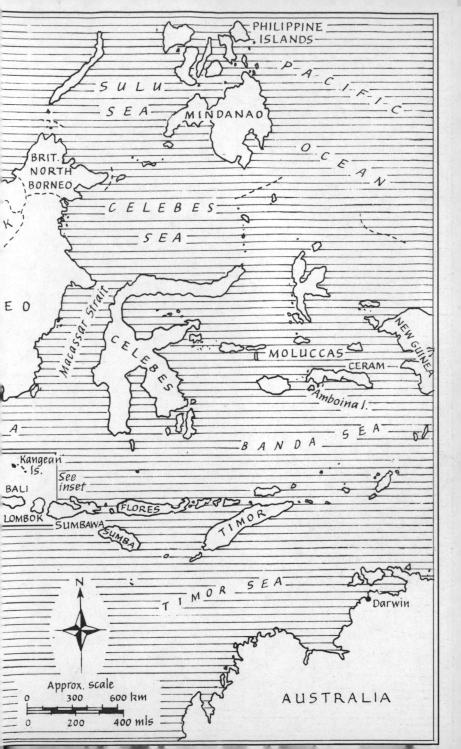

CHAPTER 1

The Surabaya Strait was a blue wedge glittering between the greens of Madura Island and the Java mainland, and as the squadron closed in towards it *Defiant*'s camouflage-painted steel ploughed water already churned by the two Dutch cruisers and the Australian and the other British one, *Exeter*. Astern of *Defiant* came the American, *Houston*, and then the mixed bag of destroyers – two Dutch, six American and three British – in a slightly ragged seaward tail.

Every damn thing, Nick Everard thought, was slightly ragged. Slightly hopeless. You had to pretend it wasn't, you had to seem to believe in this attempt to stem an avalanche that had rolled clear across the southwest Pacific in just ten weeks . . . .

Farting against thunder, Jim Jordan of the USS *Sloan* had called it.

The slaughter wasn't finished yet. Even this force now – this scratch collection of ships – well, they were steaming back into Surabaya now, but only for the destroyers to refuel. Then they'd be sailing again, to meet the invasion fleet that would be arriving within a day, possibly within hours.

De Ruyter, Rear-Admiral Doorman's flagship, had put her helm over to port a few moments ago, and her next-astern, *Java*, was following her round now. They were leaving the Jamuang rock to port, turning around it to follow the channel into that funnel-shaped approach. Nick became aware of Chevening, his navigating officer, waiting with an eye on him, wanting to know whether Nick would take over the conning of the ship now they were in pilotage waters.

The hell he would. There were still twenty miles to go, to Surabaya itself, and he'd be lunching anyway, as soon as his servant brought the tray up. He told Chevening, 'Carry on, please.'

A very proper, formal-mannered man, was Chevening, like many of these big-ship people; and it was conceivable that some of them might see their new commanding officer, Captain Sir Nicholas Everard DSO* DSC*RN, as something of an interloper. A destroyer man who'd been out of the Navy altogether between the wars certainly wasn't a typical cruiser captain; for some of them it might be difficult to imagine an RN officer leaving the Service voluntarily, unless there was something pretty odd about him . . . Chevening was a senior lieutenant, tall and prematurely balding: his light-coloured eyes reflected the sea's brightness as he waited at the binnacle for the moment when he'd turn *Defiant* in *Exeter*'s wake. Like a bloody old heron, Nick thought, watching *Perth*, ahead of *Exeter*, begin her turn. The Aussie cruiser was an old friend – from the Mediterranean, which was where he'd brought this ship from a few weeks ago. In the Med, before his own destroyer flotilla had been so reduced in numbers that it had virtually ceased to exist, he'd shared actions with *Perth* time after time: in the Greek operations, Crete, on the desert coast, in Malta convoys, she'd been through the thick of it.

Exeter, veteran of the Battle of the Plate, was turning now. But they were all, men and ships, veterans now.

Nick heard Chevening steadying *Defiant* on her new course. He lit a cigarette, squinting aft over the flare of the lighter to see *Houston*, the American, pushing her stem around inside the out-curving wake. *Houston*'s guns were eight-inch, as were *Exeter*'s; *Defiant* and the other four cruisers were armed with six-inch. With ten destroyers, they were not by any means a negligible fighting force: *would not have been*, he thought, if it weren't that they'd never fought together or even exercised together, had no joint tactical plan and no common signal code. They could communicate just about well enough to be able to follow each other around. Whereas any Jap force they came up against would be highly trained and integrated. They'd have air reconnaissance too, and their ships wouldn't be old crocks, already worked half to death. What it came down to was that any Jap force of roughly equivalent strength would be able to swallow this lot whole.

He prowled across the bridge and trained his glasses on the Java coastline, on Panka Point and the hill behind it. That strip of coast was about eight miles away, and with the binoculars you could see how the inshore waters were thickly groved with fishermen's stakes. They made what amounted to underwater corrals, by driving in bamboo stakes and lacing them together with lighter branches . . . The Japanese would take Java, all right, even if the Dutch did fight to the last man as they were promising. The Allied command had been dissolved two days ago, and General Wavell had flown back to India, leaving the island in the hands of its Dutch commanders. There was no doubt about what was going to happen now. The Japs had taken Bali to the east, Timor beyond it and Amboina north of that, and they'd raided Port Darwin in north Australia; they were in Sumatra to the west and Borneo and the Celebes to the north, they'd got Malaya and Sarawak and fighting had just about ended in the Philippines. They'd won footholds farther afield as well, at Rabaul in New Ireland and Lae in New Guinea; but the main thrust of the assault now was a pincer movement closing in on Java, which they had already isolated and which they'd want in order to close the ring on all the Indies.

It was a good thing, Nick thought, that Wavell had flown out. There was nothing he could have done here. The Japs had to be kept out of India and out of Australia: if they could be held inside that huge perimeter there'd be time to reorganize, rebuild. With the Americans in it now you could reckon that in the long term things would turn out all right. Here and now, things looked bloody awful.

There'd been an 'order of the day' issued by the Dutch governor-general. Its text ran: 'The time for destruction and withdrawal has now ended, the time for holding out and attacking has come . . . The foreign troops which are here will remain and will be maintained through a regular stream of reinforcements . . . .'

It was a nice thought, but the truth was there'd been an order that no more troops were to be landed in Java. Nick flicked his cigarette-end away down-wind and moved back to the port side of the bridge. Chevening had just ordered an increase in speed; and *Defiant* was indeed too far astern of *Exeter*. She'd lost ground somehow during that turn, he supposed. He told Chevening, 'Bit more than that, I'd say.' The navigator ducked to the voicepipe again and ordered another ten revolutions per minute, to get her back where she belonged more quickly. The last thing you wanted was a Dutchman telling you to keep proper station.

Now that was Leading Seaman Williams' voice, its Welsh lilt easy to identify, as he acknowledged the order through the voicepipe. Williams was new to the ship: he'd been drafted to her from shore duty in Singapore, and he'd left a wife there. Not many days before the end, when *Defiant* was bringing the last Australian reinforcements up through the Sunda Strait, Williams had requested a private interview and begged to be allowed ashore when they arrived. Nick had allowed it, although he'd been aware he shouldn't have; there was no question of granting shore leave, and he'd have to have *Defiant* well clear before daylight. He'd told Williams, 'I'm trusting you to be in the boat when it comes back. Whatever the situation is ashore, whatever you find out. All right?'

'Aye aye, sir. Very grateful, sir.'

Grateful, for the privilege of seeing to his own wife's safety. The town and dock area were already in chaos, thronged with desperate people who had no way out. Williams' wife was Eurasian, and the Japanese weren't behaving any less brutally to people – women particularly – of mixed blood than they were to whites, in the places they'd already over-run. The killick had come back as he'd promised he would, but in a worse state than when he'd landed: he'd failed to contact her or get any news of her. Most telephones were out of order, and the dockyard office where she'd worked had been empty, apparently ransacked. Facing Nick, he'd been stammering, helpless, a man in a waking nightmare. Nick told him that it surely meant she'd got away somehow, over to Sumatra or south to Java. Williams couldn't accept it: there was no way she could have got out, and she was there somewhere, in that panic-stricken rabble. Nick had appreciated how he'd have felt himself if Kate had been ashore there: and all he'd been able to do was tell Forbes, the chaplain, and the doctor, Sibbold, to keep an eye on him. Soon afterwards, two weeks ago, Singapore had fallen to the Japanese.

In his mind he could still smell the burning oil tanks, which had been set alight a week before the surrender. Even with Singapore island under siege, the enemy triumphant in Johore, Allied ships including *Defiant* had still been bringing troop convoys up through the Sunda Strait. You couldn't use the Malacca Strait because the Japs had established a crushing air superiority early in the battle for Malaya, and those waters were impassable. Without air power, you lost control of the sea; without that, you couldn't prevent enemy landings. The vicious circle tightened. The last troops into Singapore were the Aussie 18th Division, brought in so late they might as conveniently have marched straight into the POW camps. Evacuation had become a rout, a panic rush in anything that floated, and with Jap warships hunting close inshore. By that time there'd been a smoke-pall over Sumatra too, as the Dutch blew up their oil wells and refineries; the glow of the fires around Palembang had been visible in the sky from hundreds of miles out at sea. Nick had seen it when he'd been taking *Defiant* to meet a convoy of refugees who were being brought south from Natuna Island, a place the Japanese hadn't bothered to stop at in their first wave of assaults. The civilians had been ferried there from Miri in Sarawak and Labuan in North Borneo, just ahead of the enemy landings in those places, and at Natuna they'd been packed into a Dutch steamer which sailed with an escort of one Dutch and two American destroyers. The Dutch destroyer and one of the Americans had been sunk by Val divebombers before *Defiant* could reach them, and on the morning of the rendezvous the steamer was hit and set on fire and had to be abandoned. *Defiant* and the surviving American, USS *Sloan*, picked up most of the refugees and then fought their way down to Tanjang Priok – the port of Batavia, Java's capital – under recurrent air strikes. It had felt very much like the Crete battle: the frequent bombing, lack of air support, awareness of defeat, retreat.

A few days ago in Nick's cabin in *Defiant*, when they'd been licking their wounds in Tanjang Priok prior to sailing to join Doorman's Combined Striking Force at Surabaya, the USS *Sloan*'s captain had remarked, 'Darned strange, when you look at how things are right now, how none of us doubts we'll end up winning. Wouldn't you say so?'

Bob Gant, Nick's second in command, had glanced at Jordan in surprise. He and the American were both commanders, Gant a year or two older than Jim Jordan.

'Just as *well* nobody doubts it, I'd say.'

He'd pushed back his chair: 'If you'd excuse me now, sir. Rather a lot to see to.' Getting to his feet, Gant tried to look as if the effort didn't hurt him. He was a small man, with hair already grey although he was still under forty. He'd been in the carrier *Glorious* when she'd been sunk off Norway in June 1940, and he'd suffered some sort of damage to his spine. He wouldn't admit to it, but Surgeon Lieutenant-Commander Sibbold had said he was probably in pain twenty-four hours a day; he wouldn't admit it because if he had they'd have moved him to a desk job ashore.

Which *some* people might have preferred, Nick had thought, watching him leave the day cabin, to being where Bob Gant was

481

now. Jordan was right: you didn't have to be defeatist or a pessimist, but you didn't have to be blind or stupid either.

Jim Jordan, Commander USN, was a square-built man with ginger hair and a face that broadened at the jaw. His eyes moved back to Nick as the door shut behind Gant.

'D'you have any doubts of it yourself, Captain?'

'That we'll win, eventually?' Nick shook his head. 'None at all.'

Jordan said, 'Present circumstances are not exactly auspicious.'

'Oh, I don't know. I mean, so far as Java's concerned.' Out loud, one tended to resist the truth. 'If the Dutch can hang on ashore . . .'

'If . . .' Jordan shook his head. 'What worries me, frankly . . .'

He'd cut himself short. Nick waited: resuming, Jordan spoke more quietly. '*Everything*. As of this moment, I can't see we have a damn thing going for us. However . . .'

He'd checked again. Nick smiled. 'As you say – *however*. Let's drink to that.'

'In this whisky,' Jordan nodded at it appreciatively as his fist closed round the glass, 'I'll drink to just about anything.'

He'd come aboard to discuss details of their move to Surabaya, and stayed at Nick's invitation to sample a malt whisky, some Laphroaig that Nick had acquired in Alexandria. He added, sipping the end of it, 'I never tasted one as smooth as this.'

'Let's have one for the gangway, then.'

'No opposition . . . You married, sir? Family?'

'I'm not married now.'

He didn't want to have to think too much about it, either. There was a girl in London, Fiona Gascoyne, a young widow, to whom he felt he was more or less committed: to whom he'd *wanted* to be committed, before he'd got to know Kate Farquharson. Kate was Australian, an Army nurse, and he'd brought her out of Crete on board *Tuareg*, his destroyer. If it hadn't been for Fiona in the background he'd have proposed to Kate before she and her unit had been shipped home to Australia. In the circumstances, perhaps it was a good thing she *had* been sent home; but it was a complicated and unsatisfactory state of mind to be in.

He told Jordan, 'But family – yes. I have a son who's sort of part adopted American.'

'How come?'

'My former wife remarried, to an American. He's an industrialist, millionaire I'm told, lives in Connecticut. She had custody of our son Paul, and when the war started he ducked out of college over there and came across to join the Royal Navy. As a sailor, lower deck, but he's commissioned now and a submariner.' Nick pushed the cork back into the Laphroaigh bottle. 'Last I heard, he was being sent to Malta, to the submarine flotilla we have there.'

It was the main reason he hadn't wanted to leave the Mediterranean. With Paul in the 10th Submarine Flotilla they might have had a chance to see each other occasionally.

He'd sent Chevening down to get lunch in the wardroom; he'd already had his own, up here on the bridge. It had been corned beef, as usual. Ormrod, one of the watchkeeping lieutenants, was at the binnacle, and Nick was on his high seat in the port for'ard corner of the bridge. Glancing round, he saw Bob Gant coming forward from the ladder. Gant was in Number Sixes – tight, high-collared whites; Nick wore loose-fitting white overalls which he'd had made in Alexandria.

'Suppose we'll only get a few hours in there, sir?'

'If as much.' He offered the commander one of his black cheroots, and Gant's refusal seemed a shade defensive. Nick told him, 'They aren't as bad as they look, Bob.'

'I'll stick to my pipe, sir, thanks all the same.'

The Combined Striking Force had been patrolling north of Java since yesterday afternoon, looking for an invasion force that had been reported up there somewhere. They'd found nothing: lacking air reconnaissance, it was a matter of luck whether you bumped into an enemy or missed him. And the destroyers, with endurance strictly limited by the capacity of their fuel tanks, needed to be kept topped-up against the moment when you *might* run into the invaders.

Not 'might', though. *Would*, undoubtedly. Doorman's object would be to intercept at the earliest possible moment, and break up the convoy. To get at it, at the troopships, you'd have to sink or drive off the escorting warships first.

Gant observed quietly, stating what he knew Nick knew already but feeling he had to mention it all the same, 'Ship's company could do with some rest, sir.'

The old, old story. Exhausted men, worn-out ships. The Jap ships would be new and fast and their crews fresh, high-spirited with all the momentum of their sweeping victories. Nick asked, leaking cheroot-smoke as he glanced round to see what the officer of the watch was doing, 'Is Sandilands happy?'

Gant smiled. At the idea of Sandilands, the engineer commander, being *happy* . . .

Defiant was twenty years old. She'd been laid down as part of the War Emergency Programme – the *first* War's . . . Gant said, moving back to avoid some of Nick's smoke, 'If he can keep the wheels turning for just a while longer,' he moved one hand, indicating the other ships as well, 'we ought to give a pretty good account of ourselves, wouldn't you agree, sir?'

'Of course.' He wondered whether the commander was expressing confidence or fishing for reassurance. Remembering again the conversation with Jim Jordan, and wondering whether there was really any point in their being here at all. When there was no chance of them winning anything, except – oh, that old intangible, honour? And when you were already so short of ships that you had to keep antiques like this one running, was 'honour' worth six cruisers, a dozen destroyers?

Gant called suddenly, breaking into what was becoming a depressing line of thought, 'Yeoman!'

Pointing: at a light flashing from *Exeter*'s signal bridge. Ruddle, yeoman of the watch, had responded with a yell of 'Aye aye, sir!', and a leading signalman at the port-side lamp had already sent an answering flash.

'Captain, sir?'

Nick took his eyes off the fast sequence of dots and dashes. A messenger was beside him, with a sheet of signal-pad. He recognized the sloping scrawl of Instructor Lieutenant Hobbs, 'Schooly', who'd have deciphered this wireless message down in the plot, immediately below this bridge. Before he'd had time to read it, Ruddle called, 'Squadron stand by to reverse course in sequence of fleet numbers, sir!'

'Pass it to *Houston*.'

'Aye aye, sir!' PO Ruddle had a high screech of a voice, acquired from years of bawling down to flag-decks against high winds. *Defiant*'s lamp was already calling the American cruiser astern of her, and Nick was reading the decoded signal – which Doorman would have received in Dutch, from his Dutch senior officer at the other end of Java. There was a British rear-admiral there too, working with the Dutchman. Nick looked up from the signal, and told Gant, 'Two assault groups coming this way. Our bird's the eastern bunch. Said to be eighty miles offshore now.'

The flagship, *de Ruyter*, had begun to swing to starboard,

initiating the about-turn. No fuelling for the destroyers, after all. There wouldn't be time for it, of course. With the two forces steaming to meet each other at an aggregate speed of, say, nearly forty knots, it would be only a couple of hours before they met. He glanced again at the signal. The escort with the eastern group was reported to consist of four cruisers and fourteen destroyers. Behind them, of course, not in company with them but near enough to be whistled up when required, would be heavy striking units, battleships and carriers. However much damage you did to start with, therefore, you wouldn't be left long to gloat over it.

But – as Jim Jordan had so aptly put it – *however* . . .

CHAPTER 2

From the motor vessel *Montgovern*'s boat deck, with one shoulder against a lifeboat's davit for support as the ship rolled, Sub-Lieutenant Paul Everard RNVR gazed around at the crowd of ships bound for Malta. *Montgovern* was second in the port column of merchantmen; there were four columns, each of four ships, and all except one of them were carrying mixed cargoes consisting mainly of food, ammunition and cased petrol. The food was mostly flour. The exception, the *Caracas Moon*, was an oil tanker, and the cased petrol distributed among the other ships was there in case, with her load of aviation spirit, she did not get through. They'd all of them be targets for the Luftwaffe and for submarines' torpedoes, but tankers did tend to attract particular attention.

Ahead of the *Montgovern* steamed the *Warrenpoint*, nine thousand tons, and abeam of her, leading number two column, was the *Blackadder*, carrying the convoy commodore. Astern of the commodore's ship and thus on the *Montgovern*'s starboard beam plodded the long, low shape of the big *Castleventry*. They and the other twelve were all fine, fast ships of good capacity, specially chosen for the task ahead of them. They'd passed through the Gibraltar Strait at dawn yesterday and they were now well into the western basin of the Mediterranean, roughly south of the Balearics, steering east with rather more than six hundred miles to go.

The strength of the naval escort was a fair indication of the importance of the operation. Ahead of the solid block of merchantmen, three cruisers in line abreast stooped and swayed to the grey-blue swell. Astern of the columns another cruiser in the central position was dwarfed by two battleships, one on each side of her. Back on the starboard quarter, not visible at the moment from here on the *Montgovern*, three aircraft carriers with three more cruisers in close attendance formed a separate group. While all across the convoy's van and down its sides were the destroyers, several as close escort on each side of the square of merchant ships and another twenty forming an A/S screen on a radius of about three miles. The whole assembly covered many square miles of sea and made, Paul Everard thought, a very impressive picture.

There was a fourth carrier too, but she had a special job to do and wasn't part of the convoy's escort.

The enemy knew, by this time, that the convoy was on its way. They might have known a long time ago, when it was on its way south from the Clyde: but their spies in and around Gibraltar would certainly have reported the sudden traffic through the Strait and the warships, dozens of them, steaming in to refuel and hurrying out to sea again. On top of which there'd been several submarine alarms yesterday, contacts by destroyers out in the deep field, and a few depth charges dropped, and the submarines would have wirelessed sighting reports when they'd surfaced astern of the convoy and after nightfall. More annoyingly, and just to clinch it, yesterday evening an Algeria-bound French airliner had overflown the convoy with its radio chattering excitedly.

'Bless their little Vichy hearts!' Mackeson, naval liaison officer in the *Montgovern*, was a soft-voiced, easy-going man. Humphrey Straight, the freighter's master, had been very much more forthright. He'd growled, 'Fucking frogs . . .' and spat to leeward, which had happened to be in the direction of Algeria.

'Weather's not much cop, eh, Paul?'

Mick McCall, the freighter's second mate, was beside him, steadying himself with a hand on the lifeboat's rudder. He nodded skyward. 'Clearing, isn't it?'

It was, unfortunately; as daylight hardened you could see that grey areas were fewer and smaller than blue ones. At this time of year, you'd think you could have reckoned on some decent cloud cover . . . It was damned cold, anyway: Paul hunched into the turned-up collar of his greatcoat as McCall asked him, 'Service all right, still? Food up to standard? Sleeping well, are you? No rude noises in the night to wake you?'

Sarcasm: because Paul was a passenger and McCall had work to do, watches to keep. It was only half joking, too: part of it was the Merchant Navy man's resentment of the 'fighting' navy, the men who – McCall would have said – won all the applause, the glamour. It was an understandable resentment too: sitting on this eight-thousand-ton steamer with her explosive cargo, knowing that very soon a powerful enemy would be doing his best to see that it did explode, you could understand his point of view.

Paul told him, 'I'd have you know I was on the bridge for more than an hour last night.'

'My God, hadn't you better turn in again?'

'You're a riot, Mick . . .'

The whole convoy was altering course, turning to a new leg of the anti-submarine zigzag. Convoy manoeuvres, emergency turns and formation changes had been practised over and over again on the way down fom the Clyde to Gibraltar; the merchantmen had acted like a herd of recalcitrant cows to start with, but the admiral had drilled them until their masters must have been stuttering with Merchant Navy-type fury, and they were handling themselves quite well now. McCall said, 'I'd best be getting up there. And you ought to get below while there's still some breakfast left . . . Just look at that bloody sky!'

Paul glanced up, and agreed. The Luftwaffe would be in luck, if this weather held.

In the saloon, he found fellow passengers and ship's officers crowding the table. At first glance it looked as if he'd have to wait for someone to finish; then Mackeson called, 'Here you are, Sub!' and Paul saw there was a vacant chair beside him. He helped himself to coffee from the urn, murmured a general 'Good morning' as he squeezed in: someone pushed the cornflakes along, and Mackeson nudged the milk-jug his way. Condensed milk, of course; by this time any other kind would have tasted peculiar. Mackeson jerked a thumb towards Paul, and told a grey-haired, wingless RAF officer across the table, 'I knew this lad's father in the Navy twenty years ago. Small world, eh? Would you believe it, there are three damn generations of his family at sea now?'

The air-force man raised his eyebrows, let them fall again, chewed for a few seconds and then swallowed; he muttered, 'Remarkable.'

The three generations were Paul, his father Nick, and Nick's uncle Hugh. Admiral Sir Hugh Everard had come out of retirement to become a commodore of Atlantic convoys: a fairly arduous job, for a man of seventy. Nick Everard was – well, Paul wasn't sure where he was. Until quite recently he'd had a destroyer flotilla in the Eastern Mediterranean, but in the last letter Paul had had from him he'd given his address as HMS *Defiant* and hinted – or seemed to hint – that he was taking her elsewhere.

It had been on Mackeson's invitation that he'd spent some time on the freighter's bridge last night. Several times since they'd sailed from the Clyde the older man had said something like: 'Must have a yarn, Everard, when we get a minute's quiet. I want to hear the news of your family.' He'd known Nick in the Black Sea in 1919, and he'd known *of* Hugh Everard in the same period. He – Mackeson – had gone to sea as a midshipman RN in 1918, left the Service a few years later and rejoined as an RNR lieutenant-commander in 1939. So he was about forty-two now, Paul supposed, to Nick's forty-six.

Egg and a rasher of bacon appeared suddenly: powdered egg, as usual. The plate curved in from nowhere and more or less dropped in front of him: Paul looked round and said 'Thank you' to the retreating steward's back. Devenish, the *Montgovern*'s chief officer, advised from Paul's left, 'Wouldn't bother with the courtesies, if I were you. He's a bolshy sod . . . Did you get that Mention in Despatches in submarines?'

'No.' Devenish was squinting downwards at the small bronze oak-leaf sewn to Paul's reefer jacket. Paul told him, 'I haven't been in submarines very long. Hardly operationally at all.'

'He was at Narvik.' Mackeson spoke to Devenish across him. Mackeson seemed proud of the Everards, or of his old friendship with Nick. He added, 'Ordinary Seaman, gun's crew in one of the H-class destroyers. That's where he got it.' He asked Paul, 'Sunk, weren't you?'

Paul nodded as he began to eat. He'd been through all this last night, and the egg mixture was getting cold.

Last night in the darkened bridge, with Pratt, the third officer, in charge of the watch and Mackeson there to back him up while Captain Straight snored in the chartroom, Mackeson had suggested that Nick Everard might have taken *Defiant* to join the Eastern Fleet.

'It's as likely as anything.' He'd taken another pull at his pipe. The ship was moving rhythmically to the swell, creaking as she rolled, and the night air was cold enough to mist the glass side-windows. He'd removed the pipe from his mouth again; it made a popping sound as he took it out. 'Unless he's taken her home for refit, of course. And if you're right and she'd left the station at all. If he's still out here and you run into him, though, give him my very kind regards, will you?'

Paul said he would, of course.

'Bongo, they used to call me. Bongo Mackeson. I was a few years junior to him, of course, but I dare say he'll remember . . . I wouldn't envy him, mark you, if that's where they've sent him now. Japanese are all over us, and what've we got to stop 'em with?'

Paul really needed to see his father. Not just for the pleasure of a reunion: there was a very personal and unpleasant situation back in England which Nick Everard had to be told about, and Paul was the only person who could tell him. It wasn't anything to look forward to, and it wasn't the sort of information you'd want to put in a letter for some censor to read, either.

'Are we expecting things to warm up today, Mackeson?'

Paul emerged from his thoughts. The question had come from the other end of the table, in the high, thin tones of Lieutenant-Commander Thornton RNVR. Thornton was some kind of cipher expert: code-breaking, something of that sort. He'd made it plain that his particular expertise, for which he was urgently needed in Malta, was too secret and important to be discussed. The boy on his left, toad-like in thick spectacles, was an RNVR paymaster sub-lieutenant named Gosling; he was shy and hardly ever spoke to anyone. Thornton was staring at Mackeson, dabbing at his mouth while he waited for an answer to what Paul thought had been a damn-fool question.

Mackeson said easily, pushing his chair back from the table, 'Depends if we're referring to the weather or the enemy. Damned if I know either way.'

Thornton looked offended. 'Bongo' Mackeson was on his feet, bushy-browed and noticeably bow-legged: at fifty paces you'd guess he'd spent a lot of his life on horses. Leaning over his chair, he was telling anyone who cared to listen that the aircraft carrier that was doing the ferrying job would be flying-off her load of Spitfires later in the forenoon, and that there'd probably be a view of it from the *Montgovern*'s boat deck.

It was still cold up there at noon, when the passengers came drifting up to watch the fly-off. The ferrying carrier had hauled out to the convoy's port quarter, with two destroyers in attendance; she had forty-two Spitfires which were to fly from here to join the RAF in Malta, then this evening she'd turn and head back to Gibraltar, her job done. The other three carriers – fighter patrols from them were up and guarding the convoy now – would carry on eastward, providing air cover, Paul guessed, until the convoy came into range

490

of the Malta squadrons. Or as near to that point as possible. And come to think of it, there'd have to be a gap, a period when there'd be *no* fighter cover, and the convoy would be at its most vulnerable then. But the carriers' Sea Hurricanes had drawn first blood this morning: just after boat drill had finished, Mackeson had sent down a message that they'd shot down a shadowing Junkers 88.

Dennis Brill, a young Army doctor, had murmured as he stirred a mug of Bovril, 'So we're being shadowed . . .'

There was no surprise in it. Brill looked thoughtful, more than surprised, and Paul understood the reaction. It was only that this confirmation of the enemy's interest in the convoy brought home the reality, the certainty that before long they'd be attacked.

He and Brill had come up to the boat deck together, and Brill had stopped near Thornton and Harry Woods. Woods was a captain in the Royal Artillery and in charge of the *Montgovern*'s Army gunners. Thornton, the cipher expert, sniffed and murmured, 'Place is getting like Brighton pier.' He made room for them at the rail, though. He was tall, an inch or so taller than Paul, and he had an irritatingly high voice.

Woods pointed. 'You're just in time.'

The first Spitfire lifted from the carrier's deck, and curved skyward. Thornton turned his back on the scene, as if he now knew all about it. He asked Paul, 'Are you going to Malta to join one particular submarine, or—'

'Yeah.' Paul nodded. 'Just one.' The second Spitfire swooped away. Another stupid question, he thought. Talking to people like this one made him feel more American, more like he used to sound before the re-anglicizing process began two and a half years ago. It wasn't intentional, the reaction simply occurred, an instinctive raising of some psychological drawbridge. It reminded him, when he thought about it, that his father had said in his own younger days that *he*'d had a lot of difficulty getting along with some of his superiors.

'Not simply to the Malta flotilla for an unspecified appointment, I meant.' Thornton said it sharply, as if he thought he'd been snubbed. He had been, too. Four Spitfires were airborne now. Paul explained, 'I was in a submarine called *Ultra*. I went sick just when she was sailing for the Mediterranean, and now I'm rejoining her.'

He'd developed appendicitis a day or two before *Ultra* had been due to cast off from the depot ship in Holy Loch, where they'd been based during their work-up period. He'd had a pain in his gut and tried to ignore it, but then it had blown up and he'd had no option. After the long preparation, months of training and practising for the time when they'd be judged fit to go 'operational', it had been intensely disappointing. But his CO had come up trumps: he'd taken a spare crew sub-lieutenant out with him as a temporary replacement, and promised Paul his job back if he could get out there reasonably quickly. This convoy had been the first chance of a passage: there'd have been three weeks' wait in Gibraltar for the next supply submarine's trip to the island – even if he could have got himself to Gib and then wangled the passage in her. He was scared, even now, that if he didn't get there soon his replacement might have taken root, proved to be more useful than Paul Everard. Any submarine skipper would want the best team he could put together – particularly in the 10th Flotilla, who were fighting an extremely tough campaign in very difficult conditions. And another reason for concern was that he thought there'd probably be some spare submarine officers kicking their heels at the Malta base: several boats had been sunk or damaged in harbour by the bombing, so there'd be experienced men without sea billets.

By wartime standards Paul wasn't experienced at all. Since the submarine training course at Blyth he'd spent six months in a training boat, then the work-up months in *Ultra*. At the end of the work-up they'd done operational patrol in the North Sea – it was standard routine, a shake-down patrol – and in the course of it they'd sunk a U-boat, and that was the sum total of his submarine experience.

Woods said, watching the eighth Spitfire climb to join the others, 'That'll be the first flight. Short break for refreshments now. They go in eights, I'm told.' He asked Paul, 'What's its name?'

'What?'

'This submarine, what's—'

'*Ultra*.'

Thornton proclaimed, looking up at the Spitfires, 'Those are the only chaps who can be reasonably certain of getting anywhere *near* Malta.'

The Spits had formed up, and were flying east. They'd be on the ground in Malta in about a couple of hours . . . But this ciphering character was, truly, a jerk. You could know the odds without going around shouting them . . . Brill murmured, as Thornton stalked away, 'He's right, isn't he?'

'Is he? I guess I'm an optimist.'

492

'You'd have to be, wouldn't you?' Woods, the gunner, made a face. 'I mean, *submarines*, for God's sake.'

A lot of people reacted in that way, because they didn't know about submarines, what it was like and how it got into your blood, how you'd have hated, now, to be anything but a submariner. It wasn't worth the effort of trying to explain. He asked Woods, instead, 'D'you stay in this tub? Go back in her?'

'I stay in Malta. Relieving some character who'll make the trip home in her. Same with my blokes.'

His soldiers, he meant. He had about a dozen of them to man the four-inch gun on the stern. As well as soldiers there were some naval DEMS ratings on board to look after a forty-millimetre Bofors – it was on this boat deck, in a raised steel nest abaft the funnel – and some Oerlikons. DEMS stood for Defensively Equipped Merchant Ships. Other extra personnel on board in-cluded Mackeson's staff – an RN signalman and a W/T operator. The same kind of set-up applied in all the other ships as well.

Brill pushed himself upright. 'Anyone for a stroll?'

Woods declined. He had work to do, he said. Paul set off with the doctor, who'd been a medical student until very recently. He wondered, as they paced around the midships superstructure, up one side and down the other, how many miles of this deck he'd covered in the past week. 'Taking passage' was a dull business, after the first day or so; hence the interest in watching something as repetitive as one fighter after another taking off from a distant aircraft carrier . . . He had a novel half-read down in his cabin, but he'd found that reading palled too. It was a combination of boredom and nervous anticipation, he thought, that prevented your mind really settling to anything.

That, and a sense of impatience, the fact that all he was really interested in was getting to the Malta flotilla and *Ultra*.

After a few circuits they stopped, and leaned on the timber rail at the after end of the boat deck. There were life-rafts here between the big grey-painted ventilators, and a ladder each side led down to the after-well deck and the hatches to numbers four and five holds. Three Jeeps and a truck with RAF markings were chocked and lashed down there between the hatch-covers; in the port-side gangway off-duty crewmen were squatting to throw dice. Brill offered Paul a cigarette: 'Did old Mackeson say *three* generations of your people are at sea?'

'He missed one out. There's a sort of in-between that makes it up to four.' He stooped, shielding a match for their cigarettes. Then, straightening, 'There's me, my father, and the old guy who's a convoy commodore. That's the three. But also my father has a young half-brother called Jack. Young enough to be his son, but happens to be his half-brother – less than two years older than I am, for God's sake . . . Look, more Spits.'

A second batch had begun to take off from the carrier. She was broad on the convoy's beam now as the block of merchantmen swung to the port leg of the zigzag. There was a white embroidery on the sea: not bad conditions, Paul realized, from a submariner's point of view, with that camouflage for the feather of a periscope and the swell too low to make depth-keeping difficult. What with that and the largely clear sky that would help the Luftwaffe . . . Then he noticed something else: that the spaces between destroyers in the outer screen were wider than they had been earlier. Counting, and allowing for similar spacing in the sectors he couldn't see, he thought there weren't more than a dozen destroyers out there altogether.

The others would be fuelling, presumably – as some had done yesterday – from the oilers that were following a few miles astern. There were two fleet oilers with their own destroyer escort, and Mackeson had told him they'd be turning back for Gibraltar tonight.

He swung around, leaned on the rail beside the doctor. Brill asked him, 'Is this Jack relation in the RNVR, like you?'

'Is he hell. He was at Dartmouth. Lieutenant RN, now. He was in a cruiser that got sunk off Crete a year ago, but he got ashore and then worked with the partisans, guerrillas or whatever they call themselves. There were soldiers on the run to be got out, and weapons and stuff to be brought in for the resistance effort, and Jack was in and out of the island a couple of times by caïque. Cloak-and-dagger stuff. They gave him a DSC for it – either for that or for whatever went on earlier.'

'*Another* bloody hero.'

Brill sounded disgusted. Paul smiled, looking at him. The doctor had a triangular-shaped face, pale and with rather large, dark eyes in it. A bit like Mickey Mouse, really. Paul's smile faded as he thought of telling him, *Jack Everard's a shit. If he's a hero, give me cowards* . . . Instead he said, 'He's back in England now. Some small-ship job.'

And preparing to take part, in whatever small ship it was, in some fantastically hazardous operation. In London a couple of months ago Jack had let Paul glean that much, then he'd clammed up. And turned his attention to quite different interests.

Jack Everard, Paul thought, was a twenty-four-carat bastard: and Mrs Fiona Gascoyne, who was tipped to marry Paul's father, was a bitch of roughly the same quality.

If his father had left the Mediterranean, Paul thought, he'd *have* to put it down in writing. When you were the only person who could tell him, and personal survival couldn't exactly be guaranteed, you couldn't just wait for a chance meeting.

But of all the lousy jobs . . .

'Those aren't Sea Hurricanes, surely?'

Brill was pointing. With the convoy on this leg of the zigzag you could see back through the lines of ships, past the oil tanker *Caracas Moon*, which was number three in column three, and the American freighter *Santa Eulalia* next to her, to the group of aircraft carriers and cruisers following astern. A fighter had just taken off from one of the carriers, and a second was following it into the air now.

He told Brill, 'They're Grumman Wildcats.'

You learnt aircraft recognition with your trousers down. 'Own' and enemy aircraft shapes were displayed inside all lavatory doors in ships and training establishments, so you had them in front of your eyes for at least several minutes every day. He looked over at the ferry carrier, out on the beam: the second batch of Spitfires was high above her, formed up and departing. He said, 'Funny to think those guys'll be in Malta in time for tea.'

And we, he thought, had better be shuffling down for lunch. He glanced down to check the time, and his eyes were on his wristwatch when the deep *thump* of an explosion reached them. It had a muffled quality: an explosion under water was his first guess. Depth charge, maybe?

A second one, now – a duplicate of the first. And smoke was spreading over one of the big carriers astern. A third explosion, and a fourth. Four torpedo hits on that one carrier? She was listing, smoke pouring up. He couldn't see where the cruiser had got to, the C-class anti-aircraft cruiser that had been with the carrier. Behind the smoke, maybe. He wished he had binoculars. He muttered, trying to make his eyes do binoculars' work, 'Four hits . . . Christ, *look* at her!'

Brill was staring, gripping the rail. The smoke cleared enough to

495

show the big ship right over on her side; then it drifted across the line of sight again like a curtain. All distant, soundless and somehow unreal: it was more like watching a film, a newsreel or something, than seeing something happening in real life. Over there, at this moment, men would be dying: burning, drowning. You leaned on a rail and watched it, because there wasn't anything else you could be doing.

Smoke clearing suddenly: and it had cleared, he saw, because the carrier had gone. Sunk – just like that . . . Other passengers were crowding to the rail and asking questions. Brill asked Paul, watching a swirl of destroyer activity back there, 'How many men would there have been in her?'

'I don't know. More than a thousand.' He added, 'I guess a lot'll be picked up.'

'God, let's *hope*—'

'Yeah.' He thought, *Let's* . . . There were six hundred miles to go, and the battle had opened with the convoy losing about one third of its air defences.

CHAPTER 3

The Java Sea was a blue-tinted mirror reflecting heat, and the steel of the cruiser's bridge was hot to touch. Nick took his eyes off the ship astern and turned to face the leading seaman who'd been waiting for him here behind the lookout positions on the port side of *Defiant*'s bridge.

'Well, how's it going?'

Williams had a long, narrow jaw and a high, similarly narrow forehead. Deep-set brown eyes, rather close together, held Nick's steadily.

'Going on all right, sir.'

'I thought we might have a chat, before we get too busy.'

A smile . . . 'Can't happen too soon, sir, far's I'm concerned.'

'How d'you mean?'

'Well. Get a crack at the bastards this trip, won't we, sir?'

Nick had told them so, in a broadcast he'd made over the Tannoy. And he could understand Williams's personal desire to hit out, kill some Japanese . . . He said, 'I've been thinking about it quite a lot – about your wife, I mean – and I keep coming to the same conclusion. I honestly think she *must* have got away. When they shut down the dockyard offices they'd have cleared out to Sumatra probably, then Batavia or Bandoeng.'

Bandoeng, in the interior of Java behind Batavia, had been Wavell's headquarters and it was the Dutch headquarters now. Nick went on, 'Then they'd have evacuated – civilians, surely – from the south coast. From Tjilatjap. The odds are she's in Ceylon now, or Australia. I'd guess Ceylon.'

'She'd've left word for me, sir. I know that.'

'*If* she'd had the slightest notion that you'd be back. But for all she could have known we might've been in Australia by that time. *I* couldn't have said for sure we were coming back.'

'She'd still have left word, in case, like.'

'She might not have been given time to. Anyway, who was left – to leave word with, I mean? Must have been panic stations by that time. You saw for yourself how it was ashore then.'

Williams nodded. 'Wish I never *had* seen it . . . I'd like to see it your way, sir, but—'

'Try allowing yourself to. You aren't helping her by torturing yourself – isn't that what it amounts to?'

'Padre said something like that, sir. But it's what's in your mind, not what you'd *like* in it. It's – well, seeing things like they *are*, sir.'

'I think you should allow yourself to admit the possibility that you're wrong. Stop thinking, and just damn well hope. The way things are out here at the moment – well, for God's sake, it's not *only* you and your wife—'

'It is to me, sir.'

It would be to me, too, if I thought Kate had been stuck in Singapore. By Christ, it would. . . .

If she'd been there and disappeared, been left behind, he'd have gone half mad. Imagining it, he could admire Leading Seaman Williams's restraint. And there was substance for a different, personal reflection in that. If when you approached bedrock, the level of bare survival as a goal, it was B and not A who kept coming into your mind, didn't it tell you something?

If you let it?

Well, Kate was in this half of the world, and Fiona was ten thousand miles away. And Kate was an Army nurse who'd been on active service, she *could* have been in Singapore, so in any connection of that kind she was naturally the person you'd think of.

And here and now, in any case, it wasn't of much consequence. Williams's state of mind was, because Williams was one of about five hundred individuals in this ship for whose welfare he, Nick Everard, was responsible. He was one of five hundred moving parts of one machine.

Back in the bridge, he unslung his binoculars from the back of the high seat and put their strap over his head. There'd been no sign of an enemy yet, but there would be soon. Doorman had wirelessed a request for air support: Nick thought he might as well have asked Father Christmas for it. Some of these cruisers had carried spotter aircraft when they'd arrived out here, but they'd all been landed weeks ago. In some places if you gave the garrison an old seaplane you doubled the local air defences. But this force's first sight of the

Japs' eastern assault group might well be an enemy spotter plane scouting ahead of their ships.

And none of these Allied ships had RDF, either.

Doorman had stationed the three British destroyers ahead of the cruisers, and he'd put the Americans and Dutch astern. The cruisers were in line ahead. With inter-ship communications as limited and slow as they were, it was the simplest formation for him to control. He was leading, in his flagship *de Ruyter*; then came *Exeter*, then *Houston, Perth, Defiant, Java*. So the admiral had the two heavier-gunned ships astern of him.

'Signal, sir.'

Hobbs – 'Schooly' – had brought this one up himself. Wanting a breath of air, no doubt – understandable, because all the below-decks compartments were stiflingly hot, and the plot below this bridge, where he did his coding and decoding, had the sun beating on its steel walls from dawn to sunset. Some ovens might be cooler . . . The signal was an English-language repeat of an answer to Doorman's request for air support. All available fighter aircraft had been sent to cover a torpedo-bomber strike against the Jap transports, the troop convoy whose escort was somewhere just over the horizon now. Nick could guess what was meant by 'all available fighter aircraft' – half a dozen American-built Brewster Buffaloes. Slow, clumsy, easily out-manoeuvred by the Zekes. The Buffaloes hadn't been built for the tropics either, and in Malaya they'd suffered from carburettors that oiled up when their engines were gunned for take-off. To counter this, some bright RAF engineer designed a home-made filter stuffed with Tampax. The RAF bought up all the Tampax from all the chemists in Singapore, then, explaining that they needed it for Buffaloes.

He passed the signal back to Hobbs.

'Comfortable down there, are you?'

Schooly's sweat-running face creased in a smile. 'No danger of frost-bite, sir.'

Nick beckoned to Gant, as Hobbs left. He told the commander, 'No air support is available to us.'

'I *am* surprised, sir.'

'At least we know that anything we see is hostile.'

'Ah.' Gant nodded. 'That's a comfort.'

'See that Haskins knows it, will you?'

Haskins was the captain of marines, and at action stations he controlled the ship's air defences. The paymaster lieutenant who'd had the job when Nick had taken command hadn't been too bright at it, so there'd been a reshuffle of some action duties. Haskins had a detachment of about fifty Royal Marines under him.

'Cup o' tea, sir?'

Able Seaman Gladwill, Nick's servant, was beside him with a tray of tea and biscuits. The china, Admiralty issue, was white with pink roses around the edges; Gladwill's thumbs, hooked over the ends of the tray, were spatulate and black-rimmed. He was a bird-fancier, and kept canaries in the lobby outside the cuddy. He muttered, as Nick got up on to his high seat, 'Warming the bell a touch, sir, but I thought while the going's good, like.'

Behind Nick and to his right, on the step at the binnacle, was Charles Rowley, a lieutenant-commander who was the ship's first lieutenant and senior watchkeeper. His shaggy brown hair needed cutting; grey eyes in a deeply tanned face were watching *Perth*, their next ahead. The sea was churned white but still quite flat here in the dead centre of the other ships' wakes: *Defiant* was so steady that the only danger to the tea in the cup was the old girl's shaking, the constant vibration in her steel.

There was a certain incongruity, to be sitting here sipping tea from flowered china when there was a fair certainty of being in action within the hour. . . .

'Signal, sir.'

It was the chief yeoman, this time, CPO Howell's ruddy complexion and prematurely white sideboards. The rest of his hair was shiny black. Howell had played rugger for the Navy at one time.

'Thank you, Chief Yeoman.' He put down the cup with its awkward little handle, and now he read the signal. It duplicated a Dutch original announcing that the Jap troopships had turned away northeastward.

Only the convoy: not the cruisers and destroyers. The transports were being kept out of danger while the warship escort cleared a path for them. The report would probably have originated with the RAF torpedo-bombers that had been sent out earlier. It was a pity they had been, really.

There'd been one signal that he hadn't shown even to Bob Gant. It was an Intelligence report which had reached Doorman before they'd sailed from Surabaya yesterday, and Doorman had apprised his captains of it when they'd met on board the flagship. It had indicated that two Jap carrier divisions had been coming south towards this area and that one of them was thought to be steering

500

for the Sunda Strait, presumably to pass through it and operate *south* of Java. If this was so, there'd be enemy surface and air patrols blocking any chance of escape south to Australia or northwest to Ceylon.

A buzzer sounded, and a light was flashing on the W/T office telephone. The chief yeoman had jumped to it, pushing a messenger aside. Now he swung round to face Nick.

'From *Electra*, sir – "Enemy in sight, bearing north!"'

He glanced round. Gladwill materialized, like a rubbery-faced genie, to remove the tray. Gant, who'd been smoking his pipe on the other side of the bridge, took it out of his mouth as he pivoted and Nick told him, 'Close the hands up, Bob.' The pipe had vanished. One of Gant's hands, unbidden, rested in the small of his back, on that damaged spine of his; the other was on the red-painted alarm button sending the morse letter 'S' – 'S' for surface action stations – reverberating through all the ship's compartments. Nick saw a string of bunting run to *Perth*'s yardarm: the flags were almost edge-on from this viewpoint but there was enough flutter in them for him to read them as flag 'N' with the numerals 3-6-0 below it: 'N' meaning 'enemy in sight' and the numerals standing for the compass bearing, north. He told Rowley, who was still officer of the watch until Chevening arrived to take over, 'Warn the engine-room.' He saw Greenleaf, known as 'Guns' but more formally as the PCO, principal control officer, and told him, 'We're likely to be up against four cruisers and fourteen destroyers.'

'Aye aye, sir.' Lieutenant Greenleaf was a tubby, cheerful-looking man. He'd turned away, to climb up the ladder into the director control tower on the foremast. And Haskins, the marine, had arrived now neck-and-neck with Chevening. Moustached and burly, Haskins was also going up the ladder, to his ADP, air defence position, an open-topped platform below Toby Greenleaf's director tower. Other men, the crews of both positions, were also scrambling aloft.

Chevening had taken over from Rowley, who'd gone below to take charge of damage control. All through the compartments certain doors and hatches would be shut and clipped, hoses unrolled, emergency lighting checked, fire-fighting gear set ready.

A telephone buzzed beside the torpedo sight, and Lieutenant-Commander Swanson, arriving in the bridge at that moment, skidded across to snatch it up. Swanson was blond and bearded, a short and stocky, pugilistic-looking man. With the telephone in one hand he used the other to remove his cap, substituting the tin hat that had been hanging below the sight, and displaying in the process the bald, suntanned back of his head. He listened to a report, then hung up. He told Nick, 'All tubes' crews closed up, sir.' He had twelve torpedo tubes, in four triple mountings. He asked Nick, 'Depth charges, sir?'

'Yes. Clear the traps.'

Depth charges in the chutes aft were a danger, if an enemy shell should land on them. Mr North, the torpedo gunner, would set their pistols to 'safe' now and release them. They'd be sinking harmlessly towards the bottom as *Java* passed over them.

CPO Howell suggested, 'Battle ensigns, sir?'

'Not yet.' Only the destroyer *Electra* had seen the enemy as yet, and *Electra* was a good five miles ahead.

'Flagship's going round to port, sir.'

Chevening reported it. Nick looked ahead and saw the turn beginning, *de Ruyter*'s rather upright-looking, single-funnelled profile lengthening as her rudder gripped the sea and hauled her round. Doorman would keep the ships in this formation: all they'd have to do was follow where he led, and there'd be no need of signals. It would be limiting, though, on his choice of tactics . . . *Exeter* was following him round now. You could guess from this change of course that Doorman must have sighted the enemy and that the Jap course was something like southwestward: *de Ruyter* had steadied on three hundred and twenty degrees.

Houston, two-funnelled, and at just over nine thousand tons nearly twice *Defiant*'s size, had put her helm over; that rather strange-looking flare-topped foc's'l' was slanting into *Exeter*'s white track, gleaming in the sunshine. Greenleaf reported by telephone, 'Main armament closed up and cleared away, sir.'

'Very good.' From his high seat, Nick reached to put the telephone back on its hook. Greenleaf and his crew up there, with stereoscopic binoculars and stabilized telescopic sights, would be straining for a first glimpse of the enemy; but there were still ships ahead, and funnel-haze, to obscure their view. It would be clearer when *Perth* had turned, though, and she was swinging now as the American ahead of her steadied on the new course.

Sure enough, the director telephone was calling. Nick reached for it: 'Captain.'

'Enemy in sight, sir. Four cruisers: two heavy, and two smaller.

And two groups of destroyers, roughly six in each but it's hard to count them yet. Bearing three-five-five—'

He heard Chevening order, 'Port fifteen.' Greenleaf was continuing his report: at this extreme range he was only looking at the enemy's upperworks, masts and fighting-tops above the curve of the horizon, and it would be a while before even the eight-inch ships, *Exeter* and *Houston*, could be in gun-range of the enemy.

'Signal, *speed twenty-five*, sir!'

Flag 'G', numerals two and five: Nick said, 'Very good.' Chevening's face was already at the voicepipe, ordering the increase in revolutions, and it was Leading Seaman Williams, down in the wheelhouse, who'd be passing that order to the engine-room. Twenty-five knots was two knots short of this ship's maximum.

Japanese heavy cruisers, Nick thought, would have eight-inch guns. Almost for sure. So the forces were fairly evenly matched. Except that the Japs, with more modern ships, would have a speed advantage. Ten or twelve minutes, he worked out roughly, would bring the heavy cruisers into range of each other. *Defiant* and the other six-inch ships would be inside the Jap cruisers' range without any hope of hitting back. There'd be a frustrating period to live through, until they got in closer.

Bob Gant said, without taking the binoculars from his eyes, 'There, sir. See their foretops.'

Chevening was steadying her on the new course. Nick had his glasses at about forty degrees on the bow, and he'd got them suddenly, the fighting-tops of two heavy cruisers in line ahead. None of the smaller ships was visible yet from this level: but all right, he thought, here we go . . . He lowered his glasses and called over to Howell, 'Battle ensigns, chief yeoman.'

'Battle ensigns, hoist!'

Two of them had been bent on and ready on the flagdeck, and PO Ruddle was passing the same order aft by telephone. White ensigns ran swiftly to both mastheads, to the mainmast gaff and the port yardarm. You put up that many in case one or more should be shot away. With four ensigns flying, there'd have to be a hell of a lot of damage done before the ship displayed *no* colours. *Perth*'s were already hoisted, he saw. Astern, *Java* was settling into line; her slender foretop made the twin funnels look more massive than they were. He checked the time: eleven minutes past four. Any minute now, someone would try the range. He reached for his tin hat, glancing round at the same time to see that everyone else was wearing them: his own helmet was blue with four gold stripes on it, artistry by AB Gladwill.

Greenleaf called again on the DCT telephone. 'Enemy has a seaplane up, sir. Green six-five at the moment, looks like it's working its way round astern of us.'

In a minute, he'd got it in the circle of his binoculars. It looked from here like a black, very slow-moving mosquito, so slow that even one of the cranky old Buffaloes could have knocked it down. It was going to be a great advantage to the Jap gunners to have a spotter wirelessing fall-of-shot to them. He looked round at the OD who manned a group of voicepipes, including one to the ADP: 'Tell Captain Haskins there's a seaplane moving down the starboard side and if it comes into range I want it shot down.'

The communications number was bawling it up the pipe. When he'd finished Nick added, 'Tell him it's worth a bottle of gin.'

His gin was quite safe, he thought. Unfortunately. That seaplane would keep its distance, if its pilot had any sense.

'Enemy's opened fire, sir!'

Sixteen minutes past four. His eyes were on his watch when *Exeter*'s guns crashed out a salvo. Two seconds later, *Houston* fired. Cordite smoke and smell drifted back along the line of ships. Nick called the DCT and asked Greenleaf what the range was.

'Twenty-six thousand yards, sir.'

Thirteen miles . . .

Shells scrunched overhead. Looking out to port, he saw the splashes rise like white pillars that turned grey as they hung momentarily and then collapsed. They'd fallen well over and quite a distance ahead, probably too far right for line. But with that seaplane spotting for them the enemy gunners wouldn't need to get their salvoes in line before they could correct for range; without a spotter you did have to, because until you had the splashes in line with the target you couldn't tell whether they were short or over.

Exeter fired again. As the noise faded, Bob Gant began, 'Flagship's—'

Houston flung off a broadside. Gant was pointing, and Nick saw *de Ruyter* swinging, starting a turn to port. He'd be weaving, perhaps, 'snaking the line', which was a way of taking avoiding action – and confusing the enemy's observations – while still keeping the ships in line ahead. He'd hardly be turning parallel to the enemy at this extreme range – when only two of his ships could use their guns?

504

Being shot at wasn't fun. Being shot at when you couldn't shoot back was extremely trying.

But perhaps there was some wisdom in it: if the enemy line had been in a position to 'cross his T' – bring their full broadsides to bear on the flagship as one narrow, bow-on target – Doorman would have seen that he'd be running into trouble, and this turn would have avoided it. More Jap shells: the whistling, rushing noise of them. They went into the sea well over again, but not as far over as the first lot. Doorman was turning towards the fall of shot, which was a well-used, logical tactic: the enemy would be shortening his range setting now, while his target veered out towards the range at which the last salvo fell. *Exeter* and *Houston* had both fired, *Exeter* well out to port now in the flagship's wake; Doorman had gone round by about twenty degrees and he seemed to have steadied on that course. *Houston* had put her helm over, turning her bow into the drift of smoke from *Exeter*'s last salvo.

The flagship wasn't weaving, though. Doorman did intend, apparently, to stay out at this range. Whatever reasons he might have for it, one's own strong inclination was to get in closer, into the fight. Nick held his glasses on *de Ruyter*'s stern, hoping to see it move, see the Dutchman begin a turn towards the enemy. He was steady though, holding that course. Then there was a flash and a burst of smoke somewhere amidships: the flagship had been hit. Other shells splashed in short. Then *Exeter* fired, and *Houston*, and a yellowish haze of cordite smoke hid the flagship. *Houston* steadied now, *Perth* turning astern of her. Nick glanced round and saw Chevening ready to order *Defiant*'s wheel over. The DCT telephone called, and Gladwill passed it to him: Greenleaf reported, 'Destroyer attack developing, sir. Six of them have turned towards us on green five-oh.'

'You may get a target or two, then.'

'Certainly wouldn't mind one, sir.'

If Doorman didn't order *his* destroyers out to meet the attack, and let them foul the range. Nick was thinking that if he'd been running this show he'd have divided the cruiser force, kept the two heavy-gunned ships at about this range and sent the other four in closer, probably in two separate groups of two ships each, making three in all. Not only so as to get their guns into the action, but also to divide the Jap gunners' attention. The snag was, of course, that communications weren't up to coping with any complicated manoeuvring: Doorman would be scared of losing control. If there'd been a prearranged plan and a chance to practise it, though, that would have been the answer, and in Doorman's shoes one would have chanced it anyway.

He wasn't sending the destroyers out, at any rate. *Exeter* and *Houston* were shooting steadily, and about twice a minute an enemy salvo splashed down. There'd only been that one hit, on *de Ruyter*, so far as one could tell from *Defiant*, and despite the spotting aircraft hovering on the quarter now the fall of shot seemed haphazard. Whether the enemy ships had been hit at all one couldn't know. Nick got up higher, with his heels jammed in the strut that linked the seat's legs, and trained his glasses on the bow where the destroyer attack was supposed to be coming in. The enemy heavy cruisers were easy to see, and one light cruiser's upperworks were in sight astern of them. The smaller ships would be flanking the big ones, he guessed, one on each quarter.

'Captain, sir!'

Director telephone again: Greenleaf said, 'Destroyers closing on green eight-five, sir. Permission to open fire?'

'Open fire.'

Perth did so at that moment. Splashes from Jap eight-inch shells lifted the sea astern. In the DCT Greenleaf said into the mouthpiece of his head-set, 'All guns with full charge and SAP load, load, load!' 'SAP' meant semi-armour-piercing, as opposed to 'HE' for high-explosive. He told his team, 'Target the right-hand destroyer.' On his left Mr Nye, the gunner, began passing information over his telephone to CPO Hughes, chief gunner's mate, down in the transmitting station. He was giving him figures for enemy course and speed. Mr Nye was the rate officer, and on his estimates the rate of opening or closing range was calculated. All kinds of other data was reaching the TS and being set on dials on the Admiralty fire-control table, which would transmit its own conclusions to the guns. Below Greenleaf the director layer and trainer held their telescope sights on the enemy, the foot of his foremast being the standard aiming point, but the guns themselves would be aimed-off by the amount that had been computed from all the facts and figures fed into the machine in the TS, which was a tank-like cell of a compartment well below the waterline. Greenleaf was watching his gun-ready box, and when he saw the lights in it all glowing, a light for each of the six gun mountings, he ordered 'Shoot!' Firegongs double-clanged as the director layer, with his eye still pressed to the rubber eyepiece of his telescopic sight, squeezed his trigger.

Defiant's six six-inch guns fired: cordite smoke washed back along her decks, curled mustard-coloured over the white wake. All six guns were on the centre-line: two for'ard of the bridge, one for'ard and one aft of the twin funnels, and two aft. They were guns with shields, not turrets. *Perth* had fired again. Then the deeper crashes of broadsides from the bigger ships ahead of her. And Nick had the oncoming destroyers in his glasses, small, jumpy images in the heat-haze low on a dazzling sea, mirage-like and distant. He saw shell-splashes momentarily superimposed, a small flickering of white that vanished as suddenly as it had appeared. *Defiant* and *Perth* both fired again.

A pressure against his forearm was Gladwill offering him the director telephone. He took it and said into it, 'Captain.'

'They're turning away, sir. I think they've fired torpedoes.'

At that range? Over the line he heard the PCO's order: 'Shoot!' Then, as the echoes of the salvo died, 'Check, check, check!'

It was said that the Japanese had torpedoes called 'Long Lance' which were far better than the Royal Navy's, but however marvellous they might be they'd been wasted by being fired from such a distance. Particularly as Doorman was now altering course again. Nick hadn't been aware of it happening, but looking astern he could see the elbow in the wake and *Java* following *Defiant* round.

Exeter and *Houston* were still engaged in their long-range action. And Doorman's new course was still more or less parallel to the enemy's . . . Might Nelson, Nick wondered, have used the excuse of that torpedo attack to turn his own ship towards the enemy? The move might have been excused, explained, if with his blind eye he'd seen torpedo tracks, and turned to comb them. But *Java* wouldn't have followed Nick Everard; mightn't even have followed Horatio Nelson. And Waller of *Perth* would have had no option but to stick to *Houston*'s tail, so there'd have been only one advancing ship for the enemy to concentrate his guns on. So – no, Nelson would *not* have. It was still galling to be kept out here, non-combatant. It wouldn't improve the ship's company's morale, either. Earlier in the afternoon, soon after the force had turned and headed back out to sea from Surabaya, he'd talked to his crew over the Tannoy broadcast system, explaining what was happening and leaving no doubt that *Defiant* would soon be in action. The enemy force was about equal to their own, he'd said, and with a bit of luck and straight shooting they ought to wipe the floor with them.

There'd been cheering on the messdecks. Some of them might be wondering now what there'd been to cheer about.

What might Doorman be hoping to achieve? To have *Exeter*'s and *Houston*'s guns knock out the big ships, leaving the rest – and the convoy – as easy meat?

It wasn't happening. The time was just on 5 pm, they'd been in action for three-quarters of an hour, and the only hit Nick had seen had been that one on *de Ruyter*. He asked Greenleaf over the telephone, 'Have you seen any hits on the enemy?'

'I think so, sir. Two earlier on, and one a minute ago. Can't be positive, but—'

'All right.' He took the phone from his ear, but Greenleaf caught him with a sharp 'Captain, sir . . .' He reported, 'Looks like a new destroyer attack starting from fine on the bow.'

Enemy shells splashed down, short. *De Ruyter* at once began a turn to starboard. *Exeter* had loosed off another broadside: and now *Houston* . . . Nick heard shells arriving, that distinctive rushing, ripping sound. . . .

Exeter was hit.

She'd been out to starboard, following the flagship round and far enough out to be in sight from *Defiant*. He saw the shell strike, the flash and puff of debris and dust as it went in, and then the explosion, eruption inside the ship. *Exeter*'s helm went over the other way, reversing the direction of the turn.

Houston's guns had fired; and now she was following *Exeter*, turning to port although *de Ruyter* was going the other way, had steadied after a swing to starboard. *Exeter*, Nick realized, was slowing, losing way quite fast; he could see her bow-wave dropping as speed fell off. *Houston* must have recognized his mistake and also seen the danger of ramming the British cruiser, and she was keeping full rudder on, in order to turn inside her, under her stern. *Perth* was following *Houston*.

Shambles . . . Nick was at the binnacle, displacing Chevening, who moved to the director telephone to maintain contact with the DCT.

'Starboard five.'

'Starboard five, sir . . . Five of starboard wheel on, sir!'

Just enough wheel to take her clear of all that mess. An enemy salvo thumped into the sea, short. He called down, 'Midships.' *De Ruyter* had held on. *Houston* and *Perth* had turned with *Exeter*, but they should not have. Nothing had been all that good so far, but now it had become much worse. Only two ships had been in action, and one of them had been crippled while the other had waltzed off on her own. Another salvo scorched over and raised spouts on *Defiant*'s bow. He called down, 'Port ten.' He'd passed clear of the scrimmage and now he had to get her up astern of the admiral. *Exeter* seemed to have stopped; destroyers were circling her, laying smoke to hide her from the enemy, whose rate of fire seemed to have increased. Those were the American destroyers: the three British ones were ahead and on the flagship's bow to port, while a Dutchman was moving up on the engaged side – to starboard. Shellspouts lifted in the gap between *Exeter* and a smoke-laying American destroyer. The smoke would have very little effect, Nick realized, when the spotter was airborne and well above it; but perhaps, in this sort of mess, every contribution helped . . . He said into the voicepipe, 'Midships.'

Houston had extricated herself from the scrum: she'd opened fire again. *Sloan*, Jim Jordan's ship, was one of those laying smoke.

'Steady!'

'Steady, sir . . . Two-six-five, sir.'

'Steer that.'

It would be suffocating in the wheelhouse. The heat came out of the voicepipe in a stream you could have smoked a herring in. Flagship going round to port . . .

'Destroyers attacking from ahead, sir!'

Chevening had that report from Greenleaf in the tower. It might account for the flagship's sharp swing away: Doorman would be turning so as to bring his guns to bear. There were ships all over the place: *Houston* still firing steadily but *Exeter* right out of it, away off on the quarter and wreathed in smoke, destroyers standing by her. He stooped to the voicepipe: 'Port fifteen.' It was necessary to cut the revs too, so as to drop back and let *Houston* get in astern of *de Ruyter*. Enemy shells fell in a clump to starboard; *Houston* was shooting over her port quarter as she came up into the re-forming line. Chevening put a hand over the mouthpiece of the DCT telephone: 'PCO requests permission to engage destroyers on bearing 330, sir!'

A glance checked that bearing. 'Open fire.' Into the voicepipe: 'Midships.'

'Midships, sir . . . Wheel's amidships, sir!'

Defiant's guns let rip, over her quarter. *Perth* edging in astern of the American. *Exeter* was under way again, steering southeast with a Dutch destroyer making smoke astern of her. Nick called down for increased revs, to maintain station now on *Perth*: the Australian had opened fire, joining *Defiant* in discouraging the Jap destroyer attack. *Java* was in action too. Chevening reported, 'Enemy destroyers have turned away, sir.' They were still being shot at, anyway, but if they'd turned away you could bet they'd have fired their torpedoes on the swing. He was thinking that, and looking round at the positions of other ships, when he saw a torpedo hit a Dutch destroyer out on *Defiant*'s beam. A column of dirty water shot up over her, then smoke rose in a cloud to hide her. He heard the *boom* of it, and when the smoke dissipated he saw she'd gone. A Jap salvo fell short of *Houston*: the course was northeast now, Doorman leading his surviving cruisers across the line of *Exeter*'s retreat. Destroyers were still laying smoke, but only *Houston* was firing. Chevening told Nick, 'PCO reports destroyer targets obscured, sir.' And CPO Howell reported from the W/T office telephone, 'The admiral's ordered our three destroyers to attack with torpedoes, sir.'

The three British destroyers were *Encounter*, *Electra* and *Jupiter*. But they were widely dispersed: one a long way off on the beam, one moving over to look for survivors from the torpedoed Dutchman, and one close astern. All three were turning now, bow-waves lifting and foam piling under their sterns as they built up speed to obey Doorman's order. Widely spaced as they were, though, the attack would amount to three individual charges, which was not at all a realistic destroyer tactic. Doorman should have given them time to concentrate and make a co-ordinated attack. Nick thought, knowing precisely as a destroyer man himself how it would be for them, *He's throwing them away . . . .*

Exeter was well clear now, retiring at half speed on a course that would take her to Surabaya, with one Dutch destroyer to keep her company. With her departure the odds had worsened: in the long-range fight it was now one – *Houston* – against two.

The Jap commander seemed no keener to get to grips than Doorman was. He'd be thinking about his convoy of troop transports, of course: his job first and foremost was to protect them, get them to the Java coast and see they got their troops ashore. If he lost his cruisers he'd lose the convoy too: so his plan would be to hold Doorman off, damage him if possible but only at minimal risk to his own ships. While Doorman's thoughts would also be concentrated on the need to destroy that convoy; and he could only achieve it by remaining afloat and intact, so he wasn't keen to take risks either. On the other hand this so-called Striking Force didn't have the speed to get round the enemy and find the convoy: the speed advantage was on the Japs' side, not Doorman's.

Doorman should have split his force, and gone for bust. He'd had no luck for the simple reason that he'd taken no chances. On the other hand, it would be starting to get dark, before long: in the dark, if he got lucky and really chanced his arm, it might just be possible to slip past these Japs, find the transports.

'Pilot. Ask—'

An explosion, some distance astern. Nick's first thought was for *Java*, but it was farther away than that. Chevening had the DCT telephone at his ear: nose like a marline spike under the tin hat's rim as he looked downwards, listening. Now he'd pushed the telephone back on to its hook. He told Nick, '*Electra*'s sunk, sir. The other two are rejoining.'

And Doorman was turning to starboard: leading them southward, maintaining his distance from the enemy. Nick thought, *Turn towards the bastards, not away. Go in and support those poor bloody destroyers.* He thought it during one slow blink. With his eyes open again and no emotion showing in his face he told Chevening, 'You'd better check on how the plot's going, pilot. Put on a good DR while you're about it.' He looked at Gant. 'Keep an ear open to the tower meanwhile, Bob?'

'Aye aye, sir.'

CPO Howell reported, 'Admiral's ordered the American destroyers to attack, sir!'

Houston ripped out a broadside, thunderous over her quarter and some of the blast-effect coming back along the line of cruisers. She'd been in action for the best part of two hours now and her ammunition was likely to be getting low. A messenger standing near the W/T telephone jumped to it as it buzzed. He answered 'Bridge!' Listening, he glanced round as the chief yeoman moved towards him asking, 'What's it about, then?' The messenger said into the telephone, 'Aye aye.' He reported, 'Orders to the American destroyers cancelled, sir. They've been told to lay smoke instead.'

Now it was dark and they'd lost contact with the enemy. The cruisers were following their Dutch admiral northwestward. Doorman had turned east under cover of the smoke-screen, and after about five miles he'd led them round to port, back up towards

511

where the enemy had been – but almost certainly would not be now.

Hoping to slip past them, probably, and find the important target, the troop convoy.

At seven Nick handed over the conning of the ship to Chevening; he checked the plot and the latest signals, and then settled down on his high seat. Doorman, he thought, could only be looking for the troopers now: but the same thing would be equally obvious to the Jap admiral. The convoy wouldn't be in easy reach and it wouldn't be unprotected either.

Houston had reported that she had very little ammunition left.

Gladwill asked him, 'Tea, sir? Coffee? Kye?'

'Coffee, please.' Gladwill made excellent coffee. Bob Gant came back. You could smell him – or rather his pipe – before you saw or heard him. Nick called after Gladwill, 'And a cup for the commander, too.'

'Much obliged, sir . . . Any idea what we're up to now?'

'Looking for the invasion convoy, I imagine. Trusting to luck.'

'We might be about due for some, at that.'

They'd certainly achieved nothing yet, beyond delaying the assault on eastern Java. It could only be a temporary delay, with a weak force trying to impede a strong one, which was the situation here. Before long Java would be attacked and occupied. Any Allied ships still afloat by that time would have no base or fuelling facility, or much prospect of escape. The Java Sea would have become a Japanese lake entirely surrounded by Jap bases in Jap-occupied territory.

'Flagship's going round to starboard, sir!'

The report came from Swanson, the torpedo officer. He'd settled himself in the starboard for'ard corner of the bridge, as an extra lookout.

'Your coffee, sir.'

'Put it down there, would you?' He had his glasses on the ships ahead. He called over his shoulder to Chevening, 'Follow round, pilot.'

'Aye aye, sir.'

No difficulty in following, in the phosphorescent wakes. Doorman brought them round to a course just south of east, reckoning, Nick supposed, that he'd come far enough north to have by-passed the enemy cruisers and that a cast to the east might bring him up against the convoy which could have been disposed a few miles astern of them.

Could have. Could have been any damn place at all. Could have been on the Java coast by now. You could be sorry for Doorman. In Doorman's boots you might well be sorry for yourself.

An hour felt like two hours, dragging by.

'Captain, sir?'

Schooly, up from the plot with a decoded signal. Nick heard the voice of Leading Seaman Williams reporting up the voicepipe to Chevening that the ship was steady on the course he'd ordered. Williams would have been giving the chief quartermaster frequent spells on the wheel down there: at least that little oven of a wheelhouse would be cooling off by this time . . . He told Hobbs, 'Read it to us, will you?'

To himself and Gant, he meant. He didn't want to spoil his night vision by going to the chart-table with it. Hobbs said quietly, 'It's a Most Immediate, sir, to the effect that the enemy has reinforced his eastern assault force. Cruiser and destroyer reinforcements, it says, but no details other than that.'

'All right. Thank you.'

The Japanese eastern assault force was the group this force had been sparring with. Nothing was getting any better.

Darkness like warm velvet. The ship's rattles, her engines' thrumming, the rush of sea along her sides and wind-noise in stays and shrouds, voices night-quiet at the back of the bridge where lookouts were being changed. It was a familiar backing to one's thoughts, to the hours of waiting and expectancy and the tension that ran through them, in your nerves and brain. It had always been like this but tonight there was more, there was a feeling of being trapped, an instinct that if the night lasted long enough to end as all the other nights had done – with daylight – then the bars of the trap would be plain to see, whichever way you looked . . . He caught a whiff of pipe-smoke: Gant was still near him, propped against the side of the bridge with binoculars at his eyes. Nick asked him, 'If you were in Doorman's place, Bob, what would you be doing?'

'The answer's rather vulgar, sir.'

'Seriously.'

'Well.' Gant moved closer, and answered in a murmur that only Nick could have heard. He said, 'I'd make a dash for Surabaya, fill up with oil, then go flat-out for the Sunda Strait. Hoping to get through before they block it. Sunda or Lombok.'

It was a programme that might be hard to fault, Nick thought.

513

But it was also, for the time being, impractical; while at any later time – as Gant had rightly pointed out – it would be impossible. He said, 'Doorman can't do it, unfortunately. He's a Dutchman, and the Dutch have said they'll defend Java to the last man.'

'Just our luck, sir, isn't it?'

'Aircraft over us, sir!'

He'd heard it too, that throbbing engine sound. Then a flare broke overhead, a sudden glimmer that expanded to flood the sea and the ships on it with blindingly white light.

He had the DCT telephone in his hand and he was asking Greenleaf whether he could see anything from up there. The thought in his mind being that the ships from which the flare-dropper was operating might be close at hand.

'Horizon's clear, sir.'

The engine drone faded. But the pilot would be using his radio, triumphantly telling his master, the Jap admiral, what he'd found and where. Nick wished to God he had RDF in *Defiant*. Even destroyers were getting sets now. *Defiant* was well overdue for refit: if her docking hadn't been delayed she'd have been fitted with one by this time. All new-building and refitting ships were getting it. The Americans called it 'Radar'.

Moonrise would be in about an hour. Well – an hour and a half . . . But if that flyer could keep them marked with occasional flares till then, they'd be tracked right through the night.

Perth, ahead, ploughed on, floodlit. *Houston*, gleaming as if she had snow on her decks but with a slant of black shadow across her afterpart as the flare drifted lower on the bow and silhouetted her, blocked any sight of the flagship beyond her. *Java*'s bow-on shape, astern, was low and solid-looking. He could see two of the American destroyers: there were two on each quarter and one right astern, and the two surviving British ones were out ahead.

The flare dwindled like fading candle-light as it approached the sea; then it was out and you were blind, night vision lost. You could as well have had your head in a bucket.

'Can't hear it now. Can you, Bob?'

Gant was back from the after-end of the bridge, where he'd been exhorting the lookouts to greater efforts. He paused, listening . . . Then he nodded. 'I'm afraid I can, sir.'

Nothing anyone could do about it. That was the worst, the sense of impotence. Having located them, it was possible that the Jap

514

airman would be able to see the ships' phosphorescent wakes and have no need of more flares. In any case he'd have counted and classified the ships, reported their course and speed. It was like being blindfolded in a room full of clear-sighted enemies.

'Can't hear it now, sir.'

'Flagship's altering to starboard!'

Chevening had seen it, from the far side of the bridge, and he was telling Rowley, the first lieutenant, who'd taken over from him at the binnacle. Chevening had been down in the plot for the last half-hour. Nick put his glasses up again, watched *de Ruyter*'s black profile growing as she swung out.

'How far have we run east, pilot?'

'Ten miles, sir.'

Doorman might be hoping to get lost again, while the Jap airman wasn't looking. *Houston* turning now: the flagship had steadied on a southerly course. Nick asked Chevening, 'How far are we now from the Surabaya Strait?'

'Forty miles, sir.'

Two hours' run, say. But they were about to steer south, and the course for Surabaya would be more like south-east. The enemy troop convoy and the augmented cruiser force covering it could be north, south, east or west by this time: but the Jap admiral knew precisely where this squadron was. He could keep his transports well out of the way, and send his cruisers hunting – probably in more than one pack, now he had more of them. Nick thought again that he didn't envy Rear-Admiral Doorman his job.

Perth was in her turn, and Rowley would be putting *Defiant*'s helm over in a minute. The two American destroyers on the port quarter would be increasing speed, and the pair to starboard slowing, in order to maintain station through the turn. Doorman would have passed an alter-course signal by light, probably, to *Jupiter* and *Encounter* ahead of him.

Behind him, Nick heard Rowley's low-voiced order, 'Starboard fifteen.' And then, sickeningly, the drone of an aircraft engine. *Defiant* was heeling to her rudder when the flare broke, high up and ahead.

Bob Gant said, 'Suppose our best hope's for the bugger to run out of petrol.'

But if he did, Nick thought, there'd be another to take his place. And for that matter, what about these destroyers running out of fuel?

Cat and mouse: a seedy mouse, and a cat that knew exactly what it was doing.

At 9 pm, five miles off the Java coast, Doorman led them round to starboard: westward. At the same time he detached the American destroyers with orders to put in to Surabaya. *Sloan* had reported engine defects from a near-miss, and they were all dangerously short of oil. The Combined Striking Force now had only two destroyers, the British pair.

There'd been no flares dropped, and no sound of aircraft, since about 8.30. With any luck that snooper *had* been forced to go home and refuel, and it was just possible he'd have thought they were retiring to Surabaya. Doorman, Nick guessed, would be hoping for just that.

'Kye, sir?'

Petty Officer Ruddle, yeoman of signals, was offering him a mug of cocoa. 'Compliments of the communications department, sir.'

'Thank you, yeoman.'

It was thick, strong, sweet and hot. Thick enough to make one suspect there'd been a little custard powder mixed into the paste of cocoa, condensed milk and sugar. It was an old sailor's trick, aimed at producing a mug in which a spoon would stand vertically without support. The matelot's ideal 'kye' would also be laced with rum: this brew was non-alcoholic, but in all other respects distinctly *Cordon Bleu*.

'You wouldn't get kye like this at the Savoy, yeoman.'

'Ah – thank you, sir!'

This very night there'd be people dining and dancing at the Savoy. It was a peculiar thought, from here in the Java Sea and at this moment. He found a picture suddenly in his mind of Fiona, Fiona dancing in the arms of – he asked himself, angered by the quick flare of jealousy which was quite irrational, *Why shouldn't she dance with anyone she pleases?*

She always had gone out with anyone she wanted to go out with. She'd never made any bones about it; since her rich and much older husband had died and thus released her from a marriage in which she'd felt trapped and miserable, she hadn't wanted or pretended to be a one-man girl. It had suited him well enough, for a time. Then, about a year ago, or a bit more than that, both his and her feelings had begun to change: hers had changed, for instance, to the extent that dancing and dining was about all she *would* do, with other men. At least, this was what she'd implied, what he thought she'd

516

implied . . . But in black and white, he'd committed himself, and she hadn't – not as unequivocally as he had. There'd been one letter which as he remembered it could have been taken for commitment. But it could have been interpreted less positively too – knowing Fiona, and not having the letter now to look at again and reassess. He didn't have it because it had gone down in his destroyer *Tuareg*, halfway between Malta and Alexandria.

She'd have implied that change of attitude rather than made any clear statement of it, he realized, because to be more forthright about it would have been to admit how she'd been handling her life up to that point, and it would have been out of character for Fiona to have made any such admission. This would account for the element of vagueness, and it had allowed him to accept it as meaning what he thought she'd meant. By that time he'd known the Australian girl, Kate Farquharson, but not as well as he'd known her a few months later. He'd never told Kate that he was in love with her. He'd wanted to, but Fiona had got in the way of it, twisted his tongue and made him feel stupid to be in such a mess. Now – well . . . He thought, training his glasses slowly across the hazy line of the horizon on the bow, that in present circumstances it wasn't likely to make a pennyworth of difference to anyone at all. Perhaps this very fact was what allowed one to look at it squarely and recognize one's own blunder.

Blunders, plural. He couldn't claim to have made any roaring success of his emotional life. He'd done a fairly good job for the Navy, off and on, but he'd done very little for Nick Everard. In the personal sense – facing it *very* squarely – very little for anyone.

And *that* kind of thinking didn't help much, either.

At 9.20 they were ten miles offshore, north of a place on the Java coast called Tuban. The course was two hundred and ninety degrees. Chevening, just up from another visit to the plot, identified a dark shadow of land on the bow as Aur Aur Point, or rather high ground just inland of it. If they held to this course they'd be passing within four miles of the headland.

At 9.25 an explosion, ahead and to port, shattered the recent quiet. Greenleaf told Nick over the DCT telephone, 'It's *Jupiter*, sir. A mine, I think.' There was flashing ahead, the flagship signalling either to the stricken *Jupiter* or to the other destroyer, *Encounter*. But there were ships between *Defiant* and the flashing light, and the snatches of it that one saw weren't readable. The squadron held on, at twenty-five knots. Bob Gant and Swanson were on the port side of the bridge. Chevening was taking over at the binnacle from Rowley, who was going down to his damage control headquarters. Swanson muttered, with glasses at his eyes, 'She's sinking . . .'

'Flagship's altering course to starboard, sir.'

That dark patch – on the beam now as they passed – wasn't a ship at all, it was smoke. Broken water gleamed there too: and – boats? He had time for no more than a quick look, because he had to know what was happening ahead. All he'd seen had been vague and smoke-wrapped, and they'd passed it now, swept past and left it on the quarter. He heard Swanson ask, 'D'you reckon those are boats, sir, or floats?' He was asking Gant: but the cruisers and the one remaining destroyer were turning north, not even *Encounter* was being allowed to stop for survivors. If that had been a mine there'd as likely as not be a whole field of them, and Doorman was right not to risk another ship in it. Particularly if *Jupiter's* people had got boats or floats away, and with the Java coast in easy distance. But another passing thought was that if there was a minefield here it would be a Dutch one and it would have been laid in the last forty-eight hours. Didn't the Dutch tell their admirals where mines were being laid?

Doorman was steering north, with *Houston* already settled astern of the flagship and *Perth* turning now. *Jupiter* had been a fine, modern destroyer, with a complement of nearly two hundred men. Launched as recently as 1939. And now this 'Striking Force' had just one destroyer. The enemy assault group had had fourteen, and had since been reinforced with more.

He thought of Jim Jordan's musings a few days ago: *however* . . .

They lost *Encounter* half an hour later.

The moon had come up, and by chance Doorman had led his ships into an area of sea dotted with survivors from the Dutch destroyer which had been torpedoed during the action earlier. He ordered *Encounter* to pick them up and then take them down to Surabaya. The five cruisers continued northward, in line ahead and with no destroyers to scout for them now, across a moon-washed sea. Moon to starboard, still low but silvery-bright.

Pitching slightly: *Perth's* quartermaster had let her swing off course, and as she turned back to regain station *Defiant* had the ridges of the Australian cruiser's wash to plough through. Her bow slammed into them, one after another in quick succession, and after each impact spray swept back across the foc's'l' and rattled on

518

the gunshields. Then she was through it, settled again, and *Perth* was back in station dead ahead.

'Time now?'

'10.29, sir.'

He wondered what Kate was doing: whether she was still at home, or working in some military hospital again by now. The hospitals would be busy, he guessed, with wounded who'd been lucky enough to be brought out of places the Japs had over-run. Kate's home was a ranch in the west of Australia, not far inland from Freemantle. That was the address he'd been using for his letters. He was closer to her now than he'd been since she'd left Egypt. If she was at home now she'd be – he guessed – a mere fifteen hundred miles away.

'Alarm port, cruisers, red—'

A crash of guns from ahead as *de Ruyter* and *Houston* opened fire drowned the lookout's yell. Nick had the DCT telephone in his hand. He heard Greenleaf's order 'Shoot!' and then the firegongs, and *Defiant*'s six-inch thundered. Gun flashes puncturing the darkness to port were the enemy's: a lot of them, and they had this force silhouetted against the moon.

'Flagship's hit, sir!'

There was a glow of fire on *de Ruyter* and she was swinging away to starboard while *Defiant*'s guns blazed in a smooth and rapid rhythm. *Houston* belching out shells too as she followed the flagship round. Swanson, at the torpedo-control panel, was shouting over his telephone to Mr North, the gunner, who'd be down at the tubes. *Perth* turning now: Nick told Chevening, 'Follow round!'

'Aye aye—'

Gunfire smothered the acknowledgement. One hit on an enemy ship – on the quarter, a blossoming glow in that blackness: then, astern of *Defiant* as she approached the turning-point in *Perth*'s wake, a heavy explosion. *Java*: and if that had been a torpedo, he thought, the sooner they got round and stern-on to any more that were coming, the better. Turn now, independently? Aft, in *Defiant*, a shell struck: he'd heard a salvo coming and he'd been thinking about *Java* and torpedoes from the Jap cruisers, and then his own ship shuddered to the hit which had sounded like a muffled *thump* below decks and somewhere amidships. Gant was roaring into the telephone to damage-control HQ, wanting to know the position and extent of the damage. Astern, a shoot of flame reached skyward and the blast of an explosion was solid, buffeting: a shout from the after-end of the bridge was CPO Howell, chief yeoman, reporting that *Java* had blown up.

Defiant was slowing: engine rhythm dying, and the way falling off her. Her guns were still firing, all of them, Nick thought, hearing Chevening in a moment's comparative quiet shouting down: 'Starboard fifteen!' But ahead – impossible to know immediately which ship it was, when from this angle the leaders were so bunched together – another eruption, a burst of flames and a roar of sound. Greenleaf told him over the telephone, 'Flagship, sir. Looked like a magazine going up.' Gant chipped in, at Nick's side and raising his voice high to beat the racket of the guns, 'Shell burst in number two boiler room, sir.'

A large-calibre shell struck aft. You felt the blow of it, heard the whine of ricocheting fragments in the echo of the explosion. There was a major fire back aft. Gant yelled, 'Permission to go aft, sir?' He'd gone without waiting for it. Chevening reported from the binnacle, 'Losing steerage way, sir.' Nick told him, shouting through the noise of another salvo, 'They'll have her moving again in a minute.' In *some* minutes, he thought. He *hoped* Sandilands would get her moving. He hadn't heard that bit of Gant's report. He heard more Jap shells coming – for a second or two before gunfire drowned the unpleasant sound of them – and he knew, knew more than guessed, that this would be a straddle over the forepart of his ship. The salvo came from abaft the beam; one shell was a near-miss, short; three went over; one burst on the foc's'l and wiped out 'A' gun's crew; the last one crashed in through the port side of the bridge superstructure and burst in the plot, most of its explosive power blasting laterally into the wheelhouse and upwards through the thin deck-plating of the bridge.

CHAPTER 4

Dusk came to the Mediterranean six hours later than it had darkened the Java Sea, and clouds low on the horizon in the west were turning pink as the sun sank down into them; against the spreading brightness Paul had watched the two carriers, astern of the convoy, turn into the wind and fly-off a stream of fighters which, when they'd gained height, had moved out northward. The two carriers were back on course now. There was a lot of activity still in the destroyer screen, though: the fleet destroyers had spread themselves into a wider and more distant arc, while the smaller Hunt class had moved in closer to the four columns of merchantmen – to provide close protection with their AA weapons against the bombers when they came.

He was in the open port wing of the *Montgovern*'s bridge. So was Gosling, the little paymaster sub-lieutenant. Mackeson, who was allocating action duties to all the passengers, had told them both to wait out here.

Some of the fleet destroyers were still hurrying back after visiting the oiling group astern. At full speed, racing to overtake the convoy and get back into station ahead before the Luftwaffe arrived, one of them passing now up the port side was throwing a high, curved bow-wave tinged pink from the reflection of the western sky. Too pretty, really, to be true . . . Convoy and escort – battleships, carriers, cruisers and destroyers – were at action stations, although no alert had been signalled yet. It was coming: it might have been expected anyway, this far into the Mediterranean, but in fact there'd been a warning signal during the afternoon: intercepted enemy radio messages had made it clear that an assault was being mounted.

Gosling said, blinking at Paul through the pebble glasses that made him look like a frog, 'I wonder what jobs he's going to give us.'

'I'd guess we'll be extra lookouts.'

'What, out here?'

Mackeson had had the passengers assembled in the saloon at tea-time, told them about the probability of a dusk attack and added that he'd be expecting them to lend a hand in the ship's defence. He'd co-opted Thornton, the cipher expert, first of all, and put him in the chartroom to decode signals. But looking out, Paul thought, was about all he and Gosling could be useful at: and the short-sighted little paymaster wasn't likely to be very good at that, even. Might be better helping Thornton, he thought: not that one would wish that on someone who hadn't done one any harm . . . He asked him, 'What were you doing before you joined?'

'Accountancy. Actually I'd just qualified.'

'You've something to go back to, then.'

'Haven't you?'

'I was at college. In the United States.'

'I *thought* you sounded a bit American.'

'Admiring the sunset, lads?'

Humphrey Straight, the *Montgovern*'s master, had come out of the enclosed bridge behind them. He was a blocky, grizzled man: he had a way of staring with his head lowered, glaring at you under his eyebrows like a bull trying to decide whether or not to charge. Paul told him, 'We're waiting for Commander Mackeson, sir.'

'Oh, aye.' Straight's eyes looked bloodshot with that western light in them. 'Grand sight, eh?'

'Beautiful.'

'Aye. Beautiful . . . If you could paint that, and get it just right, folks'd say you'd laid it on too thick.' He stared around at the destroyers; then ahead, past the column leaders to the cruisers. 'Mack had best hurry up. The buggers'll be at us directly.' His eyes moved to Paul. 'Seen action, have you?'

'Some. Not air attack, though.'

'You?'

Gosling shook his head. 'None at all, I'm afraid.'

'Afraid is what we all get, betimes.' Straight rubbed the side of his jaw reflectively. 'It's never so bad as you expect, though. Least, it's as bad for them as it is for us. Helps to bear that in mind, see.'

Mackeson came out of the side-door from the bridge. Straight asked him, 'Left all this a bit late, haven't we?'

'Well, perhaps . . . Now – Gosling . . .' He asked him sharply, 'Where's your tin hat?'

'Here, sir.'

'Well, put it on, boy. And take this.' A lanyard, with a whistle on the end of it. 'Round your neck. That's it. All you have to do is stay here, right in the wing here, and keep a sharp lookout. If you see an attack coming that the guns haven't got on to, point at it and blow that thing like hell. Understand?' Gosling nodded. Mackeson asked him, 'Wearing your lifebelt, are you?'

'Under my coat, sir.'

'Right. That's you settled, then. Now, Everard.' He pointed for'ard. 'I want you up there on the foc's'l. You'll find a bunch of bloody-minded DEMS characters lolling around the Oerlikons. I want you to keep 'em on their toes, generally act as OOQ and help to put 'em on to targets. Keep an ear open for this lad's whistle, and the other one for our tame flying officer who's in the other wing. All right?'

Paul nodded. 'Except once it's dark I won't be able to see which way they point.'

With the guns in action, he doubted whether he was likely to hear whistles anyway. He didn't want to aggravate Mackeson with too many objections to his arrangements, though. Mackeson told him, 'By the time it's dark, Everard, the show will be over. That's the usual form, anyway.'

Humphrey Straight loomed closer. He said dourly, 'My second mate looks after DEMS gunnery lads.'

'Oh, yes.' Mackeson glanced round at him. 'But he can't be in more than one place at a time, can he? Don't we want all the help we can get?'

The master shrugged, and walked away. Mackeson murmured, 'He's very talkative this evening. Don't know what's got into him.'

Paul nodded. 'Minute ago, he was talking about painting the sunset.'

'Good God!'

He went down the ladderways through the bridge superstructure, out into the ship's-side gangway, down into the for'ard well deck and across it, and up the ladder to the foc'sl-head. One glance, as he reached the top of it, showed him that one of the two Oerlikon guns still had its canvas cover on.

Keep them on their toes, Mackeson had said. A covered gun – at action stations?

A red-headed sailor, about Paul's own age, stared at him inhospitably. Beyond him a heavy-set, pale-faced man of about

523

forty was fiddling with the Oerlikon that had been uncovered. There were several drums of the twenty-millimetre ammunition in a bin nearby.

Paul told the older man, 'My name's Everard. I'm taking passage to Malta, but I've been detailed to lend a hand up here. Spot targets for you, all that.'

DEMS personnel, he was remembering, were Merchant Navy men who signed on under a special system called the T. 124 agreement. They wore naval uniform – at least, they were supposed to, although the one at the gun was wearing a checked shirt under a donkey-jacket – but weren't subject to ordinary naval discipline. They got better pay, for some reason.

The fat man had acknowledged Paul's presence with a nod. The young, red-headed one was staring at the fat one as if he was waiting for a lead. The fat one said, 'Leading 'and 'ere's Ron Beale.' He nodded towards the covered gun. 'That's Ron's. Be up in 'alf a mo'.' He stooped, and hefted a drum of ammunition; he gasped, 'I'm Withinshaw. This lad—' the young one had gone to help him – 'McNaught, this is.'

'Easy now, Art . . .'

Arthur Withinshaw, then. Possibly from Liverpool, Paul guessed. Art pushed the red-headed boy aside, or tried to, with an elbow. 'Gerrout of it!'

'*There* . . . All right?'

Boots scraped on the ladder from the well deck: with them came a leading seaman cradling an ammo drum in his arms. A younger sailor behind him also carried one. Paul told him – Beale – who he was. Beale looked round at the young one: 'Get that fuckin' cover off, Wally boy.' He looked back at Paul: 'Where's Mr McCall, then?'

'I expect he'll be along.'

The wind across this unsheltered deck was bone-cutting, and it would get worse when the sun was down. He hoped Mackeson was right that the Luftwaffe went home when it got dark. It would be about fifteen minutes to sunset now, he guessed, and that would make it about zero-hour for an attack. Astern, the whole sky was crimson. He pushed his fists deeper into his greatcoat pockets, and asked Beale – who'd clamped an ammo drum to the other gun now – whether they'd been told about that signal, the warning that an attack was coming. Withinshaw said, 'Stands to reason. Why we're 'ere, like.' He stared at Paul: at his rank insignia first, the single

524

wavy stripe on each shoulder of his greatcoat. Then at his face. He asked him, 'Had a basinful before, 'ave ye?'

'Not in the Med. Up north. Narvik, that business . . . You?'

'We done a few trips, me an' Ron, Malta an' back once. Other pair's green as grass. Bloody babes in arms, right, kiddoes?'

The red-headed one growled and spat. Beale, the killick, asked Paul, 'Fuck-up, weren't it, Norway?'

'In part, I guess it was.' The two older men were at their guns, getting their feet spaced right, then leaning into the shoulder-rests, weaving a little to test their stance, settling comfortably, the gun barrels traversing and arcing. Then they were resting, waiting, and the younger men were using spare ammunition drums as stools to sit on, McNaught chewing with his mouth open, like a dog. Paul added, 'Can't say I knew much about what was going on, though. I was an OD. Gun's crew.'

Withinshaw murmured, 'Stone the crows.'

Beale asked him, 'Did all right then, did you?' Beale was about thirty, Paul guessed. Rather mean-looking. Probably good at his job so long as he was left to do it on his own. It was undoubtedly an advantage, he thought, to have served on the lower deck in action conditions. He knew these people, understood them; to him they weren't some different form of life, incomprehensible and sometimes a bit worrying, which was how he suspected some commissioned officers tended to view them. The secret – or part of it, he thought – was to accept them as they were, appreciate and make use of the qualities they had, instead of expecting to find ones they *didn*'t have.

The one called Wally jumped up suddenly, and pointed. 'Flag's up. Stand by, gents.'

A red flag for red alert – but in this light even a white one would have looked red. Mick McCall came up the ladder: it was obvious, from his look of surprise, that he hadn't known he'd find Paul here. He gave him a hard, questioning look before he turned to the Oerlikon gunners.

'You blokes all set?'

Beale's answer to the question was a wink. Withinshaw's was: 'Be better wi' a few pints inside us.' But they were ready, alert, watching the sky, the two at the guns and the others standing by with the spare drums at their feet. McCall looked at Paul again: 'Someone tell you to come up here?'

'Mackeson. Idea is to keep us all busy, I suppose. The skipper did say it was your part of ship.'

Beale muttered, 'Extra pair of eyes can't do no 'arm, can it?'

McCall visibly relaxed. Paul blessed the instinct that had made him keep his mouth shut when he'd noticed that gun still covered. If he'd been Thornton he'd have made a fuss about it, and he'd have got nowhere with this bunch.

McCall said to him, 'What a sunset, eh?' Then, somewhere out on the convoy's port bow – northeastward – a destroyer opened fire.

There was nothing to see, from here. Just the sound, the hard, cracking thuds of four-sevens. And the recognition that the attack was starting. McCall said, 'Here we go. Least, here *I* go . . . I'll be up at the Bofors, Beale.'

Ahead of the block of merchantmen, a cruiser opened fire. Then a second joined in. Here on the *Montgovern*'s foc'sl-head the two Oerlikon gunners jerked back the cocking handles on their weapons and waited with their left shoulders towards the blaze of the dying sun.

The shooting ahead, on the bow, was thickening, but those destroyers were three or four miles away from the convoy and there was no way of knowing what their target was. The cruisers had fired a few rounds and then ceased fire, and nothing had appeared anywhere near the convoy. Slow minutes crawled by: you felt an urge to be in action, get to grips with it. Paul asked Beale, watching the sky, 'Do you have tracer in those drums?'

'One in six.'

One tracer round in every six: the others would be high-explosive or incendiary.

The cruisers ahead and the Hunts to port and astern opened fire simultaneously, their gun barrels poking out on the beam, to port. The noise of it smothered the more distant sound of the barrage from the destroyers in the screen, but obviously there were two quite separate attacks being made. Now the racket astern doubled and redoubled as the two battleships and the cruiser between them added their HA armaments to the party. Most of the warships would have RDF, Paul realized: it would have been an RDF contact on approaching bombers that would have initiated the air-raid warning in the first place.

High on the port side of the convoy shellbursts were opening like black fists against the pink-flushed sky.

Beale shouted, 'There. *There*, Art. You on 'em?'

Black against that bright background, twin-engined bombers,

Junkers 88s. They were coming straight towards the convoy, undeterred by thickening groves of shellbursts in front of them and around them. Wally muttered, *''Undreds* of the bastards!'

There were dozens, though, not hundreds. Perhaps forty, Paul thought. Beale was watching them over his sights: it would be a while before close-range weapons would have any part to play. Beyond Beale and Withinshaw at the guns was the grey steel of the foc's'l with its ordered clutter of cable gear, and the gleam of surrounding sea and, a couple of hundred yards ahead, the big lumbering stern-on shape of the motor vessel *Warrenpoint*, leader of this number one column. To port, tracer was rising from destroyers in the outer screen, and the noise of gunfire was still mounting as ship after ship joined in.

Glancing over his shoulder, Paul could see figures motionless behind the glassed-in front of the bridge. Straight, that would be, and his first officer Devenish, and Mackeson no doubt. A small, pimple-like silhouette in the extremity of the port wing would be Gosling; a taller figure was visible on the other side. Mackeson's idea might have seemed good in principle, Paul thought, but either of those two could have blown their lungs out through the whistles without a single peep being audible down here.

'Stand by, Art!'

Beale had shouted the warning. The leading flight of Junkers were diving shallowly towards the convoy's centre. Others behind them, Paul saw, were banking away to their right, towards the rear. Gunfire was a solid roar and the multi-coloured tracer was thickening too, streams of it criss-crossing and converging towards the front-running bombers as they drove in, diving, holding straight courses into the explosive centre of the barrage. One was beginning to turn away, though. You saw a wing tilting as it banked; then another – and another. But others were still coming on, and Paul's nerves jumped as Beale squeezed the trigger of his gun and Withinshaw immediately followed suit, both Oerlikons blazing out intermittent, ear-shattering bursts and the tracer-streams soaring, curving. One bomber – not one that *Montgovern*'s guns were shooting at, but one that had turned and was flying towards the convoy's rear – had smoke streaming from one engine. The tracer seemed to arc away as it approached its target: the whole sky was streaked and patterned with it, multi-coloured streams of fire and, astern, the setting sun's bonfire-like glow. A bomb-splash – the first of a stick of several, probably, but he saw only one and paid no attention to it – had risen on the quarter, between this and number two column. He was looking around, remembering that his job here was to spot new targets, not simply watch the action, when he heard the commodore's siren from ahead, the lead-ship of column two, ordering an emergency turn to port. More bombs splashed in between the lines of ships, mounds of dark water leaping. The *Montgovern*'s own siren let out a preliminary hiss and then found its voice, a deep bellow of sound repeating that order: all the ships' hooters echoing it as their helms were put over and the entire convoy, lumbering merchantmen and the warships surrounding them, turned in unison with all the guns still racketing. More bombers weaving in: on the bow now instead of the beam, black and evil-looking, bombs clumping into the sea here and there and the aircraft lifting, banking away and climbing, putting their tails to the explosive streams that were reaching up for them. The barrage over the convoy was so intense that you wouldn't have thought there'd be a space a bomber could pass through without being hit: and it did, on the whole, seem to have kept them out on its fringes. But it was easing now, and shifting, most of it astern, in the general direction of the sunset. It had become a moving barrage, in fact, as the remaining bombers circled, probing for easier targets or gaps in the defence, the warships' guns following them around like a boxer with a long straight left, keeping his opponent on the end of it.

Beale and Withinshaw were standing back from their guns while their assistants changed the ammunition drums. The red-headed boy, McNaught, was needling Withinshaw: 'I didn'a see so many comin' doon in flames.'

'I'll see *you* in fookin'—'

Siren, for a turn back to starboard. All the ships acknowledging. The long days of practising such manoeuvres, in the Atlantic on the way south from the Clyde, were paying off: the convoy was in good formation as it turned back to the mean course. Firing still quite heavy astern and on the quarter. Paul was trying to look all ways at once, knowing there were still enemies around and that this failing light was perfect for surprise. The light was going fast now, leaking away as the source of the red glow retracted and dimmed . . . Gunfire ahead, suddenly: and he saw the attacker as he turned. A bomber low, wing-tilted, swooping upwards from wave-top level where it had slipped between the cruisers, who were the ones that had opened fire. The German had flames streaming from one wing's leading edge, flickering back all over it. It passed over at masthead height, the Oerlikons starting up with an aiming-point too far astern and the midships Bofors, where McCall was, only managing three or four barks at it, much too late. Tracer rising again astern, the Hunts back there giving it all they had. There was a sheet of yellow flame like the flare of a huge match, and the guns abruptly ceased firing. The barraging was all on the starboard quarter and beam now; in this area, there was peace again. Withinshaw said, 'That sod bought it, Ron. See it, did you?'

'No fault of ours, if he did.' Beale watched the sky, which was losing its last shreds of colour. The barrage was moving up the convoy's starboard side. But the convoy was back on course, no ships had been hit, so far as anyone could see, and progress was continuing Malta-ward. Beale muttered, 'I don't reckon that last 'un for an 88, any road.'

Paul didn't think it had been, either. In the few seconds that it had been over them he hadn't had time to think about it, but in retrospect it seemed to have been a Heinkel and almost certainly a torpedo-bomber. That would account for the low level at which it had come in, and it might also explain that emergency turn. The action had started with a barrage from the destroyers on the bow to port, and that could have a torpedo-bomber attack developing. They'd have been turned away by the barrage, but they'd have hung around, waiting for a chance to press in again when the escorts might be busy fending off the attack by Junkers 88s. The convoy would have been turned to avoid torpedoes, and that last effort would have been a late comer sneaking in for a solitary, surprise attack.

It hadn't done him any good. He'd almost certainly perished in that burst of flame . . . But from a position like this you could only see pieces of the action as they happened from minute to minute and in your corner of the fight; you could only guess – in lulls or when it was over – at the broader pattern of events. It was much as it had been for him as a sailor in a destroyer gun's crew: he'd hardly ever known what was happening or which way they were going or what for; he'd simply helped to serve the gun, a creature with a voracious appetite for fifty-pound shells . . . And there was a feeling of enclosure, at this level: of being surrounded, hemmed in ahead and astern and to starboard by the bulks and high bridge superstructures of the other freighters. Rather like being a cow in a herd of other cows, plodding on with that feeling of being hidden in the mass. It was an illusion, of course, because to the attackers each ship was separate and a target to be got at, and any hunter worth his salt picked his individual quarry and went after it. The comforting feeling of partial invisibility also failed when you looked out to port and saw only darkness, glimmer of sea with the shadows of the night across it. It *was* almost night now, and the only sound of guns came faintly, distantly from astern. They might be attacking the oiling group back there, he thought.

Withinshaw mumbled, 'They weren't tryin' all that 'ard, I reckon.'

Beale had pulled the drum off his Oerlikon. He dumped it into McNaught's arms and turned back to begin overhauling the gun. He worked fast and deftly, Paul noticed, working more by feel than by sight. Neither of the guns had jammed even once, as Oerlikons tended to do, and it might have been because they were well maintained.

McNaught had a spare ammo drum ready, and he'd put the two part-used ones aside; it would be his job to refill them now. He was singing quietly, about Saturday nights in Glasgow: the song broke off abruptly as a new storm of gunfire broke out astern. In seconds the Oerlikons were reloaded and the gunners were standing ready, one facing out on each quarter. Tracer astern was heavy, and far brighter now the light had gone, and as well as the interlacing streams of red, blue, green and yellow the sky flickered with the yellowish flashes of time-fused AA shells.

It stopped as suddenly as it had begun.

Withinshaw grumbled, 'What the fookin' 'ell . . .'

McCall arrived, heaving himself up the ladder from the well deck. 'All right, lads?' He put a hand on Paul's shoulder: 'Okay?'

Paul was still watching the sky astern. He said, 'Apparently it's not over yet.'

'It is, you know. That was the Fleet Air Arm coming back. Trying to get down on their carriers. Nice sort of welcome, I must say.'

The atmosphere in the saloon was already heavy with pipe and cigarette smoke. Brill said, waving some of it away, 'Wouldn't imagine this was a hospital, would you?' Until about ten minutes ago he'd had the place to himself; at action stations the saloon became his first-aid centre and operating theatre.

Mick McCall fetched two cups of coffee from the sideboard, and came to join them. He said, accepting a duty-free cigarette from Paul, 'Very gentlemanly introduction, that.'

'Be worse tomorrow, will it?'

'Christ, what do *you* think?'

'I've no idea.' Paul sipped coffee. 'Never been on a thing like this before.'

'I'd better educate you, then.' McCall used a stub of pencil and the back of a brown OHMS envelope to make a rough sketch of the western Mediterranean. 'We're about here. Halfway, roughly, from Gib to Malta. And this –' he drew a large oval shape to the north-east of their position – 'this, believe it or not, is Sardinia. By tomorrow forenoon we'll be passing to the south of it, through the narrows here with the Sardinian coast about fifty miles to port. The Germans and the Eyeties have air bases on Sardinia, don't they?'

'I suppose they would have.'

Those narrow waters would be an obvious place to have submarines waiting for them, he thought. McCall didn't mention submarines, though. He told them, 'By tomorrow evening we'll be through that stretch. With any luck, we will be. Touching wood, etcetera . . . So – tomorrow night, *here*, the battleships and the carriers leave us and turn westward, and we carry on into the Sicilian narrows. Between Sicily here to port and Cape Bon on the North African coast to starboard. Through the Skerki Channel, and down here past Pantellaria – where E-boats are based, incidentally. And Sicily, of course, is virtually one large Luftwaffe base . . .' He put the pencil away, and reached for his coffee. 'It all starts tomorrow, really.'

CHAPTER 5

Bob Gant had rattled down four flights of ladderway from
Defiant's compass platform to the level of her foc'sl deck and
turned aft to get to the next ladder, down to the upper deck and aft
– get to the fire, get it out before the enemy found it too useful as a
point of aim. *De Ruyter* and *Java* had both blown up, which left
only three targets for the Jap cruisers out there in the dark: and this
ship was slowing, stopping, as a result of the hit in number two
boiler room.

He'd reached the ladder and started down it when number three
gun – the six-inch mounting between the foremast and the funnels –
fired, on a bearing just for'ard of the beam. The blast knocked him
backwards, flash from 'flashless' powder blinded him, and for a
moment he was witless, lost. He'd cannoned backwards into his
'doggie', Ordinary Seaman Pinner, who'd been following close
behind him. It was Pinner squawking in his ear, 'Are you all right,
sir?' that brought him back to his senses. The sheer silliness of the
question – it seemed silly at the time, anyway – penetrated and
triggered annoyance, put him back in touch with events around
him. Flames aft, voices shouting, the shouting drowned in gunfire:
Defiant wallowed, rolling in the troughs of other ships' wash. A
salvo came in a hoarse rush and the top of the for'ard funnel
glowed red and disintegrated. He had to get aft, see about the fire
that was somewhere near the after tubes on the starboard side. He
was starting down the ladder again, with Pinner in close company
behind, when he heard shells going into the sea nearby. Metal
whirred and whined, clanged into the ship's side and superstructure; then a shell struck and burst for'ard, and just as *Defiant*'s own
guns sent away another salvo she was hit again: up in the bridge
superstructure, above him.

The bridge, he realized . . .

Back the way he'd come. Up the foc'sl-break ladder, in the screen door, and climbing again. Dreading what he'd find . . . The top ladder was loose, twisted, the bulkhead of the lobby outside the plot was bulged and split, its white enamel paint blackened. Shouts for help, wounded men moaning, a first-aid party with Neill-Robertsons, hardly knowing where to start. In seconds, everything had gone, changed. You were in a different century, another world. Gant was in the after-end of the bridge, which was completely wrecked. Haskins, the captain of marines, saw him and came over to him. He had come down from the ADP because all its circuits and communications had been cut so there'd been no point staying up there; he and his ADP crew who'd come down with him were trying to help the wounded, find the living . . .

The bridge deck had been blasted open from below. Rescuers were at work down there: voices and torch-beams, and the stink of smouldering cortisone. Gant didn't want to use his own torch – it was on a lanyard attached to his belt – up here in the open. He shouted, towards the for'ard end of the bridge, 'Captain, sir?'

Haskins said, 'He'd have been right where the blast came through.'

One gun fired. Number two – sometimes referred to as 'B' gun – the mounting immediately for'ard of the bridge. It was crewed by Royal Marines. Gant hadn't at this stage caught on to the fact that he was now in command, possibly because not wanting it to be so his mind rejected the obvious truth. He only remembered later being struck by the thought that Everard couldn't have been killed, because it would be too much sheer bad luck to have history repeat itself after only this short an interval. *Defiant*'s previous captain had died in that same corner of the bridge only a few weeks ago. They'd been off Mersa Matruh on the desert coast when they'd been jumped by a lone Messerschmitt fighter-bomber that had come whistling out of the sun and strafed the bridge with cannon-fire. The skipper had been the only casualty. It had been Everard's inheritance of some of the same rotten streak of luck – in retrospect you could see it as one sequence of events – that having just had a destroyer sunk under him he'd been available to replace the cruiser captain.

'In the for'ard corner there.' Haskins had started by shouting, but he'd found there was no need to, suddenly a normal tone of voice was perfectly audible . . . 'I've seen – first thing I did was – anyway, there's no point, sir, I'm sorry but—'

'All right.' He'd check for himself though, all the same. Haskins seemed to be taking personal responsibility for his captain's death. Shock, perhaps. The ship was lying stopped, rolling very slightly, and none of her guns was in action now. Gunfire from other ships was distant and sporadic. The battle had passed on, and *Defiant* was alone. Haskins stopped beside the binnacle, which was still vertical and seemed intact. He stooped, wary of what it was that he'd found here, and Chevening told him, 'I'm all right. I think I was knocked out.'

Getting to his feet. Haskins said, helping him, 'It's the navigating officer, sir. Binnacle must have sheltered him. And the deck isn't holed here. Here, steady . . .'

'You're right, I was behind the binnacle. Is the captain—'

'Not a hope . . . Look, are you sure you're okay?'

'Bit dizzy, that's—'

'Well, you're damn lucky.' The marine tried a voicepipe: 'Bridge, wheelhouse!'

'SBA Green down 'ere, sir. And a stretcher party.' The reply had come from the void below them: and that voicepipe led nowhere, as Gant's torch revealed. He'd been unwilling to switch it on until now, when it was plain there was no enemy anywhere near them. The beam of light flickered over bodies and parts of bodies enmeshed in twisted steel. The plot was open to the bridge. A pair of shoes were jammed in torn deck-plating, their soles upward: if there was a man still in them he'd be hanging head-downwards in the lower compartment. A voice from the rear of the bridge asked gruffly, 'Captain, sir?'

Mr Nye, the gunner. Down from the director tower. Gant told him, 'The captain's dead, Mr Nye. What's the state of things in the tower?'

A low groan led his torch-beam to a body and an upturned face. It was PO Ruddle, one of the signals yeomen. Gant had already seen what was left of the chief yeoman, CPO Howell. Nye told him, 'Only communications link is with number three gun, sir. PCO's sent me and Colour Sergeant Bruce to get the lads out of the TS – the circuits is all gone, sir, see – and put the other guns in local control. Not much else we *can* do, sir. Except the ACP *might*—'

'All right, carry on.' Gant called down, 'We need stretchers up here. And morphine.' Morphine for Ruddle. Gant couldn't imagine there'd be anyone alive on that lower level, where the shell had burst. 'You still there, Green?'

'I'm coming up now, sir!'

He told his 'doggie', Pinner, 'Go down to the lower steering position. Know where it is?'

'Platform deck, sir, just about under 'ere.'

'Good man. Tell them I'll be testing communications to them from the after-conning position. Then I can decide whether to steer from there or from the after position.'

Haskins joined him as he picked a way forward through jagged edges of torn plating, wreckage, bodies you didn't need to look at twice and could not afford to allow to imprint themselves on your mind. They did, however hard you tried not to let them into your consciousness; and in later days, nights and years you'd see them again, these and others . . . The full force of the shell had blown up through the middle, under these men's feet . . . He remembered, like something in a dream, Sandilands, the commander (E), saying there'd been a shell in the top of number two boiler room. It had cut steam pipes, smashed other gear, killed or wounded most of the men in the compartment. Number two was the larger boiler room, with four boilers in it, and Sandilands had said he'd be able to provide steam from number one – steam for slow speed – in roughly half an hour. But how long ago that report had been made was hard to remember: an hour, ten minutes, it was what happened in any given space of time that counted, not the time itself.

He told Haskins, 'Job for you, soldier. There was a hit aft, starboard side, and it started a fire. I want to know whether they've put the fire out, and the extent of the damage and what's being done about it. Rowley may be there. Find him anyway, and tell him I want a situation report made to me in the ACP. All right?'

'Aye aye, sir.' ACP stood for after conning position. It was abaft the funnels, near the mainmast, on a platform which also supported the searchlights.

Haskins said, 'Here, sir.'

The captain's wooden seat had been smashed against the forefront of the bridge. Splinters of its wood were mixed with the slumped body in its overall suit that had been white but was now bright red. It was in the corner, in a heap suggesting bonelessness, and the head was like raw meat.

He'd taken the torch-beam off it. Haskins had been right when he'd said there was no point in looking. The beam moved back – as if the torch had moved his hand, more than the other way about.

There was a smear of blood all down the front of the bridge, over a nest of telephones and the captain's action-alarm button and a fuse-box, right down to the body, and at the top the glass windscreen had been shattered. He must have been hurled on to it, and the half-inch glass, jagged now and bloodstained, had just about decapitated him.

'Captain, sir?'

Gant's torch-beam swung around, to blind the doctor, Sibbold. Sibbold's whites were bloodstained too. A broad, solid-looking man, capless and dishevelled, peering blinking at the torchlight and the man behind it. Morphine ampoules in his top pocket were like a railway clerk's fountain pens.

'There he is.' The light-beam acted as a pointer. 'I wouldn't think there's the slightest chance of—'

'Stretcher here, please. Quick, now!' Sibbold dropped down beside the body. Gant said, 'Not a hope. My God, *look* at him. He'd *dead*, damn it.'

He'd had to state the fact, oblige himself to face it. He didn't want Everard's job, this command, this rotten, hopeless situation. All his life he'd funked command. Now it was being thrust on him, and in the worst of all worlds. He told Sibbold, 'Petty Officer Ruddle's over there, and he's alive, so—'

'One thing at a time.' Sibbold shouted, 'Green, are you—'

'Coming, sir, coming!'

You could sympathize with the doctor's refusal to accept the truth, that Everard was dead. But he oughtn't to be wasting time that might have been spent on men with a chance of living . . . Well, it was Sibbold's business. Gant turned away, knowing that *his* job now was to get *Defiant* under command and moving, get her away before the enemy returned.

'Another quarter of an hour should do it.' John Sandilands' voice was hoarse-sounding over the telephone between engine-room and ACP. 'But then you must let us work her up very gradually. I can just about promise you revs for five knots. If we're lucky and it looks good we *might* get her up to ten.'

Gant hesitated for a moment before he answered. Anxiety made him want to shout. It was an effort to speak normally. He said, 'It's fifty miles to Surabaya, chief, and we have to get there before dawn. That calls for ten knots as an average if we were to get cracking now, this minute.'

'It wouldn't help anyone if the repairs don't hold, Bob. And they won't if you go and—'

'Now listen . . .' Everard had asked him, an hour or two ago, what he'd have been doing if he'd had Doorman's job. Now Doorman was probably dead, but the job he'd got was Everard's, not the Dutchman's, and it was just as bad. You had to shut your mind to the hopelessness of it, just get on with what had to be done immediately. Such as, now, persuading Sandilands to see the wood as well as the trees. They'd been patching steampipes, or rigging jury ones, from the for'ard boiler room through the after one where they'd been holed by blast or splinters. It was an engineering problem, Sandilands', not *his*. He had God knew how many of his own – insoluble, overwhelming problems . . . He told Sandilands, his voice thin with anxiety, 'If we don't get into Surabaya before daylight, we're finished. Ten knots, John. I'm not asking you, I'm bloody well *telling* you, d'you understand?'

He hung up. His hands were shaking, from that flare of temper. No: from taut nerves, not temper. If Sandilands had insisted that ten knots was an impossibility, he'd have been beaten, stumped. He hadn't, thank God. So it was all right, for the moment, you could press on – to the *next* problem . . . This telephone was working only because its line went straight down through the deck under the after conning position, and it hadn't therefore been cut by that shellburst near the tubes. There was no communication from here to the lower steering position, for instance. None to the after steering position either, the ASP being a closet-sized corner of the steering-engine flat. Helm orders, when they got her moving, would be passed down to it from this conning position by voice, from man to man via a chain of sailors who were already in position. And steering would be by magnetic, since although the gyro itself, which was down on the platform deck for'ard, was all right, its repeaters weren't functioning.

What if Sandilands rang back now, said no, he couldn't do it? *Christ* . . .

The hit below the bridge, or the upward blast of it, had cut all the gunnery control circuits except for the telephone connection between the tower and number three gun. As the TS was isolated, this one link wasn't of any value from the point of view of gunnery control, but it was being made use of all the same, linking the tower as a lookout position with the upper deck, and, by messengers, with the other guns and with the ACP.

Number one gun, on the foc'sl, had been knocked out in the same salvo that had wrecked the bridge.

The hit aft had killed the crew of the starboard after torpedo tubes and wrecked that triple mounting. Luckily none of the torpedo warheads had exploded. Flying debris had smashed the starboard searchlight, torn holes in the armoured side of this conning position, and the shell had blown a hole through the upper deck, cutting leads and communications to the two after guns and jamming the ammunition hoist to number four. Artificers were working on that now, but meanwhile shells were being brought up by manpower through the hatches and stockpiled near the gun. The fire which Gant had seen from the bridge hadn't been an upper-deck fire at all. Its flames had been shooting like a blow-torch's through the hole in the deck, but it was an internal fire, in the lower deck. Charles Rowley and his damage control parties had it under control now, but it had taken a lot of water to subdue it and the water couldn't be got rid of until there was steam-pressure to run the pumps.

He kept mentally cataloguing damage and the measures that were being taken to deal with it. As if there was a danger of losing some element of the overall picture and, through oversight, making some colossal blunder in a moment of emergency.

In number two boiler room, seven men had been killed and two wounded. The latest count of casualties was nineteen dead and fourteen wounded. Everard was being counted as one of the fourteen, but Sibbold wasn't holding out much hope for him. He'd glanced round from a man whose leg he'd been amputating and told Gant, 'The presence or absence of life can be a technicality, you know.' He'd proved Gant wrong in the basic fact that Everard had been alive – technically, whatever that meant – when they'd got him down to the sickbay. Since then, he'd been ready to accept the inevitable. He was single-handed and struggling to meet all the demands that were being made on him; he'd had an assistant, a younger RNVR doctor, but he'd been landed at Batavia to look after wounded British and American naval personnel in a Dutch hospital where nobody spoke English.

There wasn't much room in this ACP, and Chevening's bony length wasn't any help. The navigator squeezed out past Gant now, emerging from the little cubby-hole that held a chart-table. He said, 'Course will be south forty-eight west, sir, if our DR's reasonably accurate.'

'What's the compass error?'

'Two degrees west, sir. Variation and deviation just about cancel each other out.'

Gant had only asked the question to see what sort of an answer Chevening might give him. The navigator's manner was peculiar, as if he hadn't completely regained contact with his surroundings. Perhaps he'd always been like that: but Gant hadn't noticed it before.

'Pinner?'

'I'm 'ere, sir.'

Ordinary Seaman Pinner was on the ladder outside the ACP, slewing himself aside from it when anyone needed to go up or down it. Out of the way, but in earshot, which was the ideal disposition for a 'doggie'. Gant was impressed by young Pinner, who'd shown a lot of common sense during the past hour's unpleasant moments. He told him now, 'Go down to the sickbay, and ask the PMO that same question.'

'Aye aye, sir.'

Pinner dropped off the ladder. It was the only entrance and exit, as the starboard one had been blown off at the same time that the searchlight on that side had been smashed.

Gant asked Chevening, 'Time now?'

'11.22, sir.'

Sandilands' quarter-hour would be up at about 11.30, he supposed. There'd be time to tour the upper deck, visit the guns' crews and have a word to Greenleaf. He told Chevening, 'Hold the fort here now. If the engine-room pipes up, or anything else, send a messenger after me. I'm going to walk around the guns.'

'Aye aye, sir.'

He added from the ladder, 'Keep Pinner here when he gets back. Use him to find me if you need to.'

The ship lay motionless in black water dappled where moonlight filtered through strips of cloud. She felt dead, spiritless, and the stink of burning still hung over her. Sandilands, he thought, had better get a move on. It was getting to the point when every passing minute mattered, if they were to reach Surabaya before daylight.

What might happen after that – with the ship crippled and a Jap invasion imminent – didn't bear thinking about. At this very moment they could be ferrying their troops ashore . . . Thinking didn't help anything at all. You had to go through the motions, but when you forced your mind past them to where they'd get you in the end, you came back to that nightmare of the no-way-out. The only trick he'd found that did help him to stave off the sense of pointlessness was to ask himself, *What would Everard be doing now*? The answer was simple, each time: Everard would have been dealing with each problem as it arose, with the situation as it was at any given moment, in this minute or the next – and so on, step by step. And he'd have looked to the future, the longer term, in the same way, deciding to cope with new developments as they cropped up.

Gant found he could only look a few hours ahead. Because beyond that, eventually, he knew he'd be on a cliff-edge; and he'd have brought a whole ship's company to it with him. *That* was the thing that froze him when he let his mind loose.

The one objective that was rational and achievable – with luck – was to get the ship to Surabaya. Surabaya and not Batavia, because it was the nearest and because Sandilands' repairs obviously couldn't be relied on for more than a short distance. And there was the need to get there quickly, not to be caught at sea, alone and in this semi-wrecked condition, in daylight.

There'd be air attacks on Surabaya, of course. There'd been raids since the beginning of the month, but they'd be intensified now because the Japanese worked to a set pattern of heavy bombing before a sea or land assault. But there'd be some collective defence, with other ships there – *Exeter* and *Encounter* and the American destroyers.

Except they'd almost certainly be ordered to run for it, now . . .

One's mind flitted, sometimes recoiling from what it found.

'All right here?'

He'd stopped at number three gun, the one that had a telephone to Greenleaf in the director tower. He'd passed by number four, the gun with the jammed ammo hoist, because the telephone link made this the key position now.

CPO Hughes, chief gunner's mate, told him, 'Top line, sir. Standing by, and no problems.'

No problems, Gant thought. Weren't there? Really, *none*?

From his jaunty tone, Hughes might have been outside a drill-shed on his native Whale Island, the Navy's gunnery school. From memories of the course he'd done on Whale Island in the remote past when he'd been a sub-lieutenant Gant still shuddered mentally at the thought of it. Whale Island produced gunnery specialists, in Gant's imagination, as primeval swamps produced pterodactyls.

'Let me have a word with Lieutenant Greenleaf.' He took the telephone headset from the sightsetter, removing his own tin hat so he could slide the earphones on. 'Greenleaf?'

'Yes, sir!'

'All right, up there?'

'Well – the horizon's clear, sir . . .'

'We'll be getting under way in a few minutes, I hope. With luck we'll be in Surabaya before sunrise. But I'll have you relieved before long.'

'Any news of the captain, sir?'

'Not yet.' The question had taken him by surprise, like a blow below the belt. In an attempt to sound brisk and optimistic he'd forgotten Everard, for that moment. He told Greenleaf, 'When there is any, I'll let you know.' He handed the gear back to the sightsetter, and put his tin hat back on. 'I'll be taking a walk around, chief. Is Mr Nye—'

'Mr Nye's aft, sir, looking after five and six.'

'I'll see him there, then . . . You chaps all right?'

'Aye, sir.' The gunlayer, Jackson, answered from his seat inside the shield. 'But – the captain, sir – do they reckon he'll—'

'PMO can't say yet, Jackson. It's touch and go.'

Everard had been alive when they'd got him down from the bridge, but he'd been in a coma, lifeless-*looking*, and Sibbold had admitted that the odds were against his coming out of it. Minor damage consisted of an arm broken in two places and a lot of cuts and punctures, but the main injury was to his head where he'd been flung on to the glass windshield. And since then, well after that, Sibbold had made his remark about the presence of life being no more than a technicality. Meaning that a man in coma was alive but he didn't necessarily have to wake up? Gant had had no time, and nor had Sibbold, for any longer session of questions and answers: the simple fact was that he didn't know, could only wait and see.

Gant went for'ard, round the side of the bridge superstructure, to number two gun. Haskins was there, talking to his colour sergeant.

'How are the old donkeys, sir?'

The engines, he meant. Gant told him, 'We should have half speed any minute now . . . You chaps all right here?'

'Satisfactory, sir . . . Any gen on the skipper, sir?'

'Not yet. PMO won't even guess.'

'Let's 'ope it's a case of no news is good news, sir.'

Colour Sergeant Bruce had a voice to match his build. A very large man, taller and wider than Haskins, who was himself no lightweight. Bruce was the marine detachment's senior NCO, and as Haskins had no subaltern this made him second in command. He looked a bit like a Saint Bernard, Gant thought.

'Soon as I hear, I'll pass the word.'

How marvellous it would be, he thought as he went aft, to be number two again, to have Everard on his feet and making the decisions. Second in command was the best job of them all: you had as much responsibility and authority as any reasonable man could want, without carrying that *ultimate* burden. As a number two, one should have been more consciously aware of one's good fortune. If he got out of this and had that kind of job again, he'd revel in it!

If . . .

Number four gun: he'd passed number three and the for'ard torpedo-tube mounting, and under the raised platform that carried a four-inch AA gun on each of its wings, and now he stopped at the gun with the non-functioning ammunition hoist. He leaned with one hand on the edge of the gunshield and the other fist pressed into the small of his back, where the pain was.

'Who's in charge here?'

'I am, sir. Petty Officer Longland, sir.'

'Any progress on the hoist, GM?'

'ERAs are still at it, sir.'

'Meanwhile you've a good stock of ready-use charges and projectiles, have you?'

'Enough to be getting on with, sir. Wouldn't want too much layin' in the open, like.'

Inevitably, then, came the question about Everard. The question, and the unsatisfactory answer. Gant was providing it when a whistle shrilled from number three gun and CPO Hughes bawled 'All quarters alert! Alarm port, bearing red two-oh!'

Mr North, at the for'ard tubes, was yelling to his team at the after ones to get them turned out. From the guns, Gant heard the clangs of loading-trays slamming over, breeches thudding shut, the calls of 'Ready!' He was back at three gun, taking over the headset. The gun was loaded, trained on the alarm bearing . . . 'Commander here. What is it, Greenleaf?'

'Two ships, sir, look like cruisers, coming straight towards.

542

They're in line abreast but they could be *Perth* and *Houston*, I can't—'

'All right.' He passed the head-sct into the sightsetter's hands, and ran aft, passing over the tops of the out-turned torpedo-tubes. 'Yeoman!' He'd reached the ladder to the ACP. 'Stand by to challenge on bearing red two-oh!'

'Searchlight, sir, or—'

'Aldis.' The searchlight would show too far. Even if the ships approaching were *Perth* and *Houston*, there could still be Jap ships around. And after that damage aloft and most electrical circuits out of commission you could be sure the yardarm challenge-and-reply system, the coloured lights, weren't working.

'Port bow, ship challenging, sir!'

They'd got in first, then. Two red lights and a green: it had flashed on, off again: on-off—

'Correct challenge, sir!'

'Give him the correct answer, then. By Aldis.' There was a challenge and reply using morse letters as well. It changed every few hours, just as the masthead lights system did. 'Pinner, tell three gun to tell the tower they're friendly.'

It could only be *Perth* and *Houston*. Anything else afloat now in this sea would be Japanese. Petty Officer Morris was clashing out the letters ZS, ZS, ZS. The other ship acknowledged, and then began again: '*Defiant* from *Perth*: How are you fixed?'

Gant had read the morse for himself. He told Morris, 'Make to him, "Have action damage to boiler room and bridge. Am about to get under way with maximum speed probably ten knots and steering from aft. Hope to reach Surabaya before daylight.'

That said it all, he thought. All that needed to be said, anyway. The yeoman was scribbling it down, inside where a dim light glowed on Chevening's chart. Still scribbling, Morris told Leading Signalman Tomsett, 'Call 'im up, an' I'll give it you word by word.'

'Commander, sir?'

'Who's that – Pinner?'

'Yes, sir. Message from the surgeon commander that the captain's still in coma, sir. Still can't say more, sir.'

Sibbold was scared to make guesses, Gant thought, for fear of guessing wrongly. Surely by this time he'd have *some* notion . . . Pinner added, 'Petty Officer Ruddle's died, sir.'

So now there were twenty dead. Gant had expected Nick Everard to become the twentieth. And he hadn't: so perhaps there was

543

hope? But even if he survived, he couldn't possibly take command . . . The telephone squeaked: there was a whole bank of them but the only one working was the line to the engine-room. Gant said into it, 'ACP, commander speaking.'

'We can move now, Bob. Sorry about the delay.'

'Wait a minute.' That signal was still being passed to *Perth*. Then he thought, *Why wait, for God's sake?* He told Sandilands, 'All right. Half ahead together. Or slow ahead if you like, but I must have a minimum of ten knots within five minutes.'

'We'll do our best. But I don't suppose you'd particularly want me to blow the—'

'I don't suppose you want to be caught out here and blown out of the water, either. Get on with it, John!'

'From *Perth*, sir: "Agree Surabaya is your best bet. I am continuing with *Houston* to Batavia. See you at the – word we're not sure of here, sir" – Galleface?"'

'It's a pub in Colombo.'

A couple of thousand miles away . . .

Captains Everard and Waller were old friends, of course. Gant was glad, for a moment, that he hadn't said anything about Everard. Then he wondered if he had any right to withhold the information from a senior officer who, however informally, had asked for a report on *Defiant*'s present state. He decided he did not have, that it was a vital part of the whole picture: and secondly, that he'd continue to withhold it. The message still formed itself in his mind: *Captain Everard seriously wounded and principal medical officer is in doubt whether he will recover consciousness. Commander R. Gant Royal Navy acting in command.* It was more an instinct than a decision not to make such a signal, and he couldn't have explained, at that moment, what the reasons were for it. *Defiant* began to tremble as her engines and screws turned. The important thing was that they should continue turning, and turn faster – much, much faster . . . He checked the ship's head by magnetic and called to Pinner on the ladder, 'Starboard twenty!' The order was repeated first by Pinner and then by a sailor ten yards farther aft; and again, more faintly as one heard it here, by a man on a downward-leading ladder: to ensure there was no slip-up he'd got Flynn, one of the watchkeeping lieutenants, back there to monitor the passage of the orders. When he'd let that first one get a certain distance, he thought probably to its destination by this time, he sent another after it: 'Steer south forty-eight west.'

544

'Signal from *Houston*, sir: "Good luck".'

Houston was commanded by a Captain Rooks USN. Gant had met him once, when he and some other captains had come aboard for a meal with Everard. He told PO Morris, who was now the senior surviving signal rating, 'Reply: "Thanks and the same to you."' About as banal as one could get, he realized; and phrased as if it might have been Nick Everard answering, not a man one rank junior to the American. Once you embarked on a deception, you had to stick to it. And having kept one's mouth shut, a deception was what it had now become.

Chevening cleared his throat. 'Should we not – er – do you think we should tell *Perth* about the captain, sir?'

'What?'

Defiant was making five or six knots, and the quartermaster in that very cramped space down aft and below the waterline was steadying her on the ordered course. The other two cruisers, steering west, had already crossed astern. And there were quite a few things to be seen to now . . . Gant poked his head out of the port-side hatch, and found his 'doggie' still there on the ladder.

'Pinner, go and find Lieutenant-Commander Rowley for me. Tell him I'd like a word.'

Chevening tried again: 'Sir, d'you think we ought to report that—'

'That the captain's wounded? No, I don't . . . Are you sure *you're* quite all right now, pilot?'

'Absolutely, sir. Full working order. But I just wondered whether—'

'Is that rev counter working?'

Chevening stooped, mantis-like, to check it.

'Yes, sir. Revs on now for – seven to eight knots.'

'Let me know how we're doing in five minutes' time.'

With *Perth* and *Houston* heading for Batavia, *Exeter* badly damaged in Surabaya, *Java* and *de Ruyter* sunk and *Defiant* crippled, the so-called Combined Striking Force no longer existed. All that survived was a ragbag of ships in various states of disrepair scattered about the archipelago and waiting to be finished off. Or to attempt escape. Nothing had been achieved, because nothing had been achievable. He'd suspected this from the outset, and he thought Everard had probably seen it too. So had the American, the captain of USS *Sloan*. *Sloan*'s captain had come near to stating it out loud, and at the time Gant had felt shocked. It had been in his own mind, but at that stage only as a private thought which he'd been trying to dismiss.

Now the proof of the pudding was in the eating, and the results were in his – Gant's – lap. Whether Everard lived or died, that was the plain fact of it: this ship was in an entirely hopeless position, and it was up to him, Bob Gant, to—

To do *what*, for Christ's sake?

Well. Get the boiler room mended, then run for the Sunda Strait, or the Lombok Strait. A lot would depend on what sort of a job Sandilands would make of it.

'Commander, sir?'

Charles Rowley's head and shoulders were framed in the open hatchway. Rowley looked as if he'd been down a coalmine.

'Bloody awful about the skipper, sir.'

'Yes. But he may pull through.'

'PMO thinks it's unlikely, sir.'

'When did he say that?'

'Ten minutes ago. I was passing—'

'Did you see the captain?'

'No, just Sibbold, but—'

'Did he say if he was still unconscious?'

Rowley nodded. 'Also that he's weaker. Loss of blood and something about his heartbeat.'

'Well.' Gant took a deep breath, as if he needed more air than he was getting. 'Listen, Charles. First, you are now executive officer of this ship, and you're to act as such . . . I take it the damage-control picture's satisfactory?'

'Everything's under control, sir.'

'Well, what the ship's company must have immediately is a meal. Soup and sandwiches, something of that sort, and action-messing routine.'

'The galley's working on it now, sir.'

'Excellent. Second thing is to relieve Greenleaf in the tower. Any of the watchkeepers – it's simply a lookout job now, with a telephone link to number three gun, and that's all. But I want lookouts for'ard, and on the four-inch gundecks too. Also, stand down one gun's crew at a time, give them each a half-hour stand-easy. Then the PMO – I want a casualty list from him, as well as a report on the outlook for the captain. And finally – for the moment, that is – the dead have got to be buried, and it must be done now, before we're much closer inshore. Tell Mr Nye to organize a burial party, put someone else as OOQ on five and six guns, and ask the padre to come and see me . . . Where is he, d'you know?'

'He was – er – ministering to the wounded, sir.'

'Tell him to come and see me, anyway.'

'Aye aye, sir. We're going into Surabaya, sir, is that right?'

'Yes. ETA about dawn. And that's another thing: we can expect air attacks, when we get there, and Haskins had better sort out his AA control system. The ADP's out of action, same as the tower, and the TS isn't operating, so it'll be local control . . . Greenleaf can work out a system, with Haskins.'

'Right.' Rowley waited in case there was more to come. Then he asked, 'After we make Surabaya, sir, what'll the programme be?'

'We'll get orders. Probably to make emergency repairs and then leg it to Ceylon.'

'From what I'm told, sir, there's at least a week's hard work to be done in that boiler room. And if the Japs are about to invade?'

'The Dutch are confident of holding out, Charles.' He thought, hearing his own voice say it, *What a stupid bloody statement . . .* He was annoyed at being faced with a question he couldn't answer, when it had become his job to produce answers and there was no one else who could provide them. And he'd let Charles Rowley see both the dilemma and the irritation . . . Anyway, to call it a week's work was ludicrous: in much less time than that, Java would be Japanese.

'That's the lot, Charles. Get on to it, will you?'

He asked Chevening, 'How are the revs?'

'Coming up steadily, sir. We must be making nearly ten knots now.'

'We shan't be in the anchorage before daylight, though, would you say?'

'I'd guess we'll be in the Strait, sir.'

And it mightn't be such a bad thing, to have some daylight to help them through that quite tricky passage. He'd leave the pilotage to Chevening, anyway . . . He asked him, 'Will you be all right on your own here, pilot, for about ten minutes?'

He was sick of getting no answers out of Sibbold. He'd decided to go and see for himself.

Chevening said, smiling, 'Oh, I believe so, sir.'

The navigator had a good opinion of himself, Gant had noticed. He hoped it might be justified, at that, because he was going to have to depend on him quite a lot. He told him, 'I'll leave Pinner here. If you need me you can send him to get me. I'm going to the sickbay.'

'Aye, sir.'

'And when there's a spare moment, pilot, you'd better ask the PMO to check you over.'

On the way for'ard he stopped to chat to the tubes' crews: his last tour of the upper deck had been interrupted by the arrival of the other cruisers. He visited the two port-side mountings first, then crossed over to starboard where he also paused for a word with shipwrights working on repairs to the thirty-foot cutter. The boat's stern, rudder and transom had been damaged by flying splinters from the shellburst further aft . . . And that hit aft, the same one that had taken the lives of four torpedomen, had saved his own life. If he hadn't been hurrying aft he'd have been in the bridge . . . The whole thing was a toss-up, and you had no control over it at all. He went on for'ard, in through the door at the foc'sl break and past the seamen's galley. Bacon was frying appetizingly in enormous pans. He asked one of the cooks – a skinny man with anchors tattooed on both forearms – 'Is that for sandwiches, Gresham?'

'It is, sir. Care for a bite?'

'Not just now, thank you.'

'Cap'n be all right, sir, will he?'

'I'm on my way to find out.'

The sickbay was a large compartment with a curtain across the centre of it. In normal times the curtain divided the area that had cots in it from the outer section where medicines were issued and minor ailments treated, but now there were camp beds in this half too. There was a reek of ether and disinfectant. One SBA was working at a desk, another was winding bloodstained bandage round a stoker's torso, and Padre Forbes, who was young and fair-haired, boyish looking, was squatting beside another of the beds. He stood up when he saw Gant.

'Hello, sir.'

'Padre.' He was looking at the men in the camp beds, and they were mostly looking back at him. 'Johnson, *you* swinging the lead again?'

'Seems so, sir.' Johnson was an Asdic rating. The SBA got up from the desk and came over. He said, 'Broken ribs, sir. And there's some metal in 'is back. Mr Sibbold'll be 'aving a go at him in a minute.' He glanced round as a messenger came in: he was a writer whose action job was in one of Rowley's damage-control parties. He looked taken aback when he saw Gant; he said, 'I was to tell Mr Forbes the commander wanted a word with him.'

'Yes. All right.' Gant explained to Forbes that he'd asked Rowley to send a message, before he'd decided to come along himself. He said, 'I'll see you in a few minutes, padre.'

Burial arrangements might be better discussed elsewhere than in the presence of wounded men, he felt. The messenger said, 'I was to ask for a casualty list too.' He'd nodded towards Gant. 'For—'

The SBA said, 'I was just making it out, sir.' Then Sibbold came out, parting the blue curtain. He said, 'Come through, sir.'

All six berths, three double tiers, were occupied. Nick Everard was in a lower bunk, flat on his back and dressed in a sickberth nightgown. He looked like a corpse in a shroud, Gant thought: there was no difference between the colour of his face and of that garment. His left arm, splinted above and below the elbow, was strapped to his chest; his head was wrapped in bandages and a thick surgical dressing had been plastered to the left side of his face.

Sibbold told Gant, 'He was practically scalped. Concussion's his main problem, if he does come out of it. The arm would be all right. Whether or not he *will* emerge from coma I simply cannot say.' The doctor looked challengingly at Gant. 'I may add I've been asked at least a hundred times.'

Gant nodded.

'There are a couple of dozen stitches in his face, under that pad. It was open to the cheekbone and down as far as the corners of his mouth. Starting near the eye. About thirty stitches in the scalp. It's very fortunate the skull isn't fractured: I don't believe it is. I suppose because the glass broke. If it hadn't, his skull would have. And of course I've no way of knowing what internal damage there may be: that's the major question.'

'If he comes out of the coma, will he be – well, normal? I mean mentally?'

'I don't know.'

'Can you estimate how long it may be before there's *some* kind of change?'

'As I said' – Sibbold shut his eyes. He looked as if he was trying not to scream – 'I do not know what damage may have been done to the brain. It is impossible, at this stage—'

'All right.' Gant sighed. 'I'm sorry . . .'

'*I'm* sorry. If I could find reason to make optimistic noises, I'd be

549

making them – very happily indeed. But for the time being – frankly – the best we can do is what we're doing already, plus maybe say a prayer or two.'

Gant realized that all this time he'd been stooping, bending forward so as to look at Everard's face. He realized it because now, as he straightened, his back felt as if there was a fire in it. Sibbold was looking at him from close range, and it was an effort to keep the pain from showing in his face. He asked him, looking at the figure in the upper berth of this tier, 'Who's this?'

'Leading Seaman Williams. Quartermaster.'

'But – he was in the wheelhouse—'

'Very lucky to be alive, aren't we, Williams?'

'I'd like to write a letter, sir. Before she starts doin' her nut.'

'Well, there won't be a mail landed for some time yet, old chap. And you'd write a better letter if you waited until you were stronger. I'd just rest, if I were you.'

He told Gant, as they moved away, 'He's a concussion case too. Plus some bits of wheelhouse in his legs. He had the luck to be on the far side of the chief quartermaster, who was between him and the blast. The chief QM was a very large man, as you know. Wasn't much left of him: what there was—' He frowned, shook his head. 'Williams's concussion's nothing to worry about. But the letter he wants to write is to that wife of his who got lost in Singapore. His memory'll come back to him in a day or two – possibly even in an hour – and when it does it won't be good for him at all. Now here we have one of our prize exhibits.' The doctor's voice had risen: 'Stoker Petty Officer Arnold, sir. First degree burns: but we'll soon have him chasing the girls again. Eh, Arnold? Here's the commander to see you . . .'

A few minutes later, in the other part of the room, they gave him the list of casualties. The dead included AB Gladwill, the captain's servant; Yeoman Ruddle and Chief Yeoman Howell; Alan Swanson the torpedo officer, a bridge messenger and two signalmen and one lookout; Hobbs the schoolmaster and Newcomb who was a CW candidate and Hobbs's assistant in the plot, and Paymaster Sub-Lieutenant Bloom; four torpedomen including a torpedo gunner's mate; and the stokers who were in the boiler room. In the wheelhouse the chief QM, a stoker petty officer and an able seaman had brought the total to twenty-two.

Gant showed Padre Forbes the list. 'This is what we have to talk about.'

550

'Yes.' Forbes nodded, blinking. 'Of course.'

Gant went back through the curtain, for another quick look at his captain. He said in his mind, staring down at the bandaged, bloodless-looking face, *Come on now, come on* . . . And then, remembering Sibbold's suggestion – which might have come better from young Forbes, when one thought about it – he whispered, *Please God, may we have him back with us, well again?*

He had to admit then – and if he was in contact with a Supreme Authority his mind would anyway be open to inspection – that he was making the request for his own sake, more than for Everard's. He and the ship and all her officers and men needed Everard alive – needed his experience and leadership and luck. He had a reputation for getting into sticky situations, and for getting out of them too – so possibly, if he could remain alive and even get back on his feet . . . Gant asked humbly and self-consciously, knowing he wasn't much of a hand at the supplication routine, *If you could see your way to helping, please – to help us all?*

Reaction set in as he turned away. He wasn't a praying man: he was a churchgoer only because the Navy made it compulsory and because at home his wife expected him to set an example to the children. If God existed, He'd know this: and why should He take notice of an appeal from an agnostic, when He had real believers sending up forty thousand prayers a minute?

Gant thought that perhaps Everard had been in too many tight corners. No man's luck could last for ever . . . He nodded to Sibbold. *Defiant*'s principal medical officer was in his middle thirties, dark-jowled and brown-eyed, Mediterranean-looking. He could easily have been taken for a Greek. Gant asked the chaplain, 'Coming?'

CHAPTER 6

Something had Paul by the shoulder, pushing and pulling at it. Then Dennis Brill's voice broke through: 'What does it take to wake you up, for God's sake?' He *was* awake: remembering where he was and that this was the day the Luftwaffe was likely to pull the stops out.

'What's the time?'

'It's alive, then. I was beginning to wonder.' The doctor told him, 'Five o'clock. Just after. Half an hour to action stations, right?'

Twenty-five minutes, actually. There'd be coffee available in the saloon, it had been mentioned. Paul let himself down from the bunk – it was the top one, with Brill's under it – and began to get dressed while the doctor shaved.

'You going to be all morning with that basin?'

'So far, I've been thirty seconds.'

The hell with shaving, anyway. Who'd care – Leading Seaman Beale? Paul muttered, buttoning his battledress trousers, 'Likely to be a tough day, according to the experts.'

Brill said, glancing at him in the mirror as he scraped his Adam's apple, 'There was some news last night, after you'd left us. I'd have told you, but I didn't like to spoil the rhythm of your snores . . . Aren't you shaving?'

'Later, maybe. What's this news?'

'RAF Beaufighters from Malta made a bombing raid on some Sardinian airfield – in aid of this convoy's easier passage, one gathers – and either on the way in or on the way back they flew over Cagliari Bay and saw Italian cruisers leaving Cagliari and steaming east.'

It would have been on their way back, Paul thought. If they'd still had bomb-loads they'd have dropped them on the cruisers,

552

surely. But the news didn't seem to him to add up to much. He glanced up from pulling on his halfboots: 'That's it?'

Cleaning his teeth now, Brill nodded.

'Well, thanks for not waking me last night.'

'Steaming east, Paul, suggests they'd be on their way to rendezvous with other Italian ships. And as the Italian fleet hardly ever does leave its harbours, I'm told the natural conclusion is they're assembling a force to put between us and Malta.'

Paul smiled. 'What time does your brain start working, Doc?'

'I beg your pardon?'

'We have battleships with us, remember? And carriers?'

'But they'll turn back tonight.'

'They part company with us, sure. But McCall didn't say it all. Mackeson told me that what the big ships do then is hang around somewhere to the west, and the escort that's taking up to Malta – cruisers and destroyers – see us into Valletta but don't come in with us. They turn around and steam back to rejoin the heavy mob, who'll be waiting for them. Bit further west still, just outside flying range of the Sardinian fields, they all join up with the fleet oilers, and away they go. Because otherwise the destroyers would have to refuel in Malta, which doesn't have enough oil for itself . . . Anyway, the point is that while they wait out here somewhere the battlefleet's a threat to any Italian ships that did think about coming south.'

'A long way from us, though?'

'Near enough to put the wind up the Italians. They like to have the sea to themselves before they stick their necks out.' He'd pulled on a sweater, and now he reached for his battledress jacket. Brill wasn't even half ready yet. Paul had had a lot of practice, of course, in turning out fast to get up on watch: and in conditions a lot less comfortable than these. A destroyer's messdecks in foul weather – well, to an outsider it wouldn't seem possible that men could live like that. Brill, fresh out of medical school, wouldn't have believed it if he'd seen it. A lot of people wouldn't. Brill was standing on one leg, getting into his khaki trousers. Paul took the opportunity to slap him on the back, and he went staggering across the cabin. 'See you, Doc. I'll be where the coffee is.'

Mackeson was in the saloon, and so was Thornton and the middle-aged flying officer. Thornton, in the early morning, looked to Paul like a turkey with an egg stuck halfway out. Amused at the thought, he smiled at him, and Thornton seemed disconcerted.

You could guess he wasn't accustomed to being smiled at. Paul said 'Good morning' to Mackeson, and asked him, 'Is it true there are Italian surface ships on the move, sir?'

'Seem to be.' Mackeson was loading his pipe. 'But their destination may be the eastern basin. That'd be my guess.'

'Why would they be going east?'

'There's a dummy convoy, a diversion to take some enemy attention off this one, persuade them to hold a few squadrons of Stukas in Crete, for instance, rather than concentrate the lot on us. The dummy consists of four ships out of Port Said in ballast, with a light escort joining them from Alexandria. Might look tempting to the intrepid Latins, eh?' 'Bongo' smiled, patting his pockets in search of a match. He asked Paul, 'How did you get on with the DEMS characters?'

They were on the dismal, frozen foc's'l-head, with their Oerlikons loaded and ready, when he got up there just after 5.30. Light was seeping up from the eastern horizon, silhouetting the dark bulk of the MV *Warrenpoint* ahead of the *Montgovern*. To starboard the *Castleventry* was a grey ghost-ship hissing along on a cushion of white foam, while to port a Hunt-class destroyer was visible only by her bow-wave.

Beale said, by way of greeting, 'Nice an' peaceful.'

The four gunners were muffled in scarves, overcoats and balaclavas. Paul said, 'I always thought of the Med as a *warm* sea.'

'Gets fookin' 'orrible when it wants to.' Withinshaw took his hands out of his pockets and beat them together. 'Am I right in guessin' you're a Yank – sir?'

He'd trotted the question out so quickly that it was obvious they'd been discussing him. And it was the first time any of them had used the word 'sir' to him. Compensation, probably, for the directly personal question. But he didn't give a damn, one way or the other. He told Withinshaw, 'I'm British, but I was at school in the States for a few years. Sounds like it, does it?'

'Well, not all *that* bad.' He was being fookin' patronizing now, Paul thought. 'How come you was in Yanky-land, then?'

It was because my mother's Russian and she and my father didn't get along . . . He wasn't about to explain all that to Withinshaw, though. He said, 'Family reasons . . . Where are you lot from?'

Withinshaw had started life in Birkenhead but lived in Yarmouth. Beale had a wife and baby daughter in Nottingham. Wally was a Londoner whose parents had moved up to Preston, Lancs, and McNaught was a Glaswegian.

Bloody cold . . .

Light was increasing, reaching upwards from the horizon ahead. He wondered what might be showing on the warships' RDF screens. It was a fair bet the enemy would have reconnaissance flights out by this time, and bombers lined up on Sardinian airstrips waiting for the convoy to be pinpointed. Some of those bombers would be taking off for the last time, and some of these ships might not be afloat by sunset; but there'd be very few airmen or sailors reckoning on it being their own last day. That was strange, when you thought about it: because conversely, if you had a ticket in a lottery you *did*, surely, consider the chances of winning.

He wished he'd written to his father.

Steady pounding of the freighter's engines, swishing murmur of the sea. It was like waiting for a curtain to go up. He wondered what the odds really were, on any one of these ships in the convoy getting through. Sixteen ships: if you reckoned on four of them arriving, you might have it about right?

Funny they'd sent passengers in them, really. Except there wasn't any other way to get there. To be flown to Malta you'd need to be an admiral or a politician, and even that wouldn't be anything like safe transport.

Such an enormous effort, to sustain that one small island. The reason for it, he supposed, was that if Malta fell there'd be no base from which to attack Axis supply convoys to the desert. So they'd be able to build up their forces to any strength they needed and then keep them supplied without interruption, so they'd sweep through to take Cairo and the Canal. Then the rest of the Middle East, including the Gulf and its oil; and up into the Caucasus to link with their armies facing the Russians there. They'd have the world strangling in a Nazi noose. When you stretched the imagination that far it became understandable that the Admiralty and the War Cabinet and the Chiefs of Staff should be satisfied if just a few of these sixteen ships survived to reach Malta. You could understand it yourself, even when you happened to be sitting on top of one of them.

He doubted whether the Admiralty would sweat blood, exactly, if Sub-Lieutenant Paul Everard RNVR didn't make it to the island, either.

If he'd mustered the resolution to write that letter before he'd left

England, what would he have said in it? How did you raise a subject like this one, to your own father?

He left the DEMS group and paced for'ard, into the eyes of the ship, the narrowing stem with its furnishing of heavy anchor-and-cable gear and the waist-high steel bulwark. He stood in the curve of it, right in the very bow, and tried to frame a letter in his mind.

I wish I didn't have to tell you this, but I hope you'll see why I do have to. If I could wait until we met it might be easier to say it than to write it – well, I don't know about that either, but the fact is I'm the only person you could hear it from, and if anything happened to me before I saw you, you wouldn't ever know. Not until it was too late. So, here goes.

You'll remember telling me and Jack about the Gay Nineties Club, and that you asked Mrs Gordon to make us members of it if we went along and saw her. Well, Jack and I met in London and we did just that, and she – Phyllis Gordon – introduced us to Mrs Fiona Gascoyne . . .

Phil Gordon was a very good-looking woman and a great personality: very smart, bright, outgoing. The Gordon family, Paul had gathered from what his father had said, was well-known in the hotel business, and this probably explained the fact that here in her own club she used her maiden name, although she was actually the wife of Eric Maschwitz, the man who'd written *A Nightingale Sang in Berkeley Square*. He was in the club too on the evening Paul and Jack Everard called in, but he wasn't around for long. He had some job in or near that same square, and his wife's club was in Berkeley Street so it was very convenient for him. A tall man, genial and easy to get along with; he was in SIS or Military Intelligence, one of those outfits. He'd spent a few minutes with them, then excused himself to go through to the dining room – where the menu was chalked, in a very stylish handwriting, on a blackboard on an easel.

Phil Gordon perched herself at the bar, and patted the stools on each side of her.

'Up you get, boys.' She told the white-coated barman, 'We'll have those again, Terry.'

'Large ones, Miss Gordon?'

'Naturally.' She smiled at Paul: her eyes did most of the smiling. 'I'd have known you for a son of Nick Everard's even if you hadn't told me.' She shook her head at Jack. 'Not you, though.'

'Perhaps because I'm *not* a son of his?'

Jack was a powerful, hard-looking man now, and the way he looked at Phil suggested that the twenty years' difference in their ages wouldn't have stood in his way if he'd been in the mood. That was very much the impression he gave: that he'd take what he wanted, when he wanted it. Paul was to remember afterwards that he'd had this thought in his mind less than half an hour before Jack went right ahead and proved it . . . But the two-year interval since they'd last met had changed Jack Everard completely. Even if it had been *ten* years you wouldn't have expected such a difference. It wasn't only that he looked so much older. At Mullbergh, at Christmas of 1939, Paul had thought he was supercilious and spoilt, with a sneering, snobby manner that wasn't easy to put up with. He'd been pampered by that rather forbidding, bloodless mother of his, Nick's stepmother Sarah. And defensive, unsure of himself.

Now, the lap-dog had turned wolfish.

Phil Gordon seemed wary of him too. She'd talked mostly to Paul. He'd asked her, 'You must have known my father quite a while?'

'So much of a while I'd rather not dwell on it. How *is* the old darling?'

'Fit and strong, going by his letters. He has a destroyer flotilla, you know, out in—'

He'd stopped, before it slipped out. 'Careless Talk': there were posters on a lot of walls about it. Phyllis said, 'Wherever he is, give him my love.'

'I sure will.'

'And kisses.'

He wondered, sipping his drink, whether they'd be a brand of kisses already familiar to his father, from some time in the pre-war era. The old man could have shown worse taste, at that . . . Phil might have guessed how his thoughts were running. She'd laughed, murmured, 'Not in front of the future Lady Everard, though . . . Have you two met her?'

Neither of them had known of the existence of any such creature. Phil told them, 'Well, if you pop in here often enough I'll see you do. She's one of our regulars.'

'Well.' Paul shook his head. 'Bombshell, if there ever was one.'

Jack asked, 'Who is she?'

'Fiona Gascoyne. *Mrs* – a widow. Very pretty, young, and rather rich.' She'd added, 'Perhaps just a *little* young for him . . .' In the

557

short silence that followed, Paul thought he could see her claws retracting again. She said suddenly, 'Oh, dear. Perhaps I should have kept my trap shut. If it's a secret from the rest of the family . . .'

Jack was looking quite put out, as if the idea of Nick Everard remarrying was an affront to him. Paul suggested to Phil, 'If you introduce us to her, it might be best that none of us mentions it. Then if *she* does, you're off the hook.'

'That's a *very* smart idea.' She patted his hand where it rested on the bar. 'Thanks. And before I let any more cats out of bags, I've a few chores to see to. So I'll leave you for a while. Remember, tonight you don't pay for any drinks.'

'It's very sweet of you, but —'

'Any argument, you don't get membership. Right?'

'We surrender.'

Jack nodded. '*Force majeure.*'

'You said it.' She slid off her stool. 'Look after these two, Doris.' Doris was the second bartender. 'Terry knows – their drinks are on the house, because I'm crazy about their father.' She looked at Jack: 'Sorry. Half-brother. Enjoy yourselves, now.'

Paul remembered Jack looking after her as she threaded her way out through the crowded room. From the back, with that cloud of red hair and her slim figure in the grey silk dress, she could have been in her twenties. Jack murmured as he turned back, 'Old Nick has an eye for them, all right. I'd have said he *had* an eye for them, but apparently . . .' He frowned, without finishing the sentence. Two years ago, Paul was remembering, he'd hardly been able to look you in the eye. Now he had eyes like stones; they looked as if they wouldn't have blinked if you'd stuck your fingers in them.

He wondered why Jack disliked the idea of Nick remarrying.

Well, a fairly simple theory was that if Nick Everard was killed, he – Paul – would succeed to the baronetcy and to Mullbergh, the house and the estate. And if *he* then drowned – or whatever – that would leave Jack in line. It wasn't such a remote possibility, at that. In wartime people did get killed, and Nick Everard was invariably in the front of things. Submarining mightn't be the safest way of earning a living, either. But on the other hand, if Nick married and started a new family – well, any baby son would stand to inherit after Paul.

Something like that?

He mightn't have thought of it, except that two years ago at

Mullbergh he'd had quite a strong impression that his presence and existence didn't exactly thrill either Jack or Jack's mother, Sarah.

Jack murmured, 'Must say, I'd like to catch a glimpse of the so-called "future Lady Everard". Are you sure you didn't know it was in the wind?'

'Not a bit of it . . . But listen – you were telling me about your time in Crete?'

'I've said everything that's worth telling.'

He'd said it irritably. Bored with the subject, because he had something else on his mind now. Paul said, 'I was finding it very interesting.'

'Did I mention that my beloved half-brother, your parent, was present in his destroyer when I was sunk in *Carnarvon*?'

'Dad told me all about it, in a letter.'

Jack took a swallow of his drink. Pink gin. 'He didn't hang around for long. Did he tell you that too?'

'He described it all. It must have been pretty damned awful for him.'

'It wasn't exactly fun for the rest of us . . . Cigarette?'

'I just put one out, thank you. Care to tell me what this job is you're doing now?'

'Be difficult. I wouldn't, if I could, anyway; but to be honest I don't know *exactly* what it's in aid of – except it's something fairly extraordinary . . . I wonder who this bloody woman is?'

'Sounds like it's a special op of some kind . . .' It had to do with MLs, motor-launches; and Jack had been employed in cloak-and-dagger work in Crete, of course . . . 'Hey, we aren't talking about the Second Front, are we?'

'We aren't talking about anything at all.' Jack emptied his glass, and pushed it forward to be filled again. 'But when you hear about it over the BBC one of these days, you'll know what I was talking about.' He shrugged. 'So will I . . . Let's change the subject, shall we?'

Paul tried to, without much success. Jack had turned moody, and he was drinking faster. It was a relief when Phyllis Gordon came back. With her, was one of the most attractive women Paul had ever set eyes on.

'Now then, Everards, pay attention!' She slid an arm round the girl's shoulders. 'Fiona darling: this is Paul, Nick's son, and this is Jack, the half-brother. Jack, Paul, this is Fiona Gascoyne.'

Jack said, getting off his stool and with his eyes fixed on the girl, 'Oh, I *know* you!'

Her black dress was sleeveless, and he'd taken hold of her arms. She glanced round at Phil. 'I never saw him before in my—'

'I know *you*, though! You don't know me yet but I do know *you*!'

Fiona was the only one who didn't seem embarrassed: just amused. Then a wing commander came up on Fiona's other side, asking, 'Who are these far-from-ancient mariners, now?' Fiona looked round at him, and turned away again: Jack asked her, 'Want to hear *how* I know you?'

'Oh, everyone in London knows Fiona. Everyone who's anybody, that is.' The RAF man had an inane laugh, Paul remembered, and Phil had cut into it, telling him, 'Harry, I only borrowed her for a moment. Take her away, will you?'

'All right.' Fiona moved back a pace, and Jack's hands slid off her arms: you could see the marks where he'd been holding her. 'I give up.'

'Your portrait. In Nick's cabin in a destroyer thousands of miles away. About a year ago, it was.'

'But how sweet of him to have had—'

'The hell with *him*! *I've* lived with your face in my mind ever since! Now I know you're real, and it's incredible. I'd begun to think you were a figment of my imagination – or Nick invented you, or—'

'You're not at all like him, are you?'

'No.' He inclined his head, like someone acknowledging a compliment. 'I'm not.'

The roar of an aircraft engine blotted out the daydream. Paul and the four DEMS gunners stared upwards as a fighter swept over. No guns were firing, and there was just enough light to make out the shape of a second one as it hurtled over behind the first: they'd both been Fulmars. Memories of that evening in the Gay Nineties were like bits of an old film that he could rerun at will in his brain. And the shot of Jack as he'd uttered those three words, 'No, I'm not,' became a still, the camera holding on an expression that was a mixture of excitement and vindictiveness.

Beale said, 'Patrols goin' up.'

The two that followed were Sea Hurricanes. One pair of fighters from each of the two carriers, probably. Paul checked the time, as the noise of the last one faded: 6.22. The escorting warships would almost certainly have enemy formations on their RDF screens by now, and two of the cruisers, Mackeson had said, were equipped as fighter-direction ships, able to vector fighters on to approaching bombers.

Daylight growing. Waiting, watching. Wally and McNaught chewing gum: even in this half-light you could see the rhythmic chomping. Withinshaw yawned like a great fat cat.

The commodore's siren had blared for an emergency turn to starboard, and out on the wing of the screen destroyers were hunting and dropping depth charges: so it was obvious what the emergency turn was for. No bombers had appeared yet, but it was almost fully light and the red air-raid alert signals were flying, indicative of there being RDF contacts on the big ships' screens.

The *Montgovern*'s Willet-Bruce moaned, repeating the emergency-turn signal. Mackeson had swung round for a quick look at the destroyer activity on the bow, but his glasses were trained out on the quarter again now, at the carriers who'd turned into the wind to fly-off a batch of Sea Hurricanes. Reinforcements to those already airborne, and another sign that enemy formations couldn't be far away.

Humphrey Straight was beside his quartermaster at the steering position, conning the ship round to starboard.

Thornton came into the bridge. He'd stopped just inside the door, with a look of surprise, as if he'd expected to be welcomed. Now he'd come over to Mackeson. He cleared his throat, as the siren wheezed itself into silence, and told him, 'Signal. About a concentration – as you were, *two* concentrations – of U-boats on our track.'

He'd announced it rather pompously, as if the information derived from his own private sources.

'They're right here, never mind on our track.' Mackeson lowered his glasses and perused the signal. He murmured, 'Galitia Island, north-east and north-west of it. That's about where we'd expect them to be thickest, isn't it. But it's – what, ninety miles ahead.' He took the message over to show the master. 'I'd say it's a case of sufficient unto the moment are the U-boats thereof, captain.'

Straight told his quartermaster, 'Steady as you go.' The pipe in his mouth had gone out but he was still sucking at it. He glanced at his chief officer, Devenish, and muttered, 'I'd say it's a case of fuck the lot of 'em.' Thornton's eyebrows were raised as he left the bridge. Out on the convoy's port beam some destroyers had opened fire: before the turn, of course, that had been the bow. Now a more solid build-up of AA fire as battleships and cruisers and the Hunts on the quarter let rip too. Young Gosling, out in the exposed port wing of the bridge, was pointing astern and he had his whistle in his mouth. He was blowing it, presumably, but he might as well have been sucking it for all the use it was. Shellbursts were gathering in the sky, which was silver-bright now from the rising sun ahead, and black-brown-grey puffballs of the exploding time-fused shells had edgings of gold and silver. To the bomber pilots they'd be plain black, and more deadly than decorative. The bombers were Junkers 88s again, a pack of a dozen or fifteen planes with a similar-sized group astern of them. They were high, and they gave the impression of climbing against the background brightness as they came in, most of the shellbursts below them at first but getting closer: in fact they weren't climbing, they were flying straight and level, giving warships' HA control systems the kind of shoot they'd been designed for and didn't often get. Bursts were appearing under the Junkers' noses and all around them: and either they were dodging now or it was the percussions of the shells jarring them this way and that. Still coming, though – black wings, black crosses on white backgrounds, slicing through the drifting smoke of the shellbursts as they held on towards the centre of the convoy.

A signalman – the naval V/S rating who was one of Mackeson's team – was pointing out to starboard: 'Sir, that—' It was drowned in sharper, closer noise as the *Montgovern*'s Bofors guns opened fire. The signalman had been pointing out at the RAF man in the starboard wing. He in turn had been trying to draw Mackeson's attention to something in the sea on the starboard bow, but now he'd given up, he was leaning over to watch the 'something' as it passed.

Devenish muttered, 'Torpedo track.' There wasn't much else it could have been. But it was as well they'd turned: the escort commander must have told the commodore that torpedoes had been fired. From the *Blackadder* now another siren-signal was wailing, ordering a return to the mean course, and at the same time every gun in the convoy and in the warships surrounding it was blazing vertically or near-vertically at bombers overhead. Humphrey Straight leaned close to his quartermaster's ear and growled, 'Port fifteen degrees.' Bombs were raising dirty-looking heaps of sea between ships in the rear half of the convoy as they began the turn. Then, from the quarter, an explosion was deep, solid-sounding . . . Mackeson, still out in the wing – he'd gone to see what had been exciting the Air Force man out there – saw several bomb-splashes between the rearmost merchantmen and the battleships: it looked as if the battleships had been the targets for those bombs. But that deep *boom* hadn't been the bomb-burst: he was almost certain someone had been torpedoed. He had his glasses trained on the quarter as the whole convoy turned back towards its mean course: and one ship back there was turning the wrong way. It was the freighter on the far side – the starboard side – of the tanker *Caracas Moon*. The last ship in column four. She was swinging out to starboard, away from the rest of the convoy and across the bows of a Hunt-class destroyer which was taking sharp avoiding action. That ship was also listing. Gunfire, which had slackened, was building to a new crescendo as the second half of the bomber force came over. Mackeson, turning to go back inside the bridge, happened to glance down at the foc's'l and saw young Everard grab one gunner's arm and point. Then both Oerlikons were spitting fire. These Junkers, unlike the front-runners, had gone into shallow dives, flying faster because of that and dipping through the barrage of AA fire and across the forepart of the convoy. *This* part. But they weren't in Oerlikon range yet, he thought. Everard lacked experience, but that DEMS killick should have known better and held his fire. He went inside, shutting the bridge door quickly to keep some of the noise out. Humphrey Straight was telling the quartermaster, 'Ease to five degrees of port wheel.' He glanced around, stared bull-like at Mackeson, who told him, 'End ship in column four. Torpedo. She's dropped out.'

Straight scowled, looking at the convoy diagram on the bulkhead.

'*Agulhas Queen*. Old Vic Kerrick.'

He stared aft in the hope of a sight of her: then he'd turned back. 'Midships the wheel.' He muttered, 'Bastards.' A stick of bombs came slanting, and sea rose in a mound of white and grey not far off the port bow. The other three of the stick hit and smothered the *Warrenpoint*: sea leaped from near-misses right against her hull, and one bomb landed in her after well deck. There was a spurt of smoke and debris, then a second afterwards an explosion near the waterline on her port side. Smoke gushed out of her, enveloping her afterpart.

Humphrey Straight was leaning forward with his blunt nose

almost touching the glass front window of the bridge. He ordered, 'Port fifteen degrees. Two short blasts.'

Devenish moved that way, but the bosun was ahead of him with a hand on the lever that operated the siren. He jerked it down twice, sending two short, strong wafts of steam through the whistle, two blasts meaning, 'I am directing my course to port.' The ships astern would follow his lead.

It was close enough. The *Montgovern*'s stem was hidden in the smoke pouring out of the ship ahead. Swinging through it, swinging faster now: and they would almost certainly have carried away the *Warrenpoint*'s Cherub speed log, coming that close under her stern. Straight had ordered the wheel to be centred, then put the other way, so as not to swing his own ship's stern in a swiping blow at the *Warrenpoint* as they pounded by her. The *Warrenpoint*'s guns were still in action: all of them, even a Bofors on her stern with Army gunners manning it. You could see the rapid winking stabs of flame as it flung up its forty-millimetre shells. In her after-well deck men were struggling with hoses. The smoke seemed to be coming up from her number five hatch. Mackeson, out on the bridge wing as the *Montgovern* passed her, saw a big gash with jagged, out-turned edges just above the waterline. So that bomb must have exploded on its way out, after it had passed almost right through the ship. They'd got by her now: she was dropping astern between columns one and two. While about a mile astern of the convoy – he used his binoculars, looking back between the columns and out past the battleship on the quarter – a long way back now a Hunt-class destroyer was nosing around the bow of the *Agulhas Queen*. She was leaning right over and he could see boats in the water, and a Sea Hurricane dipping protectively overhead. So the *Agulhas Queen* was being abandoned; and from the condition of the *Warrenpoint* as she'd been when they'd passed her he wouldn't have betted on her survival either.

As he went back inside, Humphrey Straight had just ordered five degrees of starboard wheel, to edge her over into station at the correct distance from column two; he'd also glanced at the bosun and shaken his head, a negative to the man's readiness to give one short blast from the siren. He'd take her in gradually, not swerve in. He told Devenish, with a nod towards the engine-room telegraph, 'Up a touch, mister.' Devenish gave the telegraph handle a jerk, one clang of the bell in the 'ahead' direction, a private signal for a couple more revs per minute. They had a voicepipe to the engine-room, fitted specially for the requirements of convoy manoeuvring, but they weren't accustomed to it and Mackeson had noticed that they hardly ever used it. The *Montgovern* had to move up now to take the *Warrenpoint*'s station as a column leader on the commodore's port beam.

Gunfire had died away, except on the bow where a mutter of it was still following the attackers round: they'd be circling that way to get back on to their north-eastward course for home.

They'd be back later, Paul supposed. Or others like them.

Ahead of the convoy a parachute drifted slowly seaward. Beale said, 'One of our lot. On 'is own, must be.' He was probably right: the 88s had a crew of four, so from any of them there'd have been more than one parachute. Wally Short said, stepping back with an empty or part-empty Oerlikon magazine and swinging round to dump it in the bin, 'I seen four Gerries down.'

Paul had seen three bombers hit and in trouble, but only two actually go down in the sea. The others might have crashed, but they hadn't done so in his sight. Not much of a swap anyway, for two ships . . . Another depressing fact was that although they'd fired off a lot of ammunition, these Oerlikons hadn't had any targets low or near enough to have had much chance of hitting. When they'd been choking in the *Warrenpoint*'s smoke he'd thought *There but for the grace of God . . .* and then, *But there's still lots of time.* For the grace of God to be less in evidence, he'd meant. And it had become real now, it was happening just as one had been told it would. When you were lectured on things like previous convoys' losses and what was therefore certain to be in store for this one you heard it and believed it, but somehow without seeing it as applying to you directly. Until you saw it happening it was theory, talk, speculation. But it was real now. Or it *had* been, for a few minutes . . .

There wasn't anything to do now except wait, and it was a different kind of waiting. You were waiting for something you knew about, something you'd seen the shape of.

The *Montgovern* had become the leader of the port-side column, with the *Blackadder* to starboard flying the pennant of the commodore and three cruisers ahead across the convoy's front. One, a ship of the *Mauritius* class, was about four thousand yards on the port bow of the *Montgovern*, and the smaller ship in the centre of the trio – about the same distance on the freighter's other bow –

was one of the old C class who'd been converted as anti-aircraft ships. She would be just about identical to *Carnarvon*, in which Jack Everard had been navigator when she'd been sunk off Crete. And off the far (right-hand) corner of the convoy, out on the starboard beam of the C-class cruiser, was a contrastingly modern ship of the *Newcastle* class, nearly ten thousand tons of her.

Those three cruisers would be coming on with the convoy tonight when the battleships and carriers and their attendant cruisers turned back.

Paul walked for'ard, up into the narrowing stem again. With his back to the bridge and with the foremast and a cargo-derrick nicely in the way, he lit a cigarette. Mackeson might not approve of naval personnel smoking, he thought, at action stations, and he didn't want to upset old Bongo . . . He wondered what might be happening astern, with the *Warrenpoint* and that other casualty. He hadn't seen that torpedo hit. He'd heard it, and Beale had muttered, 'Some poor sod's 'ad it', and McCall had told them about it when he'd come visiting. But with the convoy plugging on eastward and the gaps where those ships had been already filled, he realized with a touch of shame that casualties tended to drop out of mind about as soon as they dropped out of station. Perhaps because these fourteen now – he was trying to rationalize it to himself – holding on for Malta and waiting for the next stage of the whittling-down process to start, were the ones that mattered . . . But would one feel like that about it if – or when – it was the *Montgovern* falling back, sinking or burning? Might this feeling that what mattered was carrying on, pushing *some* part of the convoy through, be only a manifestation of the famous sailorlike response of *Fuck you, Jack, I'm inboard*?

Translated, it meant 'I'm safe in the boat, so the hell with *you* . . .'

The odds were, he knew, that he'd get a chance to find out. So for the time being, damn the introspection too. He dropped the half-smoked cigarette, and trod on it, then made his way back to the others. Only three of them. Beale explained, 'Ginger's gone for char.'

Phyllis Gordon had broken up Jack's play for Fiona Gascoyne (or Jack's and Fiona's play for each other: she could easily have brushed him off, made a joke of it and then ignored him) by virtually pushing her into the arms of the moustached airman, the bemedalled character called Harry who'd seemed, Paul thought, pretty ineffectual . . . Harry had found Fiona's arm linked into his, because Phyllis had put it there, and they'd gone off to the dining room because she'd directed them to it. If they were hoping to get a meal tonight, she'd urged them, they'd better take up their reservation *now*.

But she hadn't realized, as Paul had, that Jack had been doing anything more than mildly flirting. Paul had sensed it: and met Jack's glance and then *known* it . . . Phyllis told Jack, after Fiona and the airman had moved off, 'Don't overdo the charm, my boy. Nick mightn't go much on it.'

'Oh, come *on*!'

As if he couldn't believe that anyone could even *imagine* he'd make a pass at his half-brother's future wife . . . And Phil accepted it on that level: as a joke they'd shared, nothing to be taken seriously. She'd patted Jack's hand, and told him, 'Nick's very much in love with her, you know.'

'Who wouldn't be?'

He'd glanced sideways at Paul. Wanting him to know, for some reason. A personal triumph over Nick Everard? Or – more simply – just because the girl attracted him?

Jack had picked up his glass and emptied it. He said, 'We'd better go and eat too, Paul.'

In order to follow the Gascoyne girl into the dining room, Paul guessed. Phil Gordon stopped that one anyway: they hadn't booked – couldn't have, in fact, as they weren't members – and the place was full. She advised them, 'When you're members, do make sure of booking. Lunches are easier, but—'

'It doesn't matter.' Paul told her, 'I hadn't thought of eating here.'

'Might as well have one for the road, then,' Jack added. 'My round. We can't possibly go on cadging—'

'Non-members can't buy drinks, they *have* to cadge.' She beckoned the barman. 'Terry?' He was coming over. Jack said, 'How *very* kind you are. But – if you'd excuse me, a moment – where's the heads or gents', around here?'

She told him. Then she was alone with Paul. She said, 'Bit of a card, your . . . half-uncle?'

'I barely know him. Since childhood – we haven't met in years. Two days two years ago was the last time, and before that I honestly don't remember when it was.'

'Mrs Gascoyne wasn't encouraging him, you know.' Terry was waiting for the order: she twiddled her finger at the three glasses. 'I wouldn't blame her, Paul.'

'Blame her for what?'

'I had the impression you didn't like her much.'

'I don't know her. But if my father wants to marry her, she must be a very nice person.' He added, 'As well as very pretty.'

'It's quite natural that she and Nick's own brother should be interested in meeting each other, anyway . . . Here's your drink, son of Nick.'

'You're very kind.' He glanced at Terry. 'Thanks.'

'Here's to all the Everards – past, present and future.'

'Hah.' Rejoining them, Jack picked up his glass. 'I'll drink to that. This is a *very* nice club, Mrs Gordon.'

'I'm glad you like it.' She asked Paul, 'Do you really have to go now?'

'Go?' Jack seemed surprised. 'Did we say we were going?'

'To eat. This was the one for the road, remember?'

'So it was.' Jack laughed, for some reason. 'I'd quite forgotten. But – how about a meal at the Wellington?'

'I don't know it.'

'It's not a bad dump. I'm a member.'

Phyllis Gordon said that if they wanted membership of the Gay Nineties, now they'd seen it, she'd make the arrangements. They both said yes, they'd very much like to join, and she suggested they might look in tomorrow or the day after. Jack told her, 'I'm going to almost live here, from now on.'

'Don't you have a war to fight?'

'Oh, there are plenty of people to keep that damn thing going.'

They were laughing as she walked away. Paul was beginning to wonder if he could have been wrong, if he'd over-reacted, earlier. He'd never liked Jack much, and perhaps his snap judgement had been influenced by this.

Jack settled himself on a stool, and lit a cigarette.

'The Wellington's towards Knightsbridge.' He sipped his drink. 'So we'll go along and have a snack. Sign you in as a member if you like it. It's open on Sunday nights, meals and dancing, which is useful sometimes.'

'Okay. Thanks.'

'But afterwards – well, I don't know what you plan to do with the rest of the evening, Paul, but personally I'm going nightclubbing. I'm joining Wing-Commander Thingummy and Mrs Gascoyne at the Embassy.'

Paul sat leaning on the bar, looking at him sideways.

'You are *what*?'

'Did you really imagine I was in the heads?' Jack fingered a card out of the top pocket of his reefer jacket. 'He invited me, believe it or not. They're in a big party, so an odd number won't really matter. *She* pointed that out. Tell you one thing, half-nephew – *I* won't be the odd man out.' He was studying the card. 'This is where she lives. Eaton Square, hum hum. Tell you another thing – *I* reckon she's a push-over.'

Paul put his glass down. He asked him, 'You don't really imagine I'd eat with you, do you?'

Jack shrugged. 'Please yourself.' He held up the visiting card. 'Better than a hole in the ground in Crete, eh?'

'Want a wet? Sorry, sir, want—'

Withinshaw was offering him a tin mug of steaming, dark brown liquid. He had a cigarette sticking to his lip. Beale was smoking too.

'Thanks.'

Paul had been sitting on the ammunition bin. He stood up now, stretching, and glancing around at sea and sky. There'd been some aircraft around during the past twenty or thirty minutes, but each time they'd turned out to be Fleet Air Arm machines either leaving for or returning from patrol. Fulmars, Martlets and Sea Hurricanes.

The tea tasted as if someone had washed his socks in it, but he could feel its warmth trickling down inside. He asked Withinshaw, 'Are you a family man?'

Beale burst into guffaws of laughter: he was staring out towards the horizon in the north, out past a nearby Hunt. The two younger DEMS men were laughing too. Withinshaw ignored it all: but he was looking at Paul in a cautious manner, as if he wasn't going to be caught out by any trick questions. He nodded. 'Aye.'

Beale said without turning round, 'Ask 'im '*ow many* families.'

'Huh?'

Withinshaw advised him, 'Don't want to take no fookin' notice o' silly fookin' sods like Ronald bleedin' Beale.'

'Great Yarmouth is where he keeps one lot.' Beale glanced round now, to wink at McNaught and Short. 'But what do they know in Yarmouth about the little loved ones in Durban, Union of South Africa? Eh, Art?'

'You can shut your fookin'—'

'Hey, up!'

Beale had turned back, and he was pointing out on the port quarter. Aircraft: fighters like silver toys closing on two larger planes. A trail of smoke was like a thin tail from one of them. It was diving, the smoke blackening and painting a curve on the sky as it went down into the sea and the fighters lifted like swallows, banking away after the other enemy, who'd turned away. Paul couldn't see that one now. But faintly, there was a second stammering of cannon-fire.

'One down, anyway. Fleet Air Arm are keeping it all away from us. No wonder we're getting a quiet forenoon.'

Beale said, 'Them'll just be recce flights, most likely, keepin' tabs on us. When they really come, they'll not be stopped that easy.'

'You said you'd been in a convoy like this one before. Malta and back – in this ship?'

'Not in this bastard, no.' Beale cocked an ear; and Paul heard it too, depth charging, on the other bow.

'Did you get hit by anything on that convoy?'

'Not a scratch.'

'Fookin' lucky we was an' all.' Withinshaw stood up. ''Ere we go again. . . .'

Another emergency turn – to port, this time. Turning away from that submarine while the destroyers' depthcharges kept it deep.

Withinshaw murmured reflectively, 'We was fookin' lucky, though, that trip. Eh, Ron?'

'You oughter get a sign painted, Art.'

'What you on about now, then?'

'A notice you could 'old up when Gerry's comin' over. Big letters sayin': "Mercy – two families to support." '

Gunfire, out in the destroyer screen, three miles ahead . . .

Paul went towards the bow, to get a clearer view. Behind him, the DEMS men went on teasing Withinshaw, Wally asking him how many papooses he'd got so far out of each squaw in his separate wigwams. Paul could see the smoke-haze of the destroyers' barrage fire ahead, but not what they were shooting at. Then two Fulmars belted over from astern, flying in that direction: and the commodore's siren bellowed like a moose at rutting-time, ordering a turn back to starboard. McCall came up the ladder from the well deck, and Paul went back to meet him.

'What's all that about?'

'Torpedo-bombers, apparently. Italians.' Beale and Withinshaw became more alert, less chatty, standing to their guns and looking out over the port bow as the ship swung to starboard. McCall added, 'Fighters from the carriers back there have shot down two Eyetie recce aircraft in the last half-hour. Savoia Marchettis.'

'Fine.'

'Sods are just keeping an eye on us, for the moment. Getting set for something big.'

'D'you think so?'

'Well.' Staring out towards where that action was, shielding his eyes against the sun, McCall said, 'That bit's over, by the looks of it.' He answered Paul, 'Very close to Sardinia, aren't we? They aren't going to just sit on their fat arses and watch us sail by, are they?'

'I guess not.'

'Right . . . Meanwhile the *Agulhas Queen*'s sunk, and the last we heard of the *Warrenpoint* was a signal telling the destroyer that was standing by her to take her blokes off and then sink her.'

Paul looked at him, and nodded. 'Come to cheer us up, have you?'

'Why should you need cheering up, for Christ's sake?' He offered Paul a cigarette, and they both lit up. Everyone did smoke at action stations, apparently. McCall was a medium-sized man with a hooked nose, deep-set blue eyes and wiry dark hair: about as Celtic-looking as you could get, Paul supposed. The second mate added, 'We've got off very easy, so far. Aren't I right, Beale?'

The killick nodded, watching the sky across the convoy's van. McCall pinched his cigarette out, and flicked it over the side. It was only half smoked, but with duty-free at twenty for sixpence you didn't have to bother much. He nodded: 'See you later.'

Forenoon wearing on . . .

There'd been several more emergency turns, and more depth charging out in the deep field, and once the Mauritius-class cruiser on the port bow of the convoy had gone hard a-port to avoid torpedoes which had narrowly missed a Hunt outside her. The Hunt had turned too and dashed out along the torpedo-tracks, picked up a submarine contact and attacked with depthcharges, but by the time another destroyer had joined her the contact had been lost.

McCall had told Paul he wasn't bound to spend the entire day on the foc's'l-head, and he'd been aft to his cabin for a shave, then down to the saloon for coffee. He'd found Brill in the saloon, reading a P.G. Wodehouse novel. There was an oilcloth cover on the mess table, and Brill had a lot of medical gear laid out on it. He'd complained, 'Trade's slow. Thought you might've been a customer.'

From the boat deck you could see that the merchantmen had been rearranged following the loss of those two ships. There were only three freighters now in columns one and four, and four in each of the two centre columns. The *Caracas Moon*, the tanker, had shifted up to become second ship in column three, so she was now on the starboard beam of the *Castleventry* and protected by having other ships all around her.

Back on the foc's'l, Paul found the DEMS team lying around smoking, dozing, chewing gum. There was no alert, no red flag flying: and in the three cruisers ahead would be RDF sets that would pick up any enemy aircraft pretty well the minute it left the ground, with Sardinia no more than seventy-five miles away.

Getting towards noon, too. Noon, according to McCall, being danger-hour, or thereabouts. Paul shut the lid of the ammunition bin and sat down on it, facing out over the port bow, north-eastward. Out to starboard, abaft the beam when the convoy was on this leg of its zigzag, two destroyers were following up an A/S contact, but it was too far away to see what was happening.

Warmer now. He took his cap off, and opened his greatcoat. Remembering how, two evenings after that first one in the Gay Nineties, he'd gone there alone, primarily to check up on the membership situation. He'd called in first at Hatchet's on the north side of Piccadilly, to visit the bar – one flight of curving stairs down towards the restaurant – and check in the submariners' book they kept there. If you were on leave in London and at a loose end you put your name in it, and where you were staying or where you'd be that evening. But none of Paul's friends was in the capital, apparently, or had bothered to record the fact. He had a beer, than went up the stairs into Piccadilly again and headed west towards Berkeley Street. The tarts were already competing for pavement space, and there were some very smart-looking girls among them. A lot of them worked in munition factories, he'd heard, in daylight hours, and now the massed bombing raids seemed to be over they flocked into the West End every evening. It was about half-seven when he got to the Gay Nineties. He called in to the office first, saw Phil Gordon and collected his membership card, then went to the bar, and he'd just got a drink when Jack arrived and joined him.

Paul wanted to ignore, forget what had happened the other evening. Jack had only been putting on a show, either to impress him or to pull his leg. If one could shut it out of mind, it might blow over, have never happened. And she – Mrs Gascoyne – with or without the help of her RAF friend might have put Jack in his place. *That* would be the best outcome of all.

Paul told him that his card was in the office, to be collected.

'Good.' Jack checked the time. 'I won't bother with it now, though. Fiona'll be along at any minute. In fact I was late, and she's later.'

There was a silence, while Paul thought about it. He cleared his throat. 'Is – er – does she really intend to marry my father?'

'I gather he's set on it. Don't blame him, either.' Jack smiled. 'In some ways, I mean.'

'And what's your relationship with her?'

'Oh, grow up, Paul!' He shook his head. 'What d'you imagine she's been doing with the bloody Air Force?'

'She's going to marry him, but she's prepared to play around meanwhile?'

Jack shrugged. 'Takes all sorts, doesn't it?'

'Where do you fit in? I mean, if my father's—'

'Now, or after?'

'After what? Their marriage? You don't surely imagine he'd still—'

'I don't care all that much.'

'Have you considered what happens when he hears about it?'

'You mean when you tell him?'

'If no one else does first, you can count on it.'

'Well, *she* wouldn't like that. Personally, I don't give a damn.'

'You want him to hear about it, is that it?'

'It doesn't matter to me, Paul. I don't bloody *care*. Can't you understand that?' He was staring at him, across his glass. 'It's pretty damn simple, if you'd—'

'Yeah.' Paul nodded. This wouldn't be a good place to start a brawl, and in any case he thought Jack could probably take him on one-handed, and enjoy it too. He muttered, 'It's just I never imagined an Everard could be such a total shit. I wouldn't have thought *anyone* could—'

'Takes people different ways. Some men leave other men to drown, some help themselves to other men's women. Which brand's the shittiest might be a matter of opinion . . . Oh, here she is!'

Fiona Gascoyne, wreathed in fur. Jack slid off his stool, and took her hands. 'Wow. Such glamour . . .'

'Only because the old bags won't let us wear our uniforms in dives like this one. Otherwise I'd wear it all the time. Day *and* night.' Paul remembered the way she'd smiled up at Jack: then she'd glanced at him. A different kind of smile: 'Hello, Paul.' He was remembering it now through other movement, action building round him, the immediate surroundings in visual if not mental focus. He remembered Jack saying blandly, 'She does look terrific in the MTC uniform. For some reason it's *verboten* when they're off-duty. Not that I'm complaining. . . .' He was showing Fiona the face of his watch, then: 'Look, we've got to skid along, I'm afraid. I mean right away.'

'Oh, damn it all!'

In hindsight and memory you could sort the exchanges into a rational sequence. At the time, it had been a blur, confused by the way he felt. Fiona complaining to Jack that she'd have liked to spend longer here, talk to Paul and get to know him, and Jack answering that if she arrived half an hour late it wasn't *his* fault . . . Paul told him, 'My leave's up tomorrow. I'll be on an early train north.'

'Too bad.' Jack nodded. 'Good luck, anyway.'

'It might be a good thing if we could talk together about that drowning angle.'

It was totally irrational, he thought: no more than an excuse. . . .

'We do truly have to run, unfortunately.' Jack's hand was in the crook of Fiona's elbow, turning her away. A lot of men looking at her: she really was quite sensational . . .

'Fookin' soddin' bastards!'

No need to look round to know who'd yelled that. Paul was on his feet between the two guns, Beale and Withinshaw closed-up at them and the loading numbers standing by. There was a red alert and the commodore's siren was calling for an emergency turn to port, there was a pack of bombers right ahead with a fighter escort

574

weaving against the sky above them, and a big force of Junkers 88s approaching on the beam. They had fighters over them too. They'd need them, with Sea Hurricanes, Martlets and Fulmars streaming up from the two carriers astern. He'd been watching the pattern of a multiple attack develop – destroyers abaft the beam to port had just opened fire, a low-level barrage which could only mean there'd be torpedo-bombers moving in on that quarter – he'd been seeing it and reacting to it while the close-up of Fiona Gascoyne, dazzlingly attractive, faded from his mind.

CHAPTER 7

The noise bewildered him. Searching for voices in it he found one inside his head, Fiona's voice telling him, 'Of *course* I'll marry you, you great oaf!' She was naked: she was striking poses, wearing his new cap, strutting around in it, playing the fool and looking absolutely sensational, shouting things like 'Hard a-port! Are *you* hard a-port again yet?' He'd been urging her to come back to bed. The cap had arrived yesterday by parcel post from Messrs Gieves of Bond Street, who'd sent it to him at this pub where they were spending a few days of his leave. It was muddling, because it seemed to be happening in the wrong war: the cap had gold oak-leaves on its peak, which made it a commander's although he was still a junior lieutenant. He'd only come back – *been brought* back – from the raid on Zeebrugge in which he'd commanded his old 'oily-wad' destroyer *Bravo*: he'd been wounded, on *Bravo*'s bridge, in the course of towing another destroyer, *Grebe*, out of trouble, and this was why he was in bed now in Sister Agnes's private hospital in Grosvenor Gardens.

The clattering and hammering made no sense either. Unless they were tearing the lead off the roof. Which wasn't likely, he thought . . . Actually, she was a Mrs Keyser. Her patients called her 'Sister Agnes', and she was a personal friend of the King. His Majesty had given her a key to some private entrance to the palace gardens, someone had told him. It might have been Sarah, his stepmother, who'd mentioned it.

Getting muddled again now. Because if he was in Mrs Keyser's establishment, how could Fiona have been here with him?

Christ, the din . . . Connected with it was an ache in his head like a slowly turning knife.

The pub was in Sussex. But that had been a leave in the *second* war. And if Sarah wanted to persuade Mrs Keyser to discharge him, it could only mean that—

Well, he'd *dreamt* the bit about the pub. That was it.

But – damn it, if this was 1918 . . .

He was panting, his own heartbeats shook him like blows inside his chest. It was the sheer effort of thinking this out, trying to get events in their right order, trying to reason with it all, make sense . . . He warned himself, *One thing at a time, now* . . .

Sarah wanted to have him in her care at Mullbergh while he recuperated. He wanted this too. Except he also knew it should be avoided, because he had some fore-knowledge of what would happen at Mullbergh, if he was alone there for long with Sarah. He didn't want it to happen. His feelings for her were protective as well as adoring: and she was his father's wife. Besides, Fiona – who'd looked tremendous in his cap, who was one of those girls who'd been designed not to wear clothes – wouldn't approve of it either. He'd told her, 'You have the most beautiful breasts I ever saw.'

'Kiss them, then.'

Cap flat-aback, soft hair flowing around her bare shoulders, which were also beautiful. She had large eyes set slightly aslant above prominent cheekbones. He'd asked her, 'What if Sarah comes?'

So she *had* been here!

He wished to God they'd stop that hammering . . .

You got to it eventually, though, if you took it step by step and didn't rush it. Everything fell into place quite naturally and simply then. The afternoon was the time for visits, and Sarah had come specially to London to get him out of Sister Agnes's place and take him to Mullbergh. He rather liked the idea of Mullbergh, because his father wouldn't be there. Sir John Everard was in the Army, in France. Fiona asked him, 'Who's Kate?'

'She's in Australia. But if I'm going to marry *you*—'

'Will Sarah object?'

He didn't see what Sarah had to do with it. It was his having married Ilyana, Paul's mother, that had turned Sarah into a block of granite . . . He *thought* that was what had done it; that more than anything else. But Kate was Crete, where the Stukas had come in screaming packs in a day-long, day-after-day-long bedlam. *Orion* had been hit again: smoke was gushing out of her and the whole armoured top of one for'ard turret had been blown off, the gun-barrels twisted and blackened, and every man in that gunhouse would be dead. He hadn't known it at the time but her captain had been dying on his bridge at that same moment. Her

577

steering had gone and she'd swung right around, reversing course and heading back towards Crete with a new Stuka swarm coming up from Scarpanto. She was the flagship and they'd crippled her, and now they'd concentrate on her and do their damnedest to finish her. You had to stay close to her, keep the bastards high, give her a chance to draw breath and fight her fires, shift to emergency steering and get back on course. All the destroyers were turning with her, closing in around her. She'd been packed with the troops they'd lifted out of Crete and he'd guessed then what it would be like inside her, in those crowded mess-decks to which Stukas' bombs had penetrated, and he'd guessed right because they couldn't make much of a job of cleaning her, in Alex. They sent her for refit, reconstruction in the States, and when she stopped at Cape Town she smelt so badly they wouldn't let her dock. She had to anchor, outside.

He told Sarah about it, when she came to take him up to Yorkshire. Sarah had brown hair and hazel eyes and an intriguing mouth: vulnerable, adorable. He told her, 'Jack's cruiser was sunk by dive-bombers, off Crete. I couldn't stay to pick up survivors because – well, you *couldn't* stop, if you did the Stukas had you nailed. If I'd have stopped I'd have only killed *more* men—'

'Did you kill Jack, then?'

'He's alive. He got ashore, and—'

'No thanks to you. And David drowned, didn't he? At Jutland? He died like a hero, trying to save other—'

'He died in a blue funk. Off his head.'

'You're lying, Nick! You killed your own father with that lie!'

'It's the truth. I heard it all from a man named—'

'*You killed your own father, Nick!*'

It was Sarah but a different Sarah. Transformed totally. Bitter, tight-faced, shrewish. Cold, harsh eyes hating him . . . 'You'd have let Jack drown, too – your father first, then your—'

'*No!*'

It wasn't true. Ordering his destroyers away had been an agonizing, terrible decision. The sea full of swimmers and the German aircraft dipping to machine-gun them in the water, murder them as they tried to swim away: you'd see a man stop swimming and lie still in the water while it turned pink around him. Jack's face, blood-stained, staring up at him from the water. Jack screamed, '*I'm your son!*'

*   *   *

'Steady. Steady, now. You'll be all right, now. Easy does it . . .'

A different voice asked quietly, 'Could we get him aft to his own cabin?'

'I suppose we could move him without doing any damage. Trouble is, looking after him. He can't be left alone, and with this lot here I can't spare an SBA.'

'His own steward full-time, plus visits from you?'

Beyond the curtain, a sailor muttered something in a voice like a groan, and an SBA told him, ' 'Ang on, Lofty. With you in a mo'.'

'Well, I suppose that's possible . . .'

The voices had dropped lower, and with the clanging and general racket from up top he couldn't hear what they were saying. It hadn't made much sense anyway, but he'd been glad to hear the voices. Such a ghastly bloody din up there: it was like being in a destroyer in dry dock, with workmen banging around here, there and everywhere . . . There was no engine vibration, he realized, her screws weren't turning. In intervals between bouts of hammering from above he could hear the whirr of a fan, but there was no draught from it that he could feel.

All he could feel was the pain in his head and a sort of confused sadness involving Sarah and Jack, the whole mess that was the past but still contaminated the present and in some way seemed to threaten the future too.

'Will I be allowed to travel up to Mullbergh?'

Silence . . . Except for the row elsewhere. Then: 'Mullbergh?'

'Sarah's running it as a sort of recuperative centre.'

Sibbold looked at Gant. 'Sounds very suitable.' He didn't smile. He paused before he added, addressing his patient, 'To start with we'll move you to your own quarters, sir.'

Whatever *that* meant.

Tired. But he didn't want to sleep if it meant slipping back into the nightmare of Sarah's accusations. It wasn't the same Sarah whom he'd loved, whose screams had woken him in the night, brought him out of bed and hurrying down that long, icy corridor. He'd been a boy then, a child: remembering it, he was a child again, dropping off to sleep. There'd been rows before, time and again he'd lain awake trying not to hear his father's drunken raving and Sarah's quiet, defensive reasoning, pleading. Misery would hold him doubled in the bed, cold from the old house and colder still inside, helpless despite his urge to protect, to love Sarah as much as his father seemed – inexplicably – to hate her. Head under the

579

bedclothes, praying for it all to end . . . But that night she'd screamed, he'd heard a crash and another scream and he'd thought, *He's murdering her*: then he'd been running, bare-footed and shaking with cold and fright . . . Sarah's dress had been ripped open, downwards from the neck. She was trying to hold it together with one hand and the other was out defensively towards Nick's father, who was in evening clothes and raving, mad-bull drunk. The top half of Sarah's bedroom door had been smashed in – he'd done it with a heavy shoecase, which was lying among the broken wood. For years and years, her voice had echoed in his skull: 'It's all right, Nick. Truly. Go back to bed.'

'Why are we stopped?'

He wondered why they didn't answer him. And then, why he was down here anyway. What the noise was, what was going on . . . He was below decks: he could feel that – sense it, smell it. Besides, all the hammering and rasping was overhead. And – that smell was ether, a hospital smell . . . Well, of course, he'd been dreaming, he'd *dreamt* he was at sea . . . He asked, 'Has my stepmother been in today?'

He wondered whether Kate might come: whether anyone had told her he was here. But he didn't like to ask about Kate, because the people here wouldn't know who he was talking about.

He wondered whether he'd told Fiona about Kate. He didn't think he had.

'All right, sir, are we?'

'Who's that?'

'SBA Green, sir. PMO'll be back in two shakes.'

'Why are we stopped?'

'Stopped, sir? Oh. Well – we're at anchor, sir.'

'Where?'

'Surabaya, sir.'

Surabaya. Java, in the Dutch East Indies . . .

Combined Striking Force. They'd sent him to join China Force and he'd got rumbled with this fellow Doorman . . . And – it came to him suddenly – there was to be a conference, a captains' meeting in the Dutch flagship *de Ruyter*, and he had to get to it. God almighty, he'd be late!

'Help me up, would you? Are my clothes here? Come on, give me a—'

'Steady on now, sir. PMO'll be back any minute, he'll explain—'

'I can't *see*!'

'Because of the bandage, sir, that's all it is. Here – easy does it, just lie back again, sir, lie still a while and – that's the way . . .'

Hands on his shoulders were holding him down.

'Look. I have to get over to the flagship. Otherwise—'

'Hello, hello.' Different voice. The first one began to whisper: then the newcomer murmured soothingly, 'All right. All right, now, all right . . .' There was something familiar about the voice, despite its tendency to repeat itself like a stuck gramophone record. Nick said, 'I have to get up and dress, because Sarah's coming for me. She's arranged it with Sister Agnes: I'm going up to Mullbergh, to recuperate.'

'That's a first-class idea, sir.'

He felt the slight pressure of the antiseptic swab and then the prick of the needle.

'There. Relax now. Rest's your best medicine now.' Sibbold straightened up. So did Green, who'd been holding Nick down on the cot. Leading Seaman Williams, on the upper berth, had his head turned to the right and he was eye to eye with the doctor. He asked, 'In a bad way, is he?'

'Not necessarily, Williams. If we're lucky, it'll turn out to be quite a temporary condition.' He pointed upwards. 'Hear that?'

'Couldn't hardly *not* hear it.'

'They're straightening out your wheelhouse for you. All we've got to do is get your legs healed up, and you'll be right back on the job.'

'D'you know how long we're staying here, sir?'

'Just long enough to get essentials working, I'd guess. Commander Gant's ashore, seeing the rear-admiral. We'll know more about it when he gets back.'

'Repairs'll take a while, sir, won't they?'

'I think just patching up, jury-rigging—'

'Any other ships in Surabaya, sir?'

'Oh, yes. *Exeter, Encounter*, five or six Yank destroyers . . . Williams, old chap, I'm sorry, but I've got to get around the other patients now. You're feeling a lot better, aren't you?'

'Except I'd as soon be dead.'

He'd said it flatly, unemotionally, and turned his head away to stare up at the deckhead, which was white-enamelled with heavy I-sectioned girders crossing it.

'Listen, Williams. Here is one fact. There is no reason or evidence to believe that your wife did not get away from Singapore.

581

Here's another. If she did get away, she'll be as anxious to find you now as you must be to find her. You'd be no use to her dead, and precious little use alive if you adopt that kind of attitude. Aren't you giving up a bit too easily?'

'I'm sorry.' His eyes stayed on the deckhead.

'Damn it, she's going to need your help, man!'

The head turned. Williams nodded. 'Sir.'

Sibbold hesitated. Then he turned away, beckoning Green to follow him out through the curtain. He told him quietly, 'Keep an eye on that one. I don't want him left alone for any length of time.'

Gant was still ashore when the first air attack came in. They were Val dive-bombers with an escort of fighters. They went mostly for the harbour front, with only a few desultory passes at the ships – like afterthoughts, as if they hadn't been briefed to expect anything afloat here and didn't have bombs to waste on them. The shore guns put up an extremely effective barrage, too, and it kept all the attackers high. Repair work in *Defiant*, even the work on the bridge, continued without interruption while her four-inch AA guns joined for a short while in the barrage; the only notice the men working with cutting-torches in the bridge paid to the enemy was to put on tin hats.

There was damage to some buildings and to an oiling jetty, where a fire was started, and there was a nearish miss on an American destroyer in dry dock. Then it was over, and the ERAs took off their tin hats. They were cutting away the wreckage, as much as needed to be removed before new beams and plates could be riveted and welded on. LTOs – electrical ratings – were re-rigging telephone and gunnery-control circuits, and shipwrights, mechanics and ordnance artificers were all working flat out, backed up by teams of less skilled assistants. The biggest job of all, of course, and the most important, was in the boiler room.

Gant returned aboard at noon. Lieutenant Flynn RNVR was officer of the watch on the quarterdeck. Gant asked him, stepping off the gangway and bringing his hand down from the salute as the thin wail of the bosun's call died away, 'Any news of the captain?'

'He's been moved to his cabin, sir. Last I heard, he was still unconscious.'

Flynn was short, dark and dapper; he was a yachtsman, one of the pre-war weekend reservists. Rowley arrived, apologetic for not having been on the quarterdeck in time to meet him.

'Sorry, sir, I was down in the—'

'This is no time for standing around gangways, Charles . . . Did any bombs come near us?'

Rowley shook his head. 'They seemed to be more interested in the hotels.'

'I know. I was in one of them, talking to the admiral.' Gant looked round at Flynn. 'Send your messenger to the engineer commander, tell him I'll be in the cuddy and I'd like to see him if he can spare a minute. Same message to the PMO, please.'

Harkness, the captain's PO steward, came out to meet him. He murmured, 'No change, sir. He hasn't moved a whisker.'

It was half dark in the sleeping cabin, and curtains were drawn over both the scuttles. Nick Everard was lying on his back, motionless as a corpse. Gant asked Harkness, 'Has he said anything?'

'No, sir.'

When he'd been up for'ard, he'd been mumbling to some imaginary woman about her breasts. With half the ship's company listening to every word. Gant said, 'He was delirious, earlier on, talking nonsense. If you hear any – you know, personal stuff—'

'I got cloth ears, sir.'

Sibbold, the PMO, tapped on the door and came in. He stopped beside Gant, and stooped to look closely at the patient. He explained, 'We changed the wrapping, you see, so when he comes round he'll be able to open his eyes. One of the question-marks, after a crack on the head like he had, is whether his sight may be affected. Hence drawn curtains, in case the light's too much for him at first.'

'Harkness here says he hasn't moved or spoken.'

Nick recognized that voice. It belonged to – Bob Gant. And Bob Gant was . . .

Damn . . . But it would come. Just for the moment, it had slid away from him. He could see the face in his mind and match it to the voice, but he couldn't follow it beyond that. He lay still, keeping his eyes shut, wanting to listen to the voice and let it trigger his memory.

There was a lot of noise – clattering and banging and scraping – but it was farther away than it had been before, and it didn't torture his skull like it had. The pain was less intense now anyway, more of an ordinary headache.

He'd had a nightmare, about Jack. 'Half-brother' Jack . . .

Sarah had been talking about him. And about Nick's father, John Everard, who'd died after a series of strokes which had been triggered by Nick telling him the truth about Jack's drowning: how he'd had to leave him – and about five hundred others – and how the German pilots had been using swimmers for target-practice.

No. Wrong, again. That had happened – one year ago. And Nick's father had died in – oh, 1931 . . . It was David, then, he'd told him about. David at Jutland. Nick's elder brother David, who right from the nursery had had a great deal wrong with him and who'd cracked, gone round the bend before he drowned. A quarter of a century ago. History. History meant pain, for some people. And complications. It was important to keep Paul clear of all that, to keep the sins of the father *to* the father. Or fathers, plural.

David had looked very much like Jack. Sarah had always denied it, but it was a fact and there was an oil painting of David in her Dower House at Mullbergh to prove it. She denied it because she knew the truth about David, although she denied that too. She certainly *had known* the truth: but she possessed this extraordinary ability to change the truth even as it existed in her own mind, turn black into white because that was how she wanted it. And having changed it, stick to the *manufactured* truth, admit no other view, no doubt . . . That way, you built your own surroundings, your own history, you justified the loyalties you wanted to give and the hates you *needed* . . . Make-believe was reality, to Sarah. Although she'd admitted, finally, that Jack was their son, hers and Nick's.

No – she had not. That was the dream he'd had, the nightmare. Sarah would never, not even if she were tied to a stake and burning alive, admit to Nick's having fathered her son. She'd wiped all that out of her mind, washed out completely any memory of how she'd loathed and feared John Everard and in one moment's – oh, weakness, aberration, love – turned to her stepson. Who hadn't been – wasn't – all that much younger than herself.

That dream, though: Jack's dead face, and the sea reddened, washing over it . . .

Nightmare. There'd been no alternative to leaving him and the others in the water: to have stayed and tried to pick them up would have done them no good at all, would only have thrown away his own ship and ship's company. And Jack was alive, anyway, and he didn't know he wasn't John Everard's son. Only he, Nick, and Sarah knew it. Sarah *had* known it.

Paul must never know it: never have an inkling of it.

He said, 'I must write to Paul.'

Sibbold leant forward, listening. He'd sent Harkness out for a smoke, and Gant was in the day-cabin talking to Sandilands. Sibbold had pulled a chair near the head of the bunk. He got up from it now and leaned over to peer through the semi-darkness at his patient's closed eyes.

'Feeling a little better, sir?'

'Who's that?'

'Sibbold, sir. PMO.'

'Oh. Sibbold.'

Silence . . . The pulse-rate was all right. He tried again: 'How do you feel now, sir?'

'Not bad.' The right hand moved, pointing. 'Head aches, but it's better.'

'You had a very nasty bang on it.'

'What about this arm?'

'Your left arm's broken in two places. I've set it and splinted it, and it's strapped to your chest to keep it still. I don't expect any problems with it.'

'Did I miss the meeting in the flagship?'

'No, sir, you—'

'Admiral Doorman's conference?'

'You attended that meeting, sir. You've had a knock on the head, you see, and it's left you with concussion, so your memory's confused. What I'd like you to do, sir, is just lie still, relax, sleep if you can. Commander Gant—'

'Did you say I *did* attend Doorman's conference?'

'Yes. And we sailed – the whole squadron – soon after that. Now we're back in Surabaya.'

He didn't see how this was possible. Sibbold explained: the conference had taken place two days ago. They'd sailed that same day, turned back yesterday to refuel the destroyers, but an enemy report had sent them hurrying north again. This time, they'd found the enemy.

'Where am I?'

'In your sleeping-cabin, sir.'

He hadn't asked yet how he'd sustained his injuries. There were still loose connections in the mental processes.

'What – time of day is it?'

'Early afternoon, sir.'

'Well, my God, I'd better—'

'Please, you really *must* lie still, sir!' Sibbold eased him down again. 'You have to rest – you have a badly damaged head and some minor wounds as well. The only way you can do anyone any good is to stay there and rest, get your strength and memory back. Now, *please* . . .'

'Why are those curtains drawn?'

'So you'd rest better, sir.'

'Where's Gant?'

It was amazing how quickly a brain that had been jolted off its gimbals could get back on them again. Even though it would, obviously, still take a while to settle, you could see and hear awareness growing every minute. Sibbold told him, 'He's been ashore to see the admiral, sir, and now he's talking to Commander Sandilands about the repairs to the boiler room. I expect he'll be in to see you in a minute – he was here earlier, but you were asleep.'

'No, I wasn't. I heard his voice.'

He hadn't picked up that mention of repairs to the boiler room. But he might at any moment, as his mind mulled over what had been said. And any such extension to what had already been a lengthy question-and-answer session would keep Sibbold even longer from his other patients . . . 'Look here. I just walked clear through the ship, didn't I? I mean, to get here. If I can do that, why shouldn't I turn out now?'

'You were brought aft on a stretcher, sir. Unconscious.'

'I've just told you, Sibbold, I came on my own two feet!'

'You're concussed, sir—'

'Who's this?'

The door had opened, and shut again very quietly. Sibbold, glancing round, was glad to see Harkness back again.

'Your PO steward, sir.'

'Petty Officer Harkness?'

'Ah, you're a lot stronger now, sir!'

'I'll be turning out, in a minute. Where's Gladwill?'

'Gladwill, sir?' Harkness looked round for Sibbold, but the doctor was retreating stealthily towards the door. Nick said, 'I can see two of you, Harkness . . . What did you say about Gladwill?'

'I – er – been seeing to 'is birds, sir. Singing away fit to bust, that littlest one is. They've eaten all their grub, though, would you believe it? Every time you look, they've wolfed the lot!'

'Why can't Gladwill look after his own canaries?'

Sibbold had come back to the bunkside. He asked Nick, 'You said you could see two of Harkness, sir. Can you see two of me now?'

'Yes.'

'Double vision. It's probably only temporary, but I'd like to take a look at it. We'll need to have those curtains open – you may find it a bit bright, at first. Harkness, would you—'

'You haven't answered my question about Gladwill.'

The curtains were open, and he was blinking at the sunlight.

'We were in action, sir.' Sibbold held up his thermometer in its metal case in front of Nick's eyes. 'Watch this, please. Follow it with your eyes as I move it . . . We were in action last night. We were hit just under the bridge, and in number two boiler room. There was a hit aft as well – starboard side here, by the after tubes. It was the shell in the bridge that did this damage to your head. Actually you smashed the glass windbreak with your forehead, and it was the glass that cut your face too. I'm sorry to say just about everyone else up there was killed. Including Gladwill. I'm *very* sorry to have to tell you this, sir . . . How many of this object are you seeing now?'

Gant told Sandilands, 'You've got until sunset tomorrow. No matter how much still needs doing then, we sail as soon as it's dark.'

A siren was howling, ashore, signalling another air-raid alert. This time, perhaps, they'd be going for the ships. *Defiant*'s alarm-buzzers were sounding, but her AA armament was already closed up and for the moment there was nothing Gant could be doing. There wasn't anything to be seen, either. He turned back from the scuttle.

'Including tonight, it gives you twenty-eight or thirty hours. Can you finish in that time?'

Sandilands was personally supervising the boiler-room job. He was in overalls, oil-stained and unshaven. He was a rugged-looking character, but here and now he also looked just about exhausted.

'In present circumstances I couldn't finish in twenty-eight *days*, let alone that many hours. We need a dockyard and shoreside facilities. There were bits falling off before any of this happened, you know . . . All I can say is we'll do what's physically and mechanically possible. If all goes well I'll have two of those four boilers back on the job.'

'Four altogether, you mean?'

Sandilands nodded.

It was better than he'd expected. He told him, '*Sloan*'s captain wanted to spend an extra day here. He's got engine parts coming by rail from Tjilatjap.'

'So?'

'We can't wait that long. Everyone's of the same opinion. Even Jordan agreed, finally. What will our own best speed be, John?'

'Twenty-three or twenty-four.'

'You'll have done damn well, at that . . . I'd say you needed some rest, though. Did you get any, last night?'

'Christ's sake, how could I?'

'You don't have to turn every nut and bolt yourself, John. You've got Murray, Holbrook, and young Benson, not to mention—'

'The boiler room isn't the only job we've got. But I will – I'll get my head down, later . . . *Sloan*'s troubles came from a near-miss, you said?'

He nodded. 'Pretty bad, too. She ground to a halt, apparently, out there in the Strait. One of the others towed her in.'

'If they don't get the spares they're hoping for—'

'They don't. But they'll manage twenty-five knots, as opposed to more than thirty. They've had artificers from all the other destroyers working with them, I gather.'

'Some people get all the luck, don't they?' Sandilands pointed upwards, as a thudding of AA guns came to them. 'Here's some more of the other kind.'

Gant followed him outside. The Jap raiders were high, over the land in the west. He couldn't see them at first, but bursts of AA shells led his eye to them, to half a dozen mosquito-like objects flying north or northwest. The smoke bursts were already fading, gunfire tailing away. Looking for'ard he saw the crew of the starboard four-inch, on the raised gun platform that straddled the ship from one side to the other between her funnels. They were already securing the gun and discarding tin hats and anti-flash gear. It was likely those aircraft had been attacking some military target inland; the enemy had been bombing road and railway junctions, so he'd heard ashore, and there'd been raids on Tjilatjap on the south coast of the island as well as on Batavia and

Bandoeng. They were preparing for the military invasion by disrupting Dutch lines of inland communication.

Pinner was waiting, at ease, near the entrance to the cuddy. He had rather a self-satisfied look about him, Gant thought. Perhaps he was thinking of himself now as the commanding officer's doggie, a step-up from being only the second-in-command's?

'Pinner, find Lieutenant-Commander Rowley, please. Tell him I'll see heads of departments in the wardroom at 1800 hours.'

Nick had been tired by his talk with Sibbold, and he'd fallen into another deep, dream-filled sleep. Kate had been with him, somewhere or other, and he'd been trying to explain why he had to go through with the idea of marrying Fiona. Kate had argued, 'You and I hadn't met at that time, had we?' It wasn't easy to explain his view that the point was irrelevant, that a man had to stand by his word. There was more to it, as well, an attitude of mind much harder to put across to her because it had roots that led right back into his youth. It was the fact that he'd already done a lot of harm to several individuals, and the prospect of adding to the list of injured parties by breaking his word to Fiona was anathema to him. He'd never set out to harm anyone, it had simply resulted from things he'd done. This time he could see likely consequences, and choose for himself.

'Do you really think you can make amends for bloomers you've made way back by messing up your own future now – and mine?'

He wasn't sure whether he was asleep and had dreamt of Kate asking him this, or whether he'd imagined it, put the words into her mouth in his own imagination as a way of arguing with himself.

Thinking about Kate was soothing to the spirit, anyway.

When she'd been with him in Alex and Cairo – after he'd brought her out of Crete – she'd never even hinted at any such thing as marriage. The Cairo interlude had been when he'd had a few days' leave, with *Tuareg* boiler-cleaning in the dock at Suez. Ostensibly, he'd gone up to see the pyramids, and that was what she'd told her people she was doing, too. And they *had* looked at them, once or twice . . . And he, Nick, had talked about the future, peacetime, and hinted at the idea of marriage. He'd felt guilty about it, having Fiona in the back of his mind and wishing he did not have; and Kate had totally ignored the openings he'd given her.

'It's too late now, isn't it? I *am* committed. I'm sorry, Kate, I'm truly—'

'A bit late to be sorry!'

He was asleep; Sarah, not Kate, had said that. They were on the steps leading up to the front entrance at Mullbergh, which had been Sir John Everard's house and had just become Nick's. They'd just come from his father's funeral. He'd said, 'I feel as if I'd killed him.' Sarah had stopped, and her dead-white face had jerked round to him, her eyes venomous.

'*Didn't you?*'

He told Kate, 'I killed my own father.' He saw the contempt in her expression before she turned her back on him. Turning slowly, like a dummy swivelling on a central pivot. Then her back was towards him: that long, slim neck and the tawny hair, her tall, slim figure. Receding, leaving him.

'Kate!'

She was going, getting smaller, leaving not only physically, in terms of distance, but out of his life for ever. Well, he'd as good as told her to. And the thought of that was suddenly horrifying, like a new crime on his conscience: he shouted, 'Kate, please, come back?' She was tiny, as if he was looking at her through the wrong end of a telescope, and the concept of her being totally and permanently out of reach was too frightful to accept. He shouted, 'Kate, I love you!'

He woke with the shout ringing in his skull. Harkness, the PO steward, said, 'Ah, you're awake again, sir. Nice little sleep, you had.'

'Was I yelling something?'

'Only muttering a bit, sir. Not what you'd call comprehensible like . . . The commander, sir, was wanting a chat. He said I was to let him know when you found it convenient. Should I—'

'Yes, please. I'd like to see him.'

Paul and Kate would get on well together, he thought. They were the same sort of people: direct, straightforward . . . He wondered where Paul was now, at this minute. If he was in the Mediterranean – as he would be, by now – there'd be a time-difference of about – what, six hours between them?

That didn't tell him much. He didn't even know what the time was here in Java.

Harkness had gone to the door. 'Shan't be gone a minute, sir.'

Nick lifted his free hand and held the forefinger in front of his eyes, like Sibbold's thermometer. He saw two fingers instead of one. Annoyed, he let the hand flop. It was called double vision,

Sibbold had said, and the odds were that it would disappear in a few days.

That wasn't good enough. It was now, today, he needed all his faculties. Somehow or other, the process of recovery would have to be speeded up. Better talk to Sibbold again. Perhaps aspirin, or some such thing. Or just keep one eye shut. And use a telescope instead of binoculars . . .

But now, before Bob Gant arrived, he set himself to remembering what Sibbold had told him about the action – last night's, or the night before that – and the damage to the ship. There'd been – *three* hits. One under the bridge, in the wheelhouse or plot: and a mental note here, *See Leading Seaman Williams as soon as possible* . . . Second hit – back here, near the starboard after tubes. Holed the upper deck and started a fire, and cut most communications from the ACP. Work in that area would account for much of the noise that he could hear now . . . Third hit had been—

Blank.

Damn.

Well, force yourself, stretch your brain . . .

Boiler room!

He relaxed again, sweating from the effort. Major damage in number two boiler room, which had cut the speed to about ten knots. And as speed was of the essence if *Defiant* was to have the faintest chance of getting away from this place, Sandilands had teams of his best men working on it flat out.

Twenty-two dead, and fourteen wounded.

Java and *de Ruyter* had blown up and sunk. Sibbold thought they'd been hit by torpedoes from Jap cruisers. *Exeter* badly damaged. *Electra* and *Jupiter* sunk.

If ever there'd been a time when a man needed to have his brain in working order . . .

'Well, sir! *Delighted* to hear you're so much better!'

Nick raised the movable hand.

'Pull up a chair, Bob. Light that foul pipe of yours if you want to.'

Gant murmured as he sat down, 'D'you know, sir, we all thought you were a goner?'

'So Palliser's leaving?'

'On Helfrich's orders. Soon as the rest of us have cleared out. But they hadn't foreseen this delay to ourselves and *Sloan*, so in fact he'll be away before us. By air to Australia.'

591

Rear-Admiral Palliser was the senior British naval officer in Java. As long as he was here he was under the orders of the Dutch admiral, Helfrich, who was at Batavia and who had been Doorman's boss.

Gant said, 'I was asked whether it would be practicable for you to be flown to Australia with him, sir.'

Australia. Kate was in Australia . . . He caught himself thinking about Kate, and pulled himself together. Keeping the mind drifting off on its own was one of the things he was going to have to work hard at. He told Gant, 'There's no question of it, of course. I imagine you told them so?'

'I said I thought you were too groggy to be moved, sir. Frankly, it never occurred to me you'd come out of it so quickly. I said I'd have a word with the PMO, then confirm it one way or the other.'

'You can forget all that. By tomorrow I'll be on my feet and *compos mentis*. Even if there's still a touch of this bloody double vision.'

'*Truly*, sir?'

Nick nodded. 'I'll be up and about, and you'll be out of a job again, you poor chap!'

'Well, my God, if you *could* be—'

'You'd like that?'

Gant smiled. 'I most certainly would, sir!'

Nick wondered about him. *Why* he'd be so eager to relinquish the responsibilities of command . . . If he, Nick, had been in Gant's shoes he'd have welcomed the opportunity to take over, he'd have grabbed at it and he'd have been bitterly disappointed, privately, to be done out of the chance once he'd thought he'd got it.

Gant wasn't feeling any disappointment, though. And it wasn't concern for Nick Everard, either. He was genuinely anxious to get 'out from under'. Looking at him intently, interestedly, seeing two of him, Nick realized that his second-in-command was very much a background figure, self-effacing, thoroughly reliable at putting someone else's orders into effect, but – scared of the idea of command? Distrustful of his own abilities?

If the job was forced on him, he'd probably have set his teeth and eventually grown into it. But crisis-time was *now*: and a second-in-command ought to be ready, eager to step up.

'Hard luck, Bob.'

'What d'you mean, sir?'

'Weren't you looking forward to becoming your own boss?'

Gant shook his head. 'Straight answer to a straight question – no, sir. If you're fit enough, I'm as pleased as Punch!'

'You can start celebrating, then.'

Even if he wasn't as fit as he hoped he'd be, tomorrow, he'd have to pretend he was, *make* himself be so. It would be better for the ship to have a captain who was slightly boss-eyed and occasionally dizzy than one who was scared of the job.

Gant was studying *him*, now. Wondering whether he was up to it, probably. That answer had been an honest one, all right. Gant had probably reconciled himself to the idea of command, stiffened his dicky spine to it. But he was relieved now – at least, hopeful.

'Tell the admiral, Bob, that I'm much better and intend to reassume command before we sail. In the meantime I have to rest, and therefore hope he'll excuse me from calling on him. And thank him for that very kind offer.'

Gant nodded. 'I'll tell the ship's company too, sir. Should have the Tannoy working soon, and I was intending to give them a pep-talk. This'll cheer them up no end . . . I've called a heads-of-departments meeting for 1800, by the way.'

'Like me to attend it?'

'Wouldn't it be better to rest, sir, as you say?'

'What?'

He'd begun to think of something else: Gant had to say it again. It was embarrassing . . . He agreed: 'You're right, of course . . . Now – thinking of future plans . . . By tomorrow morning we and *Sloan* will be the sole occupants of Surabaya?'

'Except for the Yank destroyer in dock, sir. They're going to blow her up and wreck the dock as well.'

'Tell me about the other sailings.'

'Well. Four American destroyers will leave as soon as it's dark tonight. Eastward – via Madura and the Bali Strait.'

'Good luck to them.'

'Yes. Indeed . . . *Exeter* will leave about the same time, with *Encounter* and the USS *Pope. Exeter* draws too much water to leave by the eastern exit, of course, and Palliser's routing the three of them northward and then west. The idea is to get well clear of the coast – to avoid Jap invasion forces – and then make for the Sunda Strait.'

Sunda was at the western end of Java, between Java and Sumatra. Five hundred miles away.

'Has *Exeter* made good her damage?'

Gant shook his head. 'Sixteen knots, sir.'

'Long way, at that speed.'

'Yes.' But there weren't any soft options. Gant took his pipe out, looked at it and put it away again. Nick said, 'I don't mind if you smoke.'

'Thanks. Trying to cut down a bit.'

'Now, about ourselves, Bob. The idea ashore is we should sail tomorrow night, and it's up to us to decide which way we go?'

'Yes, sir. Point being that the situation could change dramatically between now and then. And we'll have heard how the others have got on. The admiral's arranging for Bandoeng to keep us informed.'

That was good. And the freedom of action – within limits which would be established by geography, ships' speed and the enemy's deployments – was very welcome. In recent weeks there'd been no such latitude, and every move they'd made had been not only disastrous but foreseeably so. He muttered, 'Yes . . .' Tiring, losing the track again, and Bob Gant obviously worrying that he might not be up to it . . . Nick got hold of his powers of concentration again. 'I think we might have a council of war tonight, Bob. Here. I'll send an RPC to Jim Jordan – well, you do that for me, will you? Make it 1900 for 2000, and tell Harkness I've a guest for supper. Two guests – you've got to be in on all of it, in case I keel over again. All right?'

'With much pleasure, sir.'

As a signal, that would have been sent out as WMP. The RPC to Jim Jordan stood for 'Request the pleasure of your company.'

'And have Chevening standing by with some charts . . . Chevening was damn lucky, wasn't he, getting off without a scratch?'

'Very lucky indeed.'

'You did a good job, bringing the ship back.'

'That wasn't difficult, sir. But we did truly think you were dead, at first. I suppose because there was so much blood . . .'

Blood. Thoughts wandered. Nick's right hand came up, and his fingers touched the dressing on the left side of his face. Sibbold had admitted he'd have a scar from that eye to the corner of his mouth; there were a lot of stitches in it, apparently. Nick wondered whether Kate would be revolted by it: but probably not, she was a nurse, she—

Now stop that . . . He asked Gant, 'Has Sandilands said what speed we're going to be capable of?'

'He reckons twenty-three knots, sir. Maximum twenty-four.'

'And *Sloan*?'

'They hope twenty-five.'

Gant told him – he'd meant to earlier – that Jim Jordan of *Sloan* had sent a personal message, enquiring about Nick's progress.

'Very kind of him.' Nick was thinking *Twenty-three or twenty-four* . . . Even after a crack on the head he knew that engineers could invariably do better than they promised. Then they got congratulated instead of cursed. And if Jim Jordan's destroyer could make twenty-five knots, he wasn't going to ask him to make less than that for *Defiant*'s sake. Getting out of this hole was going to require a lot of luck, a lot of nerve and every knot that anyone could squeeze out.

He interrupted Gant.

'Sandilands is always a bit over-cautious. And we can't use the Madura Channel either. *Sloan* might: she wouldn't draw more than nine or ten feet, I'd guess?'

Sloan was one of the Selfridge class: not much under two thousand tons, with five-inch guns, and launched in about 1935. Those ships had been designed for thirty-seven knots, and on trials some of them had knocked up nearly forty. So Jim Jordan, who was proud of his ship, had told Nick that evening in Batavia, the evening they'd drunk Laphroaig. A week ago? Something like that . . . But this question of speed: he covered his eyes with his free hand. His brain felt heavy, he had to drive it hard to make it work. He knew, too, that he was thinking in the dark, at this stage. Without a chart in front of you, all the distances and depths and tides, the whole thing was guesswork. But the fact remained, you'd still need every ounce of steam you could get.

'Bob, listen. If *Sloan*'s likely to make twenty-five knots, that's what I want for *Defiant* too. Tell Sandilands, will you – twenty-five, *at least*.'

'Well, sir, I'm not sure—'

'*Make* sure. Just *make* sure, Bob.'

'Aye aye, sir.'

'He'll have to do better than he thinks possible, that's all. Twenty-five, tell him.'

Gant nodded. He was looking at Nick as if he thought he mightn't be thinking straight yet.

'*Perth* and *Houston* – did you tell me they *have* got to Batavia?'

'Yes, sir. The signal arrived when I was there, ashore. They got in at 1400 hours, and Admiral Helfrich has ordered them to sail at 2100, via Sunda to Tjilatjap.'

'Why not tell them to clear out altogether, I wonder?'

'I gather there are some small ships at Tjilatjap, sir, and refugees to be evacuated. He may be putting a convoy together.'

Nick's thoughts had jumped back to the speed question. He told Gant, 'If there's any argument from Sandilands about giving us twenty-five knots, bring him here to see me.'

'Aye aye, sir.'

The commander looked relieved: he had someone to fall back on . . . Nick told himself, *I was right* . . . Then he'd lost that train of thought and he was wondering what the chances were – for *Perth* and *Houston*, for *Exeter* and the two destroyers going with her, or for the four American destroyers who'd be making a dash for the Bali Strait tonight. The Bali Strait was a lot closer than any of the other gaps – and as those destroyers could slip out over the Madura shallows, the short-cut eastward, it was closer still – but it was less than two miles wide and Bali was swarming with Japanese invaders now. They had an airstrip working too, on Bali . . . There was one fact, anyway, that was beyond dispute: however slim any of those ships' chances might be tonight, *Defiant*'s and *Sloan*'s twenty-four hours later would be slimmer.

It had all been so obvious, so inevitable . . .

'Of course, we don't have all the information that Helfrich must have.'

Gant was stuffing his pipe, at last. While out of memory like a dream Nick was re-reading a signal which Admiral Doorman had shown him: about Jap aircraft carriers operating to the south of Java, across all the lines of retreat to Australia or Ceylon.

Australia, where Kate was . . .

Think about the carriers, not Kate!

He'd muttered something, angrily. Gant, thumbing loose tobacco off the top of the pipe's bowl, had glanced up and was now embarrassed, pretending he hadn't heard. Nick told himself, *Better still, don't think about the bloody carriers either* . . . What he had to coerce his wobbly mind into concentrating on was how to get this ship and Jordan's out through the straits. Through either Lombok, Bali or Alas. *If* you made it that far, then you could start worrying about Jap carrier groups. Reaching this conclusion, he nodded to himself: and at the same moment realized that he and Gant had been staring at each other . . . Gant had looked down at his pipe, obviously embarrassed again, for the second time in a minute, doubtful of Nick's fitness. And he had good reason to be doubtful, too . . .

But he could still do the job, Nick thought, better than Bob Gant would do it. Because however technically competent Gant was, he lacked confidence, lacked trust in himself at least as much as he lacked it – at this moment – in Nick Everard.

CHAPTER 8

A freighter in column four was on fire. Junkers 88s had come in from the bow, flown down the port side of the convoy and then circled round astern; then they'd turned inward and passed over high from the other quarter, releasing their bombs as they flew homeward, north-eastward. The ship that had been hit was still in her station, but she was leaking a trail of smoke. One bomber had been shot down by gunfire from the warships astern, and the last attackers, when last seen from the *Montgovern*'s bridge, had had Fleet Air Arm fighters on their tails.

Wind and sea were on the port bow, and the ships had quite a bit of movement on them. And stage two of this assault was developing now ahead: something new, by courtesy of *Superaereo*.

Mackeson said, using binoculars and trying to make out what was happening, 'Mines, of some sort.' He had his glasses on parachutes that were drifting down ahead of the convoy, out ahead of the destroyer screen. Italian bombers, s84s, had approached from ahead during the last stages of the Junkers' bombing run, and until the parachutes blossomed it had looked from here as if they were dropping huge bombs on the destroyers. Now, through binoculars, Mackeson could see that the objects were barrel-shaped, rather like depthcharges, and that they were going into the sea well ahead, beyond and not *on* the fleet destroyers. The destroyers had engaged the bombers first, but now they'd shifted target to the dangling secret weapons: and to add to their problems fighter-bombers had just appeared. Small, stubby-shaped biplanes, diving on them.

'Commodore's flying forty-five degree emergency turn port, sir!'

Turning his ships to steer them clear of the mines – or whatever those things might be. Mackeson's signalman had reported it through the window from the bridge wing; part of his job was to watch the *Blackadder*'s yardarms for signals. There were attackers coming in from other directions as well but it was this unidentified threat ahead that had to be taken care of first. Siren, now, a hoarse screaming to implement the flag-signal for the turn. Straight told his quartermaster, in a flat tone as if the whole thing disgusted him, 'Port fifteen degrees.'

An Italian bomber was flaming down into the sea. It wasn't anywhere near any of the ships, and it looked like a kill for the Fleet Air Arm, who were making interceptions at longer range, clear of the convoy's guns. The guns were as bad for the Sea Hurricanes as they were for Junkers or Savoias, but in any case the fighter pilots' object was to break up attacking formations long before they reached the convoy.

The *Montgovern* was under helm now, her motion changing as she turned head-on to wind and sea, the whole convoy swinging round to avoid the unknown danger in its path. Devenish said to Mackeson, 'Something new, strange but true.' Quoting something, presumably. Mackeson murmured, 'Secret Woppery.' Bomb-splashes near destroyers in the screen ahead seemed to be small ones, and those aircraft which had been acting like fighter-bombers – they were already invisible in the haze thrown up by the destroyers' AA barrage – had looked old-fashioned, like First War fighters.

Ships' guns were getting noisy in other sectors now.

'Midships the wheel.'

Devenish, back from a visit to the starboard wing, told Straight, 'That was the *Neotsfield* caught one. Fire'll take some putting out, I'd say.'

With the amount of smoke that was coming out of her, any U-boat waiting for this convoy would see them coming from fifty miles away. And there'd be some U-boats waiting, all right.

Torpedo-bombers had begun an approach from the quarter – which because of the turn to port had now become the beam – but they'd split up now. It had seemed at first that the destroyers' barrage-fire in the sector had broken up the attack, but in fact they'd divided into several groups each of five or six aircraft and then begun to circle outside the range of the destroyers' guns. Before long the separate groups would make simultaneous attacks from different directions. The battleship on the convoy's port quarter opened up at some of them now, using her sixteen-inch guns: the percussions were so enormous that you just about felt them as well as heard them, even from this distance. The splashes looked as high as Nelson's Column, rising grandly somewhere inside the radius of the circling Italians. Another flight was ahead of that one, had passed round astern and would now be moving up on the other quarter; groups who'd turned the other way were hanging around on the port beam and bow.

And all turning inwards . . .

Now, Mackeson thought, it would start to become real. So far, he'd felt like a spectator. You were in the middle of it all, part of the vulnerable target, but it had all been happening at a distance and on the periphery. Like being in the middle of a bar-room brawl and for some odd reason no one hitting *you* . . . But now, matters were about to change and involve one personally: of those five separate threats spread over an arc of about a hundred and eighty degrees some, surely, would get through. They were Savoia Marchettis, he thought. This whole effort seemed to be Italian: and the air bases in Sardinia *were* Italian, of course. Any Germans that showed up, like those Junkers, would be from the Sicilian bases. He remarked to Humphrey Straight as he passed behind him to take a look out on the other side, 'Nothing but Eyeties, we have now.' Straight squirmed his facial muscles as if he was about to spit, but that was as far as it got. Destroyers all round from the port bow to the starboard quarter were engaging the on-coming torpedo bombers, and so were the big ships astern. The inner screen, the Hunts, were staying in close to the block of merchantmen; they had their guns trained out on their own sectors, ready to engage any of the Savoias that got in this far.

Straight had steadied his ship on the new course. On the quarter smoke still blew thickly out of the ship that was on fire. On the starboard bow the secret-weapon-dropping had finished. It would be very annoying, Mackeson thought, to the backroom boffins and others on the Italian side to see the convoy simply stepping round the fruits of all that labour. And they'd surely have meant all the different kinds of attack to go in at once: he guessed that the Fleet Air Arm had probably disrupted their co-ordination for them. But five attacks were on their way in now, and that was enough to be going on with. Gunfire was thickening and spreading as the action drew inexorably in towards the centre, the merchant ships and their cargoes which formed the bull's eye of the target.

Devenish touched his arm, and pointed. Ahead, high against clear sky, were – he got his glasses on them – more Junkers 88s. At

600

first he saw only one small bunch of them, but then he realized there was a wide, loose scattering of such groups, threes and fours and sixes; and above them, fighters.

One torpedo-bomber had got through the fleet destroyers' barrage on the port bow of the convoy. Suddenly it was inside the screen, an enemy at close range and determined. Hump-backed, thick-bodied, ugly, low to the sea and being shot at now by the Hunts on this side and by the Mauritius-class cruiser which was fine on the *Montgovern*'s bow. Beale and Withinshaw were on their toes at the guns, catching slit-eyed glimpses of it through shellbursts, watching it over the sights of their oily-black, wicked-looking weapons. If it kept coming, at that height, it would be lovely for the Oerlikons.

Paul saw it lift as its torpedo fell away, tilted tail-down and flopped into the sea. By the time the splash went up the aircraft was already well ahead of it. The commodore's siren was shrieking for yet another emergency turn – and none too soon, with at least one torpedo in the water. To his right, on the bow, Paul saw a second attacker trailing smoke from one engine but still coming, low and deadly. The cruiser was blazing away at it: and the first one was hauling away to the right, nose up as it banked, and tracer from a Hunt's Oerlikons seemed to lick its belly. Beale saw his target escaping before he'd had a shot at it, and he tried one burst that didn't have a hope of hitting. Paul yelled in his ear, 'Watch out for that Hunt!' The Hunt destroyer had been moving up, engaging the bomber with everything she had, and as the convoy swung to port she was about to pass across these Oerlikons' field of fire. Beale might have raked her bridge with his twenty-millimetre explosive shells before he'd known what he was doing. He'd ceased fire now, and Withinshaw hadn't fired at all.

On the bow, the aircraft that still had its torpedo under it blew up. Bits of plane and torpedo sang over, ringing off the *Mont-govern*'s steel and peppering the sea with splashes. Obviously the torpedo's warhead had exploded. The echo of it was still ringing when the second crash came: deeper, softer-sounding. Paul's eyes or mental eye still registered the fire-ball of the exploding bomber as he swung round and saw the *Garelochhead* hit – a torpedo-hit, that first one probably, the one he'd seen launched. The *Gareloch-head* had been next astern of the *Montgovern* but after two emergency turns to port she was on the beam now. A spout of sea shot up across her foc's'l; but he wasn't looking at her now, he was remembering what he was here for and doing it, looking round for new attacks. He heard Withinshaw yell at Beale, 'Let's go 'ome, Ron!'

'*Which* 'ome?'

Wally Short had shouted that. Everyone except the fat man was laughing. The volume of gunfire was decreasing: there was still some action somewhere astern but the torpedo attack, at least, seemed to have played itself out.

Then he saw bombers: high up, and to starboard. He thought they were 88s. You got used to recognizing each different type without consciously looking at the details of its shape: it became like looking at a face, you just glanced at it and knew it. He hadn't realized this before, and he had to look back at them to check that his quick impression had been right. Siren blaring: the commodore was turning his convoy back to starboard. At present it was ninety degrees off course, steaming directly towards Sardinia, with wind and sea consequently fine on the starboard bow, the ship rolling as well as pitching, a ponderous corkscrewing motion that wasn't violent but still made you take care of your footing and hold on to things. He'd drawn Beale's and Withinshaw's attention to those bombers, and now he was free to look around, take stock.

Earlier on, there'd been a bomb-hit on one of the ships in column four. It had started a fire and there was still a lot of smoke back there. But one ship in each of the outer columns made a total of four casualties so far, although the ship on fire was still keeping up – so far as he could see. Turning, now. The *Garelochhead* was out of sight, lost among the crowd of freighters astern. As the convoy swung back towards its easterly course she'd be somewhere between columns two and three, and then she'd slip out astern as the rest of them forged on. So – three drop-outs, one burning; and now – gunfire from the cruisers ahead reminded one – the Junkers 88s were about to make *their* effort.

The bombers were coming over high and in their separate groups. He thought there were fewer than when he'd last looked at them. All the warships firing steadily, surrounding them with shellbursts which the wind quickly tore to shreds. They were at ten or twelve thousand feet: you got the impression, from their appearance of remoteness, that they were only passing – like migrating geese . . . Mick McCall was beside him, staring up at them. Paul hadn't noticed him arriving.

'Fleet Air Arm gave their mates a clobbering. There were half as many again, before they got stuck in.' He jerked his head. 'We get a good view of things, up top.'

'Shot them down, you mean?'

'Just broke 'em up. You could see the bomb-loads going, and they'd skip out of it. They've got the legs of our lot when they put their noses down.'

The bombers were still flying south-westward. It was the rearmost groups that the cruisers and battleships astern were shooting at now, and one was turning away to port, an engine smoking . . . Wally and McNaught cheered, and McCall said, 'Every little helps.'

Paul said, 'Going down in Tunisia, I suppose.'

'Maybe.' McCall told Short, 'Don't want to cheer too soon. It'll get worse before it gets any better.'

Withinshaw muttered, 'Be 'appier if we was carryin' wheat.' Paul asked why. The fat man said, 'Keeps you afloat, like.' McCall explained, 'Wheat expands when it gets wet. So if you get holed when you're carrying it in bulk it's like having your 'tween-decks full of kapok.'

'It don't explode, neither.'

'There.' McCall sighed. 'Buggers are turning. They'll be at us now.' He asked Withinshaw, 'Had a load of wheat on that Atlantic trip, did you?'

'Aye. Out of Halifax. Laffin', we were.'

'Does a lot o' laffin', does our Art.' Beale glanced round at McCall, then back at the 88s. 'Won't be laffin' when they catch 'im, though.'

The bombers were circling astern, maintaining the separate groups. Paul asked McCall, 'A ship on fire, is there, back there?'

'The *Neotsfield*. Last ship in column four. Her skipper reckons they're getting on top of it, though this wind can't help.'

'How about the one that was astern of us?'

'*Garelochhead*. All we know is she was holed and flooding for'ard. She won't be coming on with us, that's for sure.' He nodded, with his eyes on the bombers. 'Here we go. Here *I* go.' He told Beale and Withinshaw, 'Shoot 'em all down, lads. Wait till you see the whites of their eyes, then plug 'em up the arse.' He went to the ladder and rattled down it, on his way back to the midships Bofors. Paul checked the time: it was 1.35. Beale said, 'Stand by, Art.' Up astern, from something like ten thousand feet, the first of the 88s were putting their noses down, aiming their dives into the centre of the convoy.

You waited. There was always such a lot of waiting, Paul thought. In submarines there was a lot of it too. They sent you to patrol an area or a position where it was hoped targets would appear, and you sat and waited for them. Just as submarines on this convoy's track would be waiting now. But they'd know something was coming, they couldn't doubt it, whereas sometimes you could wait for two or three weeks, the whole duration of the patrol, and see nothing. They called those 'blank' patrols.

Here, now, you waited for bombs. For bombers diving, with men his own age at their controls. He wondered what it felt like and looked like from up there. But for those Germans the wait was over, the attack had been launched and time-fused shells were exploding in their faces.

Withinshaw was narrow-eyed, open-mouthed. You could see his thick torso heaving as his breath came and went in short gasps. Paul wondered if it was true about his double life. He walked behind him, passing between Wally Short and the ammo bin, to the rail on the port side; he leaned out over it, looking astern. A freighter had closed up in the place of the *Garelochhead*, and that one and the *Montgovern* were now the only two ships in column one. Firing was heavy astern: battleships', cruisers' and carriers' AA guns all plastering the sky with high-explosive, dark smoke-flowers opening in tight bunches that quickly loosened and smeared, disintegrating while fresh clutches of them appeared like magic under the noses of the diving bombers. He was back in his place between the guns. That was Mackeson out in the bridge wing, staring aft, up at the approaching aircraft. If Beale or Withinshaw got careless they'd wipe old Bongo off his perch. Gosling was there too, and the signalman. A stockier figure behind the glass-enclosed front of the bridge could only be Humphrey Straight.

Gunfire spreading as well as thickening. The close escort of Hunts had joined in, and Bofors from ships at the tail-ends of columns two and three. It was one roar of noise but you could pick out the different elements in snatches of solo sound: the harsh rattling stabbing fire of Oerlikons, the measured thump-thump-thump of pompoms from the Hunts and the distinctive Bofors bark, and over all of it the hard thunder of four-inch.

Explosion astern. It had sounded like a bomb hitting. Then before he'd expected, like great black bats howling across the sky—

604

Oerlikons jumping, pumping their din into your skull. Tracer soaring, and the sky a mass of shell-smoke. Withinshaw a jellyfish shaking from the pulsing of his gun, shaking like a fat woman in a slimming machine, and used shell-cases cascading. The sea rose hummocking on his left – to starboard – with the top streaming off it like confetti, and a second later, as a separate stick came down, the back end of the *Castleventry*'s bridge went up in a sheet of flame.

There were three – four – bombers over the convoy, all just about finishing their dives, pulling out, sea leaping in mounds between ships and columns, and the bone-jarring crash of another hit somewhere on the quarter. Paul wasn't looking at the *Castleventry* but that huge gush of fire was still blinding, brain-scorching, as the belly of a Junkers 88 obscenely exposed itself, black crosses on white panels and one of its engines smoking, a lick of bluish flame from the wing behind it and smoke colouring with fire all out along the wing. It was Beale's gun hitting, Beale screaming joy and Withinshaw's tracer arcing to another one, fire-beads curling away behind its tail as it roared over, lifting out of the mess of bomb-bursts and gun-smoke. Half a dozen separate streams of tracer were converging on it but it still rose, banking to port across the *Empire Dance*. Beale shouted, 'I got 'im! See me get 'im?' The first one, he meant, and Paul nodded and gave him a thumbs-up sign, but he hadn't seen it. He'd seen Beale hitting and the machine in flames; he didn't doubt that it had crashed but he hadn't seen it. There were some moments now in which to breathe, look around, confirm that this ship was still intact, still plugging on: it was simultaneously reassuring and surprising. The noise had lessened and there were no enemies for the moment within Oerlikon range; ships astern were barraging at the next flight as it started down but here in the convoy there was a surprising pause. The *Castleventry* was out on the quarter, several cables' lengths away. He was looking at her, at the flames enshrouding her superstructure and right back as far as the after well deck, when she blew up. The heat as well as the shock-wave of the explosion hit them solidly, from a distance of about half a mile. Then the *Empire Dance* and the *Blackadder* and the freighter who'd moved up into the *Castleventry*'s station all opened fire. Some of the merchantmen had Brens and other light machine guns mounted in their bridge wings and flying bridges, as well as Bofors and Oerlikons. Withinshaw had opened up, but Beale's gun had jammed as soon as he'd pressed the trigger, and he and Short were working to clear it all through that attack. They were still at it, cursing, when the third bout started. Another Junkers had gone flaming into the sea ahead, and the Hunt-class escort who'd been standing by the *Castleventry* and must have had her paint blistered in that explosion had ranged up close to port of the *Montgovern*, adding her own close-range weapons to the protective barrage. Two tin-hatted sailors on her foc's'l were ditching what looked like wreckage – probably bits of the *Castleventry* blown on to her. Paul could see her guns' crews and bridge staff – busy, smoke-wreathed, somehow like parts of the ship herself, men and weapons and ship forming one live creature. He was reminded of destroyer action of his own, of the smell and sound of it and the sudden transition to swimming with a half-dead man on his back, then swimming alone, realizing he didn't know whether he was swimming towards the shore or away from it. He'd lost his sense of direction but after an initial surge of panic it didn't seem to matter much . . . He grabbed Withinshaw's thick shoulder, and pointed. Withinshaw swung round like a heavyweight ballet dancer twirling, old twinkle-toes himself. He had his sights on the underside of the Junkers as it flattened and its bombs thumped into the sea somewhere in the middle of the convoy. The gun began its fierce clattering roar, Withinshaw a-tremble with it as he slid his thick body round, hosepiping with the tracer. Then a shell from the Hunt burst under the bomber's tail and it was a cloud of out-flying debris around the bright nucleus of its exploding petrol tanks.

Mackeson said, 'Not so good, that shemozzle.' Humphrey Straight, who'd been adjusting engine revs to maintain station on the commodore's beam, only glanced at him and sniffed. Devenish, who'd moved up front in case the master wanted him to take over the conning of the ship now that bit of action had finished, muttered, '*And* we've got tonight ahead of us.'

Tonight they'd be turning down into the Skerki Channel, towards the Sicilian Narrows. And before dark – apart from whatever might be thrown at them in the interim – there'd be the evening, sunset performance.

Mackeson thought, *And we're lucky, at that.* Because the *Castleventry* people, amongst others, did not have an evening or a night ahead of them.

The destroyers were busy with a submarine contact out on the convoy's bow. Three of them had converged there, and they'd dropped two patterns of charges. The escort commander had sent up his two reserves – Hunt-class ships which he'd stationed ahead of the cruisers for this purpose – to fill the temporary gaps in the screen.

Gunfire from ahead. Mackeson raised his binoculars. It had come from destroyers, but it had already stopped. He caught a glimpse of a single aircraft, flying low to the sea and coming in towards the convoy. He'd tensed, but relaxed again when his signalman said, 'Fulmar, sir.'

'You're right.' Devenish had his glasses on it too. 'And it's in trouble.'

It was trailing smoke, and struggling to stay airborne. But if it went down now, a destroyer would get the pilot out, with any luck – unless he was badly wounded. Quite a few of the fighters returning from intercepting enemy formations had been in difficulties, struggling to reach their carriers. And when they did make it, since this last fracas they'd found they all had to get down on just one of them, because the other had had a bomb on her flight-deck. It was an armoured deck and the bomb hadn't penetrated, but it would be a while before that carrier could operate normally. A side-effect was that the other one would be so overcrowded that her flying operations would be hampered too.

'He's going in.'

The Fulmar was belly-landing into the sea, within fifty yards of one of the Hunts.

The *Castleventry* had blown up. Like the *Montgovern*, she'd had her quota of aviation spirit stowed in her bridge deck, which was where the bomb had struck and burst. It must have blown out through the for'ard part of the bridge as well – or sprayed burning petrol right through the superstructure – because she'd gone out of control immediately, swinging off-course and under the stern of the *Empire Dance*, and by that time the whole of her afterpart had been wrapped in flame. You'd been looking at a fire, not at a ship. When she'd exploded, burning wreckage had landed on a Hunt who'd been close to her; the same Hunt was now abeam to port and had signalled the commodore via the *Montgovern* that she'd picked up two survivors.

The *Kinloch Castle*, leading column three, had been hit for'ard. Some of her deck cargo of landing-craft had been blown overboard and there'd been internal damage, in her foc'sl and 'tween-deck spaces for'ard, but she was still in station and her master had said he was all right. The Clan ship that had been number two in column four had been less fortunate: she'd dropped out, with engine defects following a near-miss. And a couple of miles astern a destroyer who'd been badly hit was being abandoned and would then be sunk.

'Emergency turn starboard, sir!'

To give a wider berth to the submarine which they were still hunting out there on the bow. Turns like this were the commodore's decision. The escort commander told him what was happening ahead, and the commodore took such action as he personally considered necessary. The flag-hoist dropped, and the siren hooted. Humphrey Straight nodded to his chief officer, and moved away to the side of the bridge; Devenish told the quartermaster, 'Starboard fifteen degrees.'

More depthcharges exploded as the convoy swung away. In this column there were still only two ships, the *Montgovern* and the *Empire Dance*, but there were three in each of the three others. A rearrangement since the end of the last bombing attack had involved moving one ship, the *Mirabar*, from column three to column four, where the Clan ship had fallen out and the *Neotsfield* – her fire was out now, and the smoke was greatly reduced – had moved up into second place astern of the *Blair Atholl*.

Mackeson counted on his fingers: out of sixteen starters, five had gone, either sunk or dropped astern. Droppers-out very often ended up by being sunk anyway. But near enough one-third of the convoy had been lost. And the worst, admittedly, was still to come, as they moved in close to the Luftwaffe bases in Sicily and the submarine and E-boat ambush territory, the narrow waters south of the Skerki Bank. But if one-third of the original convoy could be brought into Malta, he thought, it would be a triumph. One-third would mean half the number of ships surviving now.

A triumph: and perhaps a pipe-dream too. Decodings of some Malta RAF reports indicated that a strong Italian cruiser force had assembled at sea and was steering south. The two cruisers from Cagliari and the Third Cruiser Squadron out of Messina and the heavy cruiser *Trento* had been mentioned. Mackeson had decided not to think about it: and he'd told Thornton to keep the information to himself.

'By 'eck, look there!'

On the beam, a submarine had shot to the surface. The long

finger of the fore-casing was sticking up out of the sea, and the stubby conning-tower was awash like a half-tide rock.

'Ease to five degrees of wheel.' Devenish had given the U-boat one quick glance, and turned back to his job. The Hunt to port of the *Montgovern* had opened fire: she was under helm, bow-wave rising as she picked up speed. Mackeson hurried out into the bridge wing. Looking aft, he saw the Army gunners with their four-inch on the ship's stern. They'd got the gun trained round but they couldn't fire because the Hunt was in the way. The Hunt's own for'ard four-inch were firing as she tore straight in towards the submarine. She'd fired again: and splashes had gone up, over by a hundred yards. There were men visible in the conning-tower, which could only have been a couple of feet above sea-level. He'd certainly seen *one* man, and now the Hunt was in the way . . . The *Montgovern* and all the rest of the merchantmen were steadying on the new course, the Hunt and the submarine abaft the beam now. The Hunt seemed to jump in the water as she rammed, her stem smashing into the enemy craft's hull, opening it to the sea and riding over it, thrashing over and now moving slowly, wallowing, down by the bows in a welter of churned foam. The submarine had gone.

There were cheers from the gunners, Army and DEMS men. Mackeson thought the ramming had been unnecessary and rather stupid. The U-boat had already been in bad trouble, presumably from the depth-charging, and a few well-aimed shells would have finished her. Alternatively, she might have been boarded. The glimpse he'd had of at least one man in the tower had given him the impression that her crew had been about to abandon ship. It hadn't been necessary at all, he thought. A perfectly good escort destroyer had been put out of action. She might limp back to Gibraltar and eventually be repaired, but in the meantime this convoy, which needed all the protection it could get, had lost one escort. Thinking about it as he turned to go back into the bridge, Bongo Mackeson was angry. Part of it lay in the fact that while he would gladly have seen every living German and Italian burn in hell if it saved Allied lives or helped to beat them in the war they'd started, a completely unnecessary taking of lives seemed incompatible with his own ideas of why the war had to be fought anyway: and he was face to face with Humphrey Straight, who must have been standing right behind him. Scowling: reflecting Mackeson's own scowl . . .

'That were a daft bloody thing to do.' Straight stared at him challengingly, his head lowered like a bull's. 'I'd courtmartial that bugger!'

Mackeson heard himself responding to the challenge, defending his own Service.

'The submarine might have slipped under again. He just made certain of it, that's all.'

'I thought destroyers were along to look after us, not play silly buggers like—'

'That's what he was doing, captain. If that thing had got down again it might still have got some torpedoes off – or even just got away, fished you on your way home to Gib next week, or—'

'Bloody 'ell—'

Siren: for the turn back to port . . .

There'd been submarine alarms and emergency turns all through the afternoon, and now with dusk approaching it was time for the air assault to start up again. The convoy had re-formed, into two columns instead of four. The reason for it was that when they turned down into the Skerki Channel destroyers ahead would be streaming their TSDS minesweeping gear, and the merchantmen had to be in a narrower formation to keep inside the strip of cleared water.

This pair of ships, the *Montgovern* and the *Empire Dance*, had dropped back and tagged on to what had been column two. But the C-class cruiser had inserted herself in the line as well, so there were three merchantmen, then the cruiser, then the *Montgovern* and the *Empire Dance*. The starboard column consisted of the three ships who'd comprised column four – the *Blair Atholl*, the damaged *Neotsfield* and the *Mirabar* – with the *Kinloch Castle*, the tanker *Caracas Moon* and the American freighter *Santa Eulalia* completing the line of six ships.

So the *Montgovern* now had a cruiser ahead of her and the tanker abeam to starboard. Two other, heavy cruisers led the columns, and a third, who'd been with the battleships earlier on, was centrally placed astern with a Hunt-class escort on each side of her. The minesweeping destroyers were in the lead and there were three others down each side, all inside the area of swept water.

New air attacks were coming, and in strength. Mackeson's W/T operators had been listening to the chitchat between Fleet Air Arm pilots and the fighter-directing cruisers, and the Sea Hurricanes had already run into some opposition. They'd reported big formations of Italian and German bombers already up and circling in waiting areas. The Hurricanes had scored some successes and they'd suffered losses too, and among the formations they'd encountered had been some of Ju87s, Stuka dive-bombers.

Beale spat down-wind. 'Stukas is *all* we bloody need.'

'I heard they're sitting ducks to fighters.'

'Won't be no fighters, will there? Not when the flat-tops turn back.'

The carriers and their own cruisers, and the battleships, would be reversing course in about an hour's time. The light was already weakening, and by then it would be dark. The hope, Mackeson had explained, was that the enemy might not realize the forces had split until tomorrow's daylight.

Paul was hungry. Lunch, in mid-afternoon, had been corned beef and pickles, and there'd been sardines for tea. Devenish, who presided over the saloon and the messing arrangements, had said the evening meal would probably be soup and corned beef sandwiches. He'd added, 'What we're missing, thanks to you lot, is a decent breakfast.' Thanks to having passengers on board, he meant. When they had the saloon to themselves, apparently the ship's officers breakfasted on steak and onions, which rations didn't allow for now.

Withinshaw said, 'Can't abide fookin' Stukas.'

Paul told him, 'Your turn to knock one down, this time.'

'I 'ad one *last* time!' The fat man was indignant. 'I was all over the sod an' some bastard blew it in fookin' 'alf before I could shittin' finish!'

'Yeah.' Beale laughed. 'I bet. Just because I got one an' you didn't come inside 'alf a mile—'

'He did, though.' Paul confirmed it. 'I saw it. He was hitting, and a shell burst right under it.'

''Ear that?'

Withinshaw was delighted. Beale said, 'Bein' kind to you, ain't he? On account o' you're so cultural . . . What's time now?'

Paul checked. 'Just on six.'

'Light's going. If they're coming, they'll come now.'

'Fookers'll come, don't you worry!'

Paul wondered where his father was. BBC news of events east of Suez wasn't encouraging, particularly if you listened to what they *didn't* say. He hoped *Defiant* had not been sent east . . . But whether she was there or still here in the Mediterranean he wondered how his father would like it, commanding a cruiser when he was so very much a destroyer man. Funny, really: Nick Everard, destroyer man, driving a cruiser, and Paul Everard, submariner, a passenger in a freighter . . . He put a hand up and touched his forehead – an old schoolboy habit, 'touching wood', for luck. He shut his eyes: *Please let me get to Malta.*

Double-think, he knew it: prayer or wish? He doubted whether either was likely to change the course of events. Destroyers opened fire, out to starboard in light that was turning milky. The scattering of gunfire thickened into a steady barrage. Torpedo-bombers were probably the target: there were no shellbursts in the colour-washed sky, so it was a low-level barrage which almost certainly meant torpedo-carrying aircraft. This in turn was likely to mean Italians.

Sirens were wailing for an emergency turn, and he guessed torpedoes might have been dropped. Waiting again, wondering what was happening, trying to put the clues together. He'd learnt one thing: that after you'd waited a while, things did happen . . . Like the whistle which he heard now above the sound of the guns to starboard. Gosling was in the bridge wing, pointing upwards, and Beale, watching the sky ahead and to port, shouted, 'Stukas, Art!'

The destroyers ahead – cruisers too now – were engaging them. Two formations, Paul saw, at about ten thousand feet. Or eight, or maybe seven . . . If they attacked from that direction they'd be diving with the setting sun right in their eyes. Gold and pink and violet, too pretty by half, and there was a watered-down reflection of it in the sky behind the Stukas. They were on the port bow as the convoy altered course. Withinshaw was muttering at them resentfully as he settled at his gun. Paul was glad, in one way, to be seeing them. His father and Jack had written and talked about the dreaded Ju87s in connection with the Crete evacuation last year, and now he'd experience them for himself. He didn't want too much of them, just enough so that when someone started shooting a line about Stukas next time he could cut in with his recollections of this convoy.

To have any, though, you had to stay alive. To get to Malta or see your father or write a letter you didn't know how to write, you had to get through this. The first Stukas were in their dives: there were three of them, with two more behind, in this group. Flipping over sideways, rolling over and shoving their noses down . . .

No screamers: they were supposed to have sirens on their wings, and these hadn't. Gone out of fashion, he guessed, thinking of how he'd put it in a letter to his father: *Stuka sirens are now old hat* . . . The noise was the racket of their engines and the surrounding roar of gunfire. Tracer added to the overhead colour, lacing and criss-crossing its brilliant streaks, garish against the subtler colouring of the sunset through a sky that was being spoilt and dirtied by the shellbursts. For seconds at a time bombers would be hidden in them, then reappear intact, still diving, coming . . . Beale had opened fire, now Withinshaw. Both guns snarling, shaking, jetting fire: and bombs away . . . It was exactly as it had been described to him and as he'd seen it in his mind, except for the absence of the siren-shriek that was intended to affect morale. A merchantman in the other column was firing some kind of rocket that soared vertically to meet the dive-bombers and then exploded, smoke and fragments bursting outwards. He saw there were several of these things in use, now. An anti-Stuka device he hadn't heard of before. From the merchantmen alone there must have been fifty or sixty Oerlikons and a couple of dozen Bofors in action, plus a lot of lighter weapons, and when you added all the warships' four-inch AA guns and close-range weapons to that you had a sky so full it was surprising the Stukas could get through it without being torn apart. Bombs were splashing in ahead and between the columns, and he saw another go in to port, beyond the AA cruiser's bow. The action was shifting back, though, nearer the tail-end of the convoy: the second rush of Stukas seemed to be going for the cruiser. Withinshaw's gun jammed, and Beale's was temporarily silent too as Short changed its magazine. It didn't matter, the barrage was slackening, the next batch of attackers still high. And now Beale had the new magazine on and the gun cocked, ready. Paul moved over to watch the fat man and McNaught clearing their snag. They were busy at it, and on the other side Beale was staring upwards, watching for Stukas, when gunfire flared suddenly to starboard and an aircraft came lurching over the other column at only about masthead height. It was a Savoia, one of the Italian torpedo planes. It passed over the tanker, the *Caracas Moon*, with its nose coming up as its pilot fought to gain height, and all the tracer was curving away astern of it – gunners taken by surprise, shooting *at* it instead of ahead of it. Withinshaw was screaming obscenities as he wrestled with his Oerlikon. The Savoia roared over ahead of the *Montgovern* and Beale was shooting behind it, but the AA cruiser's guns were ready and right on it, blasting it as it rose across her. More Stukas had started down by this time, and Beale had shifted target to them. But the Italian was in flames, and out of the side of his eye as he turned back to pay attention to the dive-bombers Paul saw it belly-flop, burning, into the sea. That one had clearly been the cruiser's bird. But Stukas were the threat again now, four or five of them coming down together, and again every gun – including Withinshaw's, at last – blazing up at them. One was pulling out high, and looked as if it had been hit, but the others came on in near-vertical dives, and like the last few they were going for the convoy's rear. But there were others suddenly – a pair he hadn't seen until this second, although Withinshaw had been on to them, aiming at the centre: they were greenish-khaki coloured and they carried the green-white-red Italian markings. He hadn't taken it in before, but all these Stukas were Italian. Pulling out, bombs on their way, black eggs tumbling slowly at first, then accelerating, and you didn't see them after that until they splashed in or hit. More Stukas were diving now behind that pair: others swarming over high . . . The diving bombers and the stammering guns merged into one enclosing, deafening and blinding blur of action: it was more mind-dulling than frightening, it swamped your consciousness, identity, sense of time. His own problem, he knew, was mostly *in*action, and he envied the two men at the Oerlikons. If you had a weapon in your hands the whole thing became much easier – your mind as well as your hands had that weapon to hang on to, to become a part of. The weapon became an anchor holding you to reality. The Oerlikons had ceased fire, though, McNaught and Short changing ammo drums while the gunners stood back and flexed their fingers and hands, loosening taut muscles.

There was a freighter on fire, Paul saw suddenly, at the rear of the other column.

Beale was telling the two younger men to take some of the empty magazines below and bring up full ones . . . But that ship had been hit, just a few hundred yards across the water, without him having seen it happen. He wouldn't have thought that was possible. It was the ship astern of the *Caracas Moon*, who was abeam of the *Montgovern*. Straining his eyes through the rapidly fading light he saw that her flag was the Stars and Stripes: and there was only one American in the convoy, so that was who she was, the *Santa Eulalia*. The fire was in her for'ard well deck, and a Hunt had ranged up alongside with a hose jetting water over it. With night coming on – it would be dark within minutes – and enemies of

614

various kinds lying in wait ahead, prospects for a ship with a fire to light her up wouldn't be too marvellous. They wouldn't be all that good for the other ships with her, either.

There was a new outbreak of firing ahead. High-angle gunnery from the cruisers leading the two columns and from the destroyers ahead of them. Shellbursts thickening up there: a fresh assault arriving, evidently, with the last of the evening light. A hand grasped his arm: Mick McCall asked, 'All right, are we?'

Paul said, 'That American isn't all right.'

'You're telling me. She's got ammo down for'ard . . . I was coming to spread the news that it's the intention to remain closed up at action stations.' He jerked a thumb upwards. 'Now we have more visitors anyway . . . See that Savoia getting chopped?'

'What's this lot, then?'

The new attack, Beale was asking about. He didn't want to talk about the Savoia, which had been an easy target that he'd missed. McCall told him, 'Stukas again. From the Sicily direction, and the carrier boys said there were Hun Stukas as well as Wop ones, so these'll be the other kind, most likely.'

Gunfire was closing in again as the enemies droned over, high. Paul asked McCall, 'Was that the only hit they scored?' On the American, he meant. McCall yelled, 'Destroyer. One of the fleets, astern.'

'Sunk?'

He'd nodded. 'A Hunt got some survivors.'

That was the engine note of diving Ju87s, now, lacing through the noise of the guns. Quite a different note was the commodore's signal for a turn back to port. All the heaviest firing was from astern. Then he saw the burning American open fire, and from the volume of it you'd have guessed she had a gun on every square foot of desk-space. All the merchantmen's guns opened up again as a single Stuka, its dive completed, came racketing over from astern, lifting through streams of tracer, straining towards the sanctuary of the surrounding dark. With luck there might still be some Sea Hurricanes waiting for stragglers out there. The ships were all under helm, coming round to port. Heavy firing astern and the intermittent snarl of diving bombers, the rising note and then the full-throated roar as they flattened out and sped away . . . Paul was out at the ship's side, at the starboard rail, from where he hoped that if any other Stukas came this way out of the action astern he'd get an early sight of them and warn the gunners. Back there in the tracer-streaked, flash-pocked near-darkness he saw a flash bigger than all the other flickering, a flare of yellow spearing into an orange-coloured fireball that spread and then snuffed out abruptly: it had lasted about three seconds. Then, from the general roar of action astern, there was one much heavier explosion.

McCall shouted, 'They're after the carriers!'

Paul had thought the second mate had left them. He went over to him. 'Did you mean we'll be at action stations all night?'

Perhaps he hadn't heard him. The fire on the American freighter was a bright glow that brightened as the darkness gathered, and the bridge superstructure of the fire-fighting Hunt was blackly silhouetted against it. Astern, gunfire faded and died away. As your ears came back to life, you could hear the pounding of the ship's engines and the swish and thump of the sea around her stem.

With Bizerta thirty miles to starboard, the convoy had altered course to enter the Skerki Channel. Ahead, destroyers streamed mine-sweeping gear, and astern the heavy escort of battleships and carriers had turned back westward.

There was a sense of total commitment at this point. In fact the convoy had been committed to its purpose from the moment it had left the Clyde, and more deeply so again when, passing through the Gibraltar Strait into the Mediterranean, it had been joined by its heavy naval escort. But now, with only three cruisers and a dozen destroyers remaining, it was actually pushing its head into the noose – the Sicilian Narrows, where there'd be U-boats and E-boats to contend with as well as German air bases on Sicily and Italian torpedo aircraft from Pantellaria.

For the moment, things were quiet, and Paul went aft to get something to eat. The guns were to be manned all night, but the DEMS men would have stand-off periods with their number twos – Short and McNaught, for instance – taking over. Paul, unconvinced of his own value to the community on the foc'sl-head, didn't think his absence was likely to upset anyone.

The atmosphere in the saloon was cheerful, laced with tension, awareness of the crucial stage they'd reached. There was satisfaction, too, in the fact that losses so far had been light. To have eleven ships still in convoy at this point was better than anyone had expected.

Brill, the doctor, offered, 'Beer?'

'I think a large Scotch might fit the occasion better.'

'Oh, you do, do you!'

'So would you, if you poked your nose out into the cold. It's freezing, up on that damn—'

The ship trembled to the deep *crump* of an explosion.

He thought first, *Mine*? Because with the sweeping gear out ahead you were conscious of the danger of them, now the convoy was in narrow waters. A second thought was that it might be the *Santa Eulalia*, her fire reaching the ammunition in her for'ard holds.

Matt Harrison, the *Montgovern*'s second engineer, began, 'Best get up top, boys, or—'

A second explosion was closer, much louder. Movement towards the door became a rush. Up till now most of them had been listening and wondering, waiting for an explanation and not keen to leave their food and drink. Paul was on his way up to the boat deck when the third bang went off. He and Brill and John Pratt, the third mate: they'd been the last out of the saloon. The ship was under helm. He'd thought about the *Santa Eulalia* because although it had looked from the outside as if her fire had been put out, it could still have been alive inside her; but at the second crash he'd thought, *Torpedoes* . . . And the third seemed to confirm it.

Then suddenly he was up on deck, in the open, and off to starboard the *Caracas Moon* was a sheet of flame. To port of the *Montgovern*, as she swung under helm to starboard, the AA cruiser – the old C-class ship who'd been ahead of them – lay stopped with her stern deep in the sea and her bow lifting as she flooded aft. Humphrey Straight was swinging his ship around her, handling the clumsy merchantman as she'd never been designed to be handled. The whole seascape was lit by the burning tanker. She was stopped, and the *Santa Eulalia* had had to put her engines astern to avoid running into her.

They'd passed the cruiser. There were ships all over the place, as helms were flung over to avoid collisions. And on the bow another cruiser – a big one, *Mauritius*-class – was circling to port with a heavy list.

It was incredible. Two cruisers – out of a total of three – and one tanker, the convoy's *only* tanker, full of the stuff Malta needed most . . . In one salvo of torpedoes? There'd been three freighters between those two cruisers. If it had been just one salvo, picking out those particular ships and thus denuding the convoy of its protection – protection against surface attacks, *Italian* cruisers, for instance – some German or Italian submarine captain had been extraordinarily lucky. And the *Caracas Moon* was in the other column – she *had* been, she wasn't in any column now, she was a mile astern and burning – so the fish that hit her must have passed through this port column, probably between the cruiser and the *Montgovern*.

Unless that one had come from the other side, a simultaneous attack by a different submarine . . . Brill was asking him what he thought had happened. He told him, 'We've taken a beating, that's what.' Torpedoes from E-boats? It didn't seem likely: and they'd have been seen, or at least picked up on the warships' RDF screens. There'd been no alarm, no gunfire, just three hits at fairly regular intervals. It *had* been one salvo . . . He saw McCall coming down the ladder from the bridge, and moved to intercept him.

'What was it?'

'U-boat, apparently. That's the flagship and the anti-aircraft cruiser gone. The only two fighter-direction ships we had!'

So when fighters from Malta had the convoy in range, they wouldn't be able to communicate with them?

The convoy was in a mess. Ships in all directions, and they were pointing in all directions too. Some had turned one way and some another, some had put on speed and some had slowed. They were strung out and widely separated, in single and small groups. Depth-charges went off somewhere astern. A destroyer passed at high speed, bow-wave and stern-wash foaming high, close under the *Montgovern*'s stern. It was a Tribal-class destroyer, big and two-funnelled, and it was heading towards the heavy cruiser – the flagship – which was still circling slowly around out on the quarter. You could see it all in the yellowish flickering light from the burning *Caracas Moon*. Another destroyer creaming up now – you saw the bow-wave first, then the ship, and this was one of the Hunts. Its captain's voice, magnified by a loud-hailer, boomed across the gap of dark water between that slim hull and this stout, lumbering one: 'Will you step on it a bit, *Montgovern*? Close up on the *Woollongong* please, captain?' An answering shout, unamplified but strident enough to carry, was Bongo Mackeson's: 'Where *is* the bloody *Woollongong*?' But the Hunt was already surging ahead again, heeling with her rudder hard a-port as she cracked on speed, heading to round up another member of the flock, herd the stragglers together. If the enemy had an attack ready to come in now, Paul thought, they'd make hay with us . . . He'd been intending to put on an extra sweater, and he hadn't done it. Nor, he realized as he went for'ard to his action station, had he had even a sniff of whisky. He'd have settled, now, for just one good sniff . . . It was colder. And Withinshaw was belly-aching, complaining that if the destroyer screen had been doing its job that U-boat wouldn't have had such an easy shot. Paul explained that there was no A/S screen on the convoy's beams now. There couldn't be, because destroyers as well as freighters had to be inside the strip of sea that had been swept for mines.

Withinshaw still griped. Beale snarled at him to shut his face. '*You've* come to no 'arm, 'ave you, you great fat—'

'No thanks to *them*, I 'aven't!'

Gunfire: it was on the port bow and ahead. Astern, there was much less flame visible from the *Caracas Moon*: enough, though, to silhouette the convoy for the benefit of any enemy attacking from ahead. Paul blew up his lifebelt, and suggested to the DEMS men that they should do the same. The firing was thickening. And a Hunt came up between the columns at high speed, making about thirty knots and heading for where the action was. The ship ahead of them now was presumably the *Woollongong*. The one astern didn't look like the *Empire Dance*, who'd been there earlier. Abeam of the *Montgovern* now was the *Kinloch Castle*, and ahead of her – he thought – was the *Neotsfield*, and that was the *Santa Eulalia* bringing up the rear of the starboard column. So what was left of the convoy seemed to have got itself fairly well together, after all. Most of the gunnery that was in progress ahead would be from the cruiser that had been leading the starboard column, and the minesweeping destroyers and two or three other escorts . . . Then suddenly they were *all* in it – all the ships, all the Oerlikons, pompoms, Bofors, rockets, Brens, the sky hung with skeins of tracer, flashing and flickering with shellbursts. The attackers were Junkers 88s in low-level, shallow dives. A stick went down across their next-ahead – *Woollongong*, if that was her. There was a bomb-splash close on her port side, then the crash and flash of a hit amidships and the usual, now-to-be-expected leap and spread of flames; and more splashes on her other side. The *Neotsfield* had fallen away to starboard, outwards from that other column, with smoke gushing from her and the *Woollongong*'s flames illuminating it. The *Montgovern* was hauling round to port to get past the *Woollongong*; and the *Woollongong* blew up, in a spurt of fire and an ear-splitting roar of detonating explosives, debris flying through the tracer-laced darkness while bombers dipped overhead and soared upwards out of havoc. The *Montgovern* was back on course, steaming through littered water into which the Australian freighter had disintegrated. There were torpedo-bombers coming in now, as the Junkers finished. They were approaching on the other bow, and Paul saw the wide, blurred shadow of the first one like a great evil bat lifting over the lead ship of the starboard column. He knew what it must be, immediately, because it obviously wasn't an 88, and logic did the rest. Tracer was hosing at its nose and then pompoms or Bofors or both were hitting. It was a Heinkel with its port wing on fire, the black crosses of Nazi Germany floodlit as it stalled, turned nose-down and dived into the sea between the columns of merchantmen in a great fountain of black water. But a second Heinkel was over the centre too, Beale's gun amongst fifty others flinging coloured beads of explosive to meet it. Its torpedo fell away, splashed in, and the big aircraft was lifting, in a hurry to get up and away now while gunners in a dozen different ships tried to make sure it didn't. Humphrey Straight's loud-mouthed Willet-Bruce let out one short blast, meaning he was shoving his helm a-starboard. Paul thought he'd be too late if that fish *was* on course for the *Montgovern*. The ship had barely begun to swing when it hit her, abaft the stem on the starboard side.

It felt as if she'd steamed full-tilt into a stone quayside. Sea that had flung up was raining down on them now. He'd been thrown across the foc's'l and grabbed the wire rails to stop himself going over the side. Only Beale and Withinshaw, clinging to their guns, had stayed on their feet. Beale was yelling at Withinshaw to watch out for new attackers, and to the other two to stand by with more ammo. Beale was a hell of a good hand, Paul thought. The *Montgovern*'s engines had stopped, and she was settling by the head. Looking down over the side he couldn't see much except that the water seemed closer to him than it had been before. A freighter was passing, almost close enough for him to have reached out and touched her, or to have jumped, cadged a lift to Malta. She'd been their next astern but now she was overhauling them and would close up – by two spaces, one for the *Montgovern* and one for the *Woollongong* – on the leaders. Paul remembered, as the ship rolled sluggishly in the other one's overtaking wash, that he'd wondered what it might feel like to be dropping out while others – *the ships that mattered now*, was how he'd thought of them – pushed on. Now, he'd find out.

CHAPTER 9

Gant came in and shut the cabin door. Nick told him, 'Come and sit down, Bob. Like some coffee?'

'Thank you, sir, but I just had some. That was a hell of a barrage again, wasn't it?'

They'd just been visited by Val dive-bombers. *Defiant* and *Sloan* had been the targets, but the Dutch AA gunners ashore had put up such a solid umbrella barrage over them that no bombs had come anywhere near.

Now it was 7.20, and Nick was eating breakfast. Making himself eat, although he wasn't hungry. Last night's grim events were in his mind – in Gant's face too, as the commander pulled back a chair and eased himself down into it, like a dummy being let down on a rope – on account of that back of his, which he swore had nothing wrong with it.

The repair work to the boiler room and bridge superstructure had been going on all night, and you could hear them banging around now in the ACP.

Gant said, 'Let's hope no news is good news, sir.'

News of the other ships, he meant: of *Exeter* and the two destroyers with her, and of the four Americans. Nick had been up and dressed since five o'clock, waiting for it. He knew he should have been resting, and he'd every intention of leaving all today's problems to Gant, but you couldn't just lie there and wait. Perhaps some men could have. Perhaps, he thought, he ought to have more self-control. But old dogs got to know what they could or couldn't do.

Jim Jordan of *Sloan* had accepted Nick's invitation for dinner yesterday evening, and Gant had joined them. They'd known that *Perth* and *Houston* had been due to sail from Batavia at 9 pm, and when the meal had ended, at about that time, Nick had proposed a toast to them, to their safe passage through the Sunda Strait to Tjilatjap.

'*Perth* and *Houston*.' Gant put down his empty glass. It was the last of the Laphroaigh. Jim Jordan said evenly, 'May God go with them.' He was a very direct, plain-spoken sort of man, and you could tell that for him it hadn't been any mere form of words or pseudo-pious hope, that he'd meant literally, 'God, please look after them.'

God hadn't heard. Or he'd had his hands full elsewhere. Soon after eleven o'clock a telegraphist on duty in *Defiant*'s W/T office picked up a signal from *Perth* to the Dutch admiral at Batavia. She and *Houston* had run into a Jap invasion fleet in Banten Bay, troop transports with a covering force of heavy cruisers and destroyers. After that, messages were sparse and brief, scraps of information sent in the heat of battle with increasing damage and ammunition running low. What it amounted to, when that distant radio had fallen silent, was that *Perth* and *Houston* had fought like tigers and gone down still fighting. *Perth* had sunk first – just after midnight – and *Houston* had followed her within half an hour. From some of the earlier messages it seemed likely they'd taken quite a few of the transports to the bottom with them; but not even a hundred Jap troopships could make up for the loss of those two cruisers.

In the case of the American destroyers who'd run for the Bali Strait, Nick thought, it *might* be a case of no news being good news. Because that strait wasn't far, and if they had *not* got through one would surely have heard something by now. But *Exeter* and *Encounter* and the USS *Pope* – well, some time today, probably this forenoon, they'd be trying to pass through Sunda, where HMS *Perth* and USS *Houston* had been overwhelmed last night.

Gant sighed. 'They could have better luck. The fact there was a Jap cruiser squadron there last night doesn't mean it'll still be there now.'

Nick thought he was talking nonsense. The troopships had been putting men ashore in Banten Bay, at the eastern entrance to Sunda. They wouldn't get themselves unloaded in ten minutes, and while they were there they'd have warships to protect them.

And it didn't have to be in the Sunda Strait that it happened, either. There could be an encounter anywhere. Since the invasion of Java had now started, the entire coastal region was likely to be infested with Japanese, and the air would be thick with them too . . . You could only wait, hope, guess; and there was no way of guessing how far the three ships might have got at this stage. *Exeter* had sailed with a known capability of sixteen knots, after repairs here to her damage, but her engineers had been hopeful of working her up to quite a bit more than that. She'd been hurt badly, but she was a very tough old bird. At the Battle of the Plate, in December 1939, she'd played the leading part in running the *Graf Spee* to earth, and in the process she'd stood up to an incredible amount of battle damage. With two turrets out of action from direct hits by the *Graf Spee*'s eleven-inch shells, with her bridge and control tower wrecked, no internal communications and no W/T or electric power, on fire below decks and several feet down by the bow and listing ten degrees to starboard, she'd stayed in the fight – with only one turret in action, finally, and with her captain using a boat's compass to steer by.

That was what he thought of when he thought of *Exeter*. That, and the fact that she was somewhere in the Java Sea now, with Japanese forces closing in from all directions and the only exit that twelve-mile-wide Sunda Strait . . . He'd eaten all he could. He put the plate aside, and reached for a cigarette.

'I want a third funnel, Bob.'

Gant looked at him oddly. Speculatively. The doubt, suspicion in that glance was irritating. Nick said tersely, 'We have two funnels, don't we? You said the for'ard one's under repair?'

Gant had coloured. 'We're patching the top of it, yes, sir.'

'Right. And now I want a *third* funnel. It'll have to go on number four gundeck.' He pointed: 'If you'd bring over that copy of *Jane's*, I'll show you what I want us to look like.'

The shipwrights had their hands full already, of course. Gant would probably remind him of it in a minute. But this wouldn't be an intricate or delicate job of work . . . Gant brought the book, *Jane's Fighting Ships*, and Nick opened it at the page where he'd left a marker, earlier this morning.

'There. You'd better let Raikes have a sight of this, so he'll know what he's doing.' Raikes was the chief shipwright. 'Timber and canvas, hinged so it can be hauled up into place when we want it. It'll need to be done after dark and without showing any light, so the rigging must be as simple as it can be.'

He'd been thinking about it, in between periods of dozing, during as much as had been left of the night. Dozing, and struggling to think instead of dream, most of the time ending up with a cross between the two . . . But adding a third funnel would change the ship's profile from that of a Dauntless-class cruiser to a fair likeness of one of the Japanese Natori class.

Last evening he'd gone through a period which, looking back on it, he could only have described as hellish. A waking nightmare . . .

When he'd finished yesterday afternoon's conference with Gant he'd gone back to his bunk, slept heavily, and woken with the doubt already in his mind – an instinctive feeling that things weren't going to work out. It was as if it had been in his mind all the time and he'd just seen it, recognized it. He'd sent Harkness to collect a chart and some instruments and reference books from Chevening. The navigator had brought them along himself, but he'd sent him away again because he'd needed to look into this alone.

That instinct had been right. Speeds, times and distances combined to confirm the unpleasant truth that *Defiant* was locked in.

Sandilands had agreed, under protest, that he'd provide engine revs for twenty-five knots. So that was the speed you could count on, and the first basic element in this calculation. (It would have been pointless to have demanded more than twenty-five knots, because even before the recent action damage their best speed had been twenty-seven.)

The second basic was that he couldn't take her out of Surabaya before dusk. If he tried to move her in daylight and she was spotted, they'd know which way she was going and they'd be in or near the Strait, waiting for her. In effect, this meant she couldn't get under way earlier than 9 pm.

Point three was that whichever of the straits you picked on, you'd need to have passed through it and got far enough south of it by first light to have some chance of not being found and attacked at sunrise. A ship caught on her own wouldn't have a hope of surviving, because the enemy had numerous aircraft and the Allies had none.

(Well, they did. They had two, based at Bandoeng and used for reconnaissance. He thought they were Beauforts.)

Now: you had to relate those three basic points to the distances from Surabaya to the various exits. The nearest was the Bali Strait, through which the Americans were hoping to pass: and those four destroyers would get to it by the short route through the Madura Channel, the eastern way out of Surabaya, south of Madura Island. This channel was impassable to *Defiant*, because she drew fifteen feet of water. At the top of the tide she might just about have made it, but the time of high tide would have to fit in with a dusk departure, and the tide tables showed clearly that in the next few days it would not. So *Defiant*'s only way east would be around the north side of Madura; and the distances involved were such that at twenty-five knots she'd be right in the Bali Strait, or still this side of the islands if he picked on the Lombok or Alas Straits, at sunrise.

Then ship and ship's company would live – what, half an hour?

Sloan, Jim Jordan's destroyer, drew only about ten feet of water, so she could use the Madura Channel. She'd be all right. For *Defiant*, it wasn't easy to see any way out at all.

When he'd checked the distances and times again, he sat back and thought about it. He was sweating, and he could feel his pulse and heartbeat racing. The wounds in his head, face and arm pulsed too. The fear wasn't personal, it was the nightmarish suspicion, rapidly hardening, that he wasn't going to be able to get his ship out of the Java Sea.

He took some long, slow breaths, to slow the pulse-rate, and told himself to be calm and rational. There *had* to be a solution.

Think about going west, as *Exeter* was about to do?

She'd be sailing as soon as it was dark, in about two and a half hours' time. It wasn't a good prospect, he thought – not even for *Exeter* now, and certainly not for *Defiant* later. As time went on and the enemy built up naval and air strength down here it became less likely with every passing hour that an Allied ship could survive in daylight north of Java.

He murmured aloud, '*However . . .*'

Jordan's philosophic acceptance gave no comfort now, though. And Jordan would be arriving on board soon. Nick wanted desperately to have some sort of answer to the problem before he found himself having to talk about it.

He was trying too hard, perhaps. Panicking. So relax, think it out logically and calmly . . .

Well, if you discarded the idea of using the longer, western route, the choice narrowed to one of the three eastern straits. It would have to be either the narrow Bali Strait, or the much wider one between Bali and Lombok, or the more distant, medium-sized one, the Alas Strait, between Lombok and Sumbawa. And whichever one you chose, *Defiant*'s track would have to be to the north of Madura.

Those were conclusions, facts, solid and unchangeable. You

could save yourself the trouble of looking for alternatives to them, because there weren't any. Another fact – the one that crushed you – was that *Defiant* would not be able to make the trip inside any period of darkness.

He shut his eyes. It could be, he thought, that his brain wasn't working properly, that there was some oversight in his calculations.

There *had* to be!

He tried again. Checking the route on the chart first, looking for short cuts. No short cuts . . . Until now he'd assumed that the run along the north coast of Madura to the Bali Gap was within his reach. He didn't know now *why* he'd made any such assumption. Trying to think back to any earlier state of mind was like thinking about another person, one whose mental processes he didn't understand and – worse – had no faith in.

There were five hundred men in this ship – nearly five hundred – all getting on with their jobs and relying, as they were entitled to do, on their captain's competence to direct their efforts sensibly, professionally, in ways that gave reasonable chances of survival. How would they feel if they knew he was sitting here sweating with fear, *seeing no way out*?

Perhaps Gant's doubts were well-founded, and he was unfit for the command now. If he couldn't find a way out of this trap, he *was* unfit for it.

Give up? Hand over to Gant?

His head hurt, and he felt sick.

Sunda, after all? A hundred to one against making it, but the only chance there was?

No. Sunda was a locked door now. Even if it wasn't yet – you had to allow yourself to hope that *Exeter, Encounter* and *Pope* would get through – it would be barred and bolted by this time tomorrow.

Lombok, then. Sail at dusk. No – a little before that. Let them see her heading west. Then turn north in the dark, and north-east, spend the following day out of sight of land and away from obvious routes, and hope to God not to run into anything or be spotted by aircraft. Then, the following evening when it got dark, turn southward, fast, through the Lombok Strait.

Well, what alternative was there?

He stared at the chart. It would be only about twice as risky as a game of Russian roulette. It depended entirely on the sheer luck of

626

remaining undetected throughout one whole day at sea. The odds were very heavily against any such thing being possible: but long-odds bets *had* been won, before this. And it would be less foolhardy than trying to get away through Sunda . . . Ask Jordan to take *Defiant*'s wounded with him in *Sloan*? And others too: cut down to a skeleton crew, enough men to steam her and man her guns and tubes, while the rest took passage in the destroyer?

Five minutes later, still concentrating on this possible way out, he'd heard *Sloan*'s captain being piped aboard. No alternative had occurred to him, and the chances of remaining invisible for a whole day in an area that would probably be carrying a lot of enemy traffic, seaborne and airborne, were so slim that it was going to be embarrassing to spell out the plan. Another consideration was that with several thousand miles to go, Jordan wouldn't want to be cluttered up with passengers. He might take the wounded, and perhaps Sibbold or an SBA to look after them . . .

Nick gave him a pink gin. A proper one, made with iced water, no lumps of ice in it to melt and turn it into dishwater.

'All set for tomorrow night, Jim?'

'Well.' Jordan rubbed his wide jaw. 'I guess we will be.'

'Bali Strait?'

The close-cropped, ginger head nodded. 'If our guys get through it tonight, that seems the obvious way to go.' He frowned. 'Only thing is—'

'I'd say you're right. Flat out through the Madura Channel, sharp right past Bali, and you're home for breakfast.'

'Almost.' The American smiled, briefly. 'But how about you, sir?'

'I can't get over those shallows, unfortunately.'

'That's what I thought. I've been trying to work out what you might do, and frankly I don't seem to get very far.'

'Well, let's deal with your intentions first. Incidentally, Bob Gant's joining us for dinner, and afterwards my navigating officer will be available if we want him. I thought we could have half an hour's private chat first, though.'

'Sure . . . It's a – er – peculiar drink, this.'

'Don't you like it?'

'Oh, I *like* it—'

'An acquired taste, I suppose. But the malt whisky comes later.'

'Did you see me wondering about that?'

They both laughed. Nick thanked him for having sent enquiries

627

about his state of health when he'd been lying unconscious in the sickbay. Then he came back to the subject.

'I take it you'll sail at sunset, via Madura to the Bali Strait, at – did someone say twenty-five knots?'

'Right.' Jordan flicked a light to his Chesterfield. 'Only thing is – well, okay, we have to get the hell out, first chance we have. I know it. I just wish I had another twenty-four hours.'

'What for?'

'So my ship could be near as good as new.' He blew smoke at the deckhead: the draught of the fan caught it, sent it swirling . . . 'Twenty-eight, maybe thirty knots I'd have. There's some engine spares we need, coming up from Tjilatjap by railroad, due here tomorrow afternoon. If I had the time to get some bits and pieces fitted – well, listen, sir. Twenty-five knots, the way I am now, if I sail at 2100 hours by sun-up I'm out of the Bali Strait, sure, but I'm only forty miles south of that airstrip. Okay, that's the best there is, I'll do it. But if I waited, had another five knots out of her, I'd be *seventy or eighty* miles south!'

'How did you happen to have spares at Tjilatjap?'

'Another Selfridge-class ship there. Or was, yesterday. She had 'em. We swapped a couple of signals, and I struck lucky.'

Nick was nodding at him, but he'd barely heard that explanation. An idea – the germ of the possibility of an idea – had just stirred into being.

'Excuse me, Jim. I want to take a quick look at the chart.'

He pushed himself up, one-handed. Jordan asked him, 'Are you all right, to be moving around this soon?'

'Better every minute, thanks.'

He was standing, looking down at the chart, with one eye shut to cut out the double vision. And, incredibly, hope stirring. It was Jordan's idea of taking an extra day that had triggered it. It wasn't totally different, in general principle, from his earlier idea, but it was a hell of a lot sounder. He was checking now, with the dividers – one-handed, of course. You only needed one, though, except in rough weather . . . If this was a valid, pursuable plan, he'd been blind and daft during the last half-hour. Double-checking, now . . . Then he dropped the brass dividers on the chart, and went back to his chair. He picked up his glass. He knew he couldn't possibly be showing the degree of relief that he was feeling.

Not that it was going to be easy – or anything approaching easy. He raised the glass. 'Bless you, Jim. You've saved my bacon.'

'I have?'

'And I think you'd do well to wait for those spares. After all, if the Dutch can put up barrages like we've seen today and yesterday, we don't have to worry much about air attack in here.'

'No, we don't. But – well, only thing is, if they start their invasion. Paratroops ashore here – maybe surface ships outside – we could find ourselves in a real jam.'

'If you want your extra day, taking that risk's the price of it.'

'I guess I'll take it. But how does it help you?'

'I don't think it necessarily makes much odds to me, Jim. But just to clear your side of it first – obviously your plans will depend on what we hear of your people in the Bali Strait tonight. If they get through – fine, no problem. But if it goes wrong – well, I suppose with thirty knots you might just make it via Lombok.'

'Maybe. Cutting margins so fine I'd get the shivers. But for now, I'm *assuming*—'

'Yes. Assuming the Bali Strait looks good, that's your choice. I believe mine is the Alas Strait.'

'But that's a hell of a long way!'

Nick nodded. 'From here, it is. But Surabaya won't be my starting-point. It can't be, can it?'

'I – don't quite follow—'

'You'd seen the snags for yourself, before you came over. I can't do more than twenty-five knots, I can't alter the distances or extend the hours of darkness. On the other hand I have *got* to get this ship out through one of those holes. The only variable factor, therefore, is where I start from.'

'You plan to hole-up some place?'

'Exactly.' He nodded towards the chart. 'In the Kangeans. Just off the cuff, I like the look of an island called Sepanjang. We'll check all that later, in the Sailing Directions, but it looks like deep water – give or take a few rocks ... But you see – I'll sail tomorrow, as intended, at sundown. I'll have the ship hidden – tucked away, anyhow – before daylight, somewhere among those islands. I *hope* the Japs won't be looking for us: and we'll be a damn sight less visible than we would be out at sea. Then we – and you – push off the night after. You from here at thirty knots, and me from the Kangeans at twenty-five. You go through Bali, I'll take Alas.'

'Might you not as easily make it to the Bali Strait, rendezvous there with me?'

629

'I don't think so. Which gap one chooses is a toss-up; but making a rendezvous that close to the enemy on Bali, one of us perhaps having to hang around and wait for the other – *and* I'd slow you down . . . No, that doesn't appeal to me much. Lombok I don't like, either. It's too obvious, the one they'd expect us to pick on. Don't you think?'

Jordan nodded. 'But your scheme may not be as easy as you make it sound. With respect—'

'I'm not suggesting it's going to be easy, Jim.'

'No . . . Would we rendezvous down south, after we both get through?'

'I'd like to, yes. We'll make for Perth, I should think. It's a long way, and two's company. It's not impossible that in the early stages there could be air attacks – remember Doorman had information about carrier groups moving to the other side of Java?' The American nodded. Nick suggested, 'We might work out some details after we've eaten. My navigator can do the work – it's what he's paid for. He isn't seeing double, either.'

'You are, sir?'

'It's only temporary. But the rendezvous – I'd imagine we'll naturally converge about two hundred miles south, some time around noon. Then we could afford to slow down a little – we'll need to conserve fuel.'

'It'll be a great moment, making that rendezvous.'

'Yes . . . But listen. I hope to God we'll have good news early tomorrow about your four Bali Strait ships. But if it is *not* good, then you'd better forget about the spares and sail with me tomorrow evening. Otherwise you'll be in the trap *I* could've been in.'

He was tired, now. But he was also excited. Nobody would ever know, and he himself would be glad to forget, the state of mind he'd been in only an hour earlier.

Gant was taking another look at the photograph of a Japanese Natori-class light cruiser. He'd been out and told the chief shipwright what was wanted; now he was back again, in Nick's day cabin. He said, 'It's quite startling, sir. Add that funnel and we'll look very much like this. Except for the seaplane catapult on her stern.'

The disguise wouldn't have to stand up to close inspection anyway. The main thing was that when *Defiant* sailed tonight he wanted any enemy, or enemy agent ashore, to think he was

630

steering west; and when he turned her the other way after dark it would help the illusion if she looked like a different ship. It could be useful later on, as well. The deeper the water, the more readily you clutched at straws.

'How are the repairs going, Bob?'

'The bridge is finished, sir. Some parts are planked – timber bolted to the steel beams – but otherwise it's near-enough normal. Telephones and voicepipes have all been refitted, and gunnery circuits will be fixed by this afternoon. By sailing time anyway. You agreed we wouldn't try to refit the wheelhouse.'

'Did I?'

Gant gave him that suspicious look again.

'Yesterday afternoon, sir. I proposed that we should make do with the lower steering position, with telephone communication. Because of certain practical difficulties, and priorities elsewhere, and you concurred.'

'I don't remember any such conversation.'

Gant said, after a pause, 'The only other defect we can't do anything about is the starboard searchlight.'

'We can manage without it.' He looked round, as Harkness knocked and entered. The PO steward said, 'Yeoman of signals, sir.'

'Come in, Morris.'

'Signal from *Exeter* to Bandoeng, sir. Enemy report.'

The news they'd dreaded. *Exeter*'s only hope had been *not* to run into any enemies.

He took the log from Morris, and read the top signal in the clip. It was a report of sighting enemy cruisers. He handed it across the table to Gant. There was nothing to do but wait for the rest of it, for what you knew would be happening in the next few hours. Facing a superior enemy force, *Exeter*'s only hope of survival would lie in avoiding action. But she was already crippled, so she couldn't make much of a run for it, and in any case the only way she could run was into the trap of the Sunda Strait.

He nodded. 'Thank you, yeoman.'

'It's good to see you so recovered, sir.' Morris was on his way to the door. Nick asked him, 'Have we got a Japanese ensign on board, Morris? Rising Sun thing?'

'Yessir, we have.'

'Look it out, would you, and keep it handy.'

He wondered whether *Exeter* could have adopted a plan such as

631

hc had in mind now for *Defiant*. But yesterday, the escape route westward hadn't looked so hopeless. And if the Japs hadn't picked Banten Bay as their landing-place, right on the entrance to Sunda, the other two might have got away. Hindsight changed viewpoints: twenty-four hours ago, if it had been his own responsibility, *he* might have sent *Exeter* westbound. And if *Defiant* had been seaworthy then, she'd have been there now, with *Exeter*.

'Bob, tell me – if I'd remained comatose, and you had the command, how would you be getting us out of this place?'

Last night, Gant had been thoroughly alarmed at the thought of trying to hide in the Kangeans. Even when Chevening had checked in the local Sailing Directions and confirmed that there'd be water enough behind Sepanjang, he'd still looked scared of it. Nick had asked him, 'Worried, are we?'

'I was only thinking, sir – it's less than eighty miles from Bali, there'll be aircraft about, and we don't know until we see the place how much cover there'll be or how—'

'Pilot.' Nick told Chevening, 'Read out that description of Sepanjang.'

Chevening found the place, in the *Indonesia Pilot Volume II*. He read aloud, '. . . second largest island of the Kepulauan Kangean . . . wooded, and approximately two hundred feet high near its middle . . . the north coast consisting of mangroves with deep creeks forming islands—'

'That's enough.' Nick looked at Gant. 'The north coast's our billet. Doesn't it sound tailor-made?'

'Yes, on the face of it . . .'

'Do you have any alternative suggestions?'

He'd been questioning himself as much as Gant. How could you tell whether your brain was functioning as it should: how could you trust it, when it was the brain itself that told you it was trustworthy? The only thing that mattered was that *Defiant* should get away. It didn't matter a damn who did the job. It was his own responsibility to do it if he was capable of it, but alternatively to see that it was done by someone else. By Gant, for instance. He thought that he, Nick Everard, was the best man to do it: but again, the belief came out of his own brain. He asked Gant, 'Well, Bob?'

'I hope I'd have come eventually to the same conclusion you've arrived at, sir. I'm not sure, though. I *might* have opted for the Sunda Strait – taking a gamble on the situation having changed by the time we got there.'

'You'd have been wrong, if you had.'

'I agree, sir. Before, it wasn't as plain.'

One aspect bothered Nick a little. In the Crete evacuation he'd solved a problem by capturing an island and holding it for a day. One long, hot, sleepy day. If his mind was cranky now, might a symptom be that it was throwing up an old answer to a new problem?

But in fact it *wasn't* the same answer. The Milos operation had involved a deliberate penetration into enemy territory, whereas in this case they were in potentially enemy territory already and trying to get out of it. The Kangeans would be a halfway house on the way out. The similarity was that Sepanjang and Milos were both islands. Beyond that, it was a superficially similar solution to an entirely different situation.

He had to be sure. Because his mind *had* been playing tricks. And several hundred lives and this ship, possibly Jordan's as well, depended on it functioning properly.

'Do you see any weakness? Something I haven't thought of and nobody's mentioned yet?'

'No, sir, I don't.'

'You realize that if I drop dead you'll have to see it through?'

Gant nodded. 'Yes.'

'So you're happy with it?'

'I was in the chartroom at six this morning, with Chevening, and we went over every possible alternative. There isn't one that stands a hope.'

He nodded. Thinking, *You can stop dithering, now* . . . 'While we're at it, Bob, there's another question I've been meaning to ask you. About the exchange of signals you had with *Perth* when she and *Houston* came back for you after the night action. When poor old Waller asked you what state we were in, why didn't you let him know I'd been knocked out?'

'It was more instinctive than logical, sir. I was trying to put myself in your place – well, naturally, in the circumstances – and I'd say the reasoning was that if I'd reported you were out of action, Captain Waller would most likely have felt obliged to keep us with him. It would have slowed them down a lot. Also, Surabaya being so much closer seemed to me the place you'd have chosen to make for.'

'Has it occurred to you that your decision may have saved all our lives?'

'No, it hasn't.'

'We'd have gone with them to Batavia. Then Sunda Strait. I don't think anyone stands a dog's chance through Sunda.'

Exeter . . .

He was anxious for news of the American destroyers too. It was about time one heard something. There'd have to be a deadline, some time this afternoon, for Jim Jordan's decision about which way he'd go. Nick lit a cigarette. 'Is Leading Seaman Williams still in sickbay?'

'Yes. Out of concussion, but he's immobilized by his leg wounds.'

'I'll go along and see him, presently. And the others. D'you have a list of them, and their injuries?'

Williams said, 'Can't keep a good man down, sir; isn't that what they say?'

Nick told him, 'You can if you shoot him in the legs.'

'I wasn't shot, sir. Splinters. Commander Sibbold's dug 'em all out.'

'Painful?'

'You wouldn't do it for a lark, like.'

'But you'll be on your feet again soon, now.'

Williams' vague expression showed the drift of his thoughts. Nick thought, *That's how I've been looking* . . . The killick asked, 'No answer to the signal you sent, I suppose, sir?'

He'd signalled Colombo, a week or ten days ago, asking the welfare people whether a Mrs Williams was among refugees arriving there.

'They'll be up to their eyes in refugees, you know. Not only from Singapore, either. It's bound to take some time, to—'

'Take a lifetime.'

'What?'

The close-together eyes were calm. 'I reckon she's dead, sir,'

Sibbold had changed the dressings on Nick's various injuries. Nick had also been talking to the other patients, and he was leaving now. Sibbold murmured, 'You should be resting, sir. Really, it's very *important* that—'

'All right, PMO, all right . . .'

Forbes, the chaplain, joined them. 'Is he bullying you, sir?'

'Doesn't like to see anyone getting out of his clutches. Probably a hangover from the days when his patients used to pay him.'

They both came outside with him. He asked them, 'Is Williams as gloomy as that all the time?'

'I don't believe he really *is* so gloomy, now,' Forbes said. 'He's convinced himself the girl's dead. What was torturing him was the possibility of her being alive in Japanese hands. He *wants* her to be dead.'

'In his shoes, padre, one might feel the same.'

The chaplain sighed. Sibbold stared at Nick. 'As I was saying, sir – about *you* – in all seriousness—'

'I know. I'll turn in soon.'

After, he thought, some news arrived about the Bali Strait destroyers. He didn't think he'd sleep until he knew what had happened to those Americans. He could shut his mind to *Exeter*. She was doomed. It was hideous and tragic but he knew that at this moment she'd be fighting her last action, and thinking about it wasn't going to make the slightest difference to the outcome. But he did need rest: for *this* ship's sake, which was what Sibbold, he guessed, had been talking about.

'Captain, sir.'

PO Morris, the yeoman of signals, saluted. A square, pale face with a short nose and a blunt chin. Pale blue eyes blinked once. He muttered, '*Exeter*, sir.'

Nick took the signal log from him. He'd come out from under the foc's'l break into the heat of the upper deck: the steel of the bridge superstructure was a hot grey wall on his right. The signal told him that four heavy cruisers and an unspecified number of destroyers were closing in on that fine old ship. It was now – he checked his wristwatch – just on ten, and this signal's time of origin was 0940.

She'd have been trying for the last two hours to get past them, and now they'd encircled her.

'Anything else?'

'No, sir.'

'I'll be in my cabin.'

Charles Rowley, the first lieutenant, was on number four gun-deck with CPO Raikes, the chief shipwright; they were deciding how they'd rig the stays for the dummy funnel. Nick climbed up to the gundeck and joined in the discussion. As the funnel would have its base this high up, it needed to be only twenty-six feet tall for its top to be level with the others. But it was still a bulky object to accommodate in the space available, and the best idea seemed to be to stow it slantwise across the ship between that six-inch gun and the pompom mounting just abaft it.

Rowley pointed out that in either the raised or stowed position it was going to obstruct the six-inch, and when it was raised it was also going to blank off the pompoms from firing on any for'ard bearing. In addition, it seemed the wire stays supporting it would be in the way of both guns.

'It can't be helped.' Nick explained, 'The object will be to avoid action. If we have to open fire, the camouflage becomes pointless anyway.'

Raikes suggested, 'So we want to be able to ditch it good and quick, if we're going into action?'

'Yes. The gun's crew could handle it.'

The last thing he wanted was a fight. One shot, and all hopes of escape would vanish. He wanted to be silent and invisible. If he was seen at all he wanted to be taken for a Jap.

In his imagination he could hear the thunder of big guns from five hundred miles away, the other end of Java and the Sunda Strait . . .

Chevening stopped him as he went on aft.

'Have a word, sir?'

He'd been working out details for tonight and the night after and for the long run south to Australia after that. Nick had told him to have some notes of it on paper, a copy for Jim Jordan. Whichever way the Bali Strait cat jumped, Jordan would be coming aboard later for a final conference. Chevening had a rolled chart under his arm, and some queries and suggestions. They went into the cuddy – past the late AB Gladwill's noisy canaries and through to the dining cabin, where the table had room for chart display.

Chevening murmured when they'd finished, 'I'm afraid *Exeter*'s chances aren't good, sir.'

'They're non-existent.'

Chevening had improved, Nick thought. To start with he'd seemed a bit of a stuffed shirt. He asked him, 'You've no ill effects, pilot, from that smash-up?'

'None except I'm a bit deaf, sir.'

'Have you reported it to the PMO?'

'I think it'll just wear off, sir.'

'Go and see him. Tell him I sent you. But first get that signal off to *Sloan*.'

The signal was to check that the American destroyer had enough fuel for two thousand miles. It wasn't quite that mileage to Perth, but they wouldn't be taking an entirely direct route. Also, the first part of the trip would have to be made at maximum speed, which consumed oil faster. Nick wanted to start by putting as great a distance as possible between themselves and the Japanese, and it would mean steering due south and later making a dog-leg south-westward to get round North West Cape. If Jordan's ship didn't have the range to reach Perth, an alternative might be to make for Port Hedland, at about half the distance.

Perth was the obvious place, though. It was the nearest major port. The fact that Kate lived not very far from it was coincidental. 'Not very far' meant, in any case, not far by Australian standards, and it was more than likely that even from Perth – if he got to Perth – she'd be as far out of his reach as she would have been on the moon. Besides which, when one thought about Kate Farquharson, Fiona's image intruded . . . He told himself, pausing at a scuttle and looking across flat water at the heat-hazy shoreline, that it wasn't really a very urgent problem. Very soon the soldiers on that waterfront and in those buildings would be Japanese. In two days? Three?

He sat back in an armchair, and shut his eyes. The plan was set: he was sure of it, in the sense that there was no other way to get out. If he'd had to quote odds on it, he'd have put its chances at about evens. There were quite a few imponderables, and it was going to depend on luck – at least, on an absence of bad luck – at all stages. Which was a lot to ask for.

He dozed, waking occasionally to the familiar noises of the ship's routine. There were waking thoughts as well as snatches of dreams. One dream – it came back to him now with the shock of something horrible that he'd forgotten about and suddenly recalled – was that Paul was out there in *Exeter*. He shook it out of his mind, thankful that it had turned out not to be real. There was something he had to do, that he'd thought of earlier . . .

'Captain, sir?'

He focused on PO Harkness. Harkness told him, 'Made you some more coffee, sir. Petty Officer Morris says there's a signal you'd want to see.'

'Send him in.' He remembered what it was he'd been thinking about in that half-sleep: 'Harkness – pass the word to the captain of marines that I'd like a word with him, will you? And let's have another cup here for him.'

Morris had two signals to show him. The first was an answer from *Sloan* to his question about fuel for the long haul south. Jordan had replied, 'Your 10.31, affirmative.' The other was from *Exeter* to Admiral Helfrich at Bandoeng. She was stopped and on fire and taking repeated hits. Time of origin 11.20.

Haskins clicked his heels. 'Wanted to see me, sir?'

'Yes. Come in, soldier. Sit down, and don't let's be too bloody military.'

The marine grinned. 'Sorry, sir.'

'Help yourself to coffee. Is your landing organization all geared-up?'

'Top line, sir. Do you mean – d'you want us to stay behind?'

Nick looked at him. He shook his head. 'No. Even if any such thing had been suggested . . . No. The object is to get out of here, *save* our skins, not throw more of them away.'

He thought of *Exeter*, and of *Perth, Houston, Electra, Jupiter, Encounter* and *Pope*; and of *de Ruyter, Java* and that Dutch destroyer, *Kortenaar* . . . All gone, in the space of a couple of days. He was appalled at the waste, the pointlessness, the sheer stupidity . . . What he had to think about now was how not to add to the list. He told Haskins, 'As you know, we'll be sailing at dusk. But before daylight we'll be tucking ourselves into cover behind an island called Sepanjang, which is in a small group called the Kangeans about seventy-five miles north of the Lombok Strait.'

He described the plan to him, and the reasons for it.

'We'll be there from before dawn until it's dark enough to move. If you ask Chevening, he'll show you a description of the island's topography, in the Pilot. It mentions that there are two villages on Sepanjang, and local trade between it and the larger island, Kangean itself. We'll be on the north coast, up some creek – I mean literally, for once, and let's hope not figuratively as well. Mangroves and so on. The south coast has a sandy beach and that may be where the inhabitants keep their praus. Anyway, read what it says, and study it on the chart. I'd advise you to make notes, and a tracing of the island – the ship's office could run off copies for your NCOs.'

Haskins nodded. Nick went on, 'The object of putting you ashore will be to maintain security in the vicinity of the ship, and prevent any of the locals leaving the island while we're there.

So word doesn't get to the Japs. Remind me now – how many men have you got?'

'Colour Sergeant Bruce, two sergeants, four corporals, forty-one marines, sir. And me, making total strength forty-nine.'

'Organized how, for landing?'

'Five sections of eight men each, plus Platoon HQ. Sections one, two and three form a rifle group, four and five are the Bren group. Platoon HQ includes a two-inch mortar section and one PIAT.'

'What the hell's that?'

'Projector infantry anti tank, sir.'

'I think we can assume there won't be any tanks on Sepanjang.'

'Quite. We could leave the mortar on board too, I should think . . . The marines carry P.14 rifles, and section leaders have Lanchester sub machine guns.'

He thought about it . . .

'I should imagine that to police the shoreline near the ship, plus both villages and whatever beaches they keep their praus on, you'll need every man you've got. I want a lookout post established on high ground, too, but we'll use sailors for that . . . All these weapons of yours – obviously you must be armed, but let's not make a show of it. If the natives are friendly, or even just not obviously hostile, let's keep it like that. No rough stuff, women strictly taboo, and arak is not to be so much as sipped even if it's forced on thcm. See your men understand it.'

The marine said grimly, 'They'll understand it, sir.'

'They must also understand it isn't any kind of picnic. It's a very tricky operation and we'll be lucky to get away with it. One shot at the wrong moment could ditch us all. Make sure they don't load a single gun unless they're about to be attacked. Even then, I'd sooner there wasn't any noise. They're not to be seen, either – there are bound to be Jap aircraft passing over. Everyone keeps under cover and dead quiet all the time. Any sign of the enemy landing, you fall back on the perimeter around the ship. We'll discuss that contingency after we see the lie of the land, though . . . What else?'

'Rations and water for one day, I suppose?'

'Yes. And medical equipment? Snake-bite, etcetera?'

'Goes with Platoon HQ, sir. If we had an RM band, it'd be their pigeon.'

'Why don't we?'

'Very few of these small cruisers do have, sir.'

Defiant's band was a volunteer group of bluejackets. They were pretty sound on the National Anthem and on *Hearts of Oak*, but they were capable of some fairly extraordinary sounds when they strayed from that beaten track.

Nick said, 'Mosquitoes are likely to be a problem. Make sure every man has his tin of the smelly stuff . . . And I think that's about all the direction I can give you. Do your homework, brief your troops and have the gear ready . . . Did you say P.14 rifles?'

Haskins nodded.

'They had them in '14–'18!'

The marine said, 'We're lucky they don't give us pikes.'

At 11.40, *Exeter* had sunk. *Encounter* followed her a few minutes later. The report came from the American destroyer *Pope*, who at the time of her last message had been under attack by dive-bombers.

It was 12.30. A midday air-raid which had started just as the ship's company were being piped to dinner had again been driven off by the Dutch shore gunners. Work on the dummy funnel hadn't stopped, and it was still in progress now although the ship's company were at lunch. Nick had a look at it on his way for'ard: despite the promise to Sibbold that he'd turn in, he knew he wouldn't have been able to sleep. In any case, he'd have his own lunch before long. He went in through the screen door under the foc'sl, and up the ladderways to the reconstructed bridge.

He even had a reconstructed bridge seat, he saw. A solid timber job rather like the one he'd had in *Tuareg*. Up here, where so short a time ago men had died and he'd lain unconscious in his own blood, the work was finished. In fact there were improvements: his own telephone to the director tower had been sited in easier reach from the chair than it had been before, for instance. He went into the chartroom: chart 1653c was spread out on the table, with a track drawn in on it and notations of times and courses; Chevening's navigator's notebook lay open on it, with neat lists of data such as shore bearings at the turning points.

'There you are, sir!'

He looked round. 'Hello, Bob.'

'Been scouring the ship for you, sir. An SDO messenger went down to your cabin and reported you missing. And Harkness didn't know where—'

'I think you'd better stop regarding me as some kind of helpless idiot, Bob. I'm back to normal. Apart from this arm, which is a minor inconvenience—'

'You'll feel better still when you hear the news, sir. About the Yanks who were trying the Bali Strait?'

'Well?'

'Bandoeng sent out a Beaufort reconnaissance flight. It's back on the ground now. At 10.30 it found all four destroyers well clear to the south and on course for North West Cape at thirty knots.'

'Ah.' He nodded, restraining the urge to cheer. 'That was news worth waiting for.'

Sloan would be all right. Even if Jordan's engine spares didn't arrive – the railways were being bombed, and you couldn't count on it – his prospects for a fast exit via the Bali Strait were a lot better than the obstacle race *Defiant* had ahead of her. Nick wondered again about transferring his wounded to the American.

CHAPTER 10

The *Montgovern* was alone, down by the bows, making eight knots southward through a milky dawn. Her pumps had been slowly losing their battle against the inflow of sea, and she had ten feet of water in number one hold now. If her engines had been stopped it would have eased the pressure on cracked frames and leaking bulkheads. But you couldn't stop – the destination was still Malta, and a stopped ship would get sunk anyway.

The light was growing. It was only in the last few minutes that Paul had realized the heavy dampness they'd been steaming through was a sea-mist. When it lifted, she'd be exposed – to her obvious enemies, and also to the Vichy French in Tunisia, who might object to an intruder in their territorial waters.

The wind was down. There was a low swell, and the sea was loud, thumping and swishing around the damaged bow, banging in the cavity where the torpedo had hit. She sounded, right up there in the bow, like an old sow guzzling with her snout down in the trough.

The Vichy coast, he guessed, would be only a mile or two to starboard. He wondered if they had a hope in hell of reaching Malta. Or whether they'd just keep going as long as possible and then turn and run for the beach. If they ended up ashore here, the French would intern them all. A Vichy prison camp would be a truly rotten place to spend the rest of the war.

Well, you'd be able to catch up on some sleep.

He decided to go and find out, or try to find out, what was going on. It had been hours since Mick McCall's last visit, and even longer since the last flare-up of action. All through the first part of the night there'd been explosions, leaps of flame, outbreaks of gunfire and the rumble of distant battle. One ship, so heavily on fire that she'd been unrecognizable, had crossed about a mile astern of the *Montgovern*, heading for the coast and incapable of answering signals. And in the early hours of the morning a Hunt-class destroyer had appeared, exchanged shouts with Mackeson and then sheered away again into the dark, towards the running fight to the north of them. They'd stood to the guns when she'd first appeared – a small, menacing bow-on shape that could have been an E-boat, at that distance – and several other times when they'd heard the throb of engines, E-boat or aircraft.

On his last visit McCall had told them that one of the merchantmen sunk during the night attacks had been the *Blackadder*, the commodore's ship.

Beale was a dark mound recognizable as human only because you happened to know there was life inside it. Paul went over and told him he was going aft for a few minutes.

The mound grunted. Withinshaw mumbled, ''Ave one for me too.' Withinshaw was a mound with a shine on it, because he was wearing an oilskin over his other gear. Like a great seal, slumped against the ammo bin. Wally Short was horizontal under a piece of old tarpaulin hatch-cover, and McNaught was stamping about and slapping his arms against his sides, whistling between his teeth.

In the saloon Paul found Brill asleep, and Woods, the Army gunner, gulping coffee. He poured some for himself, and Woods gave him a cigarette: he'd only come down here for a moment, he explained, to thaw out.

'Are you lot paddling, up front?'

'We'll be swimming before long, I dare say.'

'Well, I don't know.' Woods yawned. 'We're still afloat and moving. If we hadn't been knocked out of the convoy we might have been cinders, by now. Real firework show, wasn't it?'

His hands were shaking, Paul noticed. Or perhaps he was only cold, still shivering.

Thornton stirred, and sat up. The cipher expert had been flaked out on the sofa. He stared at Paul as if he was wondering who he was, or about to challenge his presence here. Then he flopped down again and shut his eyes. Paul yawned, and told Woods, 'When I've drunk this I'm going up to see if Bongo's feeling sociable.'

'And I'm going back to my useless gun.'

'Useless?'

'Low-angle, so it's no good against bombers. And it's on the stern, so E-boats or what-have-you had better not attack from ahead . . . But I'm looking after a Bofors and some Oerlikons as well, so it's not a total waste of time, I suppose.'

The door opened, and the RAF man blundered in, the grey-haired flying officer. He was too old-looking for the rank, Paul thought, and now he was grey-faced as well as grey-headed. He stared at the coffee urn, then shook his head and turned away. He muttered, 'What a way to earn a living . . .'

'Seasick?'

'What do you think?'

Paul suggested, 'Try tightening your belt, and lying flat.'

'Can't lie flat, I'm on look-out. Does a tight belt help?'

He nodded. 'And don't drink any liquid.'

'Why don't they tell one these things?'

'Perhaps you didn't ask.' He put down his cup still half-full. He thought he really shouldn't have left the foc's'l. He told Woods, 'I'm off. Good luck.'

'I'd better go too,' Woods muttered as they left together. 'Sort of spooky, isn't it. Alone, and this fog . . .' He went aft, and Paul went for'ard and up to the boat deck, unaware that he and the Army man had had their last off-duty conversation. He was right, it *was* spooky. It was like being in a ghost-ship, dead men lost to the outside world. It was the fog, the enclosed, *hidden* feeling it gave you, and the lack of sleep, and the surrounding threat . . . Daylight was noticeably stronger as he made his way up to the bridge, but it was a woolly sort of light, a cocoon of it that hemmed the ship in on her patch of grey, heaving sea. Her motion was peculiar, like the lurching of a man with a heavy limp: the result of the water inside her forepart, of course, but you noticed it more up here because of the swaying of the superstructure.

Mackeson was in the front of the enclosed bridge, and Pete Devenish was in charge of the watch. No sign of the master. Devenish asked without turning his head, 'Who's that?'

'Everard, sir.'

Mackeson looked round, lowering binoculars. 'Problem?'

'The gunners are wondering what the future holds, sir. Thought I'd try to find out. I'm sorry, I suppose I shouldn't—'

'I'm no soothsayer, Everard. Anyway, no, you shouldn't. We've got twenty lookouts posted around this ship, and you're one of them.'

'Sorry, sir, I'll—'

'Need every pair of eyes we've got, in this muck. But since your father's a *very* old friend of mine, we'll overlook it this time. Eh, Pete?'

Devenish muttered, with binoculars at his eyes, 'Please yourself.'

There were lookouts in both wings, Paul saw. Gosling was one of them. There'd been others on the boat deck, he'd noticed on his way up, and of course McCall would be up in his Bofors nest. The fog was like cobweb all around the ship and the shine on the sea's humpy surface was visible through it over a radius of perhaps two or three hundred yards. Mackeson murmured, 'Wonder where he is now? If he's in the Java area, he won't be shivering like we are. And it'll be something like early afternoon, out there . . . Well, look here.' Thinking about Paul's father seemed to have made his mind up for him. 'I'll tell you what's happening, then you can go into the chartroom and take a look, and after that you can make yourself useful by going round the ship and giving them all the gist of it. All right?'

He nodded. 'Sir.'

'We're about two and a half miles off the Tunisian coast, off a place called Kurbah, which means we're inside the Kurbah Bank. Our course is two hundred and twelve degrees, and in another ten miles – just over an hour – we'll be off Ras Mohmur. That's the point at the top of the Gulf of Hammamet, and it's near the port of Hammamet, which is a Vichy French base inside the curve of the Gulf. Are you with me so far?'

He was using his binoculars all the time he was talking. He didn't move his lips much when he spoke, and you had to listen carefully to hear what he was saying.

'At that point we'll turn to port a bit and steer due south, straight across the entrance to the Gulf, for another ten miles. We're taking this inshore route for two reasons: one, to avoid the Pantellaria-based E-boats and torpedo-bombers who made hay with the convoy last night, and two, because the French have a swept channel here inside the minefields, and we hope we're in it.'

'Did the convoy lose much, sir?'

Mackeson hesitated. Then he murmured, 'Going by the signals we've seen, and what the captain of the Hunt told us – well, there may be three survivors on course for Malta.'

'Three . . .'

'That seemed to be the state of things a few hours ago. But there are also some other stragglers, like ourselves. The Hunt's trying to round us up and get us together. But information's scanty, at the moment, and obviously nobody's using his wireless much.' He took his glasses away from his eyes, blinked, put them back again.

He started a slow sweep down the starboard side. 'Now. Halfway across the Gulf of Hammamet, in about two and a half hours' time, we intend altering course to the east – actually to one hundred degrees – for the straight run to Malta. It'll take us just to the north of Linosa – that bit'll be after dark – and we'll be taking our chances as far as minefields are concerned. We'll be close to Lampedusa, too. At our present speed of about eight knots – well, call it twenty-four hours. If nothing gets any worse, we ought to stay afloat that long. Barring further enemy action, of course. So, all those things being equal, ETA Valletta some time after dawn tomorrow.'

'But that's marvellous!'

'It's also highly improbable, Everard. It's what we're aiming at, that's all. I did say, "barring further enemy action". You can't bar it, can you? We're in an extremely vulnerable state – you can see that for yourself. Once this fog goes – well . . .'

'It might not, sir?'

'Then we'd be *bloody* lucky!'

'You think it's going to lift, then?'

'My dear boy, I'm not God!'

'Steady there.' Humphrey Straight pushed up past Paul. 'Royal Navy officer admitting he ain't God?' Devenish laughed. Straight growled, 'Better watch it, Commander. They'll 'ave you for bloody sacrilege. Hey, what's—'

'Ship, green eight-oh!'

The signalman was shouting from the starboard wing, outside. Mackeson rushed out there. Straight slid a side window open and raised his glasses, cursing at Paul to get out of the way. Paul went out into the wing behind Mackeson.

Narrow, bow-on, trawler-like. A little upright ship with a small gun on its foc'sl, like a harpoon gun on a whaler. It had come from the direction of the land – from the bow, in fact, which suggested it might have come from Hammamet – and now a light was flashing from its bridge. In English, slowly spelt-out morse. He read it: 'What ship are you?'

From the bridge window Straight bellowed, 'Tell the little bugger we're Noah's Ark!'

Mackeson told the signalman, 'Make to him, "Please identify yourself."' He called to Straight, 'Better turn away, captain. We're half a mile inside his territorial waters. I'll try to stall him while we do a bunk.'

The signalman had passed that message, and the Frenchman was flashing again as the *Montgovern* began her slow and cumbrous turn to port. Paul read, 'You are in the territorial water of France. Stop your engines or I fire.'

Mackeson said, 'Make to him – slowly – "I am in international waters and I have a destroyer escort within call. Keep clear of me.'

He added, as the signalman began calling at about half his normal speed, 'In other words, piss off *s'il vous plait*.' He looked round. 'Everard, nip aft, tell the pongo to stand by with the four-inch and man his telephone.'

'Aye aye, sir!' He flew – down to the boat deck, down the length of it and down again at its after end to the well deck, across that – skirting the crated deck cargo – and up another ladder to the poop. 'Captain Woods?'

'Yup?'

'Commander Mackeson says close up the four-inch and man the telephone!'

'We *are* closed up. Try the phone, Reynolds.' He told Paul, 'We're loaded too. What's it about, anyway?'

'Vichy patrol. Told us to stop engines or it'd fire.'

Woods laughed. The soldier at the telephone shouted, 'Stand by to fire one shot under his bows, sir!'

'Set range two hundred yards, sergeant.'

'Range two hundred set, sir!'

'Report ready!'

'Ready!' Then: 'Fire!'

The gun roared, and recoiled. The breech thudded open and the empty shell-case was a yellowish streak that flew out, clanging on the steel gundeck. Another shell had gone in, the breech was shut and number two had slammed the intercepter shut.

'Ready!'

The splash of the shot they'd fired went up about twenty yards short of the Frenchman's stem. And the little ship was already slewing away to port. The soldier at the telephone barked, 'Cease fire!'

Woods muttered, 'Spoilsport.' The *Montgovern* was under helm again, coming back to her course down-coast.

Soon afterwards course was altered again, to one hundred degrees. Visibility was still low, but patchy; sometimes you could see half a mile. Attack was expected – awaited, even *wanted*, almost. To end the waiting, which was mind-wearing, exhausting

. . . It was odds-on that the Frenchman would have reported their position. Most of the Vichy people were said to be pro-German, but on top of that the patrol boat's captain had been made to look silly, which had never been the way to warm the cockles of a Frenchman's heart.

On the other hand, the French had only seen the *Montgovern* forging on southward across the Gulf. They hadn't seen the subsequent turn to port, so the enemy couldn't know where she was now. With the surviving ships of the convoy fifty miles closer to them – closer to Malta, too – and with this bad visibility as well, the Luftwaffe might not be inclined to waste time searching for stragglers.

Not that this meant the *Montgovern* could have any real chance of getting to Malta, Paul thought. Mackeson had been talking sense. A ship alone, making only a few knots, already sinking and with the best part of two hundred miles of enemy-infested sea to cover . . . You'd back a donkey to win the Derby, he thought, if you'd back those chances.

Withinshaw said, 'Once fog lifts, we've fookin' 'ad it.'

Nobody argued with him, because that was also true. The *Montgovern* was carrying out a clumsy zigzag, altering about twenty degrees each side of the mean course to make submarine attack less easy. It reduced the speed of advance, of course: but what tidal stream there was here – according to McCall – was running in their favour. McCall reckoned they'd be making-good about seven and a half knots; so ETA Malta, given some sort of magic wand to keep enemies away, could still be tomorrow forenoon.

Like an owl and a pussycat went to sea in a beautiful pea-green boat. Malta tomorrow forenoon was about *that* believable. He began to sing about the owl and the pussycat, and Beale was looking round at him as if he couldn't stand it, when they heard an aircraft engine. The droning German kind, the note with the throb in it. Paul, startled, shouted 'Stand by!'

He'd yelled it without thinking; it hadn't been at all necessary. Being tired made one stupid, and jumpy. Withinshaw had thrown him a look of mock alarm, and Beale, hunched at his gun, looked round and grinned sardonically. The sound of the plane was drawing ahead. He thought it had flown up the starboard side, and it was moving from right to left now as it crossed ahead. Then it was in sight – ahead – a big float plane, a Dornier, he thought. It could see them too, of course. Withinshaw opened fire, aiming out over the port bow with about fifteen degrees of elevation on the gun. The ship was under helm, swinging to a new leg of the zigzag, and the Dornier was already on the beam. The midships Bofors, McCall's gun, began firing at it. You saw it sporadically, flying in and out of fog patches. Then it was out of sight, and Withinshaw's gun fell silent.

Beale muttered. 'Recce plane.' The Bofors amidships and aft were still firing. Paul went to the starboard rail to look back, expecting it to appear on that other quarter, but it didn't and the after guns ceased fire now, having lost it in the fog astern.

Beale muttered, 'Know where to find us now, don't they?'

An hour later, the Ju88s came.

All hands had breakfasted. Devenish had set up a cafeteria system, so each man collected his own food from the galley and ate it at his action station. Short was the last of the foc's'l-head gang to return with his mug of tea and mutton sandwiches, and he informed them that the depth of water in number one hold was now more than eleven feet. Harry Willis, fourth mate, was the ship's officer responsible for that hold, and he'd just been along with the bosun to take soundings. They'd been in the food queue at the galley, and the bosun had said the leaking into number two was getting worse.

Everyone looked gloomy as well as tired. Paul said, echoing Woods' earlier remark, 'But we're still afloat and still moving. If we'd been with the convoy last night—'

'Ah.' Beale nodded. 'Reckon they took a clobberin', all right.'

Paul hadn't told them about there being only three ships left in the convoy. When you remembered that at sunset last night there'd been eleven . . .

McNaught grumbled. 'There's nae sugar in this fuckin' tea.'

'Sugar?' Withinshaw looked round at him. 'You're lucky there's *tea* in it, y' Scotch twit!'

He glanced at Paul, winking, inviting him to share in the joke, but Gosling's whistle shrilled from the bridge wing. They were at the guns in a rush of movement and a Ju88 from wavetop level was lifting over them in a scream of engine-noise, bombs tumbling from its racks as it swooped across the ship and banked away to the right with the mist already folding round it. One bomb struck somewhere aft, and the others went into the sea to starboard, the first one very close and the other two farther out. The guns on the ship's stern had got off a few rounds but these Oerlikons hadn't fired until the attack had been over and that first bomb had burst on her. Now a second Junkers, again from sea-level and the direction of the Tunisian coast, was roaring over with all the guns at it this time, tracer pastel-shaded in the fog and one of the bomber's engines smoking: flames too, that engine and the wing on fire, black smoke trailing, rising in the machine's own upward-curving path. Beale's and Withinshaw's guns were blazing at its tail as it tilted away to starboard: its bombs had gone into the sea. The *Montgovern* was slowing: her engines had stopped, and smoke was pouring up astern – from the area of the boat deck, he thought. That second bomber had gone into the sea nose-down and then toppled over on to its back, spray raining down in a white circle around it. Everything seemed quiet, suddenly; the regular thud-thudding of the engines had stopped, and although you hadn't noticed it before you missed it now. You were left with the noise of the sea against the ship's hull, the sound of flames as the fire took hold amidships, and the fading engine-throb of the Junkers that had done the damage.

Mick McCall was dead. Splinters or blast from that bomb had wiped out the crew of the midships Bofors, and he'd been with them at the time.

Fighting the fire would be easier now the engineers had got the ship under way again. It had been the near-miss, the second bomb in the stick, that had stopped her. She was making about six knots now. The fire would be more easily controllable, and a lot less dangerous, because the wind from ahead would hold it back. Until they'd got her moving it had been touch-and-go whether they'd manage to keep the flames from spreading into the bridge deck where the cased aviation spirit was stowed. Devenish was in charge of the fire-fighting.

Astern, smoke rose to a height of a couple of hundred feet, hung there like a marker telling the enemy where they'd find an easy target. Obviously they *were* looking for stragglers, or those two Junkers 88s wouldn't have been hunting fifty miles away from the convoy's track.

Fog hung around in patches, but visibility averaged about two miles.

The boats amidships, those near the for'ard end of the boat deck, had been turned out on their davits. Not because anyone was thinking of abandoning ship – yet – but to get them clear of the fire. Devenish had men hosing them down, so their timber wouldn't catch from sparks. Paul had seen it when he'd been back to the bridge to offer his services as a fire-fighter, but he'd been told to stay on the foc's'l-head: Mackeson had warned, 'That won't be the last attack we'll see today, you know.'

You could forget about arriving in Grand Harbour tomorrow morning. Even if there were no more attacks, at this speed it was going to take more like thirty-six hours than twenty-four. And as the ship was on fire, with twelve feet of water in her forepart, it was difficult to look far ahead.

Paul told the DEMS men, 'We're lucky, in one way. If it had been a clear day like yesterday – without this fog to cover us?'

'There's some as like to look on the bright side.' Beale said it to Withinshaw, and they both laughed. There was no malice in it: he was labelling Paul an optimist just as he'd labelled Withinshaw a bigamist. As far as Beale was concerned, either was good for a laugh. Paul passed his cigarettes round, and Short gave him a light for his own; he said, standing back from it, 'I wonder what we'll get for lunch?' Withinshaw suggested, 'Soup an' a mutton fookin' sandwich, o' course.' He added, 'Mutton-bone soup, an' all.'

There was some excitement in the bridge, activity out in the port wing. They all stood up and moved so they'd have a view of what was happening. Mackeson was out there, with his signalman. Then the signalman was out of sight but you could hear the rattle of an Aldis lamp. Humphrey Straight appeared, with binoculars at his eyes: behind and above that sturdy silhouette, smoke still billowed up.

'Some bastard's flashin'!'

McNaught was pointing out on the port bow: there was a flash there just as Paul turned to look. An answering flash – to a message that was being passed from the *Montgovern*. From down here you couldn't see what sort of ship it was, but Paul guessed it would be the Hunt which had visited them before. But then, in a patch of better visibility, he made out the outlines of a freighter, and he thought he recognized her.

'Is that the Stars and Stripes?'

It was. Which made her the *Santa Eulalia*.

Beale said, 'Got on fire, didn't she?'

She'd been on fire at one time. According to McCall, she'd been in danger of blowing up. Last night, it must have been. One memory of convoy action in the last day or two was very much like another, they'd merged in Paul's mind into a montage of guns, bombs, aircraft, dusks and dawns and stolidly plodding ships, with a mental image of Malta in the distance like a mirage . . . But it would be good to have company now, and the DEMS men were immediately much happier. As the ships drew closer to each other they were waving and cheering, and Americans on the *Santa Eulalia*'s upper deck were waving back. You could see the blackened area where the fire had been.

Mackeson sent Gosling round with the information that the American ship had been directed to this rendezvous by *Ainsty*, the Hunt who'd been looking for stragglers in this area. She was now looking for a third one, and hoped to get them all together before nightfall.

Gosling looked ill. Paul asked him, 'How about our fire, or fires?'

'Getting the better of it, they say. But my God it stinks, back there.' The smoke did seem to be thinning. But so was the mist: the circle of visibility was growing rapidly. Paul said something about it, and Gosling left, to return to his lookout job. He was seasick, Paul guessed, like the airman. This quite gentle but continuous rhythmic rolling was probably worse for them than a really rough sea might have been. As he turned back, he found Beale watching him with a peculiar, half-suppressed grin. Beale said, 'Fog's about gone. Be clear as a bell soon.'

'So?'

'Well – lucky, aren't we? I mean, we can see where we're going, like.' He began to let the laugh out: and the others, catching on, were also sniggering. Beale spluttered, choking with amusement, 'Gawd, ain't we bloody fortunate?'

Paul said, 'I don't know about fortunate, but you're a bunch of idiots, all right.' Over Beale's head, high up and still a long way off, he saw the Stukas. It was just the first glimpse of them that told him they were Stukas: there'd been nothing he could have explained in terms of shape or features, and they were no more than specks; but they were, undoubtedly, Stukas. Withinshaw was saying, 'Don't mind Ron – 'e likes to 'ave a go, like.'

'He can have a go at *them*, in a minute.' He put two fingers in his mouth, and whistled. It was a better noise than Gosling could have produced. The signalman appeared at the front of the port-side wing. Paul shouted, and pointed. Then someone else was blowing a

652

whistle; but the American was ahead of them, there was a red warning flag at that yardarm already, and men were ready at her guns. The two ships were steering the same course, parallel to each other and four hundred yards apart, and the *Montgovern* seemed to have built up her speed to something like the previous eight knots. He wished, as he pushed the strap of his tin hat under his chin and watched the *Staffel* of ten or twelve Ju87s growing very slowly up the sky, that he had a gun he could use himself.

But they were changing direction. They'd appeared on a course that would have brought them from Sicily, and now, with some miles still to cover, the mosquito-like objects were altering away . . . No – they were dividing. Some going left, some right.

'Splittin' up.' Beale glanced round from his gun. Paul nodded. They'd circle, he supposed, anyway separate, so as to attack from different directions. Against two slow-moving, virtually helpless merchantmen. The bastards had it made, the way they liked it. Nazi schoolgirls could have done it, but that lot would go home and be given Iron Crosses . . . It seemed odd, all the same, to be starting their deployment at such a distance.

Whatever tactics they adopted, a few of them were bound to land bombs on these ships. When there were only close-range weapons to fight them off with.

'Twelve, d'you make it?'

Withinshaw, to Beale. Beale answered, 'Too bloody many, any road.' He looked round at Paul again: 'Fam'ly man 'ere can't swim. Would you credit it?'

The far-off Stukas were now in two entirely separate groups, flying in opposite directions. It didn't seem to make sense. Nor did what Beale had just said. Paul asked Withinshaw, 'Is he joking again?'

'Not a fookin' stroke, I can't.'

'Did you ever try to learn?'

'Never seemed to take to it. I reckon me bones is too 'eavy.'

Beale said '*Bones!*', and laughed. Then: 'What's *this* monkey business?'

Paul was wondering, too. The Stuka group to the left had seemed to be motionless, static in mid-air: then he realized – they were circling, turning yet again, way out there over the horizon. He wondered if they might be waiting for other forces to join up with them – more of their own kind, or torpedo aircraft, for the sort of multiple attack they'd mustered once or twice before this. It would make sense, he supposed: this close to Sicily they were in enormous strength, and after their successes of last night they mightn't have so many targets left, so they could afford to make sure of each one they found.

It struck him for the first time as a serious proposition that perhaps not even one ship out of the sixteen who'd passed through the Gibraltar Strait three days ago would reach Malta. Such a huge effort, for a total loss. And what happened to Malta, then? Surrender?

It was unthinkable. He found he was looking at Withinshaw, and angry with him for not being able to swim. If that was true, and not another childish leg-pull. He told him. 'If you really can't swim, and we look like sinking, you'd better hightail it aft and make sure of getting a place in a boat.'

'These lads'll 'old me up.' The fat man's eyes stayed on the Stukas. He'd meant Short and McNaught would hold him up. McNaught said, 'Aye. Wi' a block an' tackle.'

Two of the Stukas, tiny at that distance, were plummeting like hawks. Beale shouted, 'Some other bugger they're after!'

Soundless, and remote. At the bottom of their dives they were out of sight, either over the rim of the horizon or in the haze obscuring it. More going down now. None of them reappeared: they must have flown off at low level, Paul guessed. That area of haze was darkening and swelling, like smoke.

Beale said, 'Some poor sod's copping it.'

'Bastards.' Withinshaw spat. 'Dirty fookin' *bastards*.'

The smoke-cloud rose, black, mushrooming. After what seemed to have been a long interval they heard the deep rumble of an explosion.

That quick, he thought. That easy for them. A ship alone, probably. Stopped, broken down, the easiest of targets. This one and the *Santa Eulalia* wouldn't be much different.

'Us next, d'you reckon?'

Beale was asking him. Half-turned from the Oerlikon, with a fresh cigarette in his mouth and one hand feeling for a match. Withinshaw pointed: 'Us *now*, Ron, could be.' The group of Stukas who'd separated to the right were still up there, still circling. Their movement at the moment was from right to left. Watching them, Paul saw that movement stop. They were flying either away now, or towards: from such a distance it would be a minute or two before you could be sure.

Withinshaw, his bulky frame resting against the shoulder-pieces of his gun and his eyes fixed on the Stuka formation, was mumbling a private litany: 'Fookin' soddin' murderin' *bastards* . . .' Paul detected the small upward tendency, the slight lift of those bombers against the greyish background which told him they were approaching, not departing. Beale had seen it too. He took one long drag at his newly-lit cigarette, and flicked it arcing over the starboard rail.

Mackeson counted five Stukas. In the haze out on the port beam there was nothing to see now. There'd been a glow, just before the explosion, but no outline of any ship. After the explosion, black smoke had hung there, slowly changing shape as it broke up. Now there was nothing – except five Stukas who hadn't emptied their bomb racks yet.

Straight had asked him a few minutes ago whether he still thought the Hunt, *Ainsty*, would be coming back for them. He'd answered that if she didn't he doubted if it would be her captain's fault . . . The Stukas were close now, rising overhead, as menacing and unpleasant as vultures. Any second now, the leaders would be tipping over into their dives, and he'd have given a lot to have had that Hunt here with her high-angle four-inch.

One was diving on the *Santa Eulalia*. By the sound of it, another might well be coming down on the *Montgovern*, but he couldn't see it from inside the bridge. The Oerlikons on the foc's'l-head were both engaging the American's attacker, but the guns aft had opened up as well. He muttered to Straight, 'Going to have a look at this,' and put his tin hat on as he went out into the wing. The American's guns were all in action, a roar of noise and tracer flooding up through smoke to meet the diving Junkers. Junkers plural: there were two going for her now. And there *was* another coming down astern; he'd noticed that the leading edges of its wings were painted yellow, then his attention was on the single bomb that looked as if it was rocking, wobbling in the air as it fell away, slow-moving at first as the pilot began to drag his bomber's nose up. He didn't see how it could possibly miss. Another bomb had burst in the sea ahead of the *Santa Eulalia*: her guns – rocket-launchers too – were barraging under the nose of the second attacker. Mackeson felt the shock of the bomb hitting and bursting aft. He called to Straight, telling him the ship had been hit at the after end of the boat deck. Devenish was sprinting for the ladder, and Straight had taken over the conning of the ship. A Stuka was spinning, in flames, off on the far side of the American, but two were still to come and it looked as if both had picked on the *Montgovern*. They always went for the one that was already hurt. It was the jackal mentality, and one's contempt for it was the greater for being on the receiving end of it. In fact the Stuka pilots weren't being stupid: the *Santa Eulalia*'s defensive barrage was twice as effective as this ship's. The rising note of the first bomber's engine-scream rose above the cacophony of Bofors, Oerlikons, Brens and whatever the American's light guns were: those were adding to the umbrella above the *Montgovern* now. There was a fire aft, he knew, but he was watching these last two bombers coming, and one bomb was already on its way. Staring up under the rim of his tin hat and through a mass of tracer-streams roofing the ship in a lattice-work of explosive brilliance, he saw the slant of the falling missile and shouted, 'Miss!' The shout was inaudible and he had his hands in his reefer pockets with their fingers crossed, in case he'd misjudged it. He hadn't – not that one – and it went into the sea thirty yards clear, to starboard. But the second one was a different matter: he knew in the last second before it hit that it was going to, and its bone-shaking explosion was in the after well deck. The possibility of reaching Malta changed in that moment of impact from being remote to non-existent. It was the chance of the ship's survival even until nightfall that became remote. The Stuka had been hit; it was trailing smoke and its engine was coughing in uneven bursts as it banked away to starboard, away from the American guns on the other side. The foc's'l Oerlikons followed it, and he thought one of them was hitting too. At any rate the Junkers was done for: it had jack-knifed downwards, and the sea flung up a white shroud around it as it hit and cartwheeled. The *Montgovern*'s afterpart was solid flame, the roar and crackle of it taking over as her guns and the American's fell silent.

The gunner's 'wingers' had refilled all the Oerlikon magazines; the bin was full and there were several on the deck beside it. They'd also brought up several cases of loose ammunition for late refilling operations. A bosun's store in the foc's'l had been in use as a magazine, but it had now been sealed off, like other spaces for'ard, so as to provide some buoyancy as the flooding pulled her down. So they'd got their stuff out of it while they'd had the chance.

Paul said to Withinshaw, 'Should've had some of that wheat down there.'

'Ah.' The fat man nodded. 'We'd 'a been laffin', then.' He began to tell him again about the trip he'd made from Halifax. The bulk cargo of wheat had shifted, apparently, but it hadn't stopped him laffin'.

They'd been unmolested for several hours, but dusk wasn't far ahead and nor were the island bases of Lampedusa and Linosa. *If* the ship floated long enough to get that far. Devenish and his fire-fighters had kept the fire away from the high-octane stowage, and on the starboard side they'd actually got it out, but the full-scale dousing operation meant diverting pump-power from the flooded spaces for'ard, and the rate of inflow had substantially increased. It seemed to Paul a rather silly arrangement of pumps and plumbing, that you couldn't do both jobs at the same time, but a ship like this one hadn't been designed to cope with action damage, simultaneous fire and flooding. As the third mate, Pratt, had commented, you couldn't have it both ways – 'as the bishop said to the actress' – and the choice, anyway, wasn't likely to be either the bishop's or the actress's or their own, but the Luftwaffe's. The bombers would be busy elsewhere, he supposed, but they'd surely be back. When they arrived, the only opposition they'd meet would be from the *Santa Eulalia*'s many guns and from the *Montgovern*'s foc'sl Oerlikons. All the after guns had been knocked out and their crews killed either by the bombs or in the fire that resulted from them. A few survivors, alive but suffering from first-degree burns, were in the hands of Dennis Brill in the saloon. Harry Woods was among the missing – who would have gone over the stern, Paul guessed, if they hadn't been killed outright. They'd have been either killed, or incapacitated and caught in the flames, or they'd have jumped. Jumping would have meant drowning, because nothing had been visible aft during the worst of the fire, but most men, he guessed, would choose drowning in preference to burning. It brought you back, if you had a sense of humour like Beale's, to Pratt's Alternative.

Paul hadn't been aft. He remembered very clearly, from Narvik, what the results of battle looked like, and he couldn't have helped or done anyone any good. But he felt stupid. Everyone had told him and the others how slim the chances were of getting through to Malta. You'd listened, not doubted the facts about previous convoys or that on the face of it the hazards on this trip would be the same. But you hadn't really taken it in, not in real and personal terms, you'd never recognized the *probability* that you'd burn or drown. Beale had known, though: Beale, with his dark-sided humour, knew *now*.

When he thought about Woods, he saw it very clearly. Woods had expected to be in Malta in a day or so. Right up to the last second he'd still have been expecting that. There'd be this danger, that danger, but eventually you'd get through it and you'd *be* there. But Harry Woods would *not* be there. Most likely Paul Everard wouldn't either. He told himself, *That's real, it's true.*

So there'd be no letter to his father. And that, he told himself, was the only truly ill effect his death would bring.

The weight of water in the ship's forepart, the flooded bow's resistance to forward movement, had cut her speed to about five knots. The *Santa Eulalia* had reduced speed to stay with her, and was still abeam. It was generous of the American, he thought, to be doing this. Her guns would help to shield the *Montgovern*, who was otherwise more or less defenceless, and it was comforting to know she was close by in case they had to abandon ship. (*When* they had to, Paul corrected.) But from the *Santa Eulalia*'s angle the *Montgovern*'s company was now a liability. There was smoke coming out of her, there might be a glow from her fire still showing after dark, and there was the fact that moving faster would get one out of the enemy's back yard more quickly . . . He thought that if he'd been Mackeson – or Straight, whichever of them had the decision to make – he'd have suggested to the American captain that he should push on at his best speed, leave the *Montgovern* to take her chances. It ought to be a matter of judging priorities, he thought, cutting your losses; there'd surely be a better chance of getting that one cargo into Malta if the faster, undamaged ship pressed on alone.

The smoke wasn't rising, as it had earlier, only lying in a spreading trail above the wake. There wasn't as much swell now, and there was hardly any breeze at all, but it was still extremely cold.

McNaught muttered, 'Here's y' whatyacall 'im.'

Mackeson. Old Bongo, coming for a visit. Paul stood up. Withinshaw was asleep, swathed in tarpaulin, but Beale came aft from the bow where he'd been smoking and staring down at the froth.

'Well, Everard!'

'Hello, sir.'

Mackeson nodded to Beale and the others. His eye fell on the slumbering mass that was Withinshaw. 'That one all right?'

Beale said, 'It's 'ow 'e likes to be.'

'No accounting for tastes. Deck must be damn cold.' Mackeson nodded towards the Oerlikons. He looked exhausted, ten years older than he'd looked two days ago. 'These are all we've got between ourselves and perdition, now. We're relying heavily on you chaps.'

'Reckon we'll get there, do you, sir?' Beale's grin had something behind it, Paul noticed. He'd grinned like that when he'd been taking the Micky out of *him*: it was the same line, the same amused contempt for false optimism. Mackeson said, 'The thing is, we have to keep going. As long as we're afloat and moving in the right direction, we *are* getting there.' He noticed Beale's wag of the head, wordless sarcasm saying something like *That's the stuff to give 'em* . . . 'I'm not saying we *will* get there, but I *am* saying we still have a chance.'

Withinshaw sat up, staring at him. He transferred his blinks to Beale. 'What's this, then?'

Paul said quickly, 'This is the other Oerlikon gunner, sir. Withinshaw.'

'Sorry to disturb you, Withinshaw.' Mackeson nodded to him. 'What I came for really was to say we've seen the pair of you doing some nice shooting, a few times.'

'That would 'a been me.' The fat man jerked his head, indicating Beale. 'Killick's no fookin' use.'

Mackeson laughed. He and Paul walked for'ard, up into the bow. The liaison officer stood looking down at the foam pushing out around it. 'Not much freeboard now, is there?' He was right: when the time came to leave her, it wouldn't be much of a jump. Mackeson added, 'Frankly, there's very little chance she'll last the night through. We've got to try, that's all.'

'Yes.'

'Every cargo's so darned important. And miracles *do* happen. I know, I've seen some. What seemed like miracles, anyway. So we'll stick to her as long as she'll float and move.'

'Isn't it surprising they've left us alone this long, sir?'

'Probably got targets nearer to them. Anyway at sunset, pretty soon now, we'll be less than thirty miles north of Lampedusa . . . Those fellows seem sound enough?'

'They're – very individualistic . . . Sorry about the gunners aft, sir. Woods and all his—'

'I think the only way to look at it is that the rest of us are bloody lucky, Everard.'

He thought, *So far* . . . He asked, 'Any more news of the Italian cruisers that were reported at sea, sir?'

Mackeson glanced at him sharply. Then, with a shake of the head, away again. 'No. None.'

Sunset came in technicolor: pink and gold and lilac, the pink deepening to blood red and the lilac to mauve and black. With the day fading and the air getting still colder, what had been a smoke-trail was only vapour, a shimmer against the light. There was an exchange of signals. A long message from the *Montgovern* was answered by the *Santa Eulalia* with 'Negative, and let's just keep praying.'

'What's that about, then?'

He told Withinshaw, 'I wouldn't know.' All you could know was as much as you could see around you. He didn't even know whether the fire was still a danger, aft, but he could see for himself that she was about six inches lower for'ard than she had been at the time of Mackeson's visit. He came back to the Oerlikons, from another visit to the bow. The light was leaking away and the colours astern were deepening, but the two gunners were still lounging around, smoking and chatting with the younger men. McNaught chewed steadily. Paul didn't want to have to tell Beale and Withinshaw to stand-to. Contrary to all the precepts and principles that had been dinned into him during his training, lectures on such subjects as 'Power of Command' and 'Leadership', it was plain to him that his relationship with these DEMS characters depended largely on not giving orders. They accepted him because he didn't try to, and if he'd ignored the tacit agreement they'd have responded by ignoring *him*. Then his usefulness here, small as it was, would disappear altogether.

It was a relief when Beale stood up and stretched, and told Withinshaw through a yawn, 'Best start lookin' like sailors, Art.' He threw Paul that same half-smile, the sardonic look, as he moved to his gun and unclamped it.

Mackeson heard Gosling shout, and then the whistle. He went out quickly into the starboard wing. 'What's up?'

'Surface craft – green eight-oh, sir!'

The spark of a white bow-wave caught his eye, and he settled his binoculars on it. E-boat. There was another to the left of it and both were bow-on, attacking. E-boats if they were German, Mas-boats if they were Italian, and it made not a shred of difference. He shouted at Humphrey Straight through the bridge window, 'E-boats attacking, starboard beam. Will you come hard a-starboard, captain?' Then – 'Signalman!'

'Sir?'

'Make to the Yank, "E-boats starboard." ' Over the front barrier of the wing he saw the foc'sl-head gunners standing by, alerted by Gosling's whistle. Everard looking up this way to see what was happening. Until she'd swung her bow towards the attackers, only one of those Oerlikons would bear. The *Santa Eulalia* had all the firepower: these bastards should have come from the other side. But they'd come from the Lampedusa side, of course. Even closer, just a few miles away, was the smaller island of Linosa. They'd quite likely been lurking there all day, anchored inshore in the knowledge that some easy kills were coming right towards them.

She'd begun to swing, at last. It was to avoid torpedoes as much as to bring both Oerlikons to bear that he'd suggested the turn to starboard. He had the E-boats in his glasses again. No – only one of them: and it was mostly bow-wave he was looking at. But where the hell . . . 'Ah. There you are.' He'd said it aloud. From behind him Humphrey Straight bawled: 'Midships the wheel!' He had Pratt, third mate, in there; Devenish was still occupied below decks, getting that fire out. The second E-boat had shot away eastward in a wide, sweeping turn: moving across the line of sight as it was now, you could see it was doing about forty knots.

The Oerlikons opened fire. The first E-boat was moving slightly right. It had altered to port, to put itself on the *Montgovern*'s starboard bow. The other – he swivelled, and focused on it – was creaming round on the other side, to the east. That one would be out ahead of the *Santa Eulalia*, who'd held to her course and was consequently on the *Montgovern*'s port quarter. The first one opened fire. A machine-gun firing tracer: yellow, twin streams of it lifting, slow-moving as it reached towards them, then accel-erating to meteor-like flashes as it passed – at bridge level, for'ard. It fired in short bursts, not a continuous stream like the *Mont-govern*'s starboard Oerlikon was spouting. Straight had ordered another turn to starboard, to avoid any torpedo that might already have been fired and also to bring the other gun to bear. The E-boat jinked, came on again, coming in almost on the beam. Unless its skipper was dim-witted he must have realized by now that this ship had no weapons anywhere except on her foc'sl-head. Mackeson heard the *Santa Eulalia*'s guns in action, as the *Montgovern* began responding to her rudder: slowly, and the damage for'ard wasn't making her any easier to handle. The E-boat was tearing in to close quarters, *two* double streams of tracer leaping from it. The *Montgovern*'s starboard Oerlikon found the range and began to hit. You could see the explosive shells bursting, and one of the two guns stopped firing – and so did the Oerlikon. Jammed . . . The enemy's bow-wave high, brilliant white, wide-spreading on a surface turning black with the fading of the colour in the west: the E-boat swung hard a-port, dipping its gunwale to the sea as it spun around, one machine-gun slashing viciously at the foc'sl-head at point-blank range and unopposed, and at about that moment the torpedo hit the *Montgovern* in her starboard quarter. The crash of the underwater explosion like a kick in the belly of the ship triggered a voice in Mackeson's tired brain. It was his own, and it said, *End of the road, old son* . . . The Oerlikon had started up again but the E-boat, roaring from left to right down the ship's side as she still swung, was already escaping from the field of fire. He heard water drenching down across the stern – it would be from the torpedo's explosion – then tracer was bright in his face, the glass side of the bridge shattered, Gosling collapsed and flames were licking round the paintwork at the back end of the bridge. The foc'sl gun had ceased fire, and so had the E-boat after that final, vicious burst. It had turned away, swinging its stern towards the *Montgovern*, a pile of foam moving at forty knots. At Mackeson's elbow the signalman shouted, 'One's on fire, sir. The Yank must've got it.' The *Montgovern* was listing to starboard, and her engines had stopped.

Paul was at the port-side Oerlikons, leaning into the shoulder-rests with the gun cocked, his fingers on the trigger and the weapon's long, slim snout trained out to where a feather of white had been his last glimpse of the E-boat. It might be finished, going home, but with any luck it might come back, too. The list on the ship made his stance difficult. He was a couple of feet higher than Beale was on the other side, and the slanting deck was also slippery. The listing process seemed to have stopped, for the moment: half a minute ago he'd been expecting her to carry on, roll right over. This was Withinshaw's gun. Withinshaw's head had been smashed in in that last but one burst of machine-gun fire. The fact that the E-boat had still been hanging around out there gave him hope that it would come back to finish them off. He and Beale were waiting for the flicker of bow-wave to show up again. He wanted the pleasure, the relief, the deep joy there'd be in blasting it. McNaught, at his elbow, complained that it was *his* job to take over this gun when the number one gunner copped it. Paul told him, 'Sure. Hang on. You can have it, in a minute.' He thought, *Come on, come on, or we'll sink before you get here!*

Gunfire, out there on the bow. Biggish guns, percussions cracking hard across the water. But the American was astern somewhere. Surely, this ship had reversed course and was pointing west, back the way she'd come from, and the *Santa Eulalia* had held on? Ahead, there was a flash, a yellow streak that shot upwards from sea level and then died down into a glimmer of burning on the sea. Gunfire had ceased. Now a white light sparked, expanded, lengthened into a long, harsh finger that swung and fastened on the *Montgovern*'s bow. From the north: a ship from the north, with a searchlight on them. He didn't think E-boats had searchlights, not of that size. It swung aft, touched the bridge, came back for'ard. At that moment, blinded by its glare, he felt the ship move, her stem rising in a sudden jolting lurch as the list became a steady roll to starboard.

CHAPTER 11

In the south-west Pacific it was about ninety minutes short of dawn. It was pitch dark, and Nick could smell the mangroves. He said into the telephone, 'Steady as you go.'

'Steady, sir. Oh-six-oh, sir.'

'Steer that.' He was using this telephone, not a voicepipe, because the wheelhouse was out of action and there was no voicepipe now, only the telephone line, to the lower steering position on the platform deck. Down there the new acting chief quartermaster, Petty Officer Riley, was wearing a telephone headset. Nick asked Chevening, 'Depth?'

'Eight fathoms, sir.' Chevening was in the front of the bridge, watching the echo-sounder. Nick asked him, 'Two point two miles, on this leg?'

'Yes, sir.'

'Tell me when we've done two.'

It would show up on the log, which was also under Chevening's eye, another indicator glowing softly in the dark.

'Course oh-six-oh, sir.'

'Very good.'

Very quiet, too, although at this slow speed there was more vibration than there would have been at higher revs – as well as some extra rattles from the damaged area below the bridge. And very dark, because the moon was down. It had been shining when they'd been off the Madura coast, earlier in the night, and the chances were that watchers ashore would have seen a three-funnelled light cruiser steaming eastward. Earlier, a two-funnelled one had come out of the Surabaya Strait and turned west, and the Japs might well be looking for that one at dawn, on course for the Sunda Strait.

This was going to be a very, very tricky bit of pilotage. He had the islet called Sasul in sight to starboard, but against the darker background of Sepanjang itself you wouldn't have seen it if you hadn't known it was there and looked for it. It was only a mile, two thousand yards, to starboard, and during the next five minutes that distance would be lessening. There was a reef extending all along this side of it. Ten minutes ago, from a different angle and with sky and stars as background, he'd even been able to make out the shapes of coconut palms along its spine. He had to take *Defiant* right around Sasul: steering north-east now, then south-east, to the place where he'd stop to put the first of the boats into the water. Before that he'd have to take her clear of the rocks which abounded off the islet's northern extremity, then guide her in between other rocks to starboard and a confusion of reef to port.

Reefs were self-perpetuating, self-extending. The chart showed him their positions and extent as they'd been when the last hydrographical survey had been made, but the coral could have grown out anywhere in recent years. Nobody came in here except fishermen – Kangean fishermen, at that.

The land-smell was a stench, and he guessed that before long mosquitoes were likely to become a problem.

Chevening called sharply, '*Four* fathoms, sir!'

The tone of alarm was irritating. Nick countered it by murmuring his acknowledgement, the traditional 'Very good', so gently that it might have come from someone half asleep. The sudden drop from eight to four fathoms was drastic, all right, but in fact it would have been more worrying if the sounder had produced any different reading. The figure matched chart data, and was what he'd expected. It would be fractionally *less* than four fathoms in a minute, and then it would increase again, and when they reached the turning-point they'd have about six fathoms showing. But Chevening didn't think this was going to be tricky, he thought it was going to be impossible. Chevening, Nick thought, was a bit of an old woman, and being knocked about in that engagement had *not* improved him. He'd come to see Nick last evening, half an hour before sailing time, bringing with him the chart, the Sailing Directions, and a very nervous manner.

'There's a point I seem to have overlooked, sir, about this place Sepanjang. In fact we all seem to have missed it . . . You want to get in here, on the north side: so we have to come past this off-lying bit – Pulau Sasul – then turn in here. But it says positively – here in the Pilot, but it's in the next column and I hadn't read that far –

that the whole area between Sasul and Seridi Besar – that's this bit – is foul.'

'Foul' in that context meant that it contained reefs, rocks or other underwater dangers that weren't specifiable or predictable and were therefore to be given a wide berth.

Nick had looked carefully at the chart again. There was a contradiction between that statement and the soundings that were shown. He knew there'd be foul areas which he'd have to negotiate, but this entrance point *had* to be open. He wasn't going to throw the whole plan away for the sake of three lines of small print and Chevening's worried frown.

'Whoever wrote this was simply clearing his own yardarm. All right, in general terms the whole area's rock-strewn. But look here – in here, steering clear of this lot, we've got six to eight fathoms. And right inside all this muck – reef – we've *still* got water enough to float in – right up to the bloody mangroves . . . All right?'

Chevening had licked sweat off his upper lip. He'd asked diffidently, 'Do you think we'll be able to follow that channel in the dark, sir? With no lights, and nothing to fix on?'

'What d'you mean, nothing to fix on?'

'The moon'll be down—'

'So it will, thank God.'

The navigator cleared his throat. 'You're thinking of taking bearings on this high ground – Paliat? But that's only one feature, and it's at quite a distance, and on Sepanjang itself there are no heights marked, sir, no features as such, or—'

'Pilot, tell me this. Where would you like us to go instead?'

There wasn't anywhere else that was suitable. They both knew it. The only other island they might have considered using would have been the big one, Kangean, but the one place there for *Defiant* to have berthed would have been in Ketapang Bay on its northwest coast. The objections to it were that if any Japanese were thinking of landing in the Kangeans, that was where they'd arrive. In the whole group of islands it was *the* anchorage and landing-place. Also, unlike Sepanjang's north coast, it offered no cover. In fact the bay was visually open to ships passing southward en route to Bali or Lombok. Third, Kangean was more densely populated: the Pilot listed half a dozen villages. As Nick had pointed out, exaggerating somewhat, in an earlier discussion, it would be like tying up in Piccadilly Circus. And what it came down to was that they were extremely lucky that Sepanjang existed. Also – he'd mentioned this to Chevening – the fact that nobody would have expected anything bigger than a rowing-boat to have been able to get in through those various hazards was a distinct advantage, because the Japs were unlikely to be looking for them there.

'What about these bays, sir, on Kangean – Hekla or Gedeh?'

'Look at the Pilot. The land on that coast's dead flat. Paddy-fields. Barely enough cover for a tapeworm.'

Remembering from his own earlier days how ridiculous senior officers' tantrums had often seemed, he'd tried to stifle his annoyance. And Chevening was perfectly correct, anyway, in coming along and pointing out the dangers. It was his duty, as navigator, to ensure the navigational safety of the ship. Besides which he might yet find himself in a position to shout 'I told you so!' Because the dangers were real, unquestionably so. It was only a matter of seeing the wood as well as the trees – the wood being the fact that this was the only way to get *Defiant* out of the Java Sea.

'Five fathoms!'

'Good.' He lifted the steering-position telephone again: 'Nothing to starboard.'

'Nothing to starboard, sir!'

That meant, not one yard's latitude to starboard of the ordered course. He had the chart photographed in his mind. *Defiant*'s pencilled track at this point was tangential to a dotted line surrounding Sasul's fringe of rock, and the line meant 'Keep out'. Sasul was eight hundred yards to starboard but most of that eight-hundred-yard gap was rock-strewn.

One mile to go, before the turn to starboard.

'Five and a half fathoms, sir.'

He checked the bearing of the high ground on Paliat, an island just this side of Kangean. That summit was marked as being four hundred and twenty feet high, and it was clearly distinguishable against the stars. Behind it by a distance of about five miles, and twice its height, was a peak in the spur of hills which ran along Kangean's north coast. If while the ship was on this course Paliat should fall into line with the higher, less distinct summit, he'd know he'd come too far, that he was running into danger.

He was running into danger anyway. But there was another metaphor, after the woods and trees one, about omelettes and eggs . . . Perhaps he *should* have transferred the wounded to *Sloan*. He hadn't, because Jim Jordan had made a proposal of his own which Nick had turned down, and after that it would have been difficult, to say the least, to have suggested it. *Sloan*'s spares had arrived, but by truck instead of by rail, and in the same convoy of Dutch army vehicles about forty refugees, who'd been on their way from Bandoeng to Tjilatjap for evacuation by sea, had turned up. Some railway junction had been bombed, so the Dutch had brought them to Surabaya instead. Jordan's idea had been that *Sloan* and *Defiant* should each take half of them. He'd had them all, when he'd made the signal about it, because his ship was alongside a jetty and the Dutch had found it convenient to dump them at his gangway. They were all civilians, and they included women and children. Nick had declined to take any of them, mainly because it was obvious that *Sloan*'s chances of getting away were a lot better than *Defiant*'s. A year ago in the Aegean he'd seen ships being loaded with troops only to put to sea and be sunk. He thought that if *Sloan* couldn't take them all, they'd be better left in Java. Besides, he had a day to spend lying-up in the Kangeans, and it was going to be tricky enough without having a load of women and children to complicate matters internally.

Jordan had thought Nick's attitude was unreasonable. *Defiant* was twice the size of *Sloan* and had far more room for passengers than the destroyer had. When the American had come aboard for a final conference before *Defiant* sailed, his manner had made his feelings plain. It was a pity, because Nick liked him and they'd got on well. Nick thought it was only a matter of seeing the issue clearly and objectively, and that for some reason Jordan wasn't able to. But at the last minute, everything changed. Jordan had made some remark about the passage down the Australian west coast to Perth being a hell of a long one, sixteen hundred miles, especially with overcrowded messdecks. Nick had suggested that when they were away and clear, say by the evening of the day after they cleared their respective straits, they might stop and transfer some of the refugees from *Sloan* to *Defiant*.

'In fact I'll accept three-quarters of them.'

'Well, now. That sounds like a very fair solution, sir.'

'*If* we're there to take them from you. If we aren't, you'll know I was right not to embark them.'

He and Jordan had parted on good terms. *Sloan*'s ship's company had cheered the British cruiser on her way, and *Defiant*'s sailors had returned the compliment as she'd left the anchorage. *Sloan*'s men were going to blow up the destroyer that was in the graving dock, before they themselves left. The job was to be left to

668

the last minute in order not to signal too clearly to the Japs that a naval evacuation was in progress. There'd been two enemy reconnaissance flights over Surabaya during the day, as well as one bombing raid.

'Two miles run, sir!'

'Depth?'

'Six fathoms, sir.'

He checked the bearing of the Paliat hill again. Three degrees to go. The course after this coming turn would be a hundred and thirty-five degrees. On these revs *Defiant* was making five knots, so one-fifth of a mile would be covered in two-point-four minutes. At the turning point there should still be six fathoms. He asked Chevening, 'Log reading?'

'One cable's length to go, sir.'

A cable's length was a tenth of a mile. Just over one minute. If he turned too early he'd put her on the rocks, and if he left it too late he'd be on a reef. He sighted again on that hill, and the bearing was *just* about—

'Stand by, sir!'

'Stop starboard.'

'Stop starboard, sir . . . Starboard telegraph to stop, sir.'

It would be hot, airless, really bloody awful, down in that lower steering position.

Chevening called, 'Now!'

'Starboard fifteen.'

The bearing was exactly right. Wiley confirmed over the telephone that he had fifteen degrees of starboard rudder on her. This was to be a seventy-five-degree turn, but starting it with that screw stopped she'd fairly whistle round; which was what he wanted, as opposed to letting her drift outwards on the turn.

'Midships.'

'Midships, sir.'

'Slow ahead starboard . . . Pilot, one-point-five miles to the first stop, that right?'

Chevening confirmed it.

'Steer one-three-five. We're in a narrow channel now, quartermaster.'

'Aye aye, sir. Steer one-three-five, sir. Starboard engine slow ahead.'

'Bob?' Gant moved up beside him. Nick told him, 'Man the starboard cutter. They'll be slipped in eighteen minutes' time.'

'Aye aye, sir.' Gant went to the after end of the bridge, to shout down to Charles Rowley. Haskins was down there too, and the thirty-foot cutter on the starboard side, abreast the second funnel, was already turned out in its davits and ready for lowering. One section of Royal Marines would be taken in it to land on the southeast corner of Sasul; when Nick stopped the ship, she'd be opposite the landing point. There was a village on Sasul for the marines to keep an eye on, and the northern end of it, which they were rounding now, commanded this channel; the section was landing with a Bren and the two-inch mortar, and with those they'd be able to sink anything that tried to get by. (Nobody in his right mind, Nick thought, would try to come through the channel in anything bigger than a canoe, anyway.)

The cutter was an oared boat, 'double banked', with six oars a side. *Defiant* did have two thirty-foot motorboats that might have been used, but oars were quieter and more reliable: also, this inshore water was, as Chevening had pointed out, foul, and a pulling-boat was less likely to rip her bottom out on a rock.

The cruiser was moving into the crescent-shaped hollow that was Sepanjang's northern side. Land-smell, mangrove-smell increasing, enveloping. Sasul was easily visible to starboard, its palms starkly black against the sky. The only connection between it and the main part of the island was a reef enclosing both of them, rather as if the larger island had arms tightly enfolding the smaller one. There were several smaller islets in the lagoon between them, between those coral banks. In a hundred years, or perhaps much less, the whole thing would quite likely be filled in solidly, a coral extension to Sepanjang. Kangean itself, according to the Pilot, was made of coral – coral lime erupted by volcanic action.

One and a half miles at five knots meant eighteen minutes from the last turn to the point where he'd arranged with Haskins that he'd slip the cutter. After it had landed the RM section that boat would follow on inshore, to the place he'd picked for *Defiant*'s berth. At this next stopping-point, in just a few minutes now, Sasul's south-east coast would be in a straight line to him so that it would look like one clear-cut edge of land, and there'd be a gap visibly open between it and the islands in the lagoon. From any other angle, they'd all overlap. The cutter had to make for that spot on Sasul because it was the one place with no reef to bar its approach. It was also the site of the village, and where the villagers would berth their praus. So landing the section here would kill several birds with one stone.

He settled his binoculars on it. There was no gap visible yet.

Chevening warned, 'Two cables' lengths, sir.'

He said into the telephone, 'Stop both engines.'

'Stop both, sir!'

The ship's momentum would carry her on into position. The quarter-hour had passed so quickly that he felt his thoughts might have been wandering. It was still a danger to watch out for. So far, he believed his mind had been working normally, responding normally to the stimulus of danger and tension. Anxiety, too. The knowledge that with one small act of carelessness, or one piece of bad luck over which he'd have no control, he could put his ship on a rock or across a reef: the prospect was so shocking that the mind, fit or sick, rejected contemplation of it. But it was there, it existed . . .

He saw the gap, just as Chevening called to him that the ship was in position. 'Slow astern together.' He said over his shoulder, 'Away cutter.'

Gant shouted. And from down aft Nick heard Rowley's order, 'Lower away!'

'Stop together.' He'd taken the way off her. He could hear the squeaking of the blocks as the boat was lowered, with two dozen men in her, to the black water. At the next stop he'd be sending away both whalers, but that would be a quicker process because, being sea-boats, the whalers had quick-release gear on their falls. The heavy cutter had to be lowered right into the water and the falls slacked off before they could be unhooked.

He checked the compass. The ship's head was at rest, on course: there was no drift or wind in here, and Wiley had held her steady while the screws had been running astern. He heard the clatter as the falls were unhooked, and then the orders, low-voiced but reflected from the water's surface: 'Shove off for'ard . . . Oars down!' The thumps of the oars' looms banging down on the boat's gunwales. Then: 'Starboard side oars, one stroke back-water . . .' And finally, 'Give way together!' That was Wainwright, an RNR lieutenant: Gant had detailed an officer to take charge of each boat. There was also a leadsman in the cutter's bow, to take soundings as it moved in towards the landing-place.

Gant murmured, returning, 'Cutter's well clear, sir.'

'Slow ahead together.'

The screws churned, and dark water swirled away under her counter. A mile and a half again now. He'd have preferred to have sent the whalers away here and now, but time was limited, and if he was going to have her hidden before the light came he'd have to get closer inshore before he brought her down to the speed of oarsmen. In less than an hour the sun would be dragging itself up over the eastern extremity of the island, that long spar of land with a fishing village called Kiau on the end of it. By that time he wanted to have her tucked away, and there'd still be some camouflaging to be done. Also, he wouldn't know until he got there whether the inlet he'd picked was as suitable as it looked on paper. It might be silted up, or too narrow, or someone might have felled the trees and destroyed the natural cover. It was pot luck, a gamble: and meanwhile you had also to accept this further period of risk navigationally. It was an exceptionally heavy risk, but here again he had no choice.

'Petty Officer Wiley.'

'Yes, sir.'

'Nothing either side. Steer as if you were on a tightrope.'

'Do me best, sir.'

'Depth, pilot?'

'Eight and a half fathoms, sir.'

When they stopped, *Defiant* would have her forefoot on one of those dotted lines which, on the chart, enclosed foul ground.

He thought, *I'm mad, and Chevening was right . . .*

He saw it, quite suddenly, as his navigator must have seen it – as an attempt at the impossible. The evidence, the words printed in the Sailing Directions and the patterns and symbols on the chart, all declared it. They didn't *suggest* it, they declared it unequivocally. Only an idiot could have embarked on this – could even have considered it . . . An idiot, or a desperate man, a man at his wits' end for a way out. He'd clutched at the straw and now he had it in his hand and there was nothing he could do except carry on, attempting the impossible but no longer believing it to be anything else . . . Again, it was like looking back on the workings of a mind that was not your own. He thought he must have seen the risks and subconsciously decided to ignore them, push on as if they didn't exist. But they did. They were *here*. And having come this far he had to go on with it, acting as if he'd assessed the risks and accepted them, expected to come through it . . .

If he bungled it, and got her stuck here, the Japs would bomb her into scrap.

Chevening called sharply, 'Five fathoms, sir!'

According to the chart there should have been eight, all the way through!

'Stop both engines.'

'Stop both, sir!'

The whalers' crews were going to have to pull farther than they'd expected. He was sweating. Before he spoke he paused, getting hold of his nerves, ensuring that his voice was steady.

'Bob. Pass the word to Ormrod and Brown that I'm slipping them a mile farther out than we'd intended. Man and lower both whalers, please.'

Each boat would have a leadsman taking soundings. Lieutenant Brown's boat would be *Defiant*'s guide, immediately ahead of her, while Ormrod's ranged farther ahead and from side to side across the bows to locate the channel and lead Brown to it. Each twenty-seven-foot whaler had five oars and a coxswain, so there'd be eight men in each, and the officers in charge of them had blue-shaded signal lamps for communication. *Defiant* was going to have to follow at no greater speed than the boats could be rowed, and she'd certainly be late in getting to her hiding-place. It would be a race with the sunrise, now, but it would be just a little less dangerous than it would have been to have gone ahead without having the boats down. The echo-sounder wouldn't be much use from here on. You needed to know what was ahead of the ship, not what was already under her.

She was slowing, and Gant reported that the two whalers were manned and lowered, ready to slip. There was no need to stop her this time. You could drop a seaboat from the disengaging gear even when you had quite a lot of way on. He'd only slowed her now because she'd be moving like a snail from here onwards in any case, and to start with the boats had to be allowed to get up ahead of her. He told Gant, 'Slip both whalers', heard the two crashes as they hit the water, and moved to the front of the bridge, beside Chevening, to see them both pull ahead. Like black water-beetles down there . . . It was Gant who'd picked Ormrod and Brown for the boat-work. Nick had told him he needed level-headed, steady characters who were experienced seamen and who'd use their initiative and find ways round problems when they came up against them. His own brain here would be operating through theirs – extensions of his own, well out ahead.

Brown had positioned his boat dead ahead of the cruiser: his orders were to keep about thirty to fifty yards ahead. Ormrod's whaler was pushing on, five oarblades swirling the dead-flat water at each stroke. He was to keep about fifty yards ahead of Brown, and to range over a channel-width of a hundred feet, marking it when it was narrower than that and reporting and marking hazards. He had a dozen white-painted spar buoys under his boat's thwarts, and Brown had more in case he needed them.

Nick told Wiley, 'I'll be using one screw only now, with an occasional touch ahead and then stopping. We'll be following our own boats through foul water.'

'Aye aye, sir.'

It might have made things easier if they'd had normal conning, with the wheelhouse in action and the quartermaster able to look ahead through his small window and see where he was going. From this upper bridge, Wiley and his assistants were six decks down.

'Slow ahead starboard.'

'Slow ahead starboard, sir . . .'

'Steer one degree to port.'

Down there, they'd still follow courses on the compass card, but Nick would only be keeping her stem pointing at Brown's whaler.

'Cutter's inshore, out of sight, sir.'

'Good.' Gant had been at the back end of the bridge, watching the cutter through binoculars. Nick said into the telephone, 'Stop starboard.'

'Stop starboard, sir . . . Starboard telegraph to stop, sir.'

'If you think you're losing steerage way, let me know at once.'

'Aye aye, sir.'

Creeping in. A touch ahead, then stop, drifting forward until the boats had increased their distance again. Then another shove, to push her along behind them. He wondered what he'd do if they came up against a solid barrier of coral, if the channel came to an end. It was quite possible that it would. Anchor, hope for the best, send the boats inshore for camouflaging materials? It would be a very awkward hole to be in, and even more awkward to get out of. Turning her, for instance, in this narrow channel would be quite a problem. *Defiant*'s waterline length was four hundred and sixty-five feet. He realized he'd probably have to take her out astern. God Almighty . . . But then, if you got stuck to that extent, you'd be lucky if you got as far as facing that particular extra problem, the one of getting *out* . . . Sweating again. From ahead, faintly across the water, he heard Brown's leadsman call, 'And a quarter five!'

Five and one-quarter fathoms, they had there. The mark on the leadline at five fathoms was a piece of white bunting. There was no mark at six, and such unmarked depths were called 'deeps'. In-between soundings were reported as references to the five mark, or to the seven which had red bunting. At four there was no mark on the line; at three, there were three strips of leather. How, or how long ago the peculiar system had become established, would be a question for historians in the National Maritime Museum; but Drake in his voyage of circumnavigation probably had leadlines marked like these.

'A quarter less five!'

The report was to Brown in the sternsheets of the whaler, not to Nick back here. But it was reassuring to hear it, even though they'd lost three feet of water between the last two soundings. There was still a depth of twenty-seven feet there, and *Defiant* only needed sixteen to float in.

Gant slapped his own neck, and cursed quietly. 'The bloody things . . .'

'A half less five!'

'Slow ahead starboard.'

Creeping in. So far so good, but you might be stopped at any moment. Land-smell foetid, thoroughly unpleasant. Mosquitoes were getting to be a nuisance, and all the repellent stuff they had on board had been issued to the marines. *Defiant* trembled as one screw churned, pushing her up closer to the boats. Fine on the bow, Ormrod's blue lamp flashed dot-dash-dot, 'R' for rock. He'd put a marker over it, then prospect for a wide enough, deepwater passage round it, if there was one . . . Nick wondered again what Gant would have done, if he'd been the man to decide it. Whatever he'd said when Nick had asked him, you could be fairly sure he wouldn't have tried *this* way out. On the face of it, he'd have had more sense; but even if he'd considered it, wouldn't Chevening's quiet hysterics have persuaded him to drop it? Then *Defiant* wouldn't have been in this knife-edge situation. But where *would* she have been?

Spending a day at sea, the first idea he'd had? That would be much more dangerous. And as for the idea of going west to Sunda—

'Stop starboard.'

'Stop starboard, sir!'

Stop *thinking* . . . It was something foreign to him, this doubting introspection. It was also pointless and potentially destructive. The result of that bang on the head, and high time he got over it. He thought, one hand up feeling the bandaging around his head, *You're in it, just get on with it* . . . Beyond that rock, which he'd buoyed, Ormrod was leading round to starboard. Making the buoy a starboard-hand mark, as it were. If this was the point for the turn in towards the creek, or inlet, there wasn't such a vast distance to be covered now. About – perhaps three thousand yards; something like that. But even three thousand yards at rowing pace, in boats that were also sounding as they went, would take some time to cover, and meanwhile a faint radiance eastward and overhead was a warning.

He checked the ship's head: it was on a hundred and forty-six degrees. Then the bearing of Brown's whaler. The course, he reckoned, would be about due south, and she'd need more steerage-way to make the turn, even if it brought him up a bit close behind the boats.

'Slow ahead port.'

'Slow ahead port, sir. Port telegraph slow ahead, sir.'

'Starboard five.'

'Starboard five, sir . . . Five degrees of starboard wheel on, sir.'

You felt the gentle push from that screw. And then the cruiser was bringing her bow around slowly to follow in the whaler's path.

'Midships.'

'Midships, sir. Wheel's amidships, sir.'

It was very quiet in the bridge. Chevening, Nick thought, was probably holding his breath. Not a bad idea, in this hothouse stink. He sighted across the compass again, on Brown's boat, and told Wiley to steer one-seven-eight. There was no absolute guarantee of safety in having boats out ahead, all this creepy-crawly stuff. There could well be a rock pinnacle which neither leadsman would pick up, and it wouldn't be their fault if they didn't: no one's fault, everyone's disaster. Sepanjang rose darkly ahead, blotting out a section of the lightening sky. To port, where the land was lower, the brightening was more evident. It was the first showing of the dawn, and they were running neck and neck with it. Running like a tortoise runs when it isn't in a hurry; and it was anyone's guess how long the berthing process would take.

Gant murmured, 'Another rock ahead, sir.'

Ormrod flashing 'R' again. Right ahead. So the channel leading inshore had a hazard smack in the middle of it. It could even be a reef, a barrier right across it which the chart didn't show.

'Stop port.'

Defiant was very close behind Brown's whaler, since he'd had to keep a screw going all through the turn. He said into the telephone, cutting across Wiley's acknowledgement, 'Steer one degree to starboard.'

If he couldn't find a way past that rock, Ormrod would flash 'S' for 'stop'. Or, until he was sure of it, 'W' for 'wait'. Nick focused his glasses on that more distant boat. He could see the spar-buoy in the water, and the whaler was under oars again, pulling away to the right. He could see the leadsman's upright figure in its bow.

Gant murmured, 'Getting lighter, sir.'

'Yes.'

Did Gant imagine he was blind?

Ormrod's boat was still moving to the right, oars sweeping slowly. Stopping, holding water . . .

The blue lamp flashed 'R'.

Another rock. It would be thirty, forty yards from the first one. Thirty yards was ninety feet, and *Defiant*'s beam was just on fifty. He muttered in his mind, *Check the depths between them and beyond* . . . He'd seen the second marker buoy go over the whaler's stern; the port-side oars were backing water, to turn her back across the channel. He said to Gant, 'Glad *I* don't have to pull an oar in this fug.'

Silence: the silence of surprise, he hoped. He'd wanted to show Gant that he was relaxed and confident. Brown's boat was edging across to starboard.

'Slow ahead port.' He added to Gant, 'God knows how we'll breathe when the sun gets up.' Ormrod's whaler was crossing the gap between the two spar-buoys, sounding as it went. The leadsmen weren't actually heaving their leads, only dabbing them up and down, feeling the bottom as they went along. A boat's lead weighed seven pounds and was shaped like a thin leg of mutton. It had a cavity in its end into which you could put tallow wax so as to bring up a sample of the ground and know whether it was sand or mud or what. That was important, so as to know whether or not it was good holding ground for an anchor. There was a lot to know about lead-lines: that you measured them, for instance, when they were wet, and stretched a new line by towing it astern of a ship. Drake had probably done those things too, in his time: but he wouldn't have tried to get in behind Sepanjang in a ship drawing sixteen feet.

Well, he *might* have.

'Stop port. Steer three degrees to starboard.'

Ormrod's boat had found the channel clear between the markers; it was moving on between them towards the shore. There was a veining of light overhead and a gleam of treetops, palms, along a high slope leading upwards towards blackness. Brown's boat was under way again, pulling after Ormrod's and aiming to pass exactly in the middle between the two spar-buoys. Nick heard the leadsman's hail: 'And a half, three!' Twenty-one feet. At that point, forty yards ahead, the ship would have five feet of water between her keel and the mud. Ormrod's whaler was almost impossible to see against the land's shadow; it was easy enough with binoculars, though. They were close in now, really *very* close. The picture of this bit of the chart which he had in his visual memory was of a line of reef indented like a funnel leading to the inlet, and *Defiant* would be entering it now, or soon, moving slowly towards its narrowing inshore neck. Out here the edges of the funnel were banks of coral, but right inside where he wanted to hide her – if he could get her in that far – they'd merge into mudbanks and the mangroves.

From right ahead, a blue light flashed 'W', meaning 'wait'.

She was virtually stopped already. Forty yards ahead Brown's whaler was taking soundings. The signal to wait might mean that Ormrod had come up against some obstruction, or it could mean he'd found the inlet and was investigating it. There'd be some exploration to be done. You needed the depth of water to get in there, and the length of navigable water from the mouth inwards so as to berth her right inside, and at the inner, bow end they'd have to land and find a tree stout enough to take a cable from the foc'sl. The hemp cable would be passed out through the bullring, and when it had been secured ashore the inboard end would be brought to the capstan, to warp her in.

'Boat coming up astern, sir!'

Number three lookout on the starboard side had reported it. Gant went back to take a look, but it could only be the cutter. It had made good time, but it had had the spar-buoys to follow. It would lie off now, close astern, until it was called for.

The sky in the east was turning pink and silver, and fissures of colour were like cracks spreading into the darkness overhead. This part of the island was still shadowed, four-fifths dark.

Ormrod's light flashed 'A'. A dot and a dash. 'A' stood for 'accessible'.

Incredible. You had to make yourself believe you'd seen it. If it was true, there should have been trumpets, a fanfare of triumph, celebration. There wasn't so much as a whisper until Nick said into the telephone, 'Slow ahead port.' You had to believe it, because it was happening. As well to postpone self-congratulation or thanks to the Almighty, or any told-you-so to Chevening, until you'd dealt with the dozen-odd problems that would be cropping up during the next half hour . . . Brown's whaler was pulling hard, heading inshore to catch up with Ormrod's. *Defiant* could now move in and wait where Brown's had been. And meanwhile, at the risk of spoiling one's luck by counting unhatched chickens, there were arrangements to be put in hand.

'Bob. Go aft now, please. Check that Greenleaf's ready with the stream anchor. I want it ready for letting go, and the quarterdeck telephone manned, *now*. Hail the cutter and tell Wainwright to keep clear of the wire. When you're satisfied with Greenleaf's arrangements, go for'ard and see Rowley's making sense on the foc'sl. I'd like you to gravitate between the two. All right?'

'Aye aye, sir.'

'Lieutenant Flynn?'

Flynn answered from the back of the bridge: 'Sir?'

'Stand by the depthcharge telephone, Flynn, and don't leave it.'

That was the communication line to the quarterdeck. The stream anchor – the stern one – would by now have a steel-wire rope shackled to its short swivel-length of cable; it would be let go more than a ship's length outside the inlet, and the wire would be paid out as she nosed in. When they were ready to sneak away tonight it would be brought to the after capstan and the ship would be eased out stern-first.

'Stop together . . . Pilot, how much water?'

'Two feet under the keel, sir.'

In that inlet, he guessed, she'd crease the mud. He told Chevening to stand by the foc'sl telephone. He had no other work for him now, and in this operation co-ordinating the actions on the foc'sl with those on the quarterdeck, getting the right orders and information to and fro, was vital. He said into the quartermaster's telephone, 'Slow astern together.' To take the way off her, hold her where she lay now. The cutter would wait astern until the ship was in and secured, and then it would be used for landing the other

679

sections of Royal Marines. Brown's whaler would be coming out to the ship in a minute, paying out a light line to measure the right distance for letting go the stream anchor; they'd only need to measure the distance to her stem. The same line would be passed inboard, up to the foc's'l and in through the bullring, and it would then be used to haul a heavier line from ship to shore. On the end of that one the mooring cable would be dragged over.

'Stop together.'

'Stop together, sir . . . Both telegraphs to stop, sir!'

Wiley had done an excellent job, Nick thought. So had Ormrod and Brown and their boats' crews. Now, apart from some back-breaking work ashore, the kingpins of the mooring effort would be Rowley and Greenleaf, with Gant looking over their shoulders.

Gant. Nick had been doing some thinking about Bob Gant. Not now, though . . . He glanced round as Flynn reported, 'Commander says all's ready aft, sir. He's on his way to the foc's'l.'

Dawn. With binoculars he could make out – just – the darker area that could only be the indentation in the wall of mangroves. There was a whaler halfway out, pulling towards the ship, a glistening of water flying from the dipping oars. Brown's. Behind the flat coastal mangrove area the hillside rose quite steeply: it was still in shadow and would be for some time yet, but he could make out the shapes of palms where they grew thinly or on their own. In about ten minutes it would be more or less daylight. What was needed now, he thought, was half an hour without any Jap aircraft over. She'd be hidden, by that time; in an hour, she'd be invisible.

By the afternoon it was very hot indeed. Nick had slept for an hour, after an early lunch, and he'd been woken by PO Harkness with a message about a Jap seaplane circling over the islands. He'd turned out and come for'ard, up to the director tower, to see it for himself. As he heaved himself up through the lubber's hole entrance – it was awkward, with only one arm in use – Charles Rowley turned a surprised but genial smile on him.

'Give you a hand, sir?'

He shook his head. 'This seaplane—'

'Gone, sir.' Rowley could have done with a haircut. His shaggy, gingerish head gave him the appearance of an Airedale, Nick thought. Fortunately he rather liked Airedales. Rowley gestured, encompassing a steamy area of reef-broken, shimmery sea: 'Circled

680

round and went down low over the eastern end there, then climbed and bumbled off that way.'

Towards Kangean . . .

Rowley, as senior watchkeeping officer, had reserved this look-out job for himself. It was the only place in the ship you could see anything from, but also, slight as the breeze was, you were out of the clammy stillness of the swamp below.

The seaplane pilot would have needed hawk's eyes to have spotted them, Nick thought. Branches of mangrove festooned this tower, masts, yards, upperworks and upper deck. After the ship had been secured Gant had mustered all hands and sent them ashore in teams to cut and bring back the foliage. To be sure, you'd need to fly over her yourself, but she had to be pretty well invisible. Meanwhile the marines were in control of the villages of Tanjong Kiau and Mandan, three sections were patrolling in the palms behind the long southern beach and another manned a lookout station on the hill. A field telephone had been rigged from there to a guard-post in the trees abreast the ship. This was the landing-place. Both cutters, side by side, supported a gangway which ran from the ship's side to the mudbank, and all of that brow and the boats had been strewn with foliage.

The view from the lookout hatches (one each side of the mainmast) in the after bulkhead of this tower was restricted by the shoreline to a quadrant between north-west and north-east. Blue sea, reefs and islands in the distance, shimmery in the heat-haze as if you were looking at it all through rising steam. Above the land to the left, just about exactly northwest, a bluish hump trembled in the sky. It was the hill he'd used to take bearings on during the early stages of the approach. Rowley asked him what it was.

'Island called Paliat. That's a hill, four hundred and twenty feet high. It's – roughly – fifteen miles from us.'

'Would any sea routes pass close to us here, sir?'

'Close to the islands.' He nodded. 'Anything coming down to the Lombok Strait from the Macassar Strait up north – or from Borneo or the Celebes – would pass to the east here. Fifteen or twenty miles clear, probably, because of reefs to the northeast. So we wouldn't see them – or vice versa.'

'What if they took it into their heads to land on the big island, Kangean?'

'I'd guess their hands are a bit full, at the moment. But they'd go for Ketapang Bay, on the west coast, and that's a good forty miles away.'

'So we're pretty safe from being stumbled on.'

He nodded, reaching for a cigarette. It was quite pleasant up here. He said, 'Except for aircraft. And with any luck—'

A face – head, shoulders – appeared in the open hatch, the lubber's hole entrance in the deck. The face was reddish – brown, and seamed. Able Seaman Bentley. Gant had produced him this morning as a replacement for Gladwill.

'Sorry, sir, I didn't know you was on the move. Else I'd 've—'

'It's all right, Bentley. I don't need you.' He checked the time. 'I'll be going down to turn in again in a minute, and I suggest you get your head down too. We'll be up all night and there'll be no rest tomorrow.'

A nod. A very solid, seasoned three-badger, was Bentley. 'Seen them monkeys, have you, sir?'

'Monkeys?'

Rowley pointed. The monkeys were on the cable that ran to the ship's bow from a palm-tree ashore. There were three of them, swinging around and doing acrobatics on it, hanging upside-down. Bentley said, 'I got nippers just like them.'

Rowley asked him, 'D'you mean they look like that, or behave like it?'

'Both, sir.' The AB slid feet-first into the tower and into the rate-clock operator's seat. 'Spittin' image. I could take two o' them home and switch 'em with the little 'uns and the missus'd never know no difference.' He looked at Nick: 'Wanted to say, sir, off-duty like, I'm happy to get this job, sir.'

'Fond of cage-birds, are you?'

'Ah.' He frowned. 'If I *got* to take them birds on—'

'Find another home for them, if you like, sell them and send the money to Gladwill's widow.'

'Wasn't never married, sir.'

'Nor he was . . . His mother, then.'

'Orphan, I b'lieve he was, sir.'

'There'll be a next-of-kin on record, Bentley.'

'Ah. That's a thought, sir.'

'I'm told you were cox'n to the C-in-C on the China Station at one time.'

'I was, sir. In thirty-six, that was. But I got in a spot of bother in Shanghai, and they drafted me up the perishin' Yangtze. In the old

682

Aphis. We was at Chinkiang when the Japs started bombing the Chinks in thirty-seven . . .' He pointed suddenly, squinting round over his shoulder, out through the lookout hatch: 'See there, sir!'

Floatplane: it was coming from the direction of Kangean, and it looked as if it would pass over Tanjung Kiau. Rowley said, with his glasses on it, 'Looks like the same one, sir.'

'Very likely. Been snooping round the big island, I expect.' He told Bentley, '*Aphis* is in the Med, now.'

'Turning towards us, sir.'

It was over the islet called Seridi. It was banking, making a slow turn to starboard . . . And steadying now, heading directly towards the inlet and the ship. Nick put his glasses down, and motioned to Rowley to do the same. One flash of sunlight on a lens would be enough to invite inspection . . . He asked Bentley, 'What kind of bother, in Shanghai?'

'Russian woman, sir. Holy terror, she was.'

He nodded. That expression might have described his own ex-wife Ilyana very aptly. He said, 'You have my sympathy.' He recognized surprise in the first lieutenant's quick glance at him. But you could hear the drone of the seaplane's engine now. Nick looked down through the starboard-side embrasure, down at his mangrove-smothered ship. Nobody was in sight, nothing moved. But if one man, one white cap appeared now among that greenery . . . The noise was growing as the floatplane bore in towards them.

'Think he could have spotted us, sir?'

'Unlikely.'

It might be just shaping course to pass over the centre of the island. It had looked at the other islands, so it was reasonable that it should have a look at Sepanjang as well. That it was heading for this inlet could be coincidental: and the flight-path would be about right for Bali, if that was where it was now returning. On the other hand – he woke up to this point suddenly – it was flying at only a couple of hundred feet, which would barely clear the hill at this point . . . He suggested to Bentley, 'Chief and petty officers might like to have those canaries in their mess. So might the warrant officers, come to think of it.'

'I wouldn't let the WOs have 'em, sir.' The creases deepened in the sailor's face. 'Serve 'em up for breakfast, soon as look at 'em.'

Rowley chuckled. With an anxious eye on the sky, though, as the engine-noise still increased. Nick said, 'No looking out, now.'

Deafening racket. They sat or squatted with their faces turned downward, as if the steel roof with its burden of branches might be transparent. The noise lifted to a peak: the machine couldn't have been even as much as two hundred feet up. But sound was falling away again, pulsing back from the hillside. Nick suspected that it had been losing height, actually coming down as it approached. Rowley was looking out through the for'ard observation slit that ran from beam to beam in that side of the DCT's armour. He said, 'Circling to the left now.'

'If it didn't, it'd be flying into the hill.'

Waiting . . .

Rowley shifted his position, to keep the seaplane in sight. 'Still circling. Might be coming round for another look.'

If the pilot *had* seen the ship, he'd be using his radio to call up an air strike. Vals, probably, from Bali: and they could be here in about as long as it would take to recite the Lord's Prayer. Meanwhile the seaplane would hang around, and show the bombers their target when they arrived.

If it came over for another check – shoot it down? Close up a pompom crew? But then, if you failed to knock it down – and if you were wrong and it *hadn't* seen the ship, or used its radio . . . He heard Greenleaf mutter, 'Still circling.'

So it *was* hanging round.

Bentley growled, 'Prob'ly only takin' a bit of a look-see, sir.'

This had been the only way to get the ship out. But he'd had a pretty good run of luck. There'd been at least as much luck as good judgement. It could have run out: it could be that this was as far as they were going to get.

On the other hand . . .

Forget the pompoms, he decided.

'Turning the other way. Going round to starboard.'

He joined Rowley at the hatch. The floatplane was out over the reefs to the north and banking to the right, to fly eastward. Rowley said, 'I don't believe he can have seen anything.'

'One section of marines is at the village where he's heading now. You said he came in over that point, didn't you?'

If Haskins's men had allowed themselves to be seen? Going back for another look at *them*, now?

But there were leatherneck sections at Mandar in the south-east, and on Sasul, and along the south coast as well. Wherever that thing flew you could imagine the worst, give it unpleasant reasons to be there.

'Turned south, sir.'

'To fly over the island where it's lower. Home to Bali.'

Or to swing back this way. The Vals would be lifting from their airstrip about now. Rowley told the pilot through that aperture in the armour, 'Go on home, you disgusting object.'

Able Seaman Bentley stirred. 'Well, seein' you don't need me, sir . . . What time we turnin' to, sir?'

'Sunset, or about then.'

'Aye aye, sir.' Bentley let himself down through the lubber's hole. A ladder from it led into the HACP – high angle control position – and from another manhole in the deck of that a longer ladder ran down the foremast to the rear end of the bridge.

'Can't have seen us, sir. He's gone.'

For a few minutes, things hadn't looked at all promising. Nick told Charles Rowley, 'I'm going down. If anything worries you, just let me know.'

With just one arm, the climb really was quite difficult. But you had to manage, get used to it. Much worse was the fact that his nerve wasn't as steady as it had been before he'd been wounded. When that seaplane had passed over and then begun to circle round again, he'd really thought they'd had it. It wouldn't do. He needed to pull himself together, get back to normal quickly: in fact *immediately*, because tonight wasn't going to be without its problems.

Thinking of wounds, though, reminded him that he had to visit the sickbay and get his dressings changed. Now might be as good a time as any.

'Captain, sir!'

He was on the third down-ladder from the bridge level, and the sickbay flat was close to the bottom of it. But the yeoman of signals, Morris, was rattling down the ladder after him. 'Signal to us, sir. Us and the *Sloan*.'

Nick took the clipboard one-handed, and leant against the steel handrail. 'Who deciphered this?'

'Sub-lieutenant Carey, sir.'

Carey was a paymaster. Schooly Hobbs had been in charge of decoding, but Hobbs was dead. Nick saw that the signal, addressed to him and to Jim Jordan, was an Intelligence report from Bandoeng. It read: 'Enemy naval movements southward through Lombok Strait are now heavy and continuous. Units passing through are deploying westward along south coast towards

685

Tjilatjap. A destroyer guardship is reported to have been anchored in the Alas Strait since first light this morning.'

Destroyer guardship in Alas. The cork was in *that* bottle, then.

No question of fighting your way through, either. If you fired a shot, they'd have you on toast at dawn, if not before.

Take a chance on Lombok? Trust to the dummy funnel, try to slip through without being challenged?

He took the signal off the log.

'I'll hang on to this, yeoman.'

He wanted time to think about it, before he had to discuss it with Gant or Chevening.

CHAPTER 12

Next time I'm sunk, Paul thought, *I'll drown*.

Brill had made it at the first attempt. And Mackeson had gone with him. The *Montgovern* had sunk, and Paul was on board *Ainsty*, the Hunt-class destroyer: he hadn't even got his feet wet. And at Narvik, two years ago, he'd been sunk in *Hoste*, and lived: so next time would be the third time *un*lucky . . . It was reasonable to suppose a man's personal luck couldn't last for ever; in fact it was a thought which had bothered him a few times when he'd been thinking about his father, when he'd got the feeling that that worst-of-all news was, in the long run, inevitable . . . Paul was standing, looking down at Beale, and Beale had made a remark about Withinshaw. Withinshaw's stout, dead body had been in the sea for two or three hours now, and it had been through remembering how it had looked when he'd last seen it that had triggered the presentiment, virtual certainty of his own turn coming – let alone his father's. It was logical to expect it: you couldn't go through this sort of experience often and expect to stay alive. To be alive as he was now, on board the destroyer, was something to be surprised at and grateful for. His last sight of Withinshaw's body had been after it had slithered down to the starboard side of the foc's'l-head. The sea had already been lapping across the scuppers although the ship seemed to have halted her long slide over and to be hanging, hesitating . . . The pause would be temporary, of course, and at any moment she'd decide to move again. Paul and Beale, clinging to the rail and stanchions on the high side – knowing by this time that the ship with the searchlight illuminating them was the Hunt and that she was closing in, coming to take them off the sinking freighter – had both been looking at the body, each thinking his own thoughts about it, and then happened to meet each other's eyes. Beale had shrugged, and Paul had understood him to be

687

saying that it wasn't worth trying to do anything about it, that Withinshaw was dead and what happened to his corpse didn't really matter. Paul had been considering sliding down there after it and trying to drag it up: for what purpose, what good, he couldn't remember.

What Beale had just said was, 'Soft as butter, was old Art.'

'Is it a fact he had two wives?'

Beale nodded. They were on the port side of *Ainsty*'s iron deck, abreast the pompom, which was perched up on a raised mounting abaft the funnel. It was about midnight. *Ainsty*'s wardroom, which was below the bridge, in the forepart of the ship, was stuffy with the crowd of survivors in it, and he'd come up for air; he'd walked aft down the starboard side of the ship to the quarterdeck, then back up the port side, and found Beale sitting here with Short and the Glaswegian and some other DEMS men from the *Montgovern*. Beale told him, in answer to the question about Withinshaw's marital complications, 'On account of bein' so soft. Couldn't say no to 'em, poor old sod.'

Paul put one hand up to the stem of the whaler in its davits, to steady himself. There wasn't all that much motion on the sea, but it was getting livelier. The *Santa Eulalia* was on the quarter, a dark bulk with white foam along its waterline. She'd sunk one of the E-boats, and the destroyer had bagged the other – which was cheering news, but no swap for the *Montgovern*. A ship became a home, and you grew fond of her without realizing it, and in this case the feeling of deprivation concerned people too – Brill in particular, and Mackeson as well. They'd been inside the ship when she'd slipped under. They and the wounded gunners, and four engine-room hands who'd been killed when the torpedo hit, and little Gosling who'd been shot through the throat, were the only non-survivors.

They'd known it was *Ainsty* floodlighting them, because after that first inspection she'd begun signalling. He'd read the flashing light, 'When my boats are in the water I intend putting my foc'sl alongside yours. Boats will pick up swimmers.' Boats had to be careful about getting too close to a ship that was about to sink and might roll over on them. The Hunt had slipped hers, then manoeuvred her bow up beside the freighter's stem. By that time other men were crowding for'ard, and among them was Thornton, the cipher expert. He'd told Paul that the order had been passed to abandon ship, and Mackeson had sent him up here to make them leave her quickly; the destroyer's captain had been issuing similar instructions through a loud-hailer. *Ainsty*'s foc'sl was higher now than the *Montgovern*'s partly submerged forepart. They let two jumping-ladders down, and the survivors began to swarm up them, destroyer sailors reaching down to help. Paul shouted to Thornton, while they were waiting for the others to go first, 'What about the doc and his patients?'

Mackeson was trying to get a boat alongside for them, Thornton had told him, and Brill had been trying to find a way of moving them. They were very badly burnt, and it wasn't easy; there was no possibility of getting them up to this end of the ship.

The *Montgovern*'s own boats had been incinerated, but there might have been some rafts intact, and the wounded could have been floated off in them, Paul thought. Fit men would be all right: the sea was low, the ship was taking her time about going down and the destroyer was close at hand. As long as no fresh attack developed, while they were in this vulnerable condition . . . He'd wondered about going aft to lend a hand: he was a very strong swimmer and might have made himself useful. But only the wounded needed help; Mackeson was taking charge of it and his orders to everyone up here were to clear out as fast as possible.

Thornton said, 'Go on, Everard.'

Action, emergency, had seemed to improve the cipher man. Paul had climbed over, stood for a moment with his heels hooked over the second rail and the top one against his calves, and judged his moment to jump for the ladder. A few seconds later he'd been on the destroyer's foc'sl, with Thornton clambering over behind him. They'd been the last and the destroyer had already been backing off, getting clear.

Brill and old Bongo must still have been with the wounded in the saloon when the *Montgovern* had tilted her bow up and slipped down. The doped-up wounded mightn't have known all that clearly what was happening to them, but Brill and Mackeson would have. They'd be inside her still, in several hundred fathoms. People you'd talked to only a few hours ago . . .

He said, 'The doctor drowned, with the guys he was looking after.'

Beale looked surprised. 'Doctor?'

'Army man.'

He strolled aft again, getting a good ration of fresh air before returning to the stuffy wardroom. Beale's surprised query,

689

'Doctor?' was a new sore in his mind. As if Dennis Brill had never existed.

There were some *Montgovern* survivors hanging around on the destroyer's quarterdeck; and torpedomen were hunched, muffled in coats and balaclavas, on watch near the depth-charge chutes. The crew of the after four-inch gun was one dark mass trying to keep itself warm inside the gunshield: and it wasn't so very long ago that he, Paul Everard, had kept a watch on deck like that. It did *seem* a long time ago . . . There was quite a lot of rise and fall on the ship: here on the quarterdeck you saw it as well as felt it, as the destroyer's counter rose and fell against the pile of white froth astern. Aboard the *Montgovern* he'd been thinking of the sea as more or less flat: except, remembering again, for the way it had come slopping over into the scuppers, like a live creature reaching to get at Withinshaw's body. Poor old Withinshaw, who couldn't swim and wouldn't have had to, either . . .

He went back up the starboard side, in through the door in the foc'sl break and through to the wardroom. The same crowd was in there, and the air was heavy with cigarette and pipe smoke. It was a space about twenty-seven feet long – the full width of the ship at this point – by twelve wide: the starboard half of it made a dining area, the rest was furnished with chairs and a sofa. Paul saw Pete Devenish, John Pratt and Harry Willis, and Cluny and Harrison, both engineers. Most of them had had to swim, and were in borrowed gear, dressing-gowns and blankets, while their own clothes dried out on the engine-room gratings. Thornton was here, and the RAF man, and some others. He guessed that Humphrey Straight, who'd been given the captain's day cabin, would already have turned in. When Paul arrived they were all listening to a young, cheerful-looking RN lieutenant: and he'd just said something about joining up with the *Caracas Moon* at first light.

But the *Caracas Moon* was the tanker, which when last seen had looked more like a floating bonfire than a ship.

'Excuse me, sir. Did you say the *Caracas Moon*'s afloat?'

'Astonishing, isn't it? After she left the convoy she was torpedoed, and it let in a rush of water that put the fire out. Then she was near-missed again yesterday, when we were with her, and it stopped her, but her plumbers are reckoning to get her fixed up during the night . . . Anyway, we left her to it, and came to round up your ship and the Yank. Who are you, by the way?'

He'd glanced at the single wavy stripe on the shoulder of Paul's greatcoat. Paul told him, 'My name's Everard. Taking passage to Malta to join HM Submarine *Ultra*.'

'Submariner, eh? Well, I'm Simpson, first lieutenant of this tub. How d'you do.' They shook hands. 'Did you say your name was Everard?'

He nodded.

'Any relation?'

It was ridiculous, really. The middle of the night, enemies thick all round them, and a few miles back men who'd been your friends were dead, drowned . . . Mackeson saying, *Bongo, they used to call me. I dare say he'll remember* . . . Simpson had turned back to the others: 'Now here's the point I was about to raise, gentlemen. The *Caracas Moon* people are just about dead on their feet. I suppose you've had a rough time too, but you can get a few hours' rest now, so – my CO suggests – how about some of you, or better still all of you, volunteering to move over to her when we find her?'

Dawn: with *Ainsty* zigzagging ahead of the *Santa Eulalia*, both ships rolling to a sea that had risen during the past few hours. The wind was force four gusting five, still from the north-west. White wave-crests streaked the darkness, and spray flew over the destroyer's port side and bow as she dipped her shoulder into them. Paul was on the upper deck, on the lee side of the funnel, with a group of the *Montgovern*'s officers. Thornton and the RAF man were both prostrate with seasickness, and had refused breakfast. It didn't matter: the meal had been laid on early for the benefit of those who'd be transferring to the tanker when they found her. Finding her shouldn't be difficult – if she was still afloat – as *Ainsty* was equipped with RDF.

Simpson had told Paul last night that *Defiant* had, indeed, been sent out to the East Indies. A friend of his had been in Alexandria when the cruiser had left for Port Said and the Canal.

'I didn't know your father had become a cruiser captain, though . . . Bad luck for you, anyway – you'd have been hoping to see him, I imagine.'

'Yes. I'd hoped to.'

Nobody could count on seeing anybody. From time to time, things happened to remind you of this simple truth. You had to register it, be aware of it, and then shut your mind to it. He'd woken with the uncertainties in his mind, though: uncertainties here in the Mediterranean, others more distant. The sleeping or

691

half-sleeping mind had no defence, it was only the waking one you could hope to take charge of.

He asked Harry Willis, 'What odds, d'you reckon, on getting *Santa Eulalia* and the tanker into Malta?'

Willis shifted his feet, balancing against a sudden bow-down lunge. In a destroyer, particularly a little one like a Hunt, when the wind got up you really felt it. That was something else Paul had forgotten about lately. The fourth mate suggested, 'Three to one against?'

'Steeper than that, I'd guess.' John Pratt chipped in, 'You're forgetting the Eyetie cruisers.'

Paul asked him, 'Eyetie cruisers?'

'A bunch of them's supposed to be coming to head us off from Malta. Now there are so few escorts left I suppose they reckon it's safe for them.'

Out of Cagliari, he remembered. But that had been days ago, and Mackeson had said they were probably going east, lured by some dummy convoy. This was the worst of being a passenger: you heard only bits and pieces, scraps of information that happened to come your way. The sense of ignorance and confusion was annoying and frustrating.

'You mean the two cruisers that were seen leaving Cagliari, Sardinia?'

'They've joined up with others.' Pratt said, 'Your pal Simpson was telling us.'

Willis said, 'Call it *five* to one against, then.' From above them, the pompom deck, an alarm rattler was sounding. And someone was shouting at them from the foc'sl ladder. It was a sub-lieutenant shouting through cupped hands over the racket of wind and sea, 'Passengers go below, please! Clear the upper deck!' Paul joined in the unwilling shuffle to the screen door, into the enclosure of the foc'sl. If it was true that an enemy cruiser force was coming, you could reckon the chances of reaching Malta as nil, he thought. Another thing Simpson had mentioned last night had been that the third cruiser, the last of three who'd been intended to escort the convoy on to Malta, had been knocked out on that night when the *Montgovern* had been hit and left the convoy. The cruiser had been torpedoed, and he thought they'd had to abandon her and sink her. So there was only a handful of destroyers now – most of them Hunts, escort destroyers with no torpedo armament. The sort of odds Italians might rather go for, he thought . . . In the wardroom,

Devenish was just hanging up the telephone: he told them, 'Air attack coming. They've got the bastards on RDF.'

Paul realized, looking around for somewhere to sit – and seeing Humphrey Straight arriving, standing glowering in the doorway because there was nowhere for him to sit either – that he'd never been below decks during an action before.

Ainsty began to heel to port: and stayed there, hard over. Altering course, under a lot of rudder, jolting and thumping her way round against the sea. He grabbed a cushion and sat down on it, on the deck in the corner near the pantry hatchway. Straight had done better: someone had surrendered the best of the armchairs to him. Devenish was stooping with a hand on the arm of it while he and Straight talked. Then he'd straightened, glancing round, and he was coming over to this corner.

'You with us, young Everard?'

'What d'you mean?'

'The old *Caracas Moon*. About half our DEMS blokes are coming over to her, but we'll be a bit short-handed. Might be useful to have you help organize 'em.'

He nodded. 'All right.'

'Fine.' Devenish looked round at Straight, and nodded. Straight, pleased-looking, nodded to Paul.

Christ. I've joined the Merchant Navy.

The four-inch opened fire. The mounting on the foc'sl was above this wardroom and only about thirty feet for'ard. When the guns fired, you *heard* them. There was no reason, he thought, not to go over to the tanker. Being a passenger with no job to do wasn't enjoyable. It was highly unenjoyable here, now, sitting and guessing at what was happening. It would be far less unpleasant in the open, and *much* less so if one was busy. Behind that feeling was a sense of enclosure, of being trapped – as Brill and Mackeson had been . . . There was a lot of gun-noise now, shaking the ship, but it was still all four-inch. He saw a new face in the doorway, hesitating, looking round genially as if it was about to introduce itself. It was a red face under brown curly hair, and the uniform had RNVR lieutenant's stripes on it. Then he saw there was red between the stripes. A doctor, surgeon-lieutenant.

'Hello . . . Captain Straight, is it? I'm Grant. I'm the sawbones.'

The pompoms had joined in now. Grant was a Scot, and he'd be about thirty, Paul guessed. Those thumps had been bombs bursting in the sea not very far away. The doctor was telling Straight,

693

pitching his voice up over the noise, 'Well, we have *three* twin four-inch, you see, Because we're a second-generation Hunt. The group one variety only had two twin mountings, you're right, they had a four-barrelled pompom where our number three gun is. Our pompom has its own deck up by the funnel. We have Oerlikons too, though, one each side of the signal bridge. You're safe as houses, you see, with us!'

She'd heeled again. You could hear the Oerlikons, as well as the pompoms and the four-inch. On the port side more bombs were exploding: he'd counted five, probably one stick. The doctor said, 'These are Junkers 88s annoying us. But there's good news too – we've a surface contact on the RDF and the skipper's pretty sure it's the *Caracas Moon*.'

One isolated, very loud explosion, somewhere astern. Grant said, 'Missed again. Never seem much good in the mornings, do they?' He looked at Straight: 'Rotten luck, sir, losing your ship.'

Straight glowered at him, and didn't answer. Humphrey Straight might not have been at his best in the early mornings either. And he *had* just lost his ship. Also, this doctor was a garrulous, socially ebullient type of man, the complete opposite to Straight, whose reaction to chitchat was to clam up, back off. The doctor had obviously been told by the destroyer's captain to come down here and entertain the passengers, and he was working hard at it too . . . Only four-inch now, and *Ainsty* was on an even keel for once, steering a more or less straight course, bucking and plunging to the sea. Straight was thumbing shag tobacco into his pipe: it wouldn't improve the quality of life for the seasick members of the party.

The four-inch ceased fire. The silence was ominous, leaving the imagination loose with no guidelines for guesswork. Then she was beginning to heel again: right over, turning in a tight circle with her starboard gunwale in the sea, by the feel of it. Juddering round: and everything suddenly letting loose again – four-inch and close-range guns all opening fire at once. Devenish yelled at Grant, 'Do they get air and surface contacts on the same RDF set?'

'Different set for each job.' The doctor leaned towards him. He looked glad to have something to talk about. 'The type 271's for surface work, finding submarines and so on, and the 279's for aircraft. They had a type 79 to start with, but it didn't give ranges, only bearings . . . There are new types being developed every week now, you know.'

She'd steadied, level-keeled, with all her guns still blasting.

694

Straight blurted suddenly, 'D'ye know as much about doctoring as you do about bloody RDF?'

'Lord, no.' The Scotsman raised his hands imploringly. '*Please* don't get anything wrong with you.'

Gunfire slackening. Grant was looking across at Paul. 'You must be the submariner, I take it?'

It was a surprise, ten minutes later, to find the *Santa Eulalia* still afloat and apparently unhurt, butting along at seven or eight knots while the destroyer zigzagged through grey-white sea a couple of hundred yards ahead of her. A new day had been born while they'd been listening to the guns. The sky was high grey cloud, wispy and fast-moving, and the wind was whipping the wave-crests into flat white streamers. Harry Willis tapped him on the shoulder: 'Other side. *Caracas Moon* herself!' Paul followed him in through the screen door and through to the other side of the ship: the weather side, wind gusty and laced with spray. Willis pointed: 'Load of old iron. Our new home, mate.'

The tanker was under way, but listing heavily to port. She was more than a load of old iron, though, Paul thought, she was a load of high-octane spirit, the stuff the Malta fighters needed, and diesel fuel for submarines as well. According to the late Bongo Mackeson. A light was flashing from her bridge, and he read 'Master and chief engineer will remain on board but assistance welcome and relief of crew members and gunners will be appreciated. Stopping my engines now.' The destroyer was under helm, heeling as she swung to pass under the tanker's stern. Paul heard the shrill of a bosun's call and the yell 'Away motorboat's crew!' It might be a damp crossing, he thought. But there was too much movement on the ships for them to approach each other closely. The boat would have the benefit of the bigger ship's lee. The *Caracas Moon* would provide a very solid barrier against wind and sea.

'Everard?'

Turning, he found Simpson, the first lieutenant, in seaboats and duffel-coat. 'You've volunteered to go over with the DEMS gunners, that right?'

'Yes, sir.'

'Well done.' Simpson looked round at the others. 'Better stand by, now. Motorboat's starboard side. We'll be turning that side to her when we get up in her lee, but it'll take several trips.' He said to Paul, as they filtered away aft, 'You're a glutton for punishment, Everard.'

Paul didn't see that it made much difference. This destroyer could be split open by a single bomb, torpedo or mine and go down in seconds. Tankers, being full of inflammable liquid, were feared: but the *Santa Eulalia*'s cargo – Pratt had told him – included fifteen hundred tons of high octane, five hundred tons of kerosene and two thousand tons of explosives including torpedo warheads. He didn't see that it could make much difference which deck you sat on.

Ainsty had hoisted the red warning flag, and gunners on all three ships waited, watching the sky, ready for whatever had appeared on the destroyer's RDF screen to come into sight.

In the boat – he'd come over to the *Caracas Moon* in the second boatload – he'd met Beale. Now, as the little convoy got under way, he had Beale in charge of all the guns aft while he himself looked after the four Oerlikons on the bridge deck up for'ard. He'd got one of them for himself, and fourth mate Willis had another. On the raised deck aft, around the funnel, there were two Bofors and two more Oerlikons. Beale had put Short and McNaught on the Oerlikons, and he was operating one of the Bofors and supervising the other one. From Paul's point of view, since he knew nothing about Bofors, it was a good arrangement.

The tanker was fire-blackened, her paintwork scorched and blistered. She was also listing, several feet lower in the water than she should have been, and there was some talk of her back being broken – or that there was a danger of it, if she was shaken by any more near-misses. Boarding her amidships, on to her after section of tanktops in the low part between bridge and funnel, had been simply a matter of jumping over from the boat's own level.

However, she was making about five knots now. She and the *Santa Eulalia* were abeam of each other, with *Ainsty* weaving ahead.

Malta sixty-five miles away.

High on the port beam – Stukas. Paul had only just spotted them when *Ainsty* opened fire at them with her four-inch HA guns.

Sixty-five miles at five knots: thirteen hours. It was now just after eight. So ETA Malta – Stukas and others permitting – might be 2100 hours this evening?

Stukas permitting . . . *Ainsty*'s time-fused shells, opening black against pale grey sky and turning immediately into brown smears on the wind, lined the Stukas' approach. Eight – no, ten of them, all

696

in one group. He'd looked round, checking that all the other guns were manned and pointing the right way. Now he settled at his own, straddling his feet and pressing his shoulders into the curved rests. He pulled back the cocking lever, felt and heard the first round slide and click into the breech. Eight o'clock here, he thought – remembering what Simpson had told him about *Defiant*, that she *had* gone east – would be eight hours plus six, therefore two o'clock in the afternoon, in the Java Sea. The mind reached to what one knew, in sober recognition of reality, Beale-style reality, might very soon be unreachable.

Come on, Stukas . . .

By noon he'd lost count of the number of attacks. Nearly all had been by Ju88s, only three by Stukas. There'd been plenty of near-missing. All three ships, at times, had been hidden from the others by bombs bursting around them. The red flag had just run up the *Ainsty*'s yardarm again, and Paul was remembering Jack Everard telling him that in the Crete battle there'd been occasions when ships had been under air attack continuously, with no intervals, from dawn to dusk. By that comparison, he told himself, this wasn't anything to write home about. You did get moments in which to draw breath, look around, smoke a cigarette.

It was bad enough, though. The attacks got into your mind, after a while. You had the images of diving aircraft, noise of guns and bombs there all the time, like some internal film running which you couldn't stop. Like the kind of replay-dreaming that you got sometimes, after some daytime task of a repetitive nature, the half-asleep brain playing it over and over . . .

Low on the port bow: torpedo aircraft. Real, not imagined. Italians: Savoia Marchetti 79s. Withinshaw's voice croaked in his mind, *Bastards. Fookin', soddin' bastards . . . Ainsty* was cracking on speed and heading straight out towards them, a mound of foam piling under her stern as she charged at high speed towards the closely-grouped flight of torpedo-bombers. Her for'ard four-inch opened up. She looked small from here, stern-on and with all that foam around her, twin four-inch hammering and shellbursts opening, low to the sea, under the attackers' noses.

One was in flames, slithering down; a sheet of water sprang up where it went in. Another was banking away, its torpedo falling askew. Two others bearing away to port, getting the hell out . . . Another torpedo toppled in all wrong, wasted – from any Italian way of looking at it – and there was only one Savoia left now. It had turned away to port, but not running away like that other pair. It had by-passed the destroyer and was now swinging in again to approach from the starboard bow, the *Santa Eulalia*'s side. *Ainsty* was turning back, and all her guns were concentrating on it. It was on the American freighter's bow, steadying on a low, attacking approach with the American obviously its target. The *Santa Eulalia*'s Bofors had judged the range right and opened fire. The *Caracas Moon*'s guns weren't going to get a look in, because by the time the range was short enough the *Santa Eulalia* was between them and the attacker. Frustrating. But there'd be time yet. Nine, ten hours, for sure . . . *Ainsty* was swinging hard a-starboard and her guns were cocked up, firing at maximum elevation.

Target overhead?

Ju88s were coming in shallow dives from astern: four of them, a pair going for each of the merchantmen. They'd sneaked up when everyone had been concentrating on the Italians. They were at about two thousand feet, in dives that would bring them over at about fifteen hundred, and almost right on top of their targets already. Paul aimed well ahead of the leader of the pair on this side, and opened fire, heard Beale's two Bofors banging away at about the same time. The bastards had been pretty smart, he thought, his gun deafening him and his head back from the sights now, watching the other end of his tracer-stream and hose-piping it towards the bomber's nose.

Hitting!

Bombs slanting down. All the guns in all three ships working hard. An explosion – away to starboard somewhere. Torpedo, he guessed: *Santa Eulalia*? The front Junkers was streaming smoke but he'd left it, to concentrate on the second. A bomb went into the sea close off the tanker's starboard quarter: a second and a third – horribly, unbelievably – burst on her, somewhere aft. He heard and felt the explosions, then almost immediately felt heat, flames behind him. The second Ju88 had let its load go. He knew, in physically sickening disappointment, that this would be the end of it – for the ship and for himself personally . . . There were no targets now except for that bomber leaving, the *Santa Eulalia*'s second one departing too and bomb-splashes subsiding right ahead of her. He thought – from just a quick glance – that she'd stopped. The gunners aft – where flames roared, heat so strong that even

698

right up here you wanted to take cover from it – were his responsibility, and on the port side it might just be possible to get through to them. With a coat over one's head – might be . . . Harry Willis yelled at him, but he didn't hear the words. He ran to the ladder and started down – it led down in two flights, with its base at the walkway over the after tank-tops – going down it backwards, on that port side of the ship, his back to the heat and the fire's noise. One-handed on the ladder's rail as he reached with the other for a handkerchief to hold over his nose and mouth to act as a filter. Halfway down he thought, *I shan't make it. It's impossible and they must be dead.* He'd heard of people plunging bravely into fires, but he'd just begun to appreciate that there were degrees of heat into which the human body could not be forced. He went on down. He had to, because something might change, it might become easier down there. And there could be a man or men not dead. Two more steps backward, dragging himself down into the inferno, *knowing* he wouldn't make it, paint that was already black from an earlier fire beginning to run and blister on the bulkhead and the ladder's handrail already hot to hold.

'Bloody idiot, *here!*'

Willis had come down after him. He was grabbing at his arm. They were halfway down, where at the level of the accommodation deck you had to switch from one flight of ladderway to another. It made sense. Sense mightn't have prevailed if the fourth mate hadn't been here bawling it in his face. They were off the ladder, in the after promenade of the accommodation deck, when the fire got into an after tank and the *Caracas Moon* blew up.

He didn't know it, at the time.

It wasn't clear what was happening, or had happened. He'd go on down in a minute, he thought, and get Beale out of it. The other way about, Beale wouldn't have left *him* to burn. Beale was a hard nut in a way, but he was absolutely straight, a man to count on. One knew that, instinctively, it was a basis of – he hoped – mutual respect. His father had said, 'I really do have to marry Mrs Gascoyne, old chap. Very kind of you to be so concerned, but—' Beale had laughed. 'Soft as butter, that's his trouble. Can't say no to 'em. 'When Paul came out of the dream-world he was flat on his back and staring up at a steel ceiling on which paint was bubbling and turning brown. Something was on fire beside him, the smoke of it in his eyes and throat; and Harry Willis was crawling towards him on his hands and knees but with his head up and his eyes fixed on Paul, his mouth opening as if he was shouting but no sound coming out. He looked either furious, or mad. Willis was on fire; the nearer burning was Paul's own greatcoat. There'd been some kind of cataclysm in which personal responsibility had ended, everything had cut off, finished. Willis was totally on fire: didn't he know it? Paul was crouching beside him, beating at flames with his bare hands. Then he'd wrenched his own coat off – it was only smouldering – and he tried to wrap it around Willis, to smother the flames with it. Willis struck out at him. He was a big man and he *did* seem mad, screaming like a character in a film with the sound cut off. He'd pushed Paul clear, throwing him back, and broken free – to the rail, sliding his body over it horizontally and then letting go . . . He *had* been screaming, Paul realized; because he, Paul, had shouted at him a second ago and not heard his own voice either. He was stone deaf. Burst eardrums, probably. There'd been an explosion, she'd blown up . . .

But – afloat, still . . .

Where the ladder had been, the ladder he'd come down from the deck above, flames licked over paintwork on the blackened vertical bulkhead. The ladder itself was scrap, twisted iron, and the bulkhead ran straight down to the sea. Down there now was no fire, no ship. Sea washed soundlessly six feet below him. A littered sea, all sorts of rubbish floating. No heads, no swimmers. The stern half of the ship had gone, sunk: she'd broken in two, he realized, and he was on the for'ard half, which was still afloat. It was conceivable, he supposed, that this half might *remain* afloat . . . He'd have been dead by now, he thought, if Harry Willis hadn't pulled him off the ladder. Willis: he went back to the side rail, where the fourth mate had gone over, expecting to see him swimming, getting clear of the ship's side. But he wasn't, he was close to it and spreadeagled face-down, motionless except for the sea's own movement. He'd have a lifebelt on, under his coat – should have – and for the time being the coat and his clothes would be helping to hold him up. But face-downwards in the water, unconscious, he'd drown even before they were sodden enough to drag him under. Paul climbed over the rail. Hesitating for a moment, he saw *Ainsty* – to his left – coming up astern through patches of burning oil and a scattering of wreckage. She had scrambling-nets down, and a whaler just leaving her side. But from there they wouldn't see Willis, not in time anyway. He jumped, feet-first and well out, away from the ship's side and Willis who was still close against it.

Under water – for a long time after he'd thought he ought to be coming up – he wondered about Beale and the others who'd been aft. Whether they'd got over the side. If they had, the destroyer might find them, somewhere astern. The light was blinding and his stretched lungs were hurting as he broke surface and let breath go, gulped air, tried not to gulp sea or, worse still, oil. Willis was within arm's reach. Paul got hold of the large, heavy body and turned it over: it had already begun to sink. And the forehead was bloody, pulpy. He'd hit the ship's side on the way down – because of the list, the slant, and just letting himself drop like that. He'd been on fire, for God's sake . . . Paul got behind, under him, began to swim with his legs, towing Willis backwards away from the tanker's side. Above him, in the bridge wing, someone was leaning over, pointing downward and waving either to the destroyer or the boat. Probably shouting, as well, but Paul still couldn't hear anything at all. Be no damn use in submarines, he knew, if he was deaf. No use anywhere. He stared up, through the water and salt in his eyes, at the figure on the tanker's bridge – two men there now. He was wishing he could hear a shout, hear *anything* – when, up beyond them and against pale grey sky, he saw four Spitfires in tight formation circling above the ships. He couldn't hear *them*, either.

On board the destroyer – whose whaler had picked him and Willis up, after which they'd been inboard in what had seemed about five seconds – Paul assured the doctor, Grant, that he was perfectly all right except for the fact that he couldn't hear. Grant examined him, then wrote on a signal-pad, 'Temporary flattening of the eardrums. Should correct itself quite quickly.' He didn't look as if he believed it, though. Paul took the pencil from him and wrote, 'Willis?' The answering scrawl read, 'Unconscious. Head injury. You rest now.' Willis had been in the sickbay, and Paul had been lent the navigator's cabin. He wasn't sure, and couldn't remember drinking anything except a mug of coffee, but the doctor might have given him some kind of sedative, because he did go out like a light; and Grant had been right about the eardrums, because after a short, heavy sleep he was woken by the ship's guns firing at more aircraft. Either he'd dreamt about seeing Spitfires, or they must have left . . . Wrapping himself in a blanket, he went into the wardroom: its sole occupant was Thornton, reclining on the sofa. The cipher expert woke up, and asked Paul why he wasn't on board the *Caracas Moon*.

701

He didn't mind Thornton now. When the *Montgovern* had been sinking he'd seemed quite human. Thornton asked him, 'Why are you wearing a blanket, for God's sake?'

'D'you have a cigarette?' He had to explain it all. While he was doing so, he smoked the cigarette and got dressed. There was a heap of gear in the corner, stuff that had been borrowed while the borrowers' clothes had been drying out, as Paul's were drying now. He selected grey flannel trousers, a collarless shirt and a white submarine sweater, and seaboots with seaboots stockings in them. The boots were tight, so he discarded the stockings, and the trousers were short but it didn't matter, they were tucked into the boots anyway. There was an oilskin coat on a hook outside the wardroom door, and he borrowed that too on his way out. The guns had ceased fire, by this time.

He went to the sickbay first, to check on Harry Willis, but the fourth mate was still in coma. And no other swimmers had been picked up, so far as the doctor knew. Simpson, whom Paul ran into in the lobby outside the cabins, confirmed this. There'd been no survivors from the *Caracas Moon*'s afterpart. Simpson said, 'But the good half of her's in tow now. Did you realize?'

Half a tanker: in tow from the *Santa Eulalia*. Simpson told him, 'Apparently she has seventy-five per cent of her total cargo in the for'ard tanks.'

It had taken an hour to get the tow passed – a manilla hawser from the *Santa Eulalia*'s stern to the tanker's bow, and a wire linking the *Caracas Moon*'s after end – which was now just behind her bridge, where she'd broken in two cleanly at the bulkhead, which was holding – to *Ainsty*'s foc'sl. The wire, with the destroyer's weight judiciously applied from time to time in this or that direction, made towing possible by holding the misshapen hulk on course; without it, the half-tanker swung around and pulled the *Santa Eulalia* off *her* course. The art, *Ainsty*'s captain's expertise, was to use just enough drag and no more: clumsy handling might part the bow hawser. Meanwhile, they were making-good three knots.

Simpson added, 'Except for interruptions. In the last Stuka attack we had to cast off the wire, to get room to manoeuvre. Then it takes a while to get connected up again.'

'So what speed are we averaging?'

'Well – up to now – about a knot and a half.'

'How far to go, now?'

'Thirty-eight miles.'

At a knot and a half, that would mean twenty-five hours' steaming.

His ears still felt muffled, and one of them had a persistent ringing noise in it . . . Simpson said, 'You'd better come up top. Skipper wants to say hello, anyway.'

Ainsty's captain was an unshaven, exhausted-looking man: bloodshot eyes stared at Paul from under a woollen hat with a red bobble on it. He nodded. 'I've met your father. You've got something to live up to there, sub. Glad they fished you out so you'll get a chance to.' He was watching the wire and the hulk of the *Caracas Moon*. He told Simpson, 'Let him stay up here if he wants to. Out of the way somewhere.'

Paul settled at the after end of the bridge, behind the starboard lookout position. He saw that the *Santa Eulalia*, who was towing the tanker, was herself listing about ten degrees to starboard. She'd been hit by a torpedo from a Savoia, Simpson told him. He remembered: he hadn't seen it but he'd .heard it, just as those Ju88s had been coming at them. But a cripple towing a wreck, he thought, watching the two ships lumbering ahead: how the hell anyone could think it possible to keep this lot afloat and moving for a whole day, or even half a day . . . But the American freighter's weight, her momentum through the water, did make her a far better towing vessel than the lightweight Hunt could have been. It still seemed futile – inevitable that pretty soon one or both ships would be bombed and sunk. But on the other hand it was also impossible just to give up, go home, admit defeat . . . He remembered a passage from a novel he'd read a few months ago, when he'd been in *Ultra* in and around the Clyde. It was a book called *The Empty Room* by Charles Morgan, and he'd re-read the lines until they'd stuck in his memory, and with an effort he could recall them now: 'Because the security of tomorrow was gone, the long, binding compulsion of past and future took possession of the English mind. Not to yield ceased to be heroic because to yield had become impossible.' It was exactly like that: you were in it and you had to go through with it, as long as there was strength to move. This convoy operation seemed to have become disjointed and haphazard; but this was only one fragmented section of it, there'd be other struggles elsewhere, ships like badly wounded men just managing to crawl on, with Malta like a magnet drawing them. Morgan's words hit the nail on the head: there was no question of heroics, only of a one-way street and a driving impulse.

He asked Simpson about the Spitfires. And they *had* been here – Spitfires from Malta. Simpson thought they'd be back again in the morning, probably. It had almost certainly been due to their presence earlier that there'd been an hour's respite from attack while the tow had been passed and the ships had got themselves under way again. Since the Spits had flown off there'd been two attacks, and the Stukas had come with an escort of fighters – Messerschmitts – over them. Stukas on their own made easy meat for fighters: but on that evidence, when the Spitfires did return these ships couldn't count on anything like total protection, because the bombers would probably have *their* escorts.

RDF had hostile aircraft on the screen. Simpson muttered, 'Here we go again. Keep your head down, sub.' He moved away, into the forepart of the bridge.

'Aircraft red three-oh, angle of sight one-five, Junkers 88s!'

The guns would be swinging to that bearing and elevation. He heard the captain tell Simpson, 'I'll try to keep the tow intact this time, number one.'

'Aye aye, sir.'

'Messenger – give Sub-Lieutenant Everard a battle-bowler.'

'RDF reports second formation right ahead, closing!'

Two lots of attackers now. They'd want to end it before sundown, Paul guessed. They'd be alarmed by the possibility of the ships getting under the Malta fighter umbrella by first light, perhaps. Not that it could be done, in fact – unless the *Santa Eulalia* was sent on alone?

Get one ship in, rather than lose two?

'Green nine-oh, torpedo-bombers!' The lookout in the bay below Paul had half risen from his seat, pointing. He yelled, 'Angle of sight zero!'

Someone in the bridge announced, 'They're Heinkels, sir.'

'God damn and blast it.' The skipper told Simpson bitterly, 'Slip the bloody wire.'

It might have been a month, by the feel of it, since the *Montgovern* had steamed through the Gibraltar Strait. And he'd changed, he felt, in that time. Passing Gib, he'd been younger, too hopeful, too blithely confident, too bloody ignorant.

Hadn't Beale seen that, and laughed at it?

No *laffin'* voices now. Just guns' voices, all of them familiar. The destroyer's four-inch alone, at first, and then the American freighter's heavy defensive barrage. Her gunners were US Navy men, Pratt had said at some stage. The half-tanker had only the four Oerlikons on her bridge now, but every little helped. One Heinkel III went into the sea, and the torpedoes from the other two weren't seen after they hit the water. The formation right ahead turned out to be Malta Spitfires: they arrived too late to break up the Junkers attack but shot two of them down as they flew away towards Sicily. No damage done, only time lost. Time, ammunition, fuel. That much less aviation spirit for the fighter defence of Malta: that much more time to be spent at sea – tonight, tomorrow . . . Considering that he'd had a few hours' sleep last night and another sleep after his swim, Paul felt extraordinarily tired. Perhaps Grant *had* given him some sedative. He didn't want to go below, though; he'd sleep up here, he thought, when it was dark and the dusk attacks were over. He thought he might even be able to sleep standing up, if he had to. Like a horse: lean on the back of the lookout bay, lift one foot on to its toes behind you, lower the head and sleep. Even the guns mightn't wake you.

'Hello, there. Everard, isn't it?'

Ainsty's RN sub-lieutenant shook Paul's hand. 'I'm Carnegie. How goes it? Ears okay now?'

Carnegie looked younger than Paul thought *he* looked. He also looked, if anything, more tired even than Paul felt. Everyone you looked at was in a state of near-exhaustion. These people would have been at action stations continuously, he guessed, for the last four days.

'Hear about the Italian cruisers?'

'I heard some were on their way south, or—'

'They've turned back. RAF recce planes fooled them into believing they were guiding some powerful force of battleships to intercept them. By putting out a lot of phoney signals, and so on. So the Eyeties have turned tail and they're legging it for home.'

'That was smart work.'

Carnegie nodded. '*Mare Nostrum* is Italian for Naples harbour. The *inner* harbour, actually . . . Now I've got to go down and see to that frigging wire. See you later.'

He'd gone. *Ainsty*'s gunners were training their weapons fore-and-aft and ditching empty shell-cases as she returned to her station astern of the *Caracas Moon*'s fore section. She'd nose up close, and a sailor on her foc's'l would lob a heaving-line across for the eye of the wire to be attached to it. (In the tanker they'd have hauled the wire up inboard, while the attack had been in progress.) Then the wire would be hauled in and made fast; and then on again, Malta-wards, waiting for the next assault to come in, and with possibly only thirty-*seven* miles to cover now.

CHAPTER 13

'Stop together.' Nick Everard put the telephone down and lifted his glasses for a look at the motorboat, which was lying waiting a cable's length on the port bow. Through gathering darkness he could see three men in its sternsheets: they'd be the boat's coxswain, and Lieutenant Wainwright, and probably the sergeant of that marine section. The rest of the Sasul RM party would be inside the cabin. *Defiant* was losing way, sliding up towards the stopping-point where he'd embark the marines and hoist the boat. He'd sent it over from the mangrove inlet just before he'd started to move the ship out; it had been reasonable to use the powerboat instead of a cutter this time, because the channel's hazards were marked with spar-buoys and Wainwright, who'd been in charge of the cutter this morning, knew his way in and out.

Nick wished he knew *his* way out. He'd weighed it up and made a choice, but the spin of a coin might have been as good a way to decide it. The Alas Strait or the Lombok Strait, both of them almost certainly patrolled. Heads or tails . . .

He'd begun extracting *Defiant* from her mud-hole just as the light was going. Breast-wires to the shore, hand-tended on both sides of the foc's'l and with the capstan running so they could apply tension this way or that as necessary, had kept her bow middled in the inlet while the wire to the stream anchor was being hove in on the quarter-deck. That part of it had been an awkward, inch-by-inch progress, but as soon as her stern had been out of the creek, and a leadline had confirmed that there were a few feet of water under it, he'd given her a touch astern on one screw, and she'd come out like a cork from a greasy bottle. A short churn of the same screw running ahead had stopped her then, while the stream anchor was weighed – a hose playing on it over the stern to wash half a ton of mud off it as it rose.

It hadn't been possible to turn her until she was out through the gap where, on the way in, Ormrod had buoyed a rock on each side of the channel. Nick had conned her out stern-first, very carefully and slowly, with Ormrod showing a fixed blue light from a whaler to guide him down the middle. When he'd got her out and clear of that gap he'd turned her inside her own length, using one screw ahead and one astern, while Chevening watched the bearings on the two sparbuoys to ensure that in the process of turning she remained over the same safe spot. Then the whaler shot alongside and was hooked on; as soon as it was clear of the water he'd had his ship under way, both screws slow ahead, following the marked channel to this point off Sasul.

Gant called from the after end of the bridge that the motorboat was out of the water.

'Slow ahead together. Steer three-one-five. And – Wiley – steer as fine as you did this morning.'

'Aye aye, sir. Both telegraphs slow ahead, sir.'

'Pilot, is it one and a half miles now?'

'One-point-four, sir. We overshot a little.'

'Tell me at one-point-three.'

Rounding the Sasul island and its rock surround, now, on the same track he'd come in by but in reverse. He was tempted to cut the next corner, and according to charted information he could have, but it would only have saved a few minutes. He'd been very lucky, he knew, to have got away with so much already. One should thank God for it, he told himself, not get over-confident and start taking risks that weren't essential.

There'd be risks enough that would *have* to be accepted, in the next few hours. Tonight, either the gamble paid off, or you lost everything. 'Everything' being a cruiser and her company. The personal side of it, his own, didn't count for much and wasn't an element in his thinking; except he'd like to have seen Kate again, and Paul. He'd like to have talked a lot with Paul, tried to steer him clear of some of the family complications. Paul would make out all right, though. By tomorrow's sunrise he might have become Sub-Lieutenant *Sir* Paul Everard RNVR, but he'd wear that all right too, once he got used to it.

Sunrise here tomorrow would be only midnight in the Mediterranean. By sunrise there, it would be midday here, and by that time *Defiant* would be either in the clear – or getting on that way – or under a lot of water.

Cross your fingers . . .

He could do that with his *left* hand.

'We've run one-point-three, sir!'

'Stop port.'

'Stop port, sir . . .'

The bearing on Paliat was all right. But on this course, heading almost straight towards it, the bearing didn't change much anyway. The log-reading was what you had to go by.

'One-point-four, sir!'

'Port ten.'

He had to bring her round to two hundred and forty degrees now, for a leg of two and one-fifth miles. Then due south for six miles, which would take her clear of Sepanjang's southwest corner. And *then* . . . Well, that was the crucial decision. He'd made it, for better or for worse; and he'd used Gant and Chevening to help him in the process.

He'd sent for them to meet him in the chartroom at half an hour before sunset, when the marines had been recalled to the ship and were on their way from the two villages, the hilltop and the southern beach. He'd shown Gant the signal from Bandoeng about the heavy naval traffic in Lombok and the destroyer on guard in Alas.

Gant murmured, passing it to Chevening, 'Seems to put the kybosh on both exits.'

'What's your view, pilot?'

'Don't know, sir . . . It's – well, it's not *good*, is it . . . Might we go west, try the Bali Strait?'

He shook his head. 'I don't even think much of *Sloan*'s chances there now. With a stream of enemy ships through Lombok, turning west – they're all cutting across the exit from the Bali Strait, aren't they? If they're still coming through, that is . . . Another point, though – if they've bothered to put a patrol on the Alas Strait, the odds are they'll have done the same elsewhere.'

You could just about spit across the Bali Strait. You could guard it with a rowing boat.

Gant was rubbing the small of his back, where the pain was. He asked, 'I imagine you've formed an idea or two already, sir?'

'Nothing hard and fast. That's why I'm enrolling your brains as well. As I see it, we have a straightforward choice between the Lombok Strait and the Alas Strait. This signal's time of origin was just after noon. We don't know what time the observations were made – by aircraft, submarine, or shore observations, whatever – but we must assume, I think, that it describes the position as we're likely to find it. And on that basis, Bob – what would you do?'

'I'd forget Alas, sir. Because it's narrower than Lombok and we do know it's guarded. I'd go for Lombok – with your dummy funnel up, and hoping to be taken for one of their lot.'

'Pilot?'

'I think I agree with that, sir.'

It had been his own first reaction, too, when he'd first seen the signal. It was an attractive idea because Lombok was the nearest of the straits, and the widest, and the direct, head-on approach appealed to him. But there were some aspects of it he didn't like. He said, 'The traffic through Lombok can't go on indefinitely. I imagine they're sending forces through to take Tjilatjap, cut off any evacuation and any ships that may be there. Perhaps put some troops ashore somewhere; but it's a phase that could well be over.'

He hoped it was, for Jim Jordan's sake. But he was only prodding, looking for aspects he hadn't thought about already.

Chevening nodded. 'It might be wide open, now.'

'Would you leave it wide open, if you were a Jap? While you were taking the trouble to block Alas?'

'Fair point, sir.' Gant said, 'The fact is we *know* they're blocking Alas, and we can give Lombok the benefit of a doubt. If they've been rushing ships through there, they may not have got as far as putting a watch on it yet. You'd tend to watch the holes you weren't using, wouldn't you?'

'Perhaps . . . You'd just dash through, Bob, would you?'

'Well – if one went through at about twelve or fifteen knots . . . Not too much dash, but not looking too sneaky either.'

Chevening said, 'My feeling too, sir.'

'And you may well be right.' His own mind was open to the idea, at that stage. Baulking still at the thought of all that traffic, the prospect of having Jap ships challenging him, or sending other signals that he wouldn't know how to answer. Except by shining a light on their beastly flag, which in any case he wasn't keen to fly. The thought of a challenge and having to identify himself was the real snag. There were advantages too, though. It was close, and he could travel fast through it and be a lot farther south by first light than he'd be if he took the longer route via Alas.

But the wide-open, easy-looking Lombok Strait still gave him the shivers, for some reason.

710

'Do we have a large-scale chart of the Alas Strait?'

The folio for these waters was in the top drawer of the chart table. He lit a cigarette while Chevening thumbed through the labelled front edges and then pulled out chart 3706.

Nick leaned over it, smoking and ruminating. After a few minutes, he thought he might have found the answer.

'Right. Pilot – you're captain of a Jap destroyer, and your orders are to anchor in the Alas Strait where you can cover anyone like us trying to break out of the Java Sea. Where'll you drop your hook?'

The requirements were for water shallow enough to anchor in, and to be able to see right across the Strait. He thought there was one place more suitable than any other; and two other possibles that you'd discard in favour of the first.

Chevening said, 'Either in this area – here, or here – or on this patch just north of Petagan.'

'You can only be in one of those places, though.'

'The Petagan area's ideal, sir. Good view across the entrance, ten fathoms or a bit less, and you'd be covering this Sungian Strait as well.'

'Why not here on the east side, your other possibles?'

'Because a ship could slip into the Strait through the Sungian backwater and you wouldn't see it.'

'That's true, you wouldn't. But if you were lying there near Petagan, what if a ship came hugging the east coast, down inside all these islands? Bob?'

Gant had been nodding, agreeing with the navigator's choice of anchorage. He answered, 'Because that's a complicated passage. It's not even labelled as a channel, the way the Sungian route is. Also, I think if I was a Jap, I'd be expecting any Allied ship to appear from the west, not from that way.'

'Exactly my own thought.' Nick was studying the chart again, looking for anything he might have missed. But this did look like the answer. He might kick himself when at dawn tomorrow he found himself not very far south of the islands – because it *would* take longer . . . Petagan: he felt sure that no destroyer captain in his senses and with that purpose would pick any other anchorage.

Steering south now, at twenty-five knots. In five minutes he'd be bringing her round to a hundred and twenty-five degrees, which would take her across the northern approach to the Alas Strait at a distance from it of about thirty miles. After three hours on that course, he'd turn south. An hour of that, and *Defiant* would be slipping in between the islands of Pandjang and Seringgit, then turning southwest to follow a zigzag route between the mainland of Sumbawa and the island that fringed the north-east entrance to the Alas Strait.

Nothing about this plan was foolproof or guaranteed. By now there might be a whole flotilla patrolling the strait. Or there might be Japanese ashore in Sumbawa – in the act of landing, perhaps, in Labu Beru Bay for instance, which was an inshore stretch he meant to sneak through. If there was anything like that going on, he'd run right into it – just as *Perth* and *Houston* had run into an invasion force in the Sunda entrance . . . But so far as he knew, there were no Japs on Sumbawa yet, and while they were so busy with Java they probably wouldn't have time or forces to spare. Also, Gant had been right about an approach from the east being unexpected. That destroyer would have been out there to thwart any escape attempt by one British cruiser and one American destroyer, which the Japanese had known to be in Surabaya. The cruiser had sailed yesterday at sunset – heading west – and disappeared, and the destroyer had still been in Surabaya at this last sunset. The Japs would be looking for the cruiser, and waiting for the destroyer to make her run for it, but they wouldn't be looking for anything to show up from the east.

So the cruiser that had departed westward, and since grown another funnel, *would* be slinking into Alas from the east.

And *Sloan* would be on her way now. Jim Jordan's ship would be in the Madura Channel, going flat out for China Point, then Cape Sedano and the Bali Strait. In which, please God, there would be no guardship. Fervently, Nick wished Jordan luck.

But he needed some more luck for himself too. *Now*. It wasn't only the passage through that strait that he had to worry about. If there was a lot of stuff passing through the Lombok gap, at least some of it would be coming down past the Kangeans. So right now, and at any time in the next few hours, *Defiant* might find herself in the middle of it.

Chevening warned him, 'Coming up to the turn, sir, for course one-two-five degrees.'

Guns and tubes would be closed up all night. The last thing he wanted was any kind of action, but he wasn't intending to be caught napping, either.

'Now, sir!'

'Port fifteen.' He called over his shoulder: 'Yeoman?'

'Sir?'

'I want the Rising Sun hoisted aft, Morris.'

'Rising—'

Morris had gagged on it, for a second. Recovering, he muttered, 'Rising Sun, sir, at the main gaff – aye aye, sir.'

Lack of enthusiasm: Nick shared it. Survival before scruples, though. It hadn't made him feel nearly so uncomfortable a year ago to fly the Italian ensign for a short while. It was perfectly legal, too, provided you hauled it down before you opened fire. He still thought, *Ugh* . . .

'Midships.'

'Midships, sir!'

'Steer one-two-five. Have yourself relieved at the wheel now, Wiley. I'll want you on it again in four hours' time.'

'Aye aye, sir. Steer one-two-five, sir . . .'

Nick looked round for Gant. 'If we run into anything, Bob, which God forbid, I may need to floodlight that rag. Warn them on the searchlight platform. But let them have an Aldis ready for it, not the big light.'

He didn't want to light up the whole afterpart of the ship, which would draw attention to at least one obvious difference between *Defiant* and a Japanese Natori-class cruiser.

Gant came back. 'That's organized, sir.' He added in a flatter, quieter tone, 'And we're flying the Rising Sun.'

'Not for a minute longer than we have to.'

'Course one-two-five, sir!'

'Very good.'

'If you feel like a rest, sir, I could take over.'

'Kind of you, Bob. But we'll let Chevening have her. Pilot?'

Chevening took over at the binnacle. Nick went to his new high seat, and struggled up on to it. Not too easy, with only one arm in use. Binoculars weren't easy one-handed either, for any length of time. Another source of irritation was that the wound in his face was sensitive, like a bad bruise, and he had to take care not to let the lens on that side bang against it; with one-handed clumsiness it did happen, and it hurt.

Gant moved up to the front of the bridge near him, and raised his glasses to look out ahead.

Stars, and their reflection in the water, and the phosphorescence in the ship's bow-wave and wake, were all that relieved the

713

darkness. The ship's engines rumbled steadily, a constant thrumming that you felt as well as heard. From below this bridge, in the space that had been a wheelhouse and a plot, rattles seemed to be getting louder.

This first hour was the period when they were least likely to run into an enemy. Southbound ships steering for Lombok from east of the Kangeans wouldn't be likely to cross *Defiant*'s track until she'd covered the first thirty miles of it, on account of the wide spread of reefs up north of the islands. If there was any safe time at all, or near-safe time, this was as good as they were likely to get for quite a while.

'Bob. I'd like you to make a tour of the upper deck. Check they're all on their toes and understand our situation.'

'Right, sir. I'll go round now.'

'Good man. Ormrod there?'

'Here, sir.' Lieutenant Ormrod had taken over the torpedo officer's job. Swanson's. Nick asked him, 'Tubes on a hair trigger, are they?'

'Pretty well, sir.' He added, 'And Mr North's all-about, down there.'

'You did a first-class job in the whaler, Ormrod . . . Who's that?'

'Me, sir. Bentley. Brought you a cup of coffee, sir.'

'You must be psychic, Bentley.'

Sandilands, the engineer commander, had protested about the twenty-five knots that Nick was again insisting on. He'd had his men working in the boiler room all day, while *Defiant* had been in the mangroves, and as usual he'd been working with them.

'Two-six-oh revs is putting an awful strain on our temporary repairs, sir. It really is a lot to ask for, after such a—'

'I know it is, chief. But tonight and all tomorrow, the only speed that's acceptable is flat out. If flat out's two-six-oh revs, two-six-oh's what I want. After dark tomorrow – if we live that long, and we *won't*, chief, if you fail to produce those revs – we'll ease down a bit. Twenty knots, perhaps.'

'Make it fifteen, sir?'

'This isn't an Egyptian market, chief.'

Sandilands blinked at him tiredly. He said, 'It's a very old, cranky ship, sir, and she's been knocked about pretty badly. If we can't slow down, the odds are we'll *stop*.'

He'd nodded. 'A lot will depend on *Sloan*. She'll need to conserve oil even more than we will. Let's talk about it tomorrow

714

evening, chief. Meanwhile, I'd like you and your men to know that I appreciate you've been doing a bloody marvellous job.'

Engine breakdown would be fatal, now. It was one of several things which, if any of them happened, would wipe you off the board.

It was 10.40. They were out of the partial-safety zone and the island of Lombok was about forty miles due south, on the starboard bow. And *Sloan*, he guessed, would be something like halfway to China Point.

Sloan's refugees were on his conscience. Partly because he couldn't put Jim Jordan's prospects any higher than his own now, and partly because he hadn't thought of asking whether there might be a Mrs Williams among them. He should have. Even if it was a thousand-to-one chance, when you'd been sending enquiries to places as far away as Colombo you ought surely to look at what was right under your nose.

He'd ask *Sloan* about her – he crossed mental fingers – when they joined up tomorrow. What a fluke it would be if the answer should come as affirmative. What a marvellous fluke, for Williams!

He *should* have asked about the girl. But his mind had been full – the Kangean plan, doubts whether his brain was working properly, engine repairs, the trouble with Jordan over the refugees themselves. That was what had really obscured the Williams problem . . .

Williams was mending well, anyway. All but two of the wounded, Sibbold had reported, would be back to duty before long. The other two would survive, but would need to be landed to hospital in Australia.

If . . .

To some hospital with Kate in it?

Kate: her eyes smiling at him. Eyes very much like Ingrid Bergman's. But they were better than that, they were Kate's eyes. She did have the Bergman look, though.

There was a change in himself – one, anyway – that he'd taken note of. He thought about Kate now, and hardly at all about Fiona Gascoyne. He'd wondered about this during the day, when he'd been half-sleeping in that oven of a cabin. It might be explained – unflatteringly – by the fact that the ambition now was to get to Australia: even to Perth, which was vaguely in the direction of Kate's home. Perth – Fremantle – same thing . . . So the mind – if this *was* the explanation – fastened pragmatically on what was – might be – within reach. Another possibility, less unattractive, was that when survival appeared uncertain your thoughts went to the things or people that mattered most to you. He was committed to Fiona – he *was*, he knew it and so did she – but if he was unlikely to live to do anything about it, then he could forget it because it didn't matter, he could let his thoughts loose to wander where they felt happiest.

He had one foot up on a projection in the front of the bridge, and his right elbow rested on the raised knee as a support to the hand holding the binoculars. Gant, Ormrod, Chevening, the yeoman and signalman of the watch, three lookouts in the bays on each side, the PO of the watch and a messenger and a bosun's mate, were all looking out, straining their eyes into the dark. Above all their heads were Greenleaf in the DCT and Haskins in the ADP, and their assistants. It added to a fair number of eyes.

Haskins had done a good job ashore on Sepanjang. No trouble, no casualties. Haskins was one of several officers and men who'd merited commendation in any report of proceedings that might come to be written. In the personnel area, the only problem was Bob Gant. In all respects except one, he was a very competent second-in-command. Because of that one deficiency, though, Nick had come to the conclusion that he'd be more suitably employed ashore. His damaged spine would serve as a good reason for recommending it, but—

'Ship, green one-oh!'

Gant's voice – low, urgent. And the DCT telephone buzzed. Nick had it at his ear and Greenleaf reported, 'Cruiser green oh-eight steering north, sir!'

'Stop together. All quarters alert.'

He couldn't use his glasses now because he needed the hand for the telephone link with the tower. Chevening had called down to stop engines: vibration ceased abruptly. *Defiant* still slid ahead, still showed bow-wave . . .

'Stand by all port-side tubes.'

He heard Ormrod, at the torpedo control panel, pass that order down to Mr North, the gunner (T). Down on that side of the upper deck they'd be turning out the two triple mountings. If he had to engage, Nick intended to swing the ship to starboard and fire on the turn.

'Keep her stem pointing right at him, pilot.'

'Aye aye, sir.'

716

The Jap cruiser was crossing the bow from starboard to port. As it crossed, Chevening would have to apply port wheel, the object of doing so being to present a small, end-on view of *Defiant* for the Jap lookouts to continue not to see. It was contradictory and inconvenient that if he had to engage he'd need to reverse the direction of the turn, but it couldn't be helped because that was the way he'd want to be pointing after he'd fired.

'Tell them on the searchlight platform to be ready with the Aldis, but not, repeat *not*, to switch on without my order.'

Ormrod reported, 'Tubes turned out and ready, sir.'

'Enemy is right ahead, course north, speed sixteen, range oh-three-eight.' Three thousand eight hundred yards. Less than two sea miles. Greenleaf added, 'I think he's Kako-class, sir.'

Eight-inch guns, twelve tubes, about thirty knots.

'Pilot. At the first sign he's seen us, I'll want port screw full ahead and wheel hard a-starboard. If I shout "Go!" that's what I want. Ormrod, you'll fire six fish on the turn, spread from half a length ahead to half a length astern.'

As we turn, we'll be showing him his own flag . . .

'Yeoman, have the port-side ten-inch manned.'

'Leading Signalman Tromsett's on it, sir.'

To give a delaying, gibberish-type reply to any challenge that might come flashing. The first spark of a light would be the signal to engage: as *Defiant* swung to loose-off her torpedoes there'd be a Rising Sun lit-up aft and something like *Knees Up Mother Brown* rippling out in fast morse from that lamp. Every second's bewilderment of the enemy would increase one's chances of hitting and escaping.

Chevening said quietly into the steering-position telephone, 'Port five.' To keep her bow pointing at the enemy. Greenleaf muttered through the DCT phone, 'No indication he could have seen us, sir.'

Not yet. But he might, at any moment . . . Nick thought, *I'll have to be damn quick on that turn. Get the fish on their way, then hell for leather out of it . . .*

No. You wouldn't get out of it. Not far out, anyway.

One-handed, he'd got his glasses on the enemy cruiser. Long, low, two raked funnels. He thought, *I could have blown him out of the water, by this time.*

Turn now, and fire?

No chance of getting away with it, of course. You'd never get through the straits. Or if you did, they'd nail you at first light.

717

Still – a seven-thousand-ton Jap cruiser for a five-thousand-ton British one?

But there'd be no certainty of hitting with torpedoes. Hit or miss, *Defiant* would pay for it with her life and with the five hundred lives in her. No strategic balance would be changed, no tactical advantage gained. And the orders were to get *Defiant* out of the Java Sea.

Chevening had increased the rudder-angle to ten degrees, because the ship had lost way and was less responsive to her helm now. The enemy cruiser was hard to see, even with binoculars. It was still dead ahead but almost stern-on to them now as it continued northward and the darkness swallowed it.

Half an hour after midnight, he turned her south. By that time they'd passed across the northern approach to the Alas Strait, and at a steady twenty-five knots it would be one hour's run down to the islands that lay off Sumbawa.

At 0115 hours he moved to the binnacle and took over the conning of the ship.

'Stay here, pilot. I'll need your eyes. Can't manage glasses and the telephone at once.'

They hadn't considered the complication of his being one-armed, when they'd decided to forgo the refitting of a voicepipe.

Navigation was likely to be slightly hit-or-miss, this next bit. He had to find and identify two islands, Pandjang and Seringgit, and pass through the half-mile gap between them. Both islands, according to their descriptions in the Sailing Directions, were low, without hills or other distinguishing features. Pandjang was all mangroves, Seringgit scrub-covered; and a number of other islands to the east of them were equally featureless. Depths were said to be less than those shown on the charts, and in the middle of the passage between the two islands there was a nineteen-foot shallow patch.

'According to this, it could be less than nineteen feet. So let's keep closer to Seringgit than to Pandjang. Not *too* close, mind you.'

Because Seringgit's encircling reef extended a third of a mile from its southwest corner.

'Bob. Chevening and I will be concentrating on pilotage. Looking out for Japanese is your pigeon now.'

'Aye aye, sir.'

Chevening suggested, 'Run the echo-sounder, sir?'

'Might as well. Ormrod – you look after the sounder and the log.'

At 0120 he cut the revs to a hundred and forty, ten knots. A minute after that, Chevening had land in his glasses, on the port bow. And then ahead, too; and to starboard. It was all low, unidentifiable: a rotten place to have to make a landfall in the dark.

Chevening said, 'I think we should come round to starboard, sir. If my guess is right, we're too far east.'

And if it was wrong, they'd now head out towards the top of the strait, where the guardship was thought to be . . . He brought her round, leaving all the land on her port bow. Chevening had his glasses on it, muttering to himself as he tried to sort it out, spot gaps and match the sizes of different islands to the chart-picture in his memory.

It was now 0126. Meeting the Jap cruiser had put them ten minutes behind schedule. Schedule being simply the need to get through as fast as possible, as far south as possible before daybreak. Now they were losing *more* time.

Sloan would be just about approaching the entrance to the Bali Strait. Jim Jordan would tear straight in at his full thirty knots, Nick guessed. The Strait was too narrow for any possibility of getting through craftily, unobserved. He'd take it head-on, and ready for a fight.

'On red two-oh, sir – must be it, I think! The gap's about the right size, and on the other side the land seems to go on for ever, flat as a pancake, so—'

'Pandjang.' He said it flatly, to counter the navigator's excited tone. He must have been getting worried, he realized. He was sighting across the dimly illuminated compass: 'We should come round to two-one-oh, sir.'

'Port ten.'

'Port ten, sir. Ten of port wheel on, sir.'

'Steer two-one-oh.'

'Then we'll have to turn due south to get through it, sir. Say half a mile after we cross the hundred-fathom line.'

'You'd better check that.'

Chevening went to the covered bridge chart table, and confirmed it, and Ormrod at the echo-sounder reported crossing the hundred-fathom line at 0141. Land to port, on the beam, was visible to the naked eye by this time, and after the next half-mile it was also in sight on the starboard bow. Nick brought her round to south, to put her through the gap. This was another half-mile run, and by the end of it the coastline to port, Seringgit's, looked dangerously close. But if you turned too soon you'd run into trouble presently with the reef that extended south from Pandjang's eastern end.

Chevening came back from another refresher at the chart.

'Time to alter to two-three-oh, sir. For seven and a half miles.'

'Starboard ten.'

'Starboard ten, sir . . . Ten of starboard—'

'Gets easier now, doesn't it?'

'Should do, sir.' *Defiant* was swinging to her new course, which would take her down to Kalong Island. Chevening added quietly, 'Please God.'

'Amen.' He said into the telephone, 'Two-six-oh revolutions.'

An end to dawdling. And they were only a few minutes astern of where he'd expected to be, so it wasn't too bad, so far. It was likely to be easier down there because there were some prominent hills to fix on, on the islands of Kalong, Namo and Kenawa. *Defiant* would be passing inside all three of them in the process of rounding Labu Beru Point, which was Sumbawa's northwest cape, and thus entering the Alas Strait proper. If there was a Jap destroyer anchored where he'd guessed it would be, there'd be seven or eight miles of open water between them as she rounded the point.

He'd slow down again, for that stretch. The bow-wave of a ship moving at speed was the real give-away, in the dark.

Sloan would be right in *her* strait, now. In the top of it where it was only three thousand yards or less from shore to shore.

'One-two-oh revolutions.'

Eight knots seemed about the optimum speed. Minimal bow-wave but acceptable progress, less than twenty minutes in the open. If there was an enemy there to see them . . . He glanced over towards the hunched figure that was Bob Gant: 'Bob, ask Greenleaf whether he can see anything like a Jap destroyer at anchor on bearing – what bearing would it be, pilot?'

'About three-three-five, sir.'

He raised his voice: 'Nobody else need waste time looking for it. Could be a patrol anywhere, from here on.'

The echo-sounder was switched off now. Pilotage *was* easy. They'd had the hills on those islands, and there was another right on Labu Beru, like a big pimple on a nose. Also, off the north end of Belang Island, which was flat, was a two-hundred-foot rock pinnacle called Songi. All the way down the Sumbawan west coast, which *Defiant* would be keeping close to, the chart showed hills and headlands; and a bonus was a southward-running two-knot tide.

It was time, he thought, for some *bad* luck. So be ready for it . . .

For a signal, perhaps. An enemy report, from *Sloan*. He and Jordan had agreed that if either of them ran into trouble, they'd let out a squawk, to let the other know. Then the survivor, if there was one, wouldn't waste time tomorrow looking for a partner who wouldn't be capable of keeping any rendezvous.

The DCT telephone had buzzed, and Gant had answered it. He said, 'PCO reports two ships at anchor on that bearing, sir. They do look like destroyers.'

Two, now. How many might there be elsewhere by this time? Patrolling, or waiting at the southern end. He hoped those destroyers had the same standard of watchfulness as the Kako cruiser had demonstrated . . . He said to Chevening, 'You guessed right, pilot.'

'With some prompting, sir.'

Chevening had been doing rather well, Nick thought. Finding the gap between the islands an hour ago hadn't been at all easy. Chevening had made a judgement, stuck his neck out, and he'd been proved right. He had the makings of something after all, it seemed. Nick called over to Gant, 'Tell Greenleaf to keep an eye on the destroyers and report any sign of life.'

There was a small island called Paserang to the north of Belang, and they'd have that between them and the guardships before they got behind the bigger one. A few minutes' less exposure . . . Songi, the tall rock, was abeam now, about one mile to starboard. Chevening suggested, 'We could come round, sir.'

'To what?'

'Two-one-oh, sir. It would take us all the way down to that lower point – Belusan.'

He told Wiley, 'Starboard five, steer two-one-oh.'

With the tide to help her, *Defiant* was making ten knots over the ground. In five minutes' time, when she was behind Paserang, he'd increase to revs for twenty-five knots, and she'd make twenty-seven. There'd be no cover after they left Belang Island astern. He'd just hug the coast, holding his ship against its blackness. He asked Chevening, 'Off that point we're now heading for—'

'Belusan, sir.'

'There's a small island to look out for, isn't there?'

721

'Just south of it, sir. If we turn to one-six-three when Belusan's abeam we'll be all right.'

They reached that turning-point within a few minutes of 0300. Two minutes later the little island was abeam to starboard. In fact as they passed it it turned out to be twins. The course of a hundred and sixty-three degrees led them into a bay called Talliwang, which had a good hill just behind it to take bearings on. The turn was to starboard now, for a five-mile run to the next headland, Tanjung Benete.

Sloan would be in widening water now, the opening funnel-shape of the Bali Strait as she pounded southward. If she ran into opposition Jordan's signal would be addressed to Bandoeng, but primarily for *Defiant*'s information. The same would apply the other way about. Codes could be broken, and you didn't want to advertise the fact that another ship was on the run.

'Course two-two-oh, sir.'

'Very good.' Nick told Gant, 'It gets narrower ahead. Tell Greenleaf that if there's a patrolling destroyer anywhere, this is where I'd expect it.'

It was probable that there would be. By a miracle, they'd escaped being sunk by that cruiser, and miracles were rationed. At any second, gunfire could split the darkness. You had to be on your toes, geared-up. A few seconds' hesitation, when the moment came, could finish you . . . He was taut, tense with readiness: the wound on his face itched from the irritation of sweat running down inside the dressing.

Tanjung Benete was abeam before 3.30. Right opposite it, eight miles away, was the southeast corner of Lombok. And nine miles ahead, after he'd brought her round to a course of a hundred and ninety degrees, was the south-west corner of Sumbawa. At that point, in another nine miles, *Defiant* would emerge from the Alas Strait. In fact she'd be leaving the Pacific, entering the Indian Ocean.

Nine miles could look like ninety, when they lay ahead of you.

'Pilot. If you had the same job down at this end – to anchor as guardship – where would you do it?'

'It's all deep water, sir.'

'No little bays inshore?'

'I'll check it, sir.' He went to the chart. There was a canvas hood over it, and a light you could switch on inside when the hood was lowered behind you. New, stiff canvas now. Nick guessed that those destroyers would probably have been anchored to save fuel. The Japs had come a long way south in a very short time, and until they got their fuelling arrangements set up in places like Sumatra – where the installations had been wrecked and set on fire – they'd be wanting to conserve supplies. Chevening came back and told him that there were three suitable inshore anchorages, three bays in the strip of coastline that lay immediately ahead of them.

They'd all be within two miles of *Defiant*'s track down-coast, and only after she'd passed each headland would it be possible to see into the bay. Unless Greenleaf, with the tower's extra height, might see over any of the promontories. Nick told Gant to warn Greenleaf about it.

To starboard, a sea-mist clung to the black surface. To port, the first of the headlands was already looming close. He ought to have considered this possibility before, he realized, been prepared for it. Not that there was much preparing that anyone could do. But he should still have seen it: seen those bays open to the strait, with clear views across it . . .

'DCT reports this bay's empty, sir.'

Two to go.

'What's that hill, pilot?'

'It's called Maloh, sir. Same name for the headland.' It was the next one, on the bow. Chevening added, 'The bay on the other side of it's about the most likely one, sir. Good wide entrance.'

'Be ready with torpedoes either side, Ormrod.'

'Standing by, sir.'

Overdue bad luck didn't *have* to be an ambush behind that headland. It could come from patrolling ships out to starboard. The straits were about nine miles wide at this end.

Maloh loomed black against the stars to port. It was about a thousand feet high, massive-looking on its steep-to, craggy headland. About half a mile away. *Defiant*'s wash, which was powerful at this speed, would be following in a rush of wave-action along those rocks. Passing the headland: the blackness of it abeam to port – now . . .

'Can't see anything in there, sir.'

'Bay's empty, sir!'

One more to go. The next headland was clear to see. As you passed one, there was always another. And beyond it was the third potential anchorage. The headland – Chevening said it was called Tanjung Amat – was coming up on the beam at 0342. Its rocky cliff-face was pale, yellowish-looking in the dark; and there was a group of hills behind it, a corrugation against the sky. To the south – opening to them suddenly as the light-coloured rocks drew aft and vanished in the dark – was the last of the three bays . . . Gant had his glasses trained into it. In the tower, Greenleaf's much more powerful ones would be probing too.

Gant answered the telephone. He muttered, 'Very good', and told Nick, 'This one's clear too, sir.'

Incredible . . . But there, two miles on the bow, was the last headland, tall and stark against blue-black sky, the last landmark in this Alas Strait. Relief was tinged with a feeling of surprise amounting to suspicion: the feeling that there had to be some snag, something still in store . . . That point – it was called Mangkung – formed the southern arm of the wide bay, this third one in which he'd been expecting to find enemies. Who, evidently, must have their hands full elsewhere, he thought – probably on Java's south coast . . . He said into the steering-position telephone, 'Port five. Steer one-eight-oh.'

Due south. The course to the rendezvous with *Sloan* – of whom no news was good news . . . You had first to survive the dawn, and then to live through several hours of daylight that would be spent within a few minutes' flying distance of the Bali airstrip. He'd foreseen this moment: the moment when it would occur to him that if he'd come down through Lombok he'd be twenty or thirty miles farther south by now.

Jim Jordan, by this time, ought to be right out of the Bali Strait. He'd be about a hundred and twenty miles away, steering south-east at thirty knots. The two ships' courses were converging and they'd meet at about noon, two hundred miles south.

There'd been no signal. The American destroyer *must* have got through.

Dawn, now, would be the danger time. Sunrise, and then every minute after it until the damn thing went down again tonight. For *Defiant* and for *Sloan* too, it was going to be a nervy day.

'Course one-eight-oh, sir!'

'Very good. You can hand over the wheel now, Wiley.'

'Aye aye, thank you, sir!'

Chevening said quietly, diffidently, 'I'd – like to congratulate you, sir.'

He glanced, surprised, at the tall, angular silhouette of his navigator. Chevening was congratulating him, he realized, on having brought *Defiant* out through the strait. As if that was the end of it – or *an* end, on its own. It had seemed like the biggest hurdle, of course, the real gauntlet, when they'd been on the other side of it. He'd forgotten, because that stage was done with and one's thinking moved on, ahead of whatever was happening at any given moment – let alone what had *already* happened . . . He told Chevening, 'Could be a little premature, pilot. Say it again at sunset, will you?'

Forty miles farther south, he rested in his high chair and watched a faint paling in the eastern sky. The fingertips of dawn's left hand. How did it go? 'Awake, my little ones, and fill the cup . . .'

Splice the mainbrace tonight, if the good luck lasted?

But – he thought – if it held, if they were still afloat and plugging south when the sun went down again, would there be cause for celebration? For the fact that *Defiant*'s and *Sloan*'s names had not been added to the heartbreaking list of ships and ships' companies who'd been lost – to no good purpose – in the Java Sea? Would that be a reason for self-congratulation?

It was a time for mourning, he thought. And for anger. The names of those ships ran through his mind. The destroyers whom he'd known well, shared actions with in the Mediterranean; and *Perth* and her captain, Waller, to whom the same applied; and Rooks of *Houston* . . . When he thought of *Exeter* it was like remembering someone who'd been very close, someone you'd loved who'd died.

Might that be why he'd dreamt of Paul being in her, that night?

Overhead, the director tower trained slowly round, watching the horizon as it became hard, definite. Nick had just put his own glasses up – resting that elbow on a raised knee, the only system that seemed to work – when Gant spoke quietly beside him.

'Stand-to at the guns, sir?'

Guns' crews were still closed up, but they'd been relaxed to the second degree of readiness, allowed to sleep around their weapons with one man at each mounting keeping watch. Now – Nick glanced to his left again, at the threatening dawn – Gant was right, it was time to stir them up.

'Yes, please, Bob.'

Not that you'd be able to do much about it, if the Vals did come. Except make it a bit harder for them. He sat back in the tall chair, and watched the light grow.

CHAPTER 14

They came in low on the dark surface, and from the west so as to have their fat, slow target silhouetted against the first bright streaks of dawn. Savoias. Paul couldn't see them, but the director tower's crew could. There was shouting, down for'ard and back aft, as the wires securing *Ainsty* to the tanker were slackened and cast off, and *Jouster*, the fleet destroyer who'd turned up during the night, was wheeling, on her beam-ends in a froth of sea as she turned under full rudder and increasing power to get back there and meet the bombers.

'All gone for'ard!'

Banshee-like cry from the foc'sl. And a man at a telephone reported, 'All gone aft, sir.' *Ainsty* had been secured alongside, towing as well as guiding, helping the *Santa Eulalia* with the tanker's weight and adding a knot or two to the rate of progress. But she needed her freedom of movement now. Paul heard her captain order, 'Two-seven-five revolutions!' He'd need to have her clear of the hulk before he could put his wheel over, for fear of swinging his stern into it.

The Hunt was surging ahead, diverging.

'Port ten!'

Astern, *Jouster* opened fire.

'Hard a-port! Full ahead together!'

Ainsty's four-inch opened up while she was in the turn. But the tow would slow virtually to a standstill now. The *Santa Eulalia* couldn't hold that stubby hulk to a straight course without assistance.

'Midships!'

Guns drowning other noise: voices, orders, were fragmented, sandwiched between their crashes. Pompoms were at work from *Jouster*, and Oerlikons' tracer arcing back, slow-moving, streaking the gloom. *Ainsty* picking up speed, hurling her slim hull jolting across the sea. Paul hadn't yet seen any of the attackers. He was trying to, using the tracer-streams as pointers.

Explosion: brilliant, dark-splitting, dark-into-daylight splitting. He thought – momentarily blinded by it – *Jouster* . . . And – still blind – *Don't count on seeing Malta* . . .

He'd woken half an hour ago with the question in his mind: Malta, today? He'd probably been dreaming about it. No memory of the dream, though, as he woke. His first waking thought was a realization that the motion of the ship had been entirely different. What had roused him – he believed – had been gunfire, but there'd been no more of it as he slid off the bunk – the navigator's, the same cabin he'd been allowed to use before – and groped around for boots and sweater. Thinking about the ship's changed and peculiar motion – it was jerky and unnatural – he wondered if she'd been damaged while he'd been asleep, might be under tow. But her engines were going strong . . . Might she have taken over the tow from the American? Maybe the *Santa Eulalia* had come to grief?

Shivering cold . . . He might have dreamt that gunfire, too. There'd been quite a lot of it last night, bombing attacks continuing until well after dusk and then two separate assaults by torpedo aircraft, the last one around midnight. He'd gone below and turned in at about one o'clock, four hours ago. He'd been out for the count, and he was still heavy-headed now . . . *Ainsty* had just lurched to port and come up hard, as if she'd crashed into something. She definitely was towing, he'd thought. He buttoned the borrowed oilskin on his way up to the bridge. Time, somehow, inverted and upside-down: through sleeplessness, long periods of action, uncertainty, total absence of routine, regular mealtimes and so on. Also, time was relative, if it existed at all. Time was the distance to Malta, how long since the last attack, how long before the next one.

Earlier, there'd been a moon, but he'd found that it was down now. And the reason for the strange motion became obvious as soon as he got up to bridge level and into the cold pre-dawn air: *Ainsty* had put herself alongside the hulk of the *Caracas Moon*, her starboard side against the tanker. From the place he'd occupied before, behind the starboard lookout bay, his downward view had been on to the flat tank-tops: a short way aft, the tanker's bridge was ten or twelve feet higher than the destroyer's. At about this level, back there, was the deck he'd jumped from after Harry Willis had saved his life.

That was a truth. If Willis hadn't pulled him off the ladder he'd have been either spread like jam across the bulkhead or tangled into its twisted steel. He wanted to know how Willis was. There'd been no news of him last night when he'd gone below to turn in.

It was the strain on the wires linking the destroyer and the tanker that had been producing the jerky, tugging effect. He stared aft at the black rectangle that was the *Caracas Moon*'s bridge, and imagined Humphrey Straight standing there beside the useless wheel, sucking at his pipe, thinking about whatever wordless men like Straight did think about. Gardening, or greyhounds, or something quite unlikely . . . There wouldn't be much for Straight to do, except see the wires here and up for'ard were tended, and the four Oerlikons manned and ammunitioned, and he'd have Devenish to help him with that; but he was the only master of the *Caracas Moon*'s remains now, since her own captain had been transferred to *Ainsty* last night in a condition of total exhaustion. He was below, in *Ainsty*'s captain's cabin.

'Kye, sir?'

'Why, thanks!'

Exactly what he'd needed. The sailor – it was a bridge messenger or a bosun's mate – brought him an extremely hot enamel mug. 'You're the officer as was in the 'oggin, ain't you?'

He nodded. Sipping, burning his lips. 'Was there some action, short while ago?'

'Aircraft, sir. They was on the 279, then we could 'ear 'em, but never got a good look at 'em. When we opened up they buggered off like.' He'd added, 'Be dawn soon. We'll 'ave 'em all back then, I reckon.'

They'd got them back *now* . . .

But *Jouster* was all right. The explosion had been beyond her and it had been a bomber going up, or rather the torpedo in its rack under a bomber's fuselage. The effect of a torpedo warhead exploding in the open was spectacular, and that plane's pilot wouldn't have known much about it. Paul's eyes were only just back to normal. There was another aircraft in trouble, a shoot of flame along a tilted wing, heavy-looking body stalling, tracer flowing at it in smooth bright curves and a Savoia rising across *Ainsty*'s bow, turning away to port and straining for height – there'd be a torpedo in the sea, somewhere or other. Probably

728

several. They wouldn't do much good – or harm – from astern though; if the Savoias hadn't been picked up by RDF, or seen from the director tower – whatever had happened, he hadn't heard the start of it – they'd have turned out on to the quarters, he guessed, flown up and then turned in to launch their fish from somewhere near the beams. Perhaps, if they'd seen *Jouster* guarding this side, from the south. She was over on that quarter now, still in action. *Ainsty*, lacking any target, had ceased fire, and her captain was bringing her round to port.

'Two-four-oh revolutions. Midships.'

He'd have to catch up before he could take her back alongside and get the tow moving again. They'd been making something like four to five knots, Paul thought, when he'd come up, and depending on how much ground had been covered during the night there couldn't, surely, be more than about twenty miles to go.

Jouster had ceased fire. So that was one more attack beaten off. But it wouldn't be long before the light came.

'Slow together. Steer one-oh-two.'

Ainsty was sliding up into the black shadow of the tanker. Simpson came to the back of the bridge and leaned over to shout down, 'Stand by, you down there!'

'Ready, sir!'

'What about the bloody fenders, then?' Turning, muttering angrily, he peered to see who Paul was. Then, recognizing him: 'You all right?'

'Fine, sir, thank you. Do we have far to go now?'

'About twenty-two miles. They might be bloody long ones, though.'

Six thousand miles east-southeast, Nick reached for the telephone to the director tower. It was just on 1100. If everything had gone exactly to plan, as agreed between himself and Jim Jordan, *Sloan* would now be twenty-five miles away and roughly on *Defiant*'s beam.

He asked Greenleaf, 'Still not in sight?'

'No, sir. Nothing.'

He put the phone back on its hook. Gant said, 'May have found he couldn't make his thirty knots after all, sir.'

'That could be it.'

There was no reason, he assured himself, to think the worst. Not yet. Plenty of things could have happened to cause slight delay.

As Gant had suggested, *Sloan*'s engine repairs might not have come up to expectations. Or if there'd been Japs around – south of the Bali Strait, ships coming out of Lombok and heading west across Jordan's track – he might have made a detour, or had to creep out slowly, or—

Or this, or that. The trouble was, if he'd been *much* delayed, one might conclude that he couldn't have come out of the Bali Strait by sunrise. You couldn't have it both ways, unfortunately. If he hadn't, he wouldn't be coming out of it at all.

One should be able to switch one's mind off, at times like this. Go back into what Sibbold had called a 'coma'. Specialist's word for 'unconscious' . . .

'Bob.'

'Yes, sir?'

'We can dispense with the dummy funnel now. Lower it, and have it dismantled.'

At first light, as soon as he'd been satisfied that the sky and the sea were clear, he'd told them to strike the Japanese ensign. Petty Officer Morris had asked him eagerly, 'Permission to shove it in the galley fire, sir?'

'If it'll give you any satisfaction, yeoman.'

Hardly an approved manner of disposing of Admiralty stores . . . But he should have got rid of the extra funnel sooner, he realized. American submarines were likely to be operating in these waters now, and if one of them got *Defiant* in its periscope and mistook her for a Natori . . .

Sloan. It was quite possible that a ship could be hit so suddenly and devastatingly that she'd have no chance to get a signal out. A W/T operator could bungle it, or panic, not stay long enough to tap it out . . . A mine or a torpedo: sudden, overwhelming, and immediate destruction . . . In his memory he saw Jim Jordan's shrug, and heard that laconic dismissal of all the disasters that had lain ahead and which both of them had foreseen: *However* . . .

How long ago, that conversation over a glass of Laphroaigh? Ten days? A lifetime?

Gant said, 'The funnel's coming down now, sir.'

Poor old Bob. It was rotten to like a man, have him with you, and be intending to ditch him. Bob Gant was a reliable, efficient, officer, as well as a thoroughly decent character to have around. The only thing that was wrong with him – apart from his cranky spine – was this fear of responsibility, the reluctance to take command. A number two had to be equipped and ready to become number one; it was part of his *raison d'être*. Gant wasn't up to it, for some reason. You couldn't let it pass, once you knew it. If you were Nick Everard you could turn a blind eye to the burning of a flag worth a few shillings, but you could not connive at risking a ship and a ship's company, risking their being left in the hands of someone who might let them down. To be kind to Bob Gant, you'd have to endanger others.

That back trouble of his was a liability anyway, entirely valid as a reason to recommend shore employment. Besides, he'd get used to it, and his family would be pleased. Bob had a wife and children in Hampshire somewhere.

Extraordinary that one could begin to think about this sort of thing now. Of a future, and places like Hampshire, and next month, next year . . .

Could Jim Jordan?

Not a thing in sight. Only an enormous circle of blinding-bright blue sea under a dome of clear blue sky . . . .

'Captain, sir?'

He looked round: Sibbold, the PMO, told him, 'You're about due for a change of those dressings, sir. Could you possibly come down—'

'No, I could *not!*'

Sibbold was taken aback. Gant met his eyes and very slightly shook his head, warning him to lay off. Sibbold, with his job to do, didn't see it. He suggested, 'May we do it up here, then, if you—'

'For Christ's sake—'

This time he saw the PMO's startled surprise. He told himself, *Steady, now* . . . He shook his head. 'Sorry, doctor. This isn't a good moment. I'll – contact you later. How are your other patients?'

He'd made himself ask the question. Now he made himself listen to the long and detailed answer. Thinking about *Sloan*, and the refugees he'd refused to take.

It was 11.20 when Sibbold left the bridge. Nick asked Chevening, 'Where would she be now, precisely, if she was up to time?'

Chevening went to the chart, and worked it out. He came back and told Nick, 'She'd bear two-five-five, fourteen miles, sir.'

So she'd have been in sight from this bridge, let alone the director tower.

* * *

731

The *Caracas Moon* was entirely hidden behind bomb-splashes. *Jouster* was alongside her now, with the *Santa Eulalia* still tugging doggedly ahead, *Ainsty* off the leash and placing herself wherever the current threat was coming from. Malta was in plain sight: low, stone-coloured, stretching from north to north-east seven or eight miles distant. It was now 08.00: the ships had been under attack sporadically since dawn, but it would have been a great deal worse if Spitfires hadn't been taking a lot of the pressure out of it. *Ainsty* was astern now, barraging over the linked ships with Ju88s overhead, diving, bombs coming like slanting rain and the sea rising white-topped all around the tanker's stern and starboard side. Around what *had become* her stern . . . There was a Spitfire patrol around somewhere, but these 88s had somehow avoided them. When enough approached at once, the RAF couldn't stop them all. One last bomb-load coming now, from a bomber trailing the first five. The guns were at maximum elevation and rapid-firing, *Ainsty*'s and *Jouster*'s and the Oerlikons on the tanker. The American freighter would be part of it too, but from here all you could see was the haze of gunsmoke over her. Paul was squinting up under the rim of a borrowed tin hat, but that Junkers was hidden in shellbursts. Then he saw it again suddenly, a glimpse just as the bombs left it.

'Full ahead together! Port thirty!'

This destroyer, not the tanker, had been that last one's target. The Hunt was heeling to full rudder and trembling to her screws' thrust as she cracked on power. *Ainsty*'s silent now, no targets left. Astern the sea blossomed, lifting in dark humps that broke white-topped, the Junkers' Parthian gifts. She was heeling right over, twisting away from danger. Paul heard 'Midships!' Third bomb . . . fourth . . . The fifth went in close to starboard, where seconds ago the ship had been. He felt the explosion through his feet, and the spout was so close that her stern swung into it as it folded, drowning her afterpart in foam. Her engines had stopped. Gunfire from the other ships – from the *Santa Eulalia* – petered out. *Ainsty* was back on an even keel, losing way as quickly as if she'd had brakes and slammed them on. The brake was the sea's pull, sucking at her. On her compass platform there was a lot of telephone and voicepipe talk going on: *Ainsty* wallowing, slumping in the sea as she lost all forward motion. There was already quite a distance between her and the group of ships plodding away eastward and making about six knots. But they needed her guns, the high-angle

732

four-inch, to shelter them. They were cripples helping each other along. The American had been torpedoed, bombed, and at least once she'd been set on fire, and the *Caracas Moon* was more corpse than cripple. A corpse worth a lot more than any other ship, though, to that island . . . *Ainsty* and *Jouster* had changed places earlier because *Jouster* was a bigger and more powerful ship than the lightweight Hunt, better suited to the towing job. She was about twice *Ainsty*'s displacement, in fact. They'd swapped round after the first series of Stuka attacks, just after first light. During that Stuka raid there'd been a near-miss on the *Caracas Moon*'s starboard side, and she was leaking oil, a long trail of Malta's life-blood discolouring the sea right back to where they'd been at dawn.

A signalman had gone to the starboard ten-inch lamp. *Jouster* – whose captain was senior to *Ainsty*'s – must have been waiting for a report, because at the first dot-dash of the call-up signal she flashed a go-ahead. The message that went over to her was 'Expect to get going in about thirty minutes.' *Jouster* acknowledged. The stern-on view of her with the blocky shape of the half-tanker beside her would have been baffling if you hadn't known what it was, and it was further complicated by an occasional sight of the *Santa Eulalia*'s upperworks beyond it. A haystack leaning on a Baby Austin, against a background of telegraph poles? The whole assembly was dwindling as it hauled eastward. It had to get right round the island's southern coast, then turn to port, northward, up towards Valletta, which was on the southeast coast.

Even that short haul, and with Spitfires helping, seemed more than one could hope to accomplish, with so much damage done already . . . A roar of engines overhead was sudden, startling: but they were Spitfires. Two of them, swinging to their left now to pass over the tow as well. As the racket faded, Simpson spoke beside him: 'Minesweepers are on their way to meet us, and we're told we'll have Spits over us all the way in now. Things are looking up, sub!'

And he'd just been thinking the opposite . . . He asked Simpson, 'How about us? The engines?'

'Not to worry. Some sort of blow-back, from that near miss. I don't know, but it's fixable.' He patted Paul's shoulder, and grinned: 'You'll soon be safe and sound in your little submarine, Everard!'

It was now 8.35. And there were – roughly – eleven miles to go.

He wondered if Simpson could be right, if one should allow oneself to believe in what he'd said. If the tow could continue to make five or six knots, with Spitfires to protect it and minesweepers coming out to help – might make it in about two hours? Into Grand Harbour, in *two hours*?

Bewildering. He was *believing* it. And thinking of Beale laughing, winking at old Withinshaw, telling him, *There's some as like to look on the bright side* . . .

He wondered what he'd do about getting new gear, uniform and other stuff. All he possessed were the clothes he'd been wearing when they'd pulled him and Willis into the whaler. They'd be dry by now, but they'd also be salt-stained and shrunk, and scorched too, some of them, and he had nothing else at all, not a razor or a toothbrush even. Presumably one would be able to get an advance of pay, and a Slops issue – 'Slops' being stores you paid for, Admiralty-issue stuff. You could get a battledress uniform from Slops, and socks and things. He wondered if there was a branch of Gieves in Malta. Simpson had gone back to the for'ard part of the bridge, so he couldn't ask him. He hadn't asked him about Willis either.

Spitfires were busy in the distance. Several times there were patches of action, smoke-trails plunging seaward, as attacks were intercepted and broken up. At 9.20, *Ainsty* got under way and worked up to twelve knots, steering east to catch up on the tow. Fighters still up there, winging around at a few miles' radius. Filfla Island – a rock, three miles off the coast – fell astern to port. Fifteen knots now: it took half an hour to overhaul the others, joining them just as they reached the position for the turn north, rounding the corner of the island. By this time the two minesweepers had arrived, and were turning in to take station ahead. Each of the stubby little ships had a three-inch AA gun and an Oerlikon.

Hour and a half now? No – surely – *less* than that . . . He checked the time: then glanced up, looking for'ard, where something was going on. Binoculars were being trained astern: and he heard the report, 'Large formation, closing, sir!'

RDF report. He couldn't see any Spitfires now. Perhaps Malta's fighter-direction people had already vectored them out to meet this assault.

'Port fifteen!'

Ainsty's captain was bringing her round to cut the corner and close up on *Jouster* and her charges. The *Santa Eulalia*'s and

Jouster's joint efforts had dragged the *Caracas Moon* around. They had only to follow the sweepers now, the local boys. *Ainsty* with her fifteen knots and the short cut was closing the gap very rapidly.

Cutting the corner might be taking her through mined water?

'Alarm port, red one-five-oh, angle of sight ten, Junkers 88s!'

A quieter report added, 'Fighters above them. Messerschmitts, I think.'

Lacking binoculars, it was a minute or two before he saw them. Then the picture was a confusing one. Like midges in a distant haze . . . Well, those were the fighters: ours or theirs . . . He found the bombers now, and he was watching the familiar, target's-eye view of oncoming Ju88s. He wondered if he'd seen any of this particular lot before: had seen that one, or that, overhead yesterday or this morning . . . Withinshaw could have named each one of them, he thought, the same string of names for each. He counted two groups of four and another of about eight, all at roughly five thousand feet. The Spitfires obviously had their hands full with escorting fighters, and the Junkers were about to get a clear run in. *Ainsty* had cut her speed as she came up astern of the others. Guns elevated, loaded and ready, gunners' eyes slitted under the helmets' rims. Tanned, tired, unshaven faces, red-rimmed eyes. Grey sky, weak sunshine filtering through high cloud, grey-green sea, dun-coloured island . . . The front-running party of bombers were pushing their noses down, starting into their attacking dives. *Ainsty* weaving across the stern of the tow, two cables' lengths clear of it. Over the island more fighters – Spitfires – were climbing, heading south. *Ainsty*'s four-inch crashed: the for'ard mounting was trained to an extreme after bearing to throw the shells up over her shoulder as she slanted across the tow's broad, swirling wake. *Jouster* had opened fire, and *Ainsty*'s pompoms joined in too, then Oerlikons and Vickers adding to the din just before the attackers pulled out of their dives. Bombs started on their way: in slow motion, tumbling, then speeding into streaks, invisible. The splashes went up to starboard and ahead: *Ainsty* under helm, turning back to recross the wake the other way. At this moment her stem was pointing directly at the tow but you couldn't see it for the bomb-splashes. The entire area of sea between this ship and the bunch ahead seemed to be erupting. *Ainsty*'s four-inch had shifted target – to engage the second wave of the attack, another group of four: but behind that foursome, Spitfires were dropping on the

735

larger group. The Junkers back there were shedding bomb-loads and turning away, running for it: one spiralling, trailing smoke. Gunfire at crescendo again as the next four bombers came droning over: and releasing bombs *now* . . .

Most of them went in to port. One stick fell close enough to *Jouster* to qualify as near-misses. Then ahead, an explosion, a gush of flame, smoke pluming vertically: like a gas-jet igniting.

Santa Eulalia.

'DCT reports tow parted, sir!'

Smoke, tinged with the colour of flame, billowed skyward. The guns had ceased fire. The tow was broken, stopped, *Santa Eulalia* burning. *Ainsty*'s captain had his bearded face at the voicepipe shouting orders that were inaudible as a Spitfire screamed overhead through dissipating shreds of shellbursts.

By the dog watches, afternoon growing into evening, it had become certain that *Sloan* had gone.

One more name on that list of ships: with the difference that in this case he, Nick Everard, felt largely responsible. He should have foreseen that they'd have clamped down on the Bali Strait, when they'd known there were still two ships to get away from Surabaya and the Bali gap was the nearest exit. Even if they hadn't been alerted to the fact that four US destroyers had already slipped away by that route; and the odds were they *would* have caught on to it.

From as much as one had known in Surabaya, the Madura Channel and the Bali Strait *had* looked like the best route. So it could be argued that this retrospection was a judgement based on factors which had emerged later. But mightn't clearer thought, logical analysis, have pointed to this outcome?

He'd have taken *Defiant* out by the Bali route if she'd been able to get over the Madura shallows. It had been the discovery that she couldn't make it that had provoked that brainstorm, panic . . . The fact she was here now, well south and within a few hours of safety, was sheer luck. Luck, not good judgement.

Bentley asked him, 'Coffee, sir?'

'Thank you.' He took the cup, put it on the ledge beside him, lit one of his last cheroots. Chevening met his glance: grimly, with no trace of the congratulatory mood in which he'd started this long day. Everyone felt the same: the failure, loss.

And only he, Nick, knew about the forty refugees who'd have been embarked in *Sloan*.

However ....

It didn't help. He could see Jim Jordan's wry expression, the slight twist of a grin on that wide-jawed face. He could hear him saying, 'It'll be a great moment, making that rendezvous.'

It would have been, too.

It had been a risk – he and Jordan had both recognized it – deciding to let the American wait that extra day. He should have insisted on her sailing the night before. It had seemed like a calculated risk, one well worth taking, for the sake of those few extra knots, but the entire situation had been so fraught with risks to start with that one had had no business adding to them. Twenty-four hours earlier, the Bali Strait might still have been wide open; and the big movement south through the Lombok Strait hadn't started.

You had to face up to it, accept your own share of blame, learn the lesson. In war, lessons tended to be expensive.

Face up to a courtmartial too, for not having engaged that Kako cruiser?

It wasn't inconceivable. There were individuals in certain quarters, hangers-on in high places, whose main concern was to make damning judgements from their armchairs. And it *had* been a close, difficult decision.

The DCT telephone buzzed. Greenleaf was still up there, although Nick had relaxed the ship's company to cruising stations a couple of hours ago. Greenleaf told him, 'Ship's foretop on green seven-oh, sir—'

'*What?*'

He'd started, spilt coffee. Greenleaf said, 'Looks very much like *Sloan*, sir.'

The *Santa Eulalia* was stopped, low in the water and listing dangerously to port. Smoke oozing from her internal fires drifted south-eastward, a heavy blanket on the sea. *Ainsty*, secured alongside the *Caracas Moon*'s starboard side, was sixty yards to windward of the American as they forged slowly past her. They were just getting the deadweight of the half-tanker under way again, *Ainsty* on this side and *Jouster* on the other, steel-wire ropes bartaut and quivering with strain. You kept well away from wires in that state of tension. If one parted, it could slice a man in half.

Moving, though. Just . . .

It was getting the movement started that took most time and effort.

737

The strain had to be applied carefully, increased slowly and steadily, and the two destroyers had to synchronize their efforts. To hold the hulk on course, you had to continue to strike a balance.

Tugs were said to be coming out from Valletta. They'd been coming anyway to take over the tanker, but now they'd be redirected to the *Santa Eulalia*. One of the minesweepers was standing by her meanwhile.

Looking down at the sea alongside, Paul guessed they were making about two knots. With about five miles to go. That was a guess too. But they had to get up-coast a bit and then turn to run down the swept channel to the harbour entrance, and it couldn't be much less than that.

Three knots, perhaps. Two and a half, anyway. And it was now just past noon.

Spitfires – several groups of them – were flying north, all seemingly heading in that one direction. He turned to look astern. At the end of the long shine of the oil-leak from the tanker, the *Santa Eulalia* lay motionless, bleeding smoke. It was the Spitfires' departure northward that had reminded him of her: the fact that she was alone and in very bad trouble, probably not far short of sinking, and that she seemed now to be losing the fighter cover as well as the protection of these destroyer's guns. He thought the minesweeper had gone alongside her, but it was on the other side of her, and he still didn't have binoculars. She looked very much alone, back there.

'Tugs are passing, t'other side.'

A signalman had said it, leaning over to address one of the lookouts. Paul asked him, 'How many?'

'Three, sir. Reckon it'll be a race who gets in first, them or us. If they can 'old 'er up, that is.'

In the north, a tail of smoke extending downward was a fighter destroyed. It had the look of a Spitfire, but it was too distant to be sure. Astern now he saw the three tugs from the Malta dockyard chugging down the oil-path towards the *Santa Eulalia*. It would be filthy luck, he thought, if she sank right there, after as much as she'd come through. The signalman said, nodding towards the sky ahead, '88s. Sods don't give up easy, do they?'

There were dogfights in progress, Spitfires versus others, in the northern distance. This side of that action, lower in the sky, he saw the Ju88s. But off to the left again, climbing towards them, was another batch of Spitfires. He pointed them out to the signalman.

'They aren't going to bother us this time.' Then he asked him – because signalmen saw signals, which a passenger did not – 'Have we been told anything about any other ships arriving?'

'Only them two, sir.'

'Which two?'

'The *Miramar* and the *Empire Dance*. They're both inside an' unloading.'

'And that's all?'

'Well. There's this lot, now.' He looked astern. 'Except I wouldn't bet on the Yank making it, would you, sir?'

The tugs were getting their lines into her, back there. And this tow, meanwhile, was making a good four knots. Paul said, looking back at the American and crossing fingers on both hands, 'She'll make it.'

One hour before dusk, six thousand miles away. Checking the time and glancing at the position of the sun, Nick recalled that this was the sunset he certainly had not counted on seeing.

'Message passed, sir.'

'Very good. Bring her round, pilot. And come down to two hundred revs.'

Jordan had signalled, an hour ago, 'I decided to maximize my distance from the Bali Strait by holding to a more southerly course before turning east to join you. Sorry if this departure from our original intentions has caused you concern.'

Then later, in answer to a question from Nick, he'd sent, 'There is no Mrs Williams among my passengers.'

Nick hadn't thought there would be. And Williams, not having known of there being any refugees in the American destroyer, would have no reason to be disappointed.

Sloan was abeam to starboard: turning inward now. A handsome, fine-looking ship, Nick thought. He was putting her astern of *Defiant* so as to make night station-keeping simpler; and both ships were cutting speed now to sixteen knots.

'Course one-nine-two, sir!'

'Very good.'

To call it 'very good' was putting it rather mildly, he thought. A hundred and ninety-two degrees was the course from here to North West Cape, the top-left corner of Australia. A run of about seven hundred and fifty miles: at sixteen knots, two days. Then south down the Australian west coast for about the same distance, two more days, to Perth.

Perth – or Fremantle – close to where Kate was. Or where she had been . . .

Kate, my darling, please be there.

Tugs had charge of the *Caracas Moon* now. *Jouster* was leading them and *Ainsty* followed, while four tugs dragged half a tanker into the Grand Harbour.

Just minutes ago a Ju88 had crashed in flames right in the harbour entrance. Spitfires had driven others off: Spits circled now, on guard above Valletta.

That noise: as *Ainsty* nosed in around the point, Paul suddenly caught on to what was making it. Brass bands, and people: about three-quarters of the island's population – going mad. He could see them, as the view unfolded: bands, people, playing and cheering the ships in. Wherever there was a foothold – on roofs, balconies, walls, ledges, ramparts, the terraces and battlements of ancient fortifications, the Maltese had massed to welcome them. Hordes of people: waving, shouting, howling, clapping.

Astern, the *Santa Eulalia*, with smoke still gushing out of her, was entering harbour with two tugs ahead and one alongside. She was very low in the water, and listing so hard that you'd guess she was on the point of foundering. The tugs were hauling her around to port, close in past a rocky promontory. The noise was indescribable: and it was moving, you could feel it in your throat. *Ainsty*'s crew were fallen in, in ranks for the drill of entering harbour. Two ranks of sailors on her foc'sl, some amidships on each side of the iron deck, another platoon on the quarterdeck: they'd become parade-ground sailors, suddenly. Up here on the compass platform the captain had exchanged his woollen hat for a uniform cap, and the two-and-a-half stripes on each of his reefer's sleeves were bright, new-looking. From a distance, nobody could have guessed he hadn't had more than a brief doze in a bridge chair for the last five days and nights. Paul was looking into the forepart of the bridge. Simpson saw him, and came aft to tell him quickly, 'They're taking the *Caracas Moon* into Dockyard Creek – round that next point on the left. Fort St Angelo, that heap is. The next point after it's called Senglea, and we'll be berthing in the creek – French Creek – beyond it.'

The *Empire Dance* was alongside a wharf, stern-on to them as they passed. She was unloading, all her derricks busy and men swarming all over her, a mass of cargo streaming out of her to the wharf on one side and into lighters on the other. Beyond her, higher up the creek, he had a brief glimpse of the *Miramar*, the centre of an equally frantic discharging operation.

The *Santa Eulalia* had stopped. She'd grounded, close to the rocky shore in that first bay. He guessed they'd got her into shallow water just in time. All three tugs were alongside her now. If they could contain the fire they'd most likely unload her there, into lighters. The noise of cheering and clapping and the blare of the brass bands never slackened, it was a constant roar of excitement and joy: it was marvellous, he thought, but it was also crazy. How many people here – ten thousand? More? But what they were getting was half a tanker, maybe three-quarters of that American freighter's cargo, and two other ship-loads. At the cost of twelve merchantmen, an aircraft carrier, three cruisers and some destroyers: and those were the ships he *knew* about . . . The band they were passing was playing *Rule, Britannia!* A hand fell on his shoulder. Turning, he found the doctor, Grant, where Simpson had been a moment ago. Grant shouted, 'Bad news, sub. Your pal Willis. I'm extremely sorry.'

'Dead?'

The doctor nodded. The band had switched to *Scotland the Brave*. Paul hadn't known Harry Willis well, but Willis had saved his life and now he was dead. So were Ron Beale, and Art Withinshaw, and Dennis Brill and Mick McCall and old Bongo Mackeson and young Gosling. And God knew how many others. The bands played and the people cheered and it made you want to cry: for the thrill in it, and pride, and sorrow too. But also, surprise. He wondered, *If they act like this now, what in hell will they do when we start winning?*

POSTSCRIPT

There was no cruiser *Defiant* or destroyer USS *Sloan*. In other respects the description of the Java Sea battle (27 February 1942) and subsequent events is drawn from history. The Japanese landed in Java on 1 March.

The Malta convoy is more thoroughly fictional. There was no convoy from the west in February: that month's attempt to supply the island was from Alexandria, and no ships at all got through. So it was necessary to invent one – in order to get Paul to Malta. The fictional convoy story is based loosely on the facts of Operation Pedestal, which took place a few months later. Pedestal opened with the loss of the carrier *Eagle*, and two cruisers and the tanker *Ohio* were hit in one (Italian) submarine's torpedo salvo at the entrance to the Skerki Channel. Among the fourteen ships in convoy was an American freighter called the *Santa Elisa*, but she was not among the five ships – two of them sinking – that reached Malta.